Arthur Wellington Brayley

A complete history of the Boston fire department, including the fire-alarm service and the protective department, from 1630 to 1888, arranged in three parts

Arthur Wellington Brayley

A complete history of the Boston fire department,including the fire-alarm service and the protective department, from 1630 to 1888, arranged in three parts

ISBN/EAN: 9783742833051

Manufactured in Europe, USA, Canada, Australia, Japa

Cover: Foto ©Andreas Hilbeck / pixelio.de

Manufactured and distributed by brebook publishing software (www.brebook.com)

Arthur Wellington Brayley

A complete history of the Boston fire department, including the fire-alarm service and the protective department, from 1630 to 1888, arranged in three parts

PORTRAIT OF THE AUTHOR AND OLD RELICS OF THE DEPARTMENT. — *Frontispiece.*

A

COMPLETE HISTORY

OF THE

BOSTON FIRE DEPARTMENT,

INCLUDING

THE FIRE-ALARM SERVICE AND THE PROTECTIVE DEPARTMENT,

From 1630 to 1888.

ARRANGED IN THREE PARTS.

PART ONE.

Fires, and Laws concerning their Prevention; Fire Apparatus and Members of Companies from the Settlement of the Town to the Granting of the City Charter in 1822.

PART TWO.

The Reorganization of the Department from a Volunteer to a Paid Force; Fire Records; Building Laws; Engine Companies and their Officers, up to 1873.

PART THREE.

A Complete Record from the Appointment of the Board of Fire Commissioners, in 1874, to December 31, 1888, including the Fire Record; to which is added a Roster of Companies since 1874, the Permanent Members, with a Portrait and Biographical Sketch of each, including the Ex-Chief Engineers and Fire Commissioners, Present Board of Commissioners, Maps of Districts, and Portraits of District Chiefs; together with the Repair-Shop, Fire-Alarm Service, and Boston Protective Department.

BY

ARTHUR WELLINGTON BRAYLEY,

Compiler of the "American Dramatic Directory," etc.

Illustrated.

BOSTON, MASS.:
JOHN P. DALE & CO., PUBLISHERS,
17 BOYLSTON STREET.
1889.

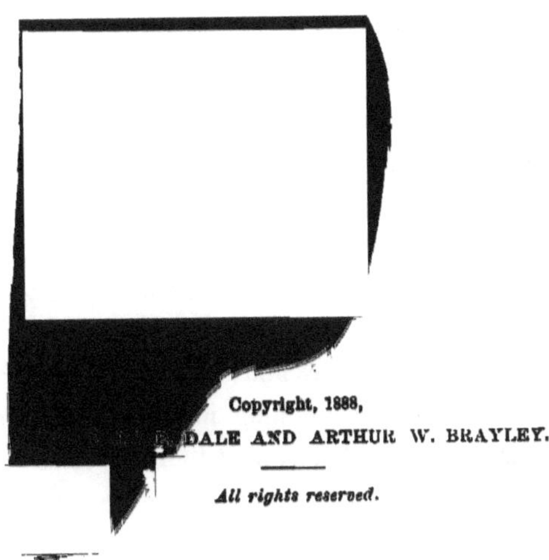

Copyright, 1888,

... DALE AND ARTHUR W. BRAYLEY.

PRESS OF
Rockwell and Churchill,
BOSTON.

INTRODUCTION.

THE information for the History of the Boston Fire Department has been very difficult to obtain, owing to the unsatisfactory manner in which the records have been left. In fact, there is no register of events made by the department in existence, the data previous to 1840 being scattered over numerous sources. In the task of research, I have given the care and patience the subject demanded, and trust I have succeeded in combining into one volume all the important matters in relation to the department that heretofore have been distributed through hundreds. The location of the various engines, hose-carriages, and ladder-trucks, and the companies attached to each, have been traced, as far as it has been possible to do so by the existing records, from their organization up to the date of closing this history, except from 1822 to 1860, at which time the membership became so large (each company having from fifty to one hundred and fifty members on the roll-book), that to mention all their names would occupy a large amount of space, and would be of no great value, as they can be obtained at the office of the Board of Fire Commissioners. I have therefore deemed it sufficient to mention only the officers.

The work of obtaining photographs and biographical sketches of members of the present department was begun during 1888, since which many changes have been made in the companies, so that by the time the portraits of one company were engraved, a member of the company represented by the plate would be transferred to other quarters, and he succeeded by another, thus making it impossible to retain a complete company for any length of time. It was found, therefore, impracticable to take notice of such changes after December 31, 1888, at which time the accompanying plates correctly represent the companies formed at that time. The work of obtaining the photographs, and grouping the entire force in its proper order, has been a task the difficulties of which only those who have had a similar experience can comprehend. I am sorry to say, in this particular, that, despite the care and attention given the matter, four errors were made (in the plates of Engine Company No. 23, Protective Company No. 1, and Ladder Companies Nos. 1 and 4) ; these are accounted for, however, in the records of the respective companies which they represent. In a few cases a portrait is omitted, and in others only brief mention is made of a member. This is entirely the fault of the parties themselves, as they would not take the trouble to furnish me with the necessary matter. There being no photograph of the first executive head, Samuel D. Harris, in existence, the plate of portraits of ex-chief engineers is necessarily incomplete. The portraits of Messrs. Sawyer and White are missing from those of the ex-commissioners, as both these gentlemen refused to furnish me with a photograph. The old relics, except the two engines illustrated in the frontispiece, are the property of the Bostonian Society. The names of members of each company since 1874 were, in most cases, furnished by the foreman of their respective commands. In some of the records the names of those who did duty only as substitutes are omitted, and where dates of appointments and resignations of members are left blank, it is owing to the fact of there being no records to supply the correct information.

The plan of this History is original with the author ; it is therefore with feeling akin to trepidation that he places it before the public ; but it will fulfil his desire should it give to the people of Boston the necessary records of a service of which they may justly feel proud, and the citizens of the United States a history of the first department organized in this country for the purpose of protection from that most gratifying servant but fearful master, fire.

A. W. BRAYLEY.

Boston, Mass, Oct. 30, 1889.

CONTENTS.

PART I.

CHAPTER I.

1627–1679.

CHAPTER II.

1680–1710.

CHAPTER III.

1711-1739.

CHAPTER IV.

1740-1759.

CHAPTER V.

1760-1763.

CHAPTER VI.

1764-1774.

CHAPTER VII.

1775-1789.

CHAPTER VIII.

1790–1797.

CHAPTER IX.

1800–1803.

CHAPTER X.

1804–1817.

CHAPTER XI.

1818–1822.

PART II.

CHAPTER I.

1822–1824.

CHAPTER IV.

1832-1834.

CHAPTER V.

1835-1842.

CHAPTER VI.

1843-1851.

CHAPTER X.

1868–1870.

CHAPTER XI.

1871–1872.

PART III.

CHAPTER I.

1873–1874.

CHAPTER II.

1875–1880.

CHAPTER III.

1881–1888.

CHAPTER IV.

CHAPTER V.

CHAPTER VI.

CHAPTER VII.

CHAPTER VIII.

CHAPTER IX.

CHAPTER X.

CHAPTER XI.

CHAPTER XII.

CHAPTER XIII.

LIST OF ILLUSTRATIONS.

HISTORY

OF THE

BOSTON FIRE DEPARTMENT.

PART I.

FROM 1627 TO 1821.

CHAPTER I.

1627–1679.

SIR HENRY ROSEWELL and Sir John Young, with their associates, near Dorchester, England, purchased of the council for New England, on March 19, 1627–8, a patent for that part of the country situated between three miles to the northward of the Merrimac river and three miles to the southward of the Charles river, and in length from the Atlantic ocean to the South sea. Under this charter "the Governor and company of Massachusetts Bay in New England" commenced the settlement of the Massachusetts colony, for which purpose they chose Matthew Cradock to be their governor, and Thomas Goffe, their deputy-governor. Capt. John Endicott and Samuel Skelton and others were first sent over to Naumkeag (Salem), which was the first town permanently settled in this colony. The company under Endicott arrived on September 6, 1628, while Skelton landed on the 29th of June the year following. Mishawum (Charlestown) was settled about this time by a few inhabitants of that town. On August 29, the same year, it was decided by the company that the government and patent should be settled in New England. At this time an agreement was entered into by the twelve leaders, who at Cambridge pledged themselves to be ready with their families on the following March to sail for these shores, during which meeting Messrs. Cradock and Goffe resigned their respective offices as governor and deputy-governor, and were succeeded by John Winthrop and John Humphrey.

On April 8, 1630, the little band sailed from Yarmouth, England, in the ship "Arbella," together with several other vessels, and after an uneventful voyage anchored in the outer harbor of Salem on Saturday, June 10, 1630, O.S. The location of Endicott did not please the new arrivals, who, after a short tour of prospecting, returned on the 19th and reported favorably for locating at Charlestown. The move was made on July 1, and the party soon safely landed. The scarcity of fresh water and other objectionable features rendered this place as undesirable as the first; they therefore accepted the invitation of Mr. William Blaxton, or Blackstone, who had settled at Boston, or Shawmut (living fountain), as it was called by the Indians (and by the people of Charlestown, Trimountain), to locate on the peninsula. The town took its present name at the meeting of the Court of Assistants held at the governor's house on Tuesday, September 7, when it was recorded that "Trimountain shall be called Boston, Mattapan, Dorchester, and the town upon Charles Ryver, Watertown."

The town of Boston at this time was compassed only by the peninsula which extended from Winnisimmet ferryways to the Roxbury line; but the old records of the colony state that on November 7, 1632, it was ordered, "that the neck of land betwixte Powder Horn Hill & Pullen Poynte shall belong to Boston, to be enjoynd by the inhabitants thereof forever," and on May 14, 1634, "the court hath ordered that Boston shall have convenient enlargement at Mount Wooleston, to be sett out by foure indifferent men." Also, "it was ffurther ordered that Winelsemet and the houses there builte and to be builte, shall joyne themselves either to Charlton or Boston as members of that towne, before the next Gen'all court." Muddy river, now part of Brookline, was also a part of "Newe Towne," September 25, 1634. Winnisimmett, Rumny Marsh, and Pullen Point were incorporated as the town of Chelsea January 9, 1738–9.

The part of Boston settled by the new-comers was bounded as follows: On the north by the Mill cove, part of the Charles river; on the south by the town of Roxbury; the west by a continuation of the Charles river or Back bay; and on the east by the Great cove and the South cove, — in all containing an area less than one thousand acres. Running from the Roxbury line to the fortification on the neck (Dover street) and north-north-east was one mile and thirty-nine yards; thence to the Winnisimmet, one mile and three-quarters and one hundred and twenty-nine yards, — a total of two miles, three quarters, and two hundred and thirty-eight yards. The breadth was very irregular: on the line of Essex and Boylston streets to the water on the west side, eleven hundred and twenty-seven yards; from Foster's wharf to south-west of Fort hill, to the north-west end of Leverett street, one mile and one hundred and thirty-nine yards. From Endicott street to the water on the east it was two hundred and seventy-five yards in breadth, but from Charles-river bridge through North square to the water it was seven hundred and twenty-six yards.

During the first ten years the town grew rapidly in wealth and population, as may be judged from the following statement: In October, 1633, of the £400 to be collected from the eleven plantations "to defray public charges," Boston paid £48, while Dorchester contributed £80; but in August, 1637, Boston paid £59 4s., while Salem, at that time second in importance, was levied £45 12s. Boston was then considered the wealthiest and most populous town in the colony.

It was not until after the first seventy-five years of the settlement that the various streets and public avenues had fixed and determined names; consequently, all the estates that bordered on them were described as bounded on "the street" or "lane" running from some well-known landmark to another. Nearly all the first houses were erected on the highway to Roxbury (Washington street) and upon the portion of Tremont street that is north of Winter street, with a few on the highway in the north end of the town, one of which was early known as "the way leading from the Orange Tree to the Ferry" (Hanover street), and the other as "the lower north highway" (North street). These were crossed by several short ones, and the whole at first bounded on the north by the present Prince street and south by Eliot street. For the first twenty years there was hardly a building west of the present Tremont street, the most populous part of the town being in the streets above mentioned, with some small houses at the Great cove, and here and there one in the vicinity of Milk and Summer streets and Cornhill (Fort hill).

Mud houses were known in the early days, but they were very few, and of course only occupied by the very poorest of the colonists. The buildings were generally of wood, although a few were of stone and brick; but until the town was at least twenty years of age these were exceptions. The first dwellings were generally of one story in height, with roofs covered with thatch or boughs of trees. But as time passed, those who could afford it built their houses of two stories in front, with a shingled roof that ran nearly to the ground in the rear, leaving but one story exposed. In time, lapped or double roofs were in order.

We do not find that any fires occurred in the town until March 16, 1630–1, when Governor Winthrop records in his journal the following:—

About noon the chimny of Mr. Thomas Sharp's house in Boston, took fire, the splinters being not clayed at the top, and taking the thatch, burnt it down. The wind being North-west, drove the fire to Mr. Coulburn's house being a [blank] rods off, and burnt that down also which were as good, and as well finished, as the most on the plantation.

Dudley adds:—

Much of their household stuff, apparell and other things, as alsoe some goods of others who soiourned with them in their house, were consumed; God so pleasing to exercise us with corrections of this kind as he hath done with others; for the prevention whereof in our new towne intended this somer to bee builded, we have ordered that noe man there shall build his chimny with wood, nor cover his house with ,thatch, which was readily assented onto; for that divers others houses have beene burned since our arrival (the fire alwaies beginninge in the wooden chimny), and some English (?) wigwams. which have taken fire in the roofes covered with thatch or boughs.

Thus the first building act was established immediately after the earliest cause. The next fire, we are informed, occurred at noon of the 18th of May the same year, when Mr. William Chesebrough, a very wealthy and influential citizen, had the misfortune to lose his house and effects by the flames; but it was not for the want of zeal on the part of the inhabitants, as the records state "all the people being present." Mr. Chesebrough soon after moved from Boston to Braintree, from which he was a representative to the General Court. Mr. Benjamin's dwelling was the next to succumb to the element, being burnt during the month of April, 1636.

A severe thunder-storm passed over the town on June 22, 1642, when lightning struck the windmill situated at the north end of the town, and did considerable damage to the building, also setting the meal-sacks on fire: and severely shocked the miller. During the latter part of March, 1645. there happened, at Roxbury, an explosion of seventeen or eighteen barrels of the town's stock of gunpowder, which was stored in the house of John Johnson. The shock shook the houses in Boston like an earthquake, and blew burning cinders beyond the meeting-house, that stood in King street (State street), and created quite a panic, for the time being, among the people. The early records of Roxbury were destroyed by this fire.

Although there are no records of any later conflagrations until the Great Fire of 1653, still, from the extensive preparations made by the citizens in 1651, it may be surmised that the inhabitants were not a little troubled with this danger as well as with the Indians.

The first action taken by the inhabitants at their regular town-meetings on the matter of fires is recorded on November 24, 1651, as follows:—

It is ordered that if any chimny be on fyer soe as to flame out of the top thereof, the party in whose possession the chemney is shall pay to the treasurer of the Towne for the Towne use, tenn shillings.

The terrible conflagration of January 14, 1653, swept over the principal section of the town, and, as Governor Winthrop states, "it was a wonderful favor of God that the whole town was not consumed." He adds:—

Mr. Wilson's house and goods, Mr. Sheaths house and goods and three young children, Mr. Shrimptons house and goods, Mr. Sellicks house and goods. Mr. Blackleech house and goods. The others I have forgotten their names, It was the most dreadfull fire that I ever Saw by reason of the barrell of Gun Powder which they had in their houses which made men fearful to come near them The Lord sanctifie his hand to us all.

From this we know that the fire raged along State and Washington streets, as the house of Mr. Henry Shrimpton, a brazier, stood on the north side of State street, near Devonshire street. Rev. John Wilson nearly adjoined him, while David Sellick dwelt south of them, near the shore line. We also find in the records of June 27, 1653, "Mr. Rob". Woodmancye to be paid 40s. as a part of his repairs of his house," which we are of the opinion was granted on account of its being pulled down to stop the progress of the flames. Woodmancy[e] was the teacher of the first school in the town, which was situated on the site of the City Hall, and from which School street was given its name. This estate was formerly owned by Thomas Scattow, who sold it to the town in 1645. Although Winthrop gives only these few names, we judge, from the district burned, that the loss must have been quite extensive and a large number of dwellings consumed, as this was the most thickly populated portion of the town. The mention of the loss of the three children of Mr. Sheaths is the first record of death from this dreadful cause.

Capt. Robert Keayne, who wrote the first part of his voluminous will on the 1st of August, this year, probably referred to this fire in the following passage ; which was also the means of establishing the conduit : —

Having thought of the want of some necessary things for the Towne of Boston, as a market place and condit; the one a good helpe in danger of fyre the want of which we have found of sad experience.

We do not wonder, after such a calamity, that the citizens were thoroughly aroused to the preservation of the town from this destroying element, and at once prepare themselves for defence.

At their meeting held March 14th, the same year, they passed the following law : —

It is ordered then that there shall be a ladder or ladders to every house within this town that shall reach to the ridg of the house, which every householder shall provid for his house by the last day of the third mo. next, one the penaltie of six shillings, eight penc, for every on that shall not by the day aforesaid be provided of such ladders, and to forfit the aforesaid sum of six shillings, 8ᵈ, for every mo'th that they shall be soe wanting, after the aforesaid last of the 3d mo.

It is ordered that every house holder shall provide a pole of above 12 foot long, with a good large swob at the end of it, to rech the rofe of his house to quench fire in case of such danger, this to be provided by the last of the next 3d mo., on the penaltie of twelve penc. forfit for every one that then shall be found defecktive, and to forfeit twelve pence per month soe long as they be so defecktive after the aforsaid last day of the 3d mo'th.

It is Ordered that the selecktmen shall forthwith provide six good and long ladders for the Towne's use, which shall hang at the outsyde of the metting house, thear to be redy in case of fier, thes ladders to be branded with the town marke.

It is Ordered that whosoever shall take away any of thes ladders, excepting in case of fier, shall forfit to the town Tresury twentie shillings.

It is Ordered that fower good strong Iron crooks, with chaines and rops fitted to them, and thes crooks fastned on a good strong pole be forwith provided by the selecktmen, which shall hang at the syd of the meeting house, thear to be ready in case of fier.

It is Ordered that no house shall be pulled downe in case of fier by any men, without the consent of the major part of the majestrats and commissioners and seleckt men of this town that ar present thear at the same time of the fier; and that noe person whoes house shall be so pulled down within this towne shall have or recover any satisfaktion by lawe for any house soe pulled downe.

The first mention of the confinement of water for use in case of fire is also mentioned in the records of this meeting : —

William Franklin and neyghbors about his howse is granted liberty to make a sisteru of 12 foot or greater, if they see cause, at the Pumpe which standeth in the hie way near to the Stats arms Tavern (corner of State and Exchange Streets), for to howld watter for to be helpful in case of fier, unto the towne. He is to make it safe from any danger of children.

The 25th of the following month Mr. Simon Ayres was the first to come under the penalties of the law regarding chimneys, and on April 25 is fined ten shillings for his chimney being on fire " contrary to an order made for prevention thereof ; " while on June 27th another order is passed : —

Foras much as sad events have bene by fire when it breaketh out beyond its due bounds. To the Damage and loss nott only of estate but of life also, for prevention wherof it is hereby ordered that no fire shall be kindled within three rod of anye barn, house or wharfe or wood pile or any other combustible matter subiect to fire, nor shall anye keepe fire in anye vessell lying in anye Dock, or to anye wharfe after nine of the clock at night or before five of the clock in the morning, in penalty of every offence tenn shillings, the one halfe to the Towne, the other halfe to the party complayning; this order to take place the First daye of the 5th month 1653.

From which we would infer that the origin of the late disaster was traced to a fire kindled in the open air near some building or wood-pile, and was the work of some evil persons to destroy the town, for the General Court, held in 1652, passed the following law, which was the first legislation on fire matters taken by that body : —

Whereas some dwelling Houses, and other Houses within this jurisdiction, have been set on Fire, and the means or occasun thereof not discovered, through some persons have been vehemently suspected to have been instrumental therin: The Court taking into consideration the danger of such a wicked practice, especially in Town where the House are near adjoyning, and there being no Law yet provided for the punishment of so hainnous a crime; Doth therefore hereby order, and be it

Enected by the Authority of this Court that any person or persons whatsoever of the age of Sixteen years and upward, that shall after the publication hereof wittingly and willingly set fire any Barn, Stable Mill, out House stack of wood Corn or Hay or any other thing of like nature shall upon due conviction by testimony or confession, pay double damage to the party damnified, and be severely whipt.

And if any person of the age aforesaid shall after the publication hereof wittingly and willingly, and felloniously, set on fire any Dwelling House Meeting House Store House, or shall in like manner set on fire any out-House, Barn, Stable, Leanto, Stack of Hay, Corn or Wood. or any thing of like nature, whereby, any Dwelling House, Meeting House or Store House, cometh to be burnt, the party or parties vehemently suspected thereof shall be apprehended by Warrant from one or more of the Magistrates and Committed to Prison, there to remain without, Baile, till the next Court of assistants, who upon legal conviction by due proof, or confession of the Crime shall adjudge such person or persons to be put to death, and to forfeit so much of his Lands, Goods or Chattels as shall make full satisfaction, to the party or parties damnified. (1652.)

The first mention of a water-engine is made in the records of March 1, 1653–4, when " the select have power and liberty hereby to agree with Joseph Jynks for Ingins to convey water in case of fire if they see cause so to do." It will be seen, therefore, that the people were thoroughly awakened to the danger to which their town was subjected, having been taught by the sad experiences of the year.

On the 25th of December, 1654, the fine for allowing chimneys to flame was reduced to five shillings, and the previous order repealed, while on January 29, 1654–5, a like penalty was inflicted on any man who carried off any of the town ladders or buckets. No doubt there was a fire during this year, as an order was passed on February 26, as follows : —

Wheras upon occayson of fire the buccetts were taken and made use of, severall of them nott yett returned, it is hereby ordered that whoever hath anie of the sayd buccetts shall forth with returne them in penalty of tenn shillings for every buccett nott returned within tenn dayes.

The fine of five shillings did not seem to satisfy the authorities, as we find an order passed November 27, 1655, that " Isaac Walker, Sam. Norden, Robt Nanny, and Xofer Gibson are fined 10s. a man, for their chymnyes being on fire, which the constables are to leavy ; " but Norden had half of his fine remitted. Robert Wyatt and William Lane were appointed chimney-sweeps. They were " to cry aboutt Streetes that they may bee knowne." March 31, 1656, James Nabors is fined five shillings for his chimney flaming, and on May 25, 1657, Isaac Cullimore was " ordered to secure a chimny in his leantoo from danger of fire within eight dayes, on penalty of 20s."

The question of a good water-supply was one of the early difficulties, and recourse was had to artificial means soon after the town was settled. The origin of the conduit or reservoir, as we have mentioned, can be traced to the provisions in the will of Capt. Robert Keayne. In 1649, during his lifetime, Mr. William Tyng gave certain privileges to Messrs. James Everell and Joshua Scottow and their associates, in a certain estate, —

With free liberty to dig, find out, erect and set up one fountain, well, headspring, or more within his land or pasture ground . . . as also from said well or wells, fountain or fountains, to dig or trench through said pasture ground, or lay down such pipes or water work conveyances as should be necessary for the carrying or conveying of water from the aforesaid fountains or wells into such place as the said neighborhood and company shall see convenient for the erecting of a conduit or water works.

Mr. Tyng died January 18, 1652–3, and subsequently the grant was confirmed by the trustees of his children, on April 29, 1656. In March of that year Mr. Everell and the neighbors were granted one of the bells which were given to the town by Captain Cromwell for a clock, to enjoy while they make use of it there; so that the conduit must have been in use at this date. The General Court, in their session of 1652, granted an act of incorporation to the inhabitants of the Conduit street in Boston to provide a fresh supply of water to their families, and especially for use in case of fire; they were annually to elect two of the proprietors to be masters or wardens of the water-works, with power to arrange for the payment of the yearly rent of the land, to make all necessary repairs, to assess the proper sums, and to admit new members. If any persons should be found guilty of wasting the water or injuring the pipes, cisterns, or fountains, the wardens for the time being might prosecute the offenders; and if any person should take water from the conduit without license the wardens might confiscate " such vessels from them `as they bring to carry such water with." This conduit was a large reservoir, about twelve feet square, made for holding water conveyed to it by wooden pipes leading from neighboring wells and springs, and was situated in a square formed by the junction of Wing's lane (now Elm street) and Union street, in the neighborhood of the present North street, and a short distance from Dock square. The street leading from the conduit to the drawbridge placed over the Mill creek (Blackstone street) was one of the first highways laid out, and was known as Conduit street.

Over the reservoir was a wooden building used for storage purposes; but later this was removed and a covering of planks was laid over the conduit, raised in the centre about two feet and sloping to the sides. On Saturdays this platform was used as a stand for a meal-market, and near this was a bell given by Captain Cromwell. (See Shurtleff's Boston.) In the records of the town after this, frequent mention is made of the conduit for repairs, permits for laying pipes, etc.; but it never fulfilled the object of its projectors, and was allowed to go into decay a few years later. We find in the records of July 28, 1657, that

Deacon Marshall and Ensigne Hull are appointed to gaine liberty in writing of Mr. Seaborne Cotton and his mother to bring water down from their hill to the conduit intended to be erected.

Also, —

Deacon Marshall Ensigne Scotto and Wm Davis and any two of them are empowered to Joyne with any one or two of the committe to treat and agree with any workmen for the erecting of and bringing water to the conduit intended to be erected.

And on March 14, 1671–2, Mr. Nicholas Page (who married Anne, a granddaughter of Captain Keayne) was granted liberty

To take away the bricks belonging to the place intended for a conduit at the end of the Town House before his door, provided he immediately fill the place even with the ground about it, for which he brought a note from the overseers of Capt Robt Keaynes will, & a discharge for his guift expended thereabout, a coppie whereof followeth & ye originall kept among the towne writings

To the Select of Bostone, Vnderstanding by Mr. Page that the place builded for a conduit is prejudicial to his house & shops and that you are Willinge he should remove and improve it to his own use, if our consent may be had thereto and being informed likewise that Capt. Robt Keaynes guift to the Towne of Boston for yᵗ end hath beene expended vpon that worke, though by the prouidence of God it hath not prooved soe, vsefull as was expected and desired, vpon these considerations Wee the ouerseers of Capt Keaynes will shall acquiesse in what is done, and not trouble the towne of Bostone any further in relation to that particular. Witness our hands the 7ᵗʰ of 1ˢᵗ Mo. 1671.

> SYMOND BRADSTREET,
> DANIEL DENISON,
> EDWARD RAWSON,
> JAMES JOHNSON.

On the approach of the cold weather the records contain one or more fires, and warnings against carelessness regarding chimneys. Ben. Gillam and James Roulstone are fined ten shillings each for making a fire on the wharf, on July 28, 1657, and on the 31st of the following month —— Graves is fined for his chimney being on fire " and his landlord for want of a ladder." On April 26, 1658, John Marshall is ordered to go through the town to see that all the houses are supplied with ladders, and report delinquents. On June 29 the following order was passed : —

Whereas many careless persons carry fire from one house into another in open fire pans or brands ends, by reason of which great damage may accrew to the towne; It is therefore ordered that no person shall have liberty to carry fire from one house to another without a safe vessell to secure itt from the winde, upon the poenalty of ten shillings to be paid by every party so fetching, and half so much by those that permitt them so to take fire.

And on January 3 : —

Itt is ordered that the Treasurer shall forthwith provi•le sixe substantiall ladders and three iron hookes, as also to gett the leather bucketts repayred for the townes use.

The law regarding the pulling down of houses was somewhat amended on March 4, 1658–9, when it was ordered that any house destroyed by the order of the authorities the owner should have their loss made good by the town. The old town-house seems to be rigidly guarded against fire, as an order was issued at this meeting that no person, whether watchman or any other, should at any time take tobacco or bring a lighted match or fire in any part of the building, except in case of military exercise and under cover, for the use of the house. The fine for disobedience was twenty shillings ; and in the orders to the town watch for the year 1662 the house was to have special care regarding persons taking tobacco or using fire.

Edward Davis and Joseph Gridley were employed as bellmen to walk through and about the town from 12 o'clock at night to 5 o'clock in the morning, and if he saw an extraordinary light or fire in any house or vessel to inspect it, and if necessary to give an alarm. They were also commanded to order out any light in vessels lying at the docks or creeks, and to caution the inhabitants whenever they saw their light burning. Thus the first fire patrol was established.

Careless citizens are warned and fined for defective chimneys, and the inhabitants make complaint of any who endanger the town by this cause, which result in large fires and a stricter watch. The wharves and vessels are also a source of care and vigilance, and in the order to the water bailiffs, April 27, 1663, we find a clause stating that no vessel lying at the dock or wharf is allowed to keep any fire between 9 P.M. and 5 A.M. on a penalty of ten shillings. John Marshal is empowered, August 28, 1665, to collect fines from delinquents of the ladder law. On March 30, 1668, an inspection of chimneys by two bricklayers occurred, which resulted in warning fifteen tenants to have them repaired within twenty-six days ; the majority of these were coopers, who were forbid firing any cask in any shop or warehouse without a sufficient chimney, otherwise to pay a fine of twenty shillings.

January 30, 1670–1, Mr. John Anderson was allowed £120 for his house and goods which were blown up in the great fire, and John Freeke and Capt Samuel Skarlet were allowed the rates of £4 8s., in consideration of their shops being pulled down to arrest the progress of the flames. Bakers came in for a share of warnings, September 21, 1670, regarding ovens with insufficient chimneys.

On the 25th of the same month the following important order was passed : —

Wheras it is found by experience that in case of fire breaking out in this towne the welfare thereof is much endangered for want of a speedy supply of water; It is therefore ordered that after the first of March next, and soe forward to the first of November in. every yeare. Every Inhabitent in this towne shall at all times duringe the said term have a pipe or a hogshead of water ready fild with the head open at or neere the dore of theire dwelling houses and warehouses upon the penaltie of 5s. for every defect.

The danger arising from explosions of gunpowder came in for the consideration of the selectmen on August 7, 1671, as this article was stored in warehouses and dwelling-houses at all parts of the town ; it was ordered therefore that all powder landed in the town should be carried to Mr. Robert Gibbs' warehouse on Fort Hill, and all powder then in the town to be removed there within six days, on a penalty of twenty shillings per barrel in both cases. The quantity allowed to be kept in any one house was restricted to twenty pounds.　Gibbs received twelve pence for every barrel stored for six months. Elisha Hutchinson was appointed a receiver of the powder.

About this time a fire occurred in the brew-house of Mrs. Ollivers, by which Nathaniel Byshop was ordered by the deputy-governor and some of the selectmen to receive £3 6s. from the town treasurer for beer delivered out of his house.　Two dwelling-houses belonging to James Hill and John Wallies, together with some warehouses, were burned July 19, 1672.　During this conflagration the wind was very high, and the houses being clapboarded and shingled with cedar, and very dry, the flames soon spread, and sparks carried to the common, which was fully a quarter of a mile distant; but the inhabitants, by their promptness and hard work, got it under control without further damage.

Thirteen coopers and others were ordered to repair their chimneys, or make no fire under them during 1673, and thereafter strict attention was paid to these matters.

The castle on Castle island, being built of timber, took fire on March 21, 1672–3, and was entirely destroyed.　The powder and a portion of the soldiers' property only were saved.　The next day the magistrates of Boston and neighboring towns issued orders for a contribution of £1,500 to repair it as soon as possible, and the General Court, on May 7, ordered that another building be erected, not exceeding sixty feet square within, or proportionate. It was finished October 7, 1674.

The conduit became a public nuisance, judging from the agreement made between the selectmen and several of the inhabitants near that section, on April 7, 1675.　This agreement was for repairing the street and making a watercourse to run the water to the bridge, and from there into the Mill creek, at one-quarter expense to the town, the balance by the citizens.　On March 9, 1676, Sewell records in his Diary: —

N.B.　The Common House on the street, called Conneys (on the north side of Sudbury street on the curve from Hanover to Portland streets) next the harbor toward the north end of the town was set on fire, about four in the morning, as is rationally conjectured, for on the middle of the roof of a lean-to were found several drops of tallow.　It was discovered by an ancient woman rising early and so prevented praise God.　On March 11 thanks were returned by the selectmen in behalf of the town for its preservation.

The principal business section of the town was at or near Bendall's dock, or Town dock, extending as far as Dock square, while along the highways lesser mercantile affairs were carried on.　There were a few brick buildings erected after the fire, the first in the town being built by Mr. Coddington. The pretty gardens and pastures made the landscape one that was in every way pleasing to the eye; the streets were laid out without regard to system,— convenience was the rule, and the path nearest leading to their place of destination became often the highways, and the cause of the crooked and winding streets of our city to-day.　Thus situated, the inhabitants were alarmed about

5 o'clock on the morning of November 27, 1676, by the terrible cry of fire, which, before the people could gather to the scene, armed with their meagre instruments of defence, had assumed most alarming proportions. It started at the house of Mr. Wakefield, occupied by Mr. Moors, situated near the Red Lion tavern, just north of Richmond street, and was occasioned by an apprentice of a tailor, who was called up before daylight; and being left alone fell asleep, and the candle set fire to the house. The district bounded by what are now Richmond, Hanover, and Clark streets, which contained forty-six dwelling-houses, several warehouses and stores, and the North meeting-house, was laid in ruins within four hours. The wind was blowing very hard from the south-east, and when the fire was at its height the wind veered to the south, and was immediately followed by a heavy downfall of rain, which we may judge was hailed with joy by the citizens, as their methods for extinguishing fire were no match for this holocaust, without which, it would have, without a doubt, consumed all that section of the town. The sparks were carried across the river, and fears for the safety of Charlestown were expressed. But the rain and the efforts of the inhabitants got it under control. The church burnt was that of the Rev. Increase Mather, of whom the following story is told by his son, in his " Remarkables : " —

In the year 1676 he had a strange impression in his mind that caused him, on November 19, to preach a sermon in these words, Zeph. iii. 7, " I said surely thou wilt fear me, thou wilt receive instructions, so their dwellings should not be cut off ; " and concluded the sermon with a strange prediction that a fire was coming that would make a deplorable desolation. After he came home, he was walking in the study ; he was exceedingly moved and melted in such a soliloquy : " Oh! Lord God, I have told this people that thou art about to cut off their dwellings, but they will not believe. Nevertheless, Oh Lord God, I beseech Thee to spair them. If it may stand with Thy holy pleasure, spare them, spare them ; " so did he walk weeping before the Lord, at the same time he earnestly urged upon his consort a speedy change of habitation, but which could not be accomplished. On the next Lord's Day, he preached, not aware of its being so, a farewell sermon in those words, Rev. iii. 3, " Remember how they have received and heard," and the conclusion of the sermon was that predictions of evil to come ought to be remembered, and that when the Lord is about to bring any heavy judgment upon his people, he is wont to stir up the heart of some servant of his to give warning of it, which warning should be remembered, that so people may be ready to entertain what must come upon them. His last words were : " People won't remember nor mind these things, but as John said unto his captain, ' Remember how the Lord laid this burden,' so, when the evil is come, you will remember what you heard concerning it." The very night following a Desolatin fire broke forth in his neighborhood. The house in which he and his flock had praised God was burnt with the fire, whole streets were consumed by the devouring flames and laid in ashes. His own house also took a part in the ruins, but by the gracious Province of God he lost little of his beloved library. Not a hundred books from above a thousand : of these also he had an immediate recruit by a generous offer which the Hon. Mrs. Bridget Hoar made him to take what he pleased from the library of her deceased husband. In less than two years also he became owner of a better house and although his flock was now scattered for several months God made it an opportunity for him to preach every Lords day in the other churches and entertain successively the whole city with his enlightening and awakening ministery.

After this fire, complaint was received, December 21, by the General Court, of the danger by fire to which the town was subjected, and praying that Messrs. Richard Callicott, John Cony, William Whitwell, Christopher Clarke, Hopestill Foster, William Ingram, Thomas Smith, and Edward Cowall should be authorized to inspect chimneys and order them repaired or swept, of which the selectmen, at their meeting December 28, highly approved, and added to the list Thomas Blithe, Thomas Fitch, and Samuel Sendall, who had power to call upon any bricklayer to pass his judgment as to the safety of the flue. In the return that was to be made for neglect, those who had not a sufficient ladder were to be included.

The following order of the town reminds us of the complaint of our citizens after the great fire of 1872 : —

Honrd. councill Dec 28 1676. Upon complaint made by the selectmen of Inconvenience of ye straightness of ye streetes latelie laid waist by the fire, it is ordered y^t noe person presume to build their again without the advise & order of ye selectmen till the next Generall Court.

Hanover street was laid out by the following order : —

January 1. 1676–7. At a meeting of the Selectmen with divers of ye inhabitents at ye North End of this town, whose houses were layd wast by the late fire the order of the Honrd Councill foregoinge was read to them, and the Selectmen staked out the Streets and declaired that any man might rebuild his house with their aprobation and consent that should observe the ensuing directions concerninge the Streete. That the West side of the strecte from Maj^r. Thos Clarkes brick wall run to a stake near the corner of Thomas Joys land in that lane wch leads to the place of ye Meeting house & from that stake alonge the s^d west side of the way as now staked out to the corner of Edmund Mountforts foundation, on ye same side of ye way and from the corner of Mr Humphrey Warrens house on the east of the way to a stake in the land of Dan'l Turine Jr. over against y^t at Thomas Joys corner, where the streete is to be 22 feet wide in breadth & soe all alonge the streete to Elmond Montfords 2 houses on each side the way. The line to run from ye stake at Dan'l Turines to another at Henry Cooleys, from thence to Edmond Montforts on the east & soe to the corner of Peter Gees house as now staked out.

The action taken by the selectmen regarding the straightness of the streets was approved by the Council by an act returned to them May 23, 1677 ; but it appears that Thomas Joy was aggrieved by the action, on account of the confiscation of some of his land. His grievance was laid before several gentlemen, who formed a board of arbitration, and they decided that the town pay him 50s. in county pay, and £20 in current money, which proved satisfactory. The widow Bastan was also allowed £5 on August 27, for part of her land, taken also for widening the street.

The selectmen found it expedient to increase the force of fire patrols, or bellmen, March 12. At their next meeting, March 26, Lieut. Richard Way was allowed £4 for the loss of his stable, or out-house, pulled down during the late fire ; and on May 19 the following entry was made : —

That some ord^r. be taken about regulatinge buildings in ye respective townes, y^t by scatteringe they expose not themselves to ye crueltie of ye natives or by their narrow streets to ye dang^r. of fire.

Gunpowder was in the late fire used probably for the first time in the town for blowing up buildings in order to arrest its progress, with what success is not stated; but as it continued to be thought a valuable agent for this purpose many years after, in fact until the present day, it must have its advantages. Captain Everden was paid £3, June 27, 1677, " for half a barrell and twenty pounds of powder used to blow up a house at the North End." Whether this quantity was used for this house alone, the records do not state. If so, it must have been pretty well shattered. The widow Kemble was allowed, on October 29, £60 recompense for her house destroyed in like manner.

About this time many daring attempts were made by incendiaries to destroy the town, and, judging from the methods adopted, they were the studied plans of some secret and determined gang of " fire-bugs."

On January 9, 1677, John Hull records in his Diary that —

A candle was fastened to the roof of a house and burnt through the roof, yet was prevented spreading through the wonderful Providence of God, but the author not known. A barn of Mr. Usher's was burnt about 1 o'clock in the morning of July 5, although his house and other property were saved. August 6. Between two small houses of Mr. Bradons, situated in Shrimpton's Lane (Exchange street), was discovered, about 10 o'clock at night, a lighted candle. About one hour later an attempt was made to set fire to a barn in Usher's Lane (near Atlantic avenue and Bedford street), but the hay, being cut on the salt marsh, smothered, and was discovered in time to prevent it bursting into a blaze.

Several other attempts were made in different sections, but were unsuccessful.

Regarding these incendiaries the General Court, on October 10, passed the following act : —

Whereas many secret attempts have been made by evil-minded persons to set fire to the town of Boston and other places tending to the destruction and devastation of the whole; this Court doth account it their duty to use all lawful means to discover such persons, and prevent the like for time to come.

It was then ordered that all persons, inhabitants or strangers, should take oath of allegiance, which oath was vastly different then to that prescribed in 1652. For this end constables and tithing men were to make a canvass of the town every three months.

Although we can find no record of the fact, it appears that the town voted to send to England for a fire-engine previous to the last large fire, as we find the following interesting order mentioned in their meeting of January 27, 1678 : —

In case of fire in yᵉ towne when there is occation to make use of yᵉ engine lately come from England, Thomas Atkins, carpenter, is desired and doth ingage to take care of the manageinge of the sᵈ engine in yᵉ worke intended & secure it yᵉ best he can from damage & hath made choyce of yᵉ seuerall psons followinge to be his Assistants which are aproved of and are promised to be paid for their pains about the worke. The persons are Obediah Gill, John Raynsford, John Barnard, Thomas Eldridge, Arthʳ Smith, John Mills, Caleb Rawlings, John Wakefield, Samˡˡ Greenwood, Edward Mortimʳ, Thomas Barnard, and George Robinson.

Thus the first engine company in Boston was organized. Thomas Atkins, the captain, was a carpenter of considerable reputation, as we find him contracting with the selectmen, on June 12, 1678, to build a wharf and highway "within five months after the date hereof." This engine was probably of the pattern illustrated on the frontispiece, as these were in use in England at that time. The location of this engine is one often disputed. We have no data concerning it, but we take it for granted that it was stationed in the most thickly settled part of the town. The Book of Possessions will show that the principal buildings were bounded by Hanover, Union, Elm, Washington, Court, Tremont, the water on the south side of State street, Devonshire, Water, the cove and the north side of Fort Hill facing the cove, while State, Court, Hanover, and Elm streets were the most thickly populated; taking these facts into consideration, and from what we can learn from subsequent records, we assume that the engine was lodged in a shed on the town's land on Queen street (Court street), near which was subsequently built the prison, and the engine was given the appellation of " yᵉ Engine by yᵉ Prison."

The terrible work of the incendiaries began to show itself early during the year 1679, which terminated before the next winter in a grand triumph of incarnate desire and ambition, by a most terrible devastation of property. The first of the series of fires began on May 8, when a fire was kindled under Capt. Ben. Edman's warehouse, but was discovered before it got under way. At midnight of the following day the ale-house of Clement Gross, sign of the Three Mariners, near the dock, was discovered to be on fire in an out-room, but was smothered with but little damage. The grand climax, however, was reached at midnight of August 8, when a second and successful attempt was made to fire that house, which in a very short time was wrapped in flames, and soon communicated to building after building, so combustible were their roofs and sides. All the warehouses, with their contents, seventy in number, were laid waste, as were eighty dwelling-houses; in fact, as Gov. Hutchinson states, "it was the most woful desolation that Boston had ever seen." So complete was its ravages that much trouble was experienced by the people in determining the bounds of their estates, as in many places the landmarks were entirely destroyed. The territory laid in ruins extended from the Mill creek, which occupied the same place Blackstone street now does, westerly to Dock square, and southerly to Oliver's dock, which was situated near the place now called Liberty square. Of this district not a single building was left complete, while the loss to shipping was also very large, as all the vessels lying at the Town dock (or Bendall's cove, as it was then called), then situated in the very centre of the district, were burnt. The efforts of the only engine possessed by the town and its company were, we can readily imagine, of very little service ; and, as the company were soon after dismissed, their work could not have been very satisfactory, meagre as it was. As the fire was twelve hours burning, the tide, which was their main dependence for the supply of water, was for a part of the time on the ebb, and the dock left dry, had it not been for the conduit in the immediate vicinity, there is no telling how far the fire would have reached.

The nearest public wells were then located, one at States Arm Tavern, Water street (State street) ; another on the highway leading to Roxbury, or, as it was later called, Cornhill (Washington street), nearly opposite to the Franklin street of to-day ; and Mr. Thomas Venner's pump, near the conduit in Union street, very near the Town dock. The building known as the old Feather Store, which until 1860 stood at the corner of North street and Dock square, was erected in 1680, immediately after the fire. The building owned by Mr. Thomas Stanbury before the fire was a wooden structure, and stood at the corner of the drawbridge facing the Conduit square ; two of its sides faced upon Fishmarket street, which separated it from the dock, but it was destroyed, and on its site the old Feather Store was built. This building was plastered outside with a cement composed, in part, of sand. gravel, and broken glass, two stories high, with a very steep roof, about equal in height to two-thirds of both stories. The timber used for sills, posts, and beams was of oak. The Triangular warehouse was another well-known building erected after this fire, at the corner of North Market street and Merchants row. It was built in 1680, and taken down by the city May 12, 1824, after having bought it from C. Miller, Jr., of New York. The computed loss at this fire amounted to £200,000, or nearly a million dollars, — a loss that would be supposed to take the ardor from the most enthusiastic colonist : but the spirit of progress displayed by them was really wonderful : with such rapidity did they rebuild that the demand for building material was so great that an order was passed, on the 18th of the month, to "prohibit the transportation of boards and other building timber out of the colony for a time." It was considered by the very pious that the destruction was a dispensation of Providence for their sins. Dr. Cotton Mather, in 1698, said in reference to it : —

Ah, Boston ! thou hast seen the vanity of all worldly possessions. One fatal morning, which laid fourscore of thy dwelling houses, and seventy of thy warehouses in a ruinous heap not nineteen years ago, gave them to read it in fiery characters.

The General Court took immediate action on the calamity by framing the following first building act, October 15, 1679 : —

The Court having a sense of the great ruin in Boston by fire and hazzard still of the same by reason of joining and nearness of their buildings, for prevention of damages and loss thereby for future. Do therefor order and enact that henceforth no dwelling-house in Boston shall be erected and set up except of stone or brick and covered with slate or Tyle, on penalty of forfeiting double the value of such buildings, unless by allowance and liberty obtained from the Magistrate, Commissioners and Selectmen of Boston or major part of them, and further the Selectmen of Boston are hereby empowered to hear and determine all controversies about properties and rights of any person to build on the land wherein now lately the housings hath been burnt down, allowing libirty of appeal for any person grieved, to the County Court.

Had this law continued in force we would not in all probability have such a large fire record for our city.

At the same date the incendiaries came in for a share of the law : —

Whereas, the persons hereafter named are under vehement suspicion of attempting to burn the town of Boston, and some of their endeavours prevailed to the burning of one house, and only by God's providence prevented from further damage ; the Court doth order that Edward Creeke, and Deborah, his wife, Hepzibah Codman, John Avis, John Easte, Samuel Doggett, Wm Renny, Richard Heath, Sypron Jarman, and James Dennis, shall depart the jurisdiction and never return, and be kept in prison until ready for their Departure.

Such was the fear of fire that the citizens, on August 18 of the same year, chose a committee, consisting of Capt. John Richards, Doct. Elisha Cooke, Capt. John Wally, Capt. Daniel Hinksman, James Whitcombe, and John Usher, to join with the selectmen to consider and draft an order for the safety of the town against conflagrations. This committee, which was composed of the militia commissioners, adopted the following excellent orders : —

Ordered that the watch of this town shall from Tuesday (26th inst.) be kept by the 8 foot com[panys] each one in theire own quarters or wards of ye towne and that the Gards in each ward be ordered by the commissioned officers of the respective Companies who are so to modell theire shouldiers that a proportionable number of carefull men be on Gard every night. That until further orders theire watch each night: Of Major Thomas Clarkes Company 6 men, of Major Thomas Saveages 6, Capt James Ollivers 5, Capt Wm Hudson 6 and 2 at the Powder Store, Capt Dan^ll Hincksman 5, Capt John Richards 6, Capt John Hull 5, and one at the powder store, and of Capt Humphrey Davies comp^y 5 men. Likewise that the select men provide a fitt man to ward at the powder store from the breaking up of the watch to the sitting thereof. That all watch in their owne persons and every one who by law are to finde arms are to watch.

That the towne be divided in to 4 quarters each one to consist of two wards, and that there be lodged in each quarter 4 Barrels of Powder and 6 hand engines & 2 crookes in each ward which the selectmen are hereby ordered to provide. That the following persons take care and dispose of premises in their respective quarters vizt. in the North quarters con^ts Major Clarkes & Capt Richards com^a, Major Thomas Clark, Capt John Richards, Capt Elisha Hutchinson and Capt Daniell Hinksman.

The conduit quarter con^t Major Tho: Savage & Capt Hinksmans com^a. Mr Wm Taylor, Lt. Danill Turill, Mr Christopher Clark & Lt. Anthony Chickley.

The center quart^r cont^s Capt Ollivers & Capt Davis comp^a, Major Thomas Savage, Mr Anthony Stoddard, Capt Thos. Brattle & Mr. Elisha Cooke.

The South quart^r con^t Capt Hu·lsons & Capt Hulls comp^a, John Joyliff, Capt. John Hull, Capt John Faireweather, Capt John Wally. And that s^d persons or any two of them shall (in case of fire) order the blowing up or pulling downe of houses in any of the quarters, and apoynt fit persons who togeath^r with the constables of each quarter shall be thereabout imployed not excludinge any superior power if present.

From the above we find the origin of the Board of Firewards, which were afterwards established by the General Court, although they are not given that title in this order. The hand-engines mentioned are no doubt some invention of Jenky's, as no water-engine except the " prison " engine was in the town at that time. The governor sat with the commissioners at their next meeting, held on the 9th of September, when they took further action on the matter of fires : —

That in every quarter of ye towne there be 20 Bucketts provided at ye Towne charge, commited to the psons that are to take care of the powder as above also 20 Swobes, 2 Scoopes, & six Axes.

That every family shall be ordered by the selectmen to have a proportion of Bucketts, swabbes, and scoopes accordinge to their estates and that each master of the familie provide the Same within 3 moneths after publication upon penaltie of doble the value of what is wantinge accordinge to this order.

That the selectmen collect all the town orders relating to fire in order to the havinge them pased and printed.

That Mr Isack Addington & John Joyliff p[er]use & put the foregoinge in a right methode fit for the presse togeather with all former orders relating to fire.

That 16 men (two out of each company) doe ward in ye towne every Sabbath day, one of wch is to be on ye top of each meetinge house, to looke abroad for preventinge spreadinge of fire y^t may break out.

A petition to the General Court was then drawn up praying for some order regarding the penalty of incendiaries; also that an abatement of the " last Rate of ye Country wh^{ch} was above 800 ld " be made, on account of the heavy loss of property sustained in the fire.

Peter Lorphelin, a Frenchman, was accused by the Court of Assistants, held September 2, of uttering " rash and insulting speeches in the time of the late conflagration thereby rendering himself justly suspicious of having a hand therein, was seased and committed to the Goale in Boston." His chest and writings were examined. In his chest were found two or three " crusables, a melting pan, a strong pair of shears to clip money, and severall clippings of the Massachusetts money and some other instruments." He denied having ever made use of any of these things, but said they were given him by a privateer. But on being remanded to jail he made up another story, by which he hoped to clear himself; all, however, to no purpose. He was " sentenced to stand two houres in the Pillory, have both ears cut off, give bond of £500 (with two securities), pay charges of prosecution, fees of court, and to stand committed till the sentence be performed." But the reign of the " fire-bugs" seemed to be in no way diminished, as we learn, from " Hull's Diary," that they made a successful attempt on the house of Lieut. Edward Creeks, about 10 o'clock, Sunday, September 7, at a time when the citizens were at church, who, at the alarm, proceeded to the scene ; but the building was entirely destroyed. Although the wind was very strong, no other damage was done. This fire was set in the garret, at a spot several feet from the chimney. The last acts of the selectmen regarding the large fire was the order to pay James Babson, of Cape Ann, twenty shillings for a " roade " taken out of his boat and used to pull down houses. Mr. Peter Sargent was paid, August 30, 1680, for six half-barrels of powder, and Samuel Jackline for three-quarters of a barrel used to blow up houses, while " James Everell and his daughter Maninge " be paid £140 for their building blown up. John Marshall received £10 for the same.

CHAPTER II.

1680–1710.

THE style of architecture after the fire was a decided improvement on the old. The houses were constructed with projecting stories, or jetties, and were ornamented at their corners with pendalls, the outside, as we have before mentioned, being plastered. Brick houses, three stories in height, with arched window-caps, were erected after the passage of the law prohibiting wooden buildings. Towers and gable roofs were introduced about this period. Jasper Dawkers and his comrades, who visited the town in 1680, said: —

> The city is large containing about twelve companies. It has three churches or meeting houses as they call them. All the houses are made of thin small cedar shingles nailed against frames and then filled in with brick and other stuff, and so are their churches. For this reason their towns are so liable to fires — as have already happened several times and the wonder to one is that the whole city has not been burnt down so light and dry are their materials.

The first fire for the year 1680 occurred about 4 o'clock in the afternoon of Sunday, September 19, being discovered in the top of the Old South Meeting-house, in the uppermost private room, or clock tower. It started on the floor and extended up the partition boards to the roof, and got to work on a principal rafter; there it was stopped, just six feet from where it originated. On the 22d of the same month a chimney flamed so as to greatly alarm the people, who, on account of their past suffering, must have been most fearful of the slightest sign of fire. No further damage was done to the building; but we are informed that " a man mounted with a pail the ladder braking," from which he no doubt received a severe shaking up.

At the close of the afternoon service on Sunday, November 16, smoke was discovered in the house of Major William Phillips, but the fire was extinguished without much damage, having only scorched the stanchions of the window. On investigation it was found that chips had been ignited on a window of the cellar, which contained wood and timber.

We do not learn of any other attempt until December 22, when the alarm rang out, about 4 o'clock in the morning, on the discovery of flames in the dwelling-house of Mr. Sampson Sheeaff. So rapidly did it spread that some of the occupants were cut off from the stairs, and had to leap from the chamber windows; but no accident occurred. Two adjoining buildings were consumed, and Goodman Dorset's house was blown up, for which act he received, on October 6, 1681, £50 from the town. Before this fire had been extinguished a ship owned by Michael Page, lying at Capt. Benjamin Gilham's wharf (Town dock), caught on fire from a defective hearth. The citizens had a hard battle, and before it was subdued, it did considerable damage to the vessel and Mr. Gilham's warehouse. A man named Jeremie Mather, who was at work in the building, was blown into the cellar, and received a broken thigh and severe contusions about the head.

The selectmen petition the Court, on February 13, 1683, for an abatement of these rates, on account of the ravages of this fire, which consumed several thousand pounds' value of property, whereby many of the former wealthy citizens were left impoverished and dependent on the town for relief. This plea was granted to all, not exceeding twenty-five pounds.

The work next accomplished by this band of criminals was on February 1, 1681, when they fired the house of Benjamin Negus, which adjoined William Kent's. This was set on the roof, near the top, about 10 o'clock in the morning; but a heavy rain falling, and the engine company, who were assisted by the members of the County Court, then sitting in the Town-House close by, being quickly on hand, it was soon quenched.

A negro woman of Mr. Lamb, of Roxbury, being indignant at some wrong done her, took revenge by setting her master's and Mr. Swan's houses on fire, at midnight of July 12, 1681. The flames spread so rapidly that all the family escaped with difficulty, except one girl, who perished in the flames. The incendiary was found guilty, and publicly burned to death, at Boston, on September 22 following. She was the first to suffer such a penalty in New England. The next serious conflagration to which the engine was called was one that occurred on October 24, 1682, in the vicinity of the dock, and burnt as far as the south of Drawbridge street (North street), which district was considered the richest in town, and did a vast amount of damage. Edward Randolph arrived on the day before, bringing with him the hated *Quo warranto*, and it was reported that the fire was the work of his tools; but it is probable that this rumor was circulated by his enemies to incite the inhabitants against him.

During the first part of December the almshouse, towards the building of which Henry Webb gave £100, on the condition that it should be rebuilt in case it was burnt down, was consumed. The selectmen, at their meeting on the 18th of that month, ordered that "a work-house be provided in some convenient place in this town."

Captain Atkins could not have continued in charge of the water-engine very long after his appointment, as on March 26, 1683, we find the following entered in the records : —

Ralph Carter moveing that he may be excused from traininge & watchinge for takinge care of and keeping the Engine in good order upon occation of fire breakinge out, he is allowed 20s. in money p. ann. upon that consideration, & he to get himselfe cleare from traininge & watching as well as he can.

Carter must have been in charge fully a year previous to the above order, as on

January 21, 1683, Ralph Carter moves to be allowed for his lookinge to the Engine formerlie. It was agreed at a meeting of all the selectmen this day that he be allowed 30s. in money for the time past until March 26ᵗʰ last and to have 20s. per an. for the time to come.

Another order, passed on May 28, says : —

Agreed with Ralph Carter that himself and 7 others (one man out of each company of the trainer bands) should take the care and charge of the water Engine to keep it in good order and be ready upon all occation, to attend the use & service thereof, when said Carter shall require it or there be any noyse of fire breaking out in any part of this town. In consideration whereof by yᵉ concent of the several captains of this town they shall be exempted from training and are to attend the said service upon the penalty the law fixeth for not training. The several persons are as follows. Ralph Carter, Edward Budd, Richard Knight, Sampson Dure, Wᵐ. Dutton, Wᵐ. Paine, —— Smith, Samuel East and Peter Oadline.

The building law of 1676 was repealed on November 7, 1683, and an act passed prohibiting the erection of any classes of buildings of wood, on penalty of £100, while the selectmen were to determine the question of boundaries of property in burnt districts. An addition was made to this law on the 3d of the month, to encourage the building of brick and stone, as follows : —

It is ordered and enacted, that whosoever shall so build shall have libirty to set half his partition-wall in his Neighbours Ground, leaving jagges on the corners of such walls for the Neighbours to adjoyn their Building to; and that when the same shall be Built unto, the Neighbours Adjoining shall pay for half the wall so far as the same shall Adjoyne. And in case of Difference, that the Select Men have power to appoint persons to make valuation or lay out the line between such Neighbours.

So sweeping were the measures in this law that the erection of necessary small buildings, such as out-houses, etc., were prohibited, so that an amendment was made January 28, 1684, making it lawful to erect buildings of wood of not more than eight feet square and seven feet high, provided permission was granted by the selectmen.

A petition from the proprietors of the land lying in the burnt district of 1682 was received by the selectmen, on which they voted favorably, March 10, 1683–4, requesting that the highway leading from the entrance to the dock to Mr. Nowell's corner on the east may be laid out at once, for the best interest of the public for the future, and not to be altered for many years, as they intended building with brick.

On account of the thorough extermination of landmarks, etc., by the fire of 1679, several disputes arose among the holders of estates within the district over which the flames swept, and the selectmen were called upon to exercise the power vested in them by the Court, November 7, 1683, " to determine controversies relating to the boundaries of land laid waist by fire." Mr. Joshua Winsor, Mrs. Joyce Hall, and Pilgram Simkins were the principals in a dispute, May 27, 1684, which was determined by the decision that Winsor had built on one-half of the land belonging to Hall and Simkins.

On March 5, 1684-5, " Priviledge were granted by the Selectmen to Capt. John Winge, Lt. Isaack Walker, Mr. Nath^ll. Williams & Mr. Thomas Stanbury, on behalf of themselves and their neighbors," to take the water from the conduit, which had overrun into the street, and convey it by pipes laid under the ground to a cistern at the head of the dock between Winge's and Stanbury's houses (Winge kept the Castle Tavern, and Stanbury had just erected the famous "old Feather Store "), for the benefit of the associates in the enterprise and for the benefit of the town in case of fire. The cost was to be defrayed entirely by the company, with the privilege that if any damage was rendered to the well while in public use it should be made good by the town.

The building law of November 7, 1683, was broken the ensuing year by Thomas Baker, who erected a wooden building, for which he was fined £100 by the County Court; but, on his petition, the fine was returned.

The several orders relating to the stopping of fire and use of gunpowder in the blowing up of buildings, acted upon by the selectmen at previous dates, were endorsed by the Council on July 22, 1686, and on September 28 Messrs. Robert Howard, William Rowse, and —— Comer were appointed to take the place of the deceased members of the committee who had charge of looking after powder, inspection of chimneys, and the blowing up of buildings.

The old engine company seemed to have trouble with the town authorities, just as did their successors nearly two centuries later; but we are at a loss to know the cause of these early difficulties. At any rate, on August 21, 1686, it was

Ordered that Ralph Carter and comp^a concerned wth him in the water Engine be discharged from any care thereof, and that John Joyliffe be desired to send for the Key of the house where ye said Engine is Kept & to demand & to receave all other things belonging to the Towne and were und^r the care and charge of s^d Carter, and that the s^d Engine & things belonginge to it be delivered and committed to the care and direction of Capt. John Faireweather & Mr. Edward Willis until further Order^s.

On Wednesday, December 8, a petition was sent in to the Council, praying for a committee to investigate and adopt some method for the relief of the many poor of the town, made so by the Indian wars, the fire, and failure of trade. Chimney-sweeps were appointed by the town, who were to be fined for neglect of duty, and to have the inspectors oversee their work; none others were to exercise that calling.

On March 24, 1689, the office of Overseer of Chimneys was created, and John Coney, Sr., William Rowse, Edward Cowell, and Nehemiah Peirce were appointed, while John Stride, Joseph Dayes, and Jeremiah the Negro were made chimney-sweeps.

Some of the towns-people must have been loth to pay the fine imposed on them for flaming chimneys, as on March 11, 1689–90, John Marshall, the constable, was to take the amount from their estates. Mr. Abraham Blish was appointed on the board of chimney inspectors on this date, and from this time until the succeeding century we find a regular election of this committee, also of chimney-sweeps.

The next extensive conflagration that the citizens were called to witness in this town was on August 11, 1690. This fire originated at a building located at the Mill bridge (Hanover, near Blackstone, street), and laid in ruins twenty buildings; three others were blown up, by which, Winthrop states, " it was stopped wonderfully." Of this fire Judge Sewall, in his Diary, says : —

Val Malum. About 2 o'clock after midnight a fire breaks out in the other side of the mill creek, which gets over to this side and consumes about 14 Dwelling Houses, besides warehouse. Madame Leverett & Mrs. Rock are great sharers in the loss.

Another, making the fifth great fire, occurred on the 15th of October of the same year, when, beginning near the Old South Meeting-house, it consumed a number of buildings, among them being the printing-office of Bartholomew Green, which he had just established. The single number of the "Public Occurrances," issued a few weeks later, speaking of it, says, "One of the considerable circumstances in the calamity of the fire," that the " best furnished printing-press of those few that we know of in America are lost — a loss not presently to be repaired." His premises, located at the corner of Avon and Washington streets, was again completed in two years, and was the first permanent press in the town. The Old South Meeting-house had a narrow escape from the flames. A youth residing in the adjoining house, where the fire started, was burnt to death.

Nearly a year later, Saturday, August 2, 1691, another disastrous fire broke out at the King's Head, near Scarlett's wharf (foot of Fleet street), about 6 o'clock, and before it was extinguished it had consumed fourteen dwellings, together with several warehouses and brewhouses, extending from the Mill bridge half-way to the drawbridge (North street). Among the sufferers of this fire were Giles Fyfeild and William Everden, the former receiving £60 and the latter £45, in payment for their buildings which were blown up, while Richard Whiteraye was paid £20 for personal injuries, besides being permitted to keep a public house and sell liquor.

In 1692 a law was passed forbidding the erection of any wooden building over eight feet in length and seven in height; and in 1700 an act recites that this provision has been constantly set aside, and while it would be too severe a punishment to destroy all that has been erected, yet that such bold and open contempt might not pass wholly unpunished, and to deter others from doing the like in future, a fine was imposed, not exceeding £50 for an offence, on all who had so offended. The gunpowder treason plot day furnished the same anxiety then that the fourth of July does now, and a proclamation was ordered, November 4, 1700, "To Prevent endangering the Town by fireworks." (Laws of the Prov. of Mass. Bay, March 23, 1696–1700.)

At the first regular town-meeting, held March 7, 1700, it was ordered "that the selectmen are desired to get the water-engin for the quenching of fire repaired as also the house for keeping the same in." Also that they "take care to procure and provide two water-engines suitable for the extinguishing of fire, either by sending for them to England or otherwise to provide them for the use of this town." These engines did not arrive until 1707. It was only two days after the order was passed that the seventh great fire startled the inhabitants. This conflagration originated in a building near the dock, and destroyed a large amount of valuable property. Three warehouses were blown up to stay its progress, for which were used six half-barrels, less six quarts, of powder, belonging to Capt. John Miles, which amount was ordered to be refunded to that gentleman by the selectmen at their first meeting after the new choice, March 13. Dr. Trasher was allowed 30 shillings for his expenses at the fire.

At the general meeting held September 22, 1701, the several rules, orders, and by-laws of the town were openly read and passed upon; among them the several orders relating to fires, which were framed at different periods, were rewritten and ordered to be printed. In the new rules we find that one shilling was the fine for carrying fire from house to house in an open vessel, while in the matter of defective chimneys they were to be repaired, or, if need be, taken down, on pain of 10 shillings per month for so long as they remain in an unsatisfactory condition. Ship-carpenters, coopers, and ropemakers were the only ones allowed to build a fire within two rods of any building, and they were to have a man standing by to attend the same. Twenty pounds of powder was the limited quantity to be kept in any building. No person was allowed to erect or burn any brick or lime kiln except in such place as allowed by the selectmen.

January 26, a new pump was ordered, and placed in the conduit by the dock, near Wing's lane, at the expense of the town, for use in case of fire; but it was not until after June 28, the year following, that it was procured. On March 30, 1702–3, the proposal offered to the selectmen for preserving the Town-House from fire was approved and recommended to the Council. Capt. Timothy Clark was appointed to examine the powder set apart by the town for use in case of fire; and Seth Perry was chosen to warn the inhabitants that they must provide themselves with the necessary fire apparatus required by the town. May 25, this same body urged their representative to the General Council to lay the circumstances of the town relating to the loss by the late fire, the decay of trade, and the extra town charge on account of the increase of poor; also to endeavor to obtain an abatement of the next provincial tax; to promote the building of one or more powder-houses, and to oblige all persons to keep their stock confined therein at a fixed rental. The bills of repairs to the engine were sent to the selectmen July 27, and they ordered James Jarvis £3, and Thomas Gold £7, for their work. Thomas Gill tried to make an extra dollar on account of the fire, by sending in a bill for twenty-nine dozen pails which he claims to have furnished; but the selectmen, on September 15, ordered him to be paid £6 for twelve dozen, which they thought was the correct number used.

The training of engine companies was adopted on December 28, 1705, by the following order : —

The several persons nominated by ye selectmen and by his Excellency the Govr by an order under his hand exempt from ordinary training & watching, upon their daily attending the service of the Towne in managing the watter engine are by the selectmen ordered to meet at the place where the say'd engine is lodged, upon the last Monday of every Month at three of the clock in the afternoon and to exercise themselves in the use of s^d Engine as the selectmen shall from time to time direct. And also that in the case of the breaking out of fires in the Towne then with all possible speed to repair unto s^d Engine and with their best skill and industry to manage the same for the extinguishing of the fires in order to the preservation of the Towne. And Henry Deering is desired and appointed as a master of s^d Comp^a to take notice and make report of any who shall neglect the due attendance of their s^d trust.

By this appointment we find the third foreman of the engine. There was some confusion regarding the proprietorship of a great amount of goods rescued from the dock fire. Owners not applying for them, they were stored, under the town's care, until April 5, when, by order of the Council, they were sold at auction, and the proceeds placed to the credit of the town, for relief of the poor.

In Sewall's Diary, under date of August 29, 1704, we find the following interesting entry : —

At South Church. Mr. Thomas Bridge pray^d; Mr. Pemberton preached : just as had done his sermon and stood up to pray a cry of fire was made, by which means the assembly was broke up, but it pleased God the fire was wonderfully quenched. The wind was so'wardly, so that if it had proceeded from the Blue Tavern [kept by George Monk on Washington Street nearly opposite Williams Court], probably the old Meeting House must have been consumed and a great part of the town beside. Ministers expressed great thankfulness in the afternoon for this deliverance.

From which it will be seen that an alarm of fire was sufficient to empty the churches of their congregation, and cause the greatest joy when it was quickly extinguished.

Messrs. Daniel Oliver, Gyles Dyer, and Thomas Fitch were appointed by the selectmen, on October 18, to agree with some person in the town to bring over one engine, together with some brass-work and other material suitable for " fixing " another, the charges to be paid by the town treasurer. The gentlemen fulfilled their trust by sending Capt. David Mason to England, on the 30th, to procure one engine and material to make another. From this we would infer that the citizens desired to try and make one themselves, and gave up their original intention of importing two that were complete.

The chimney on the building known as the Rose and Crown Tavern, situated near the Town-House, was complained of by Thomas Atkins and John Kneland, September 28, 1705. Being dangerous, it was ordered to be repaired. Atkins filled several public positions after his discharge from the engine company.

The engines arrived some time during 1707, as we find an order, dated February 18, desiring Capt. Thomas Hutchinson " to procure a hammer a lanthorne & a rope for each of the two new water-engines." The completed engines were imported, despite the agreement recorded on October 30, 1704; but as to who composed the company we cannot state, as no record of them can be found. On September 8, however, Capt. Thomas Hutchinson, Stephen Minot, and Joseph Prout were chosen to wait upon Governor Dudley, with the following petition from the selectmen : —

Whereas the Towne of Boston is now provided with three water engines commodious for the extinguishment of fires and your petitioners holding themselves conserned to appoint and improve a competent number of apt persons of the inhabitint of said town to have the principal care of managing said engine so as may best answer the use and intent whereof, and for as much as the persons so appointed to said service must necessarily spend their time in that exercise. Your petitioners do therefore pray that the number of 24 men such as they shall from time to time appoint and employ in said service may be exempt from attending duty at ordinary training and military watches as are equivallent to the ordinary duty enjoyned on them in their exercise of s^d engine.

The style of these engines was very much the same as used in the town for a number of years after. They were constructed of wood, with iron hoops. Henry Dering, during this year, offered the following motion regarding the engines : —

Wherin the Lord in his merciful Providence hath provided this Town with three engines, you may go on & be in the way of yor good and Pass a vote for about forty Pounds to be laid out for such things as are Necessary for to accommodate the said engians to facilitate the ends that they are provided for. And also to procure other things that will be necessary to use in the Quick stoping, and Preventinge the Spreadinge of fire in this Town in case it should break out.

And Likewise that you now make your choice and appoynt some men to be a committee to model a skeme of all things needfull to be done in This affaire and Present it to the Towne for their consideration And further Determination of what shall be done in the use of Means for the Safety and Good of the Towne as God shall Direct.

March 3, Capt. Timothy Clark was ordered to deliver two barrels of the town's powder to Thomas Palmer and Capt. Thomas Fitch, who were on the committee to discuss fire matters. This powder was to be kept in readiness for blowing up houses, until further orders from the authorities.

A house was built joining the north watch-house for the accommodation of one of the engines, but was ordered, on May 19, to be removed and placed to join on the north side of this house; for what purpose this trouble was incurred we cannot surmise. Inspectors were regularly appointed to examine houses, and to report in writing a breach of the town order respecting ladders, chimneys, etc., while the usual complaints were made against unsafe bakers' ovens and chimneys. Among those fined this year for the latter offence were Samuel Baley, Gilbert Burt, John Buck, William Thomas, William Obbinson, Mr. Cotton Mather, Benjamin Gallop, Peter Barbour, Edward Joseph, Davis and Mattox Bridgham, Samuel Mould, Jonathan Mountfort, Isaak Knight, which amounted to £10, one-half of which was given to James Maxwell, the inspector.

The General Court this year issued their first order regarding gunpowder, by which all of that material landed in this port — except fifty pounds in a store, and the ordinary supply of the government — be put in the powder-house, located on the common, or training field.

Sheriff Dyer took rather an unusual amount of authority on himself by appointing masters to the two new engines, for which act the selectmen became indignant, and on February 28, 1708, issued the following order: —

Whereas the water engines being the goods and chattle of this Towne, and under the care and direction of the selectmen thereof, who are now informed y^t Mr. Sheriff Dyer without the knowledge or advise of ye s^d select men hath appointed Edward Pell, and Thomas Hunt to attend the service of the s^d engines. Ordered that s^d Pell and Hunt be dismissed from ye s^d service and selectmen appoint persons thereunto.

Another fire broke forth on the morning of September 8, 1708, for an account of which Sewall's Diary is quoted: —

Last night we were alarmed between 2 & 3 in the night. I looked out of the South East window and feared that our warehouse was afire. But it proved a smithshop; Hubbards by Mr. Dastom's and a Boat-Builders shed; tis thought a hundred pounds damage is done. Blessed be God it stopped there. Mr. Pemberton's maid saw the light of the fire reflected from a black cloud and came crying to him under consternation supposing the last conflagration had begun.

We take also the account, from the same source, of a fire in his own house: —

Mid week July 13 1709. N.B Last night between 2 and 3 hours after midnight my wife complained of smoke. I presently went out of bed and saw and felt the chamber very full of smoke, to my great consternation. I slipt on my clothes except stockings and run out of one room into another, above and below stairs, and still found all well with my own bed chamber. I went into garret and roused up David, who fetched me a candle. My wife feared the brick side was afire and the children endangered. She fled thither and called me up there. While she was doing this I felt the partition of my bed chamber closet warm; which made me with fear to unlock it. And going in I found the Deal Box of wafers all afire burning lively; yet not blazing. I drew away the paper next to it and called for a bucket of water. By that time it came I had much adoe to recover the closet again. But I did and threw my water on it, and so more, and quenched it thoroughly. Thus with great indulgence God save our house and substance and the companies papers. This night as I lay down in my bed I said to my wife that the Godness of God appeared in that we had a chamber a Bed and company. If my wife had not waked me we might have been consumed. And it seems admirable that the opening of the closet door; did not cause the flame to burst out into an unquenchable flame. The Box was 18 inches over, closet full of loose papers, boxes, cases, some powder. The window curtains was of stubborn woolen and refused to burn though the iron bars were hot with the fire. Had they burnt it would have fired the pine shelves and files of paper and flasks and Bandaliers of powder. The pine floor on which the box stood was burnt deep but being well plastered between the joysts it was not burnt through. The closet under it had hundreds of reams of the companies paper in it. [Probably the paper belonging to the Society for Propagating the Gospel, for printing the Indian Bible.] The plastered wall is marked by fire as to resemble a chimney back. Although I forbid mine to cry fire; yet quickly after I had quenched it, the chamber was full of Neighbors and water. The smell of fire pressed me very much which lasted some days. We imagine a mouse might have taken our lighted candle out of the candle-stick and hearth and drag it under my closet door behind the box of wafers.

The question of flaming chimneys was one of importance, and caused the strictest vigilance on the part of the authorities, who frequently issued orders and imposed fines on the careless. On November 13, 1710, they ordered advertisments to be posted for chimney-sweeps; applicants were to meet the selectmen " on several more days following at five of the clock in the afternoon," to agree upon terms. Messrs. Richard Proctor and John Corkson were appointed to carry on the business for seven years. Sewall, writing of his chimney on November 29, says that the " Northern chimney on the new house fell a fire and blazed out extremely which made a great uprore as is usual."

" Thursday, January 17, 1711, a fire broke out in Marlborough street [Washington street], in a bakehouse at widow Gray's, and the widow Brightman's dwelling adjoining was burnt, including the bread warehouse of the former. Dr. Cutler's house was saved by hard work."

Despite the constant care and watchfulness, and the increased force of fire apparatus, the greatest and most disastrous conflagration yet witnessed in the town broke out at 7 o'clock on the evening of October 2, 1711. A poor Scottish woman, named Mary Morse, residing in a tenement owned by Capt. Ephraim Savage, situated in a back-yard in Cornhill, near the First Meeting-house, was engaged in picking over oakum, near which she used fire, and by some means the flame communicated with the combustible matter which she was handling, and before she could extinguish it or give an alarm it had got beyond control, and, being a time of great drought and the building very dry, the flames spread from building to building until both sides of Cornhill (part of Washington street) were laid in ruins. From there it extended to School street, to Dock square, the greater part of Pudding lane (Devonshire street) between Water street and Spring lane, and both sides of the upper part of King and Queen streets, sweeping everything in its path. In all, there were consumed about one hundred houses, some of which were very capacious buildings; in fact, the district was the most thickly settled and wealthiest part of the town, being filled with stores and dwellings. Among these ruins was the post-office, then located on Washington, near State, street, — it was rebuilt August 23, 1713, — and two spacious edifices which had made a most imposing appearance, because of the public relations to our greatest solemnities, in which they had stood from the days of our fathers. These were the old meeting-house (Washington, near Court, street) and the Town-House (the site of the old State-House), from which some gentlemen rescued the Queen's picture. One hundred and ten families were rendered homeless, for the relief of whom contributions were collected at the various churches, amounting to £700, £260 of which were given by the members of the Old South Church. When the old meeting-house was found to be in danger several sailors ascended to the steeple for the purpose of saving the bell; but so rapidly did the flames advance that their retreat was cut off. Just before the roof fell they were seen trying to get out, but could not, and were burned to death; their bones being found afterward. Increased horror was added to the scene by blowing up buildings, by which act several other citizens were killed, while many afterwards died from wounds received. A house of Judge Sewall, occupied by Seth Dwight, who " paid 20 pounds per annum rent," was burnt. Lieut.-Governor Taylor, who arrived the next day, said he saw the fire twenty leagues' distance; it was under control at 2 o'clock on the morning of the 3d.

> Thus the town of Boston, just going to get beyond fourscore years of age, and conflicting with much labor and sorrow, is, a very vital and valuable part of it, soon cut off and flown away!

Increase Mather improved the occasion in a sermon entitled " Burnings Bewayled." In it he said: —

> But has not God's Holy Day been prophaned in New England? Has it not been so in Boston this last summer, more than ever since there was a Christian here? Have not burdens been carried through the streets on the Sabbath day? Have not Bakers, Carpenters and other tradesmen been employed in servile work on the Sabbath day? When I saw this . . . my heart said Will not the Lord for this kindle a fire in Boston?

On the 18th of the month, in consequence of the fire and the failure of the expedition sent against Canada, a general fast was kept.

The work of clearing away the ruins was soon commenced, and the rubbish was used to fill up Long wharf, then being built. Three-story brick buildings were afterwards erected, with a garret, a flat roof, and a balustrade. Shurtleff's " Boston " says: —

The mode of laying bricks had its fashionable period. The earliest style was the old English bond, which consisted of courses of brick laid lengthwise alternating with others lying endwise. A more common style then succeeded, instead of a row of bricks laid endwise after every seventh laid lengthwise. About the time of the Revolution a very neat style was commenced known as the Flemish bond, in which every row was laid with alternate bricks lengthwise and endwise, which continued until the present century, when the present mode, that of the long edge exposed, was adopted. A style lasts a little more than a century. The olden house had a large chimney in the centre. This afforded all the rooms with a fireplace and the kitchen with an oven and an ash-pit.

Nicholas Boon and several other sufferers by the fire petitioned the selectmen, on October 1, to erect temporary wooden buildings on their land, which would enable them to carry on their business; but were refused, " for other reasons respecting the good & benefit of y* Town." The 15th of this month Edward Hutchinson was ordered to take care of the town lead saved out of the ruins, and have it cast into bullets for the town. He was also to take into his custody all uncalled-for goods saved from the flames. A proclamation was issued by the governor the day after, requesting all persons having goods rescued from the fire to send them to Arthur Jeffrey at the brick warehouse of Andrew Belcher, Esq., situated at the dock, who was in daily attendance for that purpose.

October 17 the selectmen asked for the ten barrels of powder belonging to the Province. " What was expended to save the Meeting House and Town House had not that effect, yet that it did at last obtain as a means to put a stop to the spreading of the fire to the other parts of the town which is a benefit to the public." This shows that they had great faith in this means for controlling fires. The Old Corner Bookstore located at the corner of Washington and School streets was erected immediately after this fire; it is the only building of that date standing.

On the 31st the town was divided into fire districts, under the management of firewards, which office was created by the following act of the General Court at this date : —

AN ACT *providing in case of fire for the more speedy extinguishment thereof, and for the preserving of goods endangered thereby.*

Whereas, by reason of the contiguity and adjoining of the houses and dwellings within the town of Boston, persons are under great affrightment and hurry upon the breaking out of fire, and not only the person in whose house the fire first breaks out, but the neighbourhood, are concerned to employ their utmost diligence and application to extinguish the fire and prevent the progress thereof, and to preserve their substance by the removal of their goods, being glad of the assistance of others in that regard, and divers evilminded and wicked persons, on pretence of charitable offering their help, taking advantage of such confusion and calamities to rob, plunder, embezzle, convey away and conceal the goods and effects of their distressed neighbours,

For preventing whereof,

Be it enacted by his excellency the governor council and representatives, in general court assembled, and by the authority of the same, that it shall and may be lawful to and for the justices of the peace and selectmen of the town of Boston from time to time to appoint such number of prudent persons of known fidelity not exceeding ten, in the several parts of the Town, as they may think fit who shall be denominated and called Fire-Wards, and have a proper badge assigned to distinguish them in their office, a staff of five feet in length coulered red, and headed with a bright brass spire of six inches long, and at times of the breaking forth of fire and during the continuance thereof, shall, and hereby are fully authorized and empowered to command and require assistance for the extinguishing and putting out the fire, and for removing of household stuff furniture, goods and merchandize out of any dwelling-houses store-houses or other buildings actually on fire or in danger thereof and guards to secure and take care of the same, as also to require assistance for the pulling down or blowing up of any houses or any other service relating thereto by the direction of two or three of the chief civil or military officers of the Town, as is by law provided. to stop and prevent the further spreading of the fire, and to suppress all tumults and disorder.

And the officers from time to time appointed as aforesaid are required upon the notice of fire breaking forth, taking their badge with them, immediately to repair to the place, and vigorously to exert their authority for the requiring of assistance, and using utmost endeavours to extinguish or prevent the spreading of the fire and to preserve and secure the estate of the inhabitants; and due obedience is required to be yeilded to them and each of them accordingly for that service.

And all disobedience, neglect or refusal in any, shall be informed of to some of her majesty's justice of the peace within two days next after, and the offenders therein, upon conviction thereof, before any two justices, quorum unus, shall forfeit and pay the sum of forty shillings each, to be levied and distributed by the discretion of the selectmen amongst the poor most distressed by fire, and in case the offender or offenders are unable to satisfy the fine, then to suffer ten days imprisonment.

And be it further enacted by the authority aforesaid, that if any evil minded wicked person shall take advantage of such calamity to rob plunder purloin, embezzle, convey away or conceal any goods, merchandizes or effects of the distressed inhabitants whose houses are on fire or endangered thereby and put upon removing their goods. and shall not restore and give notice thereof to the owner or owners, if known, or bring them into such publick place as shall be appointed and assigned by the governor and council, within the space of two days next after proclamation made for that purpose, the person or persons, so offending, and being thereof convicted shall be deemed thieves and suffer the utmost severities of the pain and penalties by the law provided against such.

The first board to fill this office were " Capt. Jn° Ballentine, Capt. Timothy Clark, Capt. Edw^a Winslow, Capt. Edw^a Martyn, Stephen Minot, Sam^{ell} Greenwood, John Greenough, J. Pollard, Thomas Lee, and Wm Lowder." (See autographs.)

At a meeting of the justices and selectmen, December 20, £230 was voted for the enlargement of the highway along the west district (probably to Washington street); they also determined upon the petition of the sufferers from having their buildings blown up to be recompensed as the law allowed. They, therefore, granted the following: —

Thomas Brattle, £35; Eliza Maccarthy, £60; Eliza Powning, £35; James Meers, £25; Martha Guin, £25; Mr. Smallpiece, £50; Sarah Dudley, £10; Richard Proctor, £10; and Francis Holmes, £8; and John Smallpiece, £50, for bodily hurt from buildings blowing up by powder.

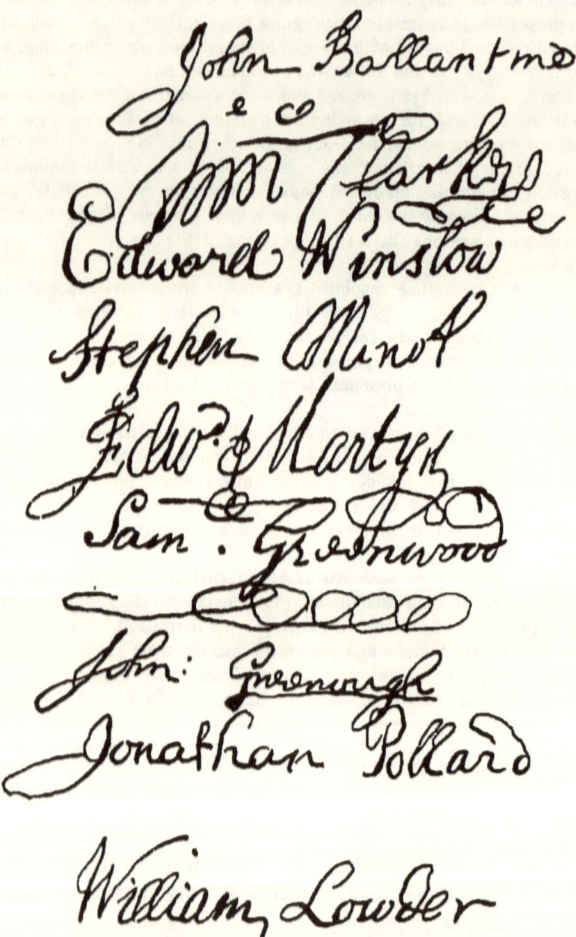

AUTOGRAPHS OF FIRST BOARD OF FIREWARDS.

CHAPTER III.

1711–1739.

A N order was given on January 21, 1711–12, for "three groce of pails for use in case of fire;" and on the 28th of the same month an order was issued by the selectmen creating the office of Superintendent or Overseer of the Fire Department.

> James Peirson to be overseer of the persons listed to attend the water engines, and that they and every one of the persons in ye said list are requested to attend their duty therein and to observe & attend the order & directions of the s^d James Peirsons in the management of s^d engines.

On the 18th of the following month it was ordered that the town-meeting be held at the house of Rev. Mr. Colman, on Monday, March 10, when action was taken regarding relief of the poor; also to grant money for rebuilding the Town-House, " and other extraordinary charges occasioned by the late fire." The Town-House was built of brick the following year. Strict measures were taken for the prevention of chimneys taking fire, and licensed sweeps were permitted to charge the following prices: For each chimney of five stories high, 18 pence; four stories, 14 pence; three stories, 10 pence; and of all other common chimneys, 8 pence. And if any servant, or any other than those permitted by the selectmen, undertook to do this work they were fined 20 shillings, while any who refused to have them swept after an inspection were fined 5 shillings for every day a fire was kept in them; and if they blazed out within fifteen days after being swept, the sweep was to pay 10 shillings.

Mr. Maryon offered the following proposal : —

> Whether it would not be convenient for the town to have as many publick Wells & as far distant from one another as the Selectmen shall see meet & y^t they be made not by any publick rate but that every man Should pay a due proportion towards them, and a good well at the East end of the Town House at a pretty good distance in the middle of the St.
>
> 2. Whether it would not be convenient that every owner of a House should provide one Bucket with his name set thereon and that men Should be chosen to look after them y^t if any Bucket should be broken or lost they should at the Town charge procure another with persons name thereon & deliver it to him, so that after every owner of an House has provided a Bucket y^t after that they should be provided at the publick charge.
>
> 3. Whether it be not convenient that the Tything Men should have the power of Constables (during the time of fire) to empty Folkes houses of their goods by a Guard & to deliver them to a Guard that shall take care of them, and in case the Fire spread to remove them (by a Guard) from one place to another.

4. Whether it would not be convenient that all Women and children should be kept out of any lane, or St. where the Fire is, only them that are concerned.

Some of those motions were afterward dismissed.

The selectmen, on November 10, 1712, offered to pay 40 shillings to the putting of the conduit in Ann street, to help defray the expense of conveying waste water underground into the dock; and on December 20, 1713, complaint was made against the conduit nigh the Mill bridge, owned by John Ballintine, a fireward, that it was open at the top, therefore dangerous: it was ordered to be covered, or to have battlements placed around it. Liberty was granted, on October 7, 1714, to Thomas Goose and William Tyler, wardens of the Ann-street conduit, to open the highway to make repairs.

Sewall, in his Diary, has the following interesting entry, under date of January 19, 1713: —

Great storm of Snow began about 3 P.M. yesterday. Last night about midnight was a dreadful cry of fire, which was stopped at Mr. Blonts work house where it began: June 30. Last night Dr. Noyes house was endangered of being burnt. About 5 in the morning there was a cry of fire: Bells rung, Mr. J. Sewell came to my bed chamber door and acquainted us. But quickly after rising the Bells left off ringing and I saw no light. Mr. Webb's malt house near Mr. Bronsdon's was burnt down. Twas a great mercy that the fire was not spread to North End. Part of the house of Mr. Bronsdon the landlord began to burn.

An advertisement was issued June 2, 1713, desiring all persons having any of the town library, or those who could give information regarding any of the books or other things belonging to the Town-House, which were removed during the fire, to notify the town treasurer. On the 16th of the month Samuel Bridge and Capt. Thomas Barnerd were appointed to make a thorough inspection regarding ladders, and to prosecute all transgressors of the law.

A house in Back street (Salem street), occupied as a tallow-chandler shop by Mr. Blunt, was entirely destroyed by fire, February 14, 1714.

A large number of fines for flaming chimneys, and orders regarding the same, were issued during the past year; and on June 14 Richard Proctor and John Cookson were empowered to make prosecution against those who should sweep chimneys without a license.

August 6, Edward Winslow and Capt. Ed. Martyn, firewards, were ordered to provide poles, with hooks and axes, and to decide on a proper place for the storage of the town's powder for use in case of fire, also as to where the town's pails should be placed; and on August 10 Henry Bridgham was appointed to prosecute the breakers of the Ladder Law. A fire at Dr. Clark's house at the North End, on October 20, nearly destroyed the building. The firewards were empowered by the selectmen, on October 25, with full control of the engines and authority at fires. These gentlemen, who were men of the highest standing, and had the town's welfare always at heart, saw the necessity of more engines to rely upon in those dangerous scenes over which they were to engineer; they, therefore, on November 30, recommended to the selectmen the purchase of another engine. A stranger in the town had one to sell, and as it was the eve of his departure for another section, the town authorities bought it for £100, which sum they were compelled to borrow, as the treasury did not contain that amount.

On Wednesday, November 3, fire entirely destroyed warehouses Nos. 18 and 19, on Long wharf, together with a large stock of valuable merchandise, the property of Walter Newbury and Ebenezer Coffin. On the morning of the 18th, between 12 and 1 o'clock, a fire broke out in the warehouse of Messrs. Oliver & Welstud, in Merchants row, which destroyed that building and the Impost Office, kept by Mr. Russell, many books of which office were lost, together with a large quantity of goods. Much difficulty was experienced in stopping the spread of the fire, and several men were injured.

Thomas Gill was allowed £10, on March 8, 1714–15, "for the payment of pails taken from him during the fire during October and November last."

Again did the firewards urge the necessity of more engines, and were supported by the selectmen; for on June 7, 1715, we find that £180 were granted to defray the expenses of two water-engines, which had already been sent after to England. An increase in the number of ladders was also ordered. These engines arrived soon after, as we find an order on June 21, as follows : —

Whereas it is though. convenient to lodge one of the water engines at the South End of the town and Saml Sewell having signified his consent that the town may have the liberty of a pece of land of his abutting on Summer Street to sett a shed on, to have the same until he or his shall see cause otherwise to improve the s^d land. The selectmen do agree that a shed be there erected for the housing of the Dock Engine there.

And on October 18 it was voted that the new water-engines be lodged in a house erected for that purpose, at the north-west side of the Old North Meeting-house. From this it will be seen that the six engines were lodged as follows: The Prison Engine, Court street; North Engine, by the North Watch-House, next to the Old North Meeting-house; the Dock Engine, moved from the Dock to Summer street; while another was placed at the Dock, another at the Old North Meeting-house, and one at the Town-House.

The General Court passed an act during 1716 making it unlawful to keep more than twenty-five pounds of powder in a building, — a fine of £5 and confiscation being imposed on every half-barrel, one-half of which was to go to the firewards, the other to the poor. It was also made unlawful to carry powder through the town, unless covered by leather or cloth. Firewards were given full power to act in these cases; also to prosecute those who threw fireworks in the streets. This body again legislated on the subject during 1719, by which no powder was to be kept on board ships lying at the wharves. This explosive was to be kept by store-keepers enclosed in a brass or tin funnel. During the following year the fine for keeping powder in a building was increased to £10 for every half-barrel.

On February 18, 1717–18, a copy of the votes regarding the authority of the firewards respecting the engines was given to each of the foremen ; also, that six large and six small ladders were provided and placed in various parts of the town. The first change in the board of firewards since their organization occurred August 21, 1718, when, on the death of Capt. Edward Martyn, Capt. John Fairweather was elected.

On September 30 the first fire society was incorporated. This society was associated "for mutual aid in case it should please Almighty God to permit the breaking out of fire in Boston where we live." The membership was restricted to twenty. Drake's "History" gives the following list of members for March 17, 1733–34: William Winter, Andrew Craige, Arthur Savage, Thomas Handasyde Peak, John Moffatt, Allen Melville, William Murray, John Cunningham, William Brattle, Thomas Tyler, Samuel Doggett, Samuel Bass, Jona Simpson, Samuel Hill, William Fairfield, Daniel Henchmen, John Tyng, David Cutler, John Hunt, Shrimpton Hunt, Thomas Marshall, Daniel Rae, Thomas Symmes, Samuel Holbrook, Thomas Fayerweather, William Andrews, Robert Williams, and Bartolemew Rand.

The societies continued to grow in popularity until after Boston became a city. We have no authentic records from which we can learn their number, but will give the names of these few that we have. One club, instituted in 1753, consisted of twenty-five members, among whom we find the names of James Otis and John Cotton. The object of these clubs was, to be at all times prepared to assist each other in case of danger by fire. Each member was to provide himself with two buckets, two clothes-bags, and one bed-key and one screw-driver. The buckets and bags were marked with the first letter of the owner's name, and with his surname at length. The buckets also had the motto of the club. A book was also provided for each in which the members' names and places of business and abode were always recorded, and was always carried in their pockets. On an alarm of fire they were to repair to the place with buckets, bags, etc., and if the property of any of their colleagues was in danger they were to exert themselves in saving it. The expenses were defrayed by quarterly assessments. Each society had a watchword, which had to be proclaimed to the secretary at the meeting; failure to do so incurred a fine of twenty-five cents. Meetings were held quarterly at the principal taverns, principally at the Concert Hall and Bunch of Grapes, non-attendance of which cost the absentees $5. At these meetings business was done only before or after dinner or supper. We have in our possession one of the bills of the society of 1753, which is made out on the back of a playing-card (the king of hearts), which we copy : —

	BUNCH OF GRAPES.	£.	s.	d.
Supper		3.	0	0
2 bottles Maderia		3.	8.	0
1 " oporto		1.	5.	0
6 Bowls of Punch		6.	4.	0
4 Bottles Porter		2.	5.	0
		15	18	0

1755 July 18   Rec^d pa contents THOS JENNOR

This, we presume, is a fair representation of the character of all the clubs that existed previous to 1826.

The Alert Fire Association was instituted November 19, 1787, with thirty-five members; they were, Ezra Whitney, William Bordman, Daniel Oliver, Samuel Sneeling, Nath. Ayers, Samuel Bradlee, John Osborn, Jos. Eaton, Jonathan Williams, Nath. Gardner, Eleazer Homer, John Cunningham, John Ballard, Eben Frothingham, Daniel Merry, D. W. Bradlee, Thomas Curtis, George Longley, William Mack, Seth Adams, Elisha Sumner, Thomas Williams, Ed. Blanchard, J. W. Blanchard, Benjamin Goddard, John Somes, Daniel Whitney, Ed. Reynolds, John Baxter, John Rice, Bar. Rand, Ed. Davis, and John Palfrey. In 1826 the society had fourteen members; T. French was president, and E. P. Hartshorn, clerk.

The Assistant Fire Society, about 1800. Its members for January 30, 1810, were T. C. Armory, Nathaniel Armory, S. Blogg, C. Bradbury, J. Chapman, S. Codman, J. Davis, Daniel Davis, Jonathan Davis, Aaron Dexter, S. Deblois, S. Elliot, E. Francis, G. Green, J. Gove, Patrick Grant, F. W. Geyer, Judiah Hayes, Jonathan Head, Jr., George Higginson, Jonathan C. Howard, S. Jones, S. May, J. May, Harrison Gray Otis, James Perkins, T. Perkins, S. G. Perkins, Isaac Parker, Jonathan Richards, J. T. Sargent, W. Sullivan, J. Tilden, R. Webster, Isaac Winslow, and D. Sargent.

The Vigilant Fire Society, instituted January 12, 1807, among the members of which we notice Otis Norcross. During 1826 J. Danforth was president and Ed. Coverley clerk; twenty-seven members. The Independent Fire Society, incorporated January 19, 1826. Suffolk Fire Society, 1826; Jos. Eveleth, president, and R. Ward, clerk. Æneas Fire Society, established September 14, 1826; Daniel Munroe, president, and Edw. Briggs, clerk; twenty-four members. Citizens' Fire Society; J. H. Adams, president, M. Amory, clerk; twenty-three members. United Fire Society, established July 17, 1826; B. M. Nevers, president, and R. Baker, clerk. Columbia Eagle Fire Society, established October 23, 1826; B. B. Appleton, president, W. Baker, clerk; twenty-seven members. Mechanics' Fire Society, established March 5, 1783; officers for 1826, John Kuhn, president, and Fred. Lane, clerk; twenty-three members. The ward companies, or "firemen," organized at the time Boston became a city, soon took the place of these old clubs.

William Wilson was ordered, on March 27, 1721, to inspect all the engines, to make any necessary repairs, in which work he was to be assisted by the members of the department; a list of the companies were to be sent in to the selectmen by the following month. Liberty was granted, on February 15, 1721–22, to place one of the engines at Long wharf, near the treasurer's warehouse.

Judge Sewall records the following, under date of March 7, 1720 : —

At night was disturbed by the cry of fire on the street so that it was past 12 before my daughter got to bed. Col. Dyer's sugar house is burned and spoiled. The weather very cold.

And on November 26, 1722, he adds : —

Friday night last a fire broke out at the Stone Goal and did considerable damage before it was extinguished.

April 12, the following year, he has another entry of fire : —

In the morning between 6 & 7 the bells rang for fire. Mr. Bridge his Kitchen in King Street near Madam Stoddards, widow, is burned down. The progress of the fire is mercifully staid.

Two warehouses on Long wharf, in which were a number of sails and a quantity of canvas, were burnt January 8, 1722.

On March 30, 1723, between 4 and 5 o'clock P.M., fire was discovered in the buildings of Elisha Cooke, Esq., situated at the lower end of King street (State street), which laid in ashes his four tenements. Another fire occurred on April 2, in a house in Leverett Lane, near the Quaker church, which was set on fire by a negro man-servant, who, upon examination, confessed that he had twice before attempted to fire the building, but only a part of the side was burnt. He was put in jail in solitary confinement.

An order was issued by the selectmen, April 19, 1723, forbidding any Indian or negro during the progress of a fire to leave his master's house, except it be on fire, on pain of being sent to jail, and being whipped for three days.

The first appointment of foremen or masters, as they were then called, of engine companies is recorded under date of March 30, 1724.

Elias Townsend is appointed to be the master of the North Engine (N°. 1) and on the 27th of the following month Joshua Townsend and Benj. Snelling were admitted enginemen, under which title members of the department were then called, they having produced their liberty from their respective captains of the militia.

The masters of each engine were ordered, on July 30, to work their engines on the last Monday of each month, and to make report to the selectmen as to their condition.

Fire originated in a warehouse near Oliver's dock, at 7 o'clock on the evening of August 10, 1724, from which it soon spread to a blacksmith shop and several other buildings near by. Several people were injured, and a large amount of damage to merchandise done.

The following order, framed October 18, 1727, cites the duty of the foreman of the engine (of course inserting his own name) : —

Orded that Elias Townsend have the charge of the Large Wooden Water Engine which is at the North end of the Town and he is allowed twelve men beside himself, and in case there should happen any difference at any time among them, that they should want to putt out or take in any one man, when Townsend that has the charge of the Engine shall give an account of the persons they want to putt out or take in to the selectmen and have their allowance or order for their so doing. At a time of fire breaking out, the said Townsend is ordered to Improve the said Engine when he thinks he may do the most service.

March 6, 1727–28, Josiah Baker was made foreman of the Copper Engine, by the North Meeting-house, No. 3, with the following company: John Adams, Thomas Demary, Joseph Roberts, Joseph Stargen, Joshua Thornton, Francis Wetaman, Samuel Pousley, Christopher Souter, and John Grant. This is the first complete company that is recorded since that of the first, with Thomas Atkins.

Beginning with March 12, 1732–33, the foreman of the engine annually sent a petition to the selectmen. The following is a copy of one forwarded a year later : —

To the Inhabitants of the Town of Boston at their General Meeting in March 1733. The Petition of the Masters belonging to the Engines and their men. Humbly sheweth, That your petitioners have for divers years belonged to the Several Engines of the time and have at all times of fire done their duty altho' frequently at the Risque of your petitioners lives and limbs. The town was pleased at their annual meetings in March last to free your petitioners from all other officers in the town the then ensuing year, and your petitioners being still willing to serve the town and comply with all the Regulations and orders in the last years vote, Humbly pray that they may be freed from the future from all other town officers, signed William Wheeler, Thomas Paine, Jon^a Bowman, Joshua Bakersen, James Read, W^m. Young and John Earle.

Bowman was appointed foreman of the Old North, August 11, 1732, Townsend having resigned; and on November 7, 1732. Thomas Ruck was appointed a fireward, *vice* Timothy Clark, who desired to be excused on account of his old age.

On July 27, 1733, the entire department was organized with the following members: The Copper Engine, No. 5, located under the Town-House (where the Old State-House now stands), with the following company:

James Read. foreman; Thomas Flagg, Samuel Duncan, Thomas Plasted Cooper, Bozone Allen, Samuel Ellis, Edward Potter, Robert Price, Thomas Goodwin. Thomas Hartley, Samuel Hastings, Peter Cotta, and Thomas Reed. In the order to the masters, the following was added after the words " when he thinks he may do the most service :" " and at no time to let the Doors of the Engine House be obstructed by Snow etc.," which was included in the orders handed to each company.

Engine at the Watch-House adjoining the Old North Watch-House, No. 1 (North street, facing Elm street) ; Jonathan Bowman. foreman, with sixteen members : Anthony Underwood, John Stephens, John Smith, Joshua Townsend, Benjamin Snelling, Richard Kent, James Dowell, Thornton Barrel, John Brown, John Beares, William Marshall, John Lowe, Thomas Kelling, Thomas Bentley. Thomas Nowell, and Richard Morgan.

Engine in Summer street, No. 9 ; William Wheeler, foreman ; thirteen members : William Cowell. Henry Howell, John Taylor, Samuel Davis. John Bowdry, William Wheeler, Jr., Abijah Adams, Joseph Wheeler, Eleazer Darby, Soloman Kneeland, Johnson Jackson, and John Lawson.

The Prison Engine, Court street, No. 7. A large shed was built in 1642 in the prison yard, which probably was used for this engine. William Young, foreman ; fifteen members : Eben Perry, Samuel Sprague, Isaac Peirce, William Ives, John Peirce, Gersham Flagg, Jarvas Young, —— Newell, John Fantel (?), Barto. Sutton, Peter Row, Stephen Parker, James Dayes, and Robert Bradford.

The Engine at the Dock. No. 4 ; Thomas Pain, foreman ; thirteen men : John Demery, Jacob Davis, Iccabod Rogers, Joseph Ricks. Jacob Varm, John Homer, John Durham, Nathaniel Goodwin, Joseph Lowdn, Thomas Atkins. William Snowden, and William Pack.

Engine No. 2, in Governor Hutchinson's buildings, near the New North Meeting-house (corner of North and Clark streets) ; John Earle. foreman, and eleven men : Thomas Person. Jr., Isaac Russell, William Haley, Jeremiah Cushing, Thomas Litton, Joshua Attwood, Joseph Burrill, James Davis, Joseph Belcher, and Daniel Merritt. This engine was loaned to the town by Lieutenant-Governor Hutchinson during 1720.

The Copper Engine, No. 3, by the North Meeting-house (head of North square) ; Joshua Baker, foreman, and nine men : Joseph Roberts, Joseph Pearson, Francis Wiltaman, Samuel Pousley, Christopher Souter, Richard Gutten, Jonathan Tarbox, Hunstable Baker, and Joseph Baker, Jr.

Some idea of the capabilities of these engines may be obtained from a notice of one contained in the " News Letter," of January 25, 1733 : —

There is newly errected in the Town of Boston, by Messieurs John and Thomas Hill, a Water Engine at there Still-house, by the advise and direction of Mr. Rowland Houghton, drawn by a horse. which delivers a large quantity of water twelve feet above the ground. This being the first of the sort in these parts. we thought taking notice of it might be of publick service, inasmuch as a great deal of labor is saved thereby.

This "Tub" must have been the first water-engine manufactured in this section, and as it was not purchased by the town, it was, no doubt, an unsuccessful experiment.

As the selectmen had the fire department under their supervision, they kept a complete record of the members and apparatus, whereby we have been able to trace, with few exceptions, the roster of each company up to the year 1800. The first change recorded is on the North Meeting-house Engine, No. 1, when, on April 10, 1734, Francis Wetaman resigned, and Walter Edmonds and Zephaniah Basset were appointed, making ten members. Edward Dumaresq was admitted a member of John Earle's company, No. 2, on October 3, 1734, *vice* Joseph Burrell, moved away. October 9, John Waters and Joshua Glidden, members, of Joshua Baker's company, No. 3, *vice* Chris. Souther and Joseph Baker, Jr., who had gone to sea. On the 23d a number of changes occur. A new company was organized for the Dock Engine, No. 4, with Joseph Ricks as foreman, and twelve members: John Dumaresq, I. Rogers, Jacob Davis, Jos. Uran, John Homer, John Durham, John Lowden, Thomas Adams, William Snowden, William Peck, Nath. Brew, and Benjaman Barnard. The Prison Engine, No. 7, is also newly manned; Barth. Sutton was appointed foreman, with fourteen men: Stephen Parker, William Ivers, John Peirce, Samuel Sprague, John Tootel, Peter Roe, James Cocks, Ebenezer Berry, James Young, Henry Newell, Jacob Green, Eliphalet Parker, and Gershom Flagg; the name of the fourteenth man is left blank. This will make the appointment of Sutton, as engraved on the plate of records of the old foreman of Engine Company No. 7, illustrated on page 43, two years ahead, as on that his appointment is recorded in 1736, when the selectmen's record enters it as above. Thomas Crafts and Peter Vergoose were appointed on this company, January 15, in place of Young and Tootel.

The town, as far as we can obtain any data, was free from fires of any importance; in fact, the only one of which we have any notice since 1731 occurred in the printing-office of Benjamin Green, January 30, 1734, which consumed his large stock of type, presses, etc.

The Summer-street Engine, No. 9, had a new foreman on February 25, 1735, when Henry Howell was appointed to that office, with the following changes in the company: George Ray and Jonathan Wheeler, *vice* William Wheeler and Samuel Davis.

Mr. Rowland Houghton, the inventor of the engine at the distil-house, must have been quite an enthusiast in the matter of extinguishing fires, as we find him in 1736 trying some arrangement to have his proposal regarding the prevention of danger by chimneys flaming pass the selectmen.

A fire occurred at the warehouse of Captain Tynge on April 6, 1736, at 2 o'clock A.M., during which three leather buckets belonging to the Dock Watch were lost; these buckets were marked with the word "Boston" and numbered, and were advertised in Thursday's newspaper, and by three writ-

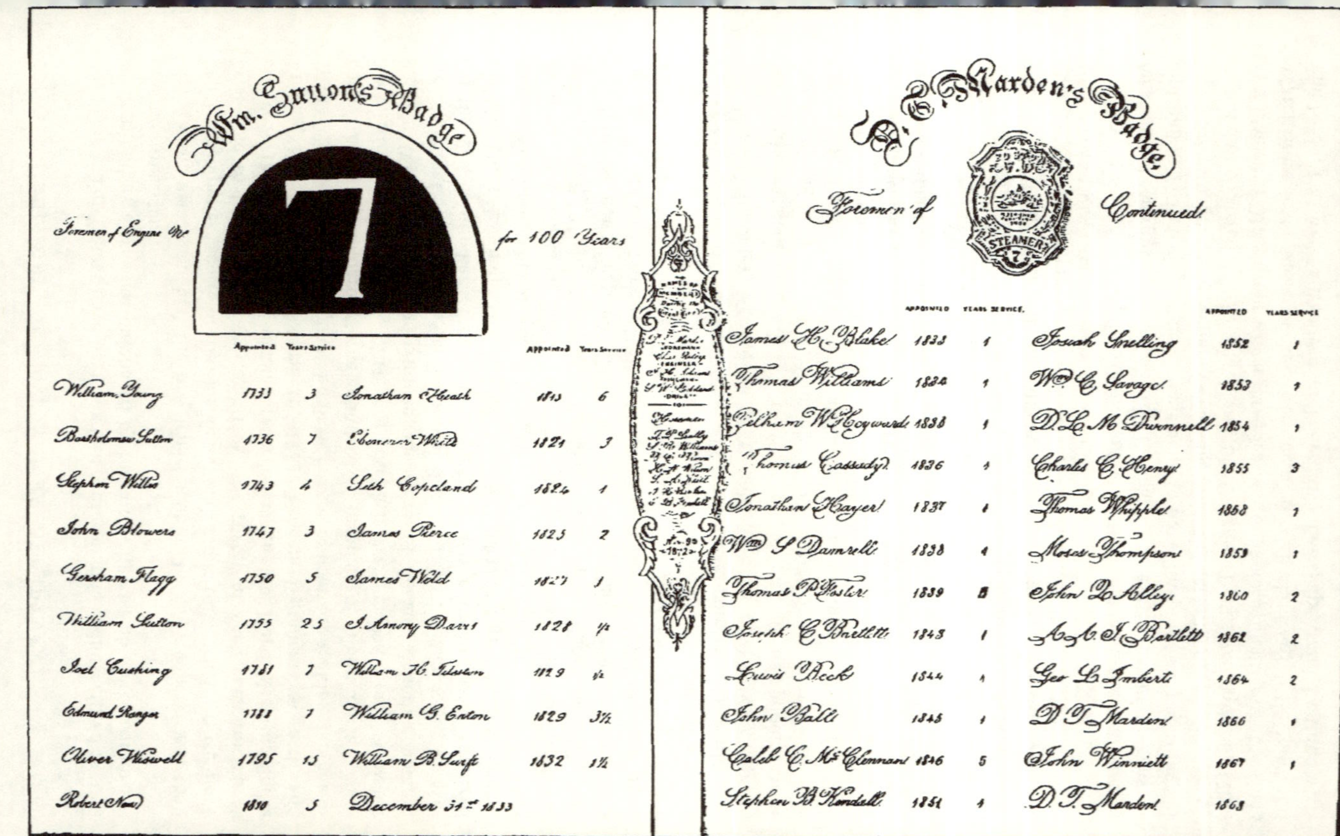

Name	Appointed	Years Service	Name	Appointed	Years Service
William Young	1733	3	Jonathan Heath	1815	6
Bartholomew Sutton	1736	7	Ebenezer White	1821	3
Stephen Willis	1743	4	Seth Copeland	1824	1
John Blowers	1747	3	James Pierce	1825	2
Gersham Flagg	1750	5	James Weld	1827	1
William Sutton	1755	25	J. Amory Davis	1828	½
Joel Cushing	1781	7	William H. Tilston	1829	½
Edmund Ranger	1788	7	William G. Eaton	1829	3½
Oliver Wiswell	1795	15	William B. Surf	1832	1½
Robert Noon	1810	5	December 31st 1833		

Name	Appointed	Years Service	Name	Appointed	Years Service
James H. Blake	1833	1	Josiah Snelling	1852	1
Thomas Williams	1834	1	Wm. C. Savage	1853	1
Pelham W. Hayward	1838	1	D. L. McDonnell	1854	1
Thomas Cassedy	1836	1	Charles C. Henry	1855	3
Jonathan Hayer	1837	1	Thomas Whipple	1858	1
Wm. S. Damrell	1838	1	Moses Thompson	1859	1
Thomas P. Foster	1839	8	John D. Alley	1860	2
Joseph C. Buellett	1843	1	A. C. J. Bartlett	1862	2
Lewis Beck	1844	1	Geo L. Imbert	1864	2
John Ball	1845	1	D. T. Marden	1866	1
Caleb C. McClennan	1846	5	John Winniett	1867	1
Stephen B. Kendall	1851	1	D. T. Marden	1868	

TABLET OF NAMES OF FOREMEN OF ENGINE COMPANY NO. 7.

ten posters placed in various parts of the town. It was probably at this fire that the North Engine was damaged.

The first mention of hose for the department is made on April 7, when Captain Sutton asked for a piece of new hose for his engine, which probably referred to a short piece for the pipe, as the regular hose was not used until after Boston became a city.

Quite an extensive fire occurred on Thursday, May 20. It broke out in the bakehouse of Mr. Brattle Oliver, near the South Battery, and in two hours laid in ashes the entire building, together with two large dwellings, a storehouse, and a cooper-shop. A large amount of flour, biscuit, and household goods were destroyed, the total loss amounting to £3,000.

A number of fire-hooks were purchased for the department on July 28, 1736, and on September 1 of the same year Nathaniel Brown and William Clark were admitted members of John Earle's company, No. 2.

September 15, Captain Bowman, of Engine No. 1, resigned his position. and recommended Anthony Underwood as a suitable person to take his place. Joseph Roberts was admitted a member of Captain Baker's company, No. 3, on October 6, *vice* Thomas Pearson. At this time Captain Underwood, of No. 1, set at work to organize a new company for his engine, and returned his list, containing the following changes : Thomas Killing, Edward Edes, James Clark, John Baker, Joseph Harley, and Joseph Wakefield.

William Weare and Isaac Vergoose were enrolled members of Captain Sutton's engine, in the place of Green and Peter Vergoose, October 20. The engine-house at the dock, No. 4, was ordered to be repaired December 1. Captain Ricks, of this engine, threw up his position on January 12, 1736–37, and was succeeded by J. Uran, who immediately appointed John Hood as a member. On April 20 William Stone was admitted a member of Engine No. 1, *vice* John Smith, deceased. Five days later David Newell was made a member of Engine No. 2, *vice* Benjamin Brown. Captain Uran made a few changes in the organization of his company, as follows : Thomas Atkins, Jr., Benjamin Eustus, William Eustus, and John Hood.

The land on which was stationed the Summer-street Engine, No. 9, belonged to Mr. Sewell, he having loaned it to the town on condition that it would be removed when the site was wanted by him or his, which request was made on March 29 ; but no place was selected to lodge the apparatus until April 5, 1738, when the trustees of Trinity Church in Summer street granted them liberty to erect the house at the back of the church, near Mr. Gooch's barn, on condition that it be removed whenever they so desired.

The laws for chimneys firing came in for a revision during 1737, when, upon a proposal by Mr. William Hainslop, who offered to take the contract of that business for the town, a set of by-laws was prepared, which were similar to those then existing, except that the prices were changed, as follows : —

For each chimney of five Stories, Three shillings, four Stories, two shillings and six-pence, Three stories Two shillings all other common chimneys Twenty pence and all Kitchen Chimneys that are above the top of the house they belong to, in proportion to the heighth of the house at the rate above.

Fire originated in a cellar under the dwelling of Mr. Benjamin Hallowell on January 13, 1738, but was extinguished without much damage. On Friday, 20th, the roof of the tavern known as the Sign of the Dream, and a house at the South End, caught on fire from defective chimneys, but did little damage. March 16, a chimney took fire near the town dock, the sparks from which caught the roofs of three other houses; but the citizens and engines, being soon on hand, extinguished them before the flames did much damage.

Isaac Russell, of Engine No. 2, becoming unable to perform duties expected of him, resigns, June 28, 1738, and his position is filled by Phillip Howell; three new screws were ordered at the same time for this engine.

Mr. Hainslop had taken the contract under bond for sweeping chimneys; employs five men; the by-laws drafted by the town on this matter passed the General Court on August 9, two hundred copies of which were ordered printed. It was not long, however, before complaints were received concerning Hain-slop's lack of employés; but that gentleman, when called upon by the select-men, informed them that he had punctually attended all orders, and that he had not sufficient work to keep what hands he had engaged in constant employment. He recommended that an inspector be appointed to look after the chimneys, and would abide by his decisions. He was again complained of, however, on April 30, 1740, and August 18 of the year following, in each of which he fully satisfied the authorities that he was carrying on the work according to his contract.

William Cowell, of Engine No. 9, having died, and E. Darby gone to sea, Joseph Birch and Thomas Foster, Jr., were appointed September 25, while on December 27 Richard Goodwin, of Engine No. 3, resigned to make room for Newman Greenough.

Isaac Vergoose, a member of Engine No. 7, was arrested by Capt. John Wendell, of the militia, for not paying his fine for absence from his company on training days; but Captain Sutton made a complaint against Wendell, as Vergoose was a member of his company, and therefore free from the charges preferred against him, which was granted.

Elijah Doubleday was admitted a member of Engine No. 1, *vice* Thomas Kelling, on August 22, 1739. A fire broke out in a joiner's shop situated at the North End, which it entirely consumed. On December 17 of this year fire was set by some person to a house belonging to the town, located on Fort Hill, and was soon destroyed. Messrs. Savell and Cowdrey were detailed to find the incendiary, also to look after the timber taken from the premises; but the author of the crime remained undiscovered.

Benjamin Snelling, of Engine Company No. 1, having died, Francis Marshall was admitted in his place.

CHAPTER IV.

1740–1759.

THE men who engaged in this department received no recompense for their labors until March 10, 1739–40, when their work was remunerated by a premium offered by the town to the most vigilant; the order is entered as follows : —

> That for the encouragement of the respective companies belonging to the several Fire Engines in this town and to stimulate them to their duty in extinguishing of Fires, as they may be occasion, There be and hereby is allowed to be payed out of the town Treasury the sum of Five Pounds to the company of such Fire Engine as shall first be brought to work upon any house or building that shall be on fire.

This custom was continued until the paid department was organized.

The firewards, since their appointment, do not appear to have been very busy, as there were but four fires of trifling importance, while no account is recorded of any difficulties regarding gunpowder until March 26, 1739–40, when William Salter, the keeper of the powder-house on the Common, informed the selectmen that they had seized six half-barrels of powder from Obediah Cookson, Jr., and three half-barrels in the house of John Carnes, which is the first seizure of this article recorded.

As the members of the engine companies had been excused from military duty, William Greenleaf, a fireward, thought it proper that these officials should be granted the same privileges ; therefore made a motion at a meeting March 9 to that effect, but it failed. On the same date an addition of two men to each engine company was made, also an order that an axe and hook be carried by each company.

Engine No. 1 was the largest apparatus in the town ; it had a company of seventeen members, while the next in size had but fifteen ; it was called at times by the town clerk in his records the " Great Fire Engine." On April 9, 1740, the captain makes application for a longer drag-chain to accommodate the number who run with it.

Gibbins Sharp was admitted a member of Engine No. 2, April 16, *vice* Thomas Litton. On the 30th, the first premium for attendance at a fire was granted to Engine No. 1, for a fire at Mrs. Rawlins', which occurred the week previous. Engine No. 2 was not far behind, as a fire broke out at the house of Mr. Holyoke the same day, and it was awarded the prize for first attendance.

The small Engine No. 3 must have been lodged in rather bad quarters at the North Meeting-house, as the captain makes complaint to the selectmen, on May 14, that the house was rotten and unfit for use, and asked that they may have another. On the 4th of the following month Stephen Greenleaf was admitted a member of Engine No. 9, *vice* John Taylor, who resigned to take charge of the work-house.

During May, 1740, seven houses were destroyed by fire at the new township, granted a few years previous to a number of inhabitants of this town, called New Boston (West End). The accident originated from fire in the woods. All the engines, as we have mentioned, were stationed in the southern and northern part of the town, which was the most thickly populated. But West Boston gradually grew in the number of people and buildings, which, as a matter of course, occasioned the calling of the engines to that section to quench fire. A petition was, therefore, on May 7, immediately after the above conflagration, presented to the selectmen, asking for an engine in their quarter ; but it was some time before their request could be complied with, as we find an entry on the year following, appointing a committee to confer with Jonas Clark concerning an engine which he had for sale, and which was purchased on November 11, 1740, for £130.

August 25, Engine No. 4 obtained the premium of £5 for a fire near the Mill bridge. Mr. Savill was instructed, on October 8, to wait on the foreman of each company and obtain a list of their members, to which list the selectmen referred when a jury was panelled, so that they knew whom to excuse. This is the first mention of the exemption of the firemen from jury duty that is made, and could not have been approved by the Court, as a bill did not pass that body to that effect until years after. On the 29th John and Henry Newell succeeded Newman Greenough and John Waters on Engine No. 3. Captain Underwood also made a change on Engine No. 1, by the appointment of Timothy Brown and Oliver Luckis. Jr., in the place of R. Kent and James Harley.

The new engine ordered for the West End was procured in January, 1740–41 ; on the 7th of the month John Pierce was appointed foreman, with nine men : Samuel Sprague, Ebenezer Messinger, Thomas Crafts, John Brown, William Russell, Samuel Emmes, Thomas Kimball, Richard Surcomb, and Thomas Barnard. It was placed in a house on Hancock street, and called the West Boston Engine ; but later on it was named Hero No. 6.

Samuel Brown was appointed a member of Captain Earle's company, *vice* Jer. Cushing, on the 21st. The firewards' office appears to have been an unimportant one, as the vacancies occasioned by death, etc., had been left unfilled for a considerable period ; on February 6, however, Mr. Henry Berry, Capt. Benjamin Pollard, and Mr. John Carnes were appointed by the trustees and selectmen, in the place of S. Minot, E. Tyler, and J. Lee.

Captain Earle obtains the premium for working at the fire of March 12, on Love street (Tileston street). Two changes were made in Engine No. 9. On April 8, William Wheeler, Jr., was again admitted, and Jonathan Chandler took the place of A. Davis. The old engine of Captain Earle at the New North Meeting-house had to have a new axle-tree and wheels on the 15th, they being very badly worn; the spear was also broken, and had to be replaced. Eleazer Newell is admitted on Captain Underwood's company, *vice* Thomas Newell, deceased. At the same date Captain Ward had a new hose added to his engine.

A fire at the rope-walk of Mr. Box in the West End during June brought the new Engine No. 6 first on the scene. Captain Underwood was obliged to resign his position as master of Engine No. 1 on June 10, on account of infirmities. He was succeeded by John Brown, who made a few changes in the company; viz., Edward Edes, Daniel Barker, Benjamin Luckis, and Ebenezer Brown admitted, *vice* J. Townsend, R. Kent, T. Barrett, J. Lowe, T. Kelling, and R. Morgan.

A fire occurred on January 30, 1741–42, at Mr. Deacon's work-house, by which Engine No. 7 received the premium. Two days later the selectmen complained of the department as not carrying out their order requiring the carrying of fire-hooks, which they found to be of excellent service; also an axe, which was to be marked with the letter " B " on the eye. Two extra men were then added to each company for that purpose, whom the foremen were to select and send their names in on the following Wednesday. Jonathan Simpson, Henry Allen, and William Beairsto were admitted on Captain Howell's company, March 29, and on April 26 the new lists of all the companies were handed in for approval. In the orders issued to the department the following clause was added : —

And that at all fires they bring with them an axe and Fire Hook and commit the same to the charge of two of their company who shall be appointed to manage the same by the selectmen, and in case either the hook or the axe be not brought they are not to be entitled to the bounty of five pounds as by the Town vote.

Mr. Jonathan Salter was appointed foreman of the engine under the Town-House, No. 5, in the place of Captain Reed, who desired to be excused, on March 29, 1742. The engine was called " Marlborough," after the street on which it stood, as this was then the name of that section of Washington street.

His company made the following changes, which are the first recorded since it was organized : Anthony Bracket, Samuel Hallowell, John Foster, Jr., John Wise, Ebenezer Knap, Brackley Read, Edward Potter, Jr., and Thomas Palfrey, *vice* Thomas Flagg, —— Duncan, T. P. Cooper, B. Allen, T. Goodwin, and S. Hastings.

Engine Company, No. 1, admitted William Edes and John Ballard. In Captain Earle's company, Nathan Brown rejoined, and John Thwing and Thomas Lawlor are added, *vice* T. Rerson, Jr., William Haley, and T. Litton. On Engine Company, No. 3, Elias Robinson, William Richards, William

Burbank, and Nathaniel Woodward were admitted, *vice* J. Robert, J. Pearson, H. Baker.

Another set of by-laws regarding chimney-sweeping was prepared on May 11, 1742, by which the rate of sweeping was reduced, as follows: Each chimney five stories high, ninepence; four stories, eightpence; three stories, sixpence; common chimneys, sixpence; and kitchen chimneys to correspond.

July 2, Captain Steele was ordered to procure three new leather buckets for Engine No. 1. A fire is recorded on September 16, which broke out at Fort Hill. On Tuesday, the 19th, about 12 o'clock, fire originated in a new building on Ann street (North street), owned by Mr. Sampson Salter, which was being fitted up for a tenement-house. Being of wood, and setting back from the street, near the Mill creek, the passage-way leading thereto was so narrow that the fire apparatus had difficulty in reaching it. One of the engines, however, was put in a boat in the creek, and landed at a small wharf in the rear of the house, where, with plenty of water, it did most excellent work, and the flames were soon extinguished. Engine No. 4 was first on hand at the fire on that day. On November 29, Captain Peirce claimed the prize for the fire at the distil-house of Mr. Sigourney at the West End.

Jonathan Brown was admitted a member of Engine No. 1 on January 12, 1742-43, and on February 16 John Seaborn and Abraham Belknap joined Engine No. 6, which made up their full equipment. On the 28th, premiums were awarded to Captain Uran for the fire at the Mill bridge, and Captain Peirce for that which occurred near the Orange Tree (a tavern at the corner of Tremont and Hanover streets).

Abraham Hallard was admitted on Captain Salter's company March 23, *vice* John Wise. May 2, the Engines Nos. 1 and 6, under the command of Captains Peirce and Brown, then known as the West and North Engines, were ordered to be repaired. William Perkins succeeded R. Price on Captain Salter's company on the 30th. This foreman was also awarded the premium for the fire at the house of Captain Davis, on School street. The fire-buckets belonging to the department were used very carelessly by some of the citizens who rendered assistance by passing them to and from the engines, and a motion was passed that some means be taken to prevent their loss and destruction. Ralph Waldo desiring to fill some casks with water, on July 27, saw the advantage to be gained by the use of the engine-hose, which on his application was allowed him, provided an engineman superintend the job and he pay for damages.

Marlborough Engine, No. 5, has another change in its foreman, on October 5, when Thomas Read is promoted to that position, in the room of Captain Salter. William Potter and Joseph Baxter were also added to the company. This foreman was awarded on the same day the prize for attending the fire at the rope-walk of Mr. Keightly.

The house of the "North Copper Engine," as Engine No. 2 was termed, was repaired on November 9, and had facilities added that would accommodate the storage of a fire-hook.

Captain Peirce having left town, was succeeded in command of the West Engine, No. 9, on December 21, by Ebenezer Messenger; he made only two changes in the membership, — that of John Box and Robert Thompson, Jr., *vice* T. Kimball and Captain Peirce.

Captain Sutton applied, December 26, for the premium for the fire at Captain Ellery's house.

On February 8, 1743-44, Captain Earl was awarded for the fire in Charter street (now North street).

About 2 o'clock, P.M., on Thursday, March 1, fire broke out in the malt-house of Mr. Jacob Sheafe, located at the South End, which was entirely destroyed, together with a large quantity of stock. The wind blowing very strong from the north-west, carried sparks a very long distance, and set fire to the barn belonging to Mr. Dwight, at the White Horse Tavern (where Hayward place now is), which was burnt to the ground. The tavern and several other houses in the neighborhood were on fire several times, but the efforts of the department, assisted by the citizens, prevented further damage. A subscription was taken up for the sufferers. The next day another fire started in a house of Hon. Samuel Welles, Esq., but was soon put out. Three days later the new meeting-house at Roxbury was burnt. Captain Brown was awarded on the 7th for a fire at the house of Mr. Hawks, near the Old South Church. Captain Messenger, of Engine No. 6, had three additions made to his company on the 21st, by the appointment of Thomas Kimball, John Ricks, and Peter Cumber. Captain Brown applied for the premium on the 26th for the fire at Dr. Kennedy's house.

On the 28th a change in the location of three of the engines was ordered. The small Engine No. 3, at the Old North Church, under Captain Baker, was removed to the Rev. Mr. Mather's meeting-house (Mr. Mather had been minister in the Old North Church for some time, but in October, 1741, he obtained his resignation, and had built the church which took his name, at the corner of North Bennet and Hanover streets, to which place the engine followed him). As the trustees of the Trinity Church had requested the removal of the Summer-street Engine, No. 9, for some time previous, the selectmen had only now succeeded in obtaining a site in which to lodge the apparatus; this was in the building occupied by Mr. Lowders; but they again failed, and it was eventually lodged on the town's land on Essex street, occupied by Mr. Solomon Kneeland. The old Prison Engine, No. 7, the first in the town, was removed from its old stand in Court street to a shed in the rear of the Old South Church (Milk street).

Captain Baker was given the prize on April 18 for the fire on the 13th at the house of George Skinner. The same company makes a change of one of its members on the 24th, — Zephaniah Basset joins Captain Sutton's company, and is succeeded by Edward Richardson, Jr. Captain Sutton has four new members beside the one recorded above; namely, John Lane, Jr., Thomas Walker, Regnell Odell, and John Blowers.

Captain Sutton was succeeded by Stephen Willis shortly after, but at what time the records do not state. On the brass tablet of the foreman of this company, on page 30, Willis is credited with taking charge in 1743 and remaining four years: but the above would show that Sutton still held command as late as April 18, 1744, and as Willis died July 8, 1747, being succeeded by John Blower, he only held the position of foreman of this company a little over three years.

The General Court, during the year, passed the following act, whereby additional duties were placed on the Board of Firewards : —

And the Fire wards aforementioned are hereby required, upon notice of the breaking forth of Fires, taking with them their badges respectively, immediately to repair to the Place and vigorously exert themselves in requiring and procuring assistance to extinguish and prevent the spreading of the fire, and for the pulling down or blowing up any houses, or any other service relating thereto, as they may be directed by two or three of the chief civil or military officers of the town, to put a Stop to the fire, and in removing household stuff, goods, and merchandize, out of any dwelling-houses, store-houses or other buildings actually on fire, or in danger thereof, in appointing guards to secure and take care of the same, and to suppress all tumults and disorders, and due obedience is required to be yielded to them and each of them accordingly for that service.

Captain Earle's engine was ordered to be repaired on July 20, and on August 15 Engine No. 5 was in the hands of the repairer. John Belcher, of Engine No. 2, being dead, Jedediah Lincoln is appointed in his place, October 3. This company was awarded the next premium for a fire at Bronsdon's wharf during the same month. Captain Baker gets the next award, on December 12, for a fire near Copp's Hill. The fire at Colonel Pollard's house on February 24, 1744–45, was attended first by Captain Read's company, while Engine No. 9 obtains the award for the fire at Mr. David Colson's buildings at the South End during the same month. This last fire was one of considerable damage. It broke out between 5 and 6 o'clock on the morning of February 11, in the leather-dressing establishment occupied by Mr. Colson, and communicated to several other buildings of his, which were entirely destroyed. Other buildings in the neighborhood were damaged, the total loss amounting to several thousand pounds.

Messrs. Belknap, Ricks, Kemball, Surcomb, and Seaborn left the service of Engine No. 6 on April 3, and Edmund Barrett and Ebenezer Messenger, Jr., are appointed, and on May 1 John Clough is enrolled on Engine No. 1, vice William Marshall. Another member is added to Engine No. 6, June 19: viz., Jonathan A. Fifield. July 29, Captain Brown received the award for the fire at Mr. Rawling's house that occurred two months previous.

The first general election of firewards, since the creation of that office, did not occur until March 10, 1745–46, when the following were chosen:

Isaac White, Robert Breck, John Carnes, John Scolley, Joseph Jackson, Col. Robert Berry, Col. Robert Pollard, Col. John Hill, and Capt. William Salter; but Colonel Pollard declining, Capt. John Russell was elected.

Again the West Engine, No. 6, has a new foreman; this time Captain Messenger gives place, on March 19, 1745–46, to Samuel Sprague, one of the old members; but Messenger does not resign his membership. Sprague adds an almost entirely new company, only one of the original members (J. Brown) being left. The new men are Daniel Ballard, Jabez Searl, Joseph Badger, Brignell Odell, Stephen Morine, John Ricks, and Benjamin Hitch, who succeeded T. Crafts, W. Russell, S. Emms, T. Kimball, T. Barnard, J. Box, R. Thompson, Jr., E. Barrett, and J. A. Fifield.

The returns for the choice of firewards for the year 1746–47 showed that John Phillips and James Day were elected, *vice* William Salter, the additional member completing the number, as required by law.

E. Messenger, former captain of Engine No. 6, over whom Sprague was promoted, was again installed in his old position on April 1, 1747, Sprague having moved to Louisburg. Nicholas Gray was then admitted a member, and on the 8th John Bowden and George Eustus were enlisted. Messenger did not continue long in the company, however, as he moved out of town on November 4. John Brown, the only one left among the original members, was promoted to fill the vacancy.

On the 9th Boston was again the scene of quite an extensive conflagration. This time the old Town-House fell a prey to the flames. In this fire many valuable records and papers were lost. We reprint the account of the fire contained in the Boston weekly "News Letter," of Thursday, December 10, 1747: —

Yesterday morning between six and seven we were exceedingly surprised by a Fire which broke out at the Court House, in this Town, whereby that spacious and beautiful building, except the bare outward walls, was entirely destroyed. As the fire began in the middle or Second Story, the Records, Books, Papers, Furniture, Pictures of the Kings and Queens, &c., which were in the Council Chamber, the Chamber of the House of Representatives and the Apartments thereof, in that story, were consumed; as were also the Books and Papers in the office of the upper story; Those in the offices below were mostly saved. In the cellars, which were hired by several persons, a great quantity of Wines and Liquors were lost. The Public Damage sustained by the sad disaster is inexpressably great and the loss to some particular persons 't is said will amount to severall thousands pounds. The Vehemence of the Flames occationed such a great Heat as to set the Roofs of some of the opposite Houses on Fire notwithstanding they had been covered with snow, and it was extinguished with great difficulty. How the Fire was occationed whether by Defect in the chimney or Hearth as some think is uncertain.

The Boston "Evening Post," on the 14th of the month, adds: —

The fine Pictures and other Furniture in the council chamber were destroyed as were also the Books Papers and Records in both the Lobbies, and those in the offices kept in the upper story; but the County Records and Papers belonging to the Inferiour Court, being deposited in a office upon the lower Floor, were most of them preserved.

The same paper printed the following extract from the " Journal of the House of Representatives : " —

12 DECEMBER A.D., 1747.

Upon a motion made and seconded, *Resolved,* that the House now make particular Enquiry how the late Fire in the Court House was first discovered, and by what Means it was occationed.   After examining the Door Keeper and Recciving a particular account of the Fire and circumstances of his leaving the House, the Evening before, and enquiring of those Gentlemen who early discovered the Fire, *Resolved,* That it appears to the satisfaction of this House, that the late Fire which consumed the Court House proceeded from the woodwork under the Hearth taking Fire, and that the Fire first broke out in the entry-way between the Council Chamber and the Representatives Room, and from thence went up the Stair Case and through the Roof, and continued until the House was consumed.

The old engine stationed in the cellar of the House was saved, and stationed at the dock while the building was being rebuilt.   A man by the name of Clough was ordered to give his assistance in extinguishing the fire by Joseph Jackson, a fireman, but refused, whereupon he was fined 20s.   This was the first fine for any offence of this kind recorded.   The walls were left by the flames standing in a very dangerous condition, and the Court issued an order to have them secured.

The Court being in session at the time of the fire, they were left without a place of meeting, but were offered the use of Faneuil Hall ; the Royal Exchange Tavern, kept by Luke Vardy, on King street, was more to their taste, however, and was used during the four days the session continued.   When they again met in February, a motion was made to have the next Court-House built at Cambridge ; but this failing, as did another to locate it at Roxbury, it was finally determined that the old one should be repaired.

The South Engine, No. 9, was again moved from the land belonging to the town to a building erected on the land owned by Hon. John Jeffries (the site of the Albion Building, corner of Tremont and Beacon streets).

Captain Brown, of Engine 1, after a service of seven years in the department, died on June 22, 1748.   He was succeeded by Thomas Bentley, the last one of the original members of the company.   In the reorganization of the company, J. Stephens, J. Dowell, J. Beares, and J. Wakefield were discharged ; they were succeeded by Richard Gooding, John Brown, John Richardson, and Samuel Bickner.

Captain Brown, of the Prison Engine, No. 7, made a considerable change in the list of members when forming his company, October 31, 1748 ; of the original company, only one, J. Young, remained.   Perry Sprague, Reine, Ivers, Newell, S. Parker Roe, Cocks, Berry, Newell, Wear, Walker, Odell, and Blowes were dismissed, and Samuel Bracket, Thomas Crafts, Jacob Cheney, Peter Roberts, Stephen Greenleafe, John Ridgaway, William Russell, William Frost, Thomas Brice, James Buck, John Glen, and Walter Motley were appointed.

A large fire occurred on October 22 in Purchase street.

The land on which Engine No. 2 was housed was owned by Governor Hutchinson, and having use for the same, he requested the selectmen, on February 15, 1748–49, to immediately remove the engine. This request was repeated on May 24, but no action was taken in the matter, although Captain Earle could obtain accommodation in a building near Mr. Webb's church.

The South Engine, under the charge of Captain Howell, did not long remain at the house on Tremont street, if indeed it was ever removed there: as when John Beaudry was promoted foreman in the place of Howell, on October 25, 1749, the records mention it as being now kept on the land belonging to the town (*sic*) taken in execution of Mr. Samuel Kneeland.

Captain Earle — with one exception the only foreman remaining who was appointed when the department was organized — died January 27, 1749–50; he was succeeded by Nathaniel Brown. Martin Grey was admitted a member on the same date.

Engine No. 5 was at this time replaced in its old stand under the Town-House. A platform and all necessary repairs were then made.

Major Nathaniel Thwing and Mr. Royal Tyler were chosen firewards during 1750–51.

Captain Blower did not long remain in the service of the Prison Engine. He sent in his resignation on February 7, and was succeeded by Gershom Flagg. On September 19, 1750, Samuel Treat is admitted on Captain Bentley's company, *vice* Doubledee, deceased, and on October 5 John Prince joins Engine No. 6; the same date Ebenezer Topliff is enrolled on Engine No. 9.

At a town-meeting held March 11, 1750–51, a vote was passed by the town whereby their representatives at the General Court be desired to use their best endeavors to have a law passed by which the number of firewards could be increased, if it be so desired, over the number now allowed; which resulted, at the next session, held in 1752, in the passage of the following law : —

Whereby from experience the Firewards who have been annually chosen by the Town of Boston have been found to be of great use and service to the said town at times of fires, and it is apprehended it would greatly serve the said Town if their number were increased. . . . Choose twelve Fire-wards who shall do the duty and be invested with the like powers and privileges as firewards in and by the said act are invested withal.

Messrs. Isaac Freeman, John Tudor, Thomas Jackson, and Newman Greenough were elected, making twelve firewards for 1752.

The last representative of the original appointment of foreman of the engines, Capt. Josiah Baker, resigns his position on Engine No. 3, on January 15, 1752–53, after a service of eighteen years. He was succeeded by Joseph Glidden, who made the following changes in the membership: John Robinson, James Barnard, William Page, and Caleb Hacker were admitted, while Pousley and W. Richards were dismissed.

The town had been quite free from fires during the past four or five years; in fact none are recorded since October 22, 1748, although there may have been some of minor importance. On February 7, 1753, the alarm was given during a dark and rainy night for a fire in an out-house on Marlborough street (part of Washington street). Although all the engines were called out and quickly on the scene, the flames spread to a stable near by, and before got under control another stable, Mr. Sellon's blacksmith shop, the dwellings of Dr. John Cutler and Dr. Edward Ellis, were left in ruins. Several people were injured by the falling of brick walls, but no lives were lost.

The growth of the southerly part of the town in population, and increase in number of buildings erected, rendered it necessary for the inhabitants to have better facilities in case of fire. They, therefore, on March 5, 1753, presented a petition to the town, praying that a suitable fire-engine be stationed in that part of the town.

Captain Hopestill Foster was chosen on the Board of Firewards for 1753, *vice* Captain Berry, resigned; and on the following year Captain Thomas J. Gruchy, Mr. Joseph Jackson, and Captain Solomon Davis were elected, *vice* Carnes, Freeman, and Tudor.

The engine was not placed in the building near the Old South Church until after July 22, 1754, as a record is made on that date that a building be erected for its accommodation, by the sanction of the committee of that church, of the following dimensions: Twenty-four feet in length, eight feet wide, and eight feet high.

For the year 1755 the choice of firewards was as follows: John Rowe and William Cooper, *vice* Davis and T. Jackson, Jr.; and in the year following Col. N. Thwing was excused, and Capt. Thomas Savage, Mr. Joseph Jackson, and Nathaniel W. Wheelwright were elected, *vice* Gerchy and Truckman.

The matters relating to the department did not claim any entries in the town records during the past two years, or were there any fires noted.

A Dutch ship, wrecked on this coast about this time, had on board a copper water-engine, which was saved and purchased by the town. A company was formed, consisting of twelve men, with James Cunningham as foreman, and stationed at the North End, as the citizens had petitioned, in a building on Newbury street (Washington street). It was subsequently called Cumberland, No. 8.

A terrible fire happened on January 13, 1756. It originated in a house on Hanover street, at the corner of Cold Lane (Portland street), and soon destroyed several tenement-houses adjoining. So rapid was the spread of the flames, that the occupants had hardly time to escape with their lives; one old lady, lodged in an upper room in the building where the fire started, was burnt to death, her remains being afterward discovered. A large amount of furniture, plate, and other household goods were destroyed.

The records are revived during 1756, beginning with May 31, when

Daniel Baker is admitted a member of Captain Bentley's company. On June 2 Captain Glidden is awarded premiums for several fires that had occurred during the past year.

During the interval mentioned, Captain Flagg was succeeded in the command of the Prison Engine by William Sutton, which appointment occurred some time during 1753, but as to the exact date we have no authentic record. Bartholomew Sutton, Jr., and John Lauton admitted in this company in the room of B. Stevens and T. Reck. A fire occurred during this month at the residence of Mr. John Welche, for which Captain Putnam of the Dock Engine was awarded the premium. Putnam was appointed to succeed Captain Uran of this company some time during 1755. On October 6 Jonathan Brown, Jr., was admitted in Captain Bentley's company, in the place of his father.

Joseph Eliot was admitted a member of Engine No. 8, *vice* Nathaniel Wales, and on March 10, 1756–57, this company won the award for a fire at Thomas Spears'.

The election of firewards for 1757 resulted in the choice of Thomas Flucker in the place of J. Hill.

Chimney-sweeps came in for a reduction of rates this year, they being allowed for each chimney five stories high 1 shilling and 4 pence ; four stories, 1 shilling and 2 pence ; three stories, 1 shilling ; all others, 8 pence ; kitchen chimneys at proportionable rates.

Joseph True succeeded Richard True on August 31 on Engine No. 3, and Joseph Peirce was admitted in the place of William Vane in the same company on December 26. No change was made in the choice of the Board of Firewards for the year 1758. Capt. John Brown, of the West End Engine, No. 6, or " New Boston," as it was sometimes called, was awarded, on March 22, the premium for a fire at that quarter of the town. On the same date the Governor excused one hundred men of the town from military duties, to man the engines, which were then numbered for the first time. By advice of the selectmen and the several foremen the men were placed as follows : —

Captain Bentley's, or the North End Engine, near the Old North Meeting-house, North square. Old North, No. 1, was allowed fourteen men. The changes being Thomas Marble, Alexander Scannell, and Joshua Bentley, *vice* E. Edes, Clark, Stone, Luckis, Jr., B. Luckis, Barker, Gooding, and Bickner.

Capt. N. Brown, old Copper Engine, by New North Meeting-house, Congress, No. 2, nine men : William Brown, John Bovey, and Thomas Atkins, *vice* Attwood, Denaresq, Clark, Newell, Howell, J. Thwing, Lawler, Lincoln, and J. True.

Capt. Elias Robinson succeeded Captain Glidden in command of the engine at the North Meeting-house, Washington, No. 3, with eight men. All of the company were old members, with the exception of Webb Pearson and Jonathan Jenkins.

Captain Putnam, of the Dock Engine Endeavor, No. 4, ten men ; an entirely new list : Joseph Bradford, Giles Brewer, Thomas Uran, Isaiah

Andbert, Benjamin Loring, Benjamin Proctor, Richard Stoper, Paul Baxter, and John Perkins.

Capt. Thomas Read, Marlborough Engine, No. 5, under the Town-House, eleven men. Of these, only four of the old members are left, — Palfrey, Holland, Baxter, and Read. The new appointments are Samuel Hallowell, Thomas Salter, John Peck, D. Wing, Thomas Read, Jr., and James Read, Jr.

Capt. J. Brown, West Boston, Engine Hero, No. 6, on Hancock street, ten men, two of whom are old members, — Cumber and Serl; the others are John Hopkins, Nicholas Tabb, Josiah Gains, Robert Bonynge, James Ridgway, Jr., William Homer, and Michial Homer.

Captain Sutton's Prison Engine, New York, No. 7, then near the Old South Church, thirteen men, five being left from the old list, — William Frost, G. Bassett, P. Roberts, B. Sutton, Jr., and J. Laughton. The new members are Garven Brown, I. Tuckerman, Adino Paddock, William Flagg, Jonathan Rogers, John Bulfinch, and James Cook.

Capt. J. Cunningham, Cumberland, No. 8, Newbury street, eleven men. J. Stimpson is the only one left out of the old staff. The others were David Wheeler, Ephraim Greens, Benjamin Wheeler, Henry Evans, Obadiah Curtiss, Moses Bastow, John Bennett, Samuel Wheeler, and Joseph Eliot.

Solomon Kneeland was appointed foreman of the South Engine Despatch, No. 9, *vice* Captain Beaudry, and had fourteen men, — Stephen Greenleaf, John Stimpson, Samuel Franklyn, John Mellege, Eben Topliff, Joseph Wheeler, Samuel Harris, John Fenno, Thomas Greenleaf, Thomas Wheeler, Stephen Wales, Richard Honeywell, and John Halding.

This company was awarded the prize on April 26 for a fire at Deacon Hill's distil-house, at the South End. On the same date Capt. J. Brown's Engine No. 6 was complained of as being so badly out of order as to be incapable of working. An order was therefore issued to have it repaired. On May 10 a fire occurred at the distil-house of Mr. Coffin, near Essex street, for which Engine No. 8 received the prize. The entire department were supplied with new buckets on July 12.

The first premium awarded for the year 1759 was given to Engine No. 9 for the fire at Mr. Johnson's house. Only two changes occurred in the Board of Firewards for this year. Capt. Solomon Davis and Mr. Samuel Austin were appointed in the place of Wheelwright and Savage.

April 11, Engine-house No. 4, at the dock, was repaired. A fire at Widow Sears', on Charter street, during this month consumed her house and barn. Engine 1 was the first to get water. While on the last of the month, Thomas Walkes' house, near the almshouse, was burnt, and Engine 7 received the money. The other fires and awards during the year were as follows : —

May 15, Rears' bakehouse, near Mill creek, Engine 4. May 30, Timothy Fitch's house, West End, Engine 6. June 25, a dispute arose between Engines 8 and 9 about a premium, which was decided in favor of No. 8. August 27,

Engine 2, for a fire at the warehouse of Foster Hutchinson, that occurred on June 28.

The largest fire that occurred in the town for several years past broke out on November 14, in a wooden building south of Oliver's bridge, at Oliver's dock. It swept everything as far as the lower end of Water and Milk streets to Hallowell's ship-yard, burning for more than two hours, during which time Governor Powell was present, and encouraged the firemen and others who were assisting in extinguishing the flames, while those who had property destroyed received his earnest sympathy. The next day the following motion was carried at the town-meeting : —

By the fire that broke out yesterday at Oliver's Dock many persons were reduced from a comfortable state to absolute want and poverty, and who need some immediate relief. That a letter be written to the ministers of the respective churches in the town desiring them to recommend it to their several churches to make a collection for the relief of such sufferers by the late Fire as may need it. That money be paid into the hands of Thos. Hancock, Thos. Hubbard, Jos. Dawes, Sam'l Grant, John Phillips, Malaliah Bounn, and Dr. G. S. Gardner, to be by them distributed to the sufferers in proportion to their late losses & their present necessities.

The last fire of the year occurred at a house near Copp's Hill, some time during December. Engine 2 was given the award.

CHAPTER V.

1760–1763.

THE month of March, 1760, is one that will be memorable for the largest fires that had occurred in New England, and which placed the great fire of 1711 in small comparison. The first of the series occurred about noon, on Monday, March 17, when a joiner's shop at West Boston took fire, and soon communicated to a large house adjoining. The entire department was quickly called out, but the very strong wind blowing from the north-east scattered the flames, so that before it was under control several other buildings in the vicinity were badly damaged. The roof of the West Meeting-house (near the corner of Lynde and Cambridge streets) took fire in several places, but after a severe struggle it was saved.

About one hour earlier on the following day the town was again alarmed by the cry of fire. This time the scene of destruction occurred in a building at the upper end of James Griffin's wharf (now Liverpool). The upper part of this house, where the fire originated, was occupied by a detachment of the Royal Artillery as a laboratory. It soon communicated to a quantity of powder, which blew up the building, resulting in wounding four or five men. One or two grenades and some small-arms exploded, the concussion from which being so great that a shock was felt over the town.

Besides Mr. Griffin's loss, which was very large, — having a quantity of merchandise stored in the lower stories, — a carpenter-shop in the lower part of the store and a blacksmith-shop near the other end of the wharf were on fire, the former being entirely destroyed. Had not the tides been high, thus providing a bountiful water-supply, the principal military stores located at the end of the wharf would have been consumed.

But these were as nothing to the scene to be witnessed on the 20th, when the great fire occurred. Regarding this conflagration, an account was written by the celebrated fireward and town clerk, William Cooper, which we copy from the Boston " Post Boy," issued March 24, 1760 : —

But the 20 of March will be a day memorable for the most terrible Fire that has happened in the town or perhaps in any other part of North America; far exceeding that of Oct. 2, 1711, till now termed the Great Fire. It began about Two o'clock in the Morning in the Dwelling House of Mrs. Mary Jackson and Son, at the Brazen Head in Cornhill [Washington street, nearly opposite Williams court] but the Accident which occasioned it is yet uncertain. The flames catched the House adjoining in the front of the St. and burnt three or four large buildings; a Stop was put to it there at the house of Mrs. West on the South, and Mr Peter Cotta on the North, but the Fire raged most violently toward the

East. All the Stores fronting Pudding Lane [Devonshire street] together with every Dwelling House, from thence Excepting those which front the South side of King-St. and a Store of Mr Spooner's on Water St. to Quaker-Lane [Congress street] and from thence only leaving a large wooden House and the House belonging to the late Cornelius Waldo, it Burnt every House, Shop Store, out-House &c. to Oliver's Dock. And an Eddy of wind carrying the Fire contrary to its Course, it took the Buil ling fronting the lower Part of King St. and destroyed the Houses from the Corner opposite the Bunch of Grapes Tavern [in State street, just below the Old State-House] to the Ware house of Messrs Box and Austin, leaving only the warehouse of the Hon. John Erwing and Dwelling House of Mr Hastings, standing. The other Brick warehouse was damaged. The fire extended from Mr Torreys the Baker in Water st. and damaging some of Mr. Daltons new shops, proceeding Mr Halls working house from there to Milk st. and consumed every house from there to Mr Calef's Dwelling house [in Milk street, corner of Congress, afterwards the famous Julien's restaurant, which stood until July, 1824] to the bottom of the street, and the opposite way, from Mr Dawes's included it carried every house from Fort Hill except the Hon Secretary Olivers and two or three Tenements along Mr. Hallowell's Shipyard his dwelling House the Sconce of the South-Battery all the Shops and Stores on Col. Wendell's wharf, and two or three Ships and a Schooner were burnt one laden with wood and another with considerable value. It consumed near 400 Dwellings Houses Stores Shops Shipping &c. together with Goods and Merchandizes of almost every kind to an incredible Value; but it is not ease to describe the Terror of that Fatal morning. The alarm was great and an Explosion of some powder soon followed which was seen and felt to a great Distance. The chief part had been removed by some hardy adventurers, just before the Explosion, the same time cinders and Flakes of fire were seen flying over that Quarter, where was reposited the remainder of the artillery stores, and combustibles which was preserved from taking fire. The people in this and the neighboring towns exerted themselves to an uncommon Degree and were encouraged by the Presence and example of the Greatest Personage amongst us, but the haughty Flames triumphed over our Engine — our Art — and our numbers. The distressed Inhabitants of those Buildings now wrapped in Fire scarce knew where to take refuge from the devouring flames; The Loss of Interest cannot as yet be ascertained or who have sustained the greatest, it is said that the damage which only one man has received cannot be made good with £2000 Sterling it is in general to great to be made in any measure by the other Inhabitants exhausted as we have been by the great Proportion this Town has borne the extraordinary Expence of the War and by a demand upon our charity to relieve a number of sufferers, and without the compassionate assistance of our Christian Friends abroad, distress and ruin may overwhelm the greatest Part of them.

In the midst of our Distress we have great cause for Thanksgiving, that notwithstanding the rage of the fire, the explosion at the Small Battery, and the falling of the walls, and chimneys, Devine Providence, who so mercifull ordered it not one life has been lost and few wounded.

The following are a list of names of the sufferers whose houses were consumed, several widows and a few others are omitted : —

Cornhill [Washington street]; Mrs. Mary Jackson & Son, Widow McNeal, Mr. Jonathan Mason, Mrs. Quick.

Pudding Lane [Devonshire street]; Wm. Fairfield, —— Rogers, John Sterling, George Glen, James Steward, Widow Marshal, Edmond Dolbear.

Upper part of Water street; Henry Laughton, jun., Mrs. Grice, an empty House of Mr. Caznean, William Palfrey, Joseph Richardson, Dinley Wing, Benj^a Jeffries, John Durant, Mr. Lawson, and a large curriers shop.

Quaker Lane [Congress street]; Wm. Hyslop, S. Salter, with a Brew-house, Robt. Jarvis, Dan Ray and Friends Meeting House.

Towards Olivers Docks; Daniel Spear, Thos. Bennet, Wm. Baker, Eben. Dogget,

Jas. Barnes, Dan Henchman, Joseph Marion, Thos. Hawkins, Shop and Barn Opposite, Widow Savel, James Thompson, Hugh Moore, Widow Davis, Nicholas Tabb, Michael Carrol, Two Tenements of Free Negroes.

Mackerel Lane [Kilby street]; John Gardner, John Powell, Vincent Mundersol, Hasleton Barber's Shop and a Gunsmith's, Edmond Perkins, James Perkins, Several chair maker's Shops, James Graham, Capt. Atherton Haugh, John Doan, Capt. B. Smith, Saul Bangs, D. Rourkes, G. Perry, Paul Baxter shop, Benj. Salisbury, Nich. Dyer, Wm. Stutely, Peter Air, Francis Warden, Benj. Phillip's store, McNeals sail Loft, Palfreys Ditto, Pulters cooper shop, Davis Blacksmith, James Graham Ditto, Fish Market, Sinsesbys shop, Reads ditto, Harris's ditto, Mellus's ditto, T. Palfrey's Sail Loft, Widow Brailesford, John Osborn, Obed Cross, Isaac Dafforn.

Lower Part of Water Street; William Torrey, Jacob Bucknam, James Beaton, Nicholas Lobden, John Rice, Blacksmith's Carpenter's & Chaisemaker's Shop, Thomas Palfrey, Thomas Hartley jun', Edmond Mann, Col. Thwing, James Thwing, Widow Noyes, Ed. Quincy Jr., Thos. Walley, Widow Parsoll, Mrs. Stevenson, Thos. Read, Thos. Read Jr., Bruelsley Read, Robt. William, Jas. Tucker, John Fullerton, Nath. Winslow, Joseph Webb Jr., Barnard & Wheelwrights Shop and Stores adjoining.

Milk St. and Battery March. — Hall's & Messis's Calif's Tan-Houses, Thomas Barnes, Widow Giffen, Jones, Waters, Nathan Foster, Thomas Speakman, Wm. Freeland, Isaac Hause, Hon. John Osborn, Widow Brown, Oliver Wiswall, Caleb Prince, Mrs. Mary Oliver, Joseph Dowse, David Burnet, Edward 'Stone, Andrew Oliver Jr., John Powell, Ed. Davis, Mr. Masters, Thos. Masters, Benj. Cobb, Jas. Orill, John Pierce, Eben Cushing, Eben Cushing Jr., Jas. Rickord, Joseph Uran, Joseph Putnam, Stephen Fullerton, John Province, Andrew Gardner, Mr. Finnesey, Andrew Lepair, Samuel Hewes, Increase Blake, Capt. Edward Blake, Benj' Hallowell, Daniel Ingersol, Two Blacksmith's and 2 Boatbuilder's and sundry other Shops, Thomas Salter, Peter Bourn, Widow Perkins, Nath Eddy, Joshua Sprigg, Zephaniah Basset, John Boyce, Jacob Ridgway, James Moore, Mr. Muggot, Wm. Fullerton, Mr. Hill, John Newell, Wm. Cox, Isaac Pierce and Distill House, a Bake House, Benj. Frothingham, Ed King, John Griffen, Mr. Bright, Thos. Spear, Capt. Killeran, Isaiah Andebert, E. B. Oliver, Math. Salter, Joshua Bowles, James Phillips, Isaac Wendell, John Allen, Wallis, Wilson, all Stores, Shops, &c., on Col. Wendell's wharf.

King-St. [State street]. — John Stevenson, the corner of Mackerel-Lane, Widow Foster, Simon Eliot, Peck, Glasier, John Green, James Lamb, Widow Checkley, John Wheatly, John Jepson, Benj^a Jepson, Thomas White, Hezekiah Cole, Goodwin shop, John Peck's shop, Messrs. Apthorp & Gardiner's warehouse, John Knight's ditto, Bart. Cheever's ditto, where the fire was stopped.

About sixty more were consumed. The light of the Fire was seen in Portsmouth, the explosion by the Gun Powder at the South Battery was heard at Hampton. The following is a copy of a vote passed the Great and General Court on the 22nd instant: —

"The House taking into Consideration that part of his Excellency's speech respecting the calamity brought on the town of Boston in the late fire, and it appearing on the best information that could in so short be obtained that there was consumed 174 dwelling houses and tenements and 175 ware houses, shops and other buildings with a great part of the furniture besides large quantities of merchandize That the loss upon moderate computation cannot be less than £100,000 sterling, that there be advanced and paid out of the Publick Treasury into the hands of the selectmen and overseers aforsaid the sum of Three Thousand pounds, out of the necessary raised by excise the year passed. The selectmen and overseers to lay an account of the money raised by the publick contribution before this court, and of their distribution thereof, and of the sum received out of the Publick Treasury. Several necessaries were sent the sufferers by the selectmen and Gentlemen of the Town."

This, then, was the great fire that had to be fought with only nine small hand-engines. It must have been anything but encouraging to the members of the department especially, as many of them had their own homes and places of business laid in ruins. Drake's History places the exact number of buildings as " one hundred and seventy-four dwellings, and one hundred and seventy-five other buildings, making a total of three hundred and forty-nine." The list of persons who applied for relief was kept in two paper-covered books, as was the list of donations, — one for the list of the wealthy and the poor, the other for the middling classes; these records are now in the office of the Fire Commissioners. From these we find that two hundred and forty-three wealthy, four hundred and sixty-eight poor, and three hundred and fourteen of the middling class were given aid, making a total of nine hundred and twenty-five applicants.

All the buildings from Pudding lane to the water-front were laid in ruins, not a single one being left excepting those above mentioned and on the side of King street.

" But it is not easy," says an eye-witness, writing an account of it which appended " Janeways' Dreadful Fire of London," " to describe the terrors of that fatal morning, in which the imagination of the most calm and steady received impression that would not easily be effaced. The distressed inhabitants of those buildings wrapped in fire scarce knew where to take refuge; numbers were confined to beds of sickness, as well as the aged and the infant, when removed from house to house, and even the dying were obliged to take one remove more before their final time."

It will be noticed that the fire broke out at nearly the same spot as did that of 1711; but the wind being in a different direction it swept over another part of the town. Although light at the commencement, the wind soon came on to blow a gale from the north-west. " There was beheld," continues the account. "a perfect torrent of fire bearing down all before it. In a seeming instant all were aflame."

There are several estimates of the value of the property destroyed: the first was £300,000; the General Court places it at £100,000. Hutchinson's History, III., 81, says : —

Others who had observed the increased value of the land upon which the houses stood estimated the loss at not more than £50,000; and judged that if the donations could have been equally distributed, no great loss would have been sustained.

Dr. Holmes' " Annals," II , 103, cites " the value of property destroyed as £73,112 7s. and 3d.," and that " collective donations amounted to £17,750 15s. and 8d." But the following petition will give the most accurate figures, besides other matters of interest : —

To the Honble the comons of Great Britain, in Parliament assembled. The Petition of Sarah Ayers, Francis Ackley &c [naming all the sufferers] of Boston in the province of Massachusetts Bay, Most humbly sheweth.

That on the 20 of March last a most terrible fire exceeding anything that ever before happened in the American colonies, broke out in the heart of the said town of Boston at the hour of two in the morning, which, increased by the wind, blowing very strong from the N. W., and the flames of many wooden buildings, raged with great violence, carrying all before it, and still widening in its progress, proceeded with such a rapid course to the waters edge, that the houses and other buildings with the movables of your petitioners, were in a very little time reduced to ashes, and some of your petitioners from affluent and others from easy circumstances to great straits and indigence.

That your petitioners, with their families, amounting to a large number of persons, being received with the greatest humanity by other inhabitants of the town, to whom for their preservation they fled in their sore distress, became burdensome to them and the whole town, whose care and kindness on this occation have been exceedingly great; but your petitioners, who when they were able cheerfully bore part of the common burden, are sensible that the inhabitants in general, however well inclined are unable to bear any considerable addition to the heavy load of taxes, which for many years has fallen upon them, far exceeding that of other colonists in consequence of their greater extortion of themselves in conjunction with the inhabitants of other parts of the province, to prevent French encroachments and prosecute war against the common enemy.

That the chief part of such of your petitioners as were the proprietors of the houses destroyed are unable to build others on the vacaut lands, and if that cannot be effected many of the distressed must of necessity soon seek their bread and habitation elsewhere, and the metropolis of the colony, which was many years the chief strength of the English interest on the continent of America, without being in the least burdensome to its mother country, will be left in a broken & declining state.

That under the direction of the government of the province, and the special care of all the proper officers of the town, an exact & particular account of the loss sustained has been taken, and is ready to be laid before this Honorable House, whereby it appears that the whole amounted to the sum of £53,334, 5s., 5.l. sterling.

That divers sums have been received for the benefit of your petitioners, amounting to the following sums in sterling money, viz., by grant of the Gen¹ Court of Mass^tts province, £2,250. By collections in the several churches in Boston, and other parts of the province £3,916, 10, 5¾. By grants of the colonies of New York, Pennsylvania, Maryland, New Hampshire, & Connecticut, £3,358, 0s. 4½l. By private donations made in the province & elsewhere including £3,000 given by Merchants of London, £3,793, 0s., 11¾d., which, amounting to £13,317, 11s., 9d. being deducted from the value of the immediate losses sustained by your petitioners, reduces them to £40,016, 13s., 8.l. sterling.

Wherefore your most humble petitioners oppressed with so heavy a loss, together with their great losses & disadvantages proceeding from their being so suddently driven from the habitation & business, most humbly pray that this Honble House will be pleased to take their calamities case into their compassionate consideration, and grant them such relief as to the great wisdom & goodness of this Honorable House shall seem proper, to assist their endeavors to support themselves and their numerous families, and to become again useful members of the commonwealth.

And your petitioners, as in duty bound shall ever pray, &c.

John Thomilson,
Wm. Bollan, in the name
and behalf of the petitioners.

Two years later, the petitioners learned that " it had been graciously received by his Majesty," but what fully became of it is not recorded. Donations continued to come in from all parts of the country until 1763, which at that time amounted to a total of £22,107 1s. 6¼d. Several private donations from gentlemen abroad were received ; among them, Mr. DeBerdh, of London, sent £100, Charles Apthorp, of New York, the same, and Christopher Kilby, £200, in gratitude for which, Mackerel lane was changed to Kilby street in his honor.

The following paragraphs were printed in the " Post Boy " after the fire : —

A woman who was overtaken in Travail and delivered in open air is doing well at the time of late Fire.

Messrs Printers

As there has been a very unhappy Fire in the Town which broke out at the House of Mrs Mary Jackson and Son, by putting hot ashes in a Hogshead which report is with out foundation for a number of Persons were in the cellar at the time the House were in Fire, and saw the Hogshead entirely sound, and not the least Fire near it, but how the Fire tooke place is uncertain but thought by the sufferers to be by accident and not by any ones neglect.

This lady and her son William soon after open another store in Washington street, a few doors from the Old State-House.

At the May session of the General Court an act was passed " for the better rebuilding that part of the Town which was laid waist by the late fire ; and for preventing fire in the future." The preamble to the act stated that the " great desolation hath been principally occationed by the narrowness of the streets, and the house being built of wood, and covered with shingles." A committee was appointed to lay out the streets anew in the district ; their plans and reports were soon after adopted. Three commissioners .were appointed to hear and settle all complaints or difficulties regarding land. They consisted of Samuel Danforth, Samuel Watts, and Jos. Williams, who, with twelve jurors (none of whom where to be residents of Boston), constituted the Court. More legislating was also passed in the matter of wooden buildings, whereby the builder of any structure of this material of more than seven feet high would be fined £50.

The buildings erected after this fire were wholly (except shops) of brick or slate. They extended from Devonshire street through Water, Congress, Kilby, the lower part of Milk streets, and around the east side of Fort Hill.

Marlborough Engine 5 was first at the fire, also at those at Griffin's wharf. Engine 6 was at that of Mr. Bowdoin's house and Mr. Eustice's dwelling on Sudbury street, all of which occurred previous to March 30.

At a town-meeting, a unanimous vote of thanks was given for all the donations received, and the donors' names were ordered printed in the paper. At the same time methods for the more speedy extinguishing of fires were adopted ; but those orders were the same as were then in force, with the addition of placing the care and inspection of the engines under the firewards, who were to use their own judgment regarding repairs, etc. Two axes and a like number of fire-hooks were given to each company instead of one, and two men were added to each engine to use them.

The only one change in the Board of Firewards occurred this year, Mr. J. M. Wendell succeeding T. Flucker. Capt. A. Brown, of Engine 2, was the first to avail himself of the increase of two members by admitting, on June 4, Joseph Balch and Joseph True. At the same date Engine 1 received the bounty for a fire a month previous at Mr. Lilley's house, near the Old North Church. This engine was ordered to be removed from its site near the Old North Meeting-house, opposite Henry Franklin's house, to the land on the square near the Watch-House (Middle street, near the Second Church). Jonathan Brown and George Rumsley joined the company on the 18th as axe-men. Captain Robinson, of Engine 3, resigns on account of bodily infirmity, and James Barnard was promoted; and four members were enrolled, — Henry Newell, Edward Burbeck, Jr., Elias Robinson, and John Adams.

August 6, Daniel Lilly was admitted on Engine 1, and on September 3 Joseph Balch was succeeded on Engine 2 by William Hill. Engine 6 was first at the fire at Iver's sugar-house, West End, during October.

On the 27th, complaint was made to the selectmen that the companies were short of men. It was ordered, therefore, that the lists of members be sent in for examination. Thomas Balter and Stephen Winter were added to Engine 7 on December 31.

The year 1761 was ushered in with another large fire. During January the weather was unusually cold, so as to render the harbor full of ice for three days, which almost stopped navigation. On the 13th, which was probably one of the coldest days, the cry was sounded about half-past 9 o'clock at night for a fire discovered in a shop opposite the north side of Faneuil Hall, in Dock square. It soon communicated to the row of wooden buildings extending to the swing bridge (Merchants row and North street), which were leased to several occupants by the town, and were soon in ashes, together with all the goods of the residents. The building on the north side escaped, but Faneuil Hall caught, and soon nothing was left of it but the brick walls. Several sailors in trying to save the bell had a very narrow escape from death. While in the cupola they were cut off, and were only reached by men going as high as they could, and resting the short ladders on their shoulders; they were by this means enabled to reach the imperilled men in the tower. The number of shops on the south side of the market soon followed. So cold was the night that the water from the engines congealed as soon as it left the pipes, and fell on the fire in particles of ice. It is no wonder, then, that the fire had its own way, as the engines were rendered almost useless, and dependence had in blowing up and pulling down buildings. The walls of Faneuil Hall, after the fire, were propped up with the ladders belonging to the town. This hall was used by the selectmen in their sessions for seventeen years, but no records or papers were lost. Their next meeting was held in the house of Mr. Robert Stover, on King street. Their old chamber at the Court-House, used before they occupied Faneuil Hall, was at times possessed by committees of the General Court, which made it very inconvenient; and unless they had a place assigned expressly to them, they could not transact their business. They, therefore, petitioned the Council, and was again given the room in the Court-House for their special use. A vote was passed at the town-meeting held March 13 for repairing Faneuil Hall, and the General Court granted a lottery for raising the necessary money. After it was rebuilt, March 14, 1763, James Otis, Esq., delivered an address on the occasion of the first meeting held in the new edifice.

After the fire the dock was filled up as far as the place where the town's shops stood; but the line near the swing bridge was left open, as being of service in case of fire. The fish-market, Engine-House No. 4, and Watch-House were ordered to be moved. Mr. Henderson Inches was elected a fireward this year, *vice* Captain Foster, resigned.

A law was passed by the town on May 12, compelling inhabitants to have their chimneys swept every three months. A regular system of entries were ordered kept by the sweeps, which were to be open at all times to the selectmen.

About this time the orders to the foremen were altered; after mentioning the engine, foreman, members, and the order regarding the appointment or dismissal of a member, it continues : —

And when ever any fire shall break out the said (foreman) and company shall immediately repair to such fire with their engines and there work and improve the same in such places as the firewards shall direct them and that they always obey such orders of the fireward in every respect as they shall give relating too fires and the extinguishing of them, and the said (foreman) and Company are not to depart from any fire or fires with their Engine until they shall have first obtained the concent of at least three of the firewards present. That no person belonging to said Engine shall leave it during the fire without liberty from one of the firewards. That if any one or more of said Company shall not be present and attend his duty by extinguishing of fires and conforming to the direction given him by the fireward unless prevented by sickness or some other unavoidable necessity, the master of said Engine shall as soon as may be given notice thereof to the selectmen, that such proceedings may be had thereupon as they shall think proper. And the said master to take care that the doors of the Engine house be not at any time obstructed or prevented being opened, by snow, ice or any other thing. And that said Engine be worked once every month from the first of May to the 1st of October, and that said Engine and pails belonging to it be kept in good order, and when at any time it shall happen that anything is out of order or wanting for said Engine the masters of some of the Company are directly to apply to the war ls for the time being for their direction concerning it, and that they carry with them at all fires that shall break out the two axes and two fire hooks, belonging to said Engine, taking care that white ropes be always fixed to said hooks and the axes fixed to said Engine. And that they at all times keep at least 15 fathoms of white rope in the engine house ready for more easy pulling down of houses to be used by them in such manner as the firewards shall direct. And that said Company may be distinguished as belonging to said Engine, the selectmen further order that each person shall at his own expense provide

and at every fire wear a black leather jockey cap with a pewter blaze in the front of it and
the number of the Engine he belongs to, of this they are not to fail on penalty of being
removed.

Then follows the clause regarding exemption from military duty and reward of £5 for the first engine at a fire. A number of ladders, making sixty,
the total number possessed by the town, were ordered on March 25. Engine
4, at the dock, was the first at the late fire, and was granted the premium on
this date; and on April 27, Engine 8, for a fire at Mr. Grindley's house, was
given a premium of thirteen shillings, from which it appears that the premium
had been reduced, although no entry is made of this fact.

The disturbances that were soon to break out in a great war and to bring
the town to the notice of the world were daily growing, so that on May 23
complaints to the selectmen became so numerous that they ordered a
detachment of fifteen men from each engine company to assist the watch
during the night in suppressing these disorders. A slight fire at the prison
this month called out Engine No. 7, next door, which consequently received
the prize. Abraham Sutman was admitted on Engine No. 3, June 3, *vice* N.
Woodward, deceased.

Captain Brown, of Engine 2, asked for an assistant on June 24, as he
was incapable, on account of bodily infirmity, to attend to all the duties of his
office. Joseph Hunt was placed in that position, he being the first to fill the
office of lieutenant or assistant. On July 22 Captain Cunningham, of Engine
8, sent in his resignation, and David Wheeler was promoted. On the same
date Aaron May, Robert Fairservice, William Wheeler, and John Lovering
were made members in the place of four others who resigned.

In the early days there stood near Powder-horn Hill, or Flagstaff Hill, on
the Common, a block-house which was burnt September 28, 1761; but it is
related, " as it is a monument of reproach and an asylum of debauchery, the
inhabitants so much noted for their agility at fires remained tame spectators
of the conflagration and allowed the destruction to go on."

Capt. N. Brown, of Engine 2, resigned on August 19, on account of
sickness; his place was filled by Gibbons Sharp, to take effect September 14,
1763. Captain Bentley, after a service of thirteen years as foreman of Engine 1, resigned his position on October 7, and John Baker was promoted.
He admitted Jonathan Lowe, Richard Green, and Joshua Pico in the company
in the place of three members who resigned.

A well or reservoir for holding salt-water was ordered to be dug at the
dock on the 8th. Engine 8, located on Newbury street, was, on December 2,
ordered to be removed to a piece of ground near Deacon Elliot's, at the South
End (corner of Essex and Washington streets, near the " Liberty Tree ").

January 6, 1762, Joel Cushing and Thomas Bracket were admitted members of Engine 7, *vice* Z. Bassett and G. Brown; and on February 3 William
Smith was made a member of Engine 3. This company was given the prize

for the fire at Rokes' sugar-house. Two premiums were given to Engine 4 for fires during March, the first being at the distil-house of Joshua Winslow, the other a barn on King street.

Five of the town ladders were lodged in the following sections of the town on April 26: North Writing school-yard; Messrs. Box & Austin's rope-walk, near Mr. Mayhew's church; Faneuil Hall market; Dr. Sewell's church; William Henshaw's yard; Mr. Bayle's church; and Mr. Checkley's church. A building near the Old North Church was on fire this month, for which Engine 1 was awarded the prize. Captain Baker appointed Timothy Atkins and Thomas Christy on Engine No. 1, June 9, in the room of Samuel Treat and Jonathan Low, and Thomas Collier was admitted on Engine 5, *vice* J. Baxter. Captain Phillips resigns his office as fireward this year, and was succeeded by Thomas Marshall.

About 1 o'clock on the 10th of June another scene of destruction by fire was witnessed by the citizens. The fire broke out in a bake-house of George Bray, at the upper end of Williams' court, and before the engines could be got to work very little of the building or stock, including one hundred and fifty barrels of flour, were left; in fact, so rapid was the spread of the flames, that the family had a narrow escape themselves. Great credit is due the department at this fire, for by their vigilance and splendid work a great conflagration was avoided, as several buildings, including barns, in the vicinity were set by the sparks, and several of them consumed, adding to the already large list of unfortunate dependents on town aid the following persons: George Bray, John Hopkins, Widow Slater, Mr. James Day (school teacher), Capt. Arthur Noble, Samuel Holbrook, Ephraim Copeland, Jr., Jacob Thayer, Benjamin Thwing, Widow Gould, and John Barker. Governor Barnard was present during the time and greatly encouraged the firemen, who were assisted in their endeavors by engines from Charlestown and Castle William, which were in excellent condition. Engine 7, of the home department, was the first to arrive, with Engine 5 as second. Eight men from the watch were stationed with Engines 4 and 5 at the ruins all night, for fear of it breaking out anew.

Engine 2 was allowed an additional man on the 15th, Gibbins Bove being appointed to fill that position. Thomas Bradford was put on Engine 1 as an extra member, June 28. July 14, Engine 2 was given the prize for a fire at Hutchinson's wharf, and on September 15 Elkonah Hayden was admitted on Engine 3, *vice* J. Loring. October 7, J. Wheeler, S. Harris, and B. Bass were succeeded on Engine 9 by William Pennyman, John Greenleaf, and Ambrose Searle. The next change in the department was on Engine 2, Samuel Brown taking the place of W. Hill, on November 17.

The advent of the year 1763 was immediately followed by the appointment of Joseph Foye on Engine 6, *vice* R. Bruyne. On the 16th of this month, about 10 o'clock in the morning, a severe fire broke out in a building on Newbury street (Washington street, from Summer to Essex streets).

Within a very short time six houses, including Engine-house 8, were burnt, while considerable damage was done to several other buildings. The snow being exceedingly deep and the weather very cold impeded the progress of the apparatus; but occurring as it did at midday, ready hands were not wanting.

Engine 5, for a fire at Mr. Storey's house, and Engine 9, for one at Deacon Jones' house, were given premiums during this month, while Ebenezer Torrey, Belcher Smith, and Samuel Shed were appointed in the place of Paddock, Cox, and Flagg on Engine 7. No change is reported on the Board of Firewards this year.

Captain Sutton, Engine 7, on April 6 asked for an addition of one man on his company, as it was one of the largest in the town. William Snowden was therefore appointed to make the sixteenth member, while John Decorter took the place of J. Bonner. Benjamin Church and William Price claimed damages for their house being pulled down during the late fire, but they were refused, on the ground that their building was actually on fire before legal orders were given for its destruction. Engine 2 was first at the fire this month at Mr. Thornton's house on Copp's Hill. Thomas Wheeler and Ebenezer Hinckley were engaged on Engine 8, April 27, *vice* A. Calson and J. Elliott. The award for a fire at Brinsley's dwelling at the South End was given to this company.

Capt. J. Barnard, of Engine 3, gave up his position on June 15, and the vacancy was filled by Jonathan Jenkins; Henry Libetts was admitted a member. Robert Pope's dwelling caught on fire during July; Engine 8 got first water.

The number of firewards was found to be inadequate to control the large force of men now in the service of the department; a petition was therefore sent during the year to the General Court, for permission to vote for an addition of four men to serve in that capacity. This petition was immediately granted by passing the following law : —

The Town of Boston may elect and appoint four more meet persons as firewards, who shall serve in that office till their anniversary meeting in March next, and from thence forward, as they shall see cause, to choose sixteen persons who shall do the duty, and be invested with the like powers, and privileges as firewards in and by the said acts are invested.

The house of Engine 9 was not rebuilt until September 9, when Mr. Wales was paid £4 for the work. The premium for the North End fire was given to Engine 3 on October 5. The election of the Board of Firewards for 1734 made no change in the old members, and William Homes, Joseph Tyler, Jonathan Williams, and Timothy Fitch were chosen as the new members, making up the sixteen.

CHAPTER VI.

1764–1774.

SMALL-POX was very prevalent in the town at this time, in consequence of which the General Court left the Town-Hall, and took up temporary accommodations at Harvard College, at Cambridge, the library room of the college being used by the Governor and Council, while the representatives had a room below. Thus occupied, a fire was discovered a little after noon on January 25, 1764, in what was then called Old College or Harvard Hall, which was in a short time entirely consumed, together with the library and philosophical apparatus. Stoughton and Massachusetts Halls were preserved from the flames with great difficulty, they having caught several times. The fire was supposed to have originated under the hearth, which was laid with timber. The files of the Court and the minutes of the Council for that session were destroyed, although there does not appear to have been any interruption to the business of the session, as it was continued in the house of Ebenezer Bradish.

Engine 7 was the first at the fire at Dr. Gardner's house during March, and on April 18 Edward Runger and Edward Bosset were admitted in the company in the place of Snowden and Shed. The same date, Engine 1 was given the award for the fire at Mr. Newell's barn. On June 6 a fire broke out near the lower end of Auchmuty lane (Essex, below South street), in a turpentine distillery, which it consumed. August 8, S. Hens was made a member of Engine 5. A fire at Mr. Scannel's house, near Dr. Pemberton's church, during September was reached first by Engine 3.

Captain Greenleaf resigned his position as foreman of Engine 9 on August 8, and was succeeded by Samuel Frankland. Benjamin Bowditch was, at the same time, made a member.

On account of the small-pox epidemic during this year, the citizens feared the terrible result should a fire break out. Advertisements were issued in the several newspapers of the town, enjoining every inhabitant to see that the law regarding chimneys was carried out. The overseers of the poor were also instructed to have the chimneys of those who could not afford the expense taken care of at the town's charge. Revisions were also made to the law on this matter, whereby the contract for sweeping chimneys was sold to the highest bidder, who was to be under bond; chimneys were to be swept only during the following time: one hour after sunrise to 11 o'clock, A.M., and 2 o'clock to sunset, and that kitchen chimneys be swept five times, and every other twice, each year. He was also to employ no less than four able-bodied men, and all fines received for neglect of the law were to go to him.

A. Putnam was permitted to rejoin Engine 3, October 10. Isaac Wiliard and Thomas Moore took the places of Crowley and Norcross on Engine 6, on November 7; the house of this engine was repaired at the same time. Timothy Pees and William Baker admitted on Engine 4, *vice* Perkins and Anderson, on the 13th.

The first complaint regarding any foreman was made the 20th, when Captain Wheeler, of Engine 8, was discharged for keeping a member of his engine named W. Wheeler on the company's list when he was ordered back to the militia " for maltreating officers on the Common." Obediah Curtis was promoted to the position of foreman. But this appointment was unsatisfactory to some of the members of that company, and the following petition was sent to the selectmen on December 12 : —

We the subscribers in behalf of this Company desire that we may have our former captain again restored to us, and that we may have the privilege of choosing or nominating a captain or members as Vacancies may arise from time to time, and as we in duty bound shall ever pray, etc. Signed John Bennett, Aaron May.

But no comfort was given by the selectmen, who, in reply, informed them that they had already appointed a suitable man to command the engine, and that they were determined not to give up their rights of nominating the captains ; in fact, they disapproved of the entire petition. Several of the members having resigned, a new company was organized on the 14th, consisting of Jos. Lovering, John Lovering, E. Hinckley, Robert Robinson, William Harking, Stephen Greenleaf, William Morse, Jr., Jos. Sumner, John McFaden, Thomas Noland, John Crosby, Jr., and Thomas Hinckley. With the usual orders to the foreman, a clause was inserted that each member wear a black-leather jockey-cap, with a pewter blaze, on which the number of the engine is engraved. By this order the first badge and fire-hat were adopted.

During January, 1765, premiums were given as follows : Engine 2, fire in Block House lane ; Engine 7, at Mr. Neal's bake-house ; Engine 8, at Widow Ferry's bake-house. John Robinson was engaged on Engine 3, in the place of his father, February 20.

The firewards elected for 1765 were Capt. Adino Paddock, James Richardson, William Taylor, William D. Cheever, James Cunningham, and Capt. Benjamin Waldo, *vice* H. Inches, R. Tyler, J. Scolly, Captain Davis, Jos. Jackson, and T. Fitch, who resigned. Engine 8 had Isaac Anmer, William Moore, Jr., and John McFaden admitted on March 20. The fire at Widow Treefor's house, below the New North Church, in May, was put out by Engine 2. John Neat succeeded T. Batter on Engine 7, on the 7th. At the same date Engine 3 was given the prize for a fire at Captain Authorberry's brigantine lying at Hancock wharf. July 17, Thomas Nolan was admitted a member of Engine 8. The ladders in the yard of Mr. Thayer, belonging to the department, were distributed at the almshouse, granary, and workhouse on August 25; and on the 28th Captains Read, Putnam, Sutton, and Curtis were called upon by the selectmen to be ready to assist the civil magistrates in their endeavors to preserve the peace.

Mr. David Wheeler, ex-foreman of Engine Company 8, is credited with being the first in the town to manufacture complete an engine to meet the requirements of the department. Wheeler was a blacksmith, and located on Newbury street (Washington street), where he had given notice in the press that there was an opportunity to encourage home industry, as he would manufacture water engines as good as any imported, and at a much lower price. He had not had his new engine finished but a few days when a chance was given him to fully test its capabilities, as on the morning of August 21 a fire was discovered in one of the six workshops that made the corner between Quaker lane and Water street (Congress street), where in a few moments the entire block was in a mass of flames; but the plentiful water-supply in the vicinity and the low wind enabled the firemen to confine it within those walls. The " home-made " engine " was found to perform extremely well." Wheeler was also probably the first to introduce lightning-rods in the town, for in an advertisement he states his purpose " to make and fix iron rods with points upon houses or any other eminence, for prevention from the effects of lightning."

The famous Stamp Act riots date from this time. In an account of one of these great disturbances we find the following : —

About twilight, on August 26, a small bonfire appeared to be kindled in King Street, and surrounded only by a few boys and children; but one of the Firewards, perceiving it to rise to a dangerous height, interpose l and use l his endeavours to extinguish, or at least to diminish it; in which salutary attempt, after several whispers from a person unknown, warning him of danger, he received a blow and such tokens of insult and outrage as obliged him to desist and take his departure. Soon after this, daylight being scarce in, the fire gradually decaying, a peculiar whoop and whistle was observed to be sounded from various quarters.

The account then goes on to detail the ravages made on the house of William Story, Esq., the rioters using the public files of the Court of the Vice-Admiralty, his private papers and accounts, to feed the dying flames of the bonfire, which they left after finishing their spoliation of the house.

Captain Green's distil-house was burned during November; Engine 7 was given the award. A. Waters and T. Wheeler resigned from Company 9, and were succeeded by George Roulston and Daniel Parks, on the 27th; and on January 22, 1766, Thomas Botter was admitted, *vice* J. Laughton.

The first fire for the year 1766 occurred during January, at Mr. Smith's house; Engine 4 arrived on the scene first. There was also a fire at John Boylston's store the same month, for which Engines 7 and 5 claimed the premium. It was given to the latter, as was a premium for a fire at Mr.

Stephens' shop. John Crosby, Jr., admitted on Engine 8, February 6, *vice* T. Hinckley. On the 19th William Dorricut and Benjamin Gottom were made members of Engine 3, in the place of W. Pearson and A. Putnam. William Brown succeeded J. Pico on Engine 1, on the 26th. The captain of this company asked for twenty members for his engine, as it was too large to be manned by eighteen. John Ballard, Jr., and John Bryant were therefore made members, March 5.

The choice of firewards for this year were John Hancock, Samuel Adams, and Francis Shaw, *vice* Joseph Jackson, James Austin, and William Taylor, resigned.

The engine constructed by David Wheeler, which, as the entry states, " does honor to the country as well as the constructor," was given to the town by the builder and his associate, Mr. John Green, on the condition that the town keep it in good order and allow the company the similar privilege as the other firemen enjoyed, which generous proposal was accepted with the above conditions on March 12. This engine was called the Green Engine, No. 10, and located in Bedford street; later on it was termed the Brooks Engine, No. 11. Wheeler was appointed foreman, with fourteen men. The first prize was given them fourteen days later for a fire at Captain Wheeler's own house in Pond lane (Bedford street). Benjamin Black joined Engine 9 on April 2.

The preparations for the celebration of great jubilation held by the town on occasion of the repeal of the Stamp Act called forth some apprehensions on the part of the authorities regarding fire. The following motions were therefore unanimously voted : —

That the Magistrates of the Town, the Selectmen Firewards Constables and Enginemen be desired to use their utmost endeavors to prevent any bonfires being made in any part of this town, also the throwing of Rockets, Squibs and other fireworks, in any part of the streets of said Town except the time that shall be appointed for general Rejoicing, and that the inhabitants be desired for the present to restrain their children and servants from going abroad on evenings. Also that the security of the Powder House on the night of general rejoicings the selectmen be desired to order two of the Fire Engines and the company to be placed near said Magazine, and that the roof thereof be well wet and that the air-holes be stop't with mortar and Bricks or otherwise.

Despite the large number of bonfires and explosion of fireworks, which was without precedent in the town, no fires were set or damage done, except it be the burning of the pyramid or obelisk, intended to be set up under Liberty Tree, but temporarily erected on the Common, by the " Sons of Liberty ; " which, by some accident, took fire about 1 o'clock on the night of the celebration. This structure was four stories high, and was illuminated with two hundred and eighty lamps. At its top was " fixed a round box of fireworks horizontally." These four compartments, or stories, exhibited each four sides. The lower story, or base, was without ornament, and is only described as " of the Doric order ; " the next was covered with cartoons ; the third, with ten verses each; and the last, with four portraits each. (See Drake's History.)

William Curtis and Joseph Ford were made members of Engine 8, May 14, and Israel Lovering and John Bacon on Engine 6. These additions were made to place the membership on the same basis as it was before the war, when a number of firemen enlisted.

Engine 2 was first at the fire in house of Rev. Mr. Checkleys, at North End; Engine 1, at Dr. Clark's barn, North End; and Engine 6, at Mr. Polland's house, — all of which occurred during June. Thomas Huntable was admitted on Engine 9, the 30th. Orcutt Shaw and James Robbins succeeded John Baker and J. Clough on Engine 1, November 5. The last fire this year occurred during December, at the potash factory, near Rev. Mr. Checkley's house; the award was given to Engine 10. On the 16th Nathaniel Corbeiny was added to Company 2.

A large fire is recorded for the beginning of 1767. It broke out about 10 o'clock on the night of February 3, in the bakehouse of Mr. Bray, located near Mill creek. About twenty-five houses were laid in ruins. The flames passed over the creek, and caught the houses in Perraway's, or Ball's, alley (Centre street), where it did most of the damage, over two-thirds of the buildings consumed being on the north side of the creek. Engine 4 was the first to throw water. The loss of real estate, as taken by the selectmen, was as follows: Mr. Jonathan Williams' mansion-house, £1,000; Capt. John Bryant's house, £175; Mr. John Griffith's house, £175; Thomas Emmon's house, £300; Capt. Robert Ball's house and five tenants, £1,000; three tenants of William Scott, £160; Jacob Emmon's house, £106 13s. 4d.; two tenants of Thomas Walker, £200; Widow Hendry's house, £100; Widow Lepson's house, £6); Widow Dodge's house, £100; tenant of Joseph Howe, £200; William Paine's house, £133 6s. 8d. Damaged property: tenant of Ed. Marion, £13 6s. 8d.; two tenants belonging to George B. Gedney, £13 6s. 8d.; storehouse of James Thompson, £66 13s. 4d.; a house of the heirs of Andrew Tyler, £40; and sundry tenants' stores, stables, etc., belonging to John Hancock, £1,490; aggregating £5,333 6s. 8d. Donations were received from various sources, the churches collecting £447 12s. 4d., and the General Court ordered, on February 28, that £400 be paid to the sufferers, who number sixty-three.

The next fire occurred during March, at Mr. Reed's sugar-house, at North End; Engine 2 was first on hand. Martin Gay, Esq., was elected a fireward during 1767, in the place of Francis Shaw. Benjamin White joined Engine 6, April 22, while B. B. Emmonds and Roland Brooks were made members of Engine 9, on the 27th; a fire in a house near Deacon Barret's gives Engine 4 a prize, June 10; and on the 17th E. Richards was enrolled on the list of Engine 9. The firewards had the public ladders replaced on August 10, and an advertisement was issued forbidding people using them except in case of fire.

Engine 3 was given the prize, on September 30, for a fire at Mr. Cowell's shop. The captain at this time complained of his engine being out of repair, and D. Wheeler, being requested to inspect it, stated that it was unfit for service, and asked that he may be allowed to build one.

On account of some trouble, the nature of which we cannot ascertain, Capt. J. Brown, of Engine 6, was called before the selectmen on September 23 ; and on the charges being preferred, he resigned, and was succeeded on October 5 by Josiah Gains ; Cable and Foy were also dismissed, and were succeeded by Mr. Pillsbury and George Newell. Wheeler was given the contract to build a new engine to take the place of No. 3, which was to be of the same dimensions as the Charlestown engine, and to be at least five inches in chamber, for which he was to be paid £57 6s. 8d. The old engine was sold to John Ruddock for £20, who kept it on his farm at the North End.

Nathaniel Wheeler took the place of J. Martin on Engine 6, October 21. Engine 4 was given the award for the fire at Mr. Goldthwait's barn, November 11.

Among the various articles placed on the list of goods to be prohibited from being imported were fire-engines, for which clause we suppose Wheeler and his friends are responsible, as he was the founder of the manufacture of these apparatus in Boston.

Captain Wheeler was dismissed from the service, December 16. He had lost one of his legs, and therefore considered by the selectmen as incapable to attend his duties ; Benjamin Wheeler succeeded him. A committee from the firewards lodged a complaint with the authorities that Captain Reed, of Engine 5, had refused to obey the direction of Captain Wendall, a late fireward ; also of several other companies, that they played their engines upon one another, which discommoded those attending to their duty. The company commanders being brought before the selectmen were acquainted with the charges, on December 23 ; but these gentlemen gave their word that they would immediately send in the name of any member who would in the future be guilty of ill-behavior. Orders were then issued to the department that every member must wear a hat with a pewter blaze, so they could be distinguished.

Captain Baker, of Engine 1, was succeeded by John Ballard on December 28, who proposed Francis Marshall, J. Walker, and Benjamin Cushing as members of his company, in the place of T. Brown, G. Rumsby, and John Ballard, Jr. G. Flagg joined Engine 6, December 30.

The initial month of 1768 did not pass without a fire. It occurred at Mr. Kneeland's house, in Kneeland's lane (Kneeland street) ; Engine 6 was on hand first. A fire at Mrs. Walles', Dock square, occurred during February, at which Engine 4 was awarded first prize ; and on March 9 Engine 2 had first water on Edes' bakehouse.

John Scollay was again elected a fireward for 1768, being chosen in the place of W. D. Cheever, and Thomas Dawes, *vice* J. Williams. After the discharge of Captain Wheeler, Engine 10 was given entirely in charge of the town, on April 25, the selectmen agreeing that in case of fire their estates to be given the preference. This engine was given the award for a fire at Mr. Deering's during the month, and Engine 6 was on hand first at Mr. Anchor's house, West End. Samuel Brenden and N. Pierce succeeded Theodore Bliss and M. Greenleaf on Engine 9. A petition was sent into the town-meeting on May 4, requesting that application be made to the General Court for an additional number of firewards; but it was not acted upon. Benjamin Burland was admitted on Engine 1, *vice* B. Brown, June 6; and Richard Cull succeeded M. Hawes on Engine 6, the 8th.

August 30, Jeffrey Richardson, Thomas Wheeler, James Blake, and Nath. Bradley were admitted on Engine 10, *vice* David Wheeler, D. Wheeler, Jr., Thomas T. Wheeler, and M. Jackson. Daniel M. Warren succeeded S. Brown on Engine 2, January 25, 1769.

The January fire for 1769 was of more importance than formerly, for a detailed account of which we reprint the report made in Snow's History : —

On Monday, January 30, 1769, at about half after 10 o'clock at night, the people adjoining the jail were alarmed by the prisoners crying fire, on which the keeper and a number of persons ran there and found part of the prison in a blaze. It was some time before the prisoners could be got out, the inner keys being lost in the confusion, and the wooden work being so strongly bound with iron that it was difficult to cut through the doors and partitions. Captain Wilson of the 59th Regiment was particularly active in extragating them. It was expected that the fire would be kept under but the great quantity of outside timber work occationed it to rage with great violence and the flames burst through the windows and reached the roof, which after burning some hours fell in, the wood-work burning all night and in the morning nothing remained but the bare stone walls. During the continuance of the fire the towns people behaved with their usual alacrity, and many of the military were very active in assisting them. The commodore was present, and a number of officers and sailors were landed from the ship and an Engine was sent from the Rumney (Chelsea). The commander of the main guard with a party, offered their services on the first alarm, which was refused, but they were afterward sent for and took charge of the prisoners. This is the only good deed we have found attributed to those persons.

According to another account, some of the prisoners had to be dragged through such small apertures that their flesh was torn in a frightful manner; two of them were considerably burned, one of them badly. Two of the prisoners escaped. On examining the others, it was found that the fire was set to the door by two of them who were confined in one room; one was a soldier, the other a young lad. Engine 5 was, as a matter of course, being next door, the first to get water on the building.

Engine 2 was at the fire in a house near the Old North Church during the month. February 1, John Fenno took T. Hinckley's place on Engine 8. The following engines were awarded premiums : Engine 7, fire at Mr. Williams, School street, in February; Engine 5, fire at Hutchins' wharf, in March; Engine 9, fire near the powder-house, at the foot of the Common, during May.

Alexander Hill was elected a fireward, *vice* Jos. Cunningham, resigned. Nicholas Deering succeeded T. Bracket on Engine 7, August 2, and Walker Turber was admitted on Engine 2, *vice* J. Turber, deceased. On Engine 6 Nathaniel Low and Nathaniel Call took the place of J. Lord, W. White, Y. Norcrost, and J. Loring. Engine 4 was first at the fire at Jacob Boyd's house, at the dock, during October; while a prize was given Engine 6 for a fire at Captain Small's house, at the West End, in December; also for one at Mr. Pallard's house. John Bound took the place of W. Darricout on Engine 3, December 27; George Cade and William Rounds succeeded R. Olle and G. Flagg on Engine 6, the same date.

The fire for January, 1770, was at the house of Mr. Eddes, at the dock; Engine 4 threw first water. A. Crown was appointed on Engine 8, *vice* W. Moore, Jr., March 11, and Thomas Button on Engine 7, *vice* J. Barrow, on the 18th. No change in the Board of Firewards occurred this year.

At the town-meeting this month the question was debated as to whether application should be made to the General Court that an act may be passed empowering a justice of the peace to convict any person who refused to obey a fireward to work at a fire; it was passed in the negative.

The great tragedy of March 5, 1770, known as the Boston Massacre, was in some respects due to the ringing of the bells; hearing which, the citizens supposed a fire was in progress, and being told that it was in King street, hurried thither. They then discovered that it was done to congregate the people around the Old State-House, where, soon after, the ever-memorable firing was committed which so inflamed the hearts of thousands of our fathers, that the great engines of power controlled by the king could not quench that fire of liberty which raged with such irresistible fury.

Nathaniel Tidmanks succeeded Mr. Lidbetter on Engine 3 in August. On the 19th Thomas Uran succeeded Captain Putnam on Engine 4. On Fast Day, this year, a fire occurred at a house in Charter street; it was put out by Engine 2.

The Old South Church was the prey for the January fire for 1771; little damage was done, however. Jos. Wheeler succeeded J. Hinckley on Engine 8, February 13. Mr. Francis Shaw succeeded William Holmes on the Board of Firewards this year. The thanks of the town were given him for his service on the board. The courtesy was extended after this to every member who, after serving for a length of time, resigned.

The care of chimneys was given less attention each year by many of the inhabitants; therefore, on May 7, the town appointed Firewards Dawes, Williams, and Austin to prepare a scheme which would benefit the town in this respect. These gentlemen, in their report, stated that, from an estimate, there were 1,800 dwelling-houses in the town, each of which have three or more funnels, which, as the law directs, must be swept four times per year, equalling 21,600 funnels, which, at the price established, amounted to more than £1,200; and as those who are careful to have their chimneys clean were in more danger from the defective flues of the neglectful than from their own chimneys, it was their opinion that it would be advantageous and economical to have the expense carried by taxation; and that a master and six sweepers be employed, at a salary of £100 per year for the foreman and £50 for the subordinates, who were to go through each ward and keep a register of the house and time when work was done. This plan was readily adopted and put in force.

The new engine for No. 3 was first mentioned on September 1 as working at a fire, when the company was given premium for those at Mr. Thornton's and Mr. Steward's dwellings, which occurred on August 22. Engine 6 was awarded for the fire at Mr. Stone's house, West End, during September. J. N. Woodward was admitted on Engine 3 on October 30, *vice* J. Brown; and on November 13 Amons These was appointed in the place of R. B. Emonds on Engine 7.

On January 15, 1772, Capt. Thomas Read, of Engine 5, after a service of twenty-nine years as foreman of that company, sends in his resignation, on account of old age. This is the longest record for service as foreman in one company recorded in the history of the Boston Fire Department. Mr. Shubael Hews succeeded him in command on the 22d.

The January fire for this year occurred in the Brick Meeting-house, for which Engine 2 was given the prize. The other fire this month occurred in Bower's building, on King street; Engine 7 was there first. John Munzie joined Engine Co. 3, *vice* J. Roberts, on February 5. On the morning of April 1 the house of Mr. Cordier on King street was destroyed by fire; Engine 5 was on hand. John Spear joined Engine 9 on the 15th. Capt. Job Prince was the only new name on the list of firewards for this year, he succeeding John Rowe.

The Honorable John Hancock presented to the town, on May 6, a very fine engine which he had imported from England. It was given with the understanding that it should be provided with a company of men by the town, who should have the same privileges as the other firemen. The machine was formally accepted at an adjourned meeting held on the 22d, which meeting was called for the especial purpose of thanking the donor, and to take proper action regarding the engine. Mr. Hancock being requested to nominate a foreman, appointed Mr. Samuel Sloan. The selectmen ordered that it was " to be placed in a house at or near Hancock wharf, and in case of fire the estate of the donor shall have the preference of its service." This engine was called Hancock No. 10, and had a company of fourteen members.

May 13, William Fenno took G. Roulston's place on Engine 9. June 3, N. Thomas succeeded T. Narnstable, and on October 11 Robert Smallpace joined the company. A fire occurred at Mr. Dalton's house during June, and at Mr. Sumner's dwelling on July 20, for which Engine 7 was given the prizes. James Sargent was admitted on Engine 7, *vice* T. Patterson,

November 27. The last fire for the year occurred at Mr. Major Lews' barn, at which Engine 8 threw first water.

The fire for January, 1773, occurred at Mr. Winter's bull-house, at which Engine 5 was the first to arrive. The company belonging to Engine 9 was increased to seventeen members on January 6. February 10, W. Manzey, W. Clark, and William Adams left Engine 3. Captain Gains, of Engine 6, was succeeded by John Norcrost on March 3, he appointing John Jackson and Hall as members. The same date William Corbin was admitted on Engine 8, *vice* J. Lovering. Capt. Edward Proctor was chosen a fireward in the place of Myer Daws, and Mr. John Coffin in the room of Mr. Richardson.

At the request of the firewards, March 9, six leather buckets were added to each engine. A committee was appointed at this meeting to make a report concerning the advisability of having pumps placed at the Mill bridge (in Hanover street over Blackstone street), to be used in case of fire. Those gentlemen urged upon the town to fix one pump on each side and two at the drawbridge (in North street), one of which they recommended being placed in the house lately erected at the Mill bridge for the engine given by Hon. John Hancock. The cost of each pump amounted to £7. They also thought it necessary to place another pump almost midway between the first bridge on the south-west side of the creek, as there were a large number of wooden buildings in that neighborhood, and as few had wells, reliance had to be had in the creek for a supply of water in case of fire.

March 24, a fire occurred at Mr. Loring's house on Middle street (Hanover street), at which Engine 2 won the premium. Engine 7 applied for this prize, but was refused. The fire at the Custom-House during March was first attended by Engine 5.

On Sunday, April 4, a fire originated in the cabinet shop of Mr. Alexander Edwards, located near the Mill pond. (The westerly part of Salem street, also Hawkins and Green streets, extended into this pond. It was filled up by the Boston Mill Corporation from soil obtained from Beacon Hill on May 14, 1804. The filling of the pond and grading of the land added about fifty acres of building lands to Boston, from which now proceeds all the railroads leading north.) Six or seven other buildings were destroyed by this fire, including the first church built by the Scandinavians, that stood at the foot of a lane "leading to the Mill Pond somewhere between the two Baptists Meeting Houses." After the burning of their church, this sect met for a time in a Latin school-house, then in Mr. S. Townsend's house, in Cross street, until a house was erected for them in the rear of Middle street. But they so diminished in numbers that in 1823 their meetings were discontinued, and the building used as a primary school.

E. Rairy took John Milladge's place on Engine 9, April 7. On May 12 John Richards succeeded J. Brown on Engine 1; June 9, C. Engelstrom joined Engine 5; at the same date Mr. Townsend took B. Burdit's place on Engine 9. The new engine, Hancock, No. 10, was granted two awards on the 2d, — one for a fire at a house in Cold lane (Portland street), the other at Ed. Shay's. Benjamin Visey, Nath. Bradlee, and Thomas Wheeler were admitted on Engine 8, August 4, *vice* J. Crowley, J. Ford, S. Haden, and J. McFadden, discharged. On the 11th John Grindly joined the company; Benjamin Houghton and John Griffith became members of Engine 7 on the 18th, *vice* J. Rogers and W. Hersey. On November 28 James Biard and Jonathan Brown took the place of Ballard, Jr., and J. Brown on Engine 1. A fire on Charter street this month gave Engine 2 the award. The last fire of the year occurred during December, at a house of Mr. Margot's, Southick's court (Howard street). Engine 6 was the lucky one.

On March 2, 1774, another change is made in the list of members of Engine 9. John Crosby, William Stevens, John Roulstom, Jr., and Samuel Breading are admitted members, and on the same date E. Thomas joins Hancock Engine 10.

The changes for this year in the Board of Firewards were Capt. John Pulling. *vice* J. M. Wendell, deceased; Mr. Caleb Davis, *vice* A. Hill, and David Cheever, *vice* John Hancock, resigned on account of ill-health.

Captain Ballard, of Engine 1, sends in his resignation as foreman of that company on April 13, as he intended moving out of town. Mr. Joshua Bentley was appointed to take command, after which he made the following change in the members: Newbury Clough, William Dwyer, and John Ballard, Jr., were admitted, and J. Richardson dismissed.

A new street was laid out this year near the ruins of the fire of 1767, which is now North Centre street. It was then called Paddy's alley.

One of the most terrible fires that is thus far recorded in the history of the department, from the extent of the loss of life, occurred on Wednesday, August 10, at about 10.30 at night. The fire was discovered in a large brick dwelling-house located on Fish street, five or six doors north of Mountfort's corner, at the foot of North square (now the corner of North and Fleet streets), and owned by Mr. Milliken and Mrs. Campbell. The lower part of the house was a mass of flames before the occupants of the upper floor were aware of their terrible danger. Several escaped by jumping from the windows, some of whom, being considerably burned, were destitute of clothing, while three women and two children perished in the flames. The house was entirely consumed, and a bakehouse adjoining was badly burned. "Earl Percy politily offered the service of some soldiers who could be depended upon, but was informed that the regulations of the town rendered their assistance unnecessary." Engine 3 was the first to throw water.

Captain Jenkins, of Engine 3, resigns his position on this company on December 7, and is succeeded by Mr. Elias Robinson.

CHAPTER VII.

1775–1789.

THE first fire for the year 1775 began in January, at the distil-house of Colonel Jackson. Engine 8 was the favored one. February 22, Thomas Jackson succeeded Ed. Reues on Engine 9. Captain Frankland, of this company, died during this month, and was succeeded by Richard Hunnewell. More changes occurred on the Board of Firewards this year than for any time since the office was established. Messrs. Ezekiel Cheever, Stephen Cleverly, Thomas Crafts, Jr., Ebenezer Hancock, Capt. Samuel Barrett, and Abiel Ruddock were elected, *vice* J. Tyler, A. Paddock, S. Adams, M. Gay, J. Coffin, and D. Cheever.

Engine 2 was first at the fire at the house of William King, at the North End, during March. Joseph Smith took John Crosby's place on Engine 9, April 5; and on the 12th Captain Shark, of Engine 2, after a service of fourteen years, resigns his position, and is succeeded by Joab Hunt. A committee, consisting of William Scollay, W. Austin, and Colonel Marshall, were ordered to inspect all the engines.

On May 17 a fire broke out on the south side of the town dock, in the building occupied as barracks by the British troops; one of the buildings belonged to John Hancock. For ten days previous there had been a report circulated that the Liberty party intended to fire the town. The general had taken the alarm, and took the engine under his care, and appointed new captains, when the engine-men took umbrage and left the service, — a fact indicative of the patriotic spirit of the firemen of 1775. " Soon as I observed the fire," says a Bostonian, " the bells not ringing, I cried ' fire ; ' but was stopped by a soldier, who said it was against orders, and who threatened to knock my brains out if I did not keep still. When I arrived at the fire there was no engine. I asked the reason of such extraordinary delay, and was told by an engine-man that he had been to his engine, but the bayonets were too thick. After the fire had been long raging the engines arrived with their new captains and military firewards, and not being used to such an enemy, they, indeed, cut a miserable figure. Upon the whole, it appears to me as plain as the meridian sun that, if the engines had been on the old footing, the fire would have been quenched and £20,000 saved. A large quantity of provisions, generously contributed by the patriotic friends of Boston for the relief of the inhabitants laboring under the oppressive Port Bill, were also destroyed." This conflagration originated from the bursting of some cartridges, and before the fire was extinguished thirty buildings were destroyed.

The fires of the Revolution are not mentioned in the town records; but we learn from other sources that the Provincials attacked and burnt a house on the Neck containing implements of war. Major Vose, of Heath's Regiment, burnt a light-house on Point Shirley, July 12, and the British, in return, routed out and burnt the George Tavern, on Dover street.

In mentioning these fires we must not omit that which happened on the 17th of June at Charlestown. On this glorious day the foe fired the town in several places, which consumed a meeting-house, a court-house, a prison, two work-houses, two school-houses, and three hundred and eighty buildings, together with a large amount of property belonging to the unfortunate citizens of Boston, who had removed it to Charlestown for safety. The people of that town lost all their furniture and household effects by this wanton and barbarous act of His Majesty's troops. We do not learn that any great efforts were made to check· the devouring element, and it is probable that the citizen soldiers of Boston and Charlestown were too seriously engaged in other and more important "fires" on Bunker Hill.

The record of this department as kept by the selectmen is an entire blank during 1776, except it be the appointment of firewards. Those chosen were Capt. Caleb Hopkins, Capt. Isaac Phillips, Paul Revere, and Thomas Tileston, in the place of F. Shaw, J. Prince, E. Cheever, and S. Cleverly.

The British evacuated the town March 17, 1776, but continued their devastations on Castle William; but it does not appear that they accomplished their work, and left the harbor several days after, as a diarist states that "on the 22 of March, five days later, Castle William was burnt to ashes and destroyed."

The first fire recorded for 1777 occurred at the house of Dr. Churches, during February, by which Engine 9 gained the premium. Maj. Andrew Symms, Capt. Gustavus Fellows, Capt. Joseph Webb, Capt. John Ballard, Mr. Francis Shaw, and Mr. John Winthrop were elected firewards for 1777, *vice* Thomas Marshall, Benjamin Waldo, Captain Barretts, A. Ruddock, C. Hopkins, and J. Phillips. On Monday, March 31, a small house at the south part of the town, used as a soap-work, was burnt.

After the evacuation of the troops the companies were ordered, on September 10, to be filled up with their usual equipment of members. It is unfortunate that we have not the names of the brave fellows of this department who lost their lives during this struggle for liberty. We know, however, that three foremen did not return to duty, — Captain Norcross, of Engine 6, who was succeeded by George Ridgway; Capt. Benjamin Wheeler, of Engine 10, having been succeeded by Jono. Champney; and Captain Hews, of Engine 5, John Holland taking his place.

Captain Uran, of Engine 4, was paid his bounty for arriving first at the fire at the jail, December 3; he was also paid for a fire at Wing's lane (Elm street). Wednesday evening, December 11, the barracks located on Cobble Hill were burned by the British prisoners who were confined there. For the fire of January, 1778, we record that which consumed the stately edifice located in Frog lane (Boylston street), built fifty years earlier by Peter Chardon, but then occupied by John Carter, Esq. The fire originated in one of the chambers about 9 o'clock on the evening of the 15th, and burnt so rapidly that very little of the furniture was saved. A barn on the premises was also destroyed, and had it not been that the snow was very deep on the roofs of the houses, a terrible conflagration would have resulted; as it was, the several buildings caught, but the flames were extinguished before much damage was done. Engine 9 was first on hand. Another fire occurred at William Sheraden's house, West End; Engine 6 was awarded the bounty.

Engine No. 10 was awarded two premiums during March, — one for a fire at E. Blanchard's house, Green lane (Salem street), the other at Widow Smith's, on Sea street (Federal street). Only one change occurred in the Board of Firewards for 1778, — Major Greenough resigned, and was succeeded by Mr. John Lowell.

The engine-men, although exempt by law from military duty, were drafted into the army of the Revolution by an act passed February 16, by which their number was reduced to one hundred and thirty men. This question was seriously taken into consideration by the firewards, who filed a petition at the town-meeting to have a committee appointed to investigate the matter. The committee being organized made the following report on January 26 : —

That they have conferred with the captains of the several engine companies and find that nothing short of a total exemption from all military duty will be sufficient to satisfy and encourage the men belonging to those companies. They would therefore propose that application be made to the General Court, that, in consideration of the great quantity of stores belonging to the States and continent stored in this town, together with the valuable Buildings the property of the State, the Enginemen necessary for the town under these circumstances may be deducted from the number of the inhabitints & not subject to raise their proportion of any draughts of men or do any Military Duty excepting in case of alarm when they are ready to appear & do their duty as the law directs. And as a further encouragement the committee propose that the premium for the engine company who first bring their engines to work upon any Fire which shall break out in any building in this town shall be advanced to Three Pounds lawful money.

Engine 11 was the first at the fire during March, at Mr. Porter's house. The next month a barn in Royal Exchange alley (Exchange street) was burned; Engine 4 was on hand. Engine 9 was first at the next fire that occurred, during May, at the house of William Newhouse, at South End. A fire at Mr. White's, at North End, during June gave Engine 3 the award. The following month Engine 9 was given the bounty for a blaze at Mrs. Clarke's house, South End. Engine 6 was at the fire at Mr. Prynghbie's house, West End.

Three fires are recorded for January, 1779. The 17th, Peter Chardon's house and a house at West End were reached first by Engine 6 ; a dwelling on Cow lane (High street) was put out by Engine 11. Maj. Thomas Melvill was chosen a fireward this year in the room of Colonel Crafts, being the only change in that board.

The small fires for the rest of this year were: January, a house at West End, Engine 6. April, Mary Wyland's house, South End, Engine 9; Mr. Tyler's house, Engine 7; and Mr. Phillips' house, near the South Church, Engine 5. June, house in Seven Star lane (Hawley street), Engine 11. Captain Curtis, of Engine 8, applies for a new house, July 14. A committee was appointed to investigate. November, fire at Mr. Bowchoton's, in Black Horse lane (Prince street), also at Captain Dudd's house, in the rear; Engine 3. December, Widow Sears' house, Engine 8; Mr. Huckley's house, Engine 9; Dr. Mather's, North End, Engine 2; and Major Cunningham's house, South End, Engine 9.

Monday, January 10, 1780, a fire broke out in the lower store on Hancock wharf, which communicated to a ship belonging to Thomas Ruffle and S. Higginson. The new frigate "Protector" also caught on fire, but was not much damaged. Another fire broke out at the jail, during January. Engine 4 was there first. The South Writing School, Mr. Holbrooks, teacher, was burned; one person was prosecuted for disobeying the firewards, and fined £4 7s., at this fire. February 28, the sign of the Lamb Tavern was also on fire. Engine 9 received both premiums.

Col. Jabez Hatch succeeded Col. Paul Revere as a fireward for 1780. Engine 10 was awarded for fires at Mr. W. Numbless' house, Middle street (Hanover street), Mr. Ballard's dwelling in Cross street, and Mr. Pulcifer's house in Middle street, during March.

The house of Engine 1 was repaired on April 19. William Darricut succeeded Thomas Atkins, Jr., on Engine No. 2, May 17. A fire at Messrs. Pain & Miller's warehouse gave Engine 3 the bounty during June.

On Wednesday, September 20, at 2 o'clock in the afternoon, a large fire broke out on Long wharf, which destroyed the warehouse of Messrs. Pitts & Call, and Mr. S. Eliot's tobacco store, the commissary store, and several other buildings. It happened at high water, otherwise the whole range of warehouses would have been consumed. October 24, the firewards complained of Captains Curtis, of Engine 8, and Holland, of Engine 5, for bad behavior, and on examination by the selectmen they declared their intention of giving no offence, on which they were excused. November 6, Joseph Daniels and Samuel Todd were admitted members of Engine 6.

No change in the Board of Firewards occurred during 1781. Joseph Pason, Jacob Gould, and E. Thayer joined Engine 8 on April 18.

On June 27 the masters of all the engines applied for a resolve to be prepared in the General Court, similar to the one applied by the military act. Engine 6 was given the prize on September 9 for the fire at Captain Crap's house, on Sudbury street.

Capt. William Sutton, after a service of twenty-six years, resigned from the department on account of old age, on October 3. Sutton is second on the record for long service as foreman in one company. He was succeeded by Joel Cushing as foreman of the company. A photograph of his badge will be seen in the engraving on page 43. The rim and figure of this badge is of pure silver, the background is of enamelled leather, size over all $4\frac{1}{2} \times 3\frac{1}{2}$ inches. It was the style adopted by the department at that time.

Engine 6 was first at the fire at Mr. Inches' house, West End, during October.

No change is reported on the list of firewards for 1782. A. Caswell joined Engine 6, *vice* S. Todd, April 24. A fire at the house of Mr. Weaver, near Liberty Tree, in September, gave Engine 9 the bounty.

On November 6 John Cade and Jacob Clough succeeded Henry Snuff and T. Badger on Engine 2. This company was at the same time awarded the prize for a fire at the house of C. Brew, in White Bread alley (Bartlett street).

Captain Curtis, of Engine 8, was again complained of by the firewards, in consequence of which he was discharged November 27, and Joseph Lovering took command of the engine.

A fire in Pudding lane during December was extinguished by Engine 9. Wednesday, the 25th, a large fire occurred at the North Spice Mills, near Charles river. The building, together with a large quantity of grain, cocoa, chocolate, ginger, etc., was entirely destroyed. The flames communicated to a barn and two stores, which were soon laid in ashes. Engine 3 had first water on this fire.

The first appointments for the year 1783 were Joner Wheeler, John Stingman, Elisa March, and Obe Curtis, on Engine 8.

Firewards Proctor and Melvill recommended, on January 29, that sleds be provided for the engines instead of wheels, as by this means they could reach a fire much quicker. This suggestion was adopted.

January 27, a fire broke out in the hat-store of Mr. Adams, opposite the sign of the Lamb Tavern (on Washington, near Milk street). Part of the stock was burnt. Engine 9 was the fortunate one. Joseph Hutchings took J. Ridgway's place on Engine 6, March 19.

Five changes occurred in the Board of Firewards this year, as follows : Capt. Isaac Phillips, Col. Josiah Waters, Mr. Jacob Rhodes, Capt. Eben Parsons, and Mr. J. Coffin Jones, *vice* J. Pulling, E. Hancock, A. Symms, I. Ballard, and J. Winthrop. Joseph Holbrook succeeded Thomas Pounds on Engine 11, on March 26. A fire at Gold's barber-house, in Southick's court, was put out by Engine 6 during April. Robert Newman took John Fuller's place in the same company, May 21, and Phillip Willdenway succeeded J. Wheeler on Engine 9, July 2.

Another order regarding chimneys was passed at the town-meeting January 13, 1783, whereby every occupant of a house must have each chimney of his house swept at least three times per year, on penalty of 10s. "They shall pay for the service to the chimney comptroiler the following rates : For each funnel of five stories, 1, 8, 6 ; four stories, 1, 8, 4 ; three stories, 1, 8, 2. For all others, 1s."

A fire occurred at Mr. Riley's store during August. Engine 3 was on hand. On the 24th, between 2 and 3 o'clock in the morning, fire broke out in a barn occupied by Mr. Crane, wharfinger, near Oliver's dock. Before assistance arrived it was levelled to the ground. The flames communicated to five other barns lying in its course, also the dwelling of Mr. Jeremiah Russell and the store of Hon. William Phillips, which were totally destroyed. Nine horses and a large quantity of merchandise were burned. The engine from Roxbury rendered assistance. Two men, — one named Moses Bailey, — having just arrived in town from Hanover, were, with their wives, passing the ruins, when a chimney fell, burying the two men, killing Mr. Bailey instantly ; the other died the next day. During the fire several men were caught trying to break into the store of William Foster. It was therefore supposed that the fire was of incendiary origin. Another fire was discovered the same day in the cellar of Mr. Townshend, carpenter, located near the Old State-House, but was extinguished without much damage.

On March 1 the Legislature passed an order forbidding the storage in buildings of loaded fire-arms as being dangerous to those who assist at a fire. The fire-arms included cannon, swivels, mortars, howitzers, Coehorns, bombs, grenades, and iron-shells, which, on seizure, would be sold at auction. On October 27 the following act was passed by the same body : —

Whereas by a Resolve of the General Court, passed Feb. 16, 1778, the number of Men exempted from military duty and allowed for the Engine in the Town of Boston was reduced to one hundred and thirty eight on account of the War, and as it is not now nessary that the said Resolve should remain in force — Therefore —

Resolved that the Resolve aforesaid be and it is hereby repealed and the number of One hundred and seventy one men allowed for the several Engines in the Town of Boston and to be subject to the same regula^tn and entitled to the same exemptions as they were before the commencement of the late War with Great Britan.

A paragraph appeared in the newspapers this year, as follows : " Method to put out a fire in a chimney : Take a bucket of water, throw it on the fire suddenly, when the damp steam or smoke will immediately put the fire all out."

A fire occurred in Mr. Riley's store during July, when Engine 3 was given the bounty ; also for one in a building near the Town-House. Engine 2 was awarded during August for a fire near Winnesimmet. The wells in the town were inspected about this time.

Some trouble must have occurred in the Board of Firewards for 1784, as we find that John Scollay, F. Shaw, E. Proctor, J. Lowell, and T. Milvill asked to be excused from further service on the board. They were succeeded by Capt. J. Ballard, Joseph Russell, Jr., Paul D. Sargent, Capt. Mungo Mackay, Mr. Joseph Clark, and Andrew Symms ; but the following year some of them being voted for, accepted, and served for a long time.

Engine 6 was first at the fire on Temple street during February. William Draker joined Engine 2, July 28. Monday, June 14, at 8 A.M., a fire broke out in the spermaceti works, erected at the bottom of Cold lane (Portland street), which, in short time, was almost wholly destroyed. Three other buildings were on fire at the same time; but by the vigilance of the inhabitants, and having plenty of water, it was soon extinguished.

January 5, 1785, Seth Webber and Thomas Page succeeded Dick and John Bouvé on Engine 2. During this month a fire occurred in a bakehouse at the North End. Engine 3 put it out. William Chester took the place of J. Foster on Engine 11, March 2.

The votes for firewards for 1785 resulted in the following choice: John Winthrop, John Lowell, Thomas Melvill, Samuel Breck, Henry Bass, and John May, *vice* C. Davis, J. Waters, E. Parsons, J. Russell, D. D. Sargent, and M. Mackay.

The chocolate mill occupied by Mr. Welch, located at the North End, was burnt with all its stock on April 15. Engine 3 was given the premium.

On May 12 a petition was sent in to the selectmen by several gentlemen relative to establishing a fire-office insurance company, which matter was referred to the Board of Firewards. These gentlemen on the 23d reported that it would not be for the advantage of the town to have such an institution established as fire insurance, which resolve was accepted. This is the first mention of an enterprise of this kind on the records. In the article under the heading Protective Department in this volume will be found the progress of fire-insurance business fully detailed.

Captain Sloan, of Hancock Engine, resigns his trust on June 1, and is succeeded by Enoch James. Monday, September 12, the roof of a building near Concert Hall caught fire by a defective chimney, but was soon quenched. September 16, the premium for the first engine at a fire was increased to twenty shillings lawful money.

John Richardson, Jr., joined Engine 2, January 11, 1786. On Engine 7 Henry Davidson and Oliver Wiswell succeeded Eben Torey and T. Ruggles, February 15. Peter McTouch, James Tate, and John Dent are appointed in the place of E. Cushing, J. Crosby, M. Eagres, on Engine 11, on the same date.

Monday, March 13, the dwelling-house of John Fenno, at the corner of Bromfield lane and Marlborough street (Bromfield and Washington streets), caught fire, but was extinguished before much damage was done. Engine 7 was on the spot first.

Captain Phillips and Captain Fellows were succeeded on the Board of Firewards by Hon. Caleb Davis and Col. P. D. Sargent. A slight fire in Royal Exchange lane during March was extinguished by Engine 5. On the 31st an old wooden tenement in Cambridge street caught on fire, but was confined to that building. It was caused by the carelessness of a negro servant. Mr. Minot's barn was also burnt this month; Engine 6 was given the award.

Engine 9 was first at the fire in Broad alley during the same month, and Engine 2 was supplied with two new pieces of hose.

For the month of April several fires are reported. A blaze in a chair manufactory on Prince street was put out by Engine 3; another at Mr. Breck's distil-house, South End, by which Engine 8 was given the money; while Horse Head Tavern, on Cross street, needed the services of Engine 2 to save it from being destroyed. Eleven ladders were ordered for the department on April 19, which were distributed to the engines; these ladders had the number of the engine to which they belonged. Thomas Green, Samuel Weeks, and Hugh Cargill were admitted on Engine 6, the 26th. Engine 8 rendered first assistance at a fire at the house of Mr. Wheeler, at the South End, during May. On the 24th Engine 10 was supplied with two new pipes.

Tuesday, June 13, a large new blacksmith shop, eighty feet long, located near Tudor's wharf, the property of Mr. James, was completely consumed by fire. Engine 1 was given the premium. Another fire broke out on Thursday night, July 9, in a building that was being erected by the town in Market square for a fish market, to be known as Pullin Building. Many carpenters lost their tools in this fire. It was supposed to have been of incendiary origin, and a reward of $100 was offered by the selectmen, which sum was increased to $500 by vote of the town-meeting, for the apprehension of the guilty person; but he was never discovered, however.

A fire at the town dock during July was extinguished by Engine 10, and one at Captain Freeman's house was put out by Engine 6 the same month. Firewards Davis and Tileston recommended to the town that long poles and buckets be provided and placed with the engine company, to be used in case of fire. These articles were supplied on August 30. Capt. E. Robinson, of Engine 3, was succeeded by William Brown on November 7, and Nicholas Pierce took command of Engine 9, *vice* Captain Hunnewell, the same date; the latter company was given a prize for a fire in Broad alley during this month. Engine 7 was at the fire in the calf tanyard at the same time. At the request of Captain Uran, of Engine 4, December 12, the engines were placed on runners.

The first change for 1787 occurred in the company of Engine 11, January 10, when John Taylor was admitted in the place of T. Foster. Fire at Mr. Gorey's house, this month, was put out by Engine 9. March 28, Benjamin Barnes succeeds R. Lash on Engine 2. Only one change is reported in the Board of Firewards for the year, — Caleb Davis resigns in favor of Mr. Ebenezer Hancock.

Sunday, February 12, the house of Mr. Torrey, located near the Common, took fire from a defective flue and was badly damaged. Much trouble was experienced in obtaining water, as the pumps were frozen. A notice was issued immediately after to owners of pumps to clear them of the chill water at 10 P.M., so they would not freeze before morning. Another fire broke out on the 19th, at the jail, it being set by some prisoners. It was put out with little damage.   On April 10 William Moat succeeded Ed. Brat on Engine 7.

The town had, by this time, almost completely recovered from the effects of the disastrous fire of 1767 and the large one preceding it, and was in a most flourishing state.   The inhabitants had ample faith in the then supposed powerful fire department, and thought that another such scene as they had witnessed at the time could not occur in their midst.   They, therefore, were wholly unprepared for the disastrous fire that burst upon them on April 19, 1787.   Dr. Belknap, in a letter to Mr. Hazard, on April 23, says of this conflagration : —

Now My Dear Sir, I will give you some account of the Fire Friday evening.   I could (as is usual in such cases) tell you of what I did, where I was, and how I worked, and waded through the Dock at low water, and all that, but I believe a general account, with a small plan or sketch will be as much as you will want to have.   I was on the spot the next day and with my pencil marked its progress, a copy of which I will enclose. [See page 91.]   The wind was a dry Northeaster and had prevailed two days, the houses with only one or two exceptions, *wooden* and *shingled*.   It began in a Malt house, and had there been no wind, the malt and dwelling house adjoining, would have silently consumed, without further Mischief, and about 100 legs of bacon which were taken in to smoke, would have been all the general damage.   But the wind carried the flakes of fire over the dock into some barns and dock houses adjoining to the Main street, and so rapid and irresistible was its progress that between six and seven [o'clock] in the evening it destroyed between 70 and 80 dwelling houses, with Mr. Wights Rectory [Ebenezer Wight, minister of the Hollis-street Church] as far as there was anything to be burned; and had the Town extended ten or twenty miles in that direction and wooden houses in the way, dry as they were, the fire would have been equally as extensive.   No lives were lost though much substance; but I have the pleasure to assure you that a very curious and valuable *Orrery*, constructed by Mr. Pope, watchmaker, was carefully and happily saved.   Dr. Byles house was in imminent danger, his hords of books, instruments, papers, prints etc were dislodged in one hour from a fifty year quietness to a helter skelter heap in an adjoining pasture.   He removed for the night to a neighbors house and returned the next day.   This morning I made him a third visit since the fire.   One of his daughters observed that her papa was the *first thing* they thought of moving; upon this he began to distinguish between persons and things, and would have brought in a long criticism, if I had not changed the discourse to some inquiries about the great fire in the year 1711, which he remembered.   You know he is a curiosity.   April 25 By an account taken by the selectmen the loss sustained by the fire was 56 dwellings, 13 stores, a Meeting House, 8 barns, and 86 families burnt out, loss of property in round numbers $20,000.

The Boston " Centinel " gives the following account : —

The loss at the late fire in house furniture, bedding and other articles, together with goods and effects was very great, and with the loss of so many valuable dwellings, loudly calls upon the benevolent and humane, to afford their aid in alleviating the distresses of the unfortunate sufferers.   We are happy however in informing the publick, that amidst the destruction a curious specimen of art and industry was luckily preserved, which does honor to the country.   We mean the Orerry, constructed by Mr. Joseph Pope.   This admirable performance, the result of many years labor and study, is near 6 feet in diameter and was almost finished when the house of the artist with most of his effects were

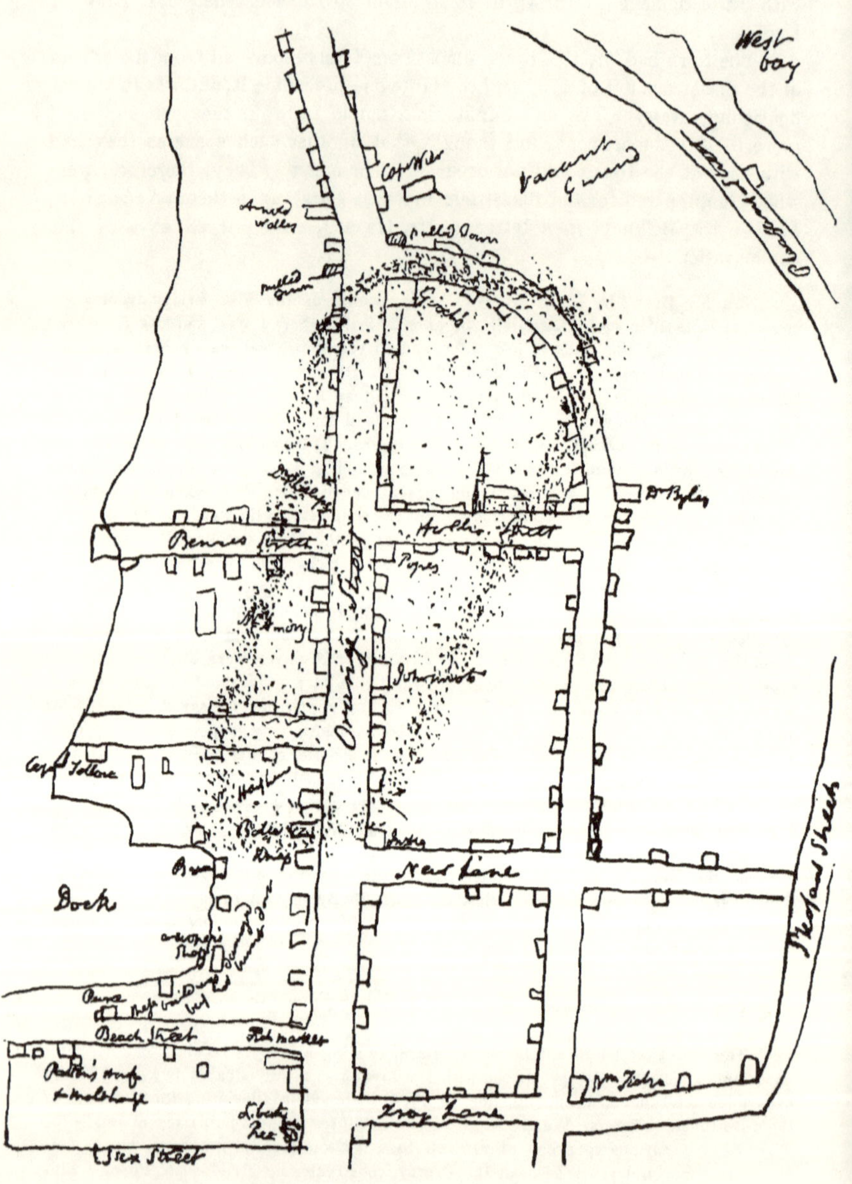

Dr. Belknap's Map of Burnt District, Fire April 19, 1787.

in a few moments reduced to ashes. Much praise is due to those gentlemen who, by their exertions preserved to the lovers of Science this curious specimen of philosophies and mechanical ingenuity, and deposited it at the house of his Excellency the Governor where we are told it still remains. The light of the fire was plainly seen at Newburyport and several towns near 50 Miles distant.

The following is a more accurate list of the persons burned out and the principal buildings that were burnt.

On the East side of Orange St. [Washington street, above Dover street.]

William Patten,	Ebenezer Waters,	Mrs. Crawford,
Samuel Heyley,	Mrs. Guyer } widows.	William Stretch,
Mrs. Searl,	Mrs. Guyer	Mrs. Swift.
Spencer Vose,	Joshua Wyette,	Ebenezer Pope,
Josiah Henshaw, Esq.	Mrs. Wyman,	Joseph Bradford,
John Fairservice,	Josiah Knapp,	Edy Vennivel,
Peter Lehr,	Daniel Bates,	Mrs. Emery,
Joseph Field,	John Fenno,	Mrs. Hopkins,
Nathaniel Phillips,	Dennis Welch,	Mrs. Wales.
Nathaniel Sheppard,	Dorothy Whorton,	Mrs. Scott,
Mrs. Segar,	Mrs. Amory,	Elijah Searl.

On the West side of Orange St.

Mrs. Inches,	Wm. Gooch,	Mrs. Cheever,
Thos. Jackson,	Fredrick Incley,	Arthur Langford,
Thos. Downing,	Thos. Stell,	Joseph Pierce,
Misses Johonnot,	Wm. Penniman, Jr.,	George Guyer,
House of the late Zechariah	Robert Price,	Joseph Clark,
Johonnot,	Mrs. Connant,	Joseph Sprague,
Joseph Lovering,	Mrs. Emmons,	Rev. Mr. Wright's Meeting
Nathaniel Bosworth,	Andrew Gardner,	house (Hollis-street Church).
House Pulled down,	Thos. Foster,	Jacob Gould,
" " "	Joseph Pope,	Spencer Bates,
Henry Stevens,	Robert Pope,	Richard Gridley,
Aaron May,	John Pope,	Josiah Goddard,
Henry Guyer,	Andrew Kalley.	Joseph Goddard.
Wm. Wyman,	Hopstill Foster,	

An account in the London (England) " Morning Chronicle " says : —

April 20, 1787, a fire broke out in Boston, N.E., in the south part of the Town, and before it could be extinguished, consumed one church and about 100 other buildings. The wind was high and wafted the blazing shingles to a great distance. Contributions were forwarded by Captain T. Barnard, of the ship Mary, which sailed May 31.

Lafayette, on June 22, wrote a letter of sympathy for Boston in her loss, and directed Samuel Beck to pay 200 guineas on his account to the sufferers. A petition was sent to the General Court by the sufferers for relief. Engine 8 had the honor of putting first water on the fire.

Other fires and the engines that were awarded for being first on hand during the year were: Messrs. Brick and Sheppard's house, Engine 2 ; a dwelling of a negro, Engine 9 ; a vessel in Mill creek, Engine 10, in July ; Mr. Croswell's meeting-house, October 11, Engine 7 ; the same engine at Lieutenant-

Governor's house, during December; liquor saloon in Back street, and Mr. Rumley's house in Middle street, Engine 10, the same month. The changes in companies were: May 16, Engine 7, James Tucker and Joseph Francis, *vice* Eben Evans and Stephen Olliver; August 22, Ed. Dolbear, *vice* J. Gray. J. Bridge, member of Engine 8, August 9. Captain Uran retired from his position as master of Engine 4, on October 10, on account of old age, and was succeeded by James Rogers.

September 19, Engine 1 was removed from North square to Hanover street, and on October 31 Engine 4 was moved from the dock to the drawbridge, in Ann street (Hanover street), and a new house built for it, the old one being too old to be removed, and was rented to a butcher for £3 per year. Engine 5 was thoroughly repaired, November 21.

Capt. J. Holland, of Engine 5, was succeeded as foreman of that company, on February 6, 1788, by Timothy Pease. The other changes in the service during the year were: Robert Pattsage, on Engine 2, *vice* D. Lilley, February 20. Captain Cushing, of Engine 7, was succeeded by Edmund Ranger, June 10. Captain Rogers, of Engine 4, also leaves the department, and Joseph Whittemore assumes command of his company, August 27.

The same Board of Firewards were elected.

Only a few fires are reported for this year; they are of very little importance. March, Mr. Davis' house, Engine 5; Widow Crowe's house, in Pleasant street. Engine 8. April, Mr. Hemmenway's house, Back street (Salem street), Engine 2. October, Mr. Adams' house, North End, Engine 3. Wednesday, November 11, a stable, the property of T. Hill, located on Essex street, was set on fire by some shavings that were lighted a short distance from it.

Engine 3 was moved from the house on North Bennett street to a house on Salem street, May 26.

In the list of firewards we find the following changes for the year 1789: Caleb Davis, Thomas Russell, Joseph Russell, Jr., David Hubbard, Samuel Parkman, *vice* Hancock, Symmes, Ballard, Sewell, and Bass; but Mr. Ballard was reappointed in the place of Colonel Sargent, and Mr. Edward Edes took Colonel Proctor's place, both of whom resigned. Tuesday, March 4, a fire was discovered in a barn near the Old South Meeting-house, the property of Rev. Mr. Exleys, but was soon extinguished by Engine 7. The other fires and premiums for the year were: May, Joseph Rugles' house, South End, Engine 8. June, a building on Averie's wharf, Engine 9; Mr. Newell's house, West End, Engine 6. December, Wentworth wharf, Mr. Ross' house, Cross street, and Mr. Phillips' house, Middle street; Engine 10 for the last three.

Forty-five pounds sterling were appropriated by the town on November 11 for a new engine, to be built by Mr. Norton, to take the place of No. 2. Engine 6 was repaired; also the engine-house at the Mill bridge, on December 7.

Only two changes in the companies occurred, — Timothy Tileston succeeded J. Stimpson on Engine 8, April 4, and Roland Campbell, *vice* D. Lilley, Engine 2, May 20.

The following advertisement appeared in the Boston " Centinel," November 14, 1789 : —

Richard Mason. Fire Engine Warranted for 7 years, and sold as cheap as can be procured in Europe, Manufactured in Philadelphia. A list of fire engines and Prices. First rate: contains 80 gals, throws water 80 feet, requires 6 men to work it. Price £40. 2nd rate contains 100 Gals throws water 100 feet, requires 8 men, cost £60. 3rd rate — contains 120 gals throws 120 feet, requires 10 men to work it. Cost £72. 4th rate contains 150 gals, throws 150 ft. requires 14 Men. cost £100.

CHAPTER VIII.

1790–1799.

THE record for the year 1790 began with the entry of the resignation of Captain Hunt, of Engine 2, who is succeeded on January 6 by Gibbon Bouvé, an old drummer in the army. On the same date Captain Ridgway, of Engine 6, is succeeded by Mr. Matthew Nazro. J. C. Burteman took the place of D. Jacobs in this company February 16, which is the only change for the year. The list, as sent in to the selectmen, of the entire department was as follows : —

Engine 1, Capt. William Brown, eighteen members : James Robbins, Orcut Shaw, Newbury Clough, William Dyer, William Alexander, Elijah Swift, William Capen, Larrabee Edes, J. Lombard, John Hutchinson, Richard Richardson. Charles Willis, Micah Orcutt, Zachariah Hall, Samuel White, Robert Allcock, and Edward Bell.

Engine 2, Capt. William Nazro, twelve men : William Darricott, John Cades, E. Nathaniel Nuttage, James Freeland, Jacob Clow, Benjamin Barns, William Lait, Seth Webber, Thomas Page, John Richardson, and Robert Partridge.

Engine 3, Capt. Elias Robertson, fourteen members : John Robertson, David Greenleaf. Nathaniel Tidmarsh, William Minzies, James Francis, Eben Chandler, Thomas Richardson, Benjamin Abrahams, William Bell, Benjamin West, John Hooton, Francis Berth, Jacob Hyler.

Engine 4, Capt. Joseph Whittemore and eleven men : Samuel Sumner, Joseph Urann, Jonathan Seargent, George Jeffers, John Garnel, William Tuckerman, Jos. Barber, William Nickels, William Baker, Ed. Allen, and Thomas Urann.

Engine 5, Capt. Timothy Pease, eleven men : Theodore Dehon, William Rice, Ed. Mannin, Nathan Glover, Charles More, James Cleverly, Philip Wentworth, Jno. Trask, Jonathan Trask, Jonathan Stoddard, and Braddock Loring.

Engine 6, Capt. Gebbins Bouvé, thirteen men : William Rouse, George Nowell, David Jacobs. Daniel Brown, James Ridgway, Elijah Caswell, Joseph Daniels, Robert Newman, James Hitchings, Samuel Weeks, Hugh Cargill, and Daniel Gealey.

Engine 7, Capt. Edmund Ranger, nineteen men : Thomas Appleton, Joel Cushing, Benjamin Horton, Joshua Bracket, Samuel Jenkins, John Bulfinch, Nathaniel Jenkins, John Neat, Stephen Winters, John Moies, William Appleton, James Tucker, Henry Davison, Jos. Francis. Oliver Wiswall, Victor Blair, William Meck, Edward Dolbear, and Henry Davidson.

Engine 8, Capt. Joseph Lovering, thirteen men: Robert Robinson, John Fenno, J. Abijah Crane, Joseph Payson, Ephraim Thayer, Joshua Wheeler, Samuel Sprague, Joseph Sprague, Enoch May, John Spear, Samuel Adams, Jeremiah Bridge, and Timothy Tileston.

Engine 9, Capt. Nicholas Pearce, fifteen men. Christian Bruzier, Jr., William Fenno, Nathan Wheeler, Thomas Stowell, Jonathan Hunnewell, Philip Wild, Edwin French, Rufus Tower, William Stevens, William Hearsey, Jr., Ebenezer French, John Clark, William White, Benjamin Fessenden, and George Rex.

Engine 10, Capt. Enoch James, fourteen men: James Tuksbury, James Worth, Clement Collins, John How, Joseph Heminway, Thomas Lewis, Gersham Thomas, William Badger, Turin Tuttle, Jacob Palley, Elijah Davis, James Calendar, Bartholomew Nason, and John Wild.

Engine 11, Capt. John Champney, fifteen men: Jeffrey Richardson, William Ellison, Levi Hersey, Nicholas Ferriter, Jireh Holbrook, Joseph Blake, Ezra Parmenter, Jared Hill, Eben Hancock, William Clouston, Peter McIntosh, John Denton, John Taylor, B. French, and James Ferriter.

Amasa Davis, Samuel Whitwell, Russell Sturgis, Jonathan Mason, Jr., and John Sweetser were chosen on the Board of Firewards for the year 1790, *vice* Bullard, May, Hubbard, Parkman, and Cooper; the latter having served in that capacity for thirty-five years, declined a reëlection.

In the Fire Commissioners' office at the City Hall are two journals of the Board of Firewards, one being a complete list of the members, beginning with 1751, also many of the laws concerning buildings and gunpowder : the other a register of their meetings from 1790. The latter begins with the following rules and regulations : —

1. If any ward neglects to attend a fire he is to pay one dollar. 2. If any ward leaves a fire without permission of two other wards, to pay one dollar. 3. If any ward is appointed to search for powder, and neglects to do so, to pay one dollar. 4. If any Engine shall be carried from the fire without orders of two of the firewards, a joint complaint to be made. 5. If any ward cannot give a satisfactory account of the condition of the engine assigned to his charge, he shall pay one dollar.

The monthly meetings of the board were held at each others' houses; after hearing the report upon the condition of the engines, and despatching what little business came before them, they spent the residue of the evening in social enjoyment, and feasting on the delicacies of the season, — thus awarding themselves, at their own expense, for the arduous and responsible duties required in the hour of danger. It is probable that the following vote was intended as a hint to some delinquent member of the board : —

March 11, 1793, Voted, that no one of the firewards, at whose house the company shall meet for the ensuing year, shall in any wise despence with the following regulations, Viz.: a sideboard to be placed in the room where the meeting is held, and covered with cold roast beef, bacon and tongue and the fruits of the season, but no pastry of any kind.

After the year 1796 their meetings were held at the various public hotels, and judging from the amount of the bills, they did not go home unrefreshed. The captains of the various engine companies, together with a town official, were always invited to their annual supper.

No large fires are reported this year, and very few small ones; of these, the following is a list: March, Mr. Thomas' house, Bennett street. June, Mr. Cooper's house, Engine 2. The ship "Lydia," Captain Tinkham, lying at Long wharf, was totally destroyed December 8; Engine 5. Only one change in the members — that of the appointment of Emerson Pierce in the place of Capt. N. Pierce as foreman of Engine 9 — is mentioned.

Engine-House 6, located on the land of Dr. Bulfinch, on Hancock street, was ordered by that gentleman, on April 14, to be removed.

Stanford's College, at West Boston, caught fire during January, 1791: Engine 6 received the prize. The other fires for the year were: February, a house in Quaker lane (Congress street), Engine 5. April, Joel Haynes' house, Engine 9. August, Mr. Raymond's house, West End, Engine 6. June 26. Mr. Sumner's house, Cold lane, struck by lightning, Engine 6. Sunday, November 9, at 3 A.M., a fire was discovered in a lot of old houses in Marlborough street (Washington street) occupied by several colored families. The buildings were entirely consumed.

General Henry Jackson succeeded J. Rhodes, and Samuel Parkman took the place of H. Sweetser, in the Board of Firewards for 1791. The following changes occurred in the department: Engine 1, Samuel Bell, Ben James, Richard Holden, *vice* W. Dyer, E. Swift, and S. Hull, July 27. Engine 7, Moses Ward, James Campbell, *vice* Muse and Bulfinch. Engine 6, Fessenden, *vice* J. Ridgway, September 20. Engine 4, Capt. J. Whittemore being dead, Mr. John Gammel was appointed foreman of the company, October 19. Engine 3, Capt. E. Robinson deceased, his son John was promoted to fill that position, December 21.

Fireward Tileston had an order passed, on August 3, to have Engine-House 11 enlarged about six feet, so that there would be room to take the engine to pieces when necessary.

The list of companies of the eleven engines sent to the selectmen met with approval. They also informed the members that hereafter they would be allowed to choose their own foremen in the month of May each year. This was the beginning of a custom that was so popular among the department for a number of years.

The January, 1792, fire occurred on Monday, the 21st, near the North Meeting-house, which, from the inclemency of the weather, threatened destruction to a considerable part of the town; but through the exertions of the departments from Charlestown and Roxbury, it extended no farther than the house in which it originated, which was owned by Mrs. Jarvis, and the building adjoining, owned by Deacon Holland. The Attorney-General and several clergymen were present and rendered assistance.

The General Court took further action in the matter of the storage of gunpowder, on January 26, by which it was ordered that after August 1, next, no powder was to be carried to or from the magazine within the town, exceeding twenty-five pounds, except in a wagon closely covered with leather or canvas, and without iron in any part; this wagon was to be approved by the firewards, and marked in capital letters, "APPROVED POWDER CARRIAGE." All powder to be landed as the firewards directed, which direction should be published in the papers for six successive weeks. The orders issued by these gentlemen on July 12 gave notice that the powder should be landed only "at the wharves of Thomas Tileston and Col. F. Hatch;" in case of fire preventing, they were to apply to the board for directions. The route the carriages were to take was through Seven Star lane and Water street, then by the most direct way to the magazine.

Monday, February 3, a large barn, the property of David Bradlee, was burned, together with a quantity of hay. Mingo Mackay and Col. William Scollay succeeded S. Whitwell and S. Breck as firewards for 1792.

Sunday, May 6, a fire was discovered in the upper story of a large house in Newbury street (Washington street), occupied by Mr. Samuel Davis, but was soon extinguished by citizens. The other small fires for the year were as follows: April, South School-house, Engine 8; Mr. Davis' house, South End, Engine 7. May, Mr. Eckley's house, Engine 7; Mr. Selim's house, Engine 3. November, house in Court street, Engine 5.

Engine 5 was repaired June 27. Firewards Melville and Davis asked for a new engine to take the place of Engine 6. October 30, a committee was appointed to investigate the matter. Joseph Fullerton and Nath. Brown succeeded N. Clough and A. Chase on Engine 1, November 7, and William Darracott was promoted foreman of Engine 2, *vice* Capt. G. Bouvé. Thursday, December 27, fire broke out in an old building belonging to the glasshouse, which was partly consumed. The same day a fire occurred in the south part of the town.

A woman was found dead in the Old South Engine-house, November 22. The cause of her death and how she came there is not known.

A civic feast was celebrated on Monday, January 21, 1793, in commemoration of the success of the Soldiers of Liberty in France. The inspector of police issued orders forbidding the lighting of bonfires, fireworks, etc. This official was also given orders to replace the town ladders, and to provide a new one for Engine 8.

Messrs. James Tisdale and Joseph May were chosen as firewards in the place of C. Davis and T. Russell, resigned.

On March 10 several of the engines were found to be very badly damaged, being the work of some unprincipled person, on account of which the selectmen ordered the following notification to be published: —

200 dollars reward. — Whereas some evil minded and disorderly persons in the course of Saturday night last did wantonly and wickedly break and injure several of the

fire engines in this town, thus exposing the property of the inhabitants to the danger of destruction by fire — a reward of TWO HUNDRED DOLLARS is hereby offred to any person who shall inform of the perpetrator of so atrocious and wanton a piece of wickedness and villany, that he or they may be brought to such punishment as their crime deserves — The above reward shall be payable on the conviction of the offender or offenders.

By order of the selectmen,

WILLIAM COOPER

Town Clerk.

BOSTON, March 10, 1793.

An investigation was held, from which it was, on July 13, found that J. McFadden, an ex-member of the department, who had been discharged during 1773, was the guilty person. He was severely punished for the deed.

Mr. William Sherburn was elected a fireward for 1794, *vice* J. Clark, resigned. A new engine was ordered to be built by E. Thayer for Engine No. 1. July 9. The same date the house of Aaron Davis was struck by lightning, and slightly damaged.

A few minutes after 4 o'clock on the morning of Wednesday, July 10, another large conflagration startled the citizens of Boston. The fire originated from an accident, in the rope-walk of Mr. Howe on Pearl street, near Milk street, a spark having caught in some hemp and tar while that gentleman was lighting a fire ; the flames were communicated to seven other rope-walks, and in three hours buried in ashes the extensive square between Milk, Atkinson (Congress), Pearl, and Purchase streets. Twenty-four shops, forty-three houses, and twenty-one barns, and the wharves of Messrs. Russell, Dawes. Somes, and Tileston were entirely consumed in the fire, together with large quantities of cordage and household furniture, making an aggregate loss, as appears by returns made to a committee of the town, of $210,000.

The flames were so rapid in their progress that several people had very narrow escapes with their lives. The losses were as follows : — Atkinson street : rope-walks of Edward Howe, John Codman, Isaac Davis, Jeffrey Richardson, Mr. McNeil. Dwellings : John Read, Captain Parker, William Cluston, Mrs. Scott, Samuel Abbott, John Kennedy, Cornelius South, and a large brick store filled with hemp ; Nathan Jenkins, Thomas Smith, George Guyer, Mrs. Bernard, J. Dodge, Mrs. Foster, row of barracks known by the name of Green's, occupied by blocks. Cow lane (High street) : Mrs. Low, two dwellings, and John White. Berry street (now a continuation of Franklin street) : Mr. Emmons, Capt. J. West, Col. John Winslow, Mrs. Crosby, M. Gray, Mr. Townsend, Mrs. Green, Solomon Cotton, his son's master's shop and several large outbuildings, two other houses, and Mrs. Quincy's barn. Purchase street : row of buildings owned by Mr. Savage and occupied by Messrs. Barry, Lincoln, Hearsey, and Francis ; the house of Mrs. Gray, Mr. Tate, Thomas Brewer, James Perkins, Daniel Bargs, Samuel Dillaway, Mrs. Brewer, block-house, Samuel Emmons. and Ferreter & Torry's rope-walk, Mr. Hill's store, several barns. hay carriages, trucks, etc., with a row of low buildings ; Thomas Lamb,

Nathaniel Appleton's house, to which the loan office of the United States was attached; John McLane, James Thwing, Mr. Clement, house and barn; Joseph Baker. Hugh Kemple. house and shop; Benjamin Gray, Mrs. McNeil, Watson Freeman, Daniel Sargent, Captain Cowel, house and shop; Mrs. Cluston, Levi Hearsay, Mrs. Brown, house and shop; Miss Kettle, Mr. Gooch, Mrs. Rand, Mr. Whitemore's cooper shop. Hon. Thomas Russell, large store; Samuel Dillaway, country house, new barn, lumber wharf. — 200,000 feet board, 100,000 shingles, timber, etc.: Hon. Thomas Dawes, store and barn on his wharf; Capt. Nehemiah Somes, country room; four stores of Mr. Tileston.

The "Centinel," in closing the account of the fire, from which these names were taken, says: "The Rope Walks will not be rebuilt, and a fine square will be open which will be an excellent place for the site of the New State House." [The proprietors of the rope-walks were permitted to rebuild in the marsh (the site of the Public Garden). The lots, six in number, were each 50 feet wide, and when bought back by the city in 1824, the first three lots measured 1,006 feet on Charles street. 1,138 feet on the west side; lots 4, 5, and 6 measured 1,138 feet each. They were again burnt and rebuilt during 1806, an account of which is given in the fires under that date.]

The town ordered a company of sixty men to watch over the fire for two days, each being paid 6s: per night. These men. with a number of engines under the charge of the firewards, proved a sufficient force to prevent the flames from again breaking out, despite the very high wind that prevailed. Sermons were preached in the several churches regarding the fire, and subscriptions were taken up for the sufferers.

Engines from Cambridge. Charlestown, Roxbury, Brookline, Milton, and Watertown came to the assistance of the Boston firemen, for which they received the following vote of thanks from the selectmen: —

The selectmen of Boston in behalf of their fellow citizens, having a more lively sence of the more timely and efficient aid offered them by their brothers of several towns in the vicinity with their Fire Engines and Personal service at the distressing fire of yesterday request them to accept their most sincere acknowledgment of the same and assure them that such benevolent and humain exertions will always excite the most kindly sensations.

Refreshments were provided them at the expense of the town. After this collation the firewards had an order passed by the selectmen, whereby the town should, in future, pay for refreshments to visiting engine companies.

The other fires for the year were: March, Lyman's wharf, Engine 1. April, Mr. Bradlee's house. South End, Engine 8. July, Deacon Jones' house. May, Engine 6, Mr. Seaver's distil-house; Engine 8, house in Bennett street; and on October 17, at Mr. Bartlett's hat-shop, South End, Engine 8.

Oliver Wiswall was appointed in command of Engine 7 during this year, *vice* Captain Ranger, resigned.

Another manufacturer of fire-engines establishes himself in the town, and issued the following advertisement: —

Fire Engines For sale of all-sorts, Made by Richard Grindley Jr. Fore St. on Capt. Goldsbury's Wharf. Any one in want of an Engine can have one at short notice, Old Engines taken as part pay.   Feb 22, 1794.

A number of citizens, taking into consideration the evils of the frequent fires, associated themselves on November 20, 1792, for the purpose of establishing a fund and applying the income to the humane undertaking of relieving the distress occasioned by the ravages of the fire-fiend. A committee was commissioned to draft a constitution for the government of the society, and a constitution was established on January 21, 1793. The society continued their meeting by adjournments until August following, when a committee was appointed to prepare an address to the several fire societies in Boston and vicinity, requesting their aid in effectually establishing the same. This resulted in a public meeting, held at the County Court-House, February 6, 1794, which was attended by committees from several fire societies; and on June 25 of the same year the society was incorporated, the name being " The Massachusetts Charitable Fire Society." Its purpose was to provide means to relieve such of the inhabitants as may suffer by and to reward the industry and ingenuity of those who may invent useful machines for extinguishing fires, or make extraordinary personal exertions in the time of such calamity, or make efforts to prevent its devastation as shall be thought worthy of their patronage. An additional act was passed February 16, 1822, whereby the society was authorized to appropriate such part of their interest accumulated from the general fund to any other charitable purpose than those mentioned in the act of incorporation, and to such benevolent institution within the Commonwealth of Massachusetts as they saw fit, provided that no appropriation exceed $300 at any one time, or to any one charitable institution. June 10, 1831, another additional act provided that the appropriation should not exceed twenty-five per cent. of the capital stock, or in no case affect the bequest of any individual. The presidents of the society were as follows: 1794 to 1800, Hon. Moses Gill; 1800 to 1802, George R. Minot; 1802 to 1817, Arnold Welles; 1817 to 1832, T. K. Jones; 1832 to 1839, John Heard, Jr.; 1839 to 1841, F. J. Oliver; 1841 to 1849, E. T. Andrews; 1849 to 1850, James Phillips; 1850 to 1854, A. W. Thaxter; 1854 to 1859, W. T. Andrews; 1859 to 1861, William Adams; 1861 to 1863, A. A. Wellington; 1863 to 1864, Enoch Hobart; 1864 to 1866, J. W. Warren; 1866 to 1868, David Kimball; 1868 to 1870, Benjamin Beal; 1870 to 1872, Moses Kimball; 1872 to 1874, Charles Leighton; 1874 to 1876, Solomon Hovey; 1876 to 1878, Uriel Crocker; 1878 to 1880, Paul Adams; 1880 to 1882, Thomas Restieaux; 1882 to 1884, Joseph F. Hovey; 1884 to 1886, Samuel P. Oliver; 1886 to 1888, F. W. Lincoln; 1888, present incumbent, William F. Davis.

Only one change occurred in the Board of Firewards for the year 1795, Maj. Andrew Cunningham succeeding T. Tileston, deceased.

On February 2, 1795, a petition was filed at the town-meeting, signed by Luther Eames, Nathan Bond, William Page, and others, praying for incorporation for bringing fresh water through subterranean pipes into the town of Boston. On the 27th a company was vested by the General Court with corporate powers for supplying the town with pure water from Jamaica Plain, in Roxbury; and by a subsequent act, passed on June 10, 1796, this corporation was empowered to assume the title of "The Aqueduct Corporation." They were authorized " to bring from any part of the town of Roxbury into the town of Boston and into any street within the same town all such fresh water as they, the said," etc., " then had or hereafter should have a right to dispose of, or to convey from the springs or sources thereof." The act gives power also to open the ground in any of the streets or highways in Roxbury and Boston as should be required for the sinking of the water-pipes, but with very prudent provisions, which prevented the aqueduct from becoming a nuisance or impairing any right of the town of Roxbury or any of its inhabitants in and to the waters of Jamaica pond. The price of the water was to be regulated by the General Court; the towns of Boston and Roxbury were to have the privilege of hydrants for extinguishing fires. It supplied about fifteen hundred houses with water, chiefly at the South End and in the neighborhood of Summer and Essex streets, and of Pleasant and Charles streets. The water was conveyed through four main pipes of pitch-pine logs (the work of boring and preparing these logs was carried on at the foot of the Common), two of four inches bore and two of three inches, the lateral pipes having a bore of one and a half inches. The lineal extent of the water-pipes in Boston was about fifteen miles, and they extended north as far as Franklin street, and branched off easterly through Harrison avenue into Congress street nearly to State street and to Broad street. They also branched of westerly through Pleasant and Charles streets, extending as far as the Massachusetts General Hospital, which was supplied with the water. This system had to give way after a few years' service, on the introduction of water from Cochituate pond on March 13, 1846.

The spermaceti factory of Mr. Nichols, and owned by Appleton & Wendall, located in Batterymarch street, was burned on Wednesday evening, February 11. Loss, £1,300.

Two large buildings were destroyed by fire on July 9, these being the houses of Isaac Durall and John Russell, and located at the West End. The occupants, Messrs. Cobb Cotton, Jr., and Benjamin Stevens, lost all their furniture.

A new engine, built by E. Thayer during the past year, was placed, February 17, 1796, between Nassau street and the building on the Neck (Washington, below Common street). It was called Eagle Engine No. 12, and Samuel Andrews was appointed foreman.

Engine 1, in Middle street, was on the land of Thomas Parker, who rented it to the town for $15 per year, the first payment being made March 28; previous to this time it was allowed to remain free of charge.

No change is reported for this year on the Board of Firewards. On the engine companies only two changes are made, — September 28, Ezra Parmenter was promoted foreman of Engine 11, *vice* Captain Champney, resigned, and —— Hanners succeeded Captain Gammel on Endeavor Engine 4.

Two buildings located near State street, the property of Messrs. Turrel Sweetser, and Diamond, a grocer, were destroyed by fire on Wednesday, March 9. During April, a building was burned on North School street; Engine 2. February 23, a fire broke out in a building on Union street occupied by Mr. Folsom, printer. Engines 4 and 10 applied for the premium. Saturday morning, 25th, 1797, the rope-walk of Messrs. Jeffrey & Russell, John Winthrop, Esq., and Messrs. Tyler & Caswell, together with several dwelling-houses owned by Messrs. Joseph Blake, Jr., Tyler, and Norcross, located at the West End, were entirely consumed by fire. Engines from Charlestown, Roxbury, Watertown, Cambridge, Brookline, and Dorchester rendered assistance. The houses of Jonathan Hastings and Samuel Blagge were several times on fire, but were saved. The loss is estimated at $100,000. Mr. Blake had $2,700 and Mr. Winthrop $4,000 insurance in the Massachusetts Fire Insurance Company. Russell and Jeffrey had their building insured in a European company. This is the first fire reported on which the loss to buildings was covered by insurance.

On account of the many distressing fires occurring during the winter, the Legislature passed a new law for regulating the proceedings at fires, also allowing towns to choose as many firewards as they thought necessary. At the town-meeting in Boston, March, 1797, it was voted to increase the number serving in that capacity to twenty-four. On the votes being assorted it was found that all the old members were reëlected. Captain Mackay resigned, and Levi Lane was chosen in his place. The new members were: Deacon William Brown, Capt. Nathaniel Fellows, Messrs. Samuel Bradford, William Shaw, Joseph Head, Thomas H. Perkins, Levi Lane, Col. John Winslow, and Col. John May.

In the act of the General Court regarding firewards, it was further ordered that when a member is elected he shall be notified within three days, and within three days after he shall, on penalty of $10, notify the town clerk of his decision, unless excused by the town. Either the selectmen or the civil officers of the town were to direct the engineers regarding their engines and all other persons they may call on for assistance, and should any citizen refuse he was to be fined $10. Regarding the building law in the same act, it prohibited any person from carrying on the business of sailmaker, rigger, or keeping livery stable, except only in such parts as the selectmen shall direct; and $10 fine was imposed for setting fire to common or wood land. The acts of 1744, entitled, " The speedy extinguishing of fires, and preserving goods endangered by it;" 1753, "To prevent fires in woods;" 1762, "Damage by fire in ye maritime towns;" and a clause in an act passed 1692, empowering "two or three chief military or civil officers to direct the pulling down or demolishing of houses,"— were repealed.

The changes in the several companies for the year were: Henry Lovering, *vice* Mr. Berry Emery, January 11, and John Thompson, Jr., *vice* Captain Hanners, Engine 4, February 1. On March 22 the firewards asked for new engines to replace Nos. 7 and 11. General Jackson, the agent for building the Continental frigate in the town (the glorious old "Ironsides"), asked for the use of one engine for watering the frigate. It was ordered "That he have liberty to use the Engine at the North End (No. 2) under the direction of the Fireward and Master of said Engine at his own expence; he also to be under engagement to make good any damage that may happen to said Engine by using it as aforesaid." We presume General Jackson richly remunerated the North Enders for their service in christening the "Constitution."

Chimney-sweeps were authorized to wear badges on this date.

The Legislature, on January 27, 1798, passed another building law, that compelled every meeting-house, school, public building, distil-house, brewery, malt-house, and livery stable to have the external walls, except doors and windows, entirely of brick or stone, with roof covered of some incombustible substance. Any dwelling-house of more than fourteen feet high should have one of its largest sides, or any two sides equal to the largest, of brick or stone, at least twelve inches thick in the lower story, and eight inches thick above. The partition walls of double houses the same, and to rise in battlements three feet above the roof. All additions made on buildings already erected contrary to this act, except on wharves or marsh, where no foundation could be obtained, buildings of more than two stories high, to be covered on all sides with slate, etc., should be subject to a fine of $50 or $500, and $50 per month until repaired according to the law. The firewards were to prosecute all offenders. Tar-kettles were to be secured by a fireplace of iron or brick, while any person carrying fire or having a lighted cigar in the street or wharf to be fined $2; among the rope-walks, $5 to $100. The act entitled "An act to secure the Town of Boston from damage by fire," passed in 1797, was repealed.

The firewards, at their meeting the next year, voted to prosecute indiscriminately all violation of this law; they also voted to support at the election the list of firewards agreed at their last meeting.

The Federal-street, or Boston, Theatre. the most elegant building of its kind in the United States, was destroyed by fire on Friday, February 2, 1798. Fire broke out about 4 o'clock of the afternoon in a dressing-room, and before the attendants could check its progress the flames were beyond control, and by 7 o'clock that night nothing was left but the brick and stone walls. Its origin was attributed by some to a rehearsal of fireworks to be exhibited in the pantomime of "Don Juan," and by others to the negligence of a servant whose duty it was to watch the fires in the dressing-rooms. Help was rendered by the citizens of Roxbury, Charlestown, and Cambridge. This was the first theatre destroyed by fire in this country. The loss was about $60,000, only one share of which was insured.

On November 27 a fire broke out and entirely consumed a tenement house in Fore street, occupied by Messrs. Branders, Wiswell, Besaute, Hogger, Evans, Mortheries, Janet, and Farmers.

Joseph Howard, Benjamin Joy, and Stephen Codman were elected fire-wards in the place of A. Cunningham, W. Shaw, and L. Lane, for the year 1798. Captain Thompson, of Engine 4, was given liberty, on August 8, to use his engine for watering the streets in the neighborhood of the engine-house, Messrs. Redley and Nolan being responsible for damages. Samuel C. May, Abner Guild, and John H. Wheeler were admitted members of Engine 8, October 19, and on January 4, 1799, Captain Thompson, of Engine 4, was succeeded by John Jarvis.

A new hose for Engine 5 was made by Mr. Fenno on February 13, being the first mention of home production of this article. A return is made of all buckets in the possession of the department on the 20th, and the 13th of the next month six pair were ordered for each company. A new engine-house for Engine 6 was erected on Dearn street, it being ordered there from the old stand on Hancock street. Andrew Cunningham and John Bray succeeded W. Little and J. Tisdale on the Board of Firewards for the year 1799.

A very large fire broke out on May 11 in a house on Washington street, which, before controlled, destroyed eleven other dwellings. A chimney on the house of Engine 10 was complained of on June 19 by Mr. Makepeice as dangerous to the town, which complaint greatly affronted the firewards, who had the building enlarged. The hose manufactured in the town did not fully satisfy the firewards, and they ordered on the 24th the following amount to be imported from London: " Eight hose, twenty feet long, 1¾ inches in diameter. Eight ditto, thirty feet and eight ditto sixty feet." They arrived on October 17, and were placed in the care of the firewards.

The new engine built by C. Thayer to take the place of No. 5 was ready on July 24 to be taken to quarters on State street. where this company had been stationed for some time. The old engine was ordered to be removed to the West End, where a house had been erected for it, and Gideon French was appointed foreman, with fifteen members. The company was called President Adams, No. 13. December 15, fire was discovered in a building No. 3 Cornhill, occupied by Mr. Hoyen, but was soon extinguished.

The lists of members of the engines sent in by the foremen were found to contain the names of too many men as allowed by law. Captains of Engines 1, 2, 3, 4, 7, and 8 were, therefore, on February 5, 1800, ordered to report, and upon investigation it was found expedient to repeal the law of 1785 restricting the number of engine-men to one hundred and thirty men, and that a bill be placed before the Legislature to increase the number and to excuse them from military duty; in consequence of which the following act was passed, March 4, 1800 : —

That the selectmen of the Towns of Boston and Charlestown be, and they hereby are respectively authorized & empowered if they shall judge it expedient, to nominate and appoint as soon as may be after the passing of this act and ever after in the month of January, annually, any number not exceeding six men to each Engine in addition to the number of men now authorized by law, and be it further enacted that all persons leagally attached to any Engine in this Commonwealth, be, and they hereby are excused from being choosen or drawn to serve as Jurors in any court within this commonwealth, in all cases where the town, to which such Engine-men belong, shall at any legal meeting of its inhabitant, by vote declare the expediency of excusing such person or persons from serving as Jurors.

CHAPTER IX.

1800–1803.

MESSRS. Thomas Dennie, Simon Elliot, and Gorham Parsons were chosen on the Board of Firewards for the year 1800, *vice* J. Hatch and J. Russell, discharged on account of ill-health, and John Winthrop, deceased.

The fires for the year were: January 19, John Hutchinson's distil-house; 29th, Capt. Amasa Stetson & Co.'s storehouse. February 1, Mr. Balcher's shop; 15th, Benjamin Thompson; 25th, Erving Botton, Cross street. March 9, Mr. Tack's shop. June 11, Mr. Carroll's shop, Washington street. July 11, Mrs. Catherine Gray's house, State street. August, Edward Edds' bake-shop. October 24, Carroll & Witherbee's workshop, Washington street. On the engine companies, Captain Nazro, of Engine 6, is succeeded by Captain Middlefield; Captain Pearce, of Engine 9. resigns in favor of Captain Hersey on October 15, and Captain Rease, of Engine 5, is succeeded by N. Glover.

Mr. Porter asked permission, on November 12, to place several upright suction pipes in the aqueduct pipe, to be used in case of fire; but he was only allowed to erect one, this being on Washington street near Dover, and was the first hydrant constructed in Boston.

Firewards E. Parsons, T. H. Perkins, Simon Eliot, and Mr. Nathan Frazier presented the town with a large and valuable engine on November 26, which they imported from Europe. This engine was called Cataract, No. 14, and was accommodated in a building back of the office of the Fire and Marine Insurance Company, 16 State street; Mr. Lephenia Spurr was appointed its commander.

Engine 7 was moved on March 25, 1801, to a site in front of the City Hall, on School street. The engines possessed by the town at this period were named as follows: Old North, No. 1; Congress, No. 2; Washington, No. 3; Endeavor, No. 4; Marlborough, No. 5; Hero-Comes, No. 6; Extinguisher, No. 7; Cumberland, No. 8; Despatch, No 9; Hancock, No. 10; Purchase, No. 11; Eagle, No. 12; President Adams, No. 13; and Cataract, No. 14,—all of which had a membership of twenty-seven, except Nos. 2, 7. and 14, which had twenty-four.

Rufus G. Amory, Jonathan Hunnewell, and Daniel Messenger filled the places made vacant during the year by the resignation of Firewards Sturgis, Fellows, and Parsons. Twenty cents per barrel of one hundred weight of powder for storage in the magazine, and ten cents per barrel per month, and twenty-five cents for each delivery of stock from the powder-house,—this amount to go toward the salary of the keeper of the magazine, — was the rate ordered to be charged by an act of the Legislature, June 19.

Several people were examined by the selectmen for setting fire to the porch of Dr. Lothrop's meeting-house during September, but no one was proven guilty. The board, however, recommended stronger vigilance on the part of the police and others.

Between 2 and 3 o'clock on the morning of December 16, a fire broke out in the rear of a wooden building, No. 95 Ann street (North street), which soon communicated to the house opposite; it then spread to the east side of Fish street (a continuation of Ann street) and to Swett wharf, laying in ashes every one of the sixteen houses. On the west side of Ann street no building was burnt, although the street was then ten feet narrower than at present; but every house from Cross street to the one opposite Swett's wharf was either burnt or pulled down. The following is a list of those who suffered by this disaster. Western side of Fish street: Alex Onek, Mrs. Read, Joseph Churchill, Jos. Martin, Mr. Morrison, Mr. Peirce, Samuel Tuttle, Mr. Loring, Mrs. Oustead, Captain Pendexter, Nich Owose, Mr. White, Mrs. Penney, and Mr. Carey. Eastern side of Fish street: Elijah Williams, Samuel Hichborn, Mrs. Besbell, Capt. S. Stetson, Stephen Emery, Widow Stodder, David Humphreys, Messrs. Bixby, Valentine, & Co., S. Gardner, David Jones, Samuel Hayden, and Samuel Sweet. Barrett's wharf: Benjamin Varney, Abner Stoddard, Frederick W. Major, Fovell & Adams, Caleb Loring, and Deacon Barret. Hichborn's wharf: Thomas Harris, Ephraim Hutchinson, B. Hichborn, Jr., Job Barnes, Samuel Hichborn, Jr., and Henry Hutchinson. Burditt's wharf: Elijah Loring, and four buildings belonging to estate of M. Burditt. Gardner wharf: Abraham Wild, Samuel Jenks, Nahum Piper, J. N. Lillie, Capt. Lemuel Gardner, also several fish-stores of his, Thomas Luckes, and a dwelling-house a little north of the wharf occupied by poor families. Gouldbury's wharf: A range of sheds and store used by Messrs. Bixby, Valentine, & Co. Vessels: "Charming Sally" (sloop), Capt. Ellmere Franklin; several other vessels were badly damaged. Insurance: Widow Stodder, $3,000; S. Hichborn, $1,500; E. Gardner, $3,000; total loss, $100,000.

The following year a brick block, called North Row, was built on Fish street. (The first block of brick buildings erected in the town was the range called the Tontine, located in Franklin street, August 8, 1793.)

The selectmen had strong reason to attribute this fire to the work of incendiaries, and for the purpose of discovering them, and to prevent further damage, they employed five additional men to each squad of police, to patrol the streets for two nights from 10 P.M. to 6 A.M., for which they were paid $1 per night. An advertisement was also issued offering $500 reward for the apprehension of the guilty persons. The selectmen promised their influence to obtain the pardon of any one concerned in this destruction who should deliver over the offender to justice.

Fires for 1801: January 9, ship at Long wharf. March 5, Nat. Appleton's house, Brattle square. April 4, Mr. Hind's house, Cambridge street; and Gay & Veazey's store, Ann street. May 11, Caleb Wheaton's store, town dock. May 6, William Andrews' shop, Marlborough street. September 20, Mrs. Doyle's house, Fitche's alley. October 7, Mr. Kendall's bakehouse: 11th, house of John Brazier, in Brazier court, occupied by several fishermen; 19th, public house of Mrs. Wheelock, Marlborough street. November 3, Mr. Eben Olive's house, Newbury street; 7th, Mrs. Bradlee's house, Ann street; 8th, Harris House, Orange street (Washington street); 13th, Captain Holland's vessel, at Russell & Inch's wharf. December 1, J. S. Lillie's house; 20th, John Winthrop, Esq.'s, house, and Goldsmith's wharf.

Captain Jarvis, of Engine 10, was succeeded this year by Joseph Hemmenway, Captain Brown, of Engine 1, by Elisha Swift, and Captain Lovering, of Engine 8, by Jonah Wheeler.

Monday, January 18, 1802, three large fires occurred, the first being at 7 o'clock in the evening, when fire was discovered in the dwelling of Messrs. Stephen and Eben Goff, on Fort Hill, which was entirely consumed; also the house adjoining, occupied by Mrs. Spear. So rapid was the progress of the flames that hardly an article of furniture was saved, and a child of Mrs. Goff, being asleep in an upper chamber, was burned to death. The next building destroyed by this element was a shop on Howard's wharf, and soon after the discovery of the fire the flames communicated to the other shop adjoining, which contained a quantity of naval stores and tools. These shops belonged to the estate of Thomas Hichborn, and were occupied by Messrs. John Howard, Jacob Libby, Thomas Hichborn, John Chesman, and Mr. Hall. A lumber yard owned by Mr. Hatch, and several stores adjacent, took fire; but by the abundant supply of water furnished from the Mill creek they were saved. At 12 o'clock the large workshop of Messrs. Webber & Page, shipwrights, on Oliver dock, was entirely consumed. Several small buildings were pulled down to stop its progress. These fires were attributed to incendiaries, as another fire was discovered in the same quarter of the town, but was extinguished without much damage.

The firewards requested the constables, on March 25, to prosecute any person they saw carrying fire in an open vessel, or smoking a pipe or cigar in the streets, for which information they were allowed the total amount of the fine. No change occurred in the list of firewards for this year.

The following act was passed by the Legislature, February 8, 1802: —

Whereas it has sometimes happened that some people from a wanton and others from a malicious disposition have injured the publick Fire Engines provided for the extinguishment of Fire which may unfortunately happen in the habitations & other buildings of the inhabitants for prevention whereof in future. Be it enacted by the Senate & House of Representatives in General Court assembled & by the authority of the same. That if any person shall wantonly or maliciously spoil, break, injure, damage, or render useless, any Engine or any of the apparatus thereto belonging prepaired by any town society

person or persons, for the extinguishment of fire, and shall be convicted thereof before
the Supreme Judicial Court, he shall be punished by a fine not exceeding five hundred
dollars or by imprisonment not exceeding two years, at the discretion of the court, And
be it further ordered to recognize with sufficient surety or surities for good behavior for
such term as the court shall order.

The engine-men were informed by the selectmen, on January 25, that it
would induce good order and effect to wear their badges and caps at fires.
The rates for sweeping chimneys were again altered this year as follows:
Kitchen chimneys, smoke-jacks, and parlor stoves, 50 cents; parlor chimneys, 40 cents, and chambers, 33 cents, each.

Another attempt was made to destroy the warehouses on the water-front.
This time the "fire-bugs" started on Spear's wharf, in the store of Joseph
Ripley. The tide being out, the water supply was very deficient, and in a
very short time the flames had spread to the stores at the head of Long
wharf, and the range of buildings from Nos. 2 to 8 were laid in ashes, while
9 and 10 were pulled down. Two on Mr. Spear's wharf were owned by
him, and were occupied by Captain Ripley and E. L. Boyd; No. 2, on Long
wharf, by Ed. Edes, Jr.; No. 3, Messrs. Oliver & Proctor; No. 4, Benjamin
Sumner; No. 5, Joseph Field; No. 6, William McKay and Josiah Bradlee;
No. 7, Stephen Codman; No. 8, Elijah and Samuel Davenport; 9 and 10,
by Ed. Blanchard, Samuel Dillaway, and George Brackett. Mr. Osborne's
new fire-proof store prevented the flames extending to State street.

A new engine for No. 7, of the same pattern as the old, was ordered on
March 24, by the firewards, from E. Thayer, which, on trial, carried water to
a greater height than was ever thrown in Boston. The committee of the
New North Church requests that the town pay a rental for the land on which
Engine No. 2 stands; but the selectmen thought it more advisable to build a
new house on the east side of the school-house on Bennet street, where the
engine was soon after lodged.

A committee of firewards, on inspecting the several engines on September
15, recommended that two new ones be made by Mr. E. Thayer, to take the
place of Engines Nos. 3 and 4; also one of the new patent engines to be
stationed as they desire. Four hundred and fifty feet of new hose was imported from England by Fireward Parkman on November 24, and placed in
charge of Mr. Cunningham, secretary of the firewards. The old hose was
given to Mr. Tilden.

Fires for 1802: January 19, Mrs. Dudley's house, Middle street, two
barns of Mr. Amory, Mr. Miller's shop, Batterymarch street, and Howard's
wharf. February 23, Samuel Hastings' house, Newbury street, and Mrs.
Dickson's house. March 8, house on Lynn street; 14th, Mrs. Bush, North
School street, and Dr. Stillman's church, Back street. April 1, building on
Spear's wharf; 8th, Mr. Gove's house, Fort Hill; 16th, Widow Butler's
house, Orange street. May 18, house of Samuel Hastings on Newbury street,
occupied by Messrs. Coltmans & Wheldon, platers. December 3, Howard's

wharf; 16th, Mr. Wilson's house, Newbury street, and Widow Pope's, adjoining. February 9, 1803, the Legislature passed an act forbidding the erection of any building over ten feet high except of brick or stone, and all buildings placed on old foundations to be governed by the same act. No building was to be moved within the town without a permit from the firewards. They were also empowered to license the erection of buildings.

A new engine was built to replace Hancock No. 10, on January 3, and the firewards were ordered to sell the several small engines that were replaced by new ones.

A man named Perkins having invented a pump for use in case of fire, recommended them for use on the wharves in Boston; but on investigation it was found that these pumps were larger and much more expensive than could be used, being impossible to accommodate them at the creek and wharves, which were of different depths. Instead of the pumps, however, the engines in the creeks were provided with a number of short ladders.

The new engine for No. 5 was finished on April 12, and was worked for the first time in the presence of the firewards, to whom it was entirely satisfactory. It was then ordered placed under the Town-House, and Jonathan Stoddard was promoted foreman.

No change occurred in the Board of Firewards for the year 1803. A new engine was built by E. Thayer, to take the place of Engine 3, on April 19. On August 23 a new house was ordered for Engine 5.

The "Centinel," on January 19, stated that the oldest persons could not recall a period when this town was so frequently alarmed by the cry of fire. Saturday evening, on January 15, the Columbian Museum, situated at the corner of Bromfield and Tremont streets, owned by Mr. Bowen, was destroyed. The flames communicated to the dwelling of Widow Polland, Mr. Bumstead, and Othello Polland, owned by Mr. Bumstead, on whose ground the museum was erected, on such terms that within a year or two the building would come into his possession. The light from the conflagration was seen at a distance of seventy miles. While the fire was in progress the alarm was given for a fire in a new store erected on Burditt's wharf, on the site of a building burned a year previous. It was occupied by Elijah Loring as a lime-store. A carpenter-shop and barn were also destroyed.

On the 17th, about midnight, another fire broke out, this time in a hay-store owned by Joshua Batchelder, located at the old Navy Yard. A large, two-story warehouse belonging to the United States and some lumber-sheds adjoining were destroyed. A few hours later a shed owned by Messrs. Starr & Washburn, near Parson's wharf, was consumed.

Monday, the 31st, between 1 and 3 o'clock, a number of inhabitants assembled in Faneuil Hall and the Old South Church for the purpose of reconsidering the vote for an application to the Legislature for a new law to prevent the erection of wooden buildings. After an animated debate, the question to reconsider the vote was rejected by a large majority, and a vote passed instructing the representatives of the town to procure a proviso and exempt those who had made contracts for building-material agreeable to the law. At a meeting of the citizens held in Faneuil Hall, January 21, the following vote was passed: —

That as the town have witnessed the exertion, prudence, and discretion of the firewards in the late distressing scenes which have fallen on this metropolis, the thanks of the Town are given unto them, and that they may be assured that the town will afford all the support necessary to such important usefulness.

The other fires for the year were: January 2, Jacob Taylor's carpenter shop, near Baldwin's Church, and a house on Back street; 7th, Thomas Page's carpenter shop, Grant's wharf; 9th, at Loring's wharf; 18th, Loring's shop, Cross street; 21st, W. H. Sumner's house, Tremont street. March, house on Milk street. June 7, soap and candle works of Mr. Lovering; 10th, house in Theatre alley. November 20, Daniel Cobb's distil-house. December 20, Wells Hunt's building, Water street.

Captain Smith succeeded Captain Stoddard on Engine 5. Joseph Burgis was made foreman of Engine 4, and Thomas Page of Engine 2.

CHAPTER X.

1804–1817.

THE beginning of 1804 was attended by a severe conflagration. On January 21 a building on State street, occupied by Maj. J. Pierce as a ship-chandler store, Messrs. Gilbert & Dean, printers of the " Weekly Magazine," and the premises of Messrs. N. & R. Freeman and E. & N. Withington, adjoining, were entirely consumed. The buildings were owned by John Parker, and his loss amounted to $20,000 ; N. & R. Freeman, $5,000 ; Withington, $500 The printers could not save a single article. Monday, 23d, a small fire occurred in the house of Mr. Merriam, at West End. Only three other fires were reported for this year, — October 4, a house on Beach street ; 25th, General Jackson's distil-house ; and December 17th, Mr. Darling's grocery store, Southwark street, West Boston.

By an act of the Legislature, passed this year, the number of enginemen on Cataract Engine 14 was increased to forty, it being the largest piece of apparatus in the town.

Ozias Goodwin was chosen a fireward during 1804, *vice* Edward Edes, deceased. This board appointed Messrs. Jackson, Melville, and Brown a committee to form a plan for ascertaining the origin of all fires that may happen within the town. Their report, on January 8, 1805, as follows, was accepted : —

That the secretary issue a commission appointing three Firewards residing in the vicinity where the fire commenced, to ascertain by a minute and particular inquiry of such persons who are able to give the best information respecting its origin, also estimating the value of the property lost or destroyed.

The secretary of the board had been paid a yearly salary of $40, but the increased amount of work occasioned by the " Building Law " was such that they voted him $100 for his services. But this did not satisfy him, as he did not wish the money to be paid by his colleagues, as he thought the town had a right to pay him ; therefore petitioned the selectmen for $200 per year, which was granted.

Messrs. Thomas Curtis, Joshua Davis, Jr., J. D. Howard, Benjamin Coates, and Judah Hays were elected firewards, *vice* Messrs. May, Brown, Howard, Gardner, and Joy, for the year 1805. The board voted that they try an American-made hose, as the last consignment from abroad was very poor. Two hundred feet was therefore ordered, as some of the engines were destitute of this article.

No large fires occurred during the year, but a great many small ones were extinguished by the department. The most serious of these were probably Gen. J. Elliott's residence, on Federal street, April 16, and Messrs. Wetherby & Needham's stable, located in Dock square, which broke out March 13, and burnt twenty-five horses, entailing a loss of $4,637. Other fires: March 2, house of Mr. Brimmer, corner of School and Washington streets, occupied by Messrs. M. & S. Thayer; 12th, Forbes & King's stable, near the market. April 4, the New York packet, lying at Long wharf; 16th, Mr. Elliott's house, Federal street; 18th, small sloop at E. Thayer's wharf. July 4, Mrs. Welsh's house, Court street; 18th, Dr. Webster's house, Ann street. November 4, bakehouse, Water street; 5th, Mr. Amsden's house, corner High street. December 11, Dr. Lloyd's house, Court street; 18th, Mr. Winslow's dwelling, Napan street; 30th, Captain Sargent's house, Atkinson street; 31st, H. J. Bean's house, Brattle square.

The following changes of foremen were made in the department during the year: William Champney, *vice* Parmenter, Engine 11; John Perry, *vice* Captain Burgis, Engine 4; and Adam Smith, *vice* Captain Stoddard, Engine 5.

A petition was granted to the inhabitants of the West End to place at the west side of the Court-House several ladders, as follows: Rev. Mr. Murray's church, West Boston Church, and Mr. Eaton's fence, on Eaton street. October 30, the American and the Amicable Fire Societies notified the selectmen that they each had provided a ladder, — that of the former to be placed at the meeting-house of Rev. Mr. Channing, the other on the wall opposite Concert Hall.

The records of the engine companies from 1800 to 1824 are not in existence, the selectmen's records ceasing to make entries of the members after 1799, and with the exception of one or two copies of the roll books of the old companies that have been left at the fire commissioners' office, no authentic data is left; therefore the list of foremen between these years is incomplete, while no mention whatever can be found of the individual members. We presume they continue in the same order as formerly, new members being admitted at each monthly meeting, and old ones leaving. Their numbers were gradually increased, and during the period of uncertainty and anxiety succeeding the French Revolution, and through our own war, the companies were harassed with applicants for membership (as engine-men were exempt from military duty), and availed themselves generally to secure a good time. Most of the companies required the payment of $10 or $15, or a company treat, as a fee of admission. This, together with the premiums and the fines exacted, created a very considerable income for the support of a system of fun and "good times." By way of illustration we give a few extracts from the records of one of these old companies: —

"December 14 1799 Mr ———— gave the company a handsome supper." "Dec 27. another handsome supper." "Jan 19 1800 ditto." "May 5. ditto." "July 10 company had a fishing voyage and spent all their stock on hand." "Oct 6, Voted to have a rump of beef roasted and brought to the Engine house." "Nov 1801 Had a supper at the Widdow's; cost $28, which was 2s 3d a head more than we had in stock." "May 1802, 3 members treated with a day on the water in lieu of a supper for each." "Aug. 1803 Voted to go on the water with women." "July 1810 Had an elegant supper at Henry Goodriches and there was a general attendance, the only one absent Mr ———. Club 75 cts each." "Feb 7 had a supper at the Engine house; all present." "April 9, Expence of evening, $3.41." "May 27, Voted to have a land frolic, and to go to Dedham."

We find among the above records a vote of $40 to a poor widow; also $40 for the Newburyport sufferers. This, we presume, is a fair sample of the records of all the fraternity. It does not appear that any of the companies under this system ever had any other than captain and clerk. They were very particular in the admission of members. The candidate was required to be of age, and show a good recommendation from the person with whom he served his time, and in some companies preference was given to married men.

The largest fire for the year 1806 was the burning of the rope-walks at the foot of the Common (on the site of the Public Garden), on February 19, where, as we have already mentioned, business was allowed to be carried on after the terrible fire of July 30, 1794. The fire originated from the boiling over of a tar-kettle in the rope-walk owned by Joseph Howe, from whence it spread to those of Messrs. Samuel Emmons, Capt. P. B. Rogers, and two others of Isaac P. Davis. The contents of the buildings were partially saved, as well as part of the hemp in Mr. Rogers' fire-proof store. Total loss, $84,000. On March 13 another fire of considerable magnitude broke out in the building owned by Deacon Tilden on the east side of Batterymarch street, occupied as a shoe-store by Mr. Mills. The flames soon spread to a building on the north side, belonging to the heirs of Mr. Cushing, and occupied by Mr. Hall, sail-maker, and Mr. Hayes, cabinet-maker. It then communicated to the houses of Widow Hickling, on the west side of the street, occupied by Mr. Grover, Mr. Billings, and Deacon Tilden, as stores, all of which were destroyed. and the house of Mr. McKean was pulled down. The other alarms for the year were: February 1, William Darricott's and Mrs. Pulsifer's houses on Charter street. March 10, Joseph Fovy's ship; 11th, Thomas Perkins' stable, H. Hicks' building, Hanover street. April 28, cellar occupied by Hall & Bates, near the market; 27th, Mr. Foster's store, owned by Samuel Richards, on Ann street, near the market. July 7, A. Gibson's distil-house. September 23. Nathan Mariam's barn. October 21, Mr. Evan's house and goldsmith shop, 50 Cornhill. November 25, in the morning, Stetson's buildings, and in the evening, Seth Thayer's building, between Faneuil Hall and Ann street.

Benjamin Smith and William Sullivan were chosen firewards for the year, *vice* R. G. Amory and J. Hays. Considerable trouble was experienced by the board from the number of engine companies leaving the town to render assistance to neighboring towns in case of fire, thus leaving their homes unprotected. A committee was therefore appointed on October 9 to make report of some permanent system. On December 11 the following rules were adopted : —

At an alarm of fire in any town in this vicinity, to whose assistance our fellow-citizens may be disposed to run, not more than four of the public engines, with their companies, shall be allowed, nor more than Eight firewards. The fireward who shall first arrive at the nearest point of the avenue leading from this town to the place intended to be succored, shall there take his stand, and when he has permitted four Engines with their companies and Eight Firewards to pass, he shall order all the other Engines with their companies back to their houses respectively; and notify all the other firewards that the number allowed to go out of town for that purpose had passed.

They also recommended that two additional men be admitted to each engine, to use the axes, saws, etc. Engine-house 7 was moved, on August 14, further back to the line of the school, about on the site where the Franklin statue now stands, and a flat composition roof put on.

The Columbian Museum, owned by Daniel Bowers and M. S. Doyle, on Tremont street, had been rebuilt of brick, three stories high, and 107×30 feet in dimensions. It again caught fire, in the upper hall, on the night of January 16, 1807, just one day following the fourth anniversary of its destruction by fire in 1803. Loss, $12,000. After the fire had been controlled, the south wall fell into the Chapel Burying-ground, and killed William Homer, 11 ; John Condon, 14 ; Henry Fullerton, 20 ; Isaac Peabody, 15 ; Joshua Urann, 17 ; and James D. Beals, 13 years of age, respectively.

Fish street was the scene of the next conflagration. This broke out on Tuesday, August 18, and before it was extinguished five dwellings were destroyed, occupied by Dr. N. Smith, I. Wakefield, Thomas Curtis, Thomas Bell, Mr. Lathrop, Francis Cleaver, Mrs. Mandville, Samuel Hallowell, Mrs. Pike, Mrs. A. Smith, Henry Hunters, and Mrs. Wade. The loss was $10,430. Owing to the narrowness of this street and the entrance to North square, the engines that ventured in these thoroughfares were soon surrounded by flames, and were burned. Fish street was widened two and one-half feet soon after.

On February 27 the rope-walk of Samuel Andrews, at West End, was burned. March 23. Timothy Tileston's building, on Pleasant street; and the house adjoining, occupied by Colonel Gardner and owned by Mr. Richardson, were destroyed ; loss, $9,000. July 20, a house in Randall's lane, and on October 25 a house in the rear of Perry May's buildings ; also Mr. Lepeau's dwelling, in Ann street, December 4, — constituted the fire record for the year.

Messrs. Ignatius Sargent, Henry Fowle, and Samuel Sweet were chosen firewards for the year in the place of Messrs. Parkman, Scollay, and Howard. At the request of the board, two hundred feet of hemp hose was imported from Holland, as the quality of this article made in this country and England was very unsatisfactory. Engine 12 house was enlarged on December 2, and Engine Company 8 asked that a meeting-room be added to their quarters. December 16, the members of Engine 11 petition for the removal of their house to the foot of Summer street, and to have it enlarged. E. Bell succeeded Captain Swift on Engine 1, and Thomas Tileston, Captain Wheeler on Engine 8. September 10, the necessary number of axes, saws, and other appliances needed for the department were procured.

A petition from inhabitants of the West End was received by the fire-wards on March 26, praying that an engine be stationed at or near Wheeler's point, and another from residents near the rope-walks at the foot of the Common, that one be placed near those buildings; but the board refused to grant either of these, as they reported that it seldom occurred that more than two-thirds of the whole number of engines were brought into operation at one time, and that, by the mode of building, the town was less exposed to extensive conflagrations than at any period within their knowledge.

The hemp hose was put to experimental purposes to test its strength, on March 11, 1808, but we do not know the results; judging from subsequent trials and reports, we take it for granted it was found wanting in quality. Three changes were made in the officers of the department during the year, as follows: Nathan Pratt, *vice* Captain Bell, Engine 1; Benjamin Coomes, *vice* Captain Page, Engine 2; and John Wild, *vice* Captain Hemmenway, Engine 10.

E. Thayer was given the contract, on November 9, for building an engine to take the place of Engine 6, and allowed $100 for the old one. The representative of the General Court was requested by the selectmen, on the same date, to have the engine-men excused from jury duty.

Messrs. Davis, Bradford, Goodwin, and Fowle were succeeded on the Board of Firewards for this year by Edward Cruft, Barker Baker, James Phillips, and Nathaniel Curtis.

The department was called out to the following fires: January 14, John Fisher's house, in Wilson's lane, or the rear of 29 Cornhill; 27th, Norcross' brewery, on Lynn street, occupied by Daniel & Chapin, and owned by Dr. Davis. February 19, Mr. Benjamin Weld's house, Newbury street, corner Suffolk place. March 7, Abigail Cowall's house; 28th, house, Fish street. May 1, William Cooledge's house, west side of Orange street, owned by B. Goddard. June 6, John Murray's dwelling and bakehouse, head of Charter street. August 15, Mr. J. C. Dyer's brick house, Franklin street, occupied by five tenants; 31st, ship "Arrow," at May's wharf. September 25, three houses on Elm street, occupied by Secretary-of-State Andrew Oliver, Mr. Bailey, and a shop owned by him; total loss, $5,500. October 19, Capt. David Cobb's building, and Dunlap's malt-house, on Washington street. November 29, store of Jonathan, Nathaniel, & Ireland, Pleasant street. December 4, John Lepeau's dry-goods store, on Ann street, building owned by Colonel Ford; 20th, William Cooledge's house, on Orange street.

An act was passed by the State, on March 8, forbidding any vessels having gunpowder on board from lying within two hundred feet of the wharves. The magazines were placed at Pine Island, Roxbury, and the fire-wards were given authority to enter buildings in search of this explosive. The law of January 26, 1792, was repealed.

Only one change occurred in the Board of Firewards for the year 1809, when Bryant P. Tilden was chosen, *vice* General Jackson, deceased. On March 23 this board had a large number of poles or staffs for their use placed at the Exchange Coffee-house. They also requested the selectmen to procure an improved powder-carriage, to be placed with the deputy police-officer, or in any other manner that would render it easily obtainable.

Captain Wiswell, of Engine 7, was succeeded by Robert New, and Captain Tileston, of Engine 8, by Mr. Wheeler. The year was also one of few fires in the town, while those that did occur were of small dimensions. January 4, Ephraim Jones' house, Pearl street. April 15, Mr. Bell's dwelling, Lynn street. May 30, Mr. Rounds' residence, Middle street. June 10, the house of Mr. Holden, on Fish street. July 2, dwelling on Hawkins street. October 26, Jacob Ganger's building, corner of Summer street.

Messrs. Nathan Webb, George Blanchard, James Robinson, Samuel M. Thayer were the successors of Firewards Perkins, Dennie, Elliot, and Baker, for the year 1810. A committee was chosen by the board to make inquiries as to whether leather could be obtained tanned in any particular manner more suitable and proper to make engine-hose. On May 10 Engine-house 7 was ordered to be moved to a place on vacant land, as the Court-House was being built; but no accommodation could be had, and a wooden house was ordered to be erected at the back of the Latin School. A new engine was ordered for Engine 2, on October 3, to be one of squirt principle, and the old apparatus was exchanged in part payment for a new one.

The most destructive fires for the year were: on Saturday, December 29, when the old Franklin house, a three-story wooden building on Milk street, the birthplace of Benjamin Franklin, was destroyed. It was then occupied by Mr. John S. Lillie. The fire was communicated to it from the livery stable situated at the corner of Hawley street, kept by Stephen L. Soper. Two houses and four barns were destroyed in this fire, the loss being $6,000. The Old South Church took fire at this time, but was saved by the exertions of Mr. Isaac Harris, for which he received a silver medal. The other was on October 19, when the bakehouse of Mr. Godfrey, on Fish street, was burnt; also his dwelling house and barn, a house on Wheeler's wharf, and a barn and two hundred cords of wood on Howard's wharf, the total value being $11,675. On the 23d the Eagle Tavern, kept by Lydia Blood and owned by William Patterson, on Back street, was destroyed; loss, $2,300. The smaller fires were: February 13, North School-house, on North Bennett street; loss, $550; 25th, Deacon Daniel Bates' house. March 30, three houses, occupied by Isaac Dupee and others, in Distil-house square. May 29, Samuel Beals' dwelling. on Fore street.   August 20, Colonel Messenger's shop.   October 9, shop of Eliah Wheeler; 26th, shop of Samuel Beaks.   December 21, building in the rear of 36 and 37 Marlboro' street, — No. 36 occupied by Messrs. Coppenhagen & Kimmer, 37 as the Indian Queen Tavern, and 35 by A. & S. Archabald; 27th, slight blaze at the Exchange Coffee-house, in the upper floor; loss, $50.   An addition was made to the Building Act on June 14, whereby it was ordered that when one building was separated from another by a partition wall, it was to be of brick or stone, so as to be capped with flat stones two inches thick.   This repealed the three-feet battlement law.

Engine-house 12 was moved on January 16, 1811, to Mr. R. S. Whitney's land, on Orange street.   The order to the members of the department to wear a badge on their hats so that they could be distinguished was unheeded by many in the strict sense of its meaning, for instead of procuring badges they marked their hats with chalk; this was copied by outsiders, who, when attending a fire, would mark the number of a certain engine on their head-wear, and in the excitement go about as they chose, often causing trouble by stealing, etc., so that the firewards•made it compulsory, on January 10, 1811, for every member to procure a proper badge, and wear it at all fires.   A communication was sent at the same time, by the board, to the religious societies in the town for them to furnish one or more ladders of sufficient length, for their respective churches, and to have them marked and placed in some convenient situation.   Messrs. Joseph Tilden, Thomas Page, Joseph Austin, and Benjamin Rich succeeded Messrs. Swett, Curtis, Davis, and Robinson on the board for 1811.   On May 27 chimney-sweeps were ordered to wear badges, and the rates for sweeping were always fixed by the selectmen.   The day following, the removal of the gun-house to Copp's Hill, as voted by the inhabitants, was complained of, and on November 27 a committee of the firewards notified the selectmen that the house was contrary to law, and should be made more secure; six months' time was given in order to render it as the law required.

Captain Francis succeeded Foreman Hersey on Engine 9.

Fires for the year: January 2, Cornhill House, occupied by Edward Martin, owned by D. D. Rogers; 29th, stables on Milk street; firemen from Medford, Charlestown, Roxbury, Cambridge, and Cambridgeport rendered assistance, and received public thanks of the wards.   March 19, Ezra Davis' store, Kilby street.   April 4, Mr. Green's house, Cornhill.   June 3, Caleb Hayward's residence, Tremont street.   July 12, Mr. Cooledge's house, Cornhill; loss, $250; 28th, house, Milk street.   September 25, glass-house.   October 13, John Bright's building on Cambridge street, occupied by J. Blainey as tin-plate shop; 18th, house of R. G. Shaw, Fore street; 23d, Asa Adams' house, Middle street, also Mr. Blood's dwelling, Back street.   November 7, Eben Oliver's residence, Newbury street.   December 2, house on Marlboro' street, house, Pleasant street; 29th, store, corner of Milk and Hawley streets.

The question of hose was again considered by the wards, and on January

16, 1812, forty feet of sewed, and the like amount of copper-riveted, leather hose was purchased from Philadelphia, and put to a severe test to ascertain which was the best. Both styles were used after, but the riveted was preferable. June 11, thirty-six staves of the wards were purchased and placed in the following buildings : Six each at the State-House, Boylston Market, Fire and Marine Insurance office, and the Massachusetts Mutual Fire Insurance office ; twelve at the Exchange Coffee-house ; four each at the First Church on Summer street and the New North Church in North street ; two each at Trinity Church in Summer street, New South Church in Summer street, Hollis-street Church, West Boston Church in Lynde street, Federal-street Church, and the Brattle-street Church ; and one each at the second Old North Church, or New Brick, in Middle street, and the Stone Chapel in School street. These poles, or staves of office, were placed as above for the purpose of having them easily accessible on alarm of fire, without going to their place of business or residence, they being much too large to carry with them, except when needed. The changes in this office for the year were Messrs. Joseph Lovering, Gidney King, Francis J. Oliver, John D. Williams, *vice* May, Head, Coates, and Sargent. Two changes occurred also in the officers of the department, Eben Oliver succeeding Captain Pratt on Engine 1, and Mr. Wilson, Captain French on Engine 13.

February 2, house at West Boston ; March 5, the White and Black House near Haskin's distil-house ; 28th, Captain Chapman's house, Salutation lane, Joshua Ellis's residence, North square.

No change in the Board of Firewards occurred for 1813, and but two fires, the least of any since the department was organized ; they were, on March 13, the glass-house, and a stable of Mr. Boyington's tavern.

Engine-house 3 was ordered on October 6 to be enlarged and a chimney built.

One of the firewards, Mr. King, being, as he claimed, " grossly insulted " at a recent fire by a Mr. J. W. Lillie, used some " degree of violence," for which Lillie commenced an action of damage. The whole board voted, on January 6, 1814, to support their colleague in the suit, but lost, and was compelled to pay damage to the extent of $68.44.

April 27, the old Engine 2 was placed at the glass-house at South Boston, and an engine company formed, but was of little service, as a new one was asked for soon after.

In 1814 the unhappy difficulty with England led to great excitement and grave fears in Boston, as at that time the British policy of coast descents was extended to New England, and the sails of English cruisers could daily be descried from our coast. The town was in a defenceless condition, the forts almost useless, and owing to the bitter quarrels with the administration, no help had been given or was to be looked for from the National Government. Our citizens, however, took every possible measure to protect themselves, one of which was the stationing of two each of the engine companies, under the command of the wards, at the various bridges, who were instructed, if deemed necessary, to cut the bridge connecting the peninsula with the mainland, to prevent the passing of the enemy. For this purpose the companies were stationed as follows: Engines 2 and 3, at Charles-river bridge, Benjamin Smith and John Winslow, Jr. ; 10 and 13, Canal bridge, A. Cunningham and Stephen Codman ; 4 and 6, West Boston bridge, Francis J. Oliver and Joseph Tilden ; 8 and 12, South bridge, James Phillips and Nathaniel Curtis. Those at Chelsea, Malden, and Brighton were to be attended to by others ; but before companies were formed the danger had subsided. Just previous to this, the entire department was cautioned by the wards not to volunteer their services in any other capacity, and that they put their engines in the best possible state of operation, and see that their complement of men was complete, and in case of alarm to rendezvous at their respective engine-houses without delay. On the 22d they applied to the selectmen for two float stages, two row boats, two tackles, blocks, and falls, ten picks, six screws, and four crow-bars, for the purpose of destroying one hundred feet of the Canal bridge, which the particular construction and material of the bridge renders necessary.   •

Messrs. William Harris and John Winslow, Jr., were admitted on the board in the place of Bray and Page, resigned.

The Legislature took further action on the subject of gunpowder on February 22, whereby officers of the United States were forbidden from keeping more than four hundred pounds of that article, and this had to be placed in an underground vault or a stone or brick building, approved by the firewards. On October 19 the same body passed an act making it unlawful to erect a stable or a building for the storage of hay within one hundred and thirty feet of any meeting-house or public building, and to have all external sides and ends of stone or brick, unless otherwise licensed by the wards. Certain lands in Back, Marlboro', and Hawley streets were exempt from this law.

Only ten alarms were responded to during the year: January 7, Mr. White's stable, Pond street. February 7, Mr. Homer's wood-house on Middle street. Engine 13 was frozen up at this fire, and rendered useless. March 13, building in Fore street, occupied by four tenants ; loss, $5,240. April 8, the Furnace Building, South Boston ; 25th, Benjamin Bass' house, Orange street ; 29th, distil-house, owned by Joshua Knap. June 30, Mrs. Lovering's house, Nausau street. July 18, house of Eben Niles. September 26, Mr. Cushing's residence, Common street. November, tenement house in Elm street.

Goose-necks for engine pipes were first used on Engine 1 by Wards Harris and King, on September 14, 1815, and proved a success. Complaint was made to the ward, by the citizens that it was impossible to comply with the law regarding the covering of roofs of buildings with slate at that time, as there were none in the market ; they consequently were given nine months' time in which to purchase these articles. Jonathan Heath succeeded Captain New on Engine 7 this year.

November 22, Engine-house 13 was ordered to have a partition put in for a meeting-room, and a fireplace, so that that they could heat water to clean their engine from frost and ice.   Mr. Leach Harris was promoted foreman of Engine 2, *vice* Captain Coomes.

Quite a number of fires are reported for the year, the largest of which was on October 4, which broke out in a barn of Nathan Call, at the bottom of Gooche's lane, which, before it was extinguished, had communicated to the other barns, and three houses were entirely destroyed, and three others were badly damaged.   The Harvard College engine company rendered assistance, and was highly complimented by the wards.   The other fires were : January 16, Mr. Bumstead's house, near the new market ; 25th, Mr. Huger's dwelling, South Bennett street ; 29th, E. Cobb's building, Washington street.   February 18, house in Richmond street ; 22d, house of Levi Harris, in Negro alley.   March 15, stable on Tremont street ; 22d. building (no particulars).   April 3, barn near Purchase street ; 4th, Mr. Hale's barn in High street ; building of Benjamin Bass on Orange street ; 28th, a tenement occupied by Mr. Lerned and others on North Bennet street.   June 13, John Gibson's store, School street.   September 23, glass-house.   November 11, Edwin Cotton's residence, Marlboro' street.

Gunpowder was again a subject of legislation at the State-House on January 18, 1816.   By an act passed on that day it was compulsory for those selling this explosive to obtain a license from the firewards at a cost of $5, and $1 for each renewal, this money to go towards the expense under which the board was placed in carrying out the law.   They also had authority to have the powder in a building removed to a place of safety, in case of an alarm of fire.   On July 3 the wards made a code of rules and regulations for those who intended keeping powder for sale, by which it was ordered that those selling at retail were restricted to twenty-five pounds, to be divided into canisters of twelve and a half pounds each, and have a sign placed near the door of the store, with the words, " Licensed to Keep and Sell Gunpowder."   The wholesale dealers were allowed one hundred pounds, to be kept in four leather bags, marked " Gunpowder," and incased in a copper chest, with two handles and closed copper cover, which was to be placed in a convenient part of the store.   This was to remain in the building six hours only during the day, when it had to be removed to the magazine at Fort Strong or South Boston, at the risk of owner.

The Massachusetts Fire and Marine Insurance Company soon after establishing their business took an interest in the engine companies, and publicly announced, during November 21, 1796, that they would give a bounty of $10 to the company first at a fire.   This was again voted upon, and recorded with the vote of the town regarding their premium of £5 on March 7, 1816.

Mr. Turner Phillips was chosen a fireward for the year, in the place of Mr. Sullivan.   Judgment was obtained against their secretary and Mr. Oliver, on July 3, for trespass and seizing gunpowder, the damages of which amounted to $110.50, which the selectmen voted should be paid out of the town treasury. Engine 13 being condemned, a new one was ordered to take its place, September 18, which was called the "Rapid 13." On December 30 four additional men were added to the list of Engine 7.

Fires: February 29, barn of Benjamin Cobb, Washington street. March 4, Mr. Bean's store, Boylston street; 21st, house in Fish street; 28th, a building occupied by Isaac Howe and others in Prince street. April 10, building at Long wharf. June 17, glass-house and lime-kiln; 26th, I. D. Howard's building, Washington street. July 16, Mr. Lovering's dwelling on Nausau street. August 22, D. Hayward's house, Newbury street. September 15, Captain Simanton's vessel, lying at Central wharf. October 20, building of Thomas B. Wales, Lloyd's wharf; 26th, stable on Nausau street, occupied by Mrs. A. C. Dorr, and owned by Joseph Lovering; 30th, Mr. Robinson's house, on Orange street. November 23, A. Willard's barn, on Washington street.

Just off the head of Long wharf, on artillery election day, 1817, there was anchored the Canton packet, "James and Thomas Handyside Perkins," a ship of three or four hundred tons burden, employed in the India trade. It was all ready to sail on the day following for the Isle of France, with a full cargo of general merchandise and $400,000 in specie. The crew went ashore to enjoy the festivities of the holiday, and left the colored steward, William Read, of Philadelphia, on board. He was so angry at this treatment, that at about 11 o'clock in the morning he took revenge by discharging a pistol in a barrel of powder stored among many others in the magazine of the ship. As a matter of course, the discharge blew the vessel into fragments. This affair was the origin of the famous byword of bygone days: "Who blew up the ship?" which was answered by the colored folks, to whom it was always addressed, by "Who put out the moon?" alluding to a famous exploit of an engine company, who once dragged their engine to the end of Long wharf to extinguish what appeared to be a large fire, but proved to be only the rising of an extraordinary bright full moon on a somewhat hazy summer evening.

On June 12, 1817, the wards made a thorough examination of all the ladders furnished by the religious societies, and had them repaired. Circulars were also sent to those societies who had neglected to provide them; and to the Long wharf, India wharf, and Central wharf corporations, for each of them to furnish a ladder as soon as possible. Orders were then issued to have the ladders returned to their proper places after being used at a fire. Baker's patent pumps were placed on the several wharves of the town for use at fires at this time. Mr. Levi Melcher was appointed keeper of the magazine at Fort Strong on Noddle's Island (East Boston), on July 12, he being placed under $5,000 bonds; but only remained in this position a few weeks, when he was discharged and prosecuted by the wards, but their action was not sustained by the Court.   Messrs. Joseph Davis and Bryant P. Tilden succeeded Firewards Craft and Winslow, Jr., this year.

Number of fires: January 8, school-house, School street; loss, $200; Major Fairbank's dwelling, owned by Mrs. Kelton, Orange street; 29th, house of Mr. Wentworth, bottom of Peck's lane; Mr. Cudworth's carpenter shop, Myrtle street.   February 12, Messrs. George Jackson & Co.'s candle-works, Washington street.   March 20, Messrs. Wood & Long's store, at the north side of Central street, West End, owned by Samuel and David Deveus, Charlestown; loss, $500.   April 7, barn in Garden street, house in Kilby street.   May 26, Messrs. Gregg & Easty's building, South Boston; a barn, chaise-house, and a shed filled with shingles, occupied by Lincoln & Jackson, on wharf near West Boston bridge, Joseph Adams, of Charlestown, owner; loss, $950.

CHAPTER XI.

1818–1822.

OWING to the trouble experienced by the wards in carrying the fire and gunpowder laws into effect, and the expense naturally attending the same, they petitioned the selectmen, on February 4, 1818, that their expenses be paid hereafter out of the town treasury. The selectmen were of the opinion that " it did comport with the honor or dignity of the town that the board of Firewards who risked their lives and health for the preservation of the lives and property of their fellow citizens without any salary or emolument from their office should be subject to the expense occurring in the discharge of their duty, Voted that in consideration of the arduous task the firewards were subjected to in carrying the Fire and Powder laws into effect and the expense materially attending the same, that they be authorized to lay their accounts before the board of allowance, deducting the sum they may receive from fires and forfeitures from the fire and powder laws, provided the expence does not exceed two hundred and fifty dollars per annum." Two changes occurred in the board for 1818, Messrs. Lemuel Shaw and John Bray succeeding Joseph Tilden and B. P. Tilden. The vote passed September 4 last, to close the magazine at Fort Strong, was rescinded on March 19, and the magazine was again placed as a deposit for powder. They employed Mr. Ephraim Thayer to examine the hose and screws of all the engines, and fit the screws so the hose would connect with each other. Each engine was also furnished with ninety feet of drag-rope. On August 12, a new brick house was ordered to be built for Cataract Engine 14 on Milk street ; but the land was found to be so very marshy that a suitable foundation could not be laid without a very great expense, therefore a wooden structure was erected by Mr. Thaxter.

The famous Exchange Coffee-house, built, as was reported, at an expense of $500,000 by Barnum, on Congress street, was discovered to be on fire, in the south-west corner of the attic, about 7 o'clock on the evening of November 3. The height of the fire, and the impossibility of getting water to reach the flames, which were rapidly making their way behind the partitions, rendered the spirited efforts of the citizens and firemen of no avail, and it was therefore consumed in about three hours. About nine o'clock the noble dome fell with a crash ; this was soon followed by the north and south walls, which damaged contiguous buildings. An immense concourse of citizens, and many from the surrounding country, were spectators to the scene. The light penetrated far into the country, so as to be clearly visible upwards of fifty miles. The following morning the front walls, ninety feet in height and eighty feet wide, stood tottering over the people's head, and threatened to crush the building opposite, but were levelled without accident. The building covered thirteen thousand square feet of ground, and contained two hundred and ten rooms. One other building at the corner of Congress and Devonshire streets was also consumed. According to the report by the committee of wards who investigated the matter, the building was not so valuable as reported. From their statement, we learn that the fire originated from a defective flue, and that the loss was as follows : the Exchange building, including the building on Devonshire street, $60,000 ; furniture and wines, $30,000. Those of the occupants of the other building were : James Prince, $4,000 ; Young & Muns, printers, $1,500 ; J. W. Taylor, Congress street, $1,500 ; D. D. Rogers, $500 ; Suffolk Insurance Company, $800 ; Rev. Mr. Bradford, $400 ; Mr. Lincoln, printer, $1,200 ; Parmenter & Martin, printers, $200 : William M. Clapp, printer, $70 ; T. Badger, printer, $550 ; Wells & Libby, $1,500 ; and miscellaneous, $179 ; total, $101,899. Fire was found in the ruins three months afterwards, and Engine 7, which was the first to arrive on the scene, was afterwards discovered to have had sufficient power to reach the fire had there been no intervening obstacle.

Immediately after this conflagration, a committee of wards, consisting of Melville, Rich, and Codman, was appointed to consider as to the advisability of increasing the number of gentlemen in that office, they reported that an addition of six men be added ; therefore, on application, the General Court authorized thirty firewards to be voted for at the next town meeting, May, 1819, when the following change occurred : Messrs. Cunningham, Winslow, Hunnewell, Rich, King, Oliver, and Harris resigned, and Messrs. Benjamin Russell, Thomas Jackson, Winslow Lewis, Amos Benney, Enoch Silsby, Isaac Harris, George W. Otis, Joseph Jones, William Howe, Jonathan Whitney, and Jeremiah Fitch were elected. Mr. John Howe declining, Samuel A. Wells was chosen in his place May 21.

Other fires for 1818 : January 26, house on North Russell street. April 2, Mr. Frost's building, Court street. June 6, Jacob Jacob's shop, Pleasant street. July 18, bakery of Eben Garrison on Back street, owned by heirs Deacon Joseph. August 5, cooper shop, Commercial street : 14th, Messrs. Austin's buildings, Hancock street ; 28th, Mr. Kelton's barn, Orange street. September, stable next to the Washington Garden. October 26, Mr. Rust's dwelling, Prince street. November 9, Messrs. Brown & Rainsford building, Marlborough street.

An act entitled " An Act to secure the town of Boston from Damage by fire " was passed by the Legislature on February 16, in which was embraced all the laws on this subject previously passed : the other acts were repealed, except such parts as may be necessary to recover fines and penalties incurred from these acts.

The first serious trouble between the wards and the engine companies occurred during 1819. A member of Engine 12 had some difficulty with a fireward, in consequence of which the former was prosecuted, but acquitted. The company, however, paid his expenses, amounting to $20, which they requested should be returned to them by the town through the wards ; but not hearing from them as soon as expected, although the committee from that body appointed to act in the matter had called on Mr. White, the clerk of the company, and informed him that they would meet them at a time and place most convenient to the members, the result was a misunderstanding, and Captain Sears of the engine, in behalf of the company, sent in a letter of resignation on January 27. This was accepted by the wards, but Capt. John Wheeler, chairman of the Associated Engine Societies of Boston, asked, on February 10, that the company be reinstated. The committee therefore met Company Commanders Wheeler, Nath. Frothingham, Jr., Joshua Vose, Jared Heath, Robert New, John Julmer, and Joel Shipley to consider the matter, which resulted in the disbandment of the company.

The competition of the companies in first throwing water on a fire resulted in the members resorting to many schemes to receive the premium. one of which was to fill the engine with water while at quarters, so as to have enough to " play away " until their engine was connected ; but this little smartness was entirely handicaped by the wards on October 28, as they issued orders stating that no prizes would be given to a company carrying water in their engines, as it was liable to freeze and render the engines useless.

A patent bolt-rope was first used at this time for dragging the apparatus. A committee, consisting of Messrs. Tilden, Phillips, and Binney, was also chosen to procure an additional number of ladders and fire-hooks, and to establish a system for getting them to fires and rendering them useful. This resulted in the appointment of the firemen, and the origin of the hook and ladder company. At their request the Legislature passed an act on February 7, 1820, authorizing the selectmen to appoint a number of men, not exceeding thirty, with the same privileges as engine-men, for the purpose of conveying to and from a fire all the ladders and fire-hooks. These men were to be called firemen, and organized into one or more companies, who were to meet some time in the month of May annually, when they should choose a foreman and a clerk. and establish rules and regulations as approved by the selectmen, and to annex penalties for the violation of the same, which could be recovered by the clerk before any justice of the peace, provided that such penalty shall exceed the sum of $6.67. They were also requested to meet once in every month to look after the apparatus in their care.

The method of giving an alarm was also considered, and a letter sent on March 8, 1820, to the secretary of each religious society requesting them not to employ any person as sexton who may be a member of the department, and to have the sextons attend their bells immediately on an alarm of fire, and continue with them until the alarm may have subsided.

February 17, 1819, additional orders were given to the town watch, whereby they were to alarm citizens as soon as they discovered fire, and one was to ring a bell while the others helped those in danger until assistance arrived, when they were to go about their own duties.

From an entry in the selectmen's report for November 15, it appears that a disastrous fire occurred at the rope-walk, which was of incendiary origin, and the selectmen were petitioned to offer a reward for their conviction, the amount to be subscribed by the citizens. We cannot find any other reference to this occurrence, the fires reported for the year being as follows: February 21, Mr. Hart's ship-yard; a wooden building on Ship street, owned by Edward Hartt, and occupied by Saul Hartt and Joseph L. Tallman as a workshop; loss, $1,750; also a small building of Mr. G. L. Williams; loss, $100; 24th, B. Wheeler's house, Newbury street; 27th, building on Swett's wharf, owned by Thomas Thompson, occupied by R. Howe, cooper, Samuel Hichborn, sailmaker, and Messrs. Adam Jennison & Chamberlain, caulkers; loss, $4,766. March 17, Mr. Pratt's building, Mill Pond street. June 22, Mrs. White's dwelling, Winter street. August, store on Dillaway's wharf. September 29, house on Warren street. October 12, building of John Moore's on the Turnpike, at South Boston. November 25, Oliver Mills' house, Mason street. December 7, distil-house in Leverett street.

March 30, 1820, the board recommended the purchase of a lantern for each engine, to be numbered and carried with the apparatus during the night; the method of attaching them was left to the discretion of the foremen. Engine-houses 1 and 2 were ordered to be enlarged on September 7. Captain Truman of Engine 4 enters a complaint against Fireward George Darricott at this time, but it was satisfactorily settled. Messrs. William Burrows, Samuel Hichborn, Jr., Jonathan Thaxter, and George Darricott were chosen wards, *vice* Messrs. Webb, Austin, Phillips, and Berry.

The first hook and ladder was organized on August 4, when the firewards provided a convenient carriage, equipped with ladders, axes, and hooks. Applicants for admission as members began to come in, and a company was rapidly formed. This was numbered 1, and lodged in a shed on Merrimac street.

On application of school committee on March 29, twenty-five fire-buckets were placed in each of the school-houses. Captain Brown was made company commander of Engine 11, Captain Sargent of Engine 1, Nathan Hammond of Engine 13, and Captain Frothingham of Engine 9, this year.

Fires: January 14, house owned by Benjamin Wild, occupied by Mrs. Green: 17th, Captain Prentiess' building, Dillaway's wharf; 23d, house in Proctor's lane; 29th, Scott & Clapp's store on Swett's wharf. February 3, Hawkins-street School-house, set on fire by boys: loss, $250; 26th, Jonathan Heath's store, State street. March 7, Jonathan Heath's store, 7 Cornhill; loss, $7,000. April 14, Mrs. White's house, Mason street. May 13, dwelling on Boylston street. June 26, the brew-house of John Snowdon & J. Cooper on Leverett street; loss, $19,650. July 23, Dr. Dix's residence, Orange street. August 23, the store of James Cook, 22 Broad street.

October 6, Capt. Winslow Lewis' rope-walk; 26th, Mrs. Payne's house, Federal and Mill streets. November 13, one of the rope-walks. December 11, house on Court street; 16th, dwelling in Wilson's lane; 22d, building occupied by John C. Proctor and C. H. Jones on Friend street.

Mr. George G. Channing was appointed by the selectmen on February 7, 1821, at which time the company went into commission, as director of the Hook and Ladder Company No. 1, which position he accepted. The company consisted of twenty-four men, as follows: Charles Leighton, foreman; John Babbit, John Reed, George Tucker, James Denton, Leonard Darling, John Kittredge, Levi L. Cushing, William Ayres, Benjamin Adlington, Levi L. Wawick, Robert Hayden, Samuel Chase, Isaac Butterfield, Elisha Goodnow, Adison Burnham, Alanda Wright, Jonathan Chamberlain, Samuel S. Crocker, William Church, Warren Lathrop, Timothy Fipander, Pelig Hayden, and William Snowdon. The directors of the Fire and Marine, the Merchants', and the Mutual Fire Insurance Companies were asked by the firewards if they would grant a premium to the ladder company, upon which they agreed to pay an annual award of $20, provided the town would pay $10, on condition that the company annually produce in the month of March or April a certificate from the wards to the effect that they had performed their work satisfactorily as firemen. A new patent life pole or ladder was purchased for the company during the year at an expense of $50.

A petition was received from the inhabitants of South Boston, on March 21, for an engine to be placed in that section; but it was not considered expedient to do so at that time, but a new one for the North End was ordered. In order to get the best that could be obtained, one each was made by Mr. Hunneman and Mr. Thayer,—the best to be bought. The selection was of the former make; but the engine proved to be an experiment, and not all the contract called for. It was, however, soon put in order and placed in a building on Lincoln wharf, South End, on February 13, 1822, where a company was organized, headed by John Foster, to take charge. It was called Boston No. 15.

Firewards Davis, Curtis, and B. P. Tilden were succeeded on the board for 1821 by Messrs. James Davis, Eliphalet Williams, and John H. Wheeler.

A most disastrous fire happened about 9 o'clock on the night of January 17, this year. It broke out in a four-story tenement, 98 Broad street, occupied by Mr. Connelly as a storage of quills, on the first floor,—the other tenants being Patrick Jackson; Elizabeth, his wife; Mrs. Ann Taylor; her son William, five years old; and Mrs. Susan Aston Dysters; their mother, Mrs. Elizabeth Brewer; and her grandchild, Eliza Palfrey, seven years old, all of whom were burned to death, except Mrs. Aston, who was killed by jumping from the third-story window. A son of Mr. Jackson escaped by the waterspout.

The other fires were: January 1, house on Pleasant street; 17th, building on Belknap street; 20th, house next to the theatre; 23d, dwelling, Thos. B.

Wales; 26th, distil-house; 30th, house on Broad street.   February 25, John Longley's soap-works, Warren street.   June 29, William Jones' house, Ann street.   July 14, six buildings in Union street; 20th, house near post-office, on Water street.   August 8, tenements in Scott's court; 13th, house in Back street.   September 23, residence in Tileston street.   December 14, Mrs. Oarney's house, 10 Grange street; 31st, Capt. Wm. Little's house.

We find the following changes in the company commanders this year: Engine 9, Captain Thaxter; Captain Sargent, Engine 1; Nathaniel Nottage, Engine 2; Captain Salmon, Engine 14; Captain Brown, Engine 11; Ebenezer White, Engine 7.

At a meeting of citizens at Merchants' Hall, on January 17, a committee of five were chosen to inquire into the probable cause and extent of an unusual number of wells having become dry in one district of the town.   On examining the state of the wells in Common, Boylston, Elliott, Warren, and Pleasant streets, and Sheafe's lane, seventy-two were found dry.   In Common street, from West to Boylston street, there were twenty-eight wells, of which twenty-one were dry, and the remainder, with the exception of one, had very little water in them.   The greater part of the wells in the other streets that had not failed, had but a limited supply, except on the west side of Pleasant street, where several wells contained six, eight, and ten feet of water, which, in the very dry season, always draughted twelve, sixteen, and eighteen feet of water. The laboratory well which had never contained less than ten feet, at this time measured only four feet of water.   One well on Boylston street, only seven inches of water was found; previously it never registered less than seven feet, — so that, in this section of the town, the water had been lowered six feet on an average.   The committee, in their report on the 24th, were unanimous in their opinion that the deficiency of water was wholly caused by the tide-water having been stopped out by the Mill Dam.

PART II.

1822-1873.

Ex-Chief Engineers. — Page 134.

PART II.

FROM 1822 TO 1873.

CHAPTER I.

1822–1824.

THE inconvenience resulting from the form of town government became apparent to the intelligent and influential citizens of Boston as early as 1784, when, during the month of May, in the petition of a large number of the inhabitants, a committee of thirteen was appointed to " consider the expediency of applying to the General Court for an act to form the town of Boston into an incorporated City, and report a plan of alteration in the present government of the police, if such be deemed elegible." On the Fourth of July ensuing, this committee reported two plans, which, being read, were ordered to be printed and distributed to each house, the town adjourning to the 17th of the same month to take them into consideration. At this meeting it was ordered that " the sense of the town be taken on the expediency of making any alterations in the present form of town government." On which question the records state : " But the impatience of the inhabitants for the question being immediately put, prevented any debate thereon, and it passed in the negative by a great majority, and the meeting was immediately dissolved."

During November, 1785, the attempt was again tried, and a committee chosen, " to state the defects of the present constitution of the town, and to report how far the same may be remedied without an act of incorporation." They reported " that they did not report any defects in the constitution." This was accepted, and leave given to the petitioners to withdraw their paper. Again was the subject renewed in December, 1791, by the petition of a number of inhabitants, " setting forth the want of an efficient police." The system reported by the committee was afterwards amended and printed and distributed in handbills. The town adjourned until January 26, ensuing, for its final consideration, when it was rejected by a vote of five hundred and seventeen for and seven hundred and one against the measure.

The matter was given a rest until January, 1804, when a committee equally selected from the two political factions, which at the time divided the town and Commonwealth, was chosen and instructed to consider and report any alterations in the town government they deemed expedient. This was done during March, but met with the same fate as those preceding it.

Again did the subject lay dormant until 1815, when Charles Bulfinch, who had been chairman of the Board of Selectmen, and superintendent of police, since 1800, together with two other members of that board, were not reëlected. This was a general surprise, much regretted, the result being that every elected member of the Board of Selectmen immediately resigned. On the second election Mr. Bulfinch and the other members of the board of the preceeding year were reinstated by decided majorities. These occurrences again directed public attention to the disadvantages of town government; and on the petition of a large number of the inhabitants, a committee formed of two individuals elected from each ward was authorized to consider the expediency of a change of the government; therefore, in October, 1815, this committee presented a bill, accompanied by an explanatory report. which was printed for general distribution, and a town meeting was called on November 13 to decide upon its acceptance. The system proposed was more to the liking of the people, being only defeated by a majority of thirty-five.

With a population upwards of forty thousand, and with seven thousand qualified votes, it was found impossible to conduct the municipal interest of the place under the form of town government. When a subject was not generally exciting, town meetings were usually composed of the selectmen, the town officers, and thirty or forty inhabitants. In assemblies thus formed by-laws were passed, taxes to the amount of $150,000 voted, on statements often general in their nature. and on reports. as it respects the majority of others present, taken upon trust, and which no one had carefully considered, except, perhaps. the chairman. The constitution of Massachusetts, which was passed in 1780, contained no express authority to establish a city organization. and in every attempt to change that of the town it never failed to be zealously contended that the Legislature of the Commonwealth possessed no such power. But by the amendments to the constitution. made by the convention of 1820, and adopted by the people, this power was expressly recognized. The question, therefore, now stood on its own merits. and independent of constitutional objections.

The first steps to the measure which finally led to this great change in the form of town government was rather incidental than preconcerted, and was the result of circumstances which might be anticipated from the complicated and ill-arranged organization of the town system. Early in the civil year 1811, votes had passed in town meeting for uniting the office of county and town treasurer in one person. The three wards constituting the committee of finance had disregarded these votes, and different persons were chosen to these offices, which, as a matter of course, created a disturbance among the populace. To add to this. great discontent arose in respect to the county expenditures, and a committee was chosen to devise measures that the town might become a county by itself. Very full reports were made by both these committees, and a very general desire became apparent that a more economical and practical management of the town concerns should be effected. Accordingly, on October 22, a committee of thirteen inhabitants were selected, to whom the two former reports were referred, with instructions to report to the town "a complete system relating to the administration of the town and county which shall remedy the present evils."

This committee made three reports in December, 1821, but did not venture to go further than to recommend some improvements in the government of the town. But this did not please many of the enthusiasts for the city charter, among whom was Mr. Benjamin Russell, a popular and distinguished politician and leader among the mechanics, who openly declared that the committee "had not gone far enough in its alterations, and, in his opinion, a great change had been effected in the minds of the inhabitants on the subject of city government," and concluding his remarks by moving "that the report should be recommitted to the same committee, with the addition of one person from each ward of the town, with instruction to report a system of the government of the town, with such powers, privileges, and immunities as are contemplated by the amendment of the constitution of the Commonwealth, authorizing the General Court to constitute a city government." This motion was accordingly adopted, and twelve persons chosen and added to the former committee.

This committee of twenty-five, on December, 1821, reported a system of municipal government conformably to their instructions, recommending indeed a change of the name of " town " for that of " city," but not venturing to introduce the names usual in city organizations, lest the ancient jealousy, which now seemed to slumber, should be awakened. In their stead the committee proposed that the executive should be called " intendant," the executive board, consisting of seven persons, " selectmen," and the more numerous branch, " a Board of Assistants," all of whom, in their aggregate capacity, should be called the " Common Council," the intendant to be elected by the selectmen; the selectmen, by general ticket; the assistants, forty-eight in number, four chosen from each ward; the overseers of the poor, fire-wards, and school committee, by the intendant, selectmen, and assistants; the State and United States officers, by general ticket.

After a debate of three days, in which the report was amended by denominating the executive board " Mayor and Aldermen," the latter to consist of eight persons, the name of the " Board of Assistants," being also changed to that of the " Common Council," and in their aggregate capacity, " the City Council," the mayor, aldermen, overseers of the poor, firewards, State and United States officers to be chosen by the citizens at large, voting in wards, report was so far accepted as to be submitted to the inhabitants for their acceptance. During the three days of debate the citizens became very excited; but the measure was finally submitted to the populace for their sanction, in the form of five resolves to be decided by ballot of yea and nay, which, being taken on Monday, January 7, 1822, was adopted by a large majority.

The assent of the inhabitants being in favor, measures were immediately taken to obtain the sanction of the Legislature of the Commonwealth, resulting in that body passing, on February 23, the same year, an act which was commonly called the "city charter," entitled "An act establishing the city of Boston." In conformity with its provisions, the inhabitants assembled in general meeting on March 4, ensuing, and accepted the act by vote, taken by ballot, by a majority of 916, the whole number being 4,778, of which 2,797 voted in the affirmative, and 1,881 in the negative.

On April 8, a meeting of the citizens was held for the election of city officers; the whole number of votes for mayor was 3,708. They were chiefly divided between Josiah Quincy and Harrison Gray Otis; but neither having a majority, no choice was effected. Immediately on this result, Mr. Otis and Mr. Quincy declined being a candidate for office. On the 16th, John Phillips was elected mayor with great unanimity.

The city government was organized for the first time on Wednesday, May 1, 1822, with a solemnity adapted to the general interest excited by the occasion. A platform was raised at the west end of Faneuil Hall, with seats for the mayor, aldermen, and City Council, the selectmen of the past year, with other town authorities, and the chief officers of the Commonwealth. The floor of the house and the galleries were filled with a crowded assembly. The city charter, enclosed in a silver case, was laid upon a table in front of the City Council. After prayer, offered by the Rev. Thomas Baldwin, D.D., the oldest settled clergyman in Boston, the oaths of allegiance and of office were administered to John Phillips, the mayor-elect, by Isaac Parker, chief justice of the Commonwealth, and afterwards by the mayor to the aldermen and Common Council. The chairman of the last Board of Selectmen, Eliphalet Williams, then arose and addressed the convention, stating the grant of a city charter by the Legislature of the State to the inhabitants of Boston, their acceptance of it, their election of the members of the legislative boards, and delivered into the charge of the new authorities the town records and title-deeds, and the act establishing the city of Boston. He was followed by a reply from the mayor, after which the meeting adjourned.

Three firewards were elected from each of the twelve wards on April 12, 1823, as follows: Ward 1, Benjamin Coomey, Eliaza Pratt, and Stephen Locke; Ward 2, John F. Truman, Joseph Stone, and Daniel Ballard; Ward 3, Robert Bacon, John Minate, and Genet Holbrook; Ward 4, Thomas Melville, James Davis, and Jeremiah Fitch; Ward 5, Jonathan Thaxter, George W. Otis, and Jonathan Whitney; Ward 6, Jered Lincoln, Joel Shipley, and Joseph H. Adams; Ward 7, Stephen Codman, Samuel M. Thayer, and William Tileston; Ward 8, Levi Brigham, James Magee, and William Tucker; Ward 9, Joseph Jones, Benjamin Darling, and Leah

Harris; Ward 10, Daniel Messenger, Thomas Jackson, and Luke Richardson; Ward 11, John L. Phillips, John H. Whuter, and Jaben Ellis; Ward 12, John D. Williams, Noah Brooks, and Samuel S. Wheeler. On the 17th substitutes were chosen in the place of those who declined the election; they were, Ward 6, Jonathan Loring; Ward 8, Bryant P. Tilden; Ward 9, Benjamin Russell; and Ward 11, Winslow Lewis. Almost the first act of this board was the repairing of Engine-house 12, at an expense of $100, and the enlargement of the ladder-house; also the purchase of some hooks for that apparatus, Mr. Charles Leighton being appointed master of the company. They voted on January to hold their meetings more often on account of the increased amount of business of which they had charge. Circulars were printed and distributed by their order regarding the erection of wooden buildings. The entire control of the apparatus and buildings belonging to the department was granted to them, with power to exchange or sell any old engine, hose, etc., as they may deem expedient. Those having charge of the several engines were to return a list of the foremen, with their address each year. The one sent in for the year ensuing was as follows: No. 1, Loring Sargent; No. 2, Nathaniel Nottage; No. 3, William Barnicoat, and J. P. Orcutt, assistant; No. 4, Samuel Hosea; No. 5, Frederick Weld; No. 6, Joel Prouty, and John Vannevar, assistant. No. 7, Ebenezer White; No. 8, William Loring; No. 9, Seth Thaxter; No. 10, Jacob Phelpes; No. 11, Jarvis Brown; No. 12, Asa Lewis; No. 13, Nathaniel Hammon, and Melzar Dunbar, assistant; No. 14, John Salmon, and David Horner, assistant; No. 15, Samuel Walker; Ladder 1, Charles Leighton. Engines 12 and 15 were allowed an additional number of members, and Engine 2 was replaced by a new machine from the works of E. Thayer on September 25.

The matter of a suitable hose was a question that was most perplexing, and experiments were frequently made by the wards and others interested in the department on the strength and durability of untanned and unprepared leather, which resulted in a great expense and risk to the town. The failure of the hose and the power of the engine at the Exchange Coffee-house was most disastrous. At one fire, nearly all the hose of three engines burst in succession. The town was put to a great expense by importing hose from England, nearly all of which were burst on the first trial, and the rest proved to be far from perfect. Had there been a suitable person who understood the matter, all this trouble could have been avoided, and they would have found out, as they did soon after, that the State of Massachusetts could furnish as good leather for the purpose, and as good workmen, as any the world afforded. The leather used by them was not stuffed or filled with a proper composition to render them impervious to water, thus preventing premature decay. At one fire the sixty feet of hose of a certain engine (which had just been proved and considered better than usual) was ruined by being packed in the engine-box without proper attention in drying, as two weeks later it was covered with slime nearly a quarter of an inch thick; so that when it was proven again, it burst in a number of places, the stitches being entirely rotten. They were then sewed together anew, and at the next trial it was proved that the leather had also perished, so that it was rent from the stitching. The hose, then, was condemned as useless; but this was not an unusual occurrence, which happened by reason of the same carelessness. The engine-men were not altogether to blame in this particular, for they had a laudable pride in keeping their engine in good order. The great part of the mischief came from an ancient custom of dignifying the younger members of an engine company by the illustrious name of the two "Catos," and then putting them to do all the drudgery, — such as looking for axes and buckets after a fire, shovelling snow, and greasing and taking care of the hose, etc. Another cause of failure in the hose was that there was not a sufficient number provided and properly prepared to be in readiness when most wanted. In consequence of this neglect, a hose was generally suffered to be wet before it was properly prepared, and also strained to the utmost power of the engine before the composition intended to preserve it and render it impervious to water would be combined and consolidated with the leather. It required some years before they had brought this important branch of the department to a satisfactory condition.

A petition was received by the selectmen, on March 6, from Asa Lewis, asking that the town vote to petition the Legislature, at their next session, so far to alter or repeal the existing laws regulating the building within the town, as to permit the citizens to erect wooden buildings. to be occupied as dwelling houses, of eighteen-feet posts, and roof of a regular pitch of one-third of the building, which in no case was to be elevated more than eighteen inches from the line of the street to the bottom of the sill, and not to have the sill to the highest point of the roof; the roof to be not more than twenty-five feet upon the ground; to be slated, and have at least one window or scuttle. Whenever two or more buildings should be joined together, there was to be a brick partition-wall of at least eight inches in thickness; and whenever such building should be erected within six feet of any other wooden building of more than ten-feet posts, to have a brick party-wall. The vote stood on the matter, 2,837 yeas, and 574 nays — so the question passed in the affirmative. and, on June 15, an act was passed by the Legislature which complied with this request.

Fires : January, Old State-House. April 20, carpenter shop, Wheeler's point : 30th, Mr. Tucker's store. Lewis wharf. May 9, building in Merchants' row. June 13, house on Sheafe street : 14th, the building on Tisdell's wharf. July 17. Lewis Burck's cabinet-makers' shop, Blackstone street. owned by Edwin Collamore : loss. $2,000 : 30th. brimstone factory of Mr. Brimley, South Boston. October, Clapp & Gulliver's store. Carver street. November 22. house on Marlborough street, Widow Thomas' house, Fort Hill ; 24th, Capt. I. W. Lewis' dwelling, Oliver street. December 1. gas-house : 4th, house of Obel Baker, State street ; 30th, Samuel Jones' store, Back street.

Neither the inclination nor the health of Mayor Phillips permitted him to become a candidate for a second election, and on May, 1823, the municipal authorities of the city of Boston were organized for the second time in Faneuil Hall, when ex-Mayor Phillips administered, as justice of the peace, the oath of office to Josiah Quincy, his successor, before the close of whose administration the department was to be so thoroughly changed.

' The fire department was sadly in need of a reform that would place it on an equal footing with the advancement made in the other departments, and to meet the transition state under which it was advancing to that period when, by the increase of population, ties of individual interest were diminished, and the duty of joining some fire company and assisting in the extinguishment of every fire was considered imperative, as was the case in the colonial days, when the inhabitants were few and the insurance system not known, the losses being sustained by the help of one another. After the establishment of this business, whereby the loss was transferred to capitalists, the inhabitants began to lose interest in the department. The members of engine companies had all the enthusiasm that men could possess, and took the greatest pride in the opinion that they were the guardians of the city against this element. Fearless, energetic, and the love of duty of the business made them most able firemen, and the premiums allowed by the city, together with admission fees and exemption from jury and military duty, were remuneration enough for their labors. To be first, nearest, and most conspicuous at fires was their greatest ambition, and the use of hose in any long length, which, of course, deprived them of this qualification, was stoutly opposed; and should one of the number, who, more far-sighted than his colleagues, express his desire for the use of this article, it was the worth of his membership and popularity. The citizens' want of interest in the matter and respect for the members and their opinions on fire matters rendered it impossible for the city government to undertake the changes which had to take place. For the time being they therefore deferred it until a more favorable moment. The mayor, in the mean time, was busily preparing for the turn of affairs by entering into correspondence with the leading members of the fire departments of New York and Philadelphia, whose systems of protection were understood to be in a high state of perfection.

Some of the citizens complained that the firewards did not exercise their authority, despotic for the emergency, with the same energy as their predecessors. The wards asserted that the citizens no longer aided them in their duties by becoming members of the fire companies; and that while the classes of population disposed to be inactive or to depreciate at fires increased, those who were willing to assist were much lessened. All acknowledged that fires were more destructive than formerly; but this was attributed, not to any defect in the system, but to the want of coöperation among the citizens. The remedies proposed and urged were, to revive the ancient volunteer fire companies, to enlarge the supply of buckets, and vest greater authority in firewards. The proposal of a fire department that should exclude instead of compel the assistance of citizens was received with indignation. " Do you think, sir," said one of the captains of the engines, " that the citizens of Boston will ever submit to be prohibited from assisting a fellow-townsman in distress? Such sort of laws may be obeyed in despotic countries or in cities where the inhabitants do not feel for one another; but this is not the case, nor ever will be, in Boston." When the advantage of the hose system was suggested, it was answered, that it was practicable in Philadelphia, from the abundance and easy command of water, but Boston possessed no such facilities. When it was stated in reply that in New York the want of a sufficient head of water was supplied by stationing engines at intervals between the water and the fire, instead of forming lines of citizens to pass the water from the well to the engines, as was practised in this city, which, by playing into each other successively, enabled the nearest to throw a continuous stream upon the fire. the answer of one of the captains was characteristic of the state of the existing prejudice on the subject: " Set engine-men at a distance from the fire! It will never be submitted to. The desire is always to be in the hottest of the battle. The nearer the fire, the higher the post of honor. The struggle is who should get to it first, and who keep the nearest. It would be more difficult to keep a Boston engine back, in order to play into its neighbor, than it would be to put out the fire." Many thoughtful and intelligent citizens had doubts also concerning the efficiency of the hose system, and the City Council concluded, after much deliberation, that it was most prudent to postpone for a time attempts to introduce improvements obnoxious to so many prejudices.

The City Council changed the amount of the premiums, on April 14, giving $15 to the first and $10 to the second engine arriving at a fire, all the rest to receive $8, with the exception of Cataract No. 14, which received $12, it having the largest company. But this was far from satisfactory to the majority of engine-men, and in June, the members, headed by Mr. Asa Lewis, petitioned the city to allow an increase in their compensation to $50 to each engine and ladder company, and $77 to Engine 14; unless this was granted, they would abandon their engines within ninety days after due notice was given. This request was renewed four times. A committee was formed in September, who interviewed two members from each of the engine companies, which resulted in a report to the effect that there should be forty members to Engine 14, and twenty-six to each of the others, making a total of four hundred and thirty; but there were only three hundred and seventy-one men attached to the department, and many of them were anxious to leave, the reason for this lack of interest being the reduction of military duty, and of the fine for non-performance of it, which rendered the military service less burdensome; the increase of the labor of engine-men by the large extent of the city, making the number of alarms more frequent, and the distance to which the engines had to be dragged much longer (the military had greatly improved its condition, which made men take some pride in that service) ; the practice of the engine-men for supping together once or twice a year, which, with other expenses incident to the service, made the amount of the whole expenses within the year equal and sometimes more than in the military. The exemption of jury duty was not considered by many as a privilege, as they were paid for this service. It was therefore considered expedient to offer them some remuneration, although there was no reason why the companies could not be filled, even should no allowance be made. The Council then voted that each company be paid $25 per year, except Cataract 14, being a large company, which was allowed $40. They were also to receive as premium $15 for the first engine at a fire, and $10 for the second, this order to take effect on January following, provided the clerk of the company file with the city clerk on the month of January next preceding a list of twenty members, and the rules and regulations governing the company, for the approval of the mayor. But this communication did not suit the members, although the firewards voted that the exemption from military duty and the compensation allowed by the city was sufficient.

The season of the year, and that which was approaching, were those in which any general derangement of the engine companies would occasion great alarm among the citizens. The members of these companies had been long in the service, and great confidence was attached to their experience. In the opinion of many citizens, the companies were composed of a class of citizens whose claims it was unsafe to deny, and in whatever spirit demanded, they ought to be conceded. On being asked if they would not be satisfied with less than $50 each, the reply of one of the foremen was : " No ; we are fixed on that point. Forty-nine dollars and ninety-nine cents will not do ! " After this evidence of feeling and opinion, a majority of the committee chosen to investigate the matter came to the conclusion that any grant made under such circumstances would be considered as an " acknowledgement of the dependence of the city upon the individuals who then composed the companies, be attributed to fear, and be only temporarily and a source of future embarrassment ; that the permanent safety of a city should never be allowed to be regarded as dependent on the capricious estimate of their own importance by any set of men ; but that general confidence should be permitted to rest on no other basis than the conviction that there exists always among the mass of its citizens talents and will adequate to self-protection."

The committee, therefore, on November 24, made a report, which was accepted by the City Council, that it was not expedient to grant the prayer of the petitioners, the present exemptions and remunerations being a sufficient compensation. On December 1, the mayor notified the board that at 1 o'clock that day all the captains of the engine companies resigned their care of the engines, as they did not accept the city ordinance. The engines were at once placed under the care of the following aldermen : Nos. 8 and 12, Baxter ; No. 5 and Ladder 1, Odiorne ; Nos. 9 and 11, Child ; Nos. 1 and 4,

Dorr; Nos. 13 and 16, Benjamin; Nos. 10 and 3, Patterson; Nos. 2 and 15, Eddy; Nos. 14 and 7, Harper. An able and active body of citizens immediately volunteered their service to man the apparatus until new companies could be formed and given the keys. On the evening of the same day the mayor communicated to the City Council that the fire department was in its usual state of efficiency. Some of the members remained, and notice was given by the Council that they were ready to receive applications for engine-men until Thursday, 4th inst., the late ordinance to be considered a basis of such membership. On December 4, Engine 1, under Samuel Jones, was the first company to be formed. Mr. B. F. Adams obtaining most of the old members to take hold was given the thanks of the board, but told they would not be accepted, as the other company was already appointed. Before the end of the month each engine had its full equipment of a regular organized company.

Before this trouble came a petition was received, on April 17, from the inhabitants of Fort Hill, signed by Israel Manson and others, for an engine and bell to be placed in that section of the city also from inhabitants of South Boston, signed by Mr. Noah Brooks and others, May 29, for an engine, both of which were purchased from Mr. Hunneman. The one at Fort Hill was placed in a house on Purchase street, and called Torrent 16 ; the other was stationed in the school-house at South Boston, and called 17, with Daniel Adams in charge of the former, and Alpheus Stetson of the latter. William Richards succeeded Captain Nottage of Engine 2 ; John Foster, Captain Sargent, Engine 1 ; and Seth Copeland, Captain White, Engine 7.

On April 10, fifteen men were added to the number of Engine 15. and twelve additional staffs were procured for the firewards. The following changes occurred in this board : Ward 1, Benjamin Dodd and Isaac Peirce, *vice* Stone and Ballard ; Ward 4, William Howe, *vice* Davis ; Ward 5, John Allan and John Hall, *vice* Otis and Whitney ; Ward 8, Bryant P. Tilden, *vice* Magee ; Ward 12, Cyrus Alger, *vice* Brooks.

The fires for the year were : January 1, Joshua Holden's store, 126 Orange street. February, house in Purchase street. May 9, building, rear 47 Cornhill. July 20, Mr. Barney's house, Garden-court street. August 27, building, Marshall street. September 11, large fire in Purchase street, in a building occupied by Charles Tileston and others ; 24th, Mrs. Myers' house, 50 Marlborough street, and John Green's dwelling, Purchase street. October 11, building owned by William Doll, and occupied by James Caswell, 10 Orange street ; 18th, Doctor Ware's residence, 20 Hanover street ; 24th, Mr. Byrnes' restaurant on Bedford street, building owned by Wentworth ; 28th, building head of North Bennett street. November 24, Louis Oliver's house. December 2, First Baptist Church, Back street. 14th, Spear's building, occupied by John Baker.

The greatest conflagration that occurred since the rope-walk fire broke out on April 7, 1824, when nearly the whole of the square between Doane,

Broad, Batterymarch, and Kilby streets was laid in ashes. The number of buildings burnt were, five in State street, six in Doane street, six in Kilby street, nineteen (every building) in Central street, four in Broad street, and thirteen in Liberty square. Many of these structures were stores, built of brick and stone, and were considered fire-proof.

This was fol owed three days later by the burning of the type foundry in Salem street, the loss being $60,000. But the members of the department were again called to another most terrible holocaust on July 7, for an account of which we reprint the article written for the " Transcript," by the late N. J. Bowditch, under the *nom de plume* of " Gleaner," during 1853, and re-printed in Vol. 5 of Record Commissioners' Report : —

Mr. Editor, — On Wednesday, July 7, 1824, just before two o'clock, the bells of Boston rang an alarm of fire, and instantly a dense mass of black smoke was seen to overhang the entire city. I have always been an amateur at fires. If the calamity must happen, I like to be present, to behold what sometimes proves a most magnificent spectacle. I was then a young man, — in my teens, — and hastened from 'Change to the corner of Park street; I saw at once that a most furious and destructive conflagration had commenced. The wind was blowing a huricane from the north-west. When I reached the bottom of the Beacon-street mall, a stream of fire was pouring through the passageway, west of Mr. Bryant's house, from carpenter shops and other combustible premises on Charles and Chestnut streets.

The flame was of the full width of the passageway, and it was curling around into the front windows of Mr. B.'s house, which was then newly finished and rea ly for occu-pancy. The outbuilding and fences of all that range of dwelling houses were then of wood, so that the fire was also making its fearful approaches in the rear. I have never seen, before or since, any similar occasion of a more appalling character. The hasty removal of household furniture, much of it being thrown from the windows, which were broken out for the purpose; the panic of the occupants, as they and their children were obliged to fly, some at a notice of a few minutes; the crackling of the flames, the intense heat, the falling of the walls of one dwelling house after another, as the fire proceeded along the street; the shouts of the firemen; the mass of spectators filling the bottom of the Com-mon and the rising ground in its centre; the jets of flame often springing over a space of several feet, the burning fragments borne aloft over our heads to remote parts of the city; the magnitude of the danger which led to the covering, with wet blankets, of houses, even as distant as Mr. Otis' and Mr. Sear's, — formed together an aggregate of sights and sounds which can never be forgotten.

As those houses which at first were not thought in great danger one after another took fire, and were consumed, owners who originally decided not to have their furniture disturbed were at last obliged to remove it so hastily that much was ruined, and much more was necessarily left behind. In some instances old family portraits and inherite l articles of furniture, rendered invaluable by the association of a lifetime, were thus reluc-tantly surrendered. On the other hand, a tin-kitchen was saved, and its viands cooking for dinner were protected from the danger of being overdone.

Extensive removals were ma'le from several houses, which were eventually saved, as in the case of Mr. William Appleton's and others. The Common presented a curious medley of miscellaneous articles; the shabbiest household utensils side by side with ele-gant drawing-room carpets and ornaments. Bottles of wine which had not seen the light for twenty years were summarily decapitate l, without any ceremonious drawing of corks, and the Juno or Elipse vintage was probably never quaffed with greater relish than when it refreshed the parched throats of the exhausted firemen; other amateurs, without having their apology, imitated their example, and the scene assumed rather a bacchanalian character. One gentleman, desirous of withholding further fuel from this conflagration, locked up his wine cellar, and left its contents to be at least harmlessly consumed.

Seven dwelling-houses on Beacon street, east of the passageway, were burnt, beside the entire range of buildings between the passageway and Charter street. The fire was at last successfully checked at the house of the late Mr. Eckley. I suppose that it always happens that in a large fire somebody's policy had *just expired*. This was, I believe, the case with the late Mr. Henry G. Rice. To many besides him that was a very sad and discouraging day. Mr. Bryant had the advantage over his neighbors of not being incommoded by any furniture or family, as he had not yet taken possession. It is satisfactory to reflect that all the pecuniary loss then sustained has, undoubtedly, been much more than made good by the greatly enhanced value of real estate in that vicinity. And, independently of all the direct and perpetual advantages, of the most inestimable character, derived by our citizens from the Boston Common, it should never be forgotten that it was solely owing to the existence of this open space on this occasion that the entire southern portion of our city was not destroyed. The range of trees at the foot of Beacon-street Mall rendered a truly important service. Suffering the flames of martyrdom, they died at their post of duty.

A burning cinder lodged in my eye, causing a violent inflammation, and bringing to an abrupt close my meditations on this striking spectacle, and a like inflammation of the same organ now brings to a like abrupt close the speculation of

GLEANER.

The closing lines of this article may be classed among the involuntary prophecies, for this proved to be the real close of these amusing and instructive series of articles. The other fires for the year were: January 23, house corner of Clark and Ship streets. February 6, Mr. Ames' sail loft, Tileston's wharf. March 28, Thomas Carns' glass factory, South Boston. April 7, house of Amos Lincoln, Middle street; 8th, Mr. Deckermary's building; 13th, house on Front street. May 31, Mr. Richardson's house, Friend street, John Dodd's dwelling, Ship street. June 20, building on Hawley street. July 7, house on Chestnut street. September 20, Mr. Huntington's building on Pond street. October 14, Oliver Chandler's blacksmith shop on Wilkinson & Pratt's wharf; 26th, house rear of 41 Back street. November 5, Mr. Foster's store, Purchase street. December 2, Baptist meeting house on Back street.

The changes in the board of firewards were: Ward 1. John P. Orcutt and Elijah Trask, *vice* Coomey and Look; Ward 2, Oliver Chandler and Thomas Reed, *vice* Truman and Dodd; Ward 3, Benjamin Smith, *vice* Minott; Ward 4, Reuben Reed and Phinehas Mitchell, *vice* Feitch and Howe; Ward 5, Joseph D. Annable, *vice* Hull; Ward 10, William H. Prentis, *vice* Richardson; Ward 12, Artimus Simonds, *vice* Alger. At their meeting on July 23, they voted to replace Engine 10 with a new machine; an order was also sent into the Council asking them to remedy the evil of a great scarcity of fire-buckets, by having the citizens furnish them when needed, and help the wards at fire. On the same date the custom of marking hose with the number of the engine to which it belonged was established.

CHAPTER II.

1825–1826.

ON January 1, 1825, the city ordinance required in its general rules and regulations of the department, that the companies should meet in the month of January ensuing to elect a captain, clerk, and two or more stewards, and make returns of the names of the members to the city clerk; the fine for absence from this meeting was $1 or not less than 50 cents; the captain to preside, in whose absence the company was to choose a temporary foreman, and was to meet once during the months of April, May, June, July, August, September, and October to look after the apparatus. On an alarm of fire, each member was to repair to the scene and assist, and not depart unless excused by the captain, on penalty of $1 or not less than 25 cents. The duties of the steward were to keep the house and apparatus in order, on penalty of $1. Not more than $5 were to be asked for admission fee.

The returns of the officers were: No. 1, Capt. John Gair; William Dillaway, clerk. No. 2, Capt. Levi Whitcomb; William Bellamy, clerk. Engine 3, Capt. Horace Fox; W. D. Bell, clerk. No. 4, Capt. Abraham Strong, who was succeeded by Rufus Eaton; Joseph A. Carney, clerk; 23 men. No. 5. Capt. B. D. Baldwin; William Parker, clerk; 26 men. Engine 6, Capt. Jabez Walcott; Augustus Reed, clerk; 26 men. No. 7, Capt. James Peirce; John Hills, clerk; 30 men. No. 8, Capt. Stephen Thayer; Isaac Spear, clerk; 20 men. No. 9, Capt. John M. Salmon; Philman Stacey, clerk; 25 men. No. 10, Capt. Joseph Veazie; James Shephard, clerk; 26 men. No. 11, Capt. Thomas Bagnell; Nathan Glover, clerk; 25 men. No. 12, Capt. Henry Adams; J. W. Lawrence, clerk; 24 men. No. 13, Capt. Nathaniel Harvard; Samuel H. Remick, succeeded by Nathaniel Cutter, clerk; 28 men. No. 14, Capt. Jerre Bird; A. H. Jennings, succeeded by William Glover, clerk; 42 men. No. 15, Capt. Joseph Ridler; J. R. Austin, clerk; 32 men. No. 16, Capt. David Adams; Hawks Lincoln, Jr., clerk; 27 men. No. 17, Capt. Alpheus Stetson; E. French, clerk; 26 men. Ladder 1, Capt. Silas Stuart; Warren Lothrop, clerk; 26 men.

On March 31, all the premiums belonging to the old companies were paid them. A new house was ordered to be built for Engine 15 on the 25th, on the site of the old one on Mr. Nathan Webb's land. A petition was received by the mayor from G. W. Otis and others, praying that they may have the aid of the city in their efforts as a fire company. The Merchants' Insurance Company also asked that the city and other insurance companies procure buckets and bags for the fire company, on condition that the city make two or more reservoirs of salt water of proper size at such places as shall be judged expedient in or near India street.

On March 11, 1825, Engine-house 11 was removed from Mr. Tileston's land on High street to the city land, situated at the south-east end of Summer street, and eight feet added to the length, and a partition built to divide the engine quarters from the meeting-room. Two new engines were ordered on the 14th from Philadelphia, Penn., one of the most approved pattern and greatest power, and a Hydraulion (a small engine with one chamber, used for forcing water through hose, as a supply to the engine), together with one thousand feet of copper-riveted leather hose; and on June 7, another powerful engine was ordered from New York, all of which were made in the most perfect manner, being different in style of construction from those used in Boston, which gave our mechanics an opportunity to compare, and if possible to improve, the construction of our engines. But these measures did not pass animadversion; the press took up the cry and asked " whether the mechanics of Boston were inferior in skill to those in Philadelphia and New York, and why the money of the city was expended in the patronage of the mechanics of other cities, rather than of its own?" But on an investigation by the mechanics themselves on the principles and effects of this policy, they were convinced of its fairness. The engine from Philadelphia arrived first, in December, and was called the Philadelphia No. 18, and was temporarily placed in a barn on Beacon street, which stood near where the north-west corner of the Tremont House now stands. Sixty men were authorized to take care of this engine, although the first fire at which it worked, Collamore's crockery-ware store, corner of Washington and Franklin streets, December 29, 1825, it was under the charge of Firewards George Darracott and Thomas C. Amory, assisted by the citizens. The first organized company was called the Associated Fire Engine and Hydraulion Company, and was under the command of William Barnicoat, foreman; Thomas C. Amory, second foreman, Almonen Holmes, third foreman, and Norman Seyer, clerk. A site was selected for the erection of a house for its accommodation on Pemberton Hill, corner of Common street (now 9 Tremont row), but the owner asked too much money for it; later, however, it was obtained for nothing (for particulars see " Boston Courier," November 9, 1825), and Dr. Shurtleff, the owner of the adjoining property, was induced to sell his land for $3,000. Soon after the engine-house was erected at a cost of $2,300. This building was of brick, with granite front, on the model of the Choragic Monument at Athens. It had a cellar for cleaning hose and a room in the upper story for meeting purposes. Land was also bought on Eliot street on November 7 from E. Marsh for $1.19 per foot, on which was built an engine and watch house combined.

On the evening of Fast Day, April 7, 1825, a destructive fire broke out in a cooper-shop in Doane street, caused by cooking a clam-chowder, the flames quickly spread to some old wooden buildings in the rear, occupied by very poor families, and was communicated at once to the surrounding stores, from State street, on the one side, and from Broad street to Kilby and Liberty streets on the other. The scene, on this occasion, was one of extreme embarrassment and confusion. The lanes formed by the wards with great difficulty were soon broken or deserted, and great depredations were committed on property, brought forth in the hurry and excitement and laid in the streets and left unprotected. Water was procured with difficulty, the engines being dragged one thousand feet to the dock and filled, after which they were drawn to the scene of the fire, and before arriving, half the water would be spilled, so that a large number of buildings were blazing at one time, rendering it impossible to check its progress, as the exertions of the citizens were first directed to the rescue of property. About fifty stores, many of which were filled with a recent importation of dry goods, were destroyed, at a loss of $1,000,000, within a few hours. Most of the property was insured at a low premium, whereby the underwriters suffered severely. They soon entered into a combination, however, and eventually recovered their loss from the public.

The next and last fire of importance we have to record under the old system occurred in Court street, on November 10, in which ten stores and a large number of lawyers' offices were destroyed. After the Kilby-street fire, the whole City Council met at the scene to consider the widening and laying out new streets, and went over the ground between Kilby, Broad, State, Central, and Doane streets.

These calamities made a deep impression upon the citizens. The want of water, and the means to bring a continuous stream of it on the flames, were apparent, and it became evident that the change in the habits and sympathies of the population, and the recent and increasing infusion of foreigners, rendered a change in the organization of a system of defence against fire and a more efficient police essential. No better opportunity could be offered the mayor for the introduction of an independent fire department, and, under the sanction of a committee of the City Council, consisting of the mayor, Aldermen Baxter, Odiorne, and Patterson, with Messrs. Goddard, S. K. Williams, Frothingham, Haskell, and William Wright, of the Common Council, made, in April, a report, stating the cause of the existing deficiency in the system of defence, and the diversity of opinion concerning the remedies, each of which was analyzed and explained. The report represented as being altogether mistaken, that it would be encouraging false hopes and a false system if the committee did not declare their opinion concerning its inadequacy to protection, and did not express themselves decidedly in favor of introducing a supply of water to the engines through the means of hose, instead of by lanes formed by bystanders. The report then submitted eight resolutions for the adoption of the City Council, to the following effect: It was expedient that a new organization of the fire department of the city should be adopted, on the principle of distinct and individual responsibility, and for this purpose a committee be appointed, in both branches of the City Council, for the purpose of arranging the details of such an organization, and that they report to the City Council as soon as possible. This was the eighth resolve; the four first had for their object to satisfy their fellow-citizens, by actual experiment, of the impracticability of reviving the ancient system of fire companies. To test the possibility of this resort, the resolutions proposed an invitation to householders and other citizens to form themselves into societies for their mutual protection against fire, and a system of organizing such societies under the sanction of the mayor and aldermen, and prescribed the number of buckets, fire-bags, and other instruments usual and proper for the service which each company should provide, and the authority which the members of such companies should exercise at fires, with an assurance that the City Council would apply to the State Legislature to invest them with all requisite powers.

This scheme, although carefully devised, when proposed to the citizens proved an absolute failure; for although some associations were formed, the attempt evidenced the utter hopelessness of any such reliance. The three remaining resolutions proposed the construction of four reservoirs of fifty thousand gallons' capacity, to be built of brick laid in Roman cement, the locations to be Liberty square, Union street, and North and South Market streets, and the purchase of the engines from New York and Philadelphia, as stated above.

The City Council adopted all the suggestions of the report, and passed the second resolution. It recommended and appointed the mayor, Aldermen Blake and Welsh, and Messrs. S. K. Williams, Barry, Boies, and Wales a committee on the eighth resolution, to arrange and report the details of a new organization of the fire department. This committee reported on May 12, as follows : —

That an organization of a fire department in this city is desirable, predicated in a systematic individual responsibility, and subordinate in all its parts. That the system adopted and for many years practised in the city of New York is of that character, and seems to approximate in point of things to the most perfect general arrangements of any system which has come to the knowledge of your committee. That it is by practical experienced men deemed *the best that can be devised*, is satisfactorily indicated by the accompanying letter from Thos. Franklin, Esq., for more than twenty years chief of the department of that city; although the committee would not recommend all the details of that department, yet the fundamental principles are sound. Resolved that it is expedient that a fire department be established in this city consisting of one Chief Engineer and as many other engineers, firewardens, engine-men, hosemen, and hook and ladder men as may from time to time be deemed necessary and as may be daily chosen and appointed by the City Council. Resolved that the mayor and aldermen be and they are hereby requested to apply to the Legislature that the officers so chosen and appointed may have all such powers and authority and enjoy all such privileges as officers of the same description now possess and enjoy under the present laws of the Commonwealth, and also that other powers and privileges may be granted to them as to their wisdom may seem expedient.

Mr. Franklin, of the New York fire department, in his letter to the mayor, recommended " that a suitable person be appointed to visit and examine our fire department, and see the operation thereof. I am persuaded it will be more effectual than any written communication." Whereupon the City Council commissioned Fireward George Darricott to visit New York and Philadelphia, and thoroughly investigate the organization of their fire departments, and to examine into the capacities and capabilities of the apparatus. Mr. Darricott's visit was most satisfactory, he being offered every opportunity by the authorities of both cities to examine and study the entire working of the systems, with which he was highly satisfied, and recommended in a letter to the mayor on the 1st of June, — which was published for the information of the citizens, — that " such is the advantage of the system in use in those cities that it could not too early be pressed upon the attention of the city authorities in Boston," adding that " although the firemen of Boston possessed as much intrepidity as any men, and risked readily both their property and persons, yet they have not been accustomed to regard favorably the hose system, and seldom make use of hose except when they cannot play from the pipe. The reverse of this is the case in New York. It there frequently happens, when a fire originates in narrow passageways, where engines cannot operate to advantage, that they are placed in the centre of one of their large squares, entirely out of view of the fire, and the hose is led through stores and houses in the vicinity. This, with the efficient organization of the various component parts of the department, and the playing of the *whole* under the supreme command of *one*, is what, in my opinion, after a minute and careful inspection of the whole system, gives the firemen of New York such a decided superiority over those of any other place. To this conclusion my mind has been irresistibly led. I have always felt a degree of pride in the character of our Boston firemen, and never could concede the point that fires were not better managed here than elsewhere. But recent events have caused doubts in my mind. These doubts are now confirmed. The fault lies not in the men, but in the system."

This was, of course, after the reorganization of the city government in May, 1825, when a joint committee, consisting of the mayor, Aldermen Blake, Marshall, and Bryant, and Messrs. Oliver, Parker, Rice, Dyer, Fisher, Wells, and Elliot, of the Common Council, were appointed on the fire department. On their report two votes were passed, — one, that a new organization of it was necessary ; the other authorizing the mayor and aldermen to apply to the Legislature of the State to invest the officers of the proposed fire department, when elected, with such power and authority as might be requisite, which was immediately attended to. But there was more abundant reason to anticipate that some of the members of that body from Boston were enemies to the bill, and would use their influence to have it thrown out without giving the citizens an opportunity to express their sentiments. The fear of such an action caused Mayor Quincy to have the following circular printed and distributed to each member of the Legislature : —

TO THE MEMBERS OF THE BOSTON SEAT IN THE LEGISLATURE OF MASSACHUSETTS.

Boston, 12th June, 1825.

Gentlemen, — Understanding that doubts are entertained concerning the principle of the bill, relative to a fire department, and that too by members of the Boston seat, I deem it my duty not to permit that bill to fail, without distinctly explaining the views of the City Council upon the subject. If the city is again made subject to destruction by the inapplicability of our present system to the existing state of population, I am desirous that the City Council shall escape the responsibility of such misfortune.

The principal object of the bill is to vest in the City Council *the power of constituting an efficient fire department, and, for this purpose, that they should have the appointment of the officers of that department and the distribution of their duties. The power to appoint and to prescribe the duties is the simple object.* If it fail, there can be no organization of an efficient fire department, and the consequences I need not portray.

The present system is, from the nature of things, inapplicable to the existing state of population, and it cannot be made applicable.

At present, thirty-six members comprise a board of firewards, and as many more as the City Council may determine. They are chosen in wards. Their power consists: 1st. In requiring, during fire, assistance in extinguishing it, or in removing goods or guarding them, and in suppressing tumults or disorders. 2d. In directing and appointing the station and operation of engines and enginemen, and of all persons in extinguishing fires. This power is supported by the sanction of a penalty of ten dollars, on refusal or neglect to obey their orders. This system had its origin in, and from the nature of things *is solely applicable* to comparatively small towns. The authority of firewards, although called *power*, is, in fact, *influence.* Of what possible use toward an efficient extinguishment of fire is the recovery of ten dollars the next day of a delinquent? Of the thousand neglects and refusals which occur at every fire, how many are prosecuted? comparatively speaking, not one!

The efficient authority of firewards, under our present system is *mere influence.* And, as such, the highest are the most influential citizens, who could be persuaded to take the office; it was the practice to make firewards, to the end that the individuals whom they required to assist, might be unwilling to refuse, either through shame or respect.

This was the real efficient power of the present system. But it is obvious that the whole of this power is annihilated when a city is grown to such a size, as that not one in ten of the firewards, let him be ever so respectable, can be known to the attendant multitude, when that multitude are, for the most part, assembled not from sympathy for the sufferers, but from idle curiosity, and many from worse motives; when from the practice of insuring, and belief prevalent that the loss will be borne by the insurance offices, indifference to them becomes more prevalent, and disinclination to incur the labor and hazard of assisting in extinguishing them more general; and that too in those very classes of the community where weight of character and property used formerly to constitute the strength of the "influence" of firewards, by coöperating in their exertion.

Is it wonderful, in such a state of population and of feeling, that the scenes which every man has witnessed of late at fires should occur? The surrounding multitude have neither shame nor fear in refusing the fireward, and running away in masses as soon as he is seen with his badge of office advancing toward them; or if a few yield a reluctant assent temporarily, yet quitting the lines, or leaving the work assigned them, as soon as the fireward's back is turned. The result of this state of things is as undeniable as it is inevitable, and the consequences and duties resulting from it are equally plain and unquestionable. The system of depending upon the aid of the surrounding multitude must be abandoned, and with it the system dependent upon mere influence or solicitation of sympathies.

A system must be adopted, suited to a large population, which every day is growing more mixed and less sympathizing with each other; in other words, discipline, subordination, and a well-marshalled arrangement, in which success is made to depend upon the organization of the department and its own efficiency, and not upon the reluctant aid of those who happen to be present. In other words, Boston, like New York and other great cities, must have a fire department based upon the principle of being adequate to self-protection in which the assistance of the mass of the citizens, so far from being solicited, is in fact prohibited; a system not of influence, but of self-dependent power. If it be denied to the present earnest application of the City Council, time needs no spirit of prophecy to foretell that it will, at no great distance of time, *be burnt into us.*

This system as it exists in New York, is founded upon the use of suction and distributing hose, in filling their engines, instead of buckets; by which it is proved that *every hundred feet of hose* is as effectual as the presence of *sixty men* with buckets; whereby the presence of the multitude is not rendered necessary. The discipline of the department applies only to those who belong to it. Great efficiency and energy is the result, and a system of influence is abandoned, and one of efficiency is substituted.

To the introduction of this system, the City Council have already authorized a great expense of engines and men, and must incur more. In order to make it effectual, discipline must be introduced, subordination established, practice in the use of the hose apparatus encouraged. For this purpose it is absolutely essential that the power possessed by this bill should be invested in the City Council.

Thirty-six men coequal in power excludes the idea of organization or subordination. How absurd is it to any efficient responsibility, that the body of men which are intrusted with the power of supplying the means and instruments should be denied the power of selecting the agents and organizing the department which is to make use of them! How fruitful in disputes and controversies must be such an attempt. This system is not theory. It is now in existence, practised and satisfactory. I submit extracts from a letter of the late Chief Engineer of New York concerning the excellence of their system, above all I subjoin a letter of George Darricott Esq. formerly a fireward of this city, who has been sent on by the city authorities to examine the actual state of things in this respect in New York.

I entreat the gentlemen of the Boston delegation so far to obtain the bill, if possible, as to be subject to acceptance or refusal, by ballot of the citizens of Boston, at a general meeting.

Considering this measure to be of the most vital importance to the prosperity and safety of this city, I have taken the liberty to address this letter to you, gentlemen, and to give it publicity, to the end that the views of the City Council might not be misapprehended, and that should this measure fail, it shall not be attributed to any neglect, indifference, or shrinking from official responsibility in them.

Very Respectfully, Yours,

JOSIAH QUINCY.

This circular had the desired effect, and on June 18, an act was passed by the Legislature "establishing a fire department in the city of Boston," which act depended for its final adoption on the votes of the citizens. On June 23, the city clerk issued a warrant for a citizens' meeting at Faneuil Hall, which was held on July 7, to consider and take the vote of yeas and nays upon the act. It may well be supposed that this was a lively gathering.

The inhabitants had been warmed to the matter by the patriotic harangues in the ward-rooms, and the warning voice of the press, on the usurpation of powers, which, it was asserted, could best be exercised by the body of the citizens, and it was publicly declared that "it would not be submitted to by the fireproof brethren of the North End." The idea of efficiency in a hose system, and of engines putting out fires by playing into one another, was treated as ridiculous. The mayor, to do everything to strengthen the popularity of the question, wrote and issued the following circular on the day previous : —

To the Citizens of Boston : —

Perceiving the acceptance or rejection of the " act establishing a fire department " is a subject of some discussion in the public prints, and being desirous wherever that question is taken, that whatever may be the event, its real nature and consequence may not be misapprehended by my fellow citizens, I deem it my duty, in the relation I stand to the city, to make a distinct development of the subject. Considering also its nature and the circumstance connected with it, I cannot deem this duty fulfilled as it ought to be unless I annex my name to this elucidation.

It will not be necessary to use any words to prove that our present system of protection against fire, is for some reason or other not satisfactory to the citizens of this metropolis. It will only be necessary to recall, on this point, the recollections of our fellow citizens to the dark discontent manifested at the conduct and result of both the last great fires, — that in Beacon and that in Central streets. On both these occasions, the inadequacy of our means of protection, or the insufficiency of their application was palpable, and the discontent expressed, little short of universal.

Great difference of opinion, however was manifested, as to the cause of the confusion, disorder and inefficiency exhibited on those occasions. Some lamented the want of water. Some the want of buckets. One set of men complained of the ward power in the firewards to command. Another of the want of willingness of the multitude to obey. And all, of the general want of fire clubs, and of those ancient associations for mutual protection on occasion of fire.

In this state of sentiment and feeling, which notoriously existed, it was the duty of the City Council to ascertain the real causes of the evils of which all complained, and apply remedies suited and adequate to the nature of the case.

Now, it was impossible to reflect upon this acknowledged state of things, with the seriousness which a sense of duty and responsibility imposed on the City Council without coming to the conclusion that all these wants or deficiencies were, more or less, founded on fact, and the resulting want of protection was not so much, if at all, attributed *to the men,* who had the control of the present system, as to that system itself; in other words, that the evils of which all complained, were attributable chiefly, if not solely, *to the inapplicability of our present system of protection against fire, to the present state and relation of the population of our city.* And as this population was every day increasing with great rapidity, our present system was every day with like rapidity growing more inadequate to effect that protection the citizens had a right to demand.

Every transient reflection on the acknowledged state of things will, I think, satisfy my fellow citizens of the justice of the conclusion, and first of the complaint of the want of water. A deficiency in this respect is unquestionable, and means are in train for remedying it, under the auspices of the City Council. Yet the truth is, that we have as much water now as we ever had in the city, and as we had in those times when the conduct of fires gave great and just complaint in our city. Assuredly also, the deficiency of water in the vicinity of Beacon street, or of Central street, could not be considered as the cause of the confusion, disorder, and inefficiency which are complained of on both these occasions. On the contrary, if our present system be sufficient, a manifest deficiency in the article of water would be a reason for order and regularity, rather than a cause of disorder and confusion. Our present system presupposes either *a will* in the surrounding multitudes at fires, to aid in forming lanes to pass water to the engines, or *a power* in the firewards to compel them to form such lanes.

Now, just in proportion as water in the vicinity of any fire is deficient, is the necessity apparent that it should be brought from a distance; and, of course, that the efficiency of the will, or the power to make lanes, should be manifested. If our present system be, therefore, in this respect, sufficient, the alacrity to form lanes and to preserve order in the multitude present, and the facility with which the firewards are enabled to form the one and preserve the other, will be increased rather than diminished, by the existence of so great an exigency. How it was on both occasions can best be answered by the firewards and the citizens present.

Again, are the evils of which we complain to be attributed to the want of buckets, of fire clubs, or any of the ancient associations for mutual protection? What is the reason of this? Why are we deficient in buckets? Why are the number of fire clubs greatly diminished? Why those ancient associations abandoned or gone into disuse? There can be but one answer. The state of things is changed in this respect. With the greatness of population a different state of feeling and of modes of protection have grown up. Formerly, one could not open the front door of the highest or the richest citizen without having his eye greeted with at least two buckets, containing fire-bags and a bed key, all duly labelled, indicating to which fire society he belonged. The same was true in relation to the house of almost every citizen, except those of the poorest class.

At this day how many doors can you open and behold the same sight? I answer, within bound, not one in fifty. Why is this? If you ask the owner, and he answers truly, nine times in ten it will be, "I am insured; why should I keep fire-buckets? Why subject myself to the rules and customs of fire clubs? Or why turn out to fire at all? I go to the expense of protecting myself. I ask no protection of others, and I mean to incur no voluntary expense, and much more, will not incur the risk of health and life in protecting them."

However cold, selfish, or calculating this language may seen, it is in the practical language of men in all great cities. In such cities, the influential classes of citizens, the householders, and men of property of every description, grow more in the habit of protecting themselves, more unwilling to incur the risk and the labor which aiding at fires makes necessary, and the number of those who are indifferent on such occasions, or who are willing to make profit by the misfortune of others, is increasing. The consequence is that in all cities, after they have obtained a certain amount of greatness, the system of depending upon the aid of all the citizens has been abandoned, and a system, self-dependent, and which so far from requiring the aid of all the citizens, excludes that aid, has been adopted.

The substantial question, therefore, presented to the citizens of Boston is this, — having become a city with a great population, will you adopt a system conformable to the state of things in which you exist? or, with a great population, will you adhere to a system adapted only, and which can be efficient only in a city with comparatively a very small population? Whatever prejudices may exist upon the subject, and whatever interests or feeling may be affected by the avowal, it is my duty to state, as the result of all the researches made under the authority of the City Council, on the subject, that *the present system of firewards is not and can not be made an efficient system of protection against fire, with a population such as at present exists in this city.* The fault is not on the men, but the system.

Thirty-six men are annually chosen, in wards, all equal in power; and in *case of fire any three have precisely the same power with every other three.* I lay aside all questions concerning the effect of choosing in wards, rather than by general ticket. I take it for granted that the men, thus chosen, are the best thirty-six men that exist in the city for this purpose, and that they always will be the best. I ask, then, what are the efficient powers of such firewards, in relation to commanding aid on those occasions, considered in the light of substantial protection? The answer, and only answer that can be given, is, that *they can require the assistance of all persons present to aid in extinguishing fires.* But, suppose the persons required refuse or neglect to obey? What then? They are liable to be prosecuted the next day for ten dollars. The penalty, indeed, is heavy; but what is it as it respects efficient protection?

Of the thousands which, at every great fire, either refuse or neglect to obey the fireward, and shrink from him, or go away as soon as he approaches, how many have ever been prosecuted, and paid their $10? Comparatively speaking, not one. This *great authority* of the firewards, on which so much reliance is placed, when looked to for efficient protection, turns out to be nothing more than *the good-will of the person present.* The firewards' orders, *if the person ordered wills, he obeys ; if he does not so will, he let it alone.* And this is the whole matter; for, unless in case of flagrant insult or outrage, he never hears any more of the business. Nor can there be any blame cast on the fireward. Amidst darkness and confusion and hurry, how can he identify the individual, much more arrest and keep him in custody?

The efficient authority of firewards turns out, then, to be, after all, *mere influence ;* and the whole system is predicated upon its *being influence, and nothing else.* It is a sufficient system in an early stage of society, and in a limited extent of population. But when society advances, when a population becomes numerous, the weight of personal character and influence is little felt; comparatively not at all. And the consequence is, that a system of influence must be abandoned, and one of efficiency adopted.

Now, a system to be efficient must be *self-dependent ;* not relying upon whim, caprice, or the accidental presence of well-disposed individuals, but possessing within itself, and by the inherent force of its own organization, the capacity of affording the protection required. By the aid of hose, of suction, and supply engines, such a system supersedes the necessity of laws, and, by the power of machines, renders only a very small number of persons sufficient for protection. This is the system of New York. The surrounding multitude, instead of being solicited to aid, are prohibited from interfering. The engineers, the firemen and hosemen, and hook and laddermen are competent to manage all the machines. The efficiency of this system is not a matter of speculation.

.　　.　　.　　.　　.　　.　　.　　.　　.　　.

The question, then, now presented to the citizens of Boston is a question *between two systems ;* and, on this point, in order that there may be no mistake in this matter, and no deception, I wish to be distinctly understood, that the existence and present relations and powers of firewards *are wholly incompatible with the system recommended and in practice in New York ; and that so long as these relations and powers subsist, this system cannot be introduced.* For although firewards make a component part of the system in New York, yet their relations and their powers are very different from those of firewards in this city. One great business, for instance, of firewardens under our system is *to make citizens assist at fires:* whereas, one great business of firewards in New York is to keep persons at a distance from them.

I know that it is urged with great warmth and vehemence in the public prints, that the object of the City Council is to wrest from the citizens the election of firewards. The truth, however, is, that the object of the City Council is of a much higher and more consequential character than the poor acquisition of any such elective power. It is an endeavor to place the safety and protection of the city against fire, upon the basis of a self-dependent, efficient system; one that does not claim for age, or manhood, or boyhood, as a duty, to turn out and give protection against fires, at the exposure of health, and often of life. On the contrary, it takes the protection of the city upon itself. It asks of the citizens, not immediately intereste l, only to keep away. It depends on its own discipline, practice, force of machinery, and engines, and relies not at all on the reluctant aid of casual bystanders.

This system is inevitable in a full-grown state of society. If our citizens do not realize. or will not a lmit the necessity of it *now*, the adoption is only postponed. Come it will. The great teacher. calamity, which has already spoken once and twice, will speak again and again, until its voice is heard. If, then, the effect of the bill is to vest in the City Council the choice of the firewards, it is because that the powers and relations of firewards, in a system destined to give protection without calling in the aid of the multitude present, and different from their powers and relations in a system like our present one, based upon depending on the aid of that multitude altogether.

Thirty-six men, coequal in power, every three of whom have a right to command, are wholly incompatible with a system which is of the nature of an organized force, having a head and members subordinate to each other, and in which responsibility is precise, direct, and individual. It will, therefore, be seen by my fellow-citizens, that the real question to be decided by them, on the acceptance and rejection of the bill, relates to the two systems, — that which now exists, and that which is recommended.

So far as the question affects the elective franchise. it depends upon another question; and that is, whether the city council. the constituted and responsible representative of all the citizens, be, or be not, the proper body to be intrusted with the organization of the fire department of the city?

Upon the general expediency of retaining the present system, which is founded on the practicability of commanding the aid of the whole multitude present at fires, I ask my fellow-citizens to consult not only recent, but also to reflect on the actual. relations of our population. Is it not becoming every day less and less homogeneous? By emigration and the constant infusion of foreigners. are not the sympathies among citizens, considered merely as such, diminishing? Has not an increased disposition to take advantage of fires as occasion for plunder been manifested of late years? Must it not be inevitable, in every city with an increasing population? What right has this city to expect an exemption from the common lot of humanity in great cities?

In making this elucidation I am sensible that I have exposed myself to the charge of unsuitable obtrusiveness. But I am willing to submit to this, or to any other like censure, rather than to have the conviction, which I should otherwise have felt, that I have failed in my duty to a people to whom I owe so many obligations for the confidence they have reposed in me. My great purpose will be answered, if I can draw the attention of my fellow-citizens to the real nature of the question, and that, when decided, an ·unequivocal expression of their opinion should be given by the number of their suffrages; and that it should not be left, as some questions have been of late, to the decision of a few individuals in the vicinity of the hall. or who had a particular interest in the subject.

The question deeply interests the fate of the whole city; only let, then, the voice of the whole city be heard.

Your fellow-citizen,

JOSIAH QUINCY.

4TH JULY. 1825.

Hon. Daniel Davis was chosen moderator of the meeting, and the poll was voted to be closed at half-past two o'clock in the afternoon. So exciting was the struggle that two thousand five hundred and eleven votes were cast, and so powerful was the opposition that the votes stood one thousand three hundred and forty-seven for, and one thousand one hundred and sixty-four against, being decided by only one hundred and eighty-three votes. Thus, after an open and hard fight, the organization of our independent fire department was accepted by the citizens of Boston. Means were now taken to carry the project into effect, with the general coöperation of the citizens. A committee of both branches of the City Council, consisting of the Mayor, Aldermen Blake and Welsh, and Messrs. William, Barry, Boies, and Wiley, of the Common Council, was chosen to prepare an ordinance in conformity with the act of Legislature. But it was not until the end of December that the details of this ordinance were settled.

The Committee on Reservoirs reported, on November 28, that the large fire was caused principally on account of the scarcity of water, and therefore recommended that twelve reservoirs be built, each to contain not less than two hundred and fifty hogsheads of water, this number being all that could be built before winter, yet three times that number in their opinion should be constructed. They were located on Liberty square ; Union street, near old State House ; new State House ; Hanover street, near new church ; near Rev. Dr. Ware's church, Hanover street ; Bowdoin square ; Old South church ; vicinity of theatre in Federal street ; Broad street, near Boylston market ; Common street, near St. Paul's church ; Summer street, and India street, — for the construction of which $6,500 were appropriated on December 1. The supply of water to feed these wells was mostly taken from the public buildings. The City Council referred the subject of " the organization of a fire department, upon the principle of distinct and individual responsibility," to the next City Council, the period of a reorganization of the city government being now approaching.

An ordinance for the regulation of chimneys and chimney-sweepers was passed December 28, 1825, by which it was made unlawful for any person to engage in the business of chimney-sweeping, unless licensed by the City Council, or for any one to employ those who were not licensed. Any person refusing to have their chimneys swept could be fined for each day they continued burning a fire. Two dollars' fine was the penalty for allowing their chimneys to fire.

The changes among the officers of the department were : No. 6, Lazarus Bowker, *vice* Captain Walcott. No. 7, J. Colby, clerk, *vice* Hills. No. 10, James Shephard, *vice* Captain Veazie ; and Thomas Furber, clerk, *vice* Shephard, promoted. No. 12, Luther Felton, *vice* Captain Adams ; and Peter B. Clark, clerk, *vice* Samuels. No. 13, Samuel H. Remick, *vice* Captain Hammond. No. 14, Alexander H. Jennings, *vice* Captain Bird. No. 17, Charles Dudley, *vice* Captain Stetson. In the board of firewards the changes were : Ward 1, William Collier, Horace H. Watson, and Henry S. Kent, *vice* Pratt, Orcutt, and Trask. Ward 2, Aaron Wallis, *vice* Chandler. Ward 3, Thomas Tivell, *vice* Holbrook. Ward 4, George Riley, *vice* Thomas Melville, who declined reëlection. Ward 5, John Hall, David Thacher, and D. C. Greenleaf, *vice* Thaxter,

Allen, and Annable. Ward 6, Samuel F. Coolidge and Daniel Brown, *vice* Adams and Shepley. Ward 7, Asa Richardson *vice* Stephen Codman. Ward 8, Thomas H. Perkins, Jr., and James Hamilton, *vice* B. P. Tilden and Brigham. Ward 9, Nathaniel Richards, *vice* Harris. Ward 12, Brewster Reynolds, *vice* Williams. As we have said, Thomas Melville declined serving for a longer period, on which occasion the board, on April 27, passed the following vote : —

That the thanks of this board, for themselves and in behalf of their fellow-citizens, be presented to Thomas Melville, Esq., for the zeal, intrepidity, and judgment with which he has on all occasions discharged his duty as a fireward of this city for forty-six years in succession, and for twenty-five years as chairman of the board. We regret his voluntary retirement, but he carries with him our best wishes that the remainder of his life may be as happy and tranquil as his public services have been useful and acceptable. Voted, that the secretary cause the above vote to be published in such of the newspapers in this city as he may deem proper.

Whereupon a committee was chosen to procure a handsome silver pitcher, at a cost of $70, and present it to him. In acknowledging the receipt of which he sent the following letter : —

BOSTON, June 22, 1825.

GENTLEMEN, — Your vote of the 27th April last, and the elegant tribute of respect which accompanied it, by the hands of your committee, on the 15th inst., have laid me under a debt of gratitude which, though I do not wish to be free from, I can never adequately repay. Memory yet lingers, and always will fondly linger, on the many happy intimacies I have formed, the many social hours I have passed, and the many heartfelt satisfactions I have experienced in your society, and while I look back on our intercourse with it, which has continued uninterrupted for nearly half a century, it is to me a consoling reflection, that I have only complied with my duty in retiring from those fatigues and labors which age would soon have rendered me incompetent, usefully and acceptably, to perform. Often as the rich libation shall be poured forth, or the invigorating draught imbibed, from the vessel you have presented, will the spirit and motives which induced the bestowment of it be remembered, and the many interesting ties which bind me to its donors be renovated and strengthened; not only so, but I trust it will be tenderly and faithfully preserved by descendants, as a testimony of *your generosity and their gratitude*, long after my silver cord of life shall be loosed and my life's pitcher broken at its fountain. My ardent wishes are directed with solicitude for your prosperity ; may your labors long prove successful, your intercourse pleasant, and your felicity be continually increasing; and when time or circumstances shall dissolve your social union, may your valuable services receive a rich reward in the approbation and blessings of a grateful community. With great consideration and respect, I am, gentlemen, your most obedient servant,

THOMAS MELVILLE.

TO THE BOARD OF FIREWARDS.

Fires for the year: January 11, North square, building owned by Mr. Andrews. April 7, Doane building, Doane wharf ; 8th, building on Lincoln wharf, near Ann street. May 21, schooner " Washington." lying at Forster's south wharf ; 26th, building in Charles street. July, building on Hobb's wharf, near Sea street : distil house, Rainsford's lane. August 5, barn of Mr.

Rogers, Beacon street; 16th, house of Joseph Nash, Fort hill; 25th, John Bannister's carpet shop, Forster's wharf. September 19, house on Purchase street; 25th, Mr. Goodwin's dwelling, corner of Ann and Fleet streets. November 12, building on Lynn street; house on Hanover street; 24th, Thomas Whitman's residence, 76 Prince street. December 13, Captain Glover's house on Purchase street, occupied by Mr. Bartholomew; 15th, Joshua Oakes' dwelling, Purchase street; 23d, building corner of Friend and Portland streets; 27th, milinery shop in Hanover street, opposite Hancock school; stable of Mr. Morton, on Hawley street.

Immediately after the reorganization of the City Council for 1826 they took measures to carry the preparatory steps for the settlement of the department, and on January 19 Samuel Devens Harris was appointed chief engineer. Mr. Harris was a man of keen judgment and prudence. He distinguished himself as a cavalry officer in almost every battle on the Canadian frontier in 1814, and was generally regarded as singularly qualified to introduce order and subordination into the department. The state of his health rendered him, at first, unwilling to accept the office, as it would subject him to great exertion and exposure; but he at length yielded to the solicitations of the mayor and City Council. He requested the mayor, soon after taking command, not to bring the subject of his salary before the City Council, assigning as a reason for this request, that, having the charge of a force consisting wholly of unpaid volunteers, he thought his usefulness would be hampered by his acceptance of a salary. On the 23d the following twenty gentlemen were appointed engineers: D. C. Bacon, George Dorricott. G. Fairbanks, S. Wilkinson, J. Chandler, T. B. Curtis. A. H. Gibbs, William Tileston, O. C. Greenleaf, T. H. Perkins, Jr., William Tucker, J. F. Cooledge, Benjamin Darling, John Farrier, Jr., H. Fox, H. Fowle, Jr., J. D. Emery, Flavel Mosely, Brewster Reynolds, and Al. Stetson. Messrs. Tucker and Greenleaf declined, and were succeeded, on the 25th, by W. H. Prentice, and Joel Prouty; Benjamin T. Reed, *vice* S. F. Cooledge, on the 14th; James Clark and Charles Wells, *vice* Farrier. Jr., and Moseley, declined, February 9. On August 28 it was ordered that all communications to the board must first pass the hands of the chief.

The changes in the board of firewards for the year before their disorganization were: Ward 1, William Barnicoat and Henry Fox, *vice* Collier and Watson; Ward 2, Robert Bacon, to fill vacancy of last year; Ward 3. Silas Stuart and Charles Mountford, *vice* Smith and Tivell; Ward 4, Abel Adams, *vice* Mitchell; Ward 6, Gridley Bryant and Lazarus Bowker, *vice* Cooledge and Brown; Ward 12, Stephen Child, Jr., *vice* Wheeler. They reported at their meeting January 13, that there was a great scarcity of men in the department. On Engines 3 and 8 all members resigned, with the exception of seven; No. 9 was disbanded and temporarily filled; No. 10, old and useless; Nos. 11 and 12. all members resigned; No. 14, only fourteen members remained, and on No. 17 only twelve. This report was sent to the Mayor, with the information that two vacancies existed in the board, viz. : Thomas H. Perkins, Ward 8, and William Barnicoat, Ward 1. A committee was formed to consider the expediency of allowing Engine 14 to employ a horse to help carry that engine to and from fires. This was allowed a short time after, the engine being drawn by a cream-colored horse, known as the "charger."

The last meeting of the wards was held at the residence of William Merriams, on May 19, at which there were present twenty-two members, with Daniel Messenger as chairman. A letter from Mayor Quincy, dated 15th inst., enclosing an order of the Board of Aldermen passed May 10, was read, when it was voted "that the late secretary inform the mayor of the receipt of this communication, and to assure him and the Board of Aldermen of the satisfaction they feel in having their conduct as firewards approved by the constituted authority of their fellow-citizens ; and the secretary is further directed, in conformity to the request of the Board of Aldermen, to deliver to Samuel D. Harris, Esq., Chief Engineer, all the records and property of the city in their possession." The balance of funds in the treasury was seventy-four dollars and fifty-six cents, which was used to defray the expense of the evening and other demands due from them. The thanks of the members were then presented to the chairman for the very acceptable manner in which he presided during his relation to them in that capacity, after which " the chairman rose and made a dignified and suitable acknowledgment, and after taking a parting glass the board formally dissolved and the members separated ;" which transaction ended the time-honored institution that had to give way to the demands of an increased population.

Fire companies in Wards 11 and 12 were appointed January 9 ; Wards 2, 4, and 5, on 17th ; Ward 7 on the 19th ; Wards 1 and 3 on the 23d ; and Ward 6, February 6. Five thousand dollars were added to the appropriation for the department on January 17. The engine from New York arrived on January 5, and was delivered to the care of Engine Company 7, and their old engine was transferred to a new company located in a house on Sea street, and named Boston No. 20. The Extinguisher Engine Company 7 was then changed to New York No. 7, and on the 9th fifty men were added to the company, and a stove and rack were placed in the engine-house. On the petition of Mr. C. C. Nichols, on the 19th, a ward-room and engine-house was erected in Ward 8, on a site of land on Franklin place, between the theatre and Josiah Bellows' property.

On the 26th the new Engine 7, Ward 18, was badly injured by some person, who drew the screws and nuts from the piston of the pump. Five hundred dollars' reward was offered for the arrest of the parties committing the act. This offer was also made for the detection of any person caught cutting hose at a fire, an act which had been committed on Engine 11 in March ; but no arrests were made. On the 30th. application was received by the committee from several of the foremen, asking for an alteration of the regulations relating to the premium as then established. They were informed that the payment was more to the encouragement of the members and the efficiency of the general system. On the same date Engine 6 was allowed six additional men to its list of members, and two hundred pairs of fire-buckets were ordered, at $4.40 per pair, which order was increased, on April 10, to three hundred pairs.

The mayor and Aldermen Bellows and Oliver were appointed on February 13 a committee on the fire department, for the year. It was ordered by the Council, on the 20th, that all engine-men must be twenty-one years of age, unless the consent of their parents, etc., be given; and on the 27th Engine 15 was surrendered by the members. James Pierce, secretary of the masters of the engines, sent the board a vote of the department commanders on March 9, to the effect that " they did not consider the company of Engine 11 as a regular engine company, and would not associate with them as such." A letter was also received from Capt. William Tucker, a fireman, stating the extreme disorganizing and disorderly conduct of Capt. Daniel Adams of Engine 16, while at a fire in Ann street on the 9th, he being at the fountain-head of the engines in line, and ordered his engine to cease playing in any of the engines forming the series. On being remonstrated with he behaved very disorderly. Acting foreman A. W. Jennings, of Engine 14, did the same. Adams was discharged, and Jennings suspended for a few days. It was resolved by the committee that the mayor address a letter to Pierce, and send a copy of the letter of Mr. Tucker's, requesting him (Pierce) to call a meeting of the engine foremen, and answer the following questions : —

1. Whether by the terms expressed in the said resolve, " that they will not coöperate with Engine 11, etc.," this Board are to understand that it is the intention of the captains to refuse all coöperation with that company in case of fire?

2. Whether the course of proceeding stated in the letters of Mr. Tucker have or not the countenance of the captains? And that the mayor request Mr. Pierce to send in the names of those who refuse to coöperate with Engine 11.

Engines Co.'s 2, 10, and several others, declared they would not receive or deliver water from Engine 11, being, as they asserted, a company of boys; but the committee informed them that the company was confirmed by the city authorities, and, unless the statement was retracted, the companies would be disbanded. Engine Co. 2 would not retract; consequently, it was disbanded, and a new one at once organized. On the discharge of Captain Adams of No. 16, the company issued a notice in the " Columbian Centinal," on March 22, stating that they would " still hold Daniel Adams their lawful captain, notwithstanding he had been dismissed by the mayor and aldermen, and they should obey him accordingly." This resolve, as a matter of course, led to their immediate dismissal.

The Columbian, Eagle, and Vigilant Fire Societies offered themselves, on March 27, to protect property, etc., and asked that they should be recognized by the city. They were highly approved of by the authorities, and the aldermen ordered that a common badge should be worn, that they may be known to the engineers, and that they should pass any line, subject to the orders of the chief and engineers. It was also resolved that any company of citizens associated for the purpose, regularly organized, with established rules, should file a list with the committee. But this would not exempt them from serving as jurors and in the militia. The Suffolk Fire Society, on the 27th, offered to take charge of any engine in the city where a company was wanted. On this date the several fire societies who had volunteered their services to take the engines when they were thrown up by the old companies were publicly thanked by the City Council.

On account of a number of false alarms that had been sounded on the bells at the North End, a new system was instituted by a committee appointed for that purpose, who reported, on April 10, that the wardens of the several churches would provide at their own expense a lock and key of the church, the key to be kept at a store opposite the church; the keeper of which would unlock the door at half-past nine at night, and lock it again in the morning. A tin sign was put on the church designating the place at which the key was kept.

Engine Co. 2 was increased to forty members. Hose company No. 1 was organized this month, with Nathan Ring, foreman; S. Sabor and I. Turner, assistants: T. F. Pratt, clerk. They were located in a building in the rear of 13 Court street. On the 24th the mayor was authorized to issue his proclamation declaring that the fire department had been duly organized agreeable to the permission of the act of Legislature and the ordinance of the City Council, the same to go into effect on the 29th. Chief Harris requested, on May 22, that the several reservoirs be filled with water; and on the first of the following month the Suffolk Fire Society was formed.

The changes in the officers during 1826 were: No. 1, Otis Munroe, *vice* John Hooton, Jr., *vice* Captain Gair; J. H. Bennett first, and S. W. Hall second foreman; Amos G. T. Ruddock, *vice* Dillaway, clerk. No. 2, James Bassett, *vice* Captain Whitcomb; Charles Gaylor, *vice* Bellamy, clerk. No. 3, Aza Swallow, *vice* Z. Sampson, *vice* Captain E. B. Green: M. Dalton, *vice* George Carpenter, clerk. No. 4, Levi Conant, *vice* William Marden, *vice* Bennett, clerk. No. 5, Benjamin D. Baldwin, *vice* Captain Torrey. No. 6, Jacob Tufts, *vice* Captain Bowker. No. 7, E. Battles, *vice* Captain Pierce, A. Parker, *vice* J. Smith, *vice* Colby, clerk. No. 8, S. N. N. Thorp, *vice* Captain Thayer. No. 9, A. W. Blanchard, *vice* Francis Trask, *vice* S. W. Stone, *vice* Captain Salmon, G. L. L. Ripper, *vice* Joseph Gibson, *vice* Stacey, clerk. No. 10, William S. Baxter, *vice* Captain Shephard. No. 11, W. T. Spear, *vice* Captain Bagnell; B. Russell, *vice* Howland, clerk. No. 12, James Barry, Jr., *vice* Captain Felton; Galvin Taylor, *vice* Clark, clerk. No. 14, Nathan Trumbull, *vice* Captain Jennings. No. 15, Henry Huxford, *vice* John Foster, *vice* Captain Ridler; Leo Hillman, *vice* Mike Dalton, *vice*

Austin, clerk. No. 16, Joseph Seaver, *vice* E. O. Hawes, *vice* Captain Adams ; T. Rand, *vice* Lincoln, Jr , clerk. No. 17, Richard Lock, *vice* Captain Dudley ; W. Haley, *vice* Clark, clerk. Associated fire engine and hydraulic company, attached to Engine 18, called the Philadelphia, and Hose Co. 18, William Barnicoat, captain ; A. Holmes, first assistant ; N. Seaver, clerk, with sixty-three men. Associated fire engine and hydraulic company attached to Hydraulion 19 ; T. C. Amory, captain ; C. N. Dennett, first-assistant foreman, and John Peirce, clerk, thirty-five men. This and No. 18 were one company.

Of the fire clubs and societies the following list is complete : Ward 1, N. C. Belton, captain ; Charles Brintnell and Nathaniel Hunt, assistants ; W. Knapp, clerk. Ward 2, B. Abrahams, captain ; D. Edes and George Lowe, assistants ; John Carnes, clerk. Ward 3, George A. Sampson, captain ; S. P. Hayward and J. P. Dupee, assistants ; B. F. Sylvester, clerk. Ward 4, G. Riley, captain ; I. Atkins and Sol Wilds, assistants ; Thomas Watman, clerk. Ward 5, George Lane, captain ; J. Hammond and W. C. Stimpson, assistants ; W. T. Waldo, clerk. Ward 6, J. Lincoln, captain ; Thomas Haviland and J. H. Belcher, assistants ; J. Holman, clerk. Ward 7, D. Brigham, captain ; J. W. Harris and William Taylor, assistants ; J. F. Haywood, clerk. Ward 8, James Horton, captain ; Ed. Hall and C. W. Thayer, assistants ; George Pemberton, clerk. Ward 9, Paul Rice, captain ; D. H. Dillaway and L. Herman, assistants ; George Witkins, clerk. Ward 10, James Crain, captain ; John Rupp assistant ; Robert T. Paine, clerk. Ward 11, John Howe, captain ; E. Watson and F. Moseley, assistants ; Otis Everett, clerk. Ward 12, Moses Williams, captain : B. Reynolds and George Jackson, assistants ; James Carey, clerk ; — each of which company had twenty-five men.

CHAPTER III.

1827–1831.

THE first report of the fire department from the hands of its chief was furnished the City Council January 15, 1827. In it he recommends the alteration of several engine-houses, and repairs of engines. This report was ordered to be printed in a single sheet, and distributed to the city government and members of the department. A committee was then appointed by the aldermen to see what alterations were necessary in the ordinance establishing the fire department; also to see about the act of Legislature whereby a member must produce a certificate from the mayor to show to the commanding officers of the militia "on or before the first Tuesday of May in each year," as the members who were admitted subsequent to that time were obliged to do both military and fire duty. The doubt as to whether the power of the firewards regarding gunpowder was transferred to the engineers was at the same time taken into consideration, and settled to their satisfaction by an act passed March 2, 1827. Messrs. N. Viles and M. Weare were appointed engineers on the 24th. On the 29th an additional story was added to Engine 9's house, on Mason street. The same date the mayor and Aldermen Loring and Savage were appointed a committee on the department.

A letter from the mayor was received by the Board of Aldermen, requesting that new engine-houses be erected where necessary, and to enlarge others, as there were no facilities for properly attending to the apparatus or drying the hose, while most of the companies had to hold their monthly meeting in public houses, resulting in useless expense, and was otherwise objectionable. The chief sent in a report to the effect that several of the engines were also in need of repairs.

The site of Engine-house 7, on School street, owned by the city, contained only four hundred and forty-seven feet of ground area, and was therefore too small for so large an engine. On February 19 arrangements were made by the city and Mr. Asa Richardson, owner of a piece of land on the west side of the county court-house, containing two thousand four hundred and five and one-half feet, whereby his land was bought for $3 per foot, while the smaller piece, on which the engine-house stood, was taken in exchange at $5 per foot. The engine-house on Mason street, despite the alterations recently made, could not be made suitable; at times over six inches of water would cover the engine floor. Plans were prepared by the members for a two-story building of brick and stone, to take the place of the old one, which arrangements were accepted by the committee, and a very fine house erected.

To carry out the extensive repairs, etc., in the department, the $10,000 appropriated by the city was found to be insufficient; consequently, on March 8, $12,000 more were added. After the authorization of this order, the mayor recommended, and the City Council ordained. that thereafter the expenditure be made under the superintendence of a joint committee of the City Council, to consist of seven persons, and three of the Board of Aldermen, and no expenditure of more than $50 be sanctioned by any committee unless the same should be previously authorized by a vote of a majority of that committee; which measure proved highly advantageous for the promotion of harmony and subordination among the chief and his assistant engineers.

Engine 10, on the Mill creek, was ordered a new house, at a cost of $800; but this was objected to by a Mr. Holbrook, as a new street was to be cut through in that section. The committee appointed to investigate the matter reported in favor of the building being erected. A building for Engine 16 was ordered erected near the gun-house on Fort Hill, but was objected to by a number of inhabitants as being dangerous. A site of land fifteen by forty-five feet in dimensions was therefore secured, on July 23, from Mr. T. P. Simpson, on Purchase street, for ten years, at $60 per year. Engine 8, on November 19, had a wooden house built on a site of land fifty by twenty feet in dimensions, situated on Warren street, — the property of Thomas Emmons, — which the city leased for five years, at $130 per annum. Previously to this the old Franklin school-house was ordered to be fitted up for their temporary accommodation. Engine 6 was ordered to have built accommodations for the drying of hose in the school-house, the tower to be " three feet wide, and four and one-half feet long, erected behind the street door." On April 23 the mayor issued certificates, to be given to each member of the department the last week in April, ensuing. At the same date the laws relating to military duty were ordered published. Engine 6 was disbanded on December 20 by the chief for allowing the hose to lay in the house five days after being in service, without being washed. A new company was organized four days later. That official issued orders soon after, requesting every engine to " take all their hose with them when going to a fire, as it might be wanted; then, after returning to the house, to spread it out and heat the room as hot as possible, so that it would be thoroughly dried."

The entire list of members of the department for the year numbered one thousand three hundred and two, all of whom worked together in entire harmony with each other. The cause of the dissensions before and during a later period was the unfortunate bickering and difficulties arising among the members, which contributed in a most powerful manner to injure the department in the public estimation. The disgraceful conduct of a few, unhappily brought dishonor on the many. The great majority, however, felt the importance of maintaining, on all occasions, the honor and respectability of the institution. They clearly understood that when any man entered the public service as a fireman he enters also into a compact, as binding as though signed and sealed, to perform the duties required by the law and its officers, to submit to the salutary rules and regulations legally established for the government of the department and the company to which he is attached; he is bound to obey the orders of his own officers by the regulations of his own company, and the engineers by the ordinance of the city and the laws of the State. If those conditions were obnoxious no one was constrained to subject himself to them, and any man, when dissatisfied with the department or any of its officers, must have known that the doors were wide open for his exit. Much of the difficulties resulted from the introduction of minors. On the rolls of some of the disbanded companies were the names of many individuals who were desirous of doing the department all the injury possible. Several of these companies formed associations for the express purpose of remaining together until an opportunity offered to get revenge. They long held nightly meetings, and on an alarm of fire were ready to rush to the scene of action, to stir up dissatisfaction, fan any flame of discord, and create and join in any row or quarrel. But as the city grew, and the department gained strength by reason of its superior system and appliances, this class of men were carefully excluded from every company, and their pretended devotion to the rights of firemen carefully examined by every member who desired to promote the harmony and welfare of an important institution, that cannot exist without law, obedience, and discipline.

The changes in the officers of the engine companies and the locations of the engine-houses, for the year, were as follows: No. 4, Ann street; George Armenege, *vice* Captain Eaton; G. B. Carreau, *vice* Dalton, clerk. No. 5, Market square; George Andrews, *vice* J. F. Foster, *vice* Captain Torrey; S. H. Hall and S. A. Andrews, assistants. Engine and Hose No. 7, School, corner Court street; W. G. Eaton, *vice* James Wild, *vice* Captain Battles; J. A. Davis, foreman of hose; Charles Fuller, *vice* Parker, clerk; seventy-five members. No. 8, 58 Warren street, near 484 Washington street; Lyman Tucker, Jr., *vice* William Willett, *vice* Captain Throope; J. T. Mulner, *vice* A. J. Dow, *vice* Blanchard, clerk. No. 10, Mill bridge, Hanover street; John Wedger, *vice* Captain Baxter; John Goodwin, assistant foreman. No. 13, discharged February 21. No. 14, Milk street; Henry Smith, *vice* Captain Trumbull; Jacob Fowle, J. A. Smith, assistants; William Lawrence, *vice* Glover, clerk. No. 15, Commercial street; C. S. Clark, *vice* Captain Foster; E. Witherell, J. M. Ball, assistants; George Clark, *vice* Hillman, clerk. No. 16, between Rowe's and Foster's wharf; James Jones, Jr., *vice* Captain Hawes; Joseph Sargent and T. H. Stibbins, assistants; C. F. Stibbins, *vice* Rand, clerk. No. 17, Hawes hall, South Boston; R. W. Lund, assistant; E. C. Blake, *vice* Haley, clerk. Ladder 1, Merrimack street; John Stevens and John Davidson, assistants; William Green, clerk; fifty members; the truck carried four ladders of sixty feet, forty-five feet, twenty-five feet, and two twenty feet long respectively; three hooks; two twenty-five, two twelve, and two six foot crotch-poles; two torches; four hammers; two lanthorns, and "tackling" for one horse. Ward companies: Ward 1, Henry Andrews, *vice* Captain Abrahams; John Holman, *vice* Edes, clerk. 4, Jacob C. Flint, *vice* Captain Riley, Thomas Waterman, *vice* Watson, clerk. 6, J. A. Ballard, *vice* Captain Lincoln; G. S. Sterns, *vice* Holman, clerk. 7, R. Warren, *vice* Hayward, clerk. 8, Thomas Baker, *vice* Pemberton, clerk. 9, George W. Williams, *vice* Watkins, clerk.

The first schedule of the location of fire-plugs inserted into the aqueduct for the use of the department was issued during the year and contained the following: 1, Washington, opposite Avery street; 2, Centre street; 3, Centre, opposite Pleasant street; 4, Centre street, near Viles & Atkins store, in the east sidewalk; 6, Pleasant street; 7, Common street; 8, Pearl, corner of Milk street, in the city drain. Reservoirs: State, Hanover, Summer, Park, Franklin, and Union streets, Hancock school-house, North square, Summer street rear of State House Bowdoin square, Old South Church, Liberty square, Mill creek and Hanover street, Mill creek and Ann street, and Frog pond on the Common.

Such was the high estimation in which the new department was held during 1828, that the very heavy appropriation allowed for the erection of buildings, repairs of apparatus, etc , were passed in both branches of the City Council without difficulty, while the presidents of several insurance companies authorized the statement that the rates of insurance against fire was reduced twenty per cent. solely on account of the efficiency of the department. Chief Harris informed the board that all the companies must be treated alike as regards apparatus, etc.; unless this was done, partiality was claimed to be shown. To treat all companies alike appropriations would be required for the erection of new houses for Engines 1, 2, 4, 5, 14, 17, enlarge 3, 13, 6, and 15, and repair Engines 1, 3, 5, 6. 8, 17, and 16. A house was erected in North Bennett street, for Engine 2, by R. G. Shaw, for $150 per year and taxes. On the same date the old house of No. 8 was sold for $8. A site for No. 14 was obtained on Water street, between Merchants' Hall and Phillips building; but, not being satisfactory, the building was erected on the land of E. B. Phillips on the same terms as that of No. 2. Engine 4 was in very poor accommodations in Ann street, the tide flowed into the house, and the engine was always rusty and damp, and, being at the bottom of a hill, the apparatus could not be moved without the aid of at least eight members. The company was moved soon after to Distil-house square, by reason of which a number of the old members resigned, being too far away; new members were then admitted, and they wanted to run the engine themselves, the result being a quarrel, and disbandment of the company on June 21. On August 19, twenty men from Engine 7, under command of W. H. Tileston, took charge.

The mayor and Aldermen Irving and Armstrong were appointed a committee on the department for 1828. Mr. J. Demary was the only new member appointed on the board of engineers for the year. At their meeting held

May 5, Captain Foster, of No. 15, was discharged on complaint of Engineer Demary, for insubordination at a fire on April 22. Mr. Seth Kingsbury, of No. 17, asked for compensation for injuries maintained at the same fire, and was allowed $40.

At a meeting of the engineers of the fire department, held January 1, 1828, the following important orders were passed : —

That a signal lantern be procured and deposited in Engine-house No. 7, and that three members be detailed from the company of said engine to take charge of, and repair with the same to all fires at which the department shall appear, taking position in front of the fire, and there remain until further orders.

That the position of the signal lantern be considered as the headquarters of the department at all fires.

That a Bugle Band be attached to the department, whose duty it shall be to repair to all fires and report at headquarters.

That twelve members of the department, one from each of the Fire Companies, be detailed to act in communicating orders and information from headquarters to the engines during the operation of the department at fire, repairing immediately on the alarm of fires to the position taken by the signal lantern, there form, and wait for orders.

That the Hose Company repair with its hose and apparatus and take position in the rear of the headquarters, or as near to the same as circumstances will admit, the officer commanding to report himself immediately on his arrival and to remain at headquarters to furnish hose when required. All requisition for hose to be sent to headquarters.

That the Hook and Ladder Company with its apparatus take position in rear of headquarters, or as near thereto as may be found convenient, the commanding officer reporting and to remain at headquarters.

That when it shall be decided for the department to retire from a fire it shall be announced by calls from the Bugle Band. The calls shall be as follows: First, for the coming in of the engineer. Second, for commanding officers of engine, hose, hook & ladder and fire companies to repair to headquarters. Third, the members of the fire companies will repair to and take position, forming in line near headquarters, when their rolls will be called by order of their respective commanding officers.

That the department then be directed to retire with the exception of such as may have been detached for further service. The fourth call of the Bugle Band will announce that movement.

Per order,
SAMUEL D. HARRIS,
Chief Engineer.

Engine-house No. 13 was burned on March 8. A few days later, on request of Captain Robbins, the engine was altered to a suction. Ten men were discharged from Engine No. 5 for insubordination, and George Andrews was appointed foreman, on September 22. There were nine hundred and seventy-three members of the department on February 27, 1828, the changes being: Engine 1, Otis Munroe, *vice* Captain Hooton; No. 5, George Andrews, *vice* Captain Andrews; No. 6, James Boyd, *vice* Captain Tufts; No. 7, Jno. Amory Davis, *vice* James Wild, *vice* Captain Eaton; Charles Fuller, foreman of hose; No. 10, Joseph Goodwin, *vice* Captain Wedger; No. 11, John F. Trull, *vice* Captain Spear; No. 13, Charles Robbins, May 15, *vice* James

Peirce, *vice* Captain Blaisdell; No. 15, Cornelius Turner, *vice* Captain Clark; No. 16, E. O. Hawes, *vice* Captain Jones; No. 17, Joseph Young, *vice* Captain Locke; Nos. 18 and 19, William Barnicoat; No. 20, Edward Battles, and Charles Tullard, captain of Hose No. 1, first put in service during the year. Firemen: Ward 2, R. T. Robinson, *vice* Captain Andrews; 3, Isaac S. Dupee, *vice* Captain Sampson; 7, J. C. Bridgman, *vice* John W. Harris, *vice* Captain Brigham; 8, George Dearborn, *vice* Captain Hoolan.

The ladders belonging to the city, besides those carried by the ladder-truck, were located in various sections of the city, as follows: one of thirty-foot and hook at Engine 15, Ann-street draw-bridge; one each at Hancock School, Engines 3 and 10, and a hook at Medical College, Mason street. Those belonging to the societies were: thirty-foot, at Boston Theatre; forty-five foot, at Old South Church; thirty-five foot, Hollis-street Church; forty foot, Mr. Lovell's church, and three under the arch on Central wharf.

On October 8 the Chief Engineer addressed a letter to the mayor, resigning his office on account of ill-health, and, after expressing " his obligations to the officers and members of the department for their prompt and willing coöperation in bringing the new system into efficiency," added, " that the department was adequate to all the purposes of its establishment, and possessed a body of men whose alacrity, zeal, and devotedness could not be improved." On December 8 the mayor, after vain attempts to induce the chief to withdraw his resignation, communicated it to the Board of Aldermen, and it having been accepted by them, he transmitted a message, highly praising Chief Harris for his work during the three years he had been in command, and that, although the chief had requested, in assuming his office, that no compensation be paid him, recommended that some proper acknowledgment should be made for his services. This message was referred to a joint committee, who on the 22d reported the following order for the adoption of the City Council: —

Whereas, the City Council hold in high estimation the services rendered this city by Samuel Devens Harris, late Chief Engineer of the Fire Department, and are convinced that the general spirit of harmony, of subordination, and efficiency which characterized that department and render it highly honorable to those who compose it, and useful to the city, is to be attributed, in a great degree, to the intelligence, the zeal. and active exertions of its late chief, — It is, therefore, ordered, That the thanks of the City Council be, and they hereby are, presented to Samuel Devens Harris, for the faithful. arduous. and highly useful services, gratuitously rendered by him for nearly three years in the office of Chief Engineer of the Fire Department.

The report being read and accepted, the order was passed by a unanimous vote in both branches of the City Council. Mr. Harris also received a complimentary vote of the department on his resignation, to which he had a fitting reply printed and distributed to the members.

On December 22, Mayor Quincy declining to be a candidate for reëlection, Mr. Harrison Gray Otis was elected without opposition. In the address of the former, on taking final leave of the office, in speaking of the fire department, he said : —

The element which chiefly endangers cities is that of *Fire*. It cannot at this day be forgotten by my fellow-citizens with what labor and hazard of popularity the old department was abolished and the new established. From the visible and active energy which members of a fire department take in the protection of the city against that element they always have been and always must be objects of general regard. Great as is the just popularity at present enjoyed by that department, the same public favor was largely enjoyed by their predecessors, who at that time composing it were a hardy, industrious, effective body of men, who had long been inured to the service, and who, having the merit of veterans, naturally imbibed the errors into which old soldiers in a regular service are accustomed to fall. They were prejudiced in favor of old modes and old weapons. They had little or no confidence in a hose system; and, above all, they were beset with the opinion that the continuance of their corps was essential to the safety of the city. More than once it was said distinctively to the executive of the city that, "if they threw down the engines, none else could be found capable of taking them up." Under the influence of such opinion they demanded of the city a specified annual sum for each company. It was refused. And in one day all the engines in the city were surrendered by their respective companies, and, on the same day, every engine was supplied with a new company by the voluntary association of public-spirited individuals.   .

From that time a regular systematic organization of the fire department was begun and gradually effected. The best model of engines was sought; the best experience consulted which our own or other cities possessed. New engines were obtained, old ones repaired; proper sites for engine-houses sought; when suitable locations were found, purchased, and those built upon; when such were not found, they were hired. No requisite preparations for efficiency was omitted, and every reasonable inducement to enter and remain in the service was extended.

The efficient force and state of preparation of this department now consists of twelve hundred men and officers, twenty engines, one hook-and-ladder company, eight hundred buckets, seven thousand feet of hose, twenty-five hose carriages, and every species of apparatus for strength of the department or for the accommodation of its members.

In this estimate also ought to be included fifteen reservoirs, containing three hundred and fifty thousand gallons of water, located in different parts of the city, besides those sunk in the Mill creek, and the command of water obtained by those connected with the pipes belonging to the aqueduct.

Of all the expenditures of the city government none, perhaps, have been so often denominated extravagant as those connected with this department. But when the volunteering of the service, its importance, and the security and confidence actually attained, are considered, it is believed they can be justified. In four years all the objects enumerated, including the reservoirs, have cost a sum not exceeding sixty thousand dollars, which is about forty-eight thousand dollars more than the old department in a like series of years was accustomed to cost. The value of the fixed and permanent property now existing in engine-houses and their sites, engines and apparatus, and reservoirs cannot be estimated at less than twenty thousand dollars. So that the expenditure of the new department beyond the old for these four years cannot be stated at more than five thousand dollars a year, or twenty thousand. Now, it will be found that, in consequence solely of the efficiency of this department, there has been a reduction of twenty per cent. on the rate of insurance within the period above specified. By this reduction of premiums alone there is an annual gain to the city on its insurable real estate of ten thousand dollars, the whole cost enumerated in two years. In this connection, let it be remembered, how great is the security in this respect now enjoyed by the city: and that, previously to its establishment, two fires — that in Kilby, Central, and Broad streets and that in Beacon street — occasioned a loss to it, at the least estimate, of eight hundred thousand dollars. Unquestionably, greater economy may be introduced hereafter into this department in modes which were impracticable at its commencement and in its earlier progress. Measures having that tendency have been suggested. These, doubtless, future City Councils will adopt, or substitute in their stead such as are wiser and better.

All the chief great expenses necessary to perfect efficiency have been incurred, and little more remains to be done than to maintain the present state of completeness in its appointment.

The committee, of which Mayor Otis was a member, appointed to make alterations in the ordinance relating to the department, reported on January 26, 1829, that the usual time for the appointment of engineers took place in this month; that, owing to the unsettled state of the nominations, the time was postponed until February, a temporary chief being chosen. At the same date a petition was rendered by the foremen to the effect that the department was hard to fill with members, and that the work was very laborious, for encouragement to engage in which they wished to be exempted forever from military and jury duty, except in case of war, after serving five years. On February 16 this was allowed, with the additional clause of seven years instead of five.

Mr. Thomas C. Amory was appointed chief of the department, February 9, and the old board of engineers was reëlected. On the 29th this body of officials, with the exception of the chief, presented a memorial to the City Council " requesting that measures may be taken, as soon as consistent with the convenience of the city authorities, to elect others to supply their places, and that, in the meantime, they will act as heretofore and give all the aid and assistance in their power in subduing the common enemy." On March 25 a vote passed the Board of Aldermen, giving their thanks to the late assistant engineers for the fidelity and alacrity uniformly manifested by them in the discharge of their arduous duties, etc. On the same day the vacancies thus created were filled by electing the following twelve citizens: Charles Brintnall, William Barnicoat, Benjamin Smith, J. C. Flint, J. D. Annabell, Thomas Haverland, J. S. Tyler, James Weld, E. O. Hawes, Benjamin Yeaton, B. M. Nevers, and J. Barry, Jr. On February 23 the chief had an office in the old State-House formerly occupied by the County Treasurer assigned to him, and on April 1 a salary of one thousand dollars per year was established by the city authorities, to be computed from February 16 preceding. Previous to this time the service of the chief had been gratuitously rendered.

The Second Baptist Church asked, on January 19, that the city give up the land on which Engine 3 was located, on Salem street, unless they intended to purchase; but the city bought a site on the same street from the Baldwin

Place Association. A new engine-house was ordered for Engine 17 at South Boston on January 6. A new two-story brick house was ordered built on April 1 for Engine 2, and one of wood for Engine 17. At the same time Engine 4 was ordered to be put in repair and transferred to a locality near the House of Reformation. Engine 17 was also removed to No. 4's old quarters, a new engine built with a suction-hose for No. 17. Francis Trask, with others, was given the charge of No. 4, or any other engine placed in Chardon street; but the company did not agree, and was kept in a constant state of insubordination, which resulted in their disbandment; but Captain Trask was soon after reinstated. A piece of land was leased from J. Chamberlin, on Cambridge street, for this engine, on November 13. On petition of Joseph Cooledge and others, May 6, $2,500 were appropriated for the erection of an engine-house on Leverett street, West Boston.

Reservoirs were placed during the year on Poplar street; Hanover street, near North Church; Washington street, near Boylston Market; a tide-reservoir in Mill creek, on Sea street; and two south of Boylston Market, to be supplied from the aqueduct, for the erection of which $10,000 were appropriated. The firemen asked the committee, on April 1, that they be allowed fire-caps, chains, and lanterns, also $100 per year. A new patent sliding-ladder was introduced in the department on April 1. On September 21 the members of the ladder company were provided with caps like those worn by the enginemen.

The city had been quite free from extensive fires during the past four years, but the one ensuing had four conflagrations placed on its record as quite disastrous. The first occurred at the Custom-House, during which Engine 5 was burnt. The Charlestown fire department rendered excellent service and were publicly thanked. On August 14 Union street was the scene of quite a blaze; on October 8, one visited Stillman street. November 29, fire commenced in a building on Summer street occupied by H. T. Salisbury; it soon spread to several adjoining buildings on Washington street, all of which were totally destroyed; loss. $30,000.

The changes in the commanding officers for the year were: Engine 1, Eben Knowlton, *vice* Captain Munroe. No. 2, David Parker, *vice* Captain Bassett; Thomas Denhurst, clerk. No. 3, Samuel Pratt, clerk. No. 6, James Riley, *vice* George Sanderson, *vice* Captain Boyd. No. 7, W. G. Eaton, *vice* William H. Tileston, *vice* Captain Davis; L. H. Huntington and J. L. Hewitt, assistants; W. B. Swift, foreman of hose; J. B. Parker, clerk. No. 10, John Chester, *vice* Captain Goodwin. No. 11, Elijah Clark, *vice* Captain Trull. No. 12, John Green, Jr., *vice* Captain James Barry, March 25. No. 13, W. T. H. Duncan, clerk. No. 14, William Lawrence, clerk. No. 15, James L. Barber, *vice* Captain Turner. No. 16, William Rhodes, *vice* Captain Hawes. No. 17, Nehemiah P. Mann, *vice* Captain Young. Hose 1, Benjamin F. Munroe, *vice* Captain Tullard. Fire companies: No. 1, William Knapp, *vice* Captain Belton. No. 2, S. W. Hall, *vice* Captain Robinson. No. 3, Franklin

Nurse, *vice* Captain Dupee. No. 4, David Kimball, *vice* Captain Riley. No. 6, Slade Luther, *vice* Captain Ballard. No. 7, Franklin Howard, *vice* Captain Bridgman. No. 8, J. Barnard, clerk. No. 9, G. W. Wilkins, clerk, promoted foreman August 9, *vice* Rich. No. 10, Richard A. Newell, *vice* Captain Cain ; A. Winchester, clerk. No. 11, Samuel Curtis, *vice* Captain Howes; W. A. B. Amiston, clerk.

The Board of Engineers for 1830 consisted of the same gentlemen as composed it the year previous, with the exception of Mr. Otis Munroe, who was elected in the place of B. Smith. N. P. Mann was also appointed from South Boston district, being the first engineer to represent that section. The report of this body of officials, sent to the City Council on February 15, proposed several changes to be made in the department. The number of engines was sufficient to protect the city, and all in good condition, except No. 11, which they recommended to be replaced with a new suction-engine, the old one to be used at the mill-dam. Nos. 1, 4, 12, and 13, from their peculiar location, were also ordered to be provided with suction-hose. The condition of the hose was reported very bad, but the two thousand feet already ordered would bring the supply to a fair standard. The useless hose was put on a reel for pump use, for filling reservoirs, etc. The ladder-service was also stated as inadequate, and the condition of the ladder-truck was almost useless. They asked that it be sent to South Boston, which was without one, and a new one of better construction be made to supply its place, equipped with more ladders, especially those for use on roofs. A ladder company was requested to be organized to take charge of another truck, which should be placed on Bedford, West, or Essex streets. The system, or want of system, of giving alarms was considered, and a change made in the ringing of the bells by having them tolled for service after sundown, instead of rung, which was mistaken by many as an alarm of fire. The number of members of the department was larger than at any other previous period, and the general state of order and discipline was highly satisfactory.

March 13, a site of land was leased by the city for Engine 20, on Sea street, at a rental or $100 per annum for ten years. At the same date $5.600 were ordered to be borrowed by the city at five per cent., to meet the expense of this department.

Engine No. 8, on Warren street, was moved to the old Franklin school-house on Tremont street, May 17, and Engine No. 10 was moved to Hanover street, July 26. $386.25 were paid by the Massachusetts Charitable Relief Association, on May 15, to a member of the department injured at a recent fire. Of this sum the association was allowed $200 by the city. On December 12 an order was passed in the Council that the association be allowed $400 per annum for five years, dating from May 1, for the relief of members injured in the service.

December 3, James Quinn, third officer of Engine No. 1, and Private E. O. Eaton were discharged for " inciting the members of that company to acts of insubordination ; " but they were reinstated in the service some time after. Twenty-nine members left the company at the time ; those who remained were thanked by the city. The fire company of Ward 7 wrote the chief that they would take charge of this engine while the company was out. Mr. J. Foster asked for permission, on July 12, to apply a gum-elastic cement to the engine-hose, which he claimed would make it water-tight.

The Charitable Association of the Boston Fire Department was instituted June 19, 1829, and incorporated February 12, 1830. Section 1 of the act of incorporation states : " That Edward E. Prescott, George Dearborn, and Jonathan A. Davis, with their associates and successors, be, and they hereby are, incorporated by the name of the Charitable Association of the Boston Fire Department, for the purpose of affording relief to such of their members as may at any time receive injury in the discharge of their duties as members of the Boston Fire Department. or to their families in the event of their decease ; and by that name may sue and be sued, and may have and use a common seal." Any fireman who received injuries while performing his duties as fireman, and who paid fifty cents annually, received assistance during the period his certificate was dated, by having all his physician's and other necessary bills paid and a sum allowed him for his lost time, not exceeding nine dollars per week, which assistance was continued as long as he was sick. An additional act was passed April 16, 1838, the first two sections of which are as follows : —

SECTION 1. Every member of the Boston Fire Department shall, at all times hereafter, have a right to be admitted a member of the " Charitable Association of the Boston Fire Department." Also, all the members of the Veteran Association of the Boston Fire Department, who shall have been, for the term of seven successive years, members of said Fire Department, shall have the right of becoming members of the said " Charitable Association " by producing to the Secretary of the Association sufficient evidence of membership, subscribing the Constitution of the Association, and paying to the Treasurer such sum, not exceeding one dollar, as the Association shall from time to time direct, which payment shall be in full for the annual contribution of the current year.

SECT. 2. The Treasurer of said Association is hereby authorized and required, after paying the debts of the Association. to invest with the Massachusetts Hospital Life Insurance Company, for a term not exceeding thirty years, the residue of the available funds of the Association, not exceeding the sum of Three Thousand Dollars, and the income thereof shall be applied by the Trustees of said Association for the time being, at their discretion, to the relief or assistance of any member of the Association or his family, or any past member who has belonged to said Fire Department for five years, and has been honorably discharged therefrom ; and any cause of distress, in these cases, shall be considered as entitled to the attention of the Board of Trustees.

The presidents of the association, from its organization to 1888, are as follows : Moses Williams, from January, 1829, to January, 1830 ; J. Weld, from January, 1830, to April, 1830 ; J. Barry, Jr.. from April, 1830, to January, 1832 ; T. C. Amory, from January, 1832, to May, 1838 ; J. Boyd, from May, 1838, to January, 1839 ; J. G. Sanderson, from January, 1839, to January,

1842 ; John Green, Jr., from January, 1842, to January, 1844 ; Jotham B.
Munroe, from January, 1844, to January, 1845 ; John C. Hubbard, from
January, 1845, to January, 1877 ; John S. Damrell, 1877, present incumbent.

Chief Amory, in reply to a letter of Mr. Neil Dow, of the Portland,
Me., fire department, asking for information regarding the system in this
city, stated that he preferred leather hose on account of its pliability and its
better regulating the distance ; that he always had a double company for each
engine,— that is, a sufficient number for relief at fires ; that the fire companies
were exempt from military but not jury duty ; the Associated Fire Engine
and Hydraulian Company was attached to Engines Nos. 18 and 19, the
latter being the suction-engine, both being under one foreman, who had three
assistants, the first and third having charge of No. 19, and the second officer
remained with the foreman at No. 18 ; but he added, " the arrangement is a
bad one, as the men are apt to have a preference for one engine or officer, or
the position of the same at a fire, over the other, and it is very troublesome
to keep each one to his particular post, having a common right in the whole,
and thus it will sometimes happen that one engine is crowded with men and the
other destitute ; besides, the Hydraulian is not always — perhaps not half the
time — employed in feeding the ' Philadelphia,' and is constantly liable, by
the orders of the engineers, to be put on other duty, either to supply or play
in some other line, or on the fire, as circumstances may occur."

The stone church on Hanover street was destroyed by fire, February 1,
this being the only important conflagration during the year.

The changes in the department were : No. 1, John Davis, *vice* Captain
Knowlton ; A. A. Adams, assistant ; A. G. Dawes, clerk. No. 2, S. N.
Cushing and John Pratt, Jr., assistants ; A. Hopkins, *vice* Denhurst, clerk.
No. 3, Luther Russell, *vice* Captain Swallow ; Samuel Pratt and George
Wilkins, *vice* William Hay and D. M. Eaton, assistants ; George Wright,
vice Pratt, clerk. No. 4, John Hammond, *vice* Captain Trask ; Thomas Polland
and James Henry, assistants ; H. N. Crane, clerk. No. 5, S. N. Hall and S.
A. Andrews, assistants ; J. Healey, clerk. No. 6, A. W. Green and Charles
Larkin, assistants ; J. B. Nason, clerk. No. 7, J. H. Blake and John Ayers,
assistants. No. 10, T. S. Pratt, *vice* Captain Chester ; John Wedger and J.
S. Low, assistants. No. 11, Gardner Wheelwright and J. Gray, assistants.
No. 12, James N. Wheeler and Thomas Gorch, assistants ; A. M. Rand,
clerk. No. 13, George F. Spooner, *vice* Captain Robbins : B. Richardson
and Benjamin Underwood, assistants ; J. A. Austin, clerk. No. 15, C. S.
Clark, *vice* Captain Barber ; James Richards, assistant ; P. B. Elliott, clerk.
No. 16, Joseph Jones, *vice* Captain Rhodes ; G. F. West, assistant ; C. W.
Stebbins, clerk. No. 17, Richard Locke, *vice* Captain Mann ; J. W. Locke
and G. F. Belser, assistants ; F. E. C. Blake, clerk. Nos. 18 and 19, C. W.
Lowett and Allen Whitman, assistants ; E. G. Austin, clerk ; seventy-five
men on engine, and sixty on hose company. Ladder No. 1, Charles Prescott
and O. Whipple, assistants ; Otis Trull, clerk. Fire companies : No. 1,

Gilbert Nurse, *vice* Captain Knapp. No. 2, C. Andrews, *vice* Captain Hail; J. Davis, clerk. No. 3, D. W. Barnes, *vice* Captain Nurse. No. 4, I. Lawrence, clerk. No. 5, Charles Hersey, *vice* Captain Hammond; Caleb Whiting, clerk. No. 6, J. A. Ballard, clerk. No. 7, Chester Daniels, *vice* Captain Howard. No. 8, I. Richardson, clerk. No. 9, G. W. Wilkins, *vice* Captain Rice; William Cassidy, clerk. No. 10, E. Haynes, Jr., clerk. No. 11, G. W. Smith, clerk. No. 12, Henry Curtis, *vice* Captain Williams; Joseph L. Richardson, clerk.

The following rules regarding the department went into force January 17, 1831 : —

RULE 1. No person under the age of 18 admitted a member. 2. No more than one-fifth part of the whole number of persons admitted into any company of firemen, hosemen, hook-and-ladder men, or enginemen, at the same time, should be persons under the age of 21. 3. That no person under the age of 21 shall be admitted into the fire department at any time, unless he shall furnish to the foreman of the company to which he may apply a written certificate of the consent of his parents, master, or guardian, which certificate shall be transmitted to the mayor and aldermen at the same time the name of such person shall be offered for admission. 4. That the age of every one under 21 years whose name shall be offered to the mayor and aldermen for admission with any company shall be stated on the list. 5. That no person under 21 shall be an officer of any engine or other company belonging to the fire department, excepting the clerk. 6. That it be recommended to the several engine and other companies of the fire department to elect five sub-assistants, being of age, whose duty shall be, according to seniority of age, to act as foremen at fires in the absence of the foreman and assistant foreman. 7. That the name of all persons hereinafter admitted into the fire department shall be returned to the board of aldermen, to the end that they may be appointed, and receive their certificate within ten days after.

Messrs. J. P. Bradlee, J. Hammond, A Tileston, H. Smith, D. Kimball, G. M. Smith, R. S. Fay, and W. G. Hodgkinson were appointed on the Board of Engineers. Mr. Bradlee declined. Messrs. Flint, Annabell, and Weld resigned. The first report of the engineers regarding the number and extent of fires for the year was sent to the City Council on January 17, in which was stated that there occurred fifty-two fires, at a loss of $54,720, being an increase of $33,295 in excess of the year previous. Twenty-seven false alarms were given.

Quite a disturbance was created on January 3 by the appointment of William Spear as foreman of Engine 10. At first several members of the company complained of his election as being illegal. This was taken up by most of the other companies, who requested his discharge. On investigation by the committee on February 21, he was dismissed. Engine 7 sent in a petition requesting his reinstatement as a member of the department; but this was not granted. The quarters of Engine 10 were set fire to during January, but the investigation by the engineers regarding its origin resulted in nothing definite. May 9, after matters had become quieted, the members asked for sufficient funds to procure furniture for the engine-house, which was granted on July 6.

Messrs. Prescott, Haskell, and Harris were appointed a committee, on June 7, to inquire regarding men injured while in the service of the department, and report a bill for legislative action necessary for their aid. An engine for No. 12 was ordered May 2, and a new house for the new ladder truck was requested by the chief to be erected on High street. A site of land thirty-five by eighteen feet in dimensions was purchased December 12, at $1.20 per foot, on Essex street, for a house for Engine No. 20.

Such was the harmony of feeling in the department after the settlement of the quarrel of Engine 10, that the entire organization dined together in February, and the City Council invited all the engineers and company commanders to meet them at the Old State-House on July 4, to " reciprocate congratulations and celebrate."

Changes in the engine department for the year: No. 1, A. H. Farnham, *vice* Captain Davis. No. 2, A. G. Dawes, T. Reed, and A. H. Wellington, assistants; Thomas Pattin, Jr., *vice* M. J. Chapin, clerk. No. 3, Mathew Hunt, *vice* Captain Parker; Stephen Wells, Peter Maire, assistants, and J. H. Pitman, clerk. No. 4, Samuel Pratt, *vice* Captain Russell; A. L. Stevens and S. E. Holbrook, assistants; S. P. Richardson, *vice* G. C. Piper, clerk. No. 5, Cambridge street, E. J. Syford and Daniel Stone discharged July 11; N. W. Richardson promoted foreman, *vice* Captain Hammond; William Story and John Withington, assistants; David Howe, clerk. No. 6, J. Lincoln, Jr., and W. B. Densmore, assistants; Patrick Riley, clerk. This company adopted new regulations, and had them printed. No. 7, T. A. Williams, *vice* L. A. Huntington on hose, and Charles G. King, assistant on engine; P. W. Hayward, clerk; Samuel Andrews, clerk. No. 8, William Willet, *vice* Captain Tucker, Jr.; Henry Drayton and A. F. Dow, assistants; T. Richardson, clerk. This company resigned on August 2. No. 9, Nathaniel Frothingham, *vice* Captain Blanchard; E. Johnson and T. D. Quincy, assistants; Thomas Frothingham clerk. No. 10, Ann street, opposite city scales, W. H. Brown, *vice* Captain Stoddard; J. Lovett, second assistant, resigned June 15; Oliver Torrey and Cyrus Bruce, assistants; Jarkin Ellingwood, clerk. No. 11, Franklin place, Charles Gaylord. *vice* C. F. Kupper, Jr., *vice* Captain Clark; Jef. Healey and F. Belser, assistants, *vice* John Dunn, Jr., and P. H. Kelley; T. C. Fernald, *vice* H. Hurst, clerk. No. 12, Franklin school-house, M. Hall, clerk; William Fernald, foreman of hose. No. 13, Leverett street, Charles Robbins, *vice* Captain Spooner; George Hammon and Francis Merriam, assistants; Henry Homer, clerk. No. 14, Water street, Jacob Fowler, *vice* Captain Smith; James Boyd and George H. Hewes, assistants; K. Whiting, clerk. No. 15, Ann street, E. Witherell and Jonathan Munroe, assistants, and J. Lothrop, clerk. No. 16, Purchase street, John Ball, *vice* Captain Jones; E. Dickerson and Joseph Jones, Jr., assistants; A. D. Smith, clerk. No. 18. Tremont street, W. R. Stacey, *vice* Captain French; Elisha Ellens and William Ulman, assistants; J. W. Frye, clerk. No. 20, J. Shelton, *vice* Captain Bridge; S. Robbins and L. Shelton, assistants, and C. S. Hunt, clerk. Ladder No. 1, Justen Cork, *vice* Captain Tillson; G. H. Cunningham and E. Southers, assistants. Ladder No. 2, organized the ensuing year, and located on High street. G. W. Wilkins, foreman; Christopher Foster, William R. Williams, and Benjamin Bourchstead, assistants; and George W. Stimpson, clerk. The truck carried five ladders, ten hooks, and ten axes. Ward companies: No. 4, A. Mitchell, *vice* Captain Lawrence; A. Jones and J. W. Lawrence, assistants. No. 6, Aaron Jaquith, *vice* Captain Luther; W. Studley, assistant; T. T. Roberts, clerk. No. 7, Charles Homer, *vice* Captain Daniels; H. Fairbanks and L. W. Sanderson, *vice* W. C. Eayes, assistants; E. A. Johnson, clerk. No. 8, N. J. Allen, assistant; Thomas Baker, clerk. No. 9, C. Foster and B. Burchstead, assistants, *vice* H. R. Coborn, clerk. No. 10, John Collamore, *vice* Captain Newell; J. Daniels and E. Foster, assistants; T. Cushing, clerk. No. 11, Dexter Dana, *vice* G. M. Smith, *vice* Captain Curtis; N. Wales, G. W. Talbott, assistants, *vice* G. Ellis, D. Dana; N. A. Thompson, clerk. No. 12, George Savage and J. L. Emmons, assistants; A. B. Batt, clerk.

A disastrous fire, from the extent of the loss of life, occurred May 4, when a bakehouse on Broad street was consumed, and five people burnt; a steamboat lying at Tileston's wharf was destroyed on June 30. Several smaller fires occurred, but they were of trifling importance.

The engineers for the year were Messrs. William Barnicoat, Thomas Haverland, B. Yeaton, B. M. Nevers, E. O. Hawes, C. Brinknall, Otis Munroe, N. P. Mann, James Barry, and John S. Tyler. Messrs. Brinknall and Barry declined, and John Green, Jr., Peter Dunbar, and William G. Eaton were appointed on March 26. Their report for the year, issued July 2, gave the number of fires from January 1 to June 30 as twenty-five; loss, $10,435, only $9,500 of which being held by insurance companies. Twenty-two false alarms were also reported.

The Legislature passed an act regarding depredation of engines and houses, which law was printed and distributed to the citizens on January 16. A list of injured firemen relieved by the city was sent to the committee on the same date.

A large quantity of gunpowder, stored at the armory in Faneuil Hall, was removed by the chief on February 16. On the 27th, at the request of Nathaniel Hammond and others, a suction-engine was placed on Leverett street, and numbered 13, and on April 13 the company had their engine named "Melville," after Mayor Thomas Melville. The basement, used as a storage for lumber, was put in order for the use of the company, and a suction-hose placed there. Engine company No. 5 got themselves in trouble over the insulting manner in which they used the chief while he was examining a member named Mr. Wood, who was charged with insubordination and disobeying rules, the result being the disbandment of the company on April 24. On the 30th a company was organized by Mr. Rufus R. Cook and thirty-four others, to whom the apparatus was given. The members of Engine No. 4 surrendered their rights as enginemen on July 16, on account of Assistant Engineer Yeaton entering a complaint against their foreman, which they believed was unjust. On December 8th Engine No. 8 had but a few members, and, in the absence of a majority of these, new members were elected, under whom the old members refused to serve. By order of the committee they were discharged. The list of men belonging to the department, with those of full age, minors, and exempt members on separate lists, was made out by the chief. A like roll was annually issued for a long period afterward.

Changes of officials for the year: Engine No. 1, James Quinn, *vice* Captain Farnham; James Hollis, W. H. Barnes, assistants, *vice* John Davis and Charles Rawson; A. M. Rice, *vice* Samuel P. Oliver, clerk. There were eighty-two members of this company. No. 2, Stephen Wells, *vice* Captain Hunt, who was elected clerk. No. 3, Salem street, A. S. Stevens, Jr., *vice* Captain Russell; George Wilkins and T. P. Foster, assistants; E. Glover, Jr., clerk. No. 5, Dock square, J. Carey, *vice* David Pulsifer, *vice* Captain Foster; R. R. Cook and Samuel Bird, assistants, *vice* James Tyler; Nathaniel Brown, *vice* Caleb Pratt, Jr., clerk. No. 6, Doane street, J. G. Sanderson, *vice* Captain Riley; Guy Bowker, assistant; A. Boyden, clerk. No. 7, William B. Swift, *vice* Captain Eaton; T. A. Williams and Oliver Jewett, assistants on engine; John Ayers and S. Andrews on hose; R. W. Haywood, clerk. This company declined the charge of the city hose on January 11. No. 8, Jacob Richardson, *vice* George W. Veasey, *vice* Captain Willet; J. Barrell and Glover Townsend, assistants, *vice* William Sears; James Blake, *vice* George H. Davis, *vice* I. R. Williams, clerk. No. 9, E. Johnson and W. B. Warren, assistants. No. 10, Union street, David C. Vaughan, *vice* Captain Brown; Robert Lord and S. F. Barrett, assistants; J. R. Farrington, clerk. No. 11, Franklin street. No. 12, J. A. Wheeler, *vice* Captain Green; J. C. Drew and M. Hall, Jr., assistants; A. Rand, clerk. No. 13, J. B. Osgood and W. Kennard, assistants. No. 14, John Tuttle, *vice* Captain Fowles; G. W. Hewes and D. Stone, assistants, *vice* J. A. Smith and John Wendell; M. B. Pierce, clerk. No. 15, C. S. Clark, *vice* Captain Barber; C. E. Gay, assistant. No. 16, Sargent Beck, *vice* Captain Ball, S. B. Merrill. No. 17, B. Lapham, *vice* Captain Mann; Augustus Develle and Fred Ballzar, assistants; J. Lapham, clerk. No. 18, Leo Matchett and M. Ollms, assistants. No. 20, one hundred and one members. Ladder No. 1, Messrs. Witherell and Woodbury, assistants; R. Abner, clerk. Ward companies: No. 1, J. R. Betts, assistant; Thomas Holbrook, clerk. No. 2, William Jameson, *vice* Captain Hall; I. Hall, T. H. Thompson, assistants; R. Restieaux, clerk. No. 4, A. Jones, *vice* Captain Lawrence; James A. Blake, J. A. Concay, assistants; I. O. Greenough, clerk. No. 5, E. Jones, *vice* Captain Hammond; Ezra Hawkes and J. A. Allen, assistants; E. Snow, clerk. No. 6, M. Warren and J. M. Doan, assistants. No. 7, H. P. Fairbanks, *vice* Captain Homer; Daniel Bates, assistant; J. H. Bufford, clerk. No. 8, F. W. Southark, *vice* Captain Allen; J. Blake, Jr., O. Briad, Jr., assistants, *vice* Theodore Baker; A. A. Lepeau, *vice* James Blake, clerk. No. 10, Josiah Daniells, *vice* Captain Collamore; Edward Haynes, assistant; J. R. Collamore, clerk. No. 12, Henry Curtis, *vice* Captain Savage; J. L. Emmons and George Savage, assistants; H. Davenport, *vice* A. B. Boss, clerk.

CHAPTER IV.

1832–1834.

SEVERAL heavy fires occurred during 1832. June 24, chemical works at South Boston; July 4, two large buildings on Commercial street; several buildings and four vessels were also burned at Spear's wharf, Fort Hill; July 7, five buildings and part of the Warren Hotel, in Friend street, were destroyed; November 21, a brick building on State street, the City Hall (Old State-House), and Post-Office were damaged by the fire to the extent of four thousand dollars; assistance was rendered by several out-of-town companies, all of whom were thanked by the City Council; December 27, the windmill on Wheeler's Point.

On April 30, 1832, the members of the department had built a suction-engine of the finest make that could be produced in this city, which they named the "Union," and sent to the citizens of Fayetteville, that city having, during the ensuing year, been almost entirely destroyed by fire. Messrs. Otis Munroe, William G. Eaton, and William Bridge constituted the committee representing the firemen.

The Board of Engineers for 1833 consisted of Messrs. William Barnicoat, Thomas Haviland, John S. Tyler, B. M. Nevens, Otis Munroe. John Hammond, N. P. Mann, Jr., David Tileston, Henry Smith, David Kimball, G. M. Smith, W. G. Hodgkinson, John Green, Peter Dunbar, William G. Eaton, and John Collamore, Jr. Their report of fires for the past year gave the number as fifty, the loss being $61,863. $24,078 being covered by insurance policies. Sixty false alarms were given.

Engine Co. 10 got in difficulty again, from neglect of duty and insubordination while at a fire on Bridge street, by which the company was disbanded, complaint being lodged by Assistant Engineer Kimball February 11th. On request of the members a hearing was given them, but the decision remained unchanged. Soon after their dismissal, the signal-lantern and parts of the engine were broken, spanners stolen, etc. A reward of $50 was offered on March 4, and increased to $500 on July 22, for the arrest of the offenders, who, growing bold at the concealment of their first offences, again entered the building and destroyed a quantity of personal property of the members; their loss being reimbursed by an order of the aldermen, issued September 3, to pay them $25. The parties who were conducting these depredations satisfied their revenge by setting fire to the building which was entirely destroyed. A reward of $1,000 was offered for the apprehension of the guilty, but they were never discovered.

The quarters of Engine 8 was used for a meeting-house, school-house, and watch-house; the result of this combination being constant discord and complaint from one room or another, proving, of course, a constant annoyance to the members of the engine company, who notified the engineers that unless they had a new house by July 4 they would give up the " machine." They changed their minds, however, and remained, as the city would not accede to their desires; but on November 18 the watchmen, who occupied a part of the building, entered complaint of the noise and disorderly conduct of the members attached to the engine. This had the desired effect, the company being dismissed on the 25th. A brick partition was then ordered to be built, to take the place of the one of plank.

Engine 4 was altered to a suction, and put in proper order on September 30, but had no company to man it. The fire of November 21, the year previous, in State street, in which the old State-House, or City Hall, as it was then called, was badly damaged, was made the subject of a sketch, which the chief submitted to the City Council as appropriate to have engraved and printed on a certificate to be given to all members who had served seven years in the department. An order was issued on March 25 to carry this plan into effect; the cost of engraving did not exceed $350. A fac-simile of this plate is still used for veterans' certificates.

A very pleasant occasion for the members was the presentation of a beautiful tortoise-shell fruit-stand by the engineers and firemen, at Concert Hall, on April 25, to Chief Engineer Amory.

On March 22 five buildings and a great quantity of lumber were burned on a wharf at the South end, this being the only fire of any note during the year.

The changes among the officers were: Engine 1, William C. Webster, clerk, *vice* Thomas Slocum. No. 2, Charles H. Porter, *vice* J. Pitts, *vice* Captain Wells; George Whitcomb and John Clark, assistants, *vice* H. Hutchinson, Jr., and William Stocker; T. P. James, clerk, *vice* William De Carteret. No. 3, J. L. Eaton, clerk, *vice* Johnson. No. 5, R. R. Cook, *vice* Captain Carey; George K. Damrill, assistant; William True, clerk. No. 6, W. B. Densmore and L. W. Dunbar, assistants; J. B. Nason, *vice* Dunbar, clerk. No. 7, James H. Blake, *vice* T. Andrews, foreman of hose; later, succeeded Captain Swift; J. E. Jones, H. C. Bird, *vice* Willet, assistants. No. 8, J. L. Drew, *vice* William Sears, *vice* Captain Richardson; S. W. Bird and James Robinson, assistants, *vice* G. H. Davis and Robert Ridgley; R. W. Hall, *vice* S. H. Hitchcock. No. 9, E. G. Richardson, *vice* Captain Johnson; T. D. Quincy and C. Ostrom, assistants; A. F. Dow, clerk. No. 10, January 7, Joseph Lovett, *vice* Captain Vaughan; Lyman Pray and G. W. Kibbie, assistants; Thomas Somes, clerk; disbanded February 11; March 20, company reorganized, T. P. Foster, foreman; succeeded by F. W. Southack, A. F. Waterman, and E. V. Glover, assistants; T. J. Cushing, clerk, *vice* J. M. Merrill, *vice* E. Parsons. July 1, Captain Southack resigns, James Blake, Jr., promoted; O. Bried and A. A. Lapham, assistants; A. Richardson, clerk. They voted on November 11 to have their house erected on the site on Merrimac street. No. 11, James Boyd, *vice* Captain Smith; P. H. Kelley and S. S. Raymond, *vice* James Bradlee, assistants; C. O. Boutelle, clerk. No. 12, F. Hooton and Charles C. White, assistants; G. W. Bird, clerk. No. 13, J. B. Osgood, *vice* Captain Robbins; F. B. Merriam, *vice* William Kennard; D. H. Hitchcock, *vice* J. C. Philbrick, *vice* E. Robbins; W. C. Webster, *vice* Henry Homer, clerk. No. 14, Nathaniel Wales, *vice* Captain Tuttle; T. D. Allen and Peter Trott, assistants, *vice* Messrs. Curtis and Cushing; Al. Bryant, clerk. No. 15, company resigned June 21. Edward Barnicoat, assistant; George Amerage, clerk. No. 16, T. P. Kendall and William A. Spear, assistants. No. 17, Augustus Dwelley, *vice* Captain Lapham; E. Ellins and B. Lapham, assistants; J. M. Mace, clerk. Nos. 18 and 19, George Matchett, *vice* Captain Stacey; A. Smith and J. Foster, assistants; W. W. Forsaith, clerk. Ladder No. 1, Joshua Jacobs, Jr., *vice* Captain Cork; John Chapin and Naph. Jepson, assistants; Charles Redding, clerk. Ladder 2, O. Trenton and N. W. Bates, assistants; J. Brisco, *vice* F. W. Stimpson, clerk. Ward companies: No. 2, John Davis, *vice* Captain Jameson. No. 3, D. W. Barnes, *vice* Capt. S. H. Barnes; A. Osgood, assistant; A. A. Rhodes, *vice* H. Beals, clerk. No. 4, C. G. King, *vice* H. H. Willard, *vice* Captain Jones; J. W. Clark and O. Rich, assistants; Caleb Marshall, *vice* G. W. Richardson, clerk. No. 6, Timothy Roberts and D. M. Bailey, assistants; J. A. Bullard, *vice* J. Roberts, *vice* John Colby, clerk. No. 7, William B. Parmenter and M. B. Spooner, assistants. No. 8, James Reck, Jr., *vice* Captain Southack; D. L. Davis, assistant; J. Cheever, Jr., clerk. No. 10, February 20, William Hardwick, *vice* Captain Daniels; A. Tolman and J. F. Green, assistants, *vice* J. McClellan and E. Haynes; Charles Dudley, clerk. August 24, James Tolman, foreman; Al. Whitcomb and Charles Andrews, assistants; F. Curtis, clerk. No. 12, J. L. Emmons, *vice* Captain Curtis; B. D. Baxter and J. P. Fairbanks, assistants; George Jackson, *vice* Henry Davenport, clerk.

The Board of Engineers appointed for 1834 were Messrs. David Tillston, William Willett, C. S. Clark, G. M. Smith, Asa Swallow, H. A. Wellington, B. M. Nevens, John Green, Jr., W. B. Swift, R. A. Newell, D. Kimball, J. G. Sanderson, Luther Russell, John Shelton. Thomas Motley declined serving, and Theodore Washburn was elected. A vote of thanks by the City Council was given to past Engineers Barnicoat, Munroe, Dunbar, Haverland, Hodgkinson, Tyler, Collamore, and Mann, for services in the department.

On a petition of the firemen from Ward 6, on January 2, a bell of more than three hundred pounds weight was placed on the English High School, and on petition of firemen of Ward 12, on June 16, a bell was also placed on the Franklin school-house. On the recommendation of the engineers, March 31, a committee was formed to frame a set of Rules and Regulations to govern the members of the department. A bill presented to the Legislature, entitled " An act for the protection of the city of Boston against fire," was amended and passed by the City Council on February 17.

Messrs. Hunting, Prescott, McLellan and Aldermen Wetmore and Leighton were constituted a committee, on April 14, to consider and report upon the expediency of adopting an act entitled " An act concerning the appointment of engineers," and such other matters relating to the act as they deemed expedient. They reported on the 31st, that it was disadvantageous to adopt the second and third section, whereby members who had done duty one year should be entitled to receive from the City Treasurer a sum equal to the poll-tax.

When General Jackson visited Boston, the firemen formed a double line across the Common, with extended ropes, between which the procession passed from West street to the State-House. They were in full-dress uniform, with the exception of No. 7, who by unanimous vote turned out in the battle-stained suits in which they had fought the last fire, and were described in one of the papers the next day as " looking like rat-catchers' dogs — rough and ready."

Quite a row occurred during the winter in Tremont Theatre over " Jim Crow " Rice, a minstrel who had, it was claimed, broken his engagement to appear at the National Theatre. For revenge, it is alleged, the manager of the latter gave one hundred tickets to truckmen to go to the former place of amusement and hiss Rice when he appeared at the benefit of H. J. Finn, who announced that he would sing a song addressed to the fire department. This, of course, had the desired effect of securing the attendance of the firemen, who desired to hear the song and see the fight which was sure to occur, for they would not allow their favorite to be interfered with. On the night of the benefit the theatre was crowded with men, not a lady being present. All went well until Rice made his appearance, when the hissing began. This was the " battle cry," when the whole audience sprang to their feet, and a fearful fight was almost instantly in progress, and continued until the " hissers " were expelled from the building. A number of people were seriously wounded during the *mêlée*, and several narrow escapes from death were reported.

Engines Nos. 7 and 14 having very large companies, and their quarters being near each other, were great rivals. When going to a fire No. 14 had the assistance of a horse which was called the " cream-colored charger," but the honors regarding the alacrity with which they arrived at a fire were about equally divided between both companies. The following lines, to the tune of " Jim Crow," appeared in one of the newspapers the day following a fishing excursion of the members of No. 7 : —

" Number Seven's gone a fishen'
For to catch de great sea snake,
And I guess as how if dey get him
Dey'll make him work de brake.

> " When dey gets him on de engine
> De team will be some larger,
> And I guess dey'll pass the Cataract
> Wid her cream-colored charger."

Engine Company 3 was dismissed, on May 5, for disorderly conduct while at a fire on May 1. The company attached to Engine 13 was, on December 1, also severely censured for going to a fire in Chelsea; a copy of the letter was sent to all the companies. In reply, a letter of apology was forwarded by Captain Quinn and his assistants. Capt. J. L. Barber, foreman of Engine 15, was suspended three months for violation of the rules. Engine 5 was surrendered by its company on November 17, on account of the refusal of the city to furnish them with a new engine. Thomas Baynell and others were appointed to take charge. Engine 11 was also given up on May 6 from the same cause. Engine Companies Nos. 17 and 18 voted, August 15, that, although they were on the best of terms with the Roxbury fire department, they would not attend fires with their engines in that section.

A return of the Ward Fire Companies was made, from which it was learned that some had several volunteers, which was against orders. The equipment of each of these companies consisted of a carriage, forty-eight large and three small buckets, one hundred feet of chain, one axe, one hammer, eleven fire-bags, ten torches, a cap and badge for each of the twenty-five members, twenty bed-keys, and a swivel ladder.

A muster of the entire department was held on the Common June 17th, at four o'clock in the afternoon, for the purpose of a general inspection and review by the Mayor and City Council. Mayor Theodore Lyman, Jr., issued orders on February 10 to the effect that the marshal, or one of his attendants, should attend every fire, where he was to inform the chief of his presence, and then assume the duties of a police-officer, wearing his badge of office while there, and give directions to the constables present. The constables were to proceed to the fire as soon as the alarm was given, and report to this officer, under whose direction they were " to use their best skill and power for the preservation of the public peace, the prevention of theft and dilapidation of property, and the removal of all suspected persons." For this service they were paid $1 for each attendance.

Changes in the service for 1834: Engine 1, J. Hollis, *vice* James Quinn, *vice* Captain Farnham; W. H. Fowl and Alexander Mair, *vice* W. Peck, assistants. No. 2, J. B. Munroe, *vice* Captain Porter; Jesse Farmer, J. Boynton, and F. W. A. Rankin, assistants; Charles Mears, *vice* Clark, clerk. No. 3, J. H. French, *vice* Capt. Washington Clapp, and Thomas Bagnell, assistant, *vice* E. Abbott, Samuel Pitts, and W. Storks; M. A. Johnson, *vice* R. Ripley, clerk. No. 4, W. E. Webster, *vice* E. V. Glover, Jr., *vice* Captain Pratt; William Marshall and R. May, assistants, *vice* W. C. Webster; M. A. Johnson, clerk. No. 5, G. R. Daniell, *vice* Captain Cook. No. 6, Luther W. Dunbar, *vice* W. B. Sanderson, *vice* Captain Cook;

Augustus Denton and J. S. Clafton, assistants; W. H. Otis, clerk, *vice* Nason. No. 7, T. A. Williams, *vice* Captain Blake; C. W. Dix and E. S. Andrews, assistants; R. W. Haywood, foreman of hose; N. R. Thomas, assistant; B. W. Fordick, clerk   No. 8, disbanded, and reorganized March 10, with George Briesler, foreman, and J. H. Foster and C. Messenger, assistants; C. H. Whitney, clerk. No. 9, A. F. Dow, *vice* Captain Richardson; T. P. Emms, H. Adams, assistants; S. H. Bean, clerk, *vice* C. B. Kingman. No. 10, B. H. Hammatt; *vice* Theodore P. Foster, *vice* Captain Blake; William Orcutt, William Waterhouse, and A. L. Frye, assistants, *vice* J. H. White; E. Parkson, Jr., clerk, *vice* C. E. Swasey. No. 11, C. F. Kupper and Henry Noyes, *vice* J. J. Eaton, assistant; Edward Wigglesworth, clerk. No. 12, G. W. Bird, *vice* Theodore C. Allen, *vice* Captain Wheeler; William Jewett, assistant; William B. Hunting, clerk. No. 13, James Quinn, *vice* Captain Osgood; William Watt, J. L. Drew, assistants, *vice* F. C. Putnam; E. Noyes, clerk. No. 14, July 7, John Ball was appointed foreman, *vice* Captain Wales, with Thomas Fernald and Thomas Stebbins, assistants, and A. R. May, clerk, for a period of one month, when George A. Curtis assumed command, with J. Ball and C. R. Banks as assistants, and A. J. Lapenn, clerk. Ball was soon after placed in charge; the company at the same time voted that the name of the company be thereafter known as "Old Cataract 14." No. 15, James L. Barber, *vice* Captain C. S. Clark; Charles H. Stearns and Benjamin Gowan, assistants; E. W. Lothrop, clerk. No. 16, G. W. Wilkins, *vice* Captain Bridge; E. L. Snow and A. D. Thayer, assistants; T. P. Kendall, clerk. No. 17, Thomas B. Warren, *vice* A. Ellms, *vice* Captain Dwelley; J. C. Crosby and J. Hammond, assistants; Josiah Dunhan, *vice* J. D. Thayer, clerk, *vice* W. V. Bail. Nos. 18 and 19 disbanded on January 20, and reëstablished under the following officers: Captain, George Malcheet; John Foster, Allen Whitman, and C. S. Russett, assistants; C. D. Chamberlain, clerk. No. 20, G. W. Prentice, *vice* Captain Shelton; J. R. Carleton and Henry F. Demster, assistants; C. S. Hunt, clerk. Ladder No. 1, J. F. Holland, clerk. Ladder No. 2, Nathaniel L. Prince, *vice* Captain Wilkins; N. N. Bates and James Mahoney, assistants; Timothy Carter, Jr. clerk. Twenty-one members resigned on August 13. Ward companies: No. 1, A. P. Young, *vice* Captain Nurse; T. C. Bacon and E. F. Fay, assistants. No. 2, Samuel Prince, *vice* Captain Davis; S. Passet, Jr., and D. W. Hill, assistants; R. Resticeaux, clerk. No. 3, George Wright, *vice* Captain Barnes; Boza Lincoln and Henry Barry, assistants; G. P. Richardson, clerk. No. 5, Charles Holbrook, *vice* Captain Jones; E. F. Hall and E. K. Lyford, assistants; E. A. Hall, clerk. No. 6, G. L. Stearns and G. Hall, assistants; O. Holman, clerk. No. 7, W. B. Spooner, *vice* Captain Fairbanks; W. C. Eayers, assistants; C. B. Hutchinson, clerk. No. 8, Joseph Lines and H. H. Goff, assistants; D. L. Davis, *vice* R. J. Brown, clerk. This company was given the command of Engine No. 11 until a company could be organized. No. 10, A.

Whitcomb, *vice* Captain Tolman ; F. Curtis and Charles Trumball, assistants, *vice* C. E. Andrews, F. Curtis, clerks. No. 11, F. D. Allen, *vice* Captain Dana ; N. A. Thompson and W. A. Barrister, assistants ; J. M. Thompson, clerk. No. 12, B. D. Baxter, *vice* Captain Emmons ; J. L. Gorham, assistant.

Mayor Lyman communicated to the chief, on May 19, his desire that the reservoirs be examined, and, when necessary, filled, the city paying the expenses. Twenty-nine additional reservoirs were constructed during the year, at the following locations : Merrimac, corner of Gouch and Lancaster streets ; Blossom, corner of McLean and Allen streets ; Thatcher street, near the pump ; Broad, near the corner of State street ; Atkinson, near High street ; Leverett, corner of Spring street ; Mt. Vernon street, near Louisburg square, opposite Willow street ; Boylston, corner of Carver street ; Dock square, between Elm and Ann streets ; Blackstone, near the corner of Charlestown and Cross streets ; Congress, between Water and Milk streets ; Essex, corner of Short street ; Tremont, corner of passageway to Mason street ; Somerset street, near Somerset place ; Cambridge, corner of Lynde street ; Salem, corner of Richmond street ; Chestnut, corner of Walnut street ; Ann, corner of Cross street ; Front, between Kneeland and Harvard streets ; Tremont, corner of Hollis street ; Dedham, half-way between Washington and Tremont streets ; Broad street, midway between Piper's wharf and Free Bridge ; Washington, corner of Northampton street ; South Boston, near the school-house, and Engine-house 17 ; Washington, near Newton street ; East Boston ; and two places fixed at the land between Canal and Haverhill streets, — one near Causeway and one near Travers street.

No event of similar character ever transpired in this country which has been the theme of so much dissension and general conversation as the destruction of the Ursuline Convent, in the Charlestown district, August 11, 1834. The facts of the case, as far as we are able to learn, are as follows : About two months previous to its destruction, rumors were afloat that several persons were confined in the nunnery against their will ; that their friends were denied the privilege of visiting, or even seeing them ; and that they were subjected to tortures of an outrageous character, as a punishment for their stubbornness and disobedience. Rumors were in circulation that one of the nuns had suddenly disappeared in a most mysterious manner ; that the interior arrangement of the convent was conducted in a manner not strictly in accordance with the moral sense of the community. Now, all these things, as is well known, only tended to create a more bitter and hostile feeling in the minds of the citizens of Charlestown against that institution ; story after story was circulated in regard to transactions which were reported as having transpired in the convent. The excitement ran very high at this time, yet nothing was done by those who had control of the convent to allay it in the slightest degree.

About a month before the burning of the building, a nun, by the name of

Harrison, made her escape from the convent at 12 o'clock, noon, and proceeded immediately to a friend's house in Cambridge. When the bishop learned of this fact, he proceeded to the house, accompanied by her brother, and had an interview, after which she consented to return, on the promise that she should be released with honor in two or three weeks. By some means, it was alleged, this promise was not kept; and when these facts came to the knowledge of the citizens of Charlestown, they had handbills of the most exciting character posted up throughout the vicinity, calling a meeting of the citizens to take into consideration the best course to be pursued in relation to the matter. So great was the excitement that the selectmen of the town, in order to preserve order and allay all trouble, proceeded to the nunnery for the purpose of investigating the truth of the matter. On ringing the bell, they were asked their business, and, when they stated their errand, were told that, if they attempted to enter within the convent, she (the lady superior) would give the alarm, and have the bishop notified, who would bring twenty thousand Irishmen, to pull their houses down over their heads. Two other visits were paid by the same gentlemen, but with the same result. They finally had an interview with the bishop, and arrangements were made for them to visit the nunnery on Monday, the 11th of August.

In the mean time, the excitement had been increased by flaring handbills, which had been posted in every direction, calling upon the citizens to assemble at the square in Charlestown, and further declaring that the selectmen would not be allowed to enter the nunnery; that Miss Harrison would not be set at liberty; and it was time the citizens should take the matter into their own hands, etc. The time appointed for the selectmen's visit to the convent was at three o'clock in the afternoon, from which time they were occupied within the convent until after six o'clock. They had a long conversation with the lady superior and Miss Harrison. When they retired it was too late to issue circulars containing full particulars of the result of this interview, giving such account of their visit as would allay the excitement then existing in the minds of the public.

About eleven o'clock on Monday night a large fire was made by burning several tar barrels upon the highest point of a hill in the vicinity of the building. Soon after, a party of from fifty to one hundred men, disguised with masks and fantastic dresses and painted faces, assembled in front of the building, and, after informing the inmates of the object of their visit, they gave them half an hour to pack up their baggage and effects and leave the convent, after which they retired a short distance from the place, to consult further with one another as to the best course to pursue in order to accomplish their purpose. When the time allowed the nuns to enable them to vacate had expired, and seeing no appearance of their intention to comply with the request, they commenced an assault upon the building. Some of the nuns were placed in carriages and taken to such place as they desired, some who were badly frightened retreated, taking with them some of the children. They left by the rear door, passing through the garden.

The distress and terror of the scenes were heightened by the solicitude of the nuns for one of their number who was confined to her bed by a disease from which she was not expected to recover. The assailants in the mean time had forced open the doors and windows of the edifice, and removed most of the furniture, among which were three pianos, a harp, and other musical instruments, into the garden, where they were destroyed. At about half-past twelve o'clock the building was set on fire in the second story of the western wing, and in a few hours it was entirely destroyed. The chapel, the bishop's lodge, the stable, and the old nunnery, a large wooden building situated a short distance from the convent, were set on fire and burnt in a short time. The work of destruction continued until daylight, when the mob dispersed, and all that remained of the famous Ursuline Convent was the blackened walls and smouldering ruins.

The burning of the main building, which was eighty feet long and four stories high, occupied about two hours. Among the other buildings were a farmhouse and a cottage. The inmates of the convent consisted of the lady superior, six nuns, three female attendants, and from fifty to sixty children who had been placed there for instruction, by their friends, many of whom were Protestants.

After the main building had been fired, an alarm of fire was given, and the firemen, with their engines, from Boston, Cambridge, Chelsea, and other near limits, repaired at once to the scene, but were prevented from throwing water on the flames.

A meeting of the citizens of Boston, by notification of the Mayor, was held on Tuesday following, at one o'clock, at Faneuil Hall. The hall was crowded to suffocation. After a brief address by His Honor, stating the object of the meeting, Josiah Quincy, Jr., Hon. H. G. Otis, and George Bond, Esq., addressed the meeting. After several speeches, the following resolutions were offered by Colonel Quincy, and adopted : —

Resolved, That, in the opinion of the citizens of Boston, the late attack on the Ursuline Convent in Charlestown, occupied only by defenceless females, was a base and cowardly act, for which the perpetrators deserve the contempt and detestation of the community.

Resolved, That the destruction of property, and danger of life caused thereby, call loudly on all good citizens to express, individually and collectively, the abhorrence they feel of this high-handed violation of the laws.

Resolved, That we, the Protestant citizens of Boston, do pledge ourselves, collectively and individually, to unite with our Catholic brethren in protecting their persons, their property, and their civil and religious rights.

Resolved, That the Mayor and Aldermen be requested to take all measures consistent with law to carry the foregoing resolutions into effect; and as citizens we tender our personal services to support the laws, under the direction of the city authorities.

Resolved, That the Mayor be requested to nominate a committee from the citizens at large, to investigate the proceedings of last night, and to adopt every suitable mode to bring the authors and abettors of this outrage to justice.

The following committee was nominated by the Mayor : —
H. G. Otis, J. D. Williams, James Austin, Henry Lee, James Clark, Cyrus Alger, John Henshaw, F. J. Oliver, Mark Healey, C. G. Loring, C. G. Green, Isaac Harris, T. H. Perkins, John Raynor, Henry Gassett, D. D. Broadhead, Noah Brooks, H. F. Baker, Z. Cook, Jr., George Darracott, Samuel Hubbard, Henry Farnham, B. F. Hallett, J. K. Simpson, John Cotton, Benjamin Rich, William Sturgis, and Charles P. Curtis.

On motion of Mr. George Bond, the committee of twenty-eight were requested to consider the expediency of providing funds to repair the damage done to the convent and other buildings.

On motion of John C. Park, Esq., it was

Resolved, That the Mayor be authorized and requested to offer a very liberal reward to any individual who, in case of further excesses, will arrest and bring to punishment any leader in such outrages.

THEODORE LYMAN, Jr., *Chairman.*
ZEBEDEE COOK, Jr., *Secretary.*

There appeared in the papers of the next morning a card from the selectmen of Charlestown, giving an account of their visit to the nunnery, and their interview.

CHAPTER V.

1835–1842.

THE department was thrown into a state of dissension during 1835, more so than ever since the reorganization. This condition was brought around by the following resolutions, passed by a committee of the Common Council : —

Resolved, That the salary now allowed and paid to the chief engineer be discontinued after the acceptance of the resignation of the present incumbent by the Board of Aldermen.

Resolved, That there be appointed a superintendent of the fire apparatus, whose duty it shall be to keep all the books, collect all bills, and perform all duties required of him by the engineers, who shall receive for his service such compensation as may be appointed by the City Council.

This measure was the result of the dissatisfaction of associated engineers, who were not willing to serve gratuitously under a paid superior. clothed with absolute power in all matters relating to the department. leaving no voice in anything relating to the service to his associates. who had always to abide by his decision. Chief Amory resigned on January 23, and was succeeded on the 26th by William II. Tileston. The aim of the Board of Engineers was to have the above resolutions go into effect at once, but a committee on the department was chosen from the City Council to thoroughly investigate the matter, after doing which they reported. on May 4, to the effect that the system ought not to be changed. that it was the choice of the citizens, and had given every satisfaction. This report led to a lengthy discussion by the engineers. who claimed it an injustice to their office to have a salaried officer, with the same powers as possessed by the former chiefs. placed at their head ; but despite their hard struggle for the cause they failed. and on February 2 the following assistant engineers were appointed : John Hammond. Henry Smith, David Kimball, George M. Smith. W. G. Eaton, Asa Swallow. James G. Sanderson. R. A. Newell, C. S. Clark, John Shelton. T. Hasburn. Henry Curtis, Rufus R. Cook, Thomas B. Warren, William Eaton, and Edward Wigglesworth.

At a meeting of the officers of the department, held May 29, it was resolved that they would support the Board of Engineers at all times in the discharge of their duty, and that their denunciation of the system was " an open and manly exposition of facts. and that the principles therein set forth meet with an unqualified approval." They also severely condemned the conduct of " certain members of Engine Company 7. in their contemptible effort to prostitute the hard-earned fame" of Assistant Engineer William G. Eaton, who. on August 24, sent in his resignation, solely on account of the unjust treatment he had received. Engine Company 8 surrendered their engine on August 3, on account of the severity of the ordinance, which, they claimed, was only fit for slaves, not for freemen who were giving their services to the city for such a slight recompense as they received. Another reason was the want of a suitable building.

An engine was ordered to be placed at East Boston on January 19, and numbered 11, and Guy C. Haynes given the command. A new engine was ordered on May 18 for Engine 14, the old one being condemned; and a new suction-engine was also ordered, to take the place of No. 5. June 8, two new suction-engines were ordered, to take the places of New York, No. 7, and Boston, No. 15. On the arrival of Engine No. 7, on September 28, the company was allowed to change the name from New York to Tiger, No. 7. Almost all the members of No. 14 resigned, and those who remained being charged with insubordination. a new company was reorganized on September 21st, under the command of Ephraim L. Snow. The name was changed, on October 5th, from old Cataract Engine No. 14 to Lion Engine No. 14. Engine Company No. 17 was also in difficulty, for disobedience of orders. It was settled, however, on December 21, by the suspension of the second officer. Ladder Company 2 petitioned for a new building on October 17, they complaining that they should be allowed as good accommodations as Ladder 1. which company had just been furnished with a handsome, new ladder-house. A contract was made with Hunneman & Co. for an engine for No. 18, to be ready in January, 1837. at a cost of $850.

A committee from the engineers being formed to procure coats for that body to wear while at fires, made a contract with the Boston and India Rubber Company, whereby each member of the board was furnished with a coat highly recommended by the corporation as impervious to water; but on trial they were found to be of no value, and were, according to the agreement, returned. Coats of pilot-cloth were then made, which proved entirely satisfactory, the cost being $232.

The schooner "Sarah," lying at a certain wharf in this city, was, on Saturday, August 22, 1835, blown to atoms. The cause of the explosion was a mystery, and created quite a public discussion, some claiming that it was the saltpetre with which the vessel was loaded, while others claimed that this was an impossibility, as that article in its virgin state could not explode, and that the explosion was caused by gunpowder. The Board of Engineers held an investigation, and reported, September 1, that their opinion was strongly in favor of the gunpowder theory, as they could find no authority, or even a single instance, where saltpetre in the state in which it was carried on board the schooner could explode.

A fire of considerable magnitude occurred on May 19. the ensuing year. It originated in the carpenter-shop of Messrs. Stetson & Smith, on Blackstone street. The flames extended to several adjoining shops, and a stable occupied by a Mr. Simmons, all of which, with their contents, were consumed. All the buildings between Blackstone, Cross, and Pond streets were entirely destroyed. On the opposite side of Pond street, the Massachusetts Hotel and several other buildings were badly damaged, and the livery-stable of Mr. Davis was laid in ashes. All the buildings on the west side of Salem street, from Cross to Hanover streets, with but one exception were consumed, and many other buildings badly damaged. Loss, $70,000. At this fire, engines from Chelsea, Charlestown, Cambridge, Roxbury, and other neighboring towns rendered assistance, for which they were thanked by the City Council. Engine 13 drafted and played on the fire through eleven hundred and fifty feet of hose.

On the recommendation of Mayor Lyman, February 14th, the order passed by the Board of Engineers at the time of the burning of the convent, the year previous, forbidding any of the apparatus of this department from leaving the city, was abrogated until a general and uniform agreement was made. Assistant Engineer John Hammond was chosen chief *pro tem.* on the resignation of Chief Tileston.

Changes of officers for 1835: Engine 1, M. A. Straw, *vice* Captain Hollis; Thomas Hammond, Jr., and A. Mair, assistants; W. H. Foule, *vice* J. R. Farrington, *vice* I. B. Smith, clerk. No. 2, Samuel Prince, *vice* Captain Munroe; Samuel Bassett, Jr., and D. W. Hill, assistants, *vice* T. C. Gould, R. Resticeaux, Jr., *vice* David Marden, Jr., clerk. No. 3, A. H. Campbell, *vice* Captain French; J. M. Merrill and T. Bagnell, Jr., assistants; S. Punchard, clerk. No. 4, W. C. Webster, *vice* Captain Glover; William Morse and R. S. May. assistants; S. P. Greenwood, clerk. No. 5, E. J. Titcomb, *vice* John White, Jr., *vice* Captain Damrill; C. A. Somerby and A. R. May, assistants, *vice* John Borrowscale, A. H. Fletcher, *vice* A. S. Lewis, clerk. No. 7, Pelham W. Haywood, *vice* Captain Williams; J. H. Colburn, clerk. No. 8, H. H. Drayton, *vice* Captain Briesler; F. Richards and William Humphrey, assistants; J. A. Drayton, clerk. No. 9, J. B. Anderson and A. H. Bean, assistants; B. W. Hall, clerk. No. 10, J. A. Norris, *vice* Captain Hammatt; S. P. Gorham and J. H. White, assistants, *vice* Henry Ide; C. E. Swasey, clerk. No. 11, at East Boston, T. C. Allen, *vice* Captain Boyd; F. A. Bailey and D. French, assistants; A. Benson, clerk. No. 13, Joseph Southark and J. P. Clark, assistants; W. H. Peirce, clerk. No. 14, E. L. Snow, *vice* Captain Ball; Thomas H. Stebbins and W. W. Classen, assistants; G. W. Billings, clerk. No. 16, A. Walcott, and W. Lewis, assistant; T. P. Kendall, clerk. No. 17, George Page, *vice* Captain Warren; J. C. Crosby and J. Young, assistants; W. B. Brooks, clerk. No. 18, and 19, J. L. Roberts, *vice* Captain Matchett; Harlow Harden, Jr., and C. P. Gould, assistants; A. S. Davis, clerk. No. 20, disbanded on May 6, organized May 22. Joseph Carlton, *vice* Captain Prentice; J. G. Hardy and G. W. Prentice, assistants; Joel Powers, clerk. Ladder 1, L.

V. R. Moore, *vice* Captain Jacobs; A. Stone and Reuben Ridler, assistants; T. P. Carvers, clerk. Ladder 2, James N. Mooney, *vice* Captain Prince; Edward Cassidy, G. W. Marsh, assistants. Ward companies: No. 3, L. L. Bates, clerk. No. 6, J. Lincoln, clerk. No. 7, W. C. Eayers, *vice* Captain Spooner; W. B. Parmenter, assistant; A. Watkins, Jr., clerk. No. 10 changed their name, on January 27, to the Amory Fire Company, No. 10, in honor of ex-Chief Amory. The company disbanded on June 19. T. J. Hobbs, assistant, A. L. Denison, clerk. No. 12, J. P. Fairbanks and J. Drew, assistants; J. L. Fairbanks, clerk. Company resigned June 19. The names of these companies were Brooks 1, Quincy 4, Melville 5, Otis 6, Tremont 7, Franklin 8, Amory 10, Boylston 11, and Vesuvius 12. Those of numbers 2, 3, and 9 we could not learn.

Five hundred dollars additional were added to the annual appropriation of the city to the charitable association on February 8, 1836, after the expiration of which time $1,000 were annually given it. Mr. Hammond resigned his office as acting chief of the department, and Mr. William Barnicoat was nominated chief on February 15, and on the 29th the following gentlemen were appointed engineers: Messrs. Henry Smith, James Sanderson, Richard A. Newell, Charles S. Clark, John Shelton, Theodore Washburn, Thomas B. Warren, James Barry, John Green, Henry Towle, Peter C. Jones, T. A. Williams, G. W. Wilkins, and Lewis Dennis. The only names of firemen that we can trace during the years 1836–37 are those on Engine No. 7. Thomas Cassidy succeeded Captain Heywood during 1836, and Jonathan Hayes was appointed to that position during 1837.

Seven thousand dollars were ordered to be paid for the exclusive use of engine-houses, which sum was withdrawn from the appropriation for the purchase of land for one school-house and the erection of two school-houses at the South End. A new engine and house were ordered, on April 25, for No. 3, while No. 9 was suspended, on December 5, for disorderly conduct. Engine-house 15, on Commercial street, was removed back to the line of the street, September 19. The house of Ladder 2 was taken down January 18, and the apparatus removed and stored in a building on Tremont street, near the Johnson school. Otis Munroe and others were given charge of Engine No. 1, which was without a company for some time.

All the apparatus in the service was inspected on September 29 and 30, resulting in the following report: Engines Nos. 1, 3, 5, 6, 7, 10, 13, 14, 15, 16, 17, and 20 were in good condition; 12 was commanded by a company of volunteers; 2 undergoing repairs, but had a full company; 4, at West Boston bridge, was removed to that house and a company formed; No. 8, on Tremont, near the junction of Washington street, in good repair, but without a company for a long time,—one was soon to be organized; No. 9 being repaired, also No. 11, at East Boston; No. 18 was complained of as being too heavy and unmanageable for the crowded and paved streets, was not used, and was for sale; an ordinary engine was temporarily used in its place, but a new engine was already ordered.   Expenses for the year: Engine-houses, $8,000; reservoirs, $10,000; repairs of houses and other expenses, $15,000.   Reservoirs filled, one each on Thatcher street and Louisburg square, the one at the corner of State and Broad streets being filled by the tide at every flood;   the whole number of reservoirs in the city being thirty-nine.   The department consisted of one hose company, with four carriages, and one thousand and six hundred feet of hose, the house being in Franklin place, — here, also, were from four to six hundred feet of extra hose, to be attached to each of the several engines;   nineteen engines, three hook-and-ladder carriages, with ladders and hooks, the third being organized during the year;   twenty-three hose-carriages, nine thousand and four hundred feet of hose, five hundred and nine feet of suction-hose;   a chief engineer, thirteen assistant engineers, a clerk to the chief engineer, and one thousand three hundred and thirty-seven firemen.

Besides several minor fires, slight fires were extinguished in the Brattle-street Church and Grace Church.

A number of new engine-houses were ordered during 1837.   House No. 8 was built on a lot in the rear of Johnson school, on Tremont street, on February 10; and April 3d, the company changed the name from " Cumberland " to " Tremont."   No. 1 was ordered to be sold, on April 17, and a new engine built at a cost of $750.   No. 12 was granted a new house on the southerly portion of land connected with the Franklin school-house. Engine No. 2 was repaired and placed at South Boston, May 22.   June 12, No. 4 was allowed new quarters.   No. 14 was not put in commission, as it was thought unnecessary.   To carry out the expenses incurred by these contracts, $3,500 were taken, on February 13, from the appropriation for repairs to the House of Correction.   On March 30 $3,000 additional were appropriated by the city, and on September 18 $25,000 were ordered to be borrowed.

Additional rules and regulations were made for the government of the department during the year; one of which was a list of neighboring towns to which the engines of Boston were allowed to render service.   Dorchester was a disputed territory, but was embraced in the list after a considerable discussion.   On October 16 a sum equal to the poll-tax was ordered to be paid each member who served for the period of one year.

On the petition of Messrs. Downer, Austin, & Co., Engine 16 was returned, on April 17, to its former stand on Fort Hill, and a company organized. An alarm-bell was placed on the engine-house, No. 11, at East Boston, February 27, and the Common Council ordered, on July 29, the establishment of a corporation yard for the repairing of engines, etc.

Engineers appointed for 1837 were: Henry Smith, J. G. Sanderson, R. A. Newell, C. S. Clark, J. Shelton, T. Washburn, T. B. Warren, J. Green, H. Towle, P. G. Jones, T. A. Williams, and G. W. Wilkins.   The only engine company to get into trouble during the year was No. 7, — it being disbanded on July 17 for disobeying the rules, and passing resolutions to persevere in so doing.

The story of the famous riot that occurred on Broad street and vicinity, Sunday afternoon, June 10, 1837, is one quite difficult to tell, as there are so many conflicting statements. From the testimonies given at the trial of those arrested as principals in the affair we glean the following: The company attached to Engine 20 had just housed their apparatus, after returning from a fire in Roxbury, and about twelve members were in the house. One of them, George Fay, went to purchase a cigar, and on his return, with it in his mouth, he passed down Broad to the foot of East street, where an Irish funeral procession was being formed. The participants in the procession were on both sides of the street, and covered the sidewalk. Fay tried to pass on the curb-stone, and by accident jostled some one, who immediately shoved him into the street, with the remark that " he had no business on the street," following it up with an effort to strike him. Fay got up and struck back. Several witnesses of the scene, standing on East street, came to help him, and were soon joined by the members of the engine. Mr. Miller, the third officer, went out and called his men back to the house, which order they immediately obeyed, but were followed up by their enemies, and several members badly beaten. He ordered out the engine. and the bell to be rung for fire, and then went for help. The funeral procession had formed, and proceeded down Broad street. Engine company 9, on their way to what they supposed, from the alarm, to be a fire, turning the foot of Summer street with their usual rush, came suddenly upon the rear of the procession, but did not touch them ; but no sooner had the mourners beheld the engine company than they left the ranks and immediately repaired to the wood-pile in the vicinity, and then the row began in earnest, at the head of J. Robinson's wharf. Engine companies 6 and 14, who arrived, were attacked by the increased force of Irishmen, and the firemen were badly beaten, and driven from their engines. They, however. quickly rallied, and, with additional numbers, drove their foes down Broad street.

A rush was made by the Irishmen to obtain possession of Purchase street, and attack the enginemen by showering down stones, etc., upon them from the more elevated position. But they were pressed upon and driven back by their opponents, who rushed up from the intervening streets and alleys, at manifest disadvantage, and, regardless of life and limb, drove them back step by step, sometimes retreating when their foes rallied or their ammunition (?) was expended, but again gaining their ground until the latter were driven into Broad street, beyond the corner of Purchase street. A house in Purchase street, near Gibb's lane, where several of their opponents had taken refuge and from where some missiles were thrown, was attacked and its windows broken ; but the principal work of destruction was carried on near the junction of this street with Broad street and the immediate vicinity.

Assistant Engineer Wilkins, being in his store, saw the head of the procession proceeding towards old Broad street, and supposed from the dust raised that the fire was near by. When he came to where the contending parties were advancing upon each other, he held up his engineer's badge, and called to the firemen to "hold on," at the same time directed the Irishmen to "keep back." Both parties then stopped. But the Irishmen again returned to the charge with shouts and yells, and the firemen were driven back. When Engineer Wilkins first arrived on the scene, he did not know the extent of the difficulty, and observed to the enginemen that their antagonists would not meddle with them, and directed them to proceed down Broad street toward State street, then to separate, and each company to take their engine home. They proceeded on in obedience to this order ; No. 6 being ahead, was immediately attacked, the men were driven from the ropes, the bell broken, and other parts of the engine injured, and the apparatus itself remained in the hands of the assailants six or seven minutes.

A gang of stout boys and loafers, who had followed the firemen at such distance that they might be protected from the dangers, and at the same time participate in the mischief of the affray, attacked the houses of the Irish in the rear of the scene of the combat, tearing to pieces and destroying everything wantonly and recklessly. The houses were sacked, their contents thrown into the streets, and everything demolished as speedily as possible. Feather-beds were ripped open, and their contents thrown out of the windows ; the fine feathers, wafted by the wind, being blown to a considerable distance. Money was stolen, stores broken open and contents destroyed and appropriated, and the most wanton spite displayed in all these depredations ; and what makes these acts more shameful was, that most of those who had suffered the loss of their little worldly goods were entirely ignorant of the cause of their suffering, taking no part whatever in the riot. A number of Irishmen who had concealed themselves in the cellars were dragged out and severely beaten with clubs and sticks. In fact, everything was in the hands of the mob. The only redeeming spirit shown by these miscreants was their conduct towards the women and children. who were let out unmolested, no one offering them harm or insult.

The Mayor was soon on the ground, and adopted, as soon as possible, measures to assemble the militia. The volunteer corps were ordered to assemble at Faneuil Hall; but the members were so dispersed — a large portion of them spending the day in neighboring towns — that it was not until six o'clock that a sufficient force could be mustered, when a strong detachment of infantry, led by the Lancers, under General Davis. marched into Broad street ; and the Irish party having by this time been driven into their houses, and about fifty being lodged in jail, the violence of the riot was exhausted. The street was soon cleared of all who did not reside there, and the military took charge by forming a cordon by posting guards at the various avenues. The citizens to the number of about ten thousand, who had been attracted by the flying reports, gradually dispersed, and quietness once more prevailed. The military continued on duty all night. The Mayor took the precaution to place a guard at every church in the city, to prevent any false alarm that might arise during the night, with a tendency to renew the affray. The Washington Light Infantry, the Boston Light Infantry, the Rifle Rangers, the New England Guards, the City Guards, the Lafayette Guards, the Montgomery Guards, the Winslow Blues, the Mechanics' Riflemen, and the Independent Fusiliers were on duty all night, and the City Guards were left in charge of Faneuil Hall the next morning. Fortunately no person was killed; but the number of wounded will never be known. Mr. Charles Sears, formerly captain of Ladder Company 2, was probably the most severe, he being knocked down on the wharf and surrounded by eight or ten of the Irish party, and almost beaten to death, after which he was about to be thrown overboard, but one of their number prevented the bloodshed. Mr. Barnes, of Engine 1, and Mr. John Russell, assistant foreman of Engine 10, were badly injured; also Capt. J. C. Tallent, of the North Watch.

The year was also remarkable for the number of attempts at incendiarism. On February 14 the Franklin Hemp and Flax Factory was destroyed. During April several efforts were made to fire the old court-house. On Saturday, June 10, the spire of the Hollis-street church was struck by lightning, the flames appearing in the pinnacle of the spire, fifty or sixty feet above the highest point at which there was any access on the outside, and far above the reach of the inside, where there was no communication with the spire after passing the bell-tower. The efforts of the firemen to get water on the blaze was fruitless, although very daring attempts were made. Ex-Captain Sears, of Ladder 2, placed a ladder on the spire above the balcony and cut at the vane; the hosemen were about to ascend when the chief ordered them down, as he saw that the top of the spire. with the vane and ball, and an iron shaft, fifteen feet long, was about to fall; they had just got to a place of safety when it came down with a crash. After that the firemen were enabled to put out the fire. June 9, the Needham Hat Factory was burnt. A shed attached to a dwelling at 48 Elliot street was set fire, on the 8th and 9th. Saturday, 10th, a number of alarms were given for incendiaries, among them being an attempt on the Park-street church, the fire being ignited in one of the pews. Two stables located at Roxbury were set on fire the next day. July 3, an endeavor was made to burn the State-House.

The orders and by-laws issued by the city from time to time were, on July 29, the ensuing year, under the administration of Mayor Samuel A. Eliot, combined under one ordinance, entitled " An act for preventing and extinguishing fires and establishing a fire department." On October 23 " twenty-seven rules and regulations for the Hose, Hook-and-Ladder, and other companies attached to the Boston Fire Department" were established. Few of these orders were entirely new to the members (see volume 1838 to 1849 of the Engineer's Report for unabridged entries). In them we find that no person not a citizen of the United States could be admitted a member of the department; substitutes were to be provided by any member absent from the city forty-eight hours. or who was sick. No person was to be engaged in the department for a shorter period than six months; if he leave before this time he was to forfeit all compensation due him.

The following engines were permitted to leave the city when a fire occurred out of town: Nos. 3 and 16, to Charlestown; No. 15, to Chelsea; 13 and 16, to Cambridge; 12 and 8, to Roxbury; and 20 and 17, to Dorchester. No other company, or hose or hook-and-ladder company, was to leave on any consideration, unless ordered by the engineer. Engine companies were not allowed to run races on returning from fires, and the use of rattles, horns, and all unnecessary noises, and the smoking of pipes or cigars, were strictly forbidden. Members were responsible for their badges or any other article; and if lost, the cost was deducted from their salary.

The engines not in use during 1838 were Nos. 1, 4, old 10. Tiger 7, and Boston 15. The first three were stored under the Hancock school-house, the next in its quarters at Water street, while Nos. 7 and 15 were in the old Franklin school-house, on Common street. Constant attention was paid to these engines, so as to render them ready for use at any moment. No. 2 was at South Boston, in charge of a company organized for that part of the city only. No. 16, which took the former company's name, was changed on January 8 from Torrent to Eliot. and was in charge of Company No. 15, and old 15 was sent to the Houses of Correction and Industry. There were three bucket-carriages in the service, having a combined capacity of one hundred and twelve buckets. All the engine companies were permitted, on April 2, to employ a horse to assist in drawing the apparatus when the streets were in such a condition from rain, etc., that their progress was impeded.

On March 5 the Mayor signed a petition to the Legislature in aid of the bill of the members of the department in relation to the funds of the Charitable Firemen's Association. The pay of the stewards of the engines was, on February 12, asked to be increased to $100 per year. On April 2 a wooden building was erected on Tremont street for the storage of the unused apparatus then housed in Franklin place. It was agreed, on September 17, by the committee. that the compensation of members discharged for neglect of duty be forfeited.

The records of the appointment of company commanders from 1835 to 1838 are lost. No data exists with which we may obtain a list of those who had charge of the apparatus during this time. The ward company records must also remain a blank from this cause, as the printed reports of the engineers (the first volume of which, issued during the ensuing year, can be found at the Chief Engineer's office at City Hall) give no mention of these companies. We believe, however, that they were all disbanded a few years later. The officers of the engines for 1838 were: Washington, No. 3, Enoch H. Snelling, captain; A. R. Campbell, assistant; C. F. Benson, steward: J. W. Ingraham, clerk. Lyman, No. 5, Artemus Ward, captain; J. K.

Hayes, assistant; W. A. Gorham, steward; Otis C. Norcross, clerk. No. 6, Wyatt Richards, captain; F. B. Winters, assistant; J. B. Nason, steward; William Learnard, clerk. Howard, No. 7, William S. Damrell, captain; Joseph Moriarty, assistant; George Runkin, steward; I. T. Smith, clerk. Tremont, No. 8, William Keith, captain; J. C. Hubbard, assistant; Isaiah Bowman, steward; Joseph Curtis, clerk. Despatch, No. 9, Jonas Fitch, captain; J. L. Sperry, assistant; Andrew McPhail, steward; B. E. Cotting, clerk. Hancock, No. 10, David Parker, captain; Jonas Forristall, assistant; C. P. Gould, steward; Fred Taylor, clerk. Maverick, No. 11, Eliazer Johnson, captain; Hosea Sargent, assistant; W. C. Fortune, steward; Samuel Brown, clerk. Eagle, No. 12, James Barry, captain; R. Lovejoy, assistant; James Ayers, steward; James Sargent, clerk. Melville, No. 13, William V. Kent, captain; George Everett, assistant; J. J. Frank, steward; William Jepson, clerk. Eliott, No. 15, Jotham B. Monroe, captain; John Cushing, assistant; T. W. Baxter, steward; William Hawes, clerk. Mazeppa, No. 17, John D. Munn, captain; William Babson, assistant; Edward Hudson, steward; Ira Drew, clerk. Lafayette, No. 18, Artemus Hammond, captain; Charles H. Keith, assistant; Fred Lane, steward; I. P. Rankin, clerk. Extinguisher, No. 20, Nahum Brigham, captain; Joseph Arnold, assistant; Jotham Twitchell, steward; Tisdale Drake, clerk. Hancock Ladder, No. 1, Joshua Jacobs, Jr., captain; H. Whittington, assistant; John Peak, steward; T. P. Carver, clerk. City Hose Co., No. 1, T. P. Foster, captain; J. W. Pierce, assistant; J. N. Randall, steward; E. R. Wormwood, clerk.

The department was called out during this year one hundred and five times; loss of property, $32,052; $20,138 being covered by insurance. On May 29, a man in a building at the corner of Suffolk and Canal streets was burned to death. Forty-nine reservoirs, holding from three to four hundred hogsheads of water, filled from the nearest building by conduits, were placed in convenient parts of the city. They were so situated as to allow three engines to draw water at the same time. Besides the above, there were thirty-three fire-plugs in the aqueducts, the location being designated by a tin sign placed on the nearest building. Twelve wells and ponds were also used to take water from in case of fire.

On February 11, 1839, a small building was ordered to be erected on a vacant lot in the vicinity of Dedham and Canton streets, at an expense not to exceed $300, for the accommodation of one of the three engines in commission. A petition was sent to the City Council, praying for an additional engine for East Boston; but the committee decided, on March 11, that the district was sufficiently protected. Engine Company No. 11 was disbanded February 11, on account of constant disturbances and quarrels among themselves. Messrs. Carlisle Brown, William Walters, and others, were given charge of the engine on the 18th. The old company was dissatisfied, and asked for an investigation; but the committee would not retract their orders, and the new company continued in service. Assistant Engineer William Barnicoat was appointed chief engineer on August 12, and Messrs. Henry Smith, G. Sanderson, R. A. Newell, C. S. Clark, J. Shelton, T. Washburne, T. B. Warren, J. Green, H. Towle, P. C. Jones, and T. A. Williams were appointed assistant engineers.

Changes in the officers for 1839 : Engine No. 3, S. W. Nichols, assistant; A. Norton, clerk.   No. 5, Otis Norcross, assistant; A. B. Butterfield, clerk. No. 6, Vera Coneday, steward.   No. 7, Thomas P. Foster, captain; George Ellis, assistant.   No. 9, George W. Bird, assistant.   No. 10, Fred Taylor, captain; Charles Hollis, assistant; Joseph Leonard, clerk.   No. 11, W. E. Bickford, clerk.   No. 12, Otis Bullard, assistant; A. W. Jones, clerk.   No. 13, Pelham Bonney, captain; William Jepson, assistant; William Cooley, steward; A. C. Hobbs, clerk.   No. 15, John Cushing, captain; Cornelius Turner, assistant.   No. 17, Isaac B. Kimball, captain; Joseph Tilton, assistant; D. B. Haynes, steward, Leander Hilton, clerk.   No. 18, Charles H. Keith, captain; Thomas Gooding, assistant; Benjamin Thurston, steward; F. A. Colburn, clerk.   No. 20, Aaron Walcott, assistant; J. W. Ferrin, steward. Ladder 1, Clement Stetson, clerk.   Hose 1, John W. Pierce, captain; J. N. Randall, assistant; Lorenzo Ames, clerk.

Only ninety-six alarms were sounded during the year.   Property destroyed amounted to $140,004, $61,711 being placed in insurance policies; the largest conflagration being on January 24, when the foundry of Messrs. Turner & Haskill, on Haverhill street, was burnt, from which it communicated to the following buildings, all of which were destroyed : Haverhill street — Messrs. Hayes, Drew, Barnard & Trull, Charles Bates, Robinson & Sinclair, E. & E. Downer, R. Barker, Bowker, Samuel Curtis, J. Ritchie, and William Shears.   Corner Market square and Beverly street — Hill and Chamberlain. Beverly street — Peak & Johnson, J. Stevens, Hutchinson, E. Russell, William Brown, S. Howland, J. Hall, S. G. Underhill, Carey & Boynton, P. Boynton, Mr. Pope.   Charlestown street — Harlow & Bowker, Mr. Hartshorn. Cooper street — Sundry persons, Reynolds & Co.   Endicott street — Catholic Society, T. Winchester, Whiteman & Newell.   Market square — S. H. Jennings, P. Deturbee, and other losses, making a total of more than $70,440. The night of the fire was extremely cold, and the firemen suffered severely, many of them being badly frost-bitten, and several of the engines were frozen up.   A large quantity of hay was destroyed by the fire.

On April 26, the Howard-street House, on Howard street, owned by Dr. Walker, was discovered on fire at about a quarter after one o'clock in the morning, and so rapid did it gain headway that the inmates barely escaped with their lives; loss, $5,700.

Another large fire occurred on September 10, when the stable attached to the City Tavern, Brattle street, was destroyed, with fourteen horses.   The Brattle-street church was injured by this fire, as were several other buildings.

On March 3, 1840, Engine Companies Nos. 3 and 10 were censured by the City Council for leaving the city and going to East Cambridge, in violation of the rules of the department, because they saw a heavy smoke. Attested copies of the ordinances were then ordered to be sent to every engine-house in the service. Application was made to the Council, on May 11, to reduce the number of assistant engineers, but they declined to act in the matter. The engine at East Boston was ordered to remain on the island, and not leave unless expressly sent for by the engineer. The company was allowed half the pay of the regular members. The order permitting horses to assist in drawing engines to fires was rescinded on March 9.

Thomas B. Warren resigned his position as a member of the Board of Engineers for 1840, and the vacancy was not filled. The change of officers for the year were: Engine 1, D. B. Fletcher, clerk. No. 5, Stephen B. Kendall, assistant; Levi P. Coburn, clerk. No. 6, Francis B. Winters, captain; T. P. Bowker, assistant; George H. Kilburn, steward; E. L. Chaffee, clerk. No. 7, Joseph Moriarty, assistant; Jeremiah Stimson, steward; George Ellis, clerk. No. 8, Milton Hall, clerk. No. 9, John S. Kimball, steward. No. 10, Joseph Leonard, captain; Oliver Welsh, assistant; George C. Jacob, clerk. No. 11, John N. Devereux, captain; John A. Spear, assistant; S. F. Sanborn, clerk. No. 12, Reuben Lovejoy, captain; David Weld, assistant; T. N. Jones, clerk. No. 13, Ezra S. Jackson, clerk. No. 15, William Hawes, clerk; D. W. Lillie, steward. No. 17, Ira Drew, captain; J. R. Button, assistant; Charles Gibson, steward; John F. Abbott, clerk. No. 18, William S. Damrell, captain; Sylvanus Denio, assistant; James Henry, steward. No. 20, Henry Evans, steward.

Four more reservoirs were added during the past two years. The department responded to one hundred and thirteen alarms during 1840, during which time $77,973 worth of property was destroyed, $58,632 being covered by insurance. The largest fire for the year occurred on August 17, when the distillery of Gardner Brewer, on Distill-house street was destroyed; loss, $14,000, fully insured. On the twenty-sixth of the following month, the distill-house of Messrs. Barnard & Trull on Distill-house square was destroyed; also the buildings of A. H. Bowman, E. Baxter, A. S. Holmes, Mrs. Moore, D. B. Badger, R. Bradshaw, C. P. Gordon, and others; total loss, $6,078.

May 10, 1841, Engine Company No. 11, at East Boston, was ordered to assemble at the engine-house at every alarm of fire in any part of the city, when the roll should be called, and, in case they saw a sufficient light to warrant them in starting for the scene, to do so, provided it was previous to 11 o'clock at night, after which time until the morning, they were not to leave the island unless especially sent for. But this measure was objected to by the company, unless they received the same compensation as the other members of the department; the result was that the entire company was discharged June 14, 1842, and on December 5th a new company was organized, the compensation being $20 per year to each member, and $50 for the steward. The number of members of the hook-and-ladder companies was increased to twenty-five, on June 8, 1844, at the request of the chief engineer.

Mr. Henry Hart was appointed clerk to the chief engineer during 1841, and the following changes in the department took place : Engine 3, Smith W. Nichols, captain ; William Dyke, assistant ; E. H. Snelling, Jr., clerk. No. 5, H. S. Gorham, steward : J. W. Easterbrook, clerk. No. 7, Royal P. Barry, assistant : J. E. F. Dixey, steward : J. C. Bartlett, clerk. No. 8, Milton Hall, Jr., captain ; William M. Wise, assistant ; Edward Wise, steward ; Francis Richards, clerk. No. 9, George W. Bird, captain ; Franklin Patch, assistant : Joseph Gormley, steward ; Curtis C. Howard, clerk. No. 11, Lewis Whitcomb, captain : John Batchelder, assistant ; W. C. Fisk, steward ; F. A. Mason, clerk. No. 12, William D. Whitney, captain : Elisha Smith, assistant : James M. Hobbs, clerk. No. 13, William Jepson, captain : James F. Holland, assistant : Samuel Hanscomb, steward ; C. P. Sanborn, clerk. No. 15, Jotham B. Munroe, captain ; Cornelius Turner, assistant : Charles Ranstead, clerk. No. 17, Jefferson Healey, captain ; C. P. Rockwood, assistant : Ira Drew, clerk. No. 18, J. P. Palmer, assistant. No. 20, Amasa Pray, captain ; J. F. Robbins, assistant : Henry Hosley, steward ; Hart Hosley, clerk. Ladder 1, Henry B. Withington, captain : Dennis Smith, assistant ; Dexter Bowker, clerk. Hose 1, Nathaniel Baker, assistant.

Of the one hundred and forty times which the department responded to alarms during the year, $102,972 worth of property was destroyed : $36,920 being held by insurance companies.

Five reservoirs and nine fire-plugs additional were added to the list of the water-supply during 1842, and thirty brass cocks were inserted in the aqueduct in various parts of the city, instead of the common plug.

There were one hundred and ninety-four alarms, during which $90,008 worth of property was destroyed, of which $44,533 was covered by insurance.

The two largest fires of the year were the burning of the new passenger-house of the Eastern Railroad Company, at East Boston, on January 25. It was ignited by sparks from a steamboat ; loss, $14,000 ; no insurance. The other occurred March 29th, when a large wooden building, used for the storage and drying of cotton, located on Atkinson street, and occupied by Mr. Oliver Tenney, was discovered to be on fire. The flames rapidly spread to a carpenter-shop and a barn adjoining, from which it communicated to the buildings of Messrs. W. & J. A. Patten, S. Mitchell, R. Robertson, M. Kramer, T. M. Coffin, E. Caldwell, J. G. Torrey. Miss Grant, S. Clark, and S. Sanford : total loss. $13,230 ; insurance, $3,480. This made the fifth time the department was called out to a fire in Mr. Tenney's building. Engine-house 17 was set fire December 30th, but was extinguished with but slight damage. Engine-houses Nos. 1 and 2, of Roxbury, were also set fire, the former August 20th, and the latter on the 26th. Two accidents by the apparatus occurred at Charlestown : a little boy was run over on August 1 by an engine and killed : and on October 2, Mr. J. Tolman, of Engine No. 8, was seriously injured by a similar accident.

Mr. R. A. Newell resigned his position as assistant engineer during

1842. The changes recorded in the companies were as follows: Engine 8, Phineas Hall, steward; F. L. Sargent, clerk. No. 6, Benjamin I. Morrill, captain; George H. Kilburn, assistant; Moses P. Moulton, clerk. No. 7, William Brown, assistant. No. 8, Daniel Smith, clerk. No. 10, Oliver Welch, captain; William H. Dole, assistant; Francis Warner, clerk. No. 12, Elisha Smith, captain; Ebenezer Foskett, assistant; Francis Hall, Jr., clerk. No. 13, James F. Holland, captain; Joseph P. Jepson, assistant. No. 15, Robert Taylor, assistant; Archibald Smith, steward; James E. Spear, clerk. No. 17, John R. Butler, captain; W. G. Reed, assistant; John Larrabee, steward; George Thomas, clerk. No. 20, Benjamin Hosley, assistant; Pardon Smith, steward. Ladder 1, Dennis Smith, captain; Dexter Bowker, assistant; Samuel Jepson, clerk. Hose 1, Nathaniel Baker, captain; William H. Barnes, assistant; Lyman Sears, clerk.

A new ordinance was passed December 12, 1842, during the administration of Mayor Jonathan Chapman, whereby it was ordered that the number of assistant engineers may be reduced to six whenever the City Council should so dispose; also, that a special meeting of a company be called for the election of officers. If there should be no officer to preside at the meeting, one of the enginemen was to do that duty, and if the person elected was not approved by the Mayor and Aldermen, the Mayor was to issue his order to the chief for a new election, after which, should the company refuse to reëlect a member, the Council would appoint a person to office. and should the company then refuse to elect any officer they were to be disbanded. On December 19, it was ordered that the term of service for members should be six months from the first of January, and no member was to be paid unless he served the whole of that period in the same company in which he entered; only for sickness or death was he excused.

CHAPTER VI.

1843–1851.

QUITE a serious fire broke out on March 25, 1843, in the building of Mr. David S. Greenough, at the corner of Washington and School streets. Before the flames were controlled they spread to the buildings of Messrs. Wilkinson & Cory, Benjamin B. Wood, W. R. & A. H. Summer, Dean & Pratt, and Bennoch, Fogg & Co., all of which were badly damaged, the loss aggregating $18,450, $14,050 being covered by insurance. Two boys, named Joseph Stark and Joseph Noble, and a man named Regan were badly injured by the falling of the gutter from the wall. Another large conflagration occurred June 4th, in the building of Timothy Carter, on Federal street, from where it spread to the estates of Mrs. S. Richards and Messrs. John Lafferty, J. & E. Walsh, J. & M. Dow, William C. Holmes, Boston Theatre Company, Patrick Murray, and the heirs of Benjamin Dearborn in Theatre alley. The fire was supposed to have originated from the careless use of a lantern in the hayloft of Mr. Carter: loss, $9,560, only $1,600 being covered by insurance companies. Two other large fires occurred, one June 24th, when fourteen buildings on Causeway street and two on Lancaster street were badly damaged; loss, $14,105. On September 10, fire was set to the same place, and eight firms were burnt out, $7,200 worth of property being destroyed. Some men smoking cigars in the carpenter-shop of S. A. Perkins, on Harrison avenue, on September 14, caused the destruction of ten buildings on that avenue and six on Washington street; loss, $7,129; $2.794 insured. The Farmers' Botanic Garden, on Western avenue, was burnt on December 6, together with a very valuable collection of plants.

Department changes: Engine 3, William Dyke, captain; G. W. Tuckerman, assistant; Edward Warren, steward; J. M. Oxford, clerk. No. 6, F. Whitney, assistant; Samuel Darling, steward. No. 7. Joseph C. Bartlett, captain; J. E. Warner, steward. No. 8, Eleazer Witherell, steward. No. 9, Samuel S. Nutting, clerk. No. 10, James Quinn. captain; Thomas Sprague, clerk. No. 11, James Kidder, Jr., captain; A. L. Foss, assistant; George H. Plummer, clerk. No. 17, George Thorn, assistant; E. H. Gardiner, clerk. No. 18, John S. Kimball, clerk. No. 20, Pardon Smith. assistant; William Pray, steward. Ladder No. 1, G. G. Wilder, assistant; W. H. Mason, clerk. Hose No. 1, R. S. Martin, captain; J. L. Wright. assistant; William Blake, clerk. Engines Tiger and Boston were sent to the House of Correction in place of Relief, 15. Two reservoirs were added to the water-supply, and the well in the street in front of 17 Dock square was taken from it. Engine Company No. 6 was disbanded September 25th, 1843, and on October 9 T. P. Bowker was placed in charge of a newly-organized company. December 4, the number of assistant engineers was reduced to seven.

Assistant Engineers Theodore Washburn and Henry Fowle resigned during 1844, and January 15 Joshua Jacobs and T. A. Williams were appointed to fill the vacancy. Department changes: Engine 3, Samuel L. Mason, assistant; Edward Warren, steward; Ira Banfield, clerk. No. 5, Solomon Reed, assistant; John S. Ryan, steward. No. 6, T. P. Bowker, captain; R. Balcom, assistant; John Balcom, steward; C. P. Daniels, clerk. No. 7, Lewis Beck, captain; William M. Lewis, assistant; C. S. McClennan, steward; J. S. Emery, clerk. This engine was moved from quarters under the City Hall to a new building on Pearl street. Captain Bartlett resigned on March 11, and the company was honorably discharged. No. 8, James M. Welch, captain; James M. Tolman, clerk. No. 11, John Pierce, captain; Thomas Brown, clerk. No. 13, Charles Carter, assistant. No. 18, Benjamin J. Morrill, captain; J. P. Palmer, assistant. No. 20, Jonathan Pierce, clerk. Ladder 1. Joseph G. Wyatt, steward; Philip Fox, clerk.

On June 6 Engine Co. No. 8 was stopped on Tremont street, by Assistant Engineer Green, while going to a fire in Roxbury, after which he left them, and proceeded to Washington street, to stop any other apparatus on their way to that section. The third officer of No. 8 put it to a vote as to whether the company would proceed, when it was found the desire was to go; but they were again stopped by Assistant Engineer Williams. The first and second officers put it to a vote the second time, and they went, contrary to the orders of their superiors, for which offence the foreman and clerk were discharged on June 24, and the members reprimanded. W. S. Damrell, who was appointed foreman of this company, was severely injured at a fire during June, and resigned on July 1. Capt. J. R. Butler, of Engine No. 17, had a charge preferred against him, September 23d, for "a decided want of energy," but it was not sustained, and he was acquitted. The pay of the members of the fire department, except those in East Boston, was increased on July 1 to $65 per month. Again was a petition sent to the City Council for another engine at East Boston, but those gentlemen gave their opinion that the value of real estate on the island did not warrant an outlay such as was necessary for a new engine, the expense for which they estimate as follows: Cost of engine, $1,000; house and land, $3,000; company per annum, $3,000; yearly outlay, about $3,000. But this did not deter the passing of the order, as an engine was sent there during the following year.

More than fifty buildings were fired by incendiaries the ensuing year, from which the loss of property was very large, while the number of alarms were two hundred and sixty-seven, — more than at any previous year since Boston was founded. The largest fire occurred August 25, at the planing-mill of Messrs. Hamilton & Co., in Groton street, when twenty buildings were destroyed or damaged, including the Franklin school-house. The loss to the city was $25,000, not a dollar being insured. The list of those burnt out were as follows: Groton street: Messrs. Lawrence Rogers, George A. Gridley, Hall & Adams, T. P. Durant, David Miller, J. W. Harris, Stephen Packard. George Archibald, J. D. Kent, Mrs. Sarah Nevens, Joseph Kent, Leonard Battelle. Dover street: Timothy C. Leeds, Abel Wyman, J. W. Gates, heirs of Ed. Tuckerman, Stanton Parker, William F. Otis, trustee, Joseph Clark. E. R. Mayo, Harrison G. Otis, J. H. Bolles, Mrs. C. K. Sargent, Rev. J. T. Sargent. Washington street: City of Boston, Samuel Appleton, Christian Tank, and J. G. Newell. Total loss, $63,766; insurance, $29.606. The other occurred on August 18, when the estate owned by the heirs of C. Taylor, on Brighton street, was ignited, by which Messrs. Bosworth & Pratt, Robert Bunton, T. Burr, Joseph Gass, M. Edgeworth, John Davis, Thomas Fairburn, Irving Peterson, R. H. Clouston, R. A. Cobb, Charles Cutler. M. King, Mrs. Edwards, and Mrs. Gear, were burnt out. Before the firemen had this blaze under control, an alarm was given from Lowell street, where a carpenter-shop was set fire, but was extinguished before it had made any progress. On the way to their respective houses. the department was called to a large conflagration on South Margin street, on which street twenty buildings were destroyed or damaged, the sufferers being Samuel Jepson. J. Kittredge, Mrs. E. Sharon, R. Ridlon, M. Smith, J. B. Jepson, John Tillson, L. Bacon. J. Wells, D. Wise, W. B. Daniels, George Mitchell, T. J. Brigham, P. Cudworth, M. L. Wallis, Dole & Hodges, Ezra Trull, C. & J. McElroy, Gray & Briggs, heirs of J. M. Dexter, A. Smith, J. F. Holland, F. D. Ware, A. A. Hill, J. B. Hancock, S. B. Heustis, C. C. Converse, William Kenneday, John Wedger, E. Corliss, Mr. Warrick, and Mr. Hayward. Loss at both fires, $55,089; insurance, $16,869. Another attempt was made August 1st, on Engine-house 17, but the fire was soon extinguished. Total loss of property during 1844, $184,083; total insurance, $95,352.

Engine No. 4 was sent to East Boston during 1845, in the place of No 11. and the latter engine given to No. 20, which was used as a relief. No. 14 was sent to the volunteer company on Suffolk street, and No. 1 was placed on the list of relief engines. Three new reservoirs of the large size were built during the year, also thirty-two with a capacity of one hundred and fifty to three hundred hogsheads; three of the former were connected with the aqueduct, making a total of one hundred reservoirs, while the fire-plugs were reduced to twenty-nine, and all the wells were crossed off the list. The Superintendent of Streets was requested. on February 10, to keep the lids of all the reservoirs in order. A new engine was ordered for South Boston, September 22, and a building erected near the Mather school-house which would be suitable for an engine-house, watch-house and armory. the latter to be occupied by the Mechanic Grays. November 15, Engine Company No. 15 was permitted to call their engine the "Boston." At the same date, Engine Company No. 20 was disbanded.

Assistant Engineer John Green, Jr., resigned, by which the board was reduced to seven members, exclusive of Chief Barnicoat. Other changes in department: Engine No. 3, Calvin Stewart. No. 5, Horace S. Gorham, captain; John S. Ryan, assistant; A. J. Hall, steward; J. R. Ellis, clerk. No. 6, Anthony Martis, steward. No. 7, John Ball, captain; John Lawrence, clerk. No. 8. Charles Carver, clerk. No. 9, William E. Hearsey, captain; S. F. Frost, clerk. No. 10, Moses F. Webster, steward. No. 11, G. E. Pierce. No. 12, E. W. W. Hawes, assistant; F. Hall, Jr., steward; Z. E. Smith, clerk. No. 15, W. H. Simonds, clerk. No. 20, John A. Rathbun, assistant; George W. Tuckerman, steward.

The ensuing year was also a prolific one for fires of an incendiary origin. One building, that of Mr. Levi T. Woodman, on Utica place, was set five times, from January 1 to February 25. Engine-house 13, on Leverett street, was entirely destroyed on April 14. The engine was saved, but in a much damaged condition; loss, $1.200. Engine-house No. 8, on Tremont street, was also damaged to the extent of $500, on May 5; and on July 26, Engine-house 18, Pemberton Hill (Tremont row), was set fire, but discovered before it got under headway. On May 11 several boys built a fire in the rear of Mr. George Newell's carpenter-shop on South Cedar street, for the purpose of roasting clams. The high wind blowing at the time blew the flames among some shavings scattered around the shop which soon communicated to the building, and before the fire was under control, the following persons were burnt out: South Margin street: Messrs. J. Bennett, Isaac Adams, Thomas Adams, Mrs. P. C. West, E. Harrington, John Morgan, A. Morgan, E. Atwood, E. L. Holt, B. Shepard, H. W. Whitney, N. Goddard, Milo Rice, Mr. Davenport, C. A. Bodge, J. Thaxter, George Sullivan, C. W. Tuttle, Asa Stearns, Lowell, Fiske, Gould, J. McGuire, Mrs. Pike, D. Hagen, C. Hutchins, M. Fisher, Mrs. E. Gardner, George R. Varney, S. Ditson, A. Fessenden, A. Brown, J. Nance, Mrs. Mary Barnes, R. Cazian, J. Bartlett, H. M. L. Whitman, Mrs. E. Kimball. Piedmont street: E. Marston, A. M. Hawkes, C. McIntire, G. Gilson, H. A. Breed, B. Foster, E. Wentworth, J. C. Wheeler, J. Tenison, Jr., E. A. Perkins, J. A. Fuller, P. O'Neil, S. O. Mason, L. Buck, Mrs. Carey, J. Alman, A. Pilgram, S. H. Hayward, F. Smith, S. Curtis, G. Martin, J. Aldrich, Ira Andrews, N. M. Morrison, Mrs. E. Roddan, M. Carr, C. P. Philbrick, Mrs. Phelps, Elisha Barnes, H. Leavett, A. Loring, and proprietors M. E. Church; loss, $41,223; insurance, $22,150.

August 15, incendiaries set fire to the building of the Fifty Associates, on Brattle square, which was entirely consumed, also that of Lucius Doolittle; loss to both buildings, $8,500. Messrs. William Roulstone, of Engine 7, and Emerson G. Thompson, of Engine 3, of Charlestown, were instantly killed by the falling of a wall; several persons were also severely burned in their endeavors to remove the horses from the stable. On September 14, the Suffolk Lead Works, Messrs. Henshaw, Ward, & Co., proprietors, in Gold street,

South Boston, consisting of five buildings, together with six dwellings were levelled to the ground, and a block of six dwellings were badly damaged; total loss, $49,050; insurance, $42,450. On December 24, the steam-boiler in the box-factory of Mr. Isaac Tirrell, on Harrison avenue, exploded, and killed Messrs. William Ford and William Tirrell. Total loss during the year, $231,191; insurance, $72,840. There were two hundred and twenty-three alarms.

The Board of Engineers was reduced to six members during 1846, Mr. Peter C. Jones having resigned. On March 30 seven were allowed for the city proper, and one each for East Boston and South Boston. On June 22 the number for the city was increased to nine. Other changes in the department: Engine 3, Jessie Farmer, assistant; A. P. Bessey, clerk. No. 5, J. S. Ryan, captain; A. R. Davis, assistant; L. L. Estabrook, clerk. No. 6, Franklin E. Whitney, captain; Samuel Darling, assistant; Albert Chandler, steward; Charles Mountford, clerk. No. 7, Caleb S. McClennen. captain; Thomas Melzar, steward; G. A. Putnam, clerk. No. 9, Franklin Patch, assistant. No. 11, Thomas Brown, captain; Jacob Barker, assistant; E. W. Hutchins, steward; D. B. Kidder, clerk: No. 12, E. W. W. Hawes, captain; Z. E. Smith, assistant; J. N. Tolman, clerk. No. 13, William Jepson, captain; Obed W. Bartlett, clerk. No. 15, Robert Taylor, captain; H. S. Ellms, assistant. Perkins Engine, 16, John Davis, Jr., captain; James Wood, assistant; James Cliff, steward; Jackson L. Stinson, clerk; forty members. No. 18, F. A. Colburn, assistant; Leonard Metcalf, clerk. No. 20. Jonathan Pierce, captain; C. B. Starkweather, assistant; N. B. Howe, clerk. Ladder No. 1, William Calder, steward.

Old North Engine was placed in charge of a volunteer company at East Boston, and old 15 at the same place, in charge of Volunteer Co. No. 4. Perkins Engine Company 16 was organized this year, and housed on Broadway, South Boston. This engine was built during 1845 by Hunneman & Co. Twenty-three additional reservoirs were also constructed during 1846. Engine Company No. 13 was disbanded on March 19; and on the 30th William Jepson and others were allowed to organize a new company to take charge of it. Engine Company No. 11 had the number of its members increased to forty on the same date. July 20, a lot was purchased on Purchase street for the building of a new house for Engine No. 7; and on November 23 a new engine-house was ordered erected on Suffolk street. The Charitable Association was appropriated $1,000 by the City Council on August 31. Capt. John Ball and Clerk S. McClennen. of Engine Company No. 7, resigned on July 27.

On January 22 the Lyman School, on Meridian street. East Boston, was burnt, together with two dwellings; loss $17,400. Engine-house 18 was again set fire, on February 1; the damage did not exceed $300. On February 23 the Howard Athenæum, owned by Messrs. Ford & Brayley, on Howard street, was burnt; loss $7,050; insurance $750. Mr. Hugh McLaughlin. employed in the rum distillery of Messrs. C. & E. Trull. on Merrimac street, was instantly killed by the bursting of a rum cistern on July 30. Engine-house No. 4 was set fire on August 26, but little damage done. A colored man named Franklin Ellick was suffocated during the fire on board the steamer "Wanderer," of Bristol, lying at Long wharf, October 12.

On October 18, 1847, it was ordered by the City Council that the term of service of members of the department should commence on the first day of every month and continue for six months, instead of the first of January and first of July, as formerly.

Assistant Engineers James G. Sanderson and Thomas A. Williams resigned during 1847, *vice* George W. Bird, Thomas French, of East Boston, and Brewster Reynolds, of South Boston. Suffolk Engine 1 was organized March 15, 1847, and housed on Suffolk street, in a building erected for the purpose, with William L. Champney as captain; W. H. Eastman, assistant; E. T. Talbot, steward; A. P. Melzarr, clerk, and thirty-eight members. Protective Engine Company No. 4 was organized June 1, the ensuing year, and placed in a building on Paris street, East Boston, with Alfred Holmes, captain; Anson Ellms, assistant; E. W. Gunnison, steward; and George Butts, clerk. No. 5, Horace S. Gorham, captain: Matthias Gorham, steward; John S. Ryan, clerk; thirty-seven members. Hose No. 6 was disbanded by the Mayor and Aldermen on August 31. A new house was built for No. 7, on Purchase street, during the year, where it was moved; William Shelton, steward; W. C. Savage, clerk. No. 9 was moved from Mason street to the City Hall. No. 10, Messrs. F. Webster, assistant; J. S. Kimball, steward. No. 11, P. Nutter, steward. No. 12, Elisha Smith, captain; Francis Hall, Jr., assistant; George W. Parshley, steward; William F. Bugbee, clerk. Cataract Engine, No. 14, was organized August 5. and placed in a building at the foot of Mt. Vernon street, with Theodore P. Bowker, captain; Solomon Reed. assistant; O. C. Whitney, steward; W. H. Palmer, clerk. No. 15, Henry S. Ellms, captain; Robert Kemp, assistant; A. Smith, steward. No. 16, George F. Hibbard, steward. No. 18, Fred A. Colburn, captain; C. C. Henry, assistant. Old North Engine Company, No. 19, was reorganized June 1, and placed in a building on Eagle Hill, East Boston, with Nathaniel Seaver, captain; Freeman Baker, assistant; Levi L. Whitcomb, steward; E. Tibbets, clerk. No. 20, Elbridge G. Damrell, captain; I. P. Thompson, assistant; H. A. Pine, steward; J. F. Milner, clerk. Ladder 1, Timothy K. Tripp, captain; Philip Fox, assistant; C. C. Bragg, clerk. Ladder 2 was moved to a building provided for it at the city stables, and kept ready for use.

The steamboat "Penobscot," the property of Messrs. Sanford, Kimball, & Page, was burnt while lying at East Boston, Jan. 7, 1847; loss $15,000; no insurance. The building in Granite place, occupied by volunteers for the Mexican war, was burnt on January 21. The same day fire originated in a wooden building used for bowling-alleys, and known as the "Neptune Bowling Saloon," from the upsetting of a stove, from where it communicated and destroyed eighty buildings, comprising dwelling-houses, carpenter-shops, stables, mechanic shops, etc., which were embraced in a square formed by Haverhill, Causeway, Medford, and Travers streets. The wind was very high, while the combustibility of the buildings, together with the scarcity of water at the commencement, rendered the efforts of the firemen unavailing; total loss $66,154; insurance, $28,001. On April 13, the building owned by H. W. Nelson, at South Boston, was burnt, and a man perished in the flames.

By an Act of March 27, 1847, and another of 1850, new building laws were framed. At the same time an ordinance regarding the same was passed by the City Council. On February 12, 1847, Engine Company No. 11 received an increase of compensation. A new engine-house was ordered to be erected on Charles street; but, instead of building a new structure, the gun-house located in the Public Garden was removed, on April 5, to the dock on a site of land in the rear of Dr. Sharp's church, on Charles street. Engine Company No. 5 was disbanded February 22, and on March 8 Mr. J. S. Ryan was appointed to take command. The members attached to Engine No. 1, on Suffolk street, being a voluntary company, were ordered, on the same date, to receive full pay. A new house was erected, on Hudson street, May 31, and an engine and ladder house was ordered built in Warren square, August 31. At the same date the members of Engine Companies Nos. 6 and 7 were discharged. Assistant Engineer James G. Sanderson resigned August 3.

The question of an adequate water-supply was one that Mayor Josiah Quincy, Jr., — who held that office from December 11, 1845, to January, 1849, — gave considerable attention. In his inaugural address, on January 5, 1846, he dealt with the water question in a way to secure the hearty coöperation of his associates in the government. The time for deliberation, he said, had passed. The time for action had come. A competent and disinterested commission had decided that Long pond was the source from which this blessing was to be derived, and the honor of beginning the important work had been conferred upon the administration then in power. He then proceeded to make a financial statement, from which it appeared that the cost of introducing water, estimated by the commissioners to be $2,651,645, was more than covered by the city lands, estimated at that time to be worth $3,175,000. The funded city debt on January 1, 1846, amounted to $1,085,200, showing a reduction of over $600,000 since 1840. This favorable exhibit of the city's financial condition had much to do with securing the approval of the citizens to the next act of the Legislature, authorizing the introduction of water. Ten days after the new government came in, the Mayor was authorized to petition for another act. It was granted in the form desired on March 30, and accepted by the citizens on April 13, the vote standing four thousand six hundred and thirty-seven in the affirmative, and only three hundred and forty-eight in the negative.

On May 4, James F. Baldwin, Nathan Hale, and Thomas B. Curtis were chosen by the City Council as commissioners under the act; and on August 20 the ceremonies of breaking ground for the beginning of the work at the lake was performed by the Mayor, assisted by his father and the venerable John Quincy Adams. At the collation which followed, the Mayor called attention to the name by which the source of supply was generally known, and said the name Long pond was like the name John Smith, without distinction. He suggested, therefore, that the Indian name " Cochituate" should be substituted, and the suggestion was immediately adopted.

On October 25, 1848, there was another celebration, this time on Boston Common. The rising of the sun was saluted with a hundred guns, and by the ringing of all the church bells. A great procession was formed, which, after marching through several streets, proceeded to the Common, where an ode, written by Mr. James Russell Lowell, was sung by the school-children, and addresses were made by the Mayor and by Mr. Nathan Hale. After these addresses the Mayor inquired of the immense throng of people assembled if it was their pleasure that water should be introduced. There was a tremendous " Yes !" and, thereupon, the gate was opened, and a column of water six inches in diameter rose to a height of eighty feet through the tall fountain in the Frog-pond. What followed is thus described by the historian of the water-works : —

After a moment of silence, shouts rent the air, the bells began to ring, cannon were fired, and rockets streamed across the sky. The scene was one of immense excitement, which it is impossible to describe, but which no one can forget. In the evening there was a grand display of fireworks, and all the public buildings, and many of the private houses, were brilliantly illuminated.

On the establishment of this water-supply, all minor institutions had to give way, and the old Jamaica-pond aqueduct ceased to be of any special use.

Assistant Engineer John Shelton resigned during 1848.

The department changes were : Engine 1, William Lovell. No. 3, A. P. Beasey, assistant ; Edward Warren, steward ; Hosea Allen, clerk. No. 4, Anson Ellms, captain ; George Butts, assistant ; Joseph Pierce, clerk. No. 5, Amos R. Davis, captain ; John S. Ryan, assistant ; Abner Gorham, clerk. No. 8, Bailey T. Mills, captain ; E. Witherell, assistant ; Jeremiah P. Ready, steward. Engine No. 9 was removed to Hudson street during the year ; David Chamberlain, captain ; J. S. Hunt, assistant ; George W. Foster, clerk. No. 10, T. M. Bartlett, steward ; J. B. Merrick, clerk. No. 11, D. B. Kidder, assistant ; F. Bucklebank, steward ; W. H. Dwight, clerk. No. 12, William F. Bugbee, assistant ; E. W. W. Hawes, steward ; Daniel Smith, clerk. No. 13, Carlon Buffum, clerk. No. 14, J. K. Adams, clerk. No. 15, W. H. Simonds, assistant ; G. H. Ames, clerk. No. 16, J. L. Stinson, assistant ; George Emmerson, clerk. No. 18, Charles C. Henry, captain ; Leonard Metcalf, assistant ; Caleb Clapp, clerk. No. 20, Charles H. White, steward.

Relief No. 15 was sent to Deer Island, and Engine 6 was placed in charge of Company No. 4.   The number of reservoirs were increased to one hundred and thirty-two.

Two hundred and eighty-two alarms were responded to by the department during 1848, during which $223,273 worth of property was destroyed. The insurance on the same amounted to $162,085.   The largest of these fires occurred March 10, when the printing office of Messrs. Damrell & Moore, 52 Washington street, was destroyed to the extent of $25,000, together with $73,100 worth of property adjoining.   The next large fire occurred July 12, in the building of Adams & Cook, on Hudson street.   This fire was set in a stable, and, before controlled, destroyed and damaged fourteen buildings, at a loss of $23,169 ; insurance, $13,645.   Engine-house 5, in Dock square, was set fire August 17 ; little damage was done ; and on October 20, Engine-house 13, on Leverett street, was also set fire, but fortunately discovered before greatly damaged ; on December 25 attempts were also made on Engine-house No. 7.   Engine 18 has the honor of first using the Cochituate water for the extinguishment of a fire, at half-past twelve o'clock, noon, November 9, at a fire in the building situated at the corner of Hanover and Cross streets, occupied by Messrs. T. R. & F. F. Raymond, grocery store ; Graves & Stevens, dry goods ; L. Warren, painter ; and Thomas Restieaux, for storage.   The hydrant from which the supply of water was received was at the corner of Hanover and Cross streets.

An attempt was made, November 28, to fire the National Theatre, on Friend street.   The burning of the Catholic church, on Broadway, South Boston, Sept. 7, 1849, was the work of incendiaries ; loss, $70,000 ; insurance, $43,000.

During 1849, Engine No. 2 was ordered to South Boston Point, but no house was provided for the company, consequently it was ordered out of service.   Engines Nos. 3, 8, and 9, were withdrawn, and hydrant or hose companies of twenty members were substituted.   Engines Nos. 3, 9, old 15, and 20 were sold.

The great power of the Cochituate water in the depressed level of the land in the vicinity of the dock, occasioned the disbandment of Engine Company No. 5, on April 30, 1849, and their engine was placed in charge of Company No. 10, whose engine was used as a relief, and the engine-house and land of the former were sold on September 22.

Assistant Engineers Thomas French and B. Reynolds resigned during 1849, and Messrs. Elisha Smith, Jr., Theodore P. Bowker, Anson Ellms, Fred A. Colburn, and Jonathan Pierce were appointed, which appointments increased the number in the board to ten.   Other department changes : Engine 1, Silas Lovell, steward ; William H. Ford, clerk.   No. 4, George Butts, captain ; B. F. Newell, assistant ; James H. Harrington, steward ; Edwin Butts, clerk.   No. 10, J. C. Jones, steward ; Charles Taylor, clerk.   No. 11, D. B. Kidder, captain ; S. Y. Chase, assistant ; P. Nutter, steward ; I. F. Crafts, clerk.   No. 12, E. W. W. Hawes, captain ; Z. E. Smith, steward.

No. 13, Charles Carter, captain; C. Buffum, assistant; J. W. Reed, clerk. No. 14. Solomon Reed, Captain; A. R. C. Lambert, assistant; H. R. Chase, steward; Alvin Vinal, clerk. No. 16, J. L. Stinson, captain; George F. Hibbard, assistant; D. C. Simpson, steward; C. R. Steiger, clerk. No. 18, Leonard Metcalf, captain; Caleb Clapp, assistant; C. C. Henry, steward; T. Gerrish, clerk. No. 19, Gilman Felch, captain; D. P. Mathews, assistant; Warren Belcher, clerk. A new house was erected for this company during the year. No. 20, David C. Meloon, captain; A. Horton, assistant; C. A. Blake, steward; E. B. Chapin, clerk. Tiger Hook-and-Ladder Co., No. 2, organized October 1, 1848, and located in Paris street, East Boston; William Hunt, captain; John H. Shattuck, clerk; ten members. The carriage had a capacity of eleven ladders of various lengths, two hooks, three crotch-poles, and four axes. Washington Hydrant Co., No. 1, organized February 1, 1849, located in old Engine 3's quarters in Salem street; William Dyke, captain; A. P. Bessey, assistant; Daniel Hardy, steward; William Lasell, clerk; sixteen members. Despatch Hydrant Co., No. 2, organized March 1, located in Engine 9's house, Hudson street; David Chamberlain, captain; John S. Hunt, assistant; N. B. Howe, steward; George W. Foster, clerk. Franklin Hydrant Co., No. 3, organized May 1, housed on Tremont row; James L. Wright, captain; William Blake, assistant; M. A. Rice, clerk; seventeen members. Tremont Hydrant Co., No. 4, organized September 1, and placed in Engine 8's quarters; Bailey T. Mills, captain; Eleazer Witherell, assistant; Edward West, steward; Charles Carver, clerk; sixteen members. Each of these companies were equipped with from eighteen to two thousand feet of leading hose, four to eight buckets, and two axes, hydrant-necks, and wrenches.

One reservoir and seven hundred and eighty-one hydrants were placed in various parts of the city during the year. The number of alarms were three hundred and thirty-seven; loss of property, $300,525; insurance, $216,992. Among these we may mention the destruction of nineteen unfinished houses on Lenox street, on February 26, the property of Trainer & Plympton. March 1, Engine-house 7, on Purchase street, was set fire and slightly damaged. Michael Harris was burned to death in a building in the rear of 12 Sea street, October 27.

By request of the City Council, the Board of Engineers, on March 8, appointed Messrs. William Barnicoat, John Davis, Jr., F. A. Colburn and C. S. Clark a committee to revise the Rules and Regulations of the department, which was accomplished, and submitted to the Mayor and Aldermen on the 22d, and approved by the latter on April 8. There were few changes of importance; but all the orders were condensed and framed in twenty articles. (See Engineer's Report, 1849).

Engines Nos. 2, 8, and 10 were sold during 1850, and Engine-house No. 18, on Tremont row, was sold at auction on August 12. The number of hydrants in the city were seven hundred and eighty-six, one hundred and forty-seven at South Boston, making a total for the use of the department of nine hundred and thirty-three.

Company changes for the year: Engine 1, William L. Champney, captain; William Lovell, assistant. No. 4, Benjamin F. Newell, captain; Joseph Pierce, assistant; William H. Perkins, clerk. No. 7, William Shelton, steward; Andrew Neville, clerk. No. 11, William Pray, steward. No. 12, Daniel Smith, clerk. No. 18, Oliver L. Roberts, captain; H. L. Champlin, clerk. No. 19, Joseph Dunbar, steward; E. B. Perry, clerk. No. 20, D. E. Knight, steward. Ladder 1, Philip Fox, captain; G. H. Lovejoy, assistant; J. S. Stevens, steward; C. C. Bragg, clerk; house on Friend street. Ladder 2, J. H. Shattuck, assistant; Andrew Leach, clerk. Hydrant No. 1, W. W. Currier, assistant. No. 3, Mason A. Rice, captain; John Colter, clerk.

Number of alarms, two hundred and forty; loss of property, $123,660; insurance, $76,197. The largest of these fires was the burning of the Boston and Maine Railroad freight depot, on Causeway street, November 5, loss, $115,332; insurance, $10,000. Messrs. Harrod & Fernald occupied part of the building as a mahogany warehouse. Twenty-three cars loaded with cotton, etc., was consumed with the depot; loss, $38,000; insurance, $20,000. Mrs. Riley, living at 4 East Orange street, was burned to death, on June 15, from explosion of a fluid-lamp.

Assistant Engineers John Davis, Jr., T. P. Bowker, and Jonathan Pierce were succeeded by Messrs. Thomas Haveland and James Wood during 1851. Engines Nos. 1, 10, 15, 18, and 20 were disbanded during the year, but were reorganized at the end of the year, and the names and numbers of each company altered. Two engines were kept in the building under the reservoir in Derne street.

On February 24 an order was passed in the City Council for a system of fire-alarms to be established, and Dr. William H. Channing submitted a plan of telegraphic alarm. On June 10, $10,000 were appropriated for establishing this system, and on December 29, $3,000 additional were expended. (See article on fire-alarm service in this volume.) Captain Quinn, of Engine No. 10, Howes, of No. 12, Hunt, of No. 2, J. Price, clerk of No. 13, and W. Lassell, clerk of No. 1, were dismissed, March 18, for insubordination and neglect of duty. Twenty-three members of Engine No. 10 asked for their discharge on April 28, whereby the company was disbanded, and Hydrant Company No. 3 substituted. An order was passed by the Aldermen, June 9, by which refreshments were furnished the members of the department while at a fire at the city's expense.

A committee was appointed on March 3 to ascertain the fitness of the Board of Engineers and members. This resulted from a hearing that took place on February 14, the ensuing year, on charges against Chief Barnicoat and several members for intoxication at the fire in the Tremont House, March 21, 1850; the neglect of duty of two of his assistants; profanity of the chief and two of his assistants at a fire in Decon street; also neglect and incompetency of the assistant engineer and some forty members. The whole statement were considered by the committee as frivolous, and they exonerated every member mentioned in the charge. On July 1 the pay of the department was fixed as follows : chief, $2,000 ; assistant, $250 ; secretary of board, $800 ; firemen, $150, except those in East Boston, who received $75 ; assistant foremen and stewards, $125 ; East Boston, $60 ; members, $100 ; East Boston, $50, per year. The chief and the assistants were paid semi-annually, the others annually.

The report for 1851 contained the following changes in the company officers : No. 4, Nathaniel Seaver, captain ; Freeman Baker, assistant ; T. B. Tilton, steward ; B. G. Prescott, clerk. No. 7, Stephen B. Kendall, captain ; Josiah Snelling, assistant ; William C. Savage, clerk. No. 11, Samuel Y. Chase, captain ; H. N. Alexander, assistant ; Aaron Brown, clerk. No. 12, John H. Clifford, captain ; Samuel N. Tucker, assistant ; J. B. Whitney, steward ; George W. Snow, clerk. No. 13, Octavius Boston, assistant ; C. B. Wilson, steward ; William Blake, clerk. No. 14, only eleven members, Otis C. Whitney, steward, the only officer. No. 16, Joshua Jenkins, captain ; D. J. Weston, assistant ; Theodore Hutchins, steward ; W. Alonzo Brabiner, clerk. No. 17, Hiram A. Bowles, clerk. No. 19, D. P. Matthews, captain ; E. Burrill, assistant ; Charles Burrill, steward ; Joseph Burrill, clerk ; Ladder No. 1, Timothy K. Tripp, captain ; N. W. Pratt, assistant ; James H. Clark, clerk. No. 2, Warren Foster, captain : T. P. Cheney, assistant ; B. C. Seaver, steward ; E. B. Lincoln, clerk. Hydrant Co. No. 1, Daniel Hardy, captain ; Peter Thompson, assistant ; Charles Jenkins, steward ; Charles E. Dunton, clerk. No. 2, John M. Butterfield, captain ; James Farnsworth, assistant ; J. C. Folsom, clerk. No. 3, J. S. Ryan, assistant. No. 4, Charles Carver, captain ; Thomas Dwyer, assistant ; David Hanson, steward ; J. W. Leatherbee, Jr., clerk.

The number of hydrants were increased to eight hundred and five in the city, one hundred and sixty-one at South Boston, and one hundred and five at East Boston, making a total of one thousand and seventy-one. Of the three hundred and thirty-three alarms at which the department responded, the loss by fire was $386,107 ; insurance, $192,937. Of these, the largest was the burning of the East Boston ferry-boat, January 5 ; loss, $18,000 ; no insurance. The Franklin school-house was set fire on August 24, and damaged to the extent of $1,500.

During the mayoralty of John P. Bigelow, June 2, 1851, the ordinances governing the department was again revised. In these it was ordered that the members should have the use of the lower room of the engine-house, but no furniture or decoration was allowed, except such as furnished by the city. Association or organized societies or clubs of firemen were prohibited, except by express permission of the City Council. No company was allowed to impose fines upon the members, but the clerk was ordered to enter in his roll-book all absences and tardiness, and to make a monthly return of the same to the engineers. For such absence, except in case of sickness, fifty cents was deducted from the member offending. If the offence was repeated at more than one-third of the alarms of fire during the month, they were discharged. In the rules established July 14, 1851, this fine was reduced to twenty-five cents. Any member wilfully neglecting or refusing to perform his duty, or guilty of insubordination, should be dismissed, and should they offend against any ordinance of the city relating to the department, they were liable to a fine of $5 or $20. Every member was obliged to sign the following statement, which was deposited with the engineers : —

I, A. B., having been appointed a member of the Boston Fire Department, hereby signify my agreement to abide by all the ordinances of the City Council, and the Rules and Regulations of the Mayor and Aldermen, and the Board of Engineers, relating thereto.

The rules were revised on December 30, so that a member should not lose his pay should he remove his residence to another part of the city, but the engineer should transfer him to an engine in the vicinity of his new place of abode. The size of the department was increased on September 27, by increasing the number of each company to forty men. A room in the basement of the eastern side of City Hall was fitted up for an engine-house on the same date. A new hose-carriage was ordered built for East Boston on September 6.

CHAPTER VII.

1852–1857.

THE changes in the Board of Engineers for 1852, were: Messrs. Lewis Beck, George S. Thorne, Nathaniel Seaver, and Richard S. Martin, *vice* Anson Ellms, Thomas Haviland, and James Wood.

Nearly all the companies were reorganized, and a new ladder company and two hydrant companies put in commission. Another engine was placed under the reservoir in Derne street, and a relief engine in Hydrant-house No. 5. The changes reported are as follows: Mazeppa Engine Co., No. 1, *vice* No. 17, Broadway, South Boston, Elijah II. Goodwin, captain; H. A. Bowles, assistant; Alpheus Gleason, clerk. Perkins, No. 2, *vice* 16, same officers. Eagle, No. 3, Washington street, *vice* Engine No. 12, same officers. Cataract, No. 4, Mount Vernon street, *vice* Engine No. 14, Samuel S. Nutting, captain; E. W. Wellman, assistant; T. Gerrish, clerk. Extinguisher, No. 5, East street, *vice* Engine No. 20, David Riley, steward; E. W. Milliken, clerk. Melville, No. 6, Leverett street, *vice* No. 13, same officers. Howard, No. 7, was the only company that retained its old number; Josiah Snelling, captain; T. A. Bridge, assistant. Boston, No. 8, Commercial street, *vice* No. 20, William A. Green, captain; Charles P. Shattuck, assistant; Benjamin Tarbox, clerk. Maverick, No. 9, Paris street, East Boston, *vice* No. 11, H. N. Alexander, captain; J. P. Somerby, assistant; Washburn Weston, clerk. Old North, No. 10, Eagle Hill, East Boston, *vice* No. 19, Joseph Dunbar, steward; Davis Damon, clerk. Ladder No. 1, N. W. Pratt, captain; J. H. Clark, assistant; Charles A. Eaton, clerk. No. 2, John Dillingham, clerk. Franklin Hook-and-Ladder Company, No. 3, house on Harrison avenue, near city stables, Otis N. Marston, captain; Z. E. Smith, assistant; Richard Mugford, clerk; seven members: the truck carried fifteen ladders of various lengths, three hooks, crotch-poles, and axes each, two guy-ropes, two rakes, and four buckets. Hydrant Company, No. 1, C. E. Danton, assistant; James E. Rich, clerk. No. 3, John S. Ryan, captain; John Colter, assistant; Andrew Tonkin, clerk. Suffolk Hydrant Company, No. 5, house on Shawmut avenue, William Lovell, captain; Samuel E. Ross, assistant; Silas Lovell, steward; John O. Fallon, clerk; ten members. Protective Hydrant Company, No. 6, Paris street, East Boston, Bradbury G. Prescott, captain; Ebenezer Higgins, assistant; T. B. Tilton, steward; I. F. Crafts, clerk; twelve members. Ten more hydrants were placed in the city, nineteen at South Boston, and twenty-five at East Boston, making a total of one thousand one hundred and twenty-five ready for use.

The alarms sounded for 1852 numbered three hundred and thirty-three, giving a total destruction to property of $386,107 ; insurance, $172,937. At the burning of Isaiah Howe's building, 20 Kingston street, on February 12, Mr. John Smith, of Hydrant Company No. 2, was killed by a falling wall, and several other members of the department were badly injured. March 31, Tremont Temple, located at 82 Tremont street, was entirely destroyed, and thirty-seven people suffered a loss $178,360 ; insurance, $45,244. During the fire a citizen named John Hall was instantly killed by a falling wall, and George Estes, of Engine 7, Charlestown, had his back broken.

About three o'clock on the morning of April 22, fire was discovered under the stairway of the National Theatre. The building being constructed of wood, the flames made such headway before the arrival of the firemen that the entire destruction of the edifice was inevitable. Despite the efforts of the department, the building was a mass of ruins within three quarters of an hour. The theatre was owned by William Sohier, Esq., and was valued at $40,000 ; properties, $6,000 ; scenery, $15,000, and music-books, $4,000 ; besides, there were two thousand volumes of prompter's books, and three thousand original manuscripts destroyed ; the loss to the actors was about $2,000. Several other buildings were injured by fire and water.

The first regular alarm given by the telegraphic system was sounded for a fire in the building of John Ward, located at the corner of Causeway and Charlestown streets, on April 29, 1852. Mr. Thomas Wise was burnt to death in the building at 102 Union street, on June 23. The largest conflagration of this year is known as the Fort Hill fire. It broke out in the building owned by the heirs of D. Packard, located on Belmont street, on July 10. The fire originated in an unoccupied stable, by some boys playing with fire-crackers, and, before being extinguished, completely destroyed the Sailor's Home, 99 Purchase street ; the Mariner's Church, near Purchase street ; the Boylston school-house, Washington place, and about thirty other buildings, including many valuable brick dwelling-houses and stores ; loss, $150,000 ; insurance, $75,000. Another authority places the loss at $400,000.

Three children of Mrs. Rogers, 29 Friend street, were burnt to death on August 3 by a lamp setting fire to their bed ; and on October 3, a child of Daniel Crowley, Maverick street, East Boston, was burnt. At the burning of the building on Purchase street, occupied by Messrs. Moses Williams and William H. Davis, October 12, Michael O'Shay was instantly killed, and Michael Lynch badly injured, by falling walls. December 1, fire, supposed of an incendiary origin, started in a building occupied by Jonas Chickering, 334 Washington street, and twenty-three tenants were burnt out : loss, $187,340 ; insurance, $86,685. Mr. Benjamin F. Foster was instantly killed, and Alvin M. Turner seriously injured, by being buried in an adjoining building, which was crushed by the falling of a wall. December 18, Mr. J. F. Plummer was burned to death from the explosion of alcohol, and on the 23d two children of Mrs. Doherty, in Block court, were suffocated by smoke.

Mayor Benjamin Seaver and the Board of Aldermen, on December 31, 1852, again revised the ordinances of the department. About the only change made, however, was the repealing of Sections 12, 18, and 28 of the act of 1851.

Assistant Engineers Joshua Jacobs, Louis Beck, and Nathaniel Seaver were succeeded during 1853 by Samuel S. Nutting, Daniel C. Melvon, and Joseph A. Dunbar. A new house was erected for Engine No. 6 and Hydrant Company No. 3. on Wall street. Despatch Engine Company, No. 11, on Court square, *vice* No. 6, and Tremont Engine Company, 12, Tremont street *vice* No. 8 were organized during the year; these were taken from the reserves in Derne street. Engine No. 10 quarters was moved to Meridian street. The engine and ladder house on Friend street, corner of North Market, was sold at auction February 24, and the ladder (No. 1), was provided quarters in a part of the primary school on Friend street, on March 14; the expense for altering the same was $1,000.

All the fines deducted from the pay of the members during a period of one year, amounting to $593, were turned over to the Charitable Fire Association on February 17. The first communication received by the City Council regarding steam fire-engines was from Mr. John Thorndike, on February 28. No action was taken in the matter at the time. The firemen were reproved by the Mayor and Aldermen. on April 11, for taking goods while at a fire. The members stated that they had no idea that any harm had been done in so doing, whereupon the statutes relating to the matter were ordered printed, and posted in each engine-house, so they could learn of the heavy penalty for stealing articles taken from a building on fire. May 31, six of the Phillips' Patent Fire Annihilators were purchased at an expense of $250. Two additional hydrants were placed in the city proper, and six at East Boston.

Changes in company officers for 1853: Engine No. 1, Ruel H. Bean, assistant; W. H. Cunningham, clerk. No. 2, Daniel Weston, Jr., captain; George Brown, assistant; A. J. Drake, clerk; No. 3, Samuel N. Tucker, captain; G. W. Snow, assistant: A. C. Wass. clerk. No. 4, Alvin Vinal, captain; John S. Damrell, clerk. No. 5, A. Horton, captain: E. W. Milliken, assistant; W. H. Rummery, steward; G. B. Chapin, clerk. No. 7, W. C. Savage, captain; G. W. Tarbox, assistant: Thomas Whipple, clerk. No. 9, Benjamin Brown, clerk. No. 10, E. Burrill. captain; Joseph Baker, assistant; J. M. Tucker, steward. Despatch Engine Company, No. 11, *vice* No. 6, house in Court square, David Chamberlain, captain: Stephen B. Kendall, assistant; H. A. Hunting. steward: H. P. Grant. clerk. Tremont Engine Company, No. 12, *vice* No. 8, house in Tremont street, Charles Carver, captain; R. D. Griggs, assistant; J. W. Leatherbee, clerk; David Hanson, steward. Ladder 1, Jeremiah S. Stevens, clerk. No. 3. Z. E. Smith, captain: R. Mugford, assistant; Lucius Cole, steward; James Kelley, clerk. Hydrant Company No. 1, C. E. Dunton, captain; J. E. Rich, assistant; G. H. Delano, steward; G. T.

Pratt, clerk. No. 2, George Newton, assistant, Jacob Smith, steward; W. W. Bass, clerk. No. 3, A. Tonkin, assistant; C. A. Sharon, clerk. No. 4, disbanded. No. 6, I. F. Crafts, assistant; Joseph Barnes, clerk.

Two hundred and five alarms were sounded during 1853; the loss to property from January, 1853, to January, 1854, being $268,621; insurance, $204,173. None of these fires were very extensive, but there were several fatal accidents. While Engine Company No. 11 was responding to an alarm on September 17, for a fire at Mrs. Nason's, Liverpool street, East Boston, Ezra J. Wiley, a member of the company, was run over by the engine, and instantly killed. April 28, the building at 127 Endicott street was destroyed, the sparks from which badly damaged the roof of the Old North Church, on Salem street. November 1, while the same engine company was on their way to a fire at 568 Commercial street, the engine run over and killed a citizen named John Little. Two children playing with matches, on November 25, set fire to a bed in the building located at 6 Sturgis place. and were suffocated; and on December 1, a bed in the house at 63 Atkinson street was set fire by an intoxicated person, and burnt to death a son of Mr. J. O'Connor.

Two new engines were built for Engines Nos. 11 and 12 by Hunneman & Co., during 1854, and the old ones were placed in reserve. under the reservoir on Derne street, with old No. 20. The old engine at the House of Correction was sold on January 23. Another new engine was built by the same firm for Webster Company No. 13, to be stationed at East Boston, on Webster street, but the company was not organized until the next year. The name of Despatch Hydrant Company, No. 2, was changed to Union, No. 2, on March 27. A new house was erected for Engine No. 7 on Purchase street, while Engine-house No. 1 was thoroughly repaired, and Despatch Engine Company, No. 11, had their name changed to Barnicoat, No. 11, on May 22. At this date permission was given the department to parade on July 4, 1854. Suffolk and Franklin Hydrant Companies were ordered, on May 10, to have a four-wheel carriage, instead of a two-wheel; and on December 14, the hydrant companies were instructed not to take their carriages out with a full complement of hose, unless there was a fire in their district. The number of members was at the same time increased to twenty.

Quite a disturbance was created in the department by the resignation of Chief Barnicoat, on April 24. There had existed for some time previous a jealousy among certain members of the Board of Engineers and members of the companies, who were supported by some of the City Councilmen. These rivals of the chief had devised several plans to remove him from office, but none had succeeded; he lived down all the charges made against him; and, on the above date, sent in a letter of resignation, immediately after which he was appointed Superintendent of Lamps, a position he held until his death. James Quinn was nominated for his successor, but his election was not concurred. On May 1, a certain Alderman made a motion that, as there was no one filling the office of chief, the position remain vacant, and the engineers should rank as follows: Quinn, 1st; Smith, 2d; Clark, 3d; Bird, 4th; Thorne, 5th; Martin, 6th; Nutting, 7th; Melvin, 8th, and Dunbar, 9th; but no action was taken in the matter. At almost every meeting of the Council some one was nominated to fill this office, but both branches could not agree until December 18, when Elisha Smith was appointed.

A committee was formed during the year to visit the machine-works of L. B. Latra, of Cincinnati, Ohio, to inspect the steam fire-engine that was in working order in that city. On their return home the committee recommended the purchase of one for this city. Therefore, on April 17, the City Council appropriated $9,000 for this purpose, and soon after a contract was made with the firm for the manufacture of the famous steamer " Miles Greenwood," named in honor of the chief of the department of that city.

Mr. James Quinn succeeded Assistant Engineer Melvin as a member of the board during 1854. Additional hydrants placed in service during the year were seven in city proper, eight at South Boston, and ten at East Boston.

Department changes: Engine No. 1, R. H. Bean, captain; W. H. Cunningham, assistant; F. Richards, clerk. No. 2, J. B. Hill, clerk. No. 3, disbanded September 4, and a new company organized. No. 4, J. S. Damrell, assistant; T. Gerrish, clerk. No. 5, John S. Maxwell, captain; W. M. Rumery, assistant; David Riley, steward; S. W. Holt, clerk. No. 7, D. L. M. Dwinell, captain; C. C. Henry, assistant; S. A. Crosby, steward. No. 9, J. P. Somerby, captain; B. Brown, assistant; D. M. R. Dow, steward; B. Varney, clerk. No. 11, John Colter, captain; H. P. Grant, assistant; H. G. Spear, clerk. No. 12, quarters moved to Warren street, B. F. Mills, captain; David Connery, assistant; R. D. Griggs, steward. Ladder No. 1, Jeremiah S. Stevens, assistant; C. H. Merritt, clerk. No. 2, J. W. Seavey, assistant; Charles Simmons, steward; S. Goodwin, clerk. No. 3, R. Mugford, captain; O. F. Marshall, assistant; John Mugford, steward; J. H. Barton, clerk. Hydrant Company No. 1, J. B. Shattuck, assistant; Alfred Williams, clerk. No. 2, S. Stone, captain; W. W. Boss, assistant; E. H. Young, steward; J. Smith, clerk. No. 3, A. Tonkin, captain; J. Nevins, assistant; J. T. Rice, steward. No. 5, W H. Ford, assistant; S. E. Ross, clerk.

The number of alarms for the year was two hundred and two, during which the loss to property was $206,836; insurance, $129,160. Probably the largest fire was the burning of the steamer " North Ocean " in the harbor on November 24. Charles C. Henry, of Engine No. 7, and J. Wentworth and W. B. Follett, of No. 6, were badly injured on February 16, at a fire in Howard street. March 2, R. S. Evans, of No. 11, was run over by the engine, and seriously injured, and on the 19th, L. K. Putney, of No. 5, fell from a ladder at a fire at 550 Washington street, and broke his leg.

New engines were building during 1855 for Engine Companies Nos. 1, 6, 10, and 13, and new houses for Nos. 8 and 13. Twenty-two additional hydrants were put in service in the city proper, five at South Boston, and eleven at East Boston. The name of Protective Hydrant Company, No. 6, was changed to Deluge, No. 6, on May 4. An act of the City Council was approved on February 3, authorizing the city to appropriate money for the relief of families of disabled firemen. The name of Ladder Company No. 2 was changed on June 20, to Washington.

Messrs. Nathaniel W. Pratt, Bailey T. Mills, and David Chamberlain were appointed on the Board of Engineers during 1855, *vice* Martin and Melvin. The changes in company officers were as follows: Engine No. 1, G. F. Gould, steward. No. 3, reorganized, E. W. Milliken, captain; G. S. Williams, assistant; A. O. Becklow, steward; C. H. Rice, clerk. No. 4, John S. Damrell, captain; J. Prince, assistant; A. H. Towne, steward; R. B. Farrar, clerk. No. 6, B. H. Bailey, steward. No. 7, Charles C. Henry, captain; Thomas Whipple, assistant; William Shelton, steward; F. L. Keay, clerk. No. 9, A. Currant, steward. The name of Old North, No. 10, was changed to Dunbar, No. 10, in honor of Assistant Engineer Joseph Dunbar, of East Boston; Joseph Baker, captain; Davis Damon, assistant; A. P. Truman, steward; John Gray, clerk. No. 11, W. H. Colburn, captain; W. D. Palmer, assistant; E. H. Dwyer, steward; F. W. Smith, clerk. No. 12, David Connery, captain; O. R. Robbins, assistant; J. H. Miner, clerk. Webster Engine Company, No. 13, house in Paris street, organized the ensuing year; Joseph H. Harrington, captain; George K. Putnam, assistant; A. C. Dyer, steward; William H. Lewis, clerk. Ladder 1, Jeremiah S. Stevens, captain; P. Collier, assistant. No. 3, O. F. Marshall, captain; E. W. Warren, assistant; E. O. Farrar, steward; J. F. Marston, clerk. Hydrant Company No. 1, A. Williams, assistant; Edward Gross, clerk. No. 2, M. C. Thompson, assistant; H. L. Houghton, steward. No. 3, J. S. Ryan, captain; H. M. Orcutt, steward; W. H. Palmer, clerk. No. 6, Joseph Barnes, captain; T. B. Tilton, assistant; Horatio Ely, steward; W. B. Rand, clerk.

One hundred and four times, during 1855, did the bells peal forth their warning notes of fire, by which $537,604 worth of property was destroyed, the insurance on the same being $361,047. The largest of these conflagrations was caused, on April 27, by a person throwing a lighted match against a bale of cotton after lighting his pipe, in a wooden building owned by Joseph W. Revere, located on Battery wharf. The wind was blowing from the northwest, and in a short time a block of wooden warehouses and a hundred bales of cotton were on fire. The flames soon extended south, across the dock, to a range of wooden buildings on Ferry avenue. The smoke was stupefying, and the heat so intense that the firemen were driven at times from their engines. The ships "Porsalia" and "Diana" were totally destroyed, and the ships " Middlesex," "General Berry," "John Bertram," brig "Fawn," schooners "Robert Stone," "Oregon," "Express," "Moses Eddy," and "General Veazie " were badly damaged. A large building on Constitution wharf was burned, also all the buildings owned by the People's Ferry Company. The fire crossed to Lincoln's wharf, where several buildings used for storing cotton and other merchandise were burned. A wood and coal yard on the wharf was on fire, and a large quantity of coal and wood destroyed. During the burning of the ship "Diana," Perkins Engine, No. 2, was stationed on board, but the heat grew so intense that the engine was abandoned; the brave "fire laddies," however, soon after rallied, and saved their machine. Engine No. 6 and a relief engine in charge of Company No. 7, also Engine No. 2, of Chelsea, were destroyed, while several of them were badly damaged. The area of ground burned over was about ten acres. Total loss, $500,000. Of this amount $298,179 was on property, of which $191,315 was covered by insurance.

In the revision of the ordinances of the department during 1855, it was stipulated that no officer, having been dismissed, should be reinstated unless by a vote of the chief and two-thirds of the assistant engineers, which vote had to be confirmed by the Board of Aldermen, and could not pass that body without a two-thirds vote. A committee, termed the Committee on Fire Alarms, was to be appointed during the month of January each year, to consist of two aldermen and three members of the Common Council, which committee was given the management of the entire plant connected with that branch of the service. They had power to nominate all persons engaged in its workings, and to establish their compensation, and determine who was to be intrusted with the care of the keys of the signal-boxes. In the month of May a Superintendent of Fire Alarms was to be appointed by the City Council. The committee had power to alter and change the rules and directions governing the system of working the alarms, and to have them printed as a city ordinance, but the City Council could annul the same. A fine of from $2 to $50 was imposed on any person who should injure the signal-boxes, wires, etc., or give a false alarm.

The steam-engine Miles Greenwood was put in service three times, during which it did not prove all that was desired. To bring it to suit the requirements of the department, it was thoroughly repaired during 1856, under the superintendence of Mr. Latra, the builder, in the shop of Messrs. Hinckley & Drury, but even after this it was found to be too cumbersome for general use. A house was built for its accommodation in the city stable yards, on Harrison avenue. Previous to this it was located at Haymarket square, and a temporary company, consisting of L. E. Smith, William Sorrell, and others, was formed May 29. The first fire at which it was of any service was on April 12, at which time Gerrish Market was consumed. Webster Engine Company, No. 13, was disbanded on April 22, but a volunteer company was formed as soon as the new house on Sumner street, East Boston, was erected. Twenty-one additional reservoirs were placed in the city proper, twenty-four at South Boston, and six at East Boston. The average distance of the hydrants from each other was about two hundred and fifty feet.

Assistant Engineers Thorn, Quinn, Colburn, and Mills resigned during 1856, and were succeeded by Messrs. David C. Melvin, R. S. Martin, George F. Hibbard, and Zenas E. Smith. F. A. Colburn succeeded Mr. Henry Hart to his former position as secretary to the board.

The death of Chief Engineer Smith was reported to the Council on November 24. All the members of the Board of Engineers and City Government attended the funeral. On December 15, Assistant Engineer George W. Bird was unanimously elected his successor. An agreement was made by the engineers of Boston and surrounding towns and cities, whereby, in case they thought the services of another department were needed, they were to send a card by a police-officer, and immediately after give the alarm. A hydrant company was located on Northampton street, opposite the Catholic church. on May 26, and the old engine on the South Bay land was removed there. Engine No. 7 had its name changed, July 7, to Tiger. On December 18, the annual parade of the department was prohibited.

Company changes for 1856: Engine No. 1, W. H. Cunningham. captain; W. H. Kakare, assistant. No. 3, H. L. Willingford, assistant; W. A. Spooner, steward; G. D. Chubbuck, clerk. No. 7, William M. Rumery. captain; S. W. Holt, assistant; E. H. Goodhue. clerk. No. 6, B. H. Bailey, captain; C. C. Geyer, assistant: William Blake, steward; C. C. Wilson, clerk. No. 7, E. L. Leavitt, clerk. No. 8, B. Tarbox. assistant; J. T. Parkhurst, clerk. No. 9, J. H. Perkins, assistant. No. 10, George Tucker, assistant; A. P. Inman, steward. No. 11, H. A. Hunting. captain; C. B. Maxfield, assistant; D. S. Newell, steward. No. 12, O. R. Robbins, captain; J. Hawkins, assistant; L. W. Shaw, clerk. Steam fire-engine Miles Greenwood, city stables, Henry H. Drayton, captain; William Lovell, assistant; T. H. Badlam, steward; Francis Hall, clerk; seven members; also an engineman at a salary of $806 per year, and a fireman at $1.50 per day: it was equipped with fifty feet of suction hose and nine hundred and fifty feet of leading hose; company disbanded on August 1. Ladder No. 1, M. Place, assistant. No. 2, Charles Simmons. captain; T. Holmes, steward; W. F. Hayes, clerk. Hydrant No. 1, Ed. Gross, assistant; A. Williams, clerk. No. 2. M. C. Thompson. captain; H. L. Houghton, assistant: J. Smith, steward; George Newton. clerk. No. 3, J. Nevins, captain: J. S. Ryan, assistant; John Colter, clerk. No. 5, George C. Fernald, assistant. No. 6, W. R. Hill, clerk.

At the one hundred and sixty-seven fires during 1856, $409.553 worth of property was destroyed. on which was $287,832 insurance. The most noticeable fire of the year broke out a few moments before one o'clock on the afternoon of April 12, in the attic of the large six-story brick building at the intersection of Sudbury, Portland, and Friend streets, known as the Gerrish Market. A high wind prevailed at the time. and the height of the building prevented the firemen from throwing any water into the upper stories. For nearly an hour the flames were unchecked in their progress from room to room, and when the fire had penetrated down into the fourth story, the upper portion of the walls were entirely hidden from view by the immense body of flame. By the aid of ladders the firemen were now able to throw a few streams of water into the third story; but it did very little service, so that the firemen turned their attention to saving the buildings in the neighborhood. Engines from Roxbury, Cambridge, Charlestown, and Chelsea rendered efficient service, while the steam-engine, Miles Greenwood, did good service, until one o'clock in the morning, when the fire was under control. The heat of the fire caused a gas cesspool at the corner of Friend and Market streets to explode, by which three men were badly hurt. Several buildings at the north part of the city took fire from the sparks carried by the wind, but were extinguished with little damage. Loss, $139,454; insurance, $86,504.

The most terrible fire, for the extent of the loss of life, that the fire department was called to witness, broke out July 29, in a large block of buildings on North street. So rapid did the flames spread that the unfortunate occupants had to make their exit by jumping from the windows, in doing which, Margaret Sweeney and Mary Collins were killed, while Ellen Kallen, Mary Kallen, Catherine Kallen. Ellen Wright, Emily Wright, and John Wright, — refusing to make the terrible leap, — were burnt to death. Charles W. Warren, a member of Ladder 3, was killed by the falling of a chimney, and Newell Harding, Jr., P. Hackett, and J. W. Ryan, members of Engine No. 21, were injured by falling bricks. Engines from Charlestown, Chelsea, Cambridge, and Medford, were on hand, and two alarms were given to bring the " Miles Greenwood " into service. Loss, $21,567; insurance, $17,750.

The court-house, in Court square, was damaged to the extent of $4,000 on April 2, by a fire caused by a lighted cigar being thrown in a wooden cuspidore filled with sawdust. James Quinn, of Engine No. 11, was run over and badly injured by the apparatus, while going to a fire at 117 Friend street, on August 31. Two children of Mrs. Andrews, of 5 Milton street, were burnt to death September 1. East Boston was the scene of a very extensive blaze on September 22, when the steam flour-mills of E. D. Brigham & Co. were destroyed; loss, $103,000, fully insured. By the falling walls the following members of the department were injured: Assistant Engineer G. W. Bird; Daniel Galencea, and Joseph Mack, Engine 7; Thaddeus Holmes, Ladder 2; and Thomas Whipple. assistant foreman No. 7. December 2, two children of Henry Chamberlain, of Athens street, South Boston, were burned to death from playing with matches.

Otis N. Marston, Esq., was appointed assistant engineer during 1857, *vice* Mr. Bird, promoted. Chief Bird, in his report for 1857, stated that the steam-engine " Miles Greenwood," besides its unreliable machinery, was heavy, its weight being between seven and eight tons; but he recommended steam fire-engines of a smaller size, and that one be built immediately, and located in the neighborhood of Pearl street. The old one was sold July 27, and the company discharged.

The question of a parade by the firemen was one that received an abundance of discussion in the City Council; some members being for abolishing the custom, as it was a useless expense, while others thought it an advantage, as the citizens could each year see the full strength of the service. The last parade occurred on Sept. 17, 1856, at the inauguration of the Franklin statue. On May 8, an order was passed repealing the law forbidding parades, and on Sept. 28, 1857, the department marched through the city.

The position of special fire-police was created April 3, and Messrs. James Goves and C. N. Chambers were appointed to fill that office. The number of men serving in Ladder Company No. 2 was increased from eighteen to twenty-four, on July 13. On December 21, Engine Company No. 12 and Hose Companies Nos. 2 and 3 were discharged for insubordination at a fire in Spring street.

A new engine and house were built for Engine Company No. 14 the following year, and located on Fourth street, between K and L streets, South Boston Point. A new house was also built for Engine No. 13, on Chelsea and Bennington streets, East Boston; the company was organized February 9, and temporarily occupied a building on Chelsea street. Several improvements were made in the equipment of the department, one of which was the introduction of springs for the engines and ladder-trucks. The chief recommended that Hydrant Company No. 3 (or hose company as they were then termed) be removed from the quarters with Engine No. 6, on Wall street, to a building in the vicinity of Brighton street, and that Engine Company 7 also be removed from that part of the city, as it was difficult to keep a good company together. Charter Hose Company, No. 4, was organized on Northampton street. The salaries of the leading hosemen, rakemen, and axemen were fixed at the same rate ($125 per year) as the other assistant officers, while the firemen at East Boston, South Boston, and Hose Company No. 4 were paid as follows: foremen, $100; other officers, $75; and members, $60 per year. Eleven additional hydrants were placed in the city proper, eight at South Boston, and four at East Boston.

At a meeting of the Board of Engineers, held July 3, 1857, an order was passed forbidding any person but members of the department to assist in drawing or working the apparatus, while each member was obliged to put on his badge previous to going on duty. Every member failing to do so was fined the same as for absence, and members or others congregating at the engine-house contrary to the ordinance were to be ordered out by the company officers; refusal by members to obey would be considered cause for discharge; substitutes were to notify the officers in charge before going on duty. These orders were approved by the City Council, August 17, 1857.

Department promotions and changes: Engine No. 1, G. O. Twiss, steward; T. H. Evans, clerk. No. 2, Peter Lincoln, clerk. No. 3, Washington, near Dover street, George D. Chubbuck, assistant; S. K. Morris, steward; W. H. Stackpole, clerk. No. 4, John Prince, captain; R. B. Farrar, assistant; W. H. Bradford, clerk. No. 5, E. M. Johnson, steward. No. 6, C. C. Wilson. captain; A. H. Jordan, assistant; C. C. Geyer, steward; J. W. D. Parker, clerk. No. 7, J. A. Allen, steward. No. 8, Benjamin Tarbox. captain: J. S. Jacobs, assistant; Daniel Rand, clerk. Engine 9 house moved temporarily to Sumner street, East Boston. No. 10, William Hall, Jr., steward. No. 11, John Tobias, clerk. No. 12, C. H. Prince, steward. Webster, No. 13. Chelsea street, East Boston. T. B. Tilton. captain; C. E. Turner. assistant; A. G. Bacon, steward; Hiram Weston, clerk. Ladder Company 1, Moses Place, captain; P. Collier, assistant. No. 2, George W. Crafts, clerk. No. 3, George W. Warren, captain; J. F. Marston, assistant; Charles Frizell, clerk. Hose No. 2, Samuel Abbott, assistant; Benjamin King, clerk. No. 3. Louis Moore, assistant; J. S. Ryan, clerk. Charter Hose Company. No. 4, Northampton street, Andrew Neville, captain; R. H. Carley, assistant; James Whittle, steward; J. W. Gamage, clerk. No. 5, W. H. Gardner, clerk. No. 6. Jonas Underwood. assistant.

The department was called out one hundred and sixty-four times during the year; the loss to property being $258,231; insurance, $233,785. King's Chapel, corner of School and Tremont streets, caught fire January 18, but was extinguished by several members of the department with buckets. Charles Litchfield. a member of Engine 8, was badly injured on February 1, while at a fire at 99 Cambridge street, by coming in contact with Ladder 1. At a fire at 8 Stillman street, May 20, David Fisher and Mrs. Fitzgerald were burned to death.

CHAPTER VIII.

1858–1862.

THE improvements made in placing the apparatus on springs was found to be of special advantage, and during 1858 the plan was adopted throughout the entire department. New hose-carriages of the double-wheel pattern were recommended by Chief Bird for general adoption, as they carried twice the amount of hose, and required five less men in a company than the single-wheel wagons, the cost of which being offset by the reduction of the number of men to pay. The subject of steam-engines was one that received an abundant amount of public controversy, the old firemen clinging to their hand-engines, claiming them to possess merits that those operated by steam could not have, while the more practical and far-sighted saw that the former machines were no match in efficiency and general utility to the latter. To convince the general public, a trial was made on August 31, under the immediate direction of the joint special committee for the City Government, which proved entirely satisfactory. The first prize of $500 was given to the Philadelphia engine, built by Messrs. Reaney & Co., of Philadelphia, Pa. ; the second of $300, to the " Lawrence," built by Messrs. Scott & Bean, of Lawrence, Mass., and the third of $200, to the " Elisha Smith," built by G. W. Bird & Co., of East Boston. The chief and a majority of the Board of Engineers were in favor of steam, and on the recommendation of the former in his report for 1858, two steamers were purchased on December 4, also one four-wheeled hose-carriage. Two small hose-carriages were placed at the Mill-dam and Washington Village, each with three hundred and fifty feet of hose, under the care of responsible parties, not in the department, to be used in case of fire in the immediate vicinity. Sixteen additional hydrants were added to the service during the year.

An appropriation was made by the City Council, on May 10. of $1,000 for a burial-lot in Forest-Hill cemetery, for firemen, and on the 22d, $1,000 was appropriated for disabled members of the department. The following engine companies were disbanded: No. 5, July 26 ; No. 11, December 16, for disobedience of orders ; and Nos. 6 and 7 to make room for the steam-engine companies, which were put in service December 16. September 13, the engine-house in Purchase street was ordered to be sold.

Assistant Engineers C. S. Clark, R. S. Martin, and O. N. Marston. were succeeded by Messrs. John S. Damrell, Charles C. Henry, and William A. Green, while George H. Allen was appointed secretary. Promotions, etc., in the department: Engine No. 1, William H. Cunningham, captain; H. H. Abbott, assistant; C. F. Karcher, steward; W. L. Pierce, clerk. No. 2, George Brown, captain; J. B. Hill, assistant; T. Hutchings, steward. No. 4, R. B. Farrar, captain; W. H. Bradford, assistant; Charles P. Stetson, clerk. No. 5, H. L. Wallingford, captain; E. M. Johnson, assistant; David Griner, steward; Thomas Merritt, clerk. No. 6, Lewis Moore, assistant; J. W. C. Prescott, clerk. No. 7, Thomas Whipple, captain; E. L. Leavitt, assistant; J. R. Symes. No. 9, J. P. Somerby, captain; Benjamin Varney, assistant; Anthony Currant, steward; Wm. Wentworth; the quarters of the company was again in Paris street. No. 10, George A. Tucker, captain; John Gray, assistant; Gershom Sherman, steward; M. H. Cross, clerk. No. 11, James Gibson, captain; Charles B. Maxfield, assistant; D. S. Newell, steward; Thomas M. Regan, clerk. No. 12, O. R. Robbins, captain; J. Hawkins, assistant; S. W. Shaw, clerk. No. 13, Hiram Weston, captain; A. M. Pollard, assistant; M. C. George, clerk; S. R. Spinney. Engine Company, No. 14, organized during the year, and located on Fourth street, between K and L streets, South Boston, James Chambers, captain; Samuel S. Lord, Jr., assistant; John H. Harrington, steward; George W. Bail, clerk. Ladder Company 2, Benjamin C. Seaver, assistant; T. Holmes, steward; W. T. Keene, clerk. No. 3, J. B. Prescott, clerk. Hose No. 1, Charles E. Dunton, captain; B. C. Brownell, assistant; George H. Delano, steward; T. S. R. Britton, clerk. No. 2, M. C. Thompson, captain; Benjamin King, assistant; J. Smith, steward; John King, clerk. No. 4, Lovering Hallett, assistant. No. 6, Joseph Barnes, captain; W. H. Poole, assistant; H. Ely, steward; W. H. Rymill, clerk.

The three largest fires for 1858 were: May 2, at 133 to 139 Federal street, the loss being $206,890; insurance, $163,440. Others on June 12, at 55 to 75 Milk street; loss, $85,950; insurance, $75,250; and December 18, the Quincy school-house at the corner of Tyler and Hudson streets; loss $50,000. At a fire in the building on Fourth street, South Boston, February 11, several persons narrowly escaped being suffocated. One woman jumped from an open window and died from its effects. Mr. H. A. Taylor, a member of the department, had his leg broken by a falling building on Third street, South Boston, on March 21. August 22, Mr. James Porter, of Engine 4 had his leg broken by the upsetting of the apparatus at a fire on Pearl street; and on December 3, a child of Mrs. Collins, at 21 Hamburg street, was smothered to death. The whole number of alarms for the year were one hundred and sixty-one; loss of property, $390,650; insurance, $316,207.

The advantage of steam-power over manual labor in the extinguishing of fires, was clearly demonstrated during the ensuing year by the excellent work performed by the two small steam-engines that were purchased last year. One of these machines was lodged in the house of Hand-engine No. 6, on Wall street, and called Eclipse, No. 6. It was built during 1858 by Messrs. Silsbee, Mynderse, & Co., of Seneca Falls, N.Y. The other was called Lawrence, No. 7, and lodged in the quarters of hand-engine of the same number, on Purchase street. It was built during 1858 by Messrs. Bean & Scott, of Lawrence, Mass.; but neither of these engines had a regular organized company, as they were only worked under a contract with the builders for one year on trial. Engine No. 8 organized with J. S. Jacobs as foreman, who was the first permanent captain of a regular organized company in charge of a steam fire-engine in this city, the company being commissioned November 1, 1859. This engine, however, was too heavy, weighing eleven thousand pounds, and was exchanged with its makers on September 1, 1860, for one of seventy-three hundred and thirty pounds, which was stationed in a house on North Bennet street. The other members of the company were J. A. Tisdale, engineer; E. C. Sholes, fireman; G. W. Brown, driver; and H. Allen, Charles H. Blake, F. R. Crane, C. H. Marks, and G. W. Sanborn, hosemen. Steam-engine Company No. 3 was regularly organized on December 1, with the following company: S. Abbott, captain; Theodore Hutchins, engineer; J. S. Young, fireman; L. P. Mayo, driver; H. E. Chase, S. D. Harrington, H. V. Hayward, F. M. Hines, and G. L. Pike, hosemen; house, on Washington street, near Dover. Steam-engine Company No. 1 organized December 19; William H. Cunningham, captain; A. H. Perry, engineer; C. W. Cheney, fireman; Amos Cummings, driver; Daniel Hallett, Robert Henderson, Appleton Lathe, N. H. Tirrell, and George O. Twiss, hosemen. The engine was built by the Boston Locomotive Works, from plans of Messrs. Bean & Stone; its weight was six thousand and eighty pounds, and was lodged in old No. 1's house, on Broadway, near Dorchester street, South Boston. Steam-engine Company No. 9 organized December 26, with J. P. Somerby, captain; C. W. Doten, engineer; Joseph Grace, fireman; S. L. George, driver; G. L. Jenkinson, Andrew Lewis, William Pray, Benjamin Varney, and Simeon Weston, hosemen. The engine was built by the Amoskeag Manufacturing Company, of Manchester, N.H., and weighed seventy-eight hundred and thirty-eight pounds, and was stationed at old No. 9's house, East Boston. Each of these engines had a hose-carriage attached, which weighed from seven hundred to thirteen hundred pounds. The engineer, fireman, and driver were the only members permanently employed, and who remained at the house.

In his report for 1859, Chief Bird states, in reference to steam-engines: —

I would recommend that, as soon as may be, the department should be reorganized by the thorough introduction of *light* steam fire-engines. I recommend this, not only because it is a matter of labor-saving, but from reasons of economy; for it can be clearly demonstrated to cost the city twenty per cent. less to support a steam fire department, than the old method has cost the past few years.

Old Melville, No. 6, was placed in the house formerly used by the " Miles Greenwood," as a relief engine, being the only one not in active use in the service. No hydrants were built during the year, being the first season passed since the water was introduced that the city did not appropriate money for a number of these water supplies.

The following engine companies disbanded : No. 8, on October 31 ; 9 and 10, December 26 ; and Hose 6 was transferred to the house occupied by Engine No. 10 on Meridian street. Soon after, the company was discharged on account of the remoteness of the residence of several of the members from the hose-house. Engine No. 3, December 8 ; Nos. 1 and 2, December 19. No. 2 was discharged on June 13, on account of disgraceful conduct. The name of Union Hose Company was changed on October 12, to Dispatch.

The compensation of the members of the steam-engine companies was fixed, on December 8, as follows : Foremen, $42 per month ; enginemen, $60 ; firemen, $40 ; drivers, $40, and $125 per year to members.

Some trouble was occasioned in the department by the unfairness of the awarding of a silver trumpet which was given to the most efficient company at the yearly muster. The matter was settled on December 23, by a vote of the Council, whereby it was deposited with the City Treasurer. Some of the engine companies, with their machines, attended the parade held in New York, October 17.

Assistant Engineer Hibbard was succeeded, during 1859, by Mr. George Brown, the changes in the companies being as follows : Engine No. 1, Oscar Dwelley, captain ; H. A. Taylor, assistant ; G. C. Bullard, clerk. No. 2, F. B. Boardman, captain ; T. C. Byrnes, assistant. No. 5, Thomas Merritt, assistant ; John Ray, clerk. Nos. 6 and 7 replaced by steam-engine. No. 8, John S. Jacobs, captain ; Albert Pearson, clerk ; no assistant. No. 11, John Tobias, captain ; John A. Fynes, assistant. No. 13, Chelsea street, East Boston, Charles E. Turner, captain ; William B. Currant, assistant ; G. W. Sargent, steward. No. 14, W. S. Locke, assistant ; G. N. Page, clerk. Hose Company No. 2, G. E. King, captain ; C. L. Melvin, assistant ; B. P. Stowell, clerk. No. 4, Irving Hallett, captain ; C. T. Coburn, assistant ; J. C. Fallon, clerk.

The largest fire that happened during 1859 broke out February 6, at the mechanical bakery of Mr. J. G. Russell, on Commercial street. Loss to this building, $160,000 ; insurance, $130,000 ; total loss of the eighteen other firms that were burnt out, $49,700, nearly covered by insurance. A $180,-000 fire occurred at the Sailors' Home, corner of Broad and Purchase streets, on the 29th of the same month. On May 12, a building on North Charles street fell, during the progress of a fire on the street, and injured a number of people. April 3 the Suffolk Flour Mills at the Eastern Railroad wharf, was consumed : loss, $38,000 ; fully insured. The House of Reformation at Deer Island was burnt July 21 ; loss, $25,000. And on October 31 the sugar-house of Mr. Seth Adams, on Gouch street, was laid in ashes ; loss, $130,000 ; insurance, $125,000.

The entire department was equipped with steam fire-engines and horse hose-carriages during 1860. Several steam-engines were in use previous to September 1, but it was not until after this date that it was an entire steam department. This, as a matter of course, resulted in a new ordinance, which was passed June 6, 1860, which repealed the ordinance of February 12. 1850, August 25, 1856, and December 26, 1856. From the new law we take the following : The Chief and nine Engineers, also a Secretary to the board were to be chosen annually by the City Council, in the months of January or February. The secretary was to perform the duty of clerk to the board, and such other duties as the Chief or Engineer, by the Rules and Regulations ordered, which were to be approved by the Board of Aldermen ; to give an account of the appropriations made by the city for the use of the department, and of the expenditures on account of the same. Also, a separate account of each company, and publish them in full in the annual report of the Chief. After the Engineers were chosen they were to organize themselves. Their Rules and Orders were always subject to the approval of the Board of Aldermen. They were responsible for the good order, etc., of the entire department. They had the control of all properties belonging to the service, and the superintendence over the officers and members, and persons at fires. When absent from a fire they were to report such to the Chief, who kept a record of the same, of which he made a report stating the facts, etc., to the City Council every three months. On the breaking out of a fire they were to take their badge of office, and exercise proper measures to arrange the engines and other apparatus in the most advantageous situation, to require and compel assistance from all persons as well as members, and to appoint guards over goods removed from a building, and to repress all disorders. In case of a fire in an adjoining town, only so many Engineers as the Chief previously designated, were to attend. The Chief Engineer was in sole command at fires. His duty was to examine into the condition of all apparatus, and houses of the apparatus, of the department, and, when repairs, alterations, etc., were to be made, he was to have it done under the direction of the City Council ; all returns of officers, members, and apparatus of the department were to be transmitted to the Board of Aldermen, as well as all other communications relating to the affairs of the same ; to keep fair and exact rolls of the respective companies, specify the time of admission and discharge, and age of each member ; critically examine all bills and accounts. and certify, in writing, their correctness. He was to issue an annual report of the entire works and condition of the department, in the month of January. Should any person refuse the orders of the Engineer, they were to be reported to the City Council. When three or more Engineers thought proper, in order to prevent the further spreading of a fire, they had power to demolish any building. Every steam fire-engine company was to consist of an engineman, fireman, and driver, — who were to be permanently employed, and at all times about the house, — and six hosemen, whose term of service continued from periods of six months each, all of whom were appointed by the Mayor, with the advice and consent of the Board of Aldermen. The number of hosemen could be increased from time to time, by the determination of that body. The enginemen were given full care of the engines, under the direction of the Board of Engineers, and all the property belonging to the city, for which they were held personally responsible. They were also accountable for the proper discharge of the duties of the firemen and drivers. The firemen were to perform all such duties as may be required of them about the engine and house, including cleaning the hose. The drivers had the care of the horse and stable, also to assist the firemen when required to do so by the enginemen. The foreman had full charge at fires, the placing of the engines, and to perform the same duty required of the clerk of a hose company. The hosemen, under his direction, were to perform such duties as were required of suction and leading hosemen of hand-engines as call-men.

The pay of the department, as established the ensuing year, was as follows: Chief engineer, $1,200 per annum; assistant engineer, $1,050; secretary to Board of Engineers, $800; enginemen of steam-engines, $60; firemen, $50; drivers, $50; foremen in city proper, $150; members, $100; foremen in East Boston, South Boston, and hose company in Northampton street, $100; assistant foremen, clerks, stewards, hosemen, axe, and rakemen in the above location, $75; members of companies in above sections, $60 per annum. (See Engineer's Report for 1860.)

Nine horse hose companies were introduced into the service during the year, in the place of the six hand companies. Twenty-six horses were purchased, with all the harnesses, blankets, and equipments complete; while the several houses were altered to accommodate the new order of things. Despite all these changes, no material increase of appropriations was required over that formerly applied to carry on the hand department, without the purchase of any new apparatus. A new house for Hose Company No. 9 was constructed on B street, South Boston, and a new house for Steam-engine No. 5, on Marion street, East Boston; the old hand company was discharged April 2, as was No. 11. Six thousand feet of two and one-half-inch hose, of Boyd's patent, were bought; the increase in size from two-inch was occasioned by the introduction of the steamers, and was used only by them, the hose companies being equipped with the smaller size. Hose-house No. 7, on River street, at the foot of Mount Vernon street, was altered so as to accommodate a steam-engine. Each police station was provided with a suitable quantity of ropes and stakes, with which to close the streets in case of large fires. These were under the care of the police department, who were requested to send a certain number of officers to each fire. Thirteen hydrants were added to the list of those in the city proper, twenty-six at South Boston, and five at East Boston.

Eight hundred dollars were appropriated by the City Council, on February 24, for the relief of the families of deceased firemen. This order did not pass the year previous. Ladder Company No. 3 was disbanded on the same date for unbecoming conduct. Old Hand-engine Companies Nos. 6 and 11 were honorably discharged July 18, and on September 17 the same order was given to Engine No. 14, while Hose Companies Nos. 1, 9, and 3 were reduced to nine members. The office of special fire police did not give satisfaction, as it was claimed to interfere with the duties of the Engineers;

therefore, on July 18, the order was rescinded, and another passed, whereby the Mayor was to appoint the Engineers as special police, to serve without extra pay. An order was also passed, on September 5, to remove the names from all engine, hose, and hook-and-ladder companies, and designate them by numbers only; this order was in force until June 2, 1868, when it was revoked. The drivers of the hose and ladder carriages protested against being subject to a less compensation than the drivers of engines; an order was therefore passed on December 8 granting them the same pay. The houses of old Hose No. 6 and Engine No. 5, in East Boston, were sold September 21.

The steam-engine companies placed in service during 1860 were as follows: No. 6, house in Wall street, organized January 1; C. C. Geyer, captain; John Travers, engineman; C. C. Wilson, fireman; George Scott, driver; Amos Cross, T. J. Davis, J. W. D. Parker, C. L. Skelton, and J. W. Tinkham, hosemen. No. 7, Purchase street, organized January 1; J. Q. Alley, captain; John Ray, engineman; F. L. Grant, fireman; Oliver Wilson, driver; G. Abercrombie, A. A. J. Bartlett, L. I. Geddings, L. Hodgdon, and George L. Imbert, hosemen; engine built by Bean & Scott, in Lawrence Machine Shop, Lawrence, Mass.; weight, ten thousand pounds. No. 4, in basement of City Hall, Court square (quarters of old No. 11), organized May 7; J. Tobias, captain; R. S. Jenness, engineman; H. A. Chase, fireman; John Lewis, driver; J. A. Fynes, P. P. Hackett, D. S. Newell, J. W. Regan, and Alexander Wilson, hosemen; they first had charge of the engine built by the Amoskeag Manufacturing Company, which was retained by them until September 17, when it was removed to the house of Engine No. 2, from which time to December 15 the steamer in charge of No. 2 was under their control, while the former engine was again returned to this company; weight, seven thousand six hundred pounds. No. 5, house on Marion street, East Boston, organized September 1; G. A. Tucker, captain; Josiah S. Battis, engineman; Gilbert Prior, fireman; Horatio Ely, driver; William Hall, Jr., C. J. Littlefield, G. Sherman, A. J. Smith, and Eben Witherell, hosemen; engine built by Amoskeag Manufacturing Co.; weight, seven thousand eight hundred and eighty-five pounds.

No. 2, house of old Spinney, No. 14, organized September 17; James Chambers, captain; Daniel Weston, engineman; J. B. Gault, fireman; M. A. Jones, driver; George W. Bail, E. H. Goodwin, J. B. Lord, William Rand, and David Smith, hosemen; engine built by the Amoskeag Manufacturing Company, and had a double steam cylinder, with a high double-action plunger pump; weight, fifty-three hundred and eighty-five pounds.

Horse Hose Company No. 1, Salem street, organized April 1; B. C. Brownell, captain; A. L. Pearson, driver; L. H. Felton, W. E. Harper, E. K. Perkins, Uzziel Putnam, F. B. Leach, R. T. Stoddard, and W. H. Weeks, hosemen. This carriage had but two wheels, with a single reel, intended to convey one thousand feet of hose. It was built, as were all the others, excepting No. 6, by Brigham, Mitchell, & Bird; weight when loaded, fifteen hundred pounds. No. 2, Hudson street, organized May 1, B.

King, captain; John Smith, driver; H. A. Barnes, John King, G. E. King, C. L. Meloon, B. P. Stowell, John H. Stevens, and G. H. Welch, hosemen; weight, fifteen hundred pounds. No. 3, house in Friend street, organized June 16; A. F. Gould, captain; R. F. Parron, driver; C. M. Babb, C. J. Carrill, Dexter R. Deering, John Gilman, A. Smith, W. H. Tyler, and H. N. Wilson, hosemen; weight, fifteen hundred pounds. No. 8, house occupied by old No. 12, on Warren near Tremont street, organized July 1; C. H. Prince, captain; William Blake, driver; M. S. Dix, G. T. Frost, William H. Flanders, P. J. Leeds, G. F. Marden, William J. McElwin, and M. H. Ridland, hosemen; the same weight as the others. No. 7, house occupied by old No. 4, on River street, foot of Mt. Vernon street, organized August 1; R. B. Farrar, captain; A. H. Town, driver; W. H. Bradford, D. F. Bartlett, E. W. Gardner, Timothy Gerrish, F. W. Gough, James Porter, and G. E. Town, hosemen. No. 4, Northampton street, organized August 18; L. Hallett, captain; B. F. Thayer, driver; J. L. Bickford, C. T. Coburn, J. C. Fallon, J. D. E. Hawkes, P. M. Marble, B. P. Norris, and John Soll, hosemen. No. 5, on Shawmut avenue, near Canton street, organized August 17, W. Lovell, captain; Silas Lovell, driver; F. A. Brigham, A. J. Emery, George C. Fernald, S. A. Green, Reuben Hanaford, H. W. Jellison, and J. A. Young, hosemen. No. 6, house occupied by old No. 13, at 391 Chelsea street, East Boston, organized September 1; J. Barnes, captain; Jacob Sherman, driver; B. F. Cowdin, J. L. Jennison, W. H. Poole, J. W. Pringle, William H. Rymill, Lincoln Stoddard, and J. L. Tewksbury, hosemen; carriage built by Messrs. Hunneman & Co., of Roxbury, Mass., February, 1857, to be run by hand, and was used in this manner until April 1, 1860, by Hose Company No. 1, when it was altered, and used by that company until No. 6 was organized. No. 9, house on B street, near Broadway, South Boston, occupied by old No. 2, organized November 1; O. P. Rowell, captain; Benjamin Donnell, driver; T. C. Byrnes, N. C. Cogley, T. W. Gowen, Peter Lincoln, Alex McKenzie, W. B. Ray, and Frederick Wakefield, hosemen. This carriage was built to run by hand, for company No. 2, and on May 1, 1860, it was altered and used by that company, until No. 9 was organized. Hose Nos. 6 and 9, were four-wheel carriages.

Ladder Company No. 1, Friend street, Moses Place, captain; Phineas Collier, assistant; C. H. Merritt, clerk; J. S. Stevens, steward; W. H. Brown, T. H. Briggs, J. L. Batcheldor, J. H. Chase, James Edwards, Asa Freeman, E. B. Hines, O. W. Knowles, John Lyman, Alvah Morse, B. Stover, George Stover, E. B. Stevens, J. H. Stevens, G. W. Thompson, D. V. Wilson, I. H. Ware, Benjamin Wright, B. T. Warren, and George Ware, members; truck built by Messrs. Stevens & Pratt, of Boston. No. 2 at old No. 10 house on Meridian street, East Boston; Charles Simmons, captain; A. S. Turner, assistant; B. H. Stimson, clerk; T. Holmes, steward; S. B. Arey, G. W. Crafts, J. H. Elliot, W. F. Hayes, D. H. Jones, W. T. Keen, John Keen, J. W. Seavey, B. C. Seaver, S. C. Stinson, and J. E.

Thayer, members; truck built by Mr. W. Hunt, East Boston. No. 3, Harrison avenue, J. B. Prescott, driver and clerk; J. F. Marston, L. M. Clifford, C. B. Corey, J. A. Collins, E. R. Chubbuck, Daniel Downes, C. H. Downes, S. L. Gowell, George Graves, A. Hutchinson, I. K. Jennings, R. M. Libby, O. W. Marston, George Mitchell, James Murray, Joseph McIntire, Ezra McIntire, N. H. Plummer, J. Runey, R. F. Ricker, Robert Spear, B. B. Wright, and J. Whitcomb, members.

Besides the above companies, hose-carriages were stationed at the following locations, for the more immediate protection of the neighborhood: Mill-dam; Washington Village; rolling-mill, South Boston: Adams School-house, East Boston: and two hundred and fifty feet of hose at Chickering's piano factory, Tremont street, and one hundred and fifty feet at the kerosene-oil works, East Boston. Old Hand-engine No. 12 was placed at the House of Correction, South Boston, and old No. 8, at Deer Island. One small fuel wagon was kept at the house of Engine 9, and two large ones in the engine-house on East street. Apparatus not in use: three hydrant-carriages, three hose-carriages, and Hand-engines Nos. 3, 4, 5, 9, 11, 13, and 14.

The number of alarms from September 1, 1859, to August 31, 1860, was one hundred and ninety-four, during which the loss of property amounted to $521,888; insurance, $471,853. From September 1 to December 31, 1860, there were fifty alarms, and $209,197 worth of property destroyed: insurance, $141,885. The largest of these occurred at 8.20 P.M., on February 5, at 42 Merchants' row, occupied by Messrs. Manning & Glover. The cause of the fire is supposed to be of an incendiary origin. The building was filled with combustible materials for filling beds, etc., and there being openings from one room to another, caused the fire to burn with great rapidity. It was a cold and stormy night, the snow driven with blinding fury, and the wind fanning the fearful blaze. At 3 o'clock the walls, previously considered safe by every member of the department, fell with a terrible crash, instantly killing Mr. Charles Carter of Ladder 1 and Capt. Charles E. Dutton of Hose No. 1. Fourteen firms were burned out, the aggregate loss amounting to $105,000, $95,000 of which were insured. February 5, Mrs. Alice O'Maley, of 3 Mechanic street, set fire to her clothing and was burned to death. At the fire of the kerosene-oil works of Page & Mitchell, on Bennington street, East Boston, March 9, a vat containing a large quantity of oil burst and set fire to a dwelling-house, which was enveloped in flames so rapidly that Mr. Francis Dunbar, who was removing goods, was suffocated. Another large fire occurred on October 6, at a building occupied by a Mr. Souther and others, in First street, South Boston; loss $43,000, fully insured. December 26, Mary Jane Geyer, of 3 Livingston street, was badly burned.

A new fire ordinance was passed August 20, 1861, and amended on November 26. In this it cites that the members were to be paid quarterly, and any member who did not serve the whole of that time, unless from sickness, death, or removal from the city, would forfeit his recompense; that each ladder company should have three or more axemen and rakemen; every engine, hose, and ladder company should have a foreman and clerk, and every ladder company an assistant foreman in addition, the foreman and assistant to be nominated annually by the members from among their members. In the absence of the foreman, the senior hoseman was to take charge. The engineers, when they considered it proper, could employ or permit one member of each company to sleep in the house where the apparatus was kept. Two weeks vacation were allowed any member on such terms as agreed upon by the Board of Engineers.

The Board of Engineers took action on the duties of stewards of ladder companies, December 16, and ordered that each ladder company having no permanent driver should have a steward, whose duty it was to keep the apparatus ready for immediate use, and the house clean. The steward of Ladder No. 2, in addition to these duties, was obliged to sleep in the house where the ladders were kept, and to have his employment in the immediate vicinity, so that he would be able to act as driver of the apparatus. A running-card was also adopted by this body on June 28, 1861, and approved by the Board of Aldermen, July 29.

On June 28, a house was erected at Washington Village for the accommodation of a hand-hose company. Within the year past, twenty-four reservoirs were thoroughly cleaned, and so arranged that water could be supplied to them from the Cochituate pipes, which enabled the department to bring more force to bear directly upon the fire through comparatively short lines.

Complaint was made by Chief Bird, in his report for 1861, of the lack of interest displayed by the police at fires, they neglecting to bring the ropes with which they were provided, or to " spring their rattles, crying ' fire,' and mentioning the district and box of the section in which fire exists."

Department changes and appointments during 1861: Engine No. 1, L. Appleton, captain; H. B. Fowler, J. W. Fowler, D. Hallett, B. F. Lucas, and F. W. Wright, members. No. 2, John Brown, W. 'E. Best, and D. H. Twiss, hosemen. No. 3, H. M. Hawkins, H. S. Hussey, and J. L. Ryan, hosemen. No. 4, J. W. Regan, captain; T. P. Bayley, P. A. Mahoney, and C. Tracey, hosemen. No. 5, C. P. Cottle and J. M. Tucker, hosemen. No. 6, John Ash, J. H. Estes, Walter Marten, and Benjamin Thomas, hosemen. No. 7, George W. Bradford, G. H. Prescott, and C. G. Smith, hosemen. No. 8, Archibald Smith, member. No. 9, S. L. Fowle, A. A. Hamblin, P. Nutter, hosemen. Hose No. 1, H. F. McDonald and E. F. Peirce, hosemen. No. 2, C. L. Ingram and R. L. Trout, hosemen. No. 3, A. P. Hawkins, captain; J. F. Bolton, A. F. Gould, G. H. Pike, John Ronamus. No. 4, W. W. Graves, hoseman. No. 5, W. H. Gardner and W. E. Manley, hosemen. No. 7, William Parker, hoseman. No. 8, Walter Dalrymple, Addison Getchel, William H. Munroe, and H. F. Young, hosemen. No. 9, T. C. Byrnes, captain; Charles Allen, G. H. Delano, and M. H. Libby, hosemen. Hand-hose Company No. 10,

Joseph Frye, captain; H. T. Bowers, steward; E. Ashcroft, J. L. Bowers, F. H. Cooper, and G. H. Sharp, members.   Ladder No. 1, George Stevens, clerk; Charles H. Merritt, D. C. Bickford, G. A. Baker, C. A. Crowell, and W. N. Young, members.   No. 2, B. H. Stinson, assistant; George W. Crafts, clerk; Austin Harding and A. S. Turner, members.   No. 3, J. F. Marston, captain; L. M. Clifford, G. L. Cooper, G. F. Clark, L. B. Clifford, L. L. Cooper, and L. Stackpole, members.

Three very large fires occurred during 1861.   The first broke out at 5 A.M., on January 5, at 72 Long wharf, owned by the Long Wharf Corporation; loss, $15,752; insurance, $11,200.   On May 6, at a fire at 235 State street, a quantity of gunpowder, kept contrary to law, was seized.   The careless use of fire-crackers in the premises of Mr. Francis Standish, 131 Albany street, at 1.18, on July 4, destroyed twenty buildings on Albany, Hudson, and Curve streets.   While most of the department were fighting this fire, another broke out at 2.17 P.M., at Nickerson's wharf, East Boston, from the same cause.   The building in which the latter originated contained a large quantity of combustible material.   When first discovered it was near being extinguished with a bucket, but for the breaking of the line when drawing the water.   On the alarm being given, only a small force of the department could be spared for this emergency.   Valuable assistance, however, was rendered by the departments of Chelsea, Roxbury, Cambridge, Malden, and Charlestown.   The loss of property, when compared with the large number of poor people who were turned from their homes and occupations, was an inconsiderable matter.   It was impossible to obtain anything like a correct return of the damage to property, but the number of people burnt out was as follows: fifteen on Nickerson's wharf, twenty on New street, twenty-one on Maverick street, two in the rear of Maverick street, seven on the corner of Border and Maverick streets, nine on Border street, fifteen on Cross street, nineteen on Liverpool street, seventeen in Erin alley, the Suffolk Salt Works of Clark & Co., A. P. Clark, Aspinwall's wharf, and ten vessels, steamboats, etc.   Gove's block, corner of Green and Pitts streets, was partly destroyed on August 3; loss, $43,758; insurance, $34,758.   Mr. and Mrs. Ezra Lincoln, Jr., of Commonwealth avenue, were severely injured by a gas explosion on November 24.   The total number of alarms during the year were one hundred and ninety-two, during which $506,075 worth of property was destroyed; insurance, $498,963.

Engine Company No. 10 was organized during May, 1862, and located in the house on River street previously occupied by Hose Company No. 1, and one was placed in Purchase street to take the place of old "Lawrence" No. 7, it being too heavy for regular service.   This engine was thoroughly repaired and placed in the old house formerly occupied by the "Miles Greenwood."   A new building was erected on Northampton street for the accommodation of Hose No. 4, which was considered the most convenient house in the department.   A new structure was also in process of building on Harrison avenue, at the junction of Malden and Wareham streets, for Ladder Company No. 3, and for the storage of one spare engine, ladder carriage, and other apparatus temporarily out of service. The old house at the westerly end of " Scollay's Building " was remodelled for the occupancy of Engine No. 4, where it was removed from the basement of City Hall. Thirty-one reservoirs — fourteen in South Boston, nine in East Boston, and the balance in the city proper — were thoroughly cleaned and arranged so that water could be supplied to them from the Cochituate water-pipes. One hose-carriage with all its equipments was located in the rear of 78 Prince street, at the distil-house of Felton & Cunningham.

The war with the South caused twenty-nine members of the department during 1862 to enter the service of the United States, — a service scarcely more dangerous than that which they left. Many of them rose to positions of honor and trust, while some few offered up their lives on the altar of devotion to their country. Mr. John W. Regan was appointed on the Board of Engineers, *vice* Otis N. Marston.

The changes and promotions in the companies for the year were as follows : —

Engine No. 1, Thomas C. Porter, hoseman. No. 3, F. M. Hines, captain ; W. N. Abbott, E. L. Barnes, J. H. Lefavor, and J. G. Pike, hosemen. No. 4, J. H. Fynes, captain ; E. H. Bright and J. S. Goodell, hosemen. No. 5, R. W. Sturtevant, fireman ; George W. Brown, driver. No. 6, J. A. Barker, hoseman. No. 7, C. H. Adams, fireman ; A. A. J. Bartlett, captain ; C. H. Hodgdon, D. T. Marden, and L. C. Smith, hosemen ; on June 1, six officers and members of this company were transferred to Engine No. 10. No. 8, H. A. Chase, fireman ; R. F. Parow, driver ; H. G. Floyd, C. A. Scott, and J. S. Young, hosemen. No. 9, Charles Hodges and I. H. Jones, hosemen. No. 10, organized May, 1862 ; F. L. Grant, engineman ; Lewis Briggs, fireman ; A. H. Towne, driver ; R. B. Farrar, captain ; W. H. Bradford, F. W. Gough, C. N. Morse, James Porter, William Parker, James Shannon, and G. E. Towne, hosemen ; weight of engine, including three members, sixty-two hundred and fifty pounds.

Hose Company No. 1, W. H. Prescott, hoseman. No. 2, N. S. Brown, Thomas Merritt, A. B. Smith, and W. W. Stevens, hosemen. No. 3, Horatio Ely, driver, and George W. Clark, hoseman. No. 4, Robert Bruce, S. C. Murray, M. C. Parcher, and J. H. Whittle, hosemen. No. 5, A. M. Hickey, hoseman. No. 6, William Classen and John Fenno, hosemen. No. 8, A. G. Shaw, hoseman. No. 9, T. W. Gowan, driver, and William Moffit, hoseman. Hand-hose No. 10, H. P. Abbott, L. F. Fluet, H. Gill, J. L. Hyde, and T. A. Harmon, hosemen.

Ladder Company No. 1, E. B. Hines, assistant ; C. H. Merritt, clerk. No. 2. J. E. Thayer, driver and steward ; Warren Foster and A. P. Inman, members. No. 3, John Demerritt, S. K. Jaquith, S. Jaquith, W. M. Norris, and N. P. Plummer, members.

The pay-roll was equalized during the year, no distinction being made between the city companies and those in East or South Boston. A new running-card was also made out by the engineers, on June 29, 1862. Four hundred dollars was paid on March 11 to the widow of Reuben Hanaford, who was killed at a fire on Commercial street, and on July 23, $600 were paid to the widow of George Abercrombie, who was killed at a fire on Sudbury street.

The year was very disastrous, both from the loss to property and the number of deaths and accidents to the members of the department. The first accident of the year occurred on January 3, when S. L. Gowell, of Ladder No. 3, was run over by the truck, and received a compound fracture of the leg. On the 14th, at 11.50 A.M., a heavy conflagration resulting from the blowing off of the head of a copper still at the establishment of Mr. J. W. Clifford, 57 Commercial street, burnt out twenty-three firms; damage unknown. Faneuil Hall market was discovered on fire at 5.16 A.M., January 28, and was almost entirely destroyed. Twenty-six occupants and others suffered by this fire; loss, $33,930; insurance, $26,325. George C. Fernald of Hose No. 5 fell from a ladder at a fire on January 31, at John H. Pray, Son, & Co.'s, 283 Washington street, and broke one leg and wrist. But the most terrible conflagration that visited Boston since it became a city occurred at 9.47 o'clock in the evening of February 24. The fire originated from some unknown cause in the store of Mr. William Mathews, on the corner of North and Commercial streets, occupied by Gove & Co., oil-clothing manufacturers, and burned with fearful rapidity, until nothing remained in the square bounded by North, Fleet, and Clark streets, to the water, including in its course the wharf property. It was an exceedingly cold night, and the wind from the westward blew with fearful violence. It is impossible to give the names or loss of many of the sufferers by this fire. The chief engineer's report gives the names of thirty-nine firms, and the loss, $702,300; insurance, $490,900. Mr. Reuben Hanaford of Hose No. 5, and some unknown person who assisted in putting out the fire in company with Mr. Hanaford, lost their lives by suffocation. Mr. H. A. Green, of the same company, was badly injured, and a young man, in endeavoring to save some property in the dark, had his boat carried by the wind to Long Island, where he was found with his feet and hands badly frozen.

At a fire in the junk store of James Powers & Co., of 392 Federal street, about sixty pounds of powder were taken from the burning building at the risk of a great sacrifice of life by the hosemen of Engine No. 7 and Hose No. 8. May 12, at 11.05 P.M., the building at 65 Broad street, occupied by Messrs. D. Webster & Co., was destroyed, together with $130.000 worth of property; insurance, $122,000. Another disastrous fire, resulting in the loss of life, broke out at 8.41 P.M., July 11, at 61 and 63 Sudbury street, occupied by Messrs. Sargent, Ham, & Co. The falling of the walls instantly killed George N. Abercrombie of Engine No. 7, and seriously injured Henry

B. Fowler and B. F. Lucas of Engine No. 1, A. Hutchinson, George Mitchell, Robert Spear, L. M. Clifford, and B. B. Wright of Hose No. 3. The loss by this fire was probably, in the aggregate, nearly $15,000, but divided among a large number of mechanics, who were unable from the nature of their loss to properly estimate the value. December 23, the Athenæum block, at 85 to 91 Pearl street, was destroyed, the loss to the occupants, etc., amounting to $65,000; fully insured.

Number of alarms from September 1, 1861, to August 31, 1862, one hundred and seventy-two; from September 1 to December 31, 1862, thirty-two; total loss, $1,242,998; insurance, $903,142.

CHAPTER IX.

1863–1867.

DURING 1863, twenty-two reservoirs in the city proper and five in South Boston were cleaned and arranged for the more advantageous use of the department. In the report of Chief Bird for that year all the statutes and ordinances that refer to this branch of the government are printed, to which we refer for the statutes enacted during 1833 relating to gunpowder; fire-arms, bonfires, and brick-kilns, July 22, 1850; fireworks, April 14, 1853; and the orders of the Board of Engineers regarding fireworks, April 29, 1853. We also refer to the Act of 1829, Chapter 44, and 1838, Chapter 131, for the incorporation of the Charitable Association of the Boston Fire Department.

The pay of the assistant engineers was increased to $350 per annum, and that of the enginemen, firemen, and drivers to $70, $60, and $55 per month, respectively, while all the other members had an increase of $25 per annum added to their salaries. Changes and promotions during 1863 were as follows: Engine No. 1, H. A. Chase, engineman; T. E. Porter, fireman; R. F. Twiss and Benjamin Twiss, hosemen. No. 2, D. E. Gilman, fireman; T. N. Page, hoseman. No. 3, M. H. Ryder, fireman. No. 4, Scollay's building, Court street, Lewis Briggs, engineman, D. R. Deering, fireman; Thomas Merritt, hoseman. No. 5, Augustus Blood, hoseman. No. 6, Cyrus Bruce, Henry Daniels, and J. W. C. Prescott, hosemen. No. 7, Charles Riley, fireman; D. A. Carney, Daniel Carter, William T. Cheswell, George E. Houghton, L. G. Howard, hoseman. The engine was built during 1862 by the Amoskeag Manufacturing Company, and had a double cylinder, also two double-acting plunger pumps; a tender to carry fuel and a water-tank for the supply of the boiler were also new additions to this engine. No. 8, E. H. Leach and Charles H. Marks, hosemen. This engine was given to Company No. 6, on June 15, until they received their new one. No. 9, Joseph Grace, engineman; J. S. Young, fireman; C. P. Wood, driver; J. D. Campbell and S. L. Fowle, hosemen. Hose Company No. 1, David Kurrus, S. P. Pool, hosemen. No. 2, John King, hoseman. No. 3, J. F. Bolton and R. Y. Young, hosemen. No. 4, R. Bruce, captain; C. F. Coburn, P. M. Marble, M. C. Parcher, hosemen. No. 8, J. T. Prescott and H. F. Young, hosemen. No. 10, J. L. Bowers, hoseman; the stewardship on this company was discontinued. Ladder Company No. 1, William Lewis, P. Collier, James Clark, Charles Kenney, Samuel Todd, and W. N. Young, members. No. 2, George W. Crafts, assistant; J. W. Seavey, clerk; B. H. Stinson, George Chilcott, Edwin Fiske, A. Lewis, L. P. Lawrence, S. C. Stinson, and J. L. Tewksbury, members. No. 3, M. H. Plummer, B. B. Wright, George F. Clarke, Henry Durant, George O. Ladd, M.

B. Rowe, C. A. Rowe, and R. E. Stannard, members. By joining the butts and tips of the ladders carried by this truck the company were able to raise them to sixty-five feet.

The Rand & Avery fire occurred on February 21 of this year. It originated in the building at 1 to 19 Washington street, occupied by F G. Tuckerman, and extended to Cornhill and Brattle street; loss, $36,137; insurance, $22,921. Rand & Avery were the heaviest losers. The National Theatre, the property of William Sohier, located on Portland street, was discovered on fire at 1.52 A.M., March 24, and in a few hours the building, with all its contents, including the actors' wardrobes, were entirely destroyed; loss, $53,468; insurance, $16,000. The first false alarm, given at 8.39 A.M., June 6, from Bowdoin square, for an exhibition, was rung in by the city government, to show the department to the city officials of Cincinnati. The Roxbury Lead Works, on Davis street, were destroyed August 20; loss, $40,000. On the 31st, the Atlantic Iron Works, Sumner street, East Boston, were burnt; five alarms were given for this fire; loss, $10,150; insurance, $4,000. Twelve horses were burnt at the stables of William McMahen, 31 Paris street, East Boston, on September 16; loss to property, $10,000; insurance, $5,500. The Bay State Rolling-Mills. on First street, South Boston, were set fire September 18; loss, $12.400; insurance, $10,000. A large number of persons were thrown out of work. November 6, Messrs. Holmes & Joy's factory at Charlestown, destroyed; loss, $75,000. Engines from Boston responded. Number of alarms from September 1. 1862, to August 31, 1863, one hundred and forty-one; from September 1, 1863, to December 31, 1863, fifty-six; total loss, $456,934; insurance, $180,477.

The most excitable time during the year was the draft riot, on Cooper street, at the North End. The city having failed to meet the requisition of men by voluntary enlistment for the war between the North and South, Mayor Lincoln found it necessary to resort to a draft. On the afternoon of July 14, two assistant provost marshals were serving notices upon the men who had been drafted for military service, and who lived in rather a disreputable quarter of the North End of the city, when they were suddenly assaulted by a woman whose husband had been numbered among the conscript. Her cries acted as a signal, and in an instant the narrow streets in that section were filled with a terrible mob, made so by the leadership of women. The marshals fled for their lives, and the local patrolmen coming to their rescue were set upon and nearly beaten to death. One officer was crippled for life. In a short time the whole North End was in a state of revolt. and an alarm was rung in on the fire-alarm service at 12.27 A.M., July 15, from District 3, Box 3, which was given for police aid. It was followed thirteen minutes later for a fire at the Cooper-street armory, which was set by the mob. but was extinguished with only $500 damage to the building. The Mayor acted with great promptness and resolution. He issued his precepts to the independent company cadets (the prescribed body-guard of the Governor), a battalion of cavalry, and a battery of light artillery, the only local military organizations in the city at that time, directing them to report to him armed and equipped for service. This force was strengthened by several military organizations then in camp at Readville, and by detachments from the heavy artillery and infantry companies on duty at the forts in the harbor. The Cooper-street armory, occupied by a light battery, was situated in the very midst of the riotous populace. It was here that the scene of bloodshed took place. The first was a citizen standing at an open window of the armory. He was shot dead by a pistol-shot. The mob took up paving-stones and bricks from the sidewalks, and threw them against the building. They attempted to effect an entrance through the doors which they had partially battered down, when a loaded cannon was fired from within. Its charge tore through the mass and demolished a part of the opposite house front. The attack was again renewed, but the firing of the infantry from the doors and windows dampened the ardor of the assailants, and a diversion was presently created by the proposition to sack Reed's gun store, in Dock square. In the mean time, the other military organizations had been brought together, and were about to march to Cooper-street armory, when word was brought Mayor Lincoln of their intent. An advance guard of policemen met the mob, and held them in check until the military force came up and effectually dispersed them. The number of the rioters killed is unknown, as the dead were in most cases conveyed away in secret, and buried without official permit. Seven hundred and thirteen men were drafted out of the twenty-six thousand one hundred and nineteen men furnished by Boston for the service.

Very few changes are reported during the year 1864. The only additional equipments to the service were the arranging of fifteen reservoirs in the city proper, and placing iron covers on the curbs of twenty-three, thus obviating the constant demands for renewals of wooden covers. Nineteen hydrants were added to the city service, five at South Boston, and three at East Boston. A new engine was built for No. 6 by the Amoskeag Manufacturing Company, December 19. All the stone floors in the engine-houses were taken out, and wood substituted. The compensation was again increased during the year. Assistant engineers received $400, while enginemen, firemen, and drivers got $80, $70, and $65 per month, respectively. The other officers and members had $25 per annum additional.

Mr. Elijah B. Hine succeeded Assistant Engineer C. C. Henry. The other changes in the department were as follows: Engine Company No. 1, John Ray, engineman; S. S. Gowen, George W. Gerrish, M. F. Holden, and F. S. Wright, hosemen. No. 2, D. E. Gilman, engineman; George O. Twiss, fireman; B. F. Lucas, driver; John Brown, captain; Robert Donelly and Edward Lamphier, hosemen. No. 4, William T. Cheswell, driver; Matthew Conley, hoseman. No. 6, John Ash and G. B. Munroe, hosemen. No. 7, Charles Riley, engineman; B. S. Flanders, fireman; George L. Imbert, captain: R. E. Flanders, J. A. Holland, and John Winniatt, hosemen. No. 8, Otis B. Hardy, engineman ; Warren Webster, fireman ; J. F. Lewis, driver ; R. J. Fortune, G. F. C. Hamilton, Erastus E. Jeffery, hosemen. No. 9. Simeon Webster, captain. No. 10, Gilman Tyng, fireman ; C. H. Kuhn and W. H. Scribner, hosemen. Hose Company No. 1, George W. Stoddard, hoseman. No. 2, Sylvester Stone, hoseman. No. 3, George W. Clark, captain ; James Mills and Henry Tracy, hosemen. This company was disbanded on August 16 for insubordination, and reorganized September 1. No. 4, J. H. Whittle, captain ; Henry Bruce, E. F. Barney, S. S. Hartshorn, Gottlieb Karcher, and J. H. Skinner, hosemen. No. 5, George F. Clark, hoseman. No. 6, John H. Weston, hoseman. No. 8, H. F. Newton, hoseman. No. 9, W. H. Godfrey, hoseman. Hand-hose Company No. 10 was not mentioned in report for this year. Ladder Company No. 1 moved to Warren street ; P. Collier, assistant ; John Lyman, Asa Freeman, M. D. Gill, R. Garland, and H. A. Ladd, members. This truck was also provided with butt ladders during the year. No. 2, Edwin Fish, member. No. 3, George H. Alexander, Charles H. Downes, L. W. Shaw, and A. C. Shaw, members.

Total number of alarms from September 1, 1863, to August 31, 1864, one hundred and eighty-eight ; from September 1, 1864, to December 31, 1864, thirty-five ; loss, $1,146,581 ; insurance, $620,669. On February 6, nine horses were burnt to death at the stables of Moses French, Jr., 374 Broad street. After the department left the building it burst out in flames the second time. Chief Engineer Bird was seriously hurt by the falling of a ladder. On the 19th, Mrs. Murphy, of No. 7 Oliver street, was burnt to death. By the explosion of ether at the establishment of Messrs. Case & Getchel, 299½ Washington street, on March 1, Mr. Eaton and Mr. Getchel were badly burnt. A large fire broke out at 2.04 A.M., March 5, at 170 Washington street, occupied by Messrs. Weeks & Potter ; loss, $189,629 ; insurance, $112,104. But the largest conflagration of the year occurred at 12.10 A.M., April 6, at Masonic Hall, located on Tremont corner of Boylston street. A large number of very valuable and almost priceless paintings were destroyed, including original portraits of Washington, General Warren, Price, the first Grand Master of the State, and also all of the Grand Masters of 1780 down to the year of the fire. All the lodges lost heavily. The painting of General Warren, owned by the Massachusetts Lodge, was lost. The Grand Lodge of this State lost a great number of original Masonic documents of the previous century, and which to them were of great value. Among them were charters and papers signed by Washington, Warren, Franklin, Paul Revere, and others, which were destroyed ; total loss over $200,000 ; insurance, $100.000. On April 15, the " Herald " office and other buildings were destroyed ; loss, $17,100 ; insurance, $10,500. On April 28, the system of fire alarms for twelve years in use was rearranged, and from that date the location of the box from which the alarm was turned was designated by the bells instead of the district.

Mary Slatterly was suffocated by fire at her house on Moon street, April

29.   An alarm was pulled in by order of the Mayor, on June 8, at 6.40 P.M., for the purpose of exhibiting the department to the Russian fleet officers.   On the 10th, at 1.06 A.M., a serious fire occurred on Rowe's wharf, occupied by A. S. & W. G. Lewis, and others ; loss, $157,000 ; insurance, $77,000.   July 5, the grain elevator of Stebbens & Anderson, on Eastern avenue, was burnt; loss, $50,000 ; insured.   Keating's saw mill on Causeway street, July 22 ; loss, $27,550.   And on September 27, the piano factory of Hallett & Davis, on Newton street, was destroyed; loss, $200,000 ; insurance, $63,000.

On Tuesday evening, October 25, the famous old Province House was destroyed by fire.   This building was erected during 1679, by Mr. Peter Sargent, as a private residence.   It was bought by the Government during 1716, and used as a Governor's house, when it was termed the Mansion House.   It had passed through the hands of several owners, and at the time of its destruction was devoted to a place of amusement.   The fire originated in an upper story of the building, and was supposed to have been the work of an incendiary.

During 1865, a new house was erected on Sumner street, East Boston, for the accommodation of Ladder Company No. 2, and for a new engine, No. 11, built by the Amoskeag Manufacturing Company.   A new building was also in process of construction on River street, for Engine No. 10.   Eighteen more iron covers were placed over the curbs of the reservoir, in the place of those removed.   One hundred and six fire-alarm boxes were in use during the year, distributed as follows : eighty-three in the city, fifteen at South Boston, and eight at East Boston, while six more hydrants were constructed in the city, and five at South Boston.

Promotions and new members in the department for 1864 :   Engine Co. No. 1, Templeton C. Twiss, driver ; T. S. Wright, captain.   No. 2, M. A. Jones, driver ; J. B. Emerson, hoseman.   No. 3, H. M. Hawkins, fireman ; H. J. Lefavor, hoseman.   No. 6, W. W. Kent, hoseman.   No. 7, Thomas Nannery, fireman ; H. T. Barnes and P. J. Mayer, hosemen.   No. 8, B. S. Flanders, engineman ; E. E. Jeffrey, fireman ; H. Allen, driver ; Eben Shapleigh and Albert Vilno, hosemen.   No. 9, William Pray, hoseman.   No. 10, James Porter, hoseman.   No. 11, Sumner street, East Boston, organized December 25.   The engine was not ready for this company until January 1, 1866 ; in the mean time they had charge of relief engine.   Ladder Company No. 1, I. N. Hodett, and Charles Sawyer, members.   No. 2, W. F. Hayes, member.   No. 3, G. P. Milliken, G. L. Cooper, H. J. Manning, James O. Stone, and G. B. Stevens, members.   Hose Company No. 1, F. B. Leach. No. 2, Thomas Merritt, captain ; F. B. Brown and B. P. Stowell, hosemen. No. 4, H. V. Haywood, captain ; D. S Knight, G. W. Lowell, and George L. Pike.   No. 5, W. A. Gaylord, hoseman.   No. 8, W. H. Munroe and W. E. Richardson, hosemen.   No. 9, Charles Allen, hoseman.   No. 10, H. E. Bradley, M. Goodale, R. Phillip, and C. E. Spiller.   Land was purchased and a suitable house erected on Dorchester street, South Boston, for this company.

The first conflagration for the year 1865 was in the office of the " Daily Evening Traveller," corner of State and Congress streets. This fire was set in several places by incendiaries and a number of offices were burnt out; loss, $20,698; insurance, $16,971. A son of Mr. Gilmore, on Highland street, was burnt to death March 18th. At 11.50 A.M., April 10, an alarm was sounded on Box 43 in the city proper and South Boston, and Box 162, East Boston, for bringing out the department on reception of the news of the fall of Richmond, Va.

April 31, at 3.17 A.M., fire was discovered on the premises of Mr. Charles Minot, corner of Sudbury and Court streets, and destroyed a large amount of property; loss, $119,700; insurance, $66,500. July 31, the premises of Mr. Silas Pierce, of 126 to 132 Commercial street, were totally destroyed; loss, $26,400; insurance, $25,300. J. A. Holland, hoseman on Engine No. 7, and R. W. Hitchcock, a substitute, were dangerously burned by an explosion. An infant of Mr. Patrick Connor, 54 Billerica street, was burned to death on August 16. Department called out by the Mayor on September 29 to exhibit the force to the commission from St. Louis. The locomotive works of Hinckley & Williams, at 418 Harrison avenue, were destroyed December 2, the fire originating in the foundry; loss, $23,290; insurance, $4,290.

Number of alarms from September 1, 1864, to December 31, 1865, one hundred and ninety-one; total loss, $625,891; insurance, $354,550. A public notice was issued giving warning to the citizens to use every care in the prevention of fire, " for should a conflagration of any magnitude break out, it might assume terrible proportion, as there were so few men in the city able to subdue it, they being engaged in the war." A series of rules were given with the order.

Assistant Engineer John S. Damrell succeeded Chief Engineer Bird, March 19, 1866. On assuming command this gentleman made several changes in the department, and recommended to the city government the purchase of two new second-size engines to take the place of those in charge of Companies Nos. 3 and 4, and that the old engines be placed, one at South Boston and the other at the south part of the city, in charge of companies then existing, and used as a reserve force. Two new horse hose-carriages and one ladder truck were also asked for, besides new houses for Engines Nos. 1 and 4 and Hose Nos. 1 and 8. He adopted a system for exercising the horses belonging to the department, which proved highly advantageous, as the animals were fast growing lame and tender from confinement and sudden exertion. Ten thousand feet of new hose were added of the following standard: pure oak, city tanned, Baltimore or Philadelphia leather, known as " over weight," the average weight not less than twenty-two pounds to the side, none less than twenty pounds, double riveted with copper wire, size known as No. 8, twenty-two rivets to the running foot; splices made with thirteen rivets of size known as No. 7 wire; finished with three loops and rings and weight not less than sixty-four pounds to each fifty feet, exclusive of the couplings, and warranted to stand a pressure of not less than two hundred pounds to the square inch. Tail-bands and tail-pieces two inches in width and length, and to be secured by three rivets. Two new small hose and one hand-hose carriage, also one with a capacity of one thousand feet of hose, were furnished the department. A steam police boat, furnished with two powerful force-pumps, was built for the protection of wharf property.

The supervision of the repairs of buildings occupied by the department, which for many years had been under the care of the chief engineer and committee on fire department, was transferred during the year to the committee on public buildings and the superintendent of that department. Twenty-seven new hydrants were constructed, — nineteen in the city, three at South Boston, and five at East Boston.

The pay-roll was also revised during 1866–67, as follows: chief engineer, $2,000; secretary, $1,000; eight assistant engineers, $450; one assistant engineer, $250 per year; enginemen, $3 per day; firemen, $80 per month; drivers, $75 per month; twenty foremen, $225, and one, $50, per year; other officers and members, $200; one steward and six hosemen, $30 per annum. The chief was also allowed a horse and wagon for his especial use.

Capt. John Stover Jacobs was appointed on the Board of Engineers, *vice* Damrell's promotion. Capt. Nathaniel W. Pratt died July 3, which left a vacancy in the board. New members and changes in the service were as follows: —

Engine Company No. 2, house between I and K streets, A. Pratt and D. H. Twiss, hosemen. No. 3, J. F. Dutton, hoseman. No. 4, Christopher Tracy, captain; M. C. Sullivan, hoseman. No. 5, George H. Morrison, fireman; Daniel Carter, driver. No. 6, Charles Harlow and E. Parker, Jr., hosemen. No. 7, J. H. Adams, fireman; D. T. Marden, captain; Frank Walker and G. F. Marden, hosemen. No. 8, C. H. Blake, captain; William Childs and Charles Dunton, hosemen. No. 9, Albert Bailey, driver; James McKown, hoseman. No. 10, Gilman Tyng, engineer; Thomas Nannery, fireman; and H. P. Hawkins, hoseman. No. 11, G. W. Brown, fireman; Andrew Lewis, captain; and C. C. Cooper, hoseman. Ladder Company No. 1, John S. Stevens, captain; W. H. Brown, steward; William Lewis, member. No. 2, John Fenno, member. No. 3, L. M. Clifford, captain; I. K. Jennings, assistant; W. H. Burrill, William H. Durling, J. F. Marston, John A. Ladd, J. W. Morrison, J. W. Randall, and N. B. Whitman, members. Hose Company No. 2, D. A. Ranking, hoseman. No. 3, R. M. Young, hoseman. No. 5, Joseph Halstick, Jr., hoseman. No. 8, Daniel Harold, hoseman. One hose-carriage, with appliances, was placed at the City Hospital, under the charge of the driver of Hose No. 4.

Total number of alarms, September 1, 1865, to December 31, 1866, two hundred and eighty-five; loss, $1,089,114; insurance, $856,871. The first large fire during this time broke out at 2.15 on the morning of February 16, in a tenement house on First and Second streets, South Boston. It was a very cold night, and before the fire was controlled forty-two families were burnt out. Bridget Downes, a widow, perished in the flames; she escaped once, but returned again for money left in her room; loss, $3,000; no insurance. March 7, Frederick Spear, of Charlestown, a lad sixteen years of age, was suffocated in the building at 126 and 128 Milk street. occupied by Means, Palmer, & Co. On May 1, at 1.15 P.M., the United States Bonded Warehouse on Boston wharf and other property were destroyed; loss, $112,150; insurance, $58,000. May 11, Snow's wharf, occupied by F. Snow & Co., burnt; loss, $43,500; insured, $39,100. The building at 407 Washington street, occupied by Messrs. Haley, Morse, & Boyden, was destroyed June 14; loss, $120,000; insured. July 1, H. S. Litchfield's Brass Foundry and other buildings on Lewis street consumed; loss, $100,000; insurance, $50,000. Philbrick & Parsons' kerosene-oil works, Chelsea street, East Boston, burnt August 7; loss, $20,000. The United States Arsenal, at Watertown, was destroyed September 2; the Boston department rendered assistance. Robert M. Young, hoseman of Hose Company 3, was seriously injured by falling from a ladder October 7, at the fire at a building corner of Milk and India streets, occupied by E. & F. King & Co. The day following. Charles E. Munroe, hoseman of Engine Company 6, was seriously hurt by falling through an open hoistway at building No. 75 Union street, occupied by A. G. Foss; loss to property, $11,300; insurance, $9,200. On November 3, at 10.30 P.M., a serious fire broke out at 41 Franklin street, occupied by Messrs. Allen, Lane, & Co. and others; loss, $208,750; fully insured.

The committee on the fire department chose a committee during 1867, consisting of Alderman Hawes and Chief Engineer Damrell, to examine the various makes of steam-engines, in order to secure the best apparatus. manufactured; the result being that contracts were awarded the Amoskeag Manufacturing Company for new engines for Companies Nos. 3, 4, and 5; also one new hose-carriage, of a capacity of one thousand feet of hose, to take the place of the one drawn by hand by Hose Company No 10. The following houses, under the control of this department, were repaired, etc. : Engine No. 3 was raised three feet, a new hose-tower erected sixty feet high, the house renovated, and fitted up with bathing fixtures at a cost of $4,500. Engine No. 5 was enlarged. a new hose-tower built, and the house fitted up with bathing tubs, at an expense of $5,000. A small house for the storage of coal-wagons and spare ladders was erected in the yard, in connection with Ladder-house No. 2; cost, $800. A new hose-tower was also put in the house of Hose No. 4, at a cost of $900. Bathing fixtures were put in the house of Hose No. 5, at an expenditure of $700. Hose No. 6 quarters were thoroughly remodelled and fitted for a tenement at a cost of $3,500, the city receiving an annual rental of $156 from the driver. Hose 10 remodelled and fitted for a horse hose-carriage; expense, $5,000. Ladder No. 3 remodelled and fitted with extra stalls for horses and a tenement for the driver, who payed $180 per year rental; expenses of repairs, $1,700.

A self-propelling engine was built during the year by the Amoskeag Manufacturing Company, which was rated as second class, and weighed about seven thousand pounds. This engine, at the solicitation of the committee on fire department, was forwarded to Boston about the 1st of October, and placed in the house of Engine 5, at East Boston, in the place of that engine, which was at the time unfit for service. At a trial on October 11 before the Board of Fire Commissioners of New York City, the self-propeller gave the utmost satisfaction. It was run from Charles street toward the toll-gate on the Mill-dam at a very fast speed. It was also run up and down Beacon and Mt. Vernon streets, stopping and starting apparently with the greatest of ease. By three or four other trips made to the Mill-dam, and through other streets, it was found capable of going at a speed of a mile in three or four minutes over the pavements with perfect safety. The propelling machinery of this apparatus consisted of a stout chain worked in slotted grooves, to which the links were fitted upon the main shaft and the hub of one of the hind wheels, smaller chains being attached to the brake and connected with the forward axle. For some reason never clearly stated, this style of engine was dispensed with until 1872, when one was placed under the charge of Engine Company No. 21, where it remained in service a number of years, when this style of apparatus was considered impractical, and the Engine formerly used by this company was taken in charge.

Liquid fuel, or what was known as hydrocarbon for steam-engines, the invention of Col. H. R. Foot, was also given a trial during the year. After an investigation of its merits by the committee, they gave Colonel Foot permission to temporarily apply his invention to Engine 3, by which he could put it to a practical test. To light the fire, a few shavings were placed under the retort, and when that was hot, the oil, which was carried in copper tanks placed over either spring at the rear of the engine, was let on, which immediately vaporizing issued from the burners; when it was lighted, the pump added the air, and the normal condition of the fire was attained. The oil was conducted from the tank to the place at the grate, or to the retort, by a common gas-pipe tube, and regulated by a stopcock, enabling the engineman to gauge the intensity of the fire at his pleasure. The result attained at the exhibition, also at the fire on Federal street, at which the engine worked six hours, gave general satisfaction. The appliance was then transferred to old Engine No. 3. The following year a committee was chosen, consisting of the enginemen of the department, to investigate the merits of the invention, also Colonel Foot's claims to propel the apparatus to a fire without noise or smoke. After a trial, May 27, 1868, the propelling attachment was found very unsatisfactory and was removed, but the appliance for firing the fuel was retained for further experiment. The engine was put in the service of the department and placed in charge of Engine Company No. 8, Mr. B. S. Flanders,

engineman, who reported after working the engine at five fires, that, " in using
the oil for fuel the heat was not confined to the fire-box, but to the flues and
top of the arch, leaving the legs of boiler entirely bare, and heating the top
of the smoke arch to a red heat, thereby making the boiler dangerous when
firing with oil, with the same amount of steam as with coal." On receipt of
this report, Chief Damrell requested, on November 7, 1868, the several engine-
men of the department to thoroughly inspect and test the matter at Engine-
house No. 8. The report of these gentlemen only substantiated Mr. Flanders'
statement, and recommended that coal instead of oil be used in the department
for fuel for steam fire-engines, which report was accepted.

On the subject of water-supply, Chief Damrell says in his report for
1867 : —

During the past three years, at large fires, much difficulty has been experienced for
the want of an adequate supply of water for our steam fire-engines. The immediate cause
of this failure is this, namely, that the hydrants, in every instance, are placed upon branch
pipes, the diameter of which varies from three to four inches, while the mains themselves,
in almost every instance, are but four inches in diameter, that supply them. In case of
fire, the hydrant upon these branch pipes will afford a supply to only one steamer; all
others on the line are useless. The steamer being at work makes a vacuum in the pipe
by drawing the water to the hydrant first tapped. The result of this difficulty is, that much
time is consumed in shifting the apparatus to lines of pipes in other streets; by reason of
which, long, continuous lines of hose have to be used to convey the water to the scene of
the conflagration; and, by this operation, the amount of friction to overcome is very great,
requiring oftentimes a water-pressure of from one hundred and eighty to two hundred
pounds to the square inch, to be effectual in our high buildings.

He then goes on to recommend that the hydrants be connected with the
main pipes of a size not less than eight inches in diameter, with a proper
outlet.

Twenty-eight hydrants were established during the year, — five in South
Boston, and the remainder in the city proper. The foreman of Hose Company
No. — had his salary increased by the City Council to $100 per year, the steward
to $80, and the members to $60, and a thorough new running-card was established by the engineers. Rules and regulations in relation to petroleum and
its products were prepared on May 24, 1866, by the committee on licenses.
(See Engineers' Report for 1867 to 1870.)

Rules and regulations regarding badges were also adopted by the Board
of Engineers on December 4 the ensuing year, whereby it was made compulsory for every member and substitute, not exceeding two for each engine and
hose company, and four for each ladder company, to wear the corporation
badge while on duty in a conspicuous manner on his coat or vest; otherwise
they should not be allowed inside the line. They were not to lend the badge
on any pretext on penalty of dismissal, and if lost, they were charged $5.
Each badge was numbered, which number should be given to any one asking
it for the purpose of making a complaint for disorderly conduct. Any

person other than a member appearing at a fire with a badge was punished for misdemeanor. Every substitute was to be approved by the chief or the engineer in the district, upon the recommendation of the foreman of the respective companies.

No change occurred in the Board of Engineers, with the exception of the appointment of Mr. Henry W. Longley as secretary. Monday, January 21, ex-Chief Engineer William Barnicoat died at his residence on Tremont street, aged seventy-eight years, one month, and nineteen days.

Promotions, new members, etc., in the department during 1867 were as follows : Engine Company No. 1, Eugene C. Phillips, hoseman. No. 3, new engine built by Amoskeag Manufacturing Company, and put in service November 7. No. 4, Joseph Pierce, hoseman. No. 6, Charles O. Davis, F. A. Bean, C. E. Wilson, F. L. Coats, L. G. Newman, and James A. Tuttle, hosemen. No. 7, T. P. Lally, Russell White, Thomas White, and P. J. Mayer, hosemen. No. 8, E. T. Smith, hoseman. No. 10, J. C. Singleton, hoseman. Hose Company No. 1, S. F. Ridler, R. E. Flanders, and Francis Reed, hosemen. No. 4, John Le Cain, William E. Barney, and T. S. Hartshorn, hosemen. No. 5, Joseph Halstick, Jr., hoseman. No. 6, C. E. Pearson and Calvin Lewis, hosemen ; William H. Rymille, deceased. No. 8, H. T. Barnes, Sinclair McDonald, and H. F. Newton, hosemen ; Daniel Harold, deceased. No. 7, William Norris, G. S. Cole, and B. B. Brown, Jr., hosemen. Ladder Company No. 1, V. C. Hausen, G. H. Gollief, and Richard Palmer, members. No. 2, George A. Brown, member. No. 3, H. D. Smith, H. A. York, and J. L. Starrett, members ; R. E. Stannard, deceased. There were also in the department Relief Engines Nos. 3, 4, 5, and 6.

Total number of alarms from January 1, 1867, to December 31, 1867, two hundred and eighty-four ; loss, $402,115 ; insurance, $340,765. The first fire of the year of any note occurred on February 20, in the old Broadway Horse Railroad Company's stables, South Boston, and destroyed, besides the building, several horses ; amount of loss not stated. March 6, at 6.40 P.M., Grace Church, on Temple street, was damaged to the extent of $16,540 : insured. Frank Walker, a member of Engine Company 7, fell from a ladder a distance of thirty-five feet, and received a broken leg and other injuries, while at a fire at Patrick Donahoe's book bindery on Franklin street, April 15 ; loss to building, etc., $4,000 ; insured. July 4, Joseph Halstrick, Jr., of Hose Company 5, was badly burned by an explosion of hot air at a fire at O. W. Esselborn & Co.'s, 33 Boylston street ; loss, $7,200 ; insured. The same day lightning struck the stable of Joseph Hale, on Hawkins street. Sixty horses were in the building, but all were saved except seven ; loss, $32,000 ; insurance, $15,000. September 20, three members of Engine Company 7 were thrown from a ladder and injured at a fire at Hon. Samuel Cooper's, Canal street ; loss, $10,300 ; insurance, $5,100. The Bay State Sugar Refinery was burned October 1 ; no return of loss. And on the 5th, a large fire occurred at 383 Federal street, building occupied by Jonas Fitch and others ;

no loss given. On the 17th a can of benzine exploded in the building owned by William Munroe, 106 Boylston street, and killed Mrs. Ware and Miss Waltz. December 15th, the store of Messrs. Barnes, Merriam, & Co., 77 Franklin street, was burned; loss, $107,000; insured.

CHAPTER X.

1868–1870.

BY the annexation of Roxbury to the city of Boston, on January 6, 1868, the department was increased by the addition of three steam-engines, one hose and one ladder carriage, which were under the command of James Munroe, chief engineer. In the act of annexation no provision was made for the continuing in service of the members of the Roxbury department. Mayor Shurtleff, on the recommendation of the Board of Engineers, presented the names of seventy-four men to take charge of the apparatus, and they were confirmed by the Board of Aldermen. By a vote of that body, the apparatus were numbered Engines 12, 13, and 14, Hose 7, and Ladder 4.

A new house was erected for Engine No. 1 at the corner of Fourth and Dorchester streets, South Boston, and the station of Engine No. 12 was thoroughly repaired. The house of No. 14 possessed a fine exterior, but no accommodations for an engine company; a school-house was in the rear, which Chief Damrell desired should be converted into a stable for the engine-house. Engine No. 8 and Hose No. 1 were located together in a new house on Salem street. Ladder 4's house had no convenience for horses, which, therefore, had to be hired from a livery stable when wanted. Coal-houses, to supply engines with fuel, were located, No. 1 on Salem street, No. 2 on Orleans street, East Boston, and No. 3 on East street. Three new hose-carriages for Hose Companies Nos. 3, 4, and 7 were purchased during the year, at a cost of $600 each, — two from the Amoskeag Manufacturing Company, and one from Messrs. Hunneman & Co. After an examination of Engine No. 8, it was found unworthy of any expensive repairs. Messrs. Junckett & Freeman, of this city, made a contract with the city to build a new engine for the sum of $3,750 and the old engine.

The chief, in his first report, had recommended to the City Council the inspection of unsafe buildings; but it was not until the ensuing year that the committee on the fire department investigated the matter, during which the following ordinance was passed : " The chief engineer of the fire department be authorized to employ some competent person, subject to the approval of the committee on that department, to inspect buildings in process of erection in this city which are, in materials or location, peculiarly liable to conflagration ; and to examine and to advise respecting the construction and location of steam boilers in this city, whenever application is made therefor, the expenses to be charged to the appropriation for the fire department." This order was passed and approved March 24, 1868, and Chief Damrell recommended for the position ex-Chief Engineer George W. Bird, who was unanimously confirmed by the committee, and he at once entered upon his duties. There was no statute law or ordinance of this city that recognized this office, he only accomplishing his work by appealing to the good judgment of those of whom the complaint was made.

Another improvement made in the same year, was the reorganization of the insurance protective department of the Board of Underwriters, by Engineer Green. A company was formed, who received their appointment from the chief engineer, being subject to the rules and ordinance of the city governing the fire department. At fires the company was placed under the direction of the Board of Engineers ; but Engineer Green made this his special duty. The whole expense of this service was paid by the Board of Underwriters.

One hundred and twenty-two hydrants were established during the year, — eleven in the city proper, seven in South Boston, ten in East Boston, and one hundred and two in Roxbury. Previous to this there were twenty hydrants and forty-three reservoirs in the latter district, the " Lowry hydrant " being adopted, which patterns were recommended by the chief to be used when additional hydrants were built in the city proper. Twenty-five signal boxes were also added to the list in the fire-alarm service by the annexation.

Four additions were made to the Board of Engineers during 1868 by the appointment of Messrs. Phineas D. Allen, Rufus B. Farrar, James Munroe, and John Colligan, engineers of the Roxbury department. All the companies throughout the service received names in addition to their numbers. The new members, promotion, etc., occurred in them during the year as follows : Mazeppa, No. 1, no change. S. R. Spinney, No. 2, no change. Eagle, No. 3, no change. Barnicoat, No. 4, Charles E. Wadleigh, hoseman. Elisha Smith, No. 5, Andrew P. Fisher, hoseman. Melville, No. 6, no change. Thomas C. Amory, No. 7, Benjamin Brown, James S. King, George R. Williams, and James H. Rankin, hosemen. Northern Liberty, No. 8, Theo. J. Munroe, hoseman. Maverick, No. 9, no change. Cataract, No. 10, George Demary, hoseman. No. 11, no name, Henry R. Demary and Thomas Barnes, hosemen. Warren, No. 12, house corner of Warren and Dudley streets, Roxbury district ; engine built by L. Button, Waterford, N.Y., and put in service September 9, 1864 : James T. Cole, engineman ; Thomas W. Bradlee, fireman ; J. M. Huggins, driver of engine ; O. J. Booker, driver of hose ; M. N. Hubbard, captain ; B. F. Applebee, J. H. Baxter, L. L. Cheswell, A. F. Choate, G. W. Downes, William H. Jones, Charles E. Jones, M. H. Jones, and Thomas C. Soesman, hosemen. Tremont, No. 13, house on Cabot street, Roxbury district ; engine built by Messrs. Campbell, Whittier, & Co., of Roxbury, and put in service April 6, 1865 ; Richard Eaton, Jr., engineman ; Francis Swift, fireman ; Charles E. Clark, driver of engine ; W. F. Booker, driver of hose ; G. F. Decatur, captain ; Anthony Atwood, Bartlet Burgess, H. B. Day, J. W. Hall, J. C. Hewes, C. H. Lincoln, George E. Orrok, F. C. Pratt, and C. L. Rosemen, hosemen. Dearborn, No. 14, house on Centre street, Roxbury ;

engine built by J. M. Stone, of Manchester, N.H., and put in service December 17, 1860; George F. Worcester, engineman; C. M. Raymond, fireman; William B. Richards, driver of engine; C. W. Bates, driver of hose; Calvin A. Vose, captain; J. H. Barutio, F. K. Houseman, G. D. Kemp, J. G. Smith, A. A. Snow, Jefferson Stimpson, Lewis P. Webber, Jabez Watkins, and John R. Yendley, hosemen. Washington Hose Company, No. 1, no change. Union, No. 2, no change. Franklin, No. 3, no change. Chester, No. 4, Benjamin P. Norris, hoseman. Suffolk, No. 5, D. A. Noble and R. J. Ryder, hosemen. William Woolley, No. 6, no change. Elliott, No. 7, house on Cabot street, Roxbury; carriage built by the Amoskeag Manufacturing Company, and put in service July 4, 1868; Walter S. Orrok, driver; Thomas A. Scott, captain; T. H. Bill, James Boss, C. G. Green, H. S. Kendall, C. E. Morrill, A. H. Perry, J. W. Sweat, J. A. Stockman, G. M. Schell, and G. W. Stimpson, hosemen. Tremont, No. 8, Charles R. Classen, hoseman. No. 9, no name; no change. Bradlee, No. 10, B. F. Donnell, driver; G. H. Putnam, hoseman. Warren Ladder Company, No. 1, William J. Hicks, James Edwards, and G. F. Griffin, members. Washington, No. 2, Samuel F. Ellis, member. Franklin, No. 3, George P. Milliken, D. W. Sampson, George E. Thomas, and John Darling, members. No. 4, no name, house on Eustis street, Roxbury; truck built by Messrs. Hunneman & Co., Roxbury, and put in service May 1, 1845; number of ladders, sixteen; four fire-hooks, four crotch-poles, three rakes, six forks, eight baskets, four axes, five lanterns, eight ladder-dogs, two hammers, and four shovels; William Farray, captain; Daniel Crockett, assistant; I. H. Randall, clerk; Thomas Jennings, steward; Frank Hutchins, B. L. Randall, Edward Whiting, Frank Upton, Lawrence Rees, Richard Hinckly; John Trull, Edward Bartlett, H. L. Bartlett, Charles Fales, Daniel Cochran, Daniel Nicholas, Jacob Schmidters, J. H. Kelly, George S. Fogg, and Gilbert S. May, members.

One fuel-wagon was kept at the old engine-house on East street, one at the old house on Salem street, one at Engine No. 11 house, one at Ladder No. 3 house, one at Engine No. 14 house, and one at Engine No. 13 house, all of which were capable of conveying about two tons of coal each.

The pay-roll of the department was again revised during the year, as follows: chief, $2,500; secretary, $1,300; assistant engineers, $500; foremen, $300; assistant foremen and others, $275 per year; enginemen, $3.50; firemen, $3.25; and drivers, $3 per day. An ordinance in relation to the fire department was passed February 26 and September 10, 1869, also one on September 17, referring to the manufacture, storage, and sale of petroleum and its products.

The year was quite noticeable for the number of serious accidents to the members of the department. The first fire of note occurred on February 7 in a block of wooden buildings at the corner of Glover and Woodward streets, Washington Village, South Boston. Twenty-one families occupied the premises, most of whom lost all their furniture and household effects, while many had a narrow escape by being cut off by the flames and smoke; loss not stated. On the 23d, the Suffolk Planing Mills of Munson & Paterson, corner of Liverpool and Decatur streets, East Boston, were destroyed; loss not stated. The Methodist church on Warren street and four dwelling-houses were partly destroyed on March 29; loss on church, $12,000; insurance, $6,900. William Farry, foreman of Ladder No. 4, while at this fire was severely injured by being struck with the iron points of a ladder. On the day following, the steamboat "Island City," lying at T wharf, caught fire from a slight explosion of a small quantity of petroleum; loss to the steamer slight. E. E. Jeffries, fireman of Engine No. 8, was run over by Hose-carriage No. 1 and severely injured in his back and hips. Charles Hubbard, engineer of the wool-drying establishment of J. F. Paul, on Wareham street, was badly burned in putting out a fire on those premises, May 5th. On the 11th, Mr. George H. Golliff, a member of Ladder No. 1, while going to a fire at the corner of Cork place and Commercial place, was run over by the truck and instantly killed. "Old Charley," a valuable horse attached to Engine No. 8, had one of his hoofs torn off while going to a fire on Dover place on July 28, and had to be killed. On November 14, at 12.25 P.M., at a fire in the establishment of McNeil Bros., on Albion street, Capt. William Lovell, George C. Fernald, W. A. Gaylord, William H. Gardner, and Levi Gaylord, members of Hose No. 5, were seriously injured by the falling of a portion of a building. At 2.14 on the afternoon of the same day, fire broke out in a block of wooden buildings on Bennett avenue and Prince street, containing a number of poor families. Mr. McCormick, an occupant of a room in the upper part of the building, was burnt to death. On the 21st, at the burning of the kerosene-oil works at South Boston, a young man named Hyde was seriously injured. December 8, a three-story block containing nine houses on Sweet street, Roxbury, was destroyed, together with most of the furniture of the sixty families who occupied the same. At 2 o'clock in the afternoon, the varnish factory of W. C. Hunneman, on the same street, caught fire and was entirely consumed. Mr. E. F. Barney, of Hose No. 4, was injured by the falling of the walls. On the 9th, the premises of A. B. Wilbur, corner of Bulfinch and Court streets, were destroyed. The upper part of the building was occupied as offices and sleeping apartments; several of the occupants had barely time to escape, leaving everything, which was destroyed. A large conflagration occurred in Lynn, Mass., on the 26th. Assistance was asked of this department, and Engines Nos. 10 and 4, and Hose No. 1, were despatched to the scene. Total number of alarms from January 1, 1868, to December 31, 1868, two hundred and ninety-three; loss, $401,106; insurance, $314,706.

By order of the Board of Aldermen, March 16, 1868, districts were assigned to the engineers as follows: District 1, East Boston; first alarm, Chiefs Dunbar, Green, and Jacobs; on the second alarm, Captain Hine was called. District 2, north section of the city, line from Leverett, Green, Court, and State streets to the end of Long wharf; first alarm, Chiefs

Green, Hine, Regan, Jacobs, and Farrar; on the second, Chamberlin and Dunbar responded. District 3, line south of Leverett, Green, Court, and State streets, North End, west of Boylston and Beach streets; first alarm, Chiefs Regan, Hine, Chamberlin, Green, and Farrar; second, Jacobs and Brown attended. District 4, line south of Boylston and Beach streets, and north of Dover and Berkeley to Boylston streets; first alarm, Chiefs Chamberlin, Regan, Farrar, Smith, and Green; second, Brown and Hine. District 5, line south of Dover and Berkeley to Boylston streets, and north of Northampton to Sweet street; first, Chiefs Smith, Munroe, Green, Chamberlin, and Colligan; second, Brown and Allen. District 6, line all south of Northampton street; first, Chiefs Munroe, Allen, and Colligan; second, Mr. Smith responded. District 7, South Boston; first, Chiefs Brown, Chamberlin, Green, Smith, and Regan; second, Chamberlin and Regan were on duty.

During 1869, there were erected the following new houses: Engine No. 7, on East street, at a cost of $24,000; Hose No. 3, on North Grove street, at an expense of $13,556.51; Hose No. 8, on Church street, at an outlay of $21,786.08; and one for Ladder No. 5, on Fourth street, near Dorchester street, South Boston, at a cost of $15,530.25. The houses occupied by Engines Nos. 9 and 13 and Ladders Nos. 1 and 4 were thoroughly remodelled, and adapted to the wants of the several companies occupying them, at an expense of $26,908.28.

A new ladder-truck was built by Messrs. Hunneman & Co. for No. 1, for the sum of $1,300; a hose-carriage for No. 1, by the same firm, May 1, and a new engine for a new company, to be organized January 1, 1870, was built by Amoskeag Manufacturing Company, for $4,250. There were also purchased during the year, thirty-six America Fire Extinguishers, — one for each engine, hose, and ladder house and police station in the city; the right to use Ballamy's Patent Hose Bridge Protector, for enabling horse-cars to pass over lines of hose without injury; also circulating water-heaters for each engine. This latter contrivance was the invention of Mr. James W. Sutton, of Detroit, Mich., one of the fire commissioners for that city. Previous to the introduction of this appliance fire had to be lighted under the boiler before starting, which issued volumes of smoke as the engine proceeded along the streets, and was a source of complaint to pedestrians and others. Three thousand six hundred and thirty-one feet of two and one-half inch hose were added to the department, also three horses. During the winter season the force of horse were increased to the number of twenty, at an expense to the city of keeping only.

During the great Peace Jubilee, held in this city during 1869, there were detailed from this department one hundred men to take part in the anvil chorus. This force was under the command of Captain Bagley of Engine No. 4. Their appearance was always greeted with the greatest enthusiasm from the vast audience of fifty thousand people. In addition to this number of men, there were detailed from the service twelve hosemen, with Engine No. 10, fully equipped, with an extra hose-carriage and one thousand feet of hose, to remain on duty during the time of the completion of the building and through the jubilee week. A room was fitted up in the Coliseum building for the engine and hose-carriage and horses; also one for the accommodation of the men. This was furnished with twelve beds. This force was under the command of Engineer Tyng, of Engine No. 10, and was detailed for duty night and day. In addition to the labors assigned them, the men was most efficient in caring for the large number of people who fainted, while the wives of these " fire laddies " rendered most valuable assistance to this class of persons.

On the recommendation of Chief Damrell, the parade and review of the department. that for years took place on July 4, was discontinued, and an order passed by the City Council, whereby the parade would occur on September 17, the anniversary of the settlement of Boston: Mr. Joseph Barnes was appointed on the Board of Engineers during the year, which increased the number serving in that office to thirteen. New members, changes, etc., in the department during 1869 were as follows: —

Engine Company No. 1, H. B. Farnham and J. C. Healey, hosemen. No. 2, H. F. Ferrin, hoseman. No. 3, W. S. Lawrence, hoseman. No. 4, J. G. Duffy, hoseman. No. 5, John G. Phillips, hoseman. No. 6, Thomas Young, hoseman. No. 7, George W. Stoddard, hoseman. No. 8, engine built by Messrs. Jucket & Freeman, and put in service April 26, 1869; J. D. Brown, D. N. Jeffery, and M. B. White, hosemen; G. F. C. Hamilton died June 5. No. 10, William H. Skimmings, Jr., hoseman. Engine No. 11 was named the " John S. Damrell," in honor of the chief engineer. L. F. Merrill, hoseman; engine built by the Amoskeag Manufacturing Company, and put in service, September 17, 1870. No. 14, Jefferson Stimpson, died August 10. Walter E. Hawes, Engine No. 15; they were temporarily located in the house of Ladder No. 5 until their building was erected; the engine was built by the Amoskeag Manufacturing Company, and put in service during December, 1869; David E. Gilman, engineman, transferred from Engine No. 2; James Kain, fireman; E. C. Phillips, driver, transferred from Hose No. 1; Nicholas C. Cogley, captain, transferred from Hose No. 9; James Bennett, Alonzo Donnells, D. P. Leonard. A. E. Marshall, Charles E. Reed, B. P. Stowell, transferred from Engine No. 2, and O. L. Wood, hosemen. Hose Company No. 1, Thomas E. Golding, hoseman. No. 2, Frank Walker, driver; Ambrose Gariboldi, hoseman. No. 4, P. M. Marble, hoseman. No. 5, E. H. Bright, hoseman. No. 6, J. M. Colby, hoseman; John H. Weston, captain, *vice* Barnes, elected assistant engineer; I. W. Campbell, hoseman; Benjamin F. Cowden died May 10. Hose No. 9 was named the " Lawrence," George W. Stone, hoseman. No. 10, A. P. Hawkins, driver; H. T. Bowers and L. F. Fluet, hosemen. Ladder Company No. 1, George W. Thompson, driver; Jerome Carleton, C. H. Knox, and R. A.

Kimball, members. No. 3, L. M. Clifford, transferred to Ladder No. 5; R. B. Riley, member. Ladder 4 was named "Washington," George W. Frost, member. Hancock Ladder Company, No. 5, house on Fourth street, near Dorchester, South Boston; the carriage under their charge was the old No. 1, until their own truck was ready; Benjamin F. Donnell, driver; transferred from Hose No. 10; J. B. Hill, captain; L. M. Clifford, assistant, transferred from Ladder No. 3; A. E. Goodwin, R. R. Jones, Appleton Lathe, David Kurrus. A. W. McKenzie. E. A. Perkins, J. J. Bell, Humphrey Choate, T. C. Dunn, H. B. Fowler, J. H. Howard, J. A. Hodgkins, Lyman Locke, Charles Spear, William Sheene, F. B. Sibley, and Daniel Weston, members.

The pay-roll of the department was revised during 1869–70, as follows: chief engineer, $3,000: secretary, $1,500; assistants, $500; foremen, $300; all other members, $275 per year; enginemen, $3.50; firemen, $3.25; and drivers, $3 per day. The number of hydrants established during the year were thirty-nine in city proper, six in South Boston, four in East Boston, and one hundred and ninety-seven in Roxbury district.

The number of alarms from January 1, 1869, to December 31, 1869, was three hundred and eighty-five; loss, $437,723; insurance, $335,975. The first fire of importance broke out on January 2, at the warehouse of W. F. Weld & Co., 40 Central wharf: a large quantity of nutmegs was destroyed; loss, $15,500; insured. Hotel Pelham had a number of rooms damaged by a fire on the 27th; loss, $2,800; insured. On February 9, a block of six wooden houses at the corner of Swan and Colony streets, South Boston, was destroyed: owned by Mrs. Mary Hennessey; no loss returned. March 5, Engineman W. H. Sturtevant, of Engine No. 11, had two of his fingers so badly crushed during a fire at 81 Meridian street as to render amputation necessary. The lumber-yard of D. N. Skillings & Co., of East Cambridge, was destroyed on the 8th; assistance being asked from the department. Engines Nos. 4, 6, 7, 8, and 10, Hose Nos. 1 and 3, and Ladder No. 1, were despatched. The cordage warehouse of Sewall, Day, & Co., at 83 Commercial street, was damaged on March 25; loss, $137,000. May 13, the establishment of Freeman, Snow, & Co., rear of Federal street and Mt. Washington avenue, was badly damaged: twenty horses were saved; loss, $12,000; insured, $10,000. The East Boston ferryboat "Lincoln" was discovered on fire by the captain just as it was entering the slip on the Boston side, July 25; loss not stated. On September 8, Engines 4, 6, 8, and 10, and Hose 1 and 3 were despatched to a large fire at East Cambridge. Mr. J. M. Tucker of Engine No. 5 had two of his fingers taken off by unreeling the hose at a fire in Winthrop, Mass., on October 7, to which assistance had been sent from the East Boston service. The Belcher House on Purchase street was on fire November 14th. Assistant Engineer Jacobs was badly injured by the falling of a wall. The ruins of the immense Coliseum building were discovered on fire at 10.32 on November 20; loss not stated. The Boston Flour Mills, at

47 to 52 Commercial street, were destroyed on December 7. On account of the heavy fall of snow, much difficulty was experienced by the department in responding to the alarm. George C. Fernald of Hose 5 was ruptured at this fire. On the 10th, a wooden building on Chapel place occupied by several families was destroyed. Two children of Cornelius Sullivan were smothered. The Carney Hospital was badly damaged on December 25. The fire was confined to the basement of the chapel, and was caused by an explosion of the boiler; and at 2.08 A.M., the same day, the cottage attached to the Insane Asylum at South Boston was badly damaged.

On June 4, 1869, the inhabitants of Dorchester and Boston voted to accept an act of the Legislature uniting the two corporations, and on January 3, 1870, the ancient town became the sixteenth ward of the city. By this annexation there was turned over to the Boston department by S. H. Hebard, chief engineer of Dorchester, all the property in possession of that department belonging to the town. The organized force of that territory was as follows: six steam fire-engines, two hand-hose carriages, and two hook-and-ladder carriages fully equipped for service, with seventeen horses. The number of men enrolled as members was one hundred and five, classified as follows: one chief engineer, five assistant engineers, six enginemen, six firemen, ten drivers, who acted as clerks of the companies, eight foremen. and sixty-nine members. The houses were the finest in the department. By a vote of the City Council in the month of May that force was reduced to one assistant engineer and eighty-four members, being a reduction of twenty men. Mr. Sylvester H. Hebard, the chief, was appointed on the Board of Engineers in charge of that district, which was numbered 8.

New engines were purchased for the department to take the places of Nos. 7, 10. 13, and 14, a hose-carriage for No. 2, and a new ladder-truck for No. 3, while the houses occupied by Engine Companies Nos. 2, 5, 11, and 14, and Ladder Company No. 1, were thoroughly remodelled. The building occupied by Engine No. 4 was taken down and the engine was removed to J. B. Smith's stable on Bulfinch street until a new building could be erected. Ten thousand one hundred and fifty feet of two and a half inch hose was also added to the service, one thousand one hundred and nineteen feet of which was entirely burnt in the large fire of July 25 and 27. The amount of repairs to the apparatus occasioned by this conflagration amounted to one-third the whole sum paid for repairs during the year. Three additional fuel-wagons were provided, — one at Hose-house No. 3, one at Engine-house No. 16, and one at Engine-house No. 17. The spare apparatus now consisted of old Engines Nos. 3, 4, 5, 7, and 10, Ladder No. 1, one hand-engine at the house of Ladder No. 3, and Hose-carriages Nos. 1, 2, 3, 5, and 8.

Mr. Charles R. Classen was appointed assistant secretary to the Board of Engineers. The changes in the companies for 1870 were as follows: Engine Company No. 2, George J. DeLuce, hoseman. No. 3, Nathan L. Hussey, hoseman; James F. Dutton died June 19. No. 5, Lewis Keen, hoseman. No. 7, engine built by the Amoskeag Manufacturing Company, was put in service September 25, 1870, Chandler Griffin, hoseman.   No. 10, engine built by Amoskeag Manufacturing Company, was put in service February 1, 1870 ; it was of the newest pattern, with crane-neck frame, so that the engine could be turned around within its length ; Jackson L. Stinson and George W. Andrews, hosemen.   No. 13, built by Messrs. Jucket & Freeman of Boston, was put in service April, 1870.   No. 14, engine built by the Amoskeag Manufacturing Company, was put in service September 17, 1870.   S. H. Hebard Engine Company, No. 16, house on Temple street, Dorchester ; engine was built by Mr. William Jeffers, of Pawtucket, R.I. ; put in service October 20, 1869 ; Eugene H. Freeman, engineman ; Samuel O. Hebard, driver ; John Hutchinson, captain ; W. W. Carsley, William Shields, M. B. Thayer, T. Strangman, Jedediah Strangman, H. N. Plummer, John Bawmister, and Jacob H. Taylor, hosemen.   Protector Engine Company, No. 17, house on Meeting-house Hill, Dorchester ; engine built by Messrs. Hunneman & Co., of Boston, and put in service March, 1866 ; C. C. Lane, engineman ; Patrick Freeman, driver ; John F. Greenwood, captain ; Albert F. Lake, Thomas J. Hatch, Alexander Glover, Jr., William Jones, Stephen H. Howe, Rastus Gordon, James F. Finley, and Nathaniel H. Bird, hosemen.   Torrent Engine Company, No. 18, house on Harvard street, Dorchester ; engine built by Mr. William Jeffers, of Pawtucket, R.I., and put in service January, 1870 ; B. Howard Warren, engineman ; William H. Cooper, driver ; J. Foster Hewins, captain ; George L. Pitman, W. T. Woodward, John Connell, M. Hallihan, Timothy Donahue, Henry Forbes, F. W. Broad, Jr., and David Ripley, hosemen.   Alert Engine Company, No. 19, house on Norfolk street, Dorchester ; engine built by William Jeffers, and put in service January 1, 1870 ; Ezra B. Hebard, engineman ; Luther N. Knox, driver ; George H. Bird, captain ; Charles E. Stephenson, I. A. Williams, H. B. Tucker, John D. Scannell, E. D. Tower, Jonathan Baker, George F. Fenno, and Warren Berry, hosemen.   Independence Engine Company, No. 20, house on Walnut street, Dorchester ; engine built by William Jeffers, and put in service January, 1870 ; Franklin Muzzy, engineman ; George Simpson, driver ; Horace A. Allyn, captain ; William G. Blanchard, F. C. P. Emery, William R. Pillsbury, George W. Richardson, John E. Tuttle, Fred H. Bronsdon, George G. Dennison, and William O. Swan, hosemen.   J. H. Upham Engine Company, No. 21, house on Boston street, Dorchester ; engine built by William Jeffers, and put in service December 27, 1869 ; J. R. Gilbert, engineman ; S. H. Bridgham, driver ; J. B. Graham, captain ; J. F. Williams, A. E. Richardson, R. T. Glidden, James Crosby, C. O. Stinson, T. Hersey, J. E. Caswell, and Oliver Davenport, hosemen.

Hose Company No. 2, carriage built by Messrs. Hunneman & Co., Boston, and put in service September 17, 1870.   No. 3, Robert M. Young died December 27, 1870.   No. 4, J. L. Gilbert, hoseman.   No. 5, carriage built by Messrs. L. B. Button of Waterford, N.Y., and put in service September 17, 1870 ; George C. Fernald, captain ; Charles H. Morse, hoseman. No. 6, James T. Cummings, hoseman.   No. 7, William E. Hamnett.   No. 8, carriage built by the Amoskeag Manufacturing Company, and put in service September 17, 1870; W. S. Leighton and H. McLaughlin, hosemen; W. S. Leighton died August 22. Ladder Company No. 1, Asa Freeman, M. D. Gill, J. C. Brofield, O. B. Bussey, Thomas E. Fennelly, and Martin Hathaway, members. No. 3, truck originally built by George Bruce & Co., June 1, 1860, but rebuilt by Messrs. Hunneman & Co. during 1870; James Fennity, member. Hancock, No. 5, truck built by Hunneman & Co., and put in service March 3, 1870; George H. Vinal and S. H. Whitney, members. General Grant Ladder Company, No. 6, house on Temple street, Dorchester; truck built by Messrs. Chapman & Strangman, of Milton Lower Mills, Mass., and put in service December, 1869; David S. Black, driver; Henry Crane, captain; Samuel Bridget, assistant; James H. Bourne, E. B. Smith, Henry Crane, Jr., C. E. Skinner, S. B. Locklin, and Elijah Piper, members. Everett Ladder Company, No. 7, house on Meeting-house Hill, Dorchester; truck built by Messrs. Jucket & Freeman, Boston, and put in service January, 1869; Jason Gordon, driver; Hartford Davenport, captain; Lewis P. Bird, assistant; Edmund Truran, J. P. Curtis, W. L. Moulton, R. N. Elmes, George Haffernill, and George F. Oliver, members.

Additional signals were made during the year by the committee on fire alarms, whereby second alarms were given by striking ten blows, and third alarm, twelve blows; general alarm, twelve blows three times. In case ladder companies only were wanted, the signal was given by striking ten blows once, with the number of the company wanted struck twice. If more than one company, the number to be struck twice. Twenty-five additional signal-boxes were added by the annexation of Dorchester. The number of new hydrants were twenty-two in the city, twelve in South Boston, three in East Boston, ninety-nine in Roxbury, and fourteen in Dorchester.

More alarms of fire were rung in during the year than at any other time since the department was organized, there being four hundred and ninety-seven. But the loss by fire was not so much in comparison; it was $855,571; insurance, $786,463. The number of accidents and deaths was also very large. The first fire of note occurred on January 14, at 197 to 199 Portland street, occupied by retail merchants; loss, $12,700; insurance, $9,000. While in the act of coupling a hose at this fire, Mr. Thomas Young, a member of Engine 6, was struck by a passing team, which threw him upon his face, breaking his lower jaw. The most terrible conflagration for the extent of life lost broke out at 10.30 A.M., March 2, at the cotton-drying establishment of Mr. George McBride, at Granite bridge, Adams street, Dorchester. Six women employed in the upper story picking over cotton were burnt to death. Loss to building, $6,700; insured. On the 7th, three small children were locked in a room in a building at 297 Athens street, South Boston, when it caught fire. The children were reached just in time to save them from a terrible death. On the 19th, the building known as Gore block, at the corner of Green and Pitts streets, and occupied by a number of manufacturing firms, was destroyed; loss, $49,594; insured. While at work at this fire, Mr.

George Demary, of Engine 10, was severely burned. A very large fire broke out on April 30 in a building at the corner of Canal and Travers streets, occupied by N. P. Duty, which communicated to a number of others. Assistant Engineer Jacobs and J. A. Fynes had a narrow escape from death; they were seriously injured. During the fire some flying cinders set fire to C. P. Vinal's stable on Charles street, but it was extinguished without an alarm. There was also a fire in the junk store of William Boyle, 107 Merrimac street, but it was extinguished by Engine 13, which was stationed there. The Bay State Wood-Moulding Mill, at 411 Tremont street, owned by J. F. Paul & Co., was consumed on April 19; loss, $13,800; insured. The Bay State Collar Company's premises, at the corner of Lincoln and Essex streets, were destroyed May 29. On July 17, a building on Mindora street, occupied by several families, was destroyed. While going to this fire the hose-carriage belonging to Engine 13 was overturned at the corner of Tremont and Culvert streets, and Mr. Francis Swift, who was driving, was thrown to the ground and severely injured. The grain elevator of the Boston & Lowell Railroad fell in on the 25th, and buried three men in its ruins.

At 3.21 P.M. July 25 fire broke out in the dwelling occupied by R. Wright on London and Border streets, East Boston, and damaged a number of buildings on those streets. Eight alarms were rung in for this fire; loss, $145,000. At 6.29 P.M. the bookstore of Messrs. Little, Brown, & Co., 110 Washington street, together with several other stores, was burnt out; loss, $24,298. Mr. William Lewis of Ladder 1 fell through a scuttle a distance of five stories and sustained serious injuries. On the 27th the ropewalk of Joseph Nickerson & Co., at the corner of Harrison avenue and Hunneman street, together with eleven dwelling-houses, was consumed; loss not returned. A building at the corner of Hanover and Battery streets fell down, August 5, killing one man and wounding several others. On September 21, at a fire at 1 Otis street, Mr. Thomas Merritt of Engine 4 fell from the hose-carriage and broke his leg, and Charles H. Dutton of Engine 8 was run over by a buggy. On the 28th, Mr. A. P. Hawkins, driver of Hose 10, received severe injuries by the breaking of hose-carriage while going to a fire on Seventh street. Mr. Lewis Briggs, engineman of Engine 4, while going to a fire at 10 Beach street, on October 13, was run over by the hose-carriage, which severely injured both of his legs. Engine No. 11, while going to a fire at 31 Pembroke street on the 21st, ran over a boy, severely bruising both his legs. The Boston Lead Works, at the corner of Albany and Hamden streets, owned by J. H. Chadwick & Co., were destroyed on November 5; loss, $166,361. Assistant Engineer Allen, while at this fire, was severely injured by a portion of the falling *débris;* also Mr. M. M. Esdale of Hose No. 10 had his finger taken off while reeling up the hose. Messrs. Hall & Draper's stable, on West Dedham street, fell in on the 12th, killing a man by the name of French.

The enginemen in Ward 16 received a salary of $1,000; driver, $800; foremen, $40; assistants and members, $35 per annum.

CHAPTER XI.

1871–1872.

BESIDES the chief engineer and Assistant Engineer Hibard, Captain Allen was put in charge of District No. 8. during 1871. Seven horses and twelve thousand nine hundred and thirty-two feet of two and a half inch hose were purchased during the year. The salary of the chief was increased to $3,300; secretary, $1,800; foremen in certain wards, $325 and $300; in Ward 16, $175. The number of additional hydrants established were, South Boston, twenty; East Boston, sixteen; Roxbury, sixty-eight; Dorchester, two hundred and twenty-six, — making a total of two thousand three hundred and seventy-five supplying the department at a cost of $18 each, or a total of $44,478. The charge of keeping these hydrants and the ninety-seven reservoirs in repair was $29,652; total for water-supply, $74,130.

Boston, in common with other large cities in the United States, was visited with an unusual large number of fires during 1871, many of which threatened to be quite serious; but by the prompt action and energy of the members, the city was saved from any serious conflagration. The number of fires was five hundred and forty-nine; loss, $704,329.06, which was a decrease over the loss of the year previous. The first fatal accident happened on January 8, when Mary A. Clinch, living at 22 Lancaster street, was burnt to death from the explosion of a kerosene lamp. The Sherman House, on Court square, was damaged to the extent of $7.80 on the 10th. Messrs. Hecht Bros., and others, 120 to 126 Pearl street, were burnt out on the 25th; loss, $20,000; insured. Mr. M. D. Gill was severely cut by glass thrown out by the explosion of a torpedo at a fire at Foss & Merrill's, 47 Charlestown street, on the 27th. The Adelphia Theatre, on Central court, was discovered on fire at 11.29 P.M., February 4, and before it was extinguished several other buildings were in flames; loss, $47,000; insured. Mr. George W. Stone of Hose 9, while driving home after the fire, had his hands and feet badly frozen. On the 25th, the chapel and workshops of the House of Correction, on First street, South Boston, were destroyed; loss, $78,000; no insurance.

March 11, Mr. R. G. Philips of Hose 10 had a finger taken off by being caught in the chain-gearing of hose-carriage, at a fire on First street, South Boston. The works of the Suffolk Glass Company, and several other buildings on Lowland street, South Boston, were burnt on the 24th; loss, $32,000; insured. John G. Duffy of Engine 4 was severely cut in the foot by falling glass at a fire at 55 Charlestown street, April 4. On the 13th, Capt. C. H. Blake of Engine 8 was run over by hose-carriage and slightly injured, while going to a fire at 42 Cross street. A block of five tenement houses on First street, South Boston, was destroyed on the 20th; loss, $23,726; insured. While going to a fire at Jamaica Plain on the 21st, Ladder Truck 4, in turning a corner, ran into a buggy driven by J. T. Eldridge, thereby breaking it, and killing the horse; Mr. and Mrs. Eldridge were slightly bruised. The Sailors' National Home at North Quincy was destroyed on May 17. Mr. James Gordon, driver of Ladder 7, while driving out of the house to attend this alarm, was brought in contract with the doors, and severely injured. A block of seven tenement houses on Hamburg street was burnt on the 20th. Three alarms were given for a fire in the building, stables, etc., at the corner of Canal and Market streets, on the 24th; loss, $7,000; insured. Mr. J. M. Littlefield, substitute on Hose 7, had the forefinger of one hand taken off by the chain-gearing of the carriage, while at a fire on Fellows *street, June 22. A general alarm was given on July 17 for a fire in several buildings at the corner of First street and Dorchester avenue, South Boston; loss not given. A. P. Hawkins, driver of Hose 10, had his hand badly burnt. On the 21st, at a fire of Greesey & Noyes, on the corner of Wareham and Plympton streets, Messrs. Gaylord and Ryder of Hose 5, and Dalrymple and McLaughlin of Hose 8, had their hair, eyebrows, and whiskers badly burnt. The Lyman School on Paris street, East Boston, was destroyed on August 2; loss, $35,000; no insurance. William Sheene of Ladder 5 had one of his feet badly injured by a spike in the end of a ladder, while at a fire on First street, corner of Dorchester street, South Boston. In answering the second alarm at a fire at J. McElroy's, rear of 17 Eustis street, the axle of Engine 21 broke, throwing the driver, T. H. Bridgham, to the ground, cutting a very severe gash in his head. On the 10th, on the same street, Assistant Engineer Allen was struck in the face with a brick thrown by some rascal in the crowd, which inflicted a severe contusion. In going to a fire on Paris street, East Boston, on the 29th, William Hall, Jr., of Engine 5, was run over by the hose-carriage and badly injured. Henry A. Tracy of Hose 3 was nearly suffocated by smoke at a fire at the Crystal Glass Company's building, 143 Washington street, November 29. The house occupied by Engine No. 7, on East street, was damaged to the extent of $4,500 on December 1. The Warwick House, 1023 Washington street, burned on the 3d; loss, $13,465; insured. Frank S. Parsons of Engine 7 fell through an open hatchway while at a fire at 411 Broad street, and received severe injuries. Mr. Joseph Crosby, fireman of Engine 21, received a bad cut on his face, and had two teeth knocked out, by the Lowery chuck, while taking it off the engine at a fire on Pleasant street, on the 24th. On the 25th, a building at 20 Blossom street was burnt. Mrs. Myers, aged seventy-three, a resident, was unable to effect her escape, as the fire had obtained possession of the stairway. Mr. Chandler Griffin of Ladder 1 managed to effect an entrance from the outside, and succeeded in saving her from a most horrible death, but not, however, until both were badly burned about the face and arms. Mr. Charles E. Wilson, driver of the extinguisher wagon, made a misstep, and fell down a flight of stairs (with the extinguisher on his back), breaking some of the ligaments of his arm. Mr. J. A. Fynes of Engine 4, and George P. Kingsley of the Insurance Brigade, were both badly burned about the face and hands in trying to get up the stairs to the rescue of Mrs. Myers.

The changes and new members during 1871 were as follows: Engine Company No. 1, Loring D. Shaw, fireman. No. 4, D. R. Deering, engineman; W. T. Cheswell, fireman; Russel White, driver; Joseph Pierce, captain; Russel White, hoseman. Lewis Briggs transferred to Engine 18. No. 6, L. G. Newman, driver of hose; Henry Daniels, captain; E. A. Whitehead and Charles Hodgdon, hosemen. No. 7, George W. Stoddard, driver; H. N. Wilson, S. A. Neal, and F. S. Parsons, hosemen. C. Griffin transferred to Ladder 1. No. 9, Samuel L. Fowle, captain. No. 10, William Parker, captain; W. B. Lottridge, William Dixon, C. H. Skimmings, and J. C. Singleton, hosemen. W. H. Bradford died August 31. No. 13, W. F. Booker, driver of engine; C. C. Clark, driver of hose; C. L. Rosemere, captain; George W. Hord, G. W. Gilman, and H. S. Kendall, hosemen. No. 14, Thomas Nannery, engineman, *vice* George F. Worcester, died August 26. No. 15, Alonzo Donnels, driver, *vice* E. C. Phillips, died January 4. No. 16, William Shields, fireman; R. L. Mason, hoseman. No. 17, N. H. Bird, fireman. No. 18, David Ripley, fireman; Edward Brigham and Lewis Briggs, hosemen. No. 19, I. A. Williams, fireman. No. 20, W. O. Swan, fireman; Thomas F. Temple, captain; George W. Berry, hoseman. No. 21, James Crosby, fireman.

Hose Company No. 2, A. C. Scott, hoseman. No. 3, E. A. Blonde, *vice* R. M. Young, died December 27; E. F. Barney, captain. No. 6, Charles Brooks, driver, *vice* J. D. Sherman, died March 14; J. M. T. Burke, hoseman. No. 7, B. F. Ansart and J. M. Littleton, hosemen. No. 9, J. J. Conley and S. H. Luther, hosemen. Ladder Company No. 1, D. C. Bickford, assistant foreman; T. B. Flanagan, C. Griffin, and W. J. Hicks, members. No. 3, George A. Kennison and F. A. W. Gay, members. No. 4, J. M. Powers, *vice* R. Hickley, died September 4, and G. W. Morse, *vice* G. S. Fogg, died September 28. Ladder 5, Anthony Martin, member.

There were added to the department one fire-extinguisher wagon, equipped with ten extinguishers, and three hundred feet of one and a half inch hose, also axes, rakes, lanterns, etc. Charles E. Wilson, driver, and J. A. Fynes, member.

Three new engines were purchased during 1872, — No. 1, put in service September 17; No. 2, August 7; and No. 9, October 14; the former from the works of the Amoskeag Manufacturing Company, the other two from Messrs. Hunneman & Co. These engines were built under the immediate supervision of Enginemen Cole, Traver, and Ray, who were appointed by the chief as inspectors of steam fire-engines. Two hook-and-ladder trucks were also purchased on April 13, from Messrs. Hunneman & Co., — one for Ladder

Company 4, the other for No. 6, to be located in the Dorchester district. Two extinguisher wagons were placed in commission, — No. 2 on April 1, and located in Ladder-house No. 3, Williston A. Gaylord, driver, and W. I. Jacobs, member; No. 3 on August 24, and located in Engine-house No. 9, George Fowle, driver. These wagons were built by Joseph T. Ryan, of Boston, and carried twenty-five extinguishers each. Two new coal-wagons — one for East Boston, and one for the city proper — were placed in service. A new house was erected for the accommodation of Engine Company No. 4 and Extinguisher No. 1 on Bulfinch street, at an expense of $54,723.54, and cost of land of $55,000. The building was also used by the Insurance Brigade and the National Lancers. The spare apparatus were Engines Nos. 1, 2, 7, 9, and 10, — the latter was thoroughly rebuilt as good as new, — Ladders 1 and 4, and Hose-carriages Nos. 1, 2, 3, 5, and 8. One hand-engine, known as "Boston," No. 8, was stationed at the Highlands. Two hundred and seventeen hydrants were established during the year, as follows: fifty-one in the city, eleven in South Boston, fifteen in East Boston, seventy in Roxbury, and seventy in Dorchester.

There was also an iron fire-boat placed in the service January 1, 1873. This fire-boat was about fifty-five tons measurement, and measures seventy-five feet in length, fifteen feet beam, and seven feet in depth. Her hull was built of iron, the keel, stem and stern posts being of hammered metal, and the frames, which were of reverse angle-iron, spread twenty-one inches between centres, were stiffened by vertical floor-plates. Three keelsons extend the entire length of the boat. The forecastle below deck was fitted with berths, table, seats, and lockers for the accommodation of the men. The house on deck had a cabin, engine, boiler, cook, and hose rooms, all of which were finished in a substantial and workmanlike manner. The pilot-house was on top of the main house over the hose-room, and was fitted with seats and mahogany steering-wheel; a hand-rail extended around the house to prevent accident, and the top was covered with tin to insure safety from fire. The main engine was vertical, direct acting, high pressure, with link motion and independent cut-off valve. Its diameter of cylinder was seventeen inches, and seventeen-inch stroke. The propeller was six feet in diameter, with five inches of wrought-iron shaft; two force-pumps driven from the main shaft, and one steam-pump for feeding the boiler, and a steam siphon-pump for the bilge. The boiler was an upright tubular, with cylindrical fire-box, twenty-four feet grate surface. The whole power of the fire-engine machinery was equal in capacity to four first-class fire-engines, and with all in action would play eight streams at one time. This machinery was built by the Amoskeag Manufacturing Company, and of the same design as their steam fire-engines. The boat, main engine, machinery, and boiler were built by the Atlantic Works, East Boston. The total cost of this boat was $19,893.95. It was named the "William M. Flanders," in honor of a member of the Common Council of that name.

During the concerts at the Coliseum building during 1873, there were stationed in a building built expressly for the purpose and adjoining that of the main building, Engines Nos. 12 and 21, which were kept in constant readiness for immediate use. The hose was coupled to the engines and run over the building at different points; steam was constantly kept up by means of the circulatory water-heaters. In the day-time, during the concerts, members of this department were stationed upon the roof with the lines of hose from the engines. There were daily detailed from the service nineteen men, who did patrol duty in and about the building, watching for fire, and who took charge of the sick and fainting. The anvil chorus was, as in the Peace Jubilee, one of the features of the concert. Mr. H. W. Longley, secretary of the Board of Engineers, led the one hundred firemen in this performance. After the concerts were discontinued, one engine and five members were stationed there until the building was removed.

There had been much sickness among the horses in this service during the year previous to the appearance of the epidemic so generally prevalent; yet up to that time no death had occurred among them. On October 28, the disease known as the epizootic, or influenza catarrh, attacked them, and so rapid was its spread, that on the 4th of November the entire force was prostrated. The services of Dr. Very were secured, the horses placed under his charge, and every attention given. The disease assumed several forms; in some, the typhoid type; in others, pneumonia; and many with kidney troubles and dropsy. At this time nearly all the horses in this locality were so badly affected that but few were to be seen upon the streets. Business was almost suspended for lack of transportation, and such conveyances as necessity absolutely demanded had to be done by men. The horses in this department were seriously affected, their feet and legs being cold and badly swollen, and so weak they could hardly be backed out of their stalls. Upon the appearance of this sudden and sweeping calamity, the Board of Engineers, after careful deliberation, voted that the force of the department be doubled, and that steps be taken immediately to supply the force, so that no unreasonable delay should occur in the transportation of the apparatus in case of fire. In addition to the doubling of the force, it was voted, should the exigency arise, to levy upon and press into the service of the city, in their several fire districts, any horses that were available. The vote was approved by the committee on fire department, and the proceedings published in the daily papers. The direct loss to the department by death from this disease was one horse each from Engines Nos. 3, 4, and 17, and Ladder 3. Twelve others were rendered unfit for the service and were exchanged.

Mr. Levi W. Shaw and George W. Clark were appointed on the Board of Engineers. The changes, etc., in the department for 1872, were as follows: Engine Company No. 1, H. L. Wallingford, hoseman. No. 2, Robert J. Tagen, hoseman. No. 3, J. H. Lefavor, driver; W. T. Hines, hoseman. No. 4, house in Bulfinch street, Matthias Conley, captain; W. M. Blood, hoseman, *vice* J. A. Fynes, transferred to Extinguisher Company No. 1.

No. 5, J. E. Wharton, hoseman, *vice* G. Sherman, appointed driver Hose 11. No. 6, J. W. Groves, E. T. Wilson, *vice* T. Young, killed November 5, and T. W. Freeman, hoseman, *vice* C. E. Wilson, appointed driver Extinguisher No. 1. No. 7, Joseph H. Rankin, *vice* F. S. Parsons, transferred to Hose 9; E. B. Haskell, hoseman. No. 9, George W. Brown, engineman, *vice* James Grace, resigned; J. W. Smith, hoseman. No. 10, William Hudson, fireman; J. S. King, *vice* W. B. Lottridge, transferred to Hose 1. No. 11, George L. Imbert, fireman; John Bickford, driver, *vice* G. W. Brown, transferred to Engine 9. No. 12, William H. Gay, hoseman. No. 13. Francis Swift, engineman; W. F. Booker, fireman; E. B. Burgess, driver; and Francis Freeman, driver of hose; Edward J. Roe and S. T. Hoen, hosemen. No. 14, C. W. Bates, driver; A. D. Snow, driver of hose; Dennis Kilduff, *vice* J. Watkins, died January 29; George White and M. J. Slattery, hosemen. No. 15, Benjamin W. Carpenter, fireman, *vice* J. Cain, resigned. No. 16, E. R. Merrill, hoseman. No. 19, George F. Fenno, captain; Joseph Abenzeller, hoseman. No. 21, R. E. Flanders of Hose 1, foreman; G. W. Richardson, hoseman.

Hose Company No. 1, W. B. Lottridge of Hose 1, *vice* R. E. Flanders, transferred to Engine 21. No. 2, Charles Ingersol, hoseman. No. 3, Thomas H. Kyte, *vice* George Clark, appointed assistant engineer. No. 4, Joseph H. Le Cain, captain; Edward Martin and W. B. Marshall, hosemen. No. 5, H. D. Fernald, *vice* W. A. Gaylord, transferred to Extinguisher 2; George E. Gardner, hoseman. No. 6, Edward A. Misener, hoseman. No. 7, A. H. Perry, W. A. Copeland, *vice* J. W. Sweat, died August 10, and Charles Miller, *vice* T. A. Scott resigned, hosemen. No. 8, William Blake, driver; S. H. T. Houghton, hoseman. No. 9, T. S. Parsons, transferred. No. 10, A. P. Hawkins, driver; J. L. Bowers, captain; John Rae, R. W. Kane, and A. E. Cluff, hosemen; R. W. Kane died October 21. No. 11, Gershom Sherman, driver. Ladder Company No. 1, I. H. Ware, assistant; V. C. Hanson and O. F. Severance, members. No. 2, A. C. Turner, assistant. No. 3, I. K. Jennings, captain; B. B. Wright, assistant; J. W. Chase, L. L. Cooper, and G. W. Warren, members; ex-Captain Marston was elected to the Common Council, and L. W. Shaw appointed assistant engineer. No. 4, E. R. Bartlett, driver; C. O. Allen and F. W. Munroe, members; Frank Upton died December 31, 1871. No. 5, George F. Horn, member. No. 6, E. B. Smith, captain. No. 7, Edmund Fruean, captain.

On account of the distemper among the horses in the city, the committee on fire department had the force of men in the department increased one hundred per cent. These were immediately enrolled, and placed on the pay-roll of the city, to remain on duty from 6 o'clock at night until 7 o'clock in the morning at the several stations to which they were assigned. Under this arrangement many alarms were responded to, the apparatus being drawn by hand, and the alacrity with which they worked called forth praise from the press as well as from the people, who, with watches in their hands, timed the apparatus on its way to the scene of action, and manifested their approval of this old-time custom by cheers and the clapping of hands.

Such was the condition of the city, — its horses down with the epizootic, its business blocked, its citizens nervous and impatient, the fire department greatly crippled, especially in the suburban districts — when it was visited by a conflagration so extensive in dimensions and appalling in result that all others fade into insignificance. November 9, 1872, was one of those beautiful autumnal days so common in New England; the air was clear and exhilarating; not a cloud obscured the sun, and the gentle breeze, veering occasionally two or three points between north and north-west, did not exceed seven miles an hour. As the day went out, and twilight settled over the valleys, a more beautiful sunset was never seen. Sick horses were convalescent and on the road to ultimate recovery. The fear which had hung over the city or a week, like a cloud, was gradually lifting, and showed a silver lining. The wholesale business centre of the city had been deserted and surrendered to the guardians of its peace and safety, the owners and occupants of the great mercantile houses of brick, stone, and iron having gone hours before to their respective homes with no warning or thought of impending danger. The city had for a long time enjoyed freedom from the fire-fiend's depredations, which fact was universally credited to the vigilance and *esprit de corps* which characterized the *personnel* of the department. But at the close of this beautiful day the enemy appeared, and attacked the very citadel of the city's strength, built of obdurate metal and mineral, and it succumbed at the first onslaught.

At 7.20 P.M. Box 52 was sounded. This was followed by four alarms in rapid succession, calling the entire working force of the department. The force of the city proper consisted of six engines, six hose companies, two hook-and-ladder companies, a chief, and seven assistant engineers, and a total of one hundred and eighty-five men. There was a fearful delay in sounding out the first alarm. This was caused by the fact that Engine No. 7 and Hose No. 2 were already at work, which impressed the officers on that beat with the idea that the alarm had already been turned in by some person who had discovered the fire. Hence the largest portion of the department was first notified by the brilliant pyrotechnic display which illuminated the entire city, and the apparatus hastened to the scene. It was fifteen minutes after the fire was discovered by the men of Engine No. 7 before the alarm was sounded on the bells, by which time the fire assumed fearful proportions. This was a terrible misfortune, and just who was to blame investigation failed to show.

The fire originated in a six-story granite building on the corner of Summer and Kingston streets, and occupied on the first floor by Tebbetts, Baldwin, & Davis, dry good jobbers; A. K. Young, on the third and fourth stories as a manufacturer of skirts and corsets: on the second floor. Damon, Temple, & Co., fancy goods. Opposite this building Engine No. 4 had taken

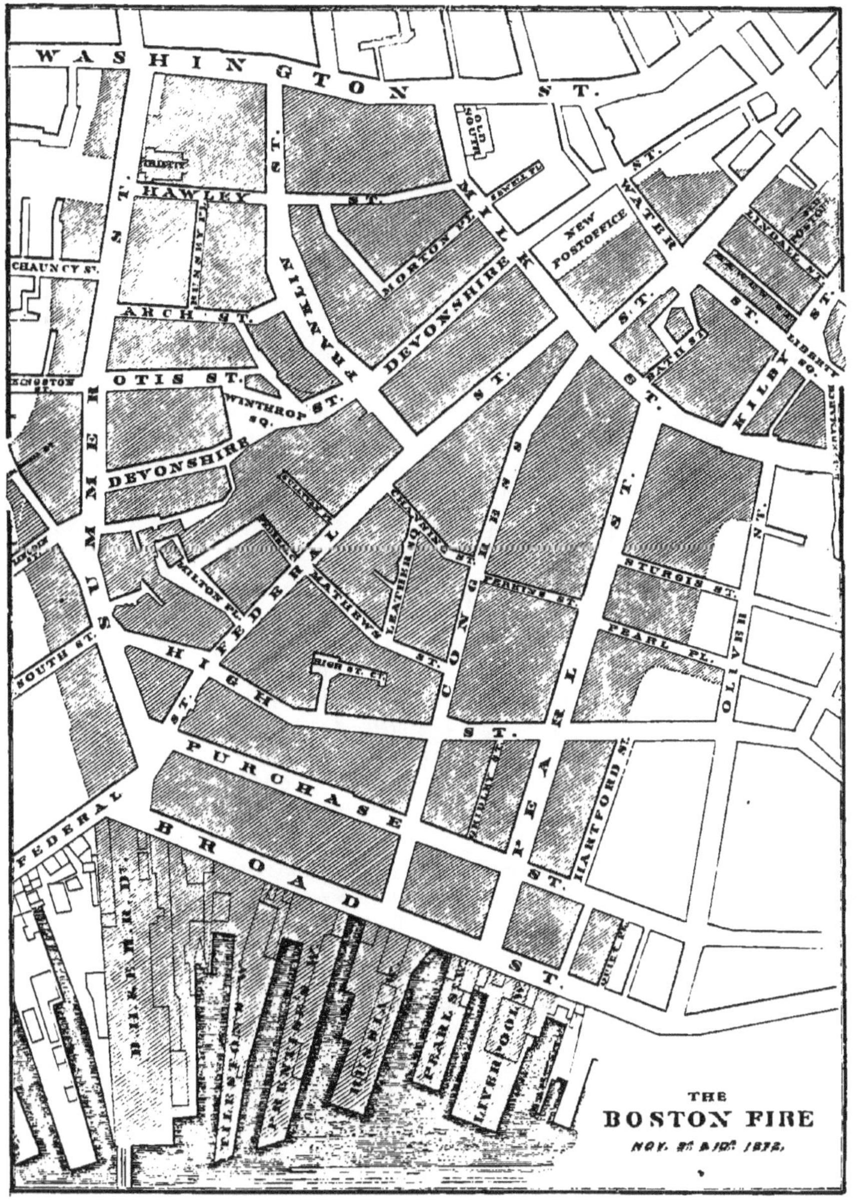
WASHINGTON ST.
OLD SOUTH
MILK ST.
NEW POSTOFFICE
WATER ST.
LINDALL ST.
BATTERYMARCH ST.
CHAUNCY ST.
HAWLEY ST.
ARCH ST.
OTIS ST.
FRANKLIN ST.
MORTON PL.
DEVONSHIRE ST.
BATH ST.
KILBY ST.
LIBERTY SQ.
KINGSTON ST.
WINTHROP SQ.
WINTHROP ST.
DEVONSHIRE
SUMMER ST.
MILTON PL.
FEDERAL ST.
MATHEWS ST.
CHAUNCY
LEATHER SQ.
CONGRESS ST.
PEARL ST.
PEARL PL.
STURGIS ST.
OLIVER ST.
SOUTH ST.
HIGH ST.
HIGH ST. PL.
PURCHASE ST.
KINGSTON ST.
HARTFORD ST.
PEARL ST.
FEDERAL ST.
BROAD ST.
DIVER PL.
FRANKLIN
PEARL
LIVERPOOL
THE
BOSTON FIRE
NOV. 9 & 10, 1872.

its position, — although at the time of the alarm the heat was so intense that it was extremely dangerous to locate any piece of apparatus within a hundred feet of the actual seat of fire, — and was taking water from a flush hydrant, the kind used in the city, and located within five feet of the ashlar line of the buildings. So intense was the heat, that the stone coping of the building, sixty feet distant from the fire, began to burst and crumble, and a piece of it fell and severed the suction, compelling the engine to retire to another source of supply. So rapid was the spread of fire that at the moment of giving the alarm, six other equally large granite buildings were enveloped in flames, and the building where it originated was a roaring furnace.

About an hour from the time the alarm sounded, assistance was summoned from every point within a radius of fifty miles, and every municipality nobly responded. Couriers were despatched to all suburban towns that could not be reached by telegraph. Hose in the several warehouses of the city was seized by order of Chief Damrell, taken to the City Hall, and from there distributed as emergency required, and all was duly accounted for. The engines in use being of the Amoskeag pattern, Governor Straw, superintendent of the Amoskeag Manufacturing Company, was telegraphed to send a corps of workmen with duplicate parts of the engines, to meet every crisis that might occur.

The key of the fire was well understood, and the departments of Boston, Cambridge, Charlestown, and the Navy Yard, were massed in a battery at this point, which embraced Arch, Devonshire, and Summer streets, and Winthrop square, and the territory bounded by them. Owing to the diminished supply of water, all outlying draughts upon pipes and mains were ordered closed, and the full power of the battery concentrated at this point. It was a fight for the city and for life. But in a moment, as it were, when success bid fair to be achieved, the water-supply failed, and the force was obliged to retire, not whipped, but driven back by overwhelming odds. This determined the fate of the fire district, and from this moment the power of the elements defied description. Granite fronts and walls burst out and fell, breaking the principal water and gas mains and the several branches which supplied the hydrants and buildings. Cellars and sewers were permeated with gas, and water was wasting and flowing in every direction. By 9 o'clock the citizens were becoming wild and frantic, making unreasonable demands on the one hand, and on the other offering fabulous sums for the desertion of one position for the defence of another. Some, in the whirl of excitement, opened their stores and invited the people to help themselves to the contents. This was a fearful and demoralizing act, and tended to inflame the thirst of that class which is ever ready to make the most of others' misfortunes. From this hour onward, the Board of Engineers fought the fire upon a principle so thoroughly understood, that the orders of the chief were often anticipated.

Currents and counter-currents of rarified air rushed in every direction with the power of a tornado, and new heat-centres were constantly produced, rendering human power impotent to resist the Niagara of destruction.

Volumes of flame held full possession of both sides of the street, while gas and air explosions, and the crash of falling walls, followed each other in such rapid succession as to resemble the crack of cannonading from a hundred field-pieces. It was impossible to mass or consolidate the engines, for the water-supply would not admit of it; therefore the force was divided into small detachments. By 10 o'clock, engines from the suburbs began to arrive, and were assigned to the reservoirs, as their couplings would not connect with the hydrants. The induced currents were carefully studied, and the air was found to be highly rarified with a strong rush upwards, which formed a terrible vacuum, and to fill this gave a velocity to the in-rushing oxygen of thirty miles an hour, and drew the heat from the outward boundary of the fire to its base or centre. From these facts it was evident to the experienced what the boundary of the fire would be. At 11 o'clock, members of the city government and leading citizens became so terrified, that all sorts of irrational demands were made on those upon whom the responsibility of this terrible battle devolved. Among the methods recommended was the use of gunpowder as an auxiliary to the work which was now being performed by the department. This was depreciated by some members of the department as being impracticable, extremely dangerous, and tending to demoralize the working force of the city, by reason of the narrow streets, lined with high buildings, and these stored with inflammable merchandise; for it was felt that the use of explosives would tumble these buildings and their contents into confused heaps of combustibles, which would not be defended as well as if they stood intact, while the thoroughfare would be blockaded by the *débris*. Besides all this, it was urged that the plans of the battle, now well arranged and understood among the generals in command, would be interfered with by the desires of inexperienced and excited men. But the powder was brought into requisition and used, and with the effect anticipated by those who opposed its use.

The fire raged for eighteen hours with relentless fury. The streets became veritable blow-pipes, by reason of their narrowness and the height of the buildings upon them, causing such intense heat that blocks of granite stores would melt, as it were, and fall before the flames had approached within five hundred feet of them. At last, the working force had been so augmented by the reënforcements from out of town, that the adequate supply of water from the tide reservoirs along the southern, eastern, and northern boundaries of the fire could be made available, and at 3 o'clock in the morning a continuous line of battle was formed, the right resting on Washington near Bromfield street, and continuing through Washington, State, and Broad, to Oliver street. This line embraced forty-two steam fire-engines, which advanced with an ardor and pluck that evinced their determination to stop and conquer further devastation. The work here performed demanded and evoked the commendation and admiration of those competent to judge of its efficacy, and by it the flames were driven to a common centre, the army holding every point gained in the attack.

At 10 o'clock Sunday morning the fearful strain to which the men had been subjected had brought them to the verge of complete exhaustion, and the reënforcements that had arrived during the morning hours were most opportune, bringing temporary relief and rest to those who had been engaged in such a long superhuman struggle. The limits of the fire were now defined, and the further spread being out of the question, the work was directed to the interior of buildings partially destroyed on the boundaries of the fire. The military organizations were doing magnificent work in keeping the curious-minded back from dangerous positions, details of the grand army of firemen were posted to take care of the ruins, and tranquillity again took possession of the city.

But on midnight on Sunday the city was again aroused by a terrific report occasioned by a gas explosion on Summer street, near Washington street, which caused a general alarm to be sent in. This explosion took place in a block occupied by W. R. Storms & Co. and R. S. Stern & Co., which had successfully resisted all advances of the fire-fiend the previous night. The front external wall was blown into the street, the merchandise with which the building was stored ignited, and a terrific fire was again in full blast, in close proximity to the two largest dry-goods stores in the city. The excitement caused by this fire was even greater than that of the night before; but the excellent work of the military in keeping the people at a proper distance enabled the department and its out-of-town allies to fight with courage and success, and after four hours of hot endeavor the fire was under control. By the explosion one life was lost, — that of the mother of Mrs. Martha Hudson, a lady residing on the premises; and during the fire a number of firemen were injured.

A summary of the work of destruction in the great Boston fire shows that it burned over sixty-five acres of land, the value of which was placed by the Board of Assessors at $24,365,000, consumed buildings assessed at $12,745,-000, and destroyed merchandise assessed for $38,434,000; add to this $10,000,000 as a fair estimate of the value of consigned goods, and we have a grand total in buildings and merchandise of $60,000,000. The Report of the Board of Fire Commissioners place the total loss at $75,000,000. The buildings numbered 776, of which 709 were brick and stone, and 67 wood; five hundred and fifty were owned by separate estates, and were occupied by over one thousand business firms. The following table shows the value of property as destroyed on the streets: —

STREETS.	Value of Land.	Value of Buildings.	Personal.	Square Feet of Land.
Arch	$136,000	$78,000	$191,800	9,995
Bath	51,000	19,000	15,300	4,500
Broad	1,040,000	116,000	295,000	391,129
Bussey place	30,500	20,500	5,000	5,345
Channing	32,000	11,000	10,000	8,910
Columbia	100,000	24,500	. . . .	8,560
Congress	2,086,000	1,230,000	3,009,900	176,135
Devonshire	1,051,000	575,000	2,561,800	55,880
Federal	2,402,000	1,356,000	3,367,300	208,801
Federal court	30,000	8,000	. . . .	6,510
Franklin	2,222,000	1,401,000	5,841,600	111,355
Gridley	17,000	9,000	. . . .	3,456
Hawes	5,000	500	. . . .	500
Hawley	174,000	73,000	54,000	16,644
High	1,389,500	1,021,000	3,326,100	118,514
Kilby	554,000	195,500	1,243,400	27,473
Leather square	10,000	4,000	. . . .	2,500
Lincoln	37,000	45,000	8,500	5,069
Lindall	154,000	68,000	53,500	12,057
Matthew	36,500	46,500	40,000	6,012
Merchants' Exchange	450,000	100,000	. . . .	1,700
Milk	1,991,000	910,000	2,944,600	103,144
Milton place	69,000	36,000	10,000	15,230
Morton place	64,000	45,000	14,900	14,680
Oliver	126,000	87,000	150,000	12,358
Otis	339,000	216,000	1,056,500	19,720
Pearl	2,466,000	1,531,000	7,251,800	218,590
Pearl place	66,700	41,800	2,000	15,388
Carried forward	$17,129,200	$8,965,300	$31,453,000	1,575,155

STREETS.	Value of Land.	Value of Buildings.	Personal.	Square Feet of Land.
Brought forward	$17,129,200	$8,965,300	$31,453,000	1,575,155
Purchase	427,000	153,000	71,000	50,152
South	177,000	33,000	....	21,658
Sturgis	8,000	4,000	....	1,125
Sullivan place	10,000	4,000	....	2,280
Summer	3,616,000	2,023,000	4,042,700	225,590
Washington	1,930,000	766,000	1,794,100	73,433
Water	725,000	242,000	170,400	31,169
Winthrop square	343,000	255,000	922,600	18,963
Total........	$24,365,200	$12,745,300	$38,453,800	1,999,525

By comparing the map of the burnt district on page 274 with one of the present day, the changes in location of streets made after the fire may be seen.

The cost of these improvements amounted to over $5,000,000. The old streets were so narrow and crooked that it was at first proposed to lay out the territory on an entirely new plan; but it was found on examination that the city could not give a good title to the land included in the old streets, and the improvement was therefore restricted to the widening and straightening of the old ways.

As a matter of course, the insurance companies were heavy losers, twenty of which were bankrupted, and on December 18, 1872, an act was passed by the Legislature respecting the formation of insurance companies.

The following is a statement of the number of engines, hose, and hook-and-ladder carriages, with the number of men and amount of hose, that attended the great fire of November 9, 1872, from out of town : —

Chief Engineer.	City or Town.	Engines.	Hose.	Hook & Ladder.	Men.	Feet of Hose.
P. H. Raymond	Cambridge, Mass.	3	2	1	75	1,500
William E. Delano	Charlestown, "	2	3	. .....	60	2,000
Samuel Hutchins	Chelsea, "	1	2	....	85	1,000
W. W. Kimball	Lynn, "	2	2	. ...	27	1,400
D. B. Lord	Salem, "	2	1	....	67	2,000
Luther Ladd	Lawrence, "	1	1	....	11	700
Alfred Kenrick, Jr.	Brookline, "	1(h)	1	1	69	1,100
C. A. Belford.	W. Roxbury, "	2	1	....	21	1,200
James R. Hopkins	Somerville, "	1	3	....	60	1,200
A. D. Drew	Watertown, "	1	1	....	21	800
R. M. Lucas	Newton, "	2	2	....	51	1,750
S. E. Combs	Worcester, "	2	3	....	60	3,800
Thomas J. Borden	Fall River, "	2	4	... ...	60	2,200
Onslow Gilmore	Stoneham, "	1	1	....	18	850
T. W. Hough	Malden, "	1	2	....	54	2,000
John R. Norton	Melrose, "	2	1	....	15	400
Benjamin H. Simmin.	Medford, "	1	2	....	40	1,000
Charles H. Davis	Wakefield, "	2(h)	.. ....	....	88	750
William H. Temple	Reading, "	1(h)	1	....	105	500
A. H. Howland, Jr.	New Bedford, "	1	1	... ..	26	700
Marshall Parks	Waltham, "	1	1	....	14	700
Oliver E. Green	Providence, R.I.	3	3	......	30	1,700
A. C. Hendrick	New Haven, Conn.	1	1		22	900
Daniel A. Delamoy	Norwich, "	2	3	....	166	2,300
S. L. Marston	Portsmouth, N.H.	1	1	....	45	1,100
B. C. Kendall	Manchester, "	2	2	....	63	1,200
....	Biddeford, Me.	......	2	..... .	175	3,000
E. G. Parrott, Com .	Charlestown N. Yard.	2	2	1	81	1,000
T. T. J. Laidley, "	Watertown Arsenal .	1	2	... .	25	1,100
E. P. Davis	Hyde Park, Mass. .	1	1	....	55	1,200
		45	52	3	1,689	41.050

The list of killed and wounded at this fire is as follows : —

William Farry, Foreman of Hook and Ladder Company No. 4, Boston, killed.

Daniel Cochrane, Assistant Foreman of Hook and Ladder Company No. 4, Boston, killed.

Henry Rogers, Volunteer, Engine Company No. 6, Boston, killed.

Michael Fitzgerald, Citizen, Boston, killed.

Lewis P. Abbott, Ex-member of Fire Department, Charlestown, killed.

William S. Frazier, Volunteer, Cambridge, killed.

Frank D. Olmstead, Volunteer, Cambridge, killed.

John Connelly, Hook and Ladder Company No. 1, West Roxbury, killed.

Walter S. Twombly, Hose Company No. 2, Malden. killed.

Thomas Maloney, Member of Fire Department, Worcester, killed.

Lewis C. Thompson, Citizen, Worcester, killed.

Thomas Mooney, Volunteer, Engine Company No. 9, Boston, slightly injured.

Martin Turnbull, Hose Company No. 3, Charlestown, killed.

Thomas M. Paine, Volunteer, Charlestown, seriously injured.

Charles T. Walden, Volunteer, Charlestown, slightly injured.

Albert C. Abbott, Ex-member. Charlestown, killed.

Francis P. Scanlan, Engine Company No. 1, Cambridge, slightly injured.

Richard F. Tobin, Engine Company No. 2, Cambridge, slightly injured.

William H. Jenness, Ex-member, Cambridge, seriously injured.

———— Murphy, Volunteer, Cambridge, slightly injured.

Lewis C. Clark, Hook and Ladder Company, Cambridge, slightly injured.

George H. Smith, Member of engine connected with Watertown Arsenal, slightly injured.

Assistant Engineer Angier, Fire Department, Somerville, slightly injured.

E. P. Small, Member of Fire Department, Somerville, slightly injured.

John Richardson, Volunteer, New Haven, seriously injured.

A. N. Cotton, Assistant Engineer, Medford, slightly injured.

Benjamin D. Griggs, Member of Fire Department, West Newton, slightly injured.

R. E. Extell, Member of Fire Department, Worcester, seriously injured.

Thomas McCann, Member of Fire Department, Worcester, seriously injured.

Jacob E. Hook, Member of Fire Department, Malden, seriously injured.

A large number of citizens met at the Mayor's office, City Hall. and coöperated with the city government in such action as was necessary. They adopted resolutions expressive of its sympathy for the sufferers by the fire, and appointed a committee for the purpose of extending immediate aid to those needing assistance, and also tendered a vote of thanks to the firemen. Generous offers of aid were received from all parts of the country, and work for the immediate relief of the distressed was begun. Before the fire had ceased burning, and while everything was unsettled, a large number of merchants secured new quarters and resumed business on Monday morning. Others commenced the erection of temporary buildings, some on the ruins of their warehouses, on the Common, and on the site of Fort Hill. An act was passed by the Legislature to enable the city of Boston to make and issue its bonds for certain purposes, for an amount not exceeding $20,000,000, bearing an interest of not more than five and six per cent., for no more than fifteen years. This was under the management of a board of three commissioners, who were to determine the amount of loan to be given to those who were burnt out during the conflagration, which loan was secured by notes or bonds of such owners, secured by first mortgages of the land, on condition that building be commenced upon the land within one year from January 1, 1873.

On December 14, 1872, an act was also passed by the same body, entitled "In addition to an act to provide for the regulation and inspection of buildings, the more effectual prevention of fire, and the better preservation of life and property in Boston."

Hardly had the limits of this terrible fire been established, when the department was made the recipient of checks ranging from $1,000 to $10,000 each, until the magnificent sum of $100,000 and upwards was realized for the benefit of firemen who lost their lives or who were injured at this fire. Of this amount, over $80,000 was placed in the hands of a Board of Trustees, of which the Hon. Martin Brimmer was president. There was also sent to the chief engineer over $20,000, $5,000 of which was paid, as requested, to the Charitable Association of the Boston Fire Department, the balance to be used for the benefit of the firemen who were injured, and the families of those who were killed, according to the judgment and discretion of the chief.

An order from the City Council was received, asking the Board of Engineers to consider and report what steps were necessary to be taken to insure the lives of the members of the Boston Fire Department. After careful deliberation on the part of the board, it was deemed inexpedient to recommend action to the City Council. The lowest estimate of those obtained from several life insurance companies would cost the city the sum of $20,000 annually to insure the lives of the members of the department in the sum of $1,000 each. It was recommended by the Board of Engineers that the department mutually insure themselves. This recommendation was adopted, and an organization was accordingly completed on the 3d of February, 1872. The plan adopted was, that each member be insured to an amount equal to $2 from each member of the organization. This organization is known as the Boston Firemen's Mutual Relief Association, to which it is compulsory for every member of the department to belong.

On November 19, the Mayor was ordered by the City Council to appoint a scientific commission, consisting of five persons, to investigate the cause of the fire and the efforts made for its suppression. The commission, consisting of Messrs. Thomas Russell, Charles G. Green, Samuel C. Cobb, A. Firth, and E. S. Philbrick, were appointed on November 26, and organized on the day following. They held forty-two sessions, during which two hundred and thirty witnesses were examined, their evidence being given *verbatim* in their printed report, containing six hundred and sixty-two pages.

Many criticisms were passed upon the ability of Chief Engineer Damrell, in the management of this conflagration, the most severe coming from parties who knew comparatively nothing concerning the methods adopted in the extinguishing of fire. To counteract these, resolutions were passed by the Board of Engineers of this city, expressing their approval of the action of their chief. A convention of Engineers of the various departments in the vicinity of Boston, was held, and the following resolutions passed : —

Engineers' Office, City Hall,
Charlestown, Mass., Nov. 22, 1872.

Convention of Engineers of the several Fire Departments in the vicinity of Boston, held on the evening of the above date, it was unanimously voted that the following preamble and resolutions be adopted : —

Preamble. Boston having been visited by one of the largest and most destructive conflagrations in the annals of its history, — such a conflagration as is liable at any moment to occur in our great cities, — and which was doubly disastrous in the case of Boston, by reason of the narrow streets and peculiarity of its stately granite warehouses connected for whole blocks by wooden copings, and surmounted with such aids to spreading a fire as the Mansard roofs, with their elaborate and profuse trimmings of wood far above the reach of any solid stream of water; and some persons have, not only in private, but by means of the press, made unjust criticism upon and circulated false reports concerning the course pursued by Chief Engineer John S. Damrell, in engineering the flames :

Resolved, That the ability, coolness, indomitable courage and perseverance displayed by Chief Engineer John S. Damrell, in his efforts to arrest the progress of the fire, merits and receives our earnest and unqualified approbation; also, his assistants, whose untiring efforts to assist their chief, are entitled to the highest praise and gratitude of the whole community.

Resolved, That, in our opinion, the use of gunpowder, as applied at the fire, did not materially arrest the progress or extension of the fire.

Resolved, That the expediency of the use of gunpowder to arrest the progress of a conflagration is a question upon which there is a wide difference of opinion; and, in our judgment, if used at all, it should be under the direction of the Engineers and by a Board created for that purpose; a Board qualified by experience to judge its effects, of the quantity necessary to be used, and the manner in which it should be used, and a sufficient quantity should be kept in packages prepared for use, and to which access could be had without delay.

Resolved, That we recommend to the different cities and towns throughout the country to have manufactured for their different fire departments hydrants and hose-couplings of a size with each other, as, at the Boston fire, several engines from out the city were delayed in going to work, being unable for a long time to take water.

Resolved. That the sympathetic letter of Capt. J. H. Roberts, Chief Engineer of the Savannah Fire Department, to Capt. Damrell, meets with our entire approbation, expressing, as he does, his views with a clearness of perception which does him great honor for his nobleness of heart and generous spirit, and its reception by Capt. Damrell must have been a source of great consolation.

Resolved, That we extend to Capt. Damrell an expression of our unwavering confidence in his ability as an Engineer, our earnest sympathy and our best wishes for his speedy and complete restoration to health and strength, and for his future happiness and prosperity.

Resolved, That a copy of these resolutions be presented to Chief Engineer John S. Damrell, of the Boston Fire Department.

Voted, On motion, voted that each Engineer of the Fire Department represented sign the foregoing preamble and resolutions.

Voted, On motion, voted that Chief Engineer Delano, of Charlestown, Raymond, of Cambridge, Sampson, of Milford, and Assistant Engineer Simond, of Melrose, be a committee to present these resolutions.

This paper, was signed by five officers each from the Departments of Charlestown, Cambridge, Somerville, and Navy Yard; four each from Melrose and Malden; six from Medford; three each from Chelsea, Lynn, and Brookline; and one from Waterford. James W. Poor was Secretary of the Convention.

The other serious fires during the year were, January 6, the Oxnard Sugar Refinery, 239 Broad street; loss to stock, $11,330; insured. 15th, D. Lyons & Co., gents' furnishing goods, 64 Summer street; loss, $36,350; insured. During the progress of this fire, Assistant Engineer E. B. Hine, was severely cut in the thigh with a piece of plate glass. M. C. Sullivan was thrown from the tender of Engine 4 and run over by the hose-cart. While going to a fire at the ship-building works of Messrs. Curtis & Smith, on Border street, East Boston, Hose No. 9 ran over a man at the corner of Border and Eutaw streets; loss at this fire, $43,500; insured. At the fire of the building occupied by Mrs. David Reed, on Brainbridge street, on March 5, several of the firemen were severely frost-bitten. Among the worst was Capt. C. L. Rosemere of Engine No. 13, and Engineer Farrar. Loss to property, $10,000; insurance, $8,000. Captain Hewins of Engine 18 had both his ears badly frozen at a fire on Washington street the same day. On the 7th, G. L. Putnam was badly injured by a falling beam at a fire on Seaver street. The St. Elmo Hotel, 25 to 29 Washington street, and other buildings, were burnt on the 11th. On the 20th, a block of tenement houses on Quincy street was destroyed; also the steam-shovel works of John Souther & Co., on Granite street, South Boston; loss, $11,800; insured. At this fire D. E. Connors of Hose 9 and James McAllister were injured. April 25, at a fire at 147 South street, W. H. Durling was badly cut in the head by a stone which fell from an upper story. At 8.17 o'clock on Friday, the 26th, Box 81 was rung in for the blowing down of the Coliseum building. Mr. D. W. Appleton was severely burnt at a fire in Walnut street on May 13. June 23, the wood store of D. D. Sparhawk & Co., at the corner of Milk and Congress streets, was burnt; loss, $25,530. The planing-mill of W. W. Bennett, and other property on Border street, East Boston, was burnt July 12; loss not given.

At the burning of the Boston City Flour Mill, 45 to 52 Commercial wharf, on the 26th, the following accidents occurred: Messrs. G. Sherman and E. Witherell of Engine No. 5, J. G. Duffy and M. C. Sullivan of Engine No. 4, were on a forty-foot ladder when it broke in the middle, thereby throwing the men to the ground. Messrs. Duffy and Sullivan escaped with a few slight bruises. Sherman broke his arm and ankle, and sustained several other injuries. Mr. Witherell broke his arm. E. H. Bright, a member of Hose 5, was severely cut upon the arm by falling slate. Loss of property, $19,500; insured.

Mr. O. B. Bussey of Ladder Company No. 1 was injured by a falling hose at a fire on August 7, at 156 Blackstone street. At 9.06 P.M. the same day, the works of the Continental Sugar Refinery, at the corner of First and A streets, South Boston, were destroyed; loss, $243,000; insured. Eighteen wholesale boot and shoe stores, numbering 80 to 92 Pearl street, were destroyed on the 7th; loss, $54,155; insured. On the 20th, the wool and cotton warehouse of T. Remick & Co., Russia wharf, was burnt; loss, $32,696; insured. Mr. N. L. Hussey of Engine No. 3 fell through a scuttle-way, a distance of fifteen feet, at a fire at 133 Congress street, on the 26th. J. McInnes & Co., wool dealers, 147 Congress street, had their building consumed on September 26; loss, $267,800; insurance. $217,000; four other firms; loss, $11,300; fully insured. The Boston Drug Mills and two other houses, 5 to 7 Sargent's wharf, were consumed on October 7; loss, $12,558; insured. D. Eddy & Son, refrigerator factory, on Gibson street, Ward 16, was burnt on the 18th; loss, $5,000; insured. The dry-goods establishment of S. S. Houghton, 55 and 57 Tremont street, was badly damaged on the 22d; loss not returned. Mr. Thomas Corrigan, an employee of the Boston Oakum Company, 86 Norfolk avenue, was burnt to death at a fire in that building, November 8. Five alarms were given for the fire in the building known as State-street block, on the 18th; loss, $60,000; insurance, $49,000. On the 20th, at 6.20 o'clock in the evening, the alarm from Box 18 was sounded, and repeated until a general call was given, for a fire in the building at 3 Cornhill, occupied by Rand & Avery, printers and book-binders. The twelve firms that suffered by this conflagration lost $198,000; insurance, $152,250. On December 23 another large fire occurred. This time the building 317 Washington street, occupied by Mrs. Charlotte M. Adams, was destroyed, together with the stores of eleven other firms, on 57 to 61 Temple place, and 311 to 313 Washington street; loss, $141,900; insurance, $94,711. During the progress of this fire, Assistant Engineer John Calligan was struck with a stream of water, by which he was seriously injured. The small-pox hospital at Swett street, Highlands, was burned on the 26th; loss, $18,440; insurance, $10,000. On the 27th, several sheds used for the storage of freight by the Portland and Boston Steamship Company, on Long wharf, were consumed; loss, $20,000; no insurance.

Number of alarms, six hundred and forty; loss, not including the great fire, $1,516,549; insurance, $1,298,983.

PART III.

1873-1888.

EX-FIRE COMMISSIONERS. — Page 290.

PART III.
FROM 1873 TO 1888.

CHAPTER I.

1873–1874.

DURING the early part of 1873 a petition was sent to the City Council, signed by a number of citizens and tax-payers, praying for the appointment of an independent board to have the control and management of the fire department. A series of public hearings were given to the petitioners, as well as to the remonstrants against the proposed measure, at the City Hall, June 24, before a joint special committee. As a matter of course the discussions were very earnest, and the representatives on either side gave very strong reasons for the acquirement of their cause. The committee representing the majority report consisted of Messrs. Samuel M. Quincy, Alanson Bigelow, William H. West, George A. Shaw, George P Denny, and Charles E. Powers. They offered the following recommendation and suggestions concerning the reorganization of the department, which it was proposed to commit and intrust to a permanent board of three commissioners, in accordance with the prayer of the petition : —

I.   Such immediate increase of the permanent force of the department, both in men and apparatus, as shall in the opinion of the commissioners suffice for the present protection of the city.

II.   The establishment and maintenance, throughout the entire command, of a system of strict military discipline and responsibility, together with such instruction, training, and drill, theoretical as well as practical, as shall bring it to the highest state of efficiency, together with the adoption, so far as necessary for this purpose, of a military form of organization.

III.   The division of the city into fire districts, in each of which an assistant engineer or other officer should reside, held to a knowledge of the character of all buildings and their contents in relation to the possible origin or spread of fires — such engineer or officer to have command in such district in the absence of the chief.

IV.   The establishment of a fire patrol in each district by detail from the department, who shall make daily reports of their tour of duty to the engineer or officer in charge, to be by him transmitted to headquarters. Such patrol to be empowered to make all investigations necessary to enable them to report all changes in use of buildings, storage of merchandise, character or habits of occupants, and all other matters which may in any manner bear upon the danger of origin or spread of fire within the district. Such a system would give those in command constant information of the state of the lines and the points of danger most necessary to be strongly covered.

V.   The establishment of a body of fire police, in accordance with the prayer of the petitioners, whose duty it shall be to take charge of the streets and keep the lines at fires. If it shall be found impracticable or unadvisable to detail this body from the regular force, we recommend its appointment in addition thereto, and that legislative authority, therefore, be obtained, if necessary, without delay.

VI.   The amount of water-supply necessary and available at different points should, of course, receive the immediate and earnest attention of the board. Whether all hydrants and water-apparatus are in proper order for instant use should form part of the daily patrol report before alluded to, together with the condition of the fire alarm and boxes.

VII.   In view of the surprisingly large expenditures now incurred for the repair of engines and fire-apparatus, the committee would suggest that the establishment of a city repair shop, with skilled workmen in regular employ, would, in the long run, be found to be a measure of economy, as has been shown in the case of railway corporations.

VIII.   The committee have provided in the ordinance that a report containing such information concerning fires as is most interesting and useful to the public, be made monthly instead of annually. The facts will thus be known before the interest of the matter has died out, and the lesson which they inculcate will be more likely to be remembered.

The committee, therefore, recommend the passage of the following ordinance, which was adopted October 13, 1873: —

AN ORDINANCE TO ESTABLISH A FIRE DEPARTMENT.

SECTION 1.   The Fire Department of the City of Boston shall consist of a Board of three Fire Commissioners, a Chief Engineer, a Superintendent of Fire Alarms, ten Assistant Engineers, and other Officers, Engine-men, telegraph operators, and other members, to the number of five hundred and fifty men.

SECT. 2.   In the month of October, in the year 1873, or as soon thereafter as may be, the Mayor shall appoint, subject to the approval and confirmation of the City Council, three persons, who shall constitute said Board of Fire Commissioners of the City of Boston, and who shall have and exercise the powers and duties hereinafter designated. One member of said Board shall be appointed to hold his office until the first Monday of May in the year one thousand eight hundred and seventy-four, one until the first Monday of May in the year one thousand eight hundred and seventy-five, and one until the first Monday of May in the year one thousand eight hundred and seventy-six. In the month of April in the year one thousand eight hundred and seventy-four, and thereafterwards annually in the month of April, the Mayor shall appoint, subject to like confirmation and approval, one person to be one of said Fire Commissioners for the term of three years from the first Monday of the following May. The persons so appointed shall devote their time to the duties of the office, and shall not actively engage in any other business. Any member of said Board shall, at any time, be subject to removal by the Mayor for cause, and all vacancies occurring in said Board, from any cause, shall be filled in the same manner in which the original appointments are herein directed to be made. No member of either branch of the City Council shall hold the office of Fire Commissioner. For their services the Fire Commissioners shall receive such compensation as the City Council may from time to time determine.

SECT. 3.   The said Board shall organize forthwith upon the first appointment of its

members, and thereafterwards annually on the first Monday of May, by the choice of one
of their members as chairman.   They shall also choose a clerk, who shall not be a member
of the Board; and they shall make such rules and regulations for their own government
and for the government of all other officers and members of the fire department, including
the fire-alarm telegraph, as they may deem expedient, provided that said rules and regulations shall not be inconsistent with the ordinances of the city.

SECT. 4.   The duty of extinguishing fires and protecting life and property in case of
fire, shall within the City of Boston be intrusted to the said Board of Commissioners; and,
to enable them to perform that duty in the most efficient manner, the said Board is hereby
authorized to appoint all other officers and members of the Fire Department, including the
fire-alarm telegraph, and fix their compensation; to discharge any of said officers or members at any time for cause; to divide the city into fire districts; to organize companies and
battalions to work the apparatus; to establish a Fire Patrol by detail from the permanent
force of the department, which shall render such services in connection with the police and
the department for the survey and inspection of buildings as the said Commissioners may
direct; to purchase horses, steam-engines, extinguishers, hose-carriages, hook-and-ladder
carriages, and all other apparatus and supplies necessary for the complete equipment of
the said department, or conducive to the proper performance of its duties; provided, however, that the expenditures for the purposes herein named shall not exceed in the aggregate
the sums previously appropriated by the City Council for the maintenance of said Fire
Department.

SECT. 5.   The said Board of Fire Commissioners shall, annually, on or before the
fifteenth day of February, send to the City Auditor an estimate in detail of the appropriations
required for the maintenance of the Fire Department during the next financial year.   All
bills for expenditures from the appropriations for the Fire Department shall be drawn for
by the said Board, examined by the Auditor, and approved by the Committee on Accounts,
before they are paid by the Treasurer.

SECT. 6.   The said Board shall, on or before the tenth day of each month, present to
the City Council a report made up to, and including, the last day of the preceding month,
containing a chronological statement of the number of fires in such month, with the causes
thereof, a general description of the property destroyed or injured at each fire, with the
names of the owners or occupants and the amount of insurance, if any, specifying
the portion of the force and apparatus called into action at each fire, with the name of
the officer in command; also a statement of all fatal or serious accidents to members of the
department or others on account of fires, or alarms of fires, during the month, together with
such other information or suggestions as they may deem proper.   They shall also, annually,
in the month of May or June, present to the City Council a report made up to, and including, the thirtieth day of the preceding April, containing, in addition to a consolidated statement of the facts contained in the monthly reports of the preceding year, a list of the
causes of fire, alphabetically arranged, a statement of the income and expenditures on account of the department during the preceding year, a schedule of all the property belonging to the department, with a statement as to its condition on the date of the report, and an
estimate of its value; also a statement of the number and location of the fire-alarm boxes,
together with such other information or suggestions as they may deem proper.

SECT. 7.   The Chief Engineer and the Assistant Engineers appointed by the Fire
Commissioners as hereinbefore provided, shall constitute the Board of Engineers of the
City of Boston, and shall have and exercise all the powers conferred upon such officers by
the Statutes of the Commonwealth and by the ordinance in relation to the manufacture,
storage, and sale of petroleum, camphene, and burning-fluids.   And they shall also have
authority, under the direction of the Fire Commissioners, to inquire for and examine into
all shops and other places where shavings or other such combustible materials are collected
or deposited, and report to said commissioners from time to time the condition in this

respect of the district to which they are assigned; and whenever, in the opinion of said commissioners, the same may endanger the security of the city from fires, they shall direct the tenant or occupant of said shops or other places to remove such shavings or other combustible materials; and in case of such tenant's or occupant's neglect or refusal so to do, they shall cause the same to be removed at the expense of such tenant or occupant, who shall, in addition, be liable to a penalty of not less than five nor more than fifty dollars for such neglect or refusal; and any person who shall obstruct the said commissioners or engineers or any of them in carrying out the provisions of this section shall also be liable to a penalty of not less than five nor more than fifty dollars.

SECT. 8.   It shall be the duty of the members of the Police Department to aid the Fire Department by giving alarms in case of fire in such manner as the Fire Commissioners may direct, and in clearing the streets or grounds in the immediate vicinity of the fire so that the members of the Fire Department shall not be hindered or obstructed in the performance of their duties.   If any policeman refuses or neglects to give an alarm, as directed in the manner aforesaid, or refuses to obey the orders of the chief officer in command at a fire, he shall forfeit and pay a fine of not less than five nor more than twenty dollars.

SECT. 9.   The said Board of Fire Commissioners shall make suitable regulations, under which the officers and men of the Fire Department shall be required to wear any appropriate uniform and badge, by which, in case of fire and at other times, the authority and relations of such officers and men in said department may be known, as the exigency of their duties may require.

SECT 10.   There shall be appointed annually in the month of January, a Joint Committee of the City Council on the Fire Department, consisting of two members of the Board of Aldermen and three members of the Common Council.   It shall be the duty of said committee to examine, as often as once in each month, the records and accounts of the Board of Commissioners on the Fire Department, and also to examine all applications for appropriations for the said department, and report thereon to the City Council.

SECT. 11.   The ordinance in relation to the Fire Department, printed in the revised ordinances adopted the thirty-first day of December, A.D. 1869, and all the amendments and additions thereto, are hereby repealed, said appeal to take effect upon the organization of the Board of Fire Commissioners as herein designated.   All officers and members of the department at the time of such repeal shall hold their several offices until their successors are appointed, at the salaries established by the City Council; and, until otherwise ordered by the Fire Commissioners, shall be subject to the rules and regulations now in force governing the officers and members of the Fire Alarm and Fire Departments; and the present Joint Standing Committee of the City Council on the Fire Department shall perform the duties provided in Section 10 during the remainder of this municipal year.

The committee representing the minority report consisted of Messrs. James Power and Benjamin Dean.   Their objections to a commission were as follows : —

First.   It is unnecessary.   We already have something like a commission in the Board of Engineers.   They have such full control of the department that the committee on the department meets but once a month.

Second.   The expense would be inordinate for the duties performed.   All the executive duties of the department would be done by the engineers, leaving no necessity for the expense of a commission.

Third.   The commission, if independent, and of the powers asked for by the majority of the committee, having the complete control of five hundred voters, and all their influence, would be a political power, capable of controlling almost any municipal election

In the city of Boston. The appointment of a commission, therefore, would not take the department out of politics.

Fourth. Such a commission, independent, having absolute control of the large expenditures of the department, would be likely to become corrupt, and we might have a repetition of the frauds which have so recently disgraced New York. Whatever may be said of the Committee of the Fire Department, it has never been charged with corruption.

It required no additional legislation on the part of the State to enable the City Council to place the department under a paid commission; therefore no time was lost in carrying the ordinance into effect, and appointing the following gentlemen to fill that office: Timothy T. Sawyer for three years; Alfred P. Rockwell, chairman, for two years; and David Chamberlin for one year. These officers organized and entered upon their duties November 20. Mr. Frederick W. Smith was appointed clerk.

Previous to the organization of the Board of Commissioners, the Joint Standing Committee made the following changes from January 1 to November 1, 1873. Engine-houses built: —

Engine Company No. 12, corner of Winslow and Dudley streets, Highlands; this house was built to take the place of the old one, situated on the corner of Warren and Dudley streets, which was taken down on account of the widening of Warren street. Engine Company No. 22, Parker street, Highlands; this building was for temporary use only. Engine Company No. 24, corner of Quincy and Warren streets, Highlands. Engine Company No. 25, Washington square; for temporary use. A new building was in course of construction for the accommodation of this engine and Ladder 8. Hose-house No. 4, Northampton street, enlarged so as to accommodate a steam fire-engine and horse hose-carriage. Hose Company No. 12, corner of Fourth and O streets, South Boston. Hook and Ladder Company No. 6, corner of River and Temple streets, Ward 16. The building known as the " Normal School-house," on Mason street, was remodelled so as to accommodate a permanent steam fire-engine company. Engine No. 26 was placed in this house.

A building for Hook and Ladder Company No. 4, on Dudley street, Highlands, was contracted for. Horse hose-carriages were placed in engine-houses numbered 4, 7, 8, 9, and 25, to run in connection with the engines, in place of the small hose-tenders formerly used. In accordance with the order of the City Council, horse hose-carriages were placed in all the other engine-houses as soon as completed. Several of the horse hose-carriages were remodelled so as to convey the firemen to fires. The apparatus purchased or contracted for was as follows: —

One steam fire-engine each from Hunneman & Co., Amoskeag Manufacturing Company, and Clapp & Jones.

Four horse hose-carriages from Amoskeag Manufacturing Company.

One horse hose-carriage from William Gilchrist.

One hook-and-ladder carriage from Hunneman & Co.

Four coal-wagons from Joseph T. Ryan.

One self-acting fire-engine (Babcock) from New England Fire Extinguisher Company.

One steam fire-engine from Amoskeag Manufacturing Company.

One self-acting fire-engine from Holloway, Baltimore.

The following additions were made to the working force of the department :—

Engine companies numbered 4 and 7 were reorganized by the appointment of the foremen and hosemen for constant service, making twelve permanent members in each company.

Hose Company No. 1 was changed to an engine company (No. 25), and twelve members appointed for constant service, making an addition to the department of five men.

Hose Company No. 4 was reorganized and made an engine company (No. 23), on Northampton street, making an addition of two men to the department.

A new hook-and-ladder company, located on Washington square, and known as No. 8, was organized with fifteen permanent men.

A new hose company was organized in South Boston, and known as No. 12, thereby adding to the department nine men. Also two new engine companies in the Highland district, and known as Engine Company No. 22, on Parker street, and Engine Company No. 24, on Warren street, thus giving to the department twenty-two additional men; making a total of fifty-three men added to the service during the year. The company in Parker street was added in response to petitions from citizens of Wards 6 and 9, to cover the recently occupied lands in those wards.

The task of reorganization imposed upon the Board of Fire Commissioners was one of great importance; the changes had to be made without in the least diminishing the efficiency of the force then existing. The annexation of Charlestown, West Roxbury, and Brighton, on January 5, 1874, complicated the problem, and materially increased their labors. Under the new organization the officers were held to a strict responsibility for their companies. The men were drilled and disciplined in such a way as to secure the greatest efficiency practicable, and all who should have public property in charge were held to a personal accountability for its proper care. All the companies within the city proper — consisting of Engine Companies Nos. 1, 3, 4, 6, 7, 8, 10, 23, and 25; Ladder Companies Nos. 1, 3, and 8; Chemical No. 1; and fire-boat — were placed on a permanent basis, while the others consisted of call-companies. The actual force on April 30, 1874, was seven hundred and twelve men, consisting of one chief engineer and eleven assistant engineers, permanently employed, and two assistant engineers on call-duty. The permanent engine companies consisted of a foreman, assistant foreman, engineman, assistant engineman, and eight hosemen; ladder companies : foreman, assistant foreman, and twelve ladder-men; chemical engine: driver, chemical engineman, and one hoseman; fire-boat: captain, mate, engineer, assistant engineer, steward, stoker, and one deck-hand; call-engine companies: engineman, assistant engineman, and driver of engine, permanent (and when separate hose-carriages were used, the foreman was permanently employed, and drove the hose-carriage) foreman, and seven hosemen on call-duty; ladder companies: the drivers only were permanent, the foreman, assistant foreman, and seventeen ladder-men did duty only at fires.

The number of alarms from January to October, 1873, was three hundred and twenty-seven, and one hundred and ninety-eight still, making a total of five hundred and twenty-five. The loss to buildings and stock was $2,548,346.24; insurance, $1,920,394.67. The first large conflagration of the year broke out on January 8 at 52 Wareham street, occupied as a furniture factory; loss, $10,000; insured. This was soon followed by one of the most disastrous fires, from the extent of the loss of life, that had occurred for years. This fire was discovered at 10.06 o'clock on the morning of February 27, in the mattress factory of Mr. G. A. Sammett, located at the corner of Hanover and Blackstone streets. While at work at this fire, the front wall fell, thereby killing Messrs. Brown P. Stowell and James Starks of Engine Company No. 15, and John Prince, Jr., substitute, of Engine Company No. 11, and wounding the following members quite severely: A. C. Scott, T. Merritt, Charles Ingersoll, and S. Stone of Hose Company No. 2; G. Le Cain and W. B. Marshall of Hose Company No. 4; H. Demary of Engine No. 11; O. L. Woods and C. H. Smith of Engine No. 15; while E. Martin of Hose No. 4, W. Baker of Engine No. 11, M. W. Hayes, substitute, of Engine No. 15, S. D. Harrington of Engine No. 3, and M. A. Packard of Insurance Brigade were slightly injured. Misses Lizzie J. Hanks and Mary Babb, who were employed by Mr. Sammett, were burned to death, and Miss Mary Ellen Moore was severely injured by jumping from the window. The loss to property was $36,197; insurance, $33,197.

Three alarms were sounded April 12 for a fire in a block of brick buildings on Wareham street, occupied as wood-working shops; loss, $43,077; insurance, $38,372. A general alarm was rung in, May 3, at midnight, for a fire in a block of wooden buildings at the corner of Causeway and Portland streets, used for wood-working factories; loss, $42,232; insurance, $18,132.

A fire second to the great conflagration of the year previous broke out on the morning of May 30, in the furniture factory of Haley, Morse, & Co., 411 Washington street. Before the alarm was given the fire had made terrible progress, and when the department arrived it was apparent to all that the scenes of the great fire were to be in the main enacted. Panic and fear seized all who dwelt in the vicinity. Building after building and block after block of immense granite and brick structures were levelled by the relentless flames, until the buildings situated on Washington, Essex, and Boylston streets, Fayette and Bumstead courts, and Brimmer place were ingulfed in a seething mass of fire. Besides the many large warehouses destroyed, the Globe Theatre, owned by Arthur Cheney, was burned, the loss being $237,000. The total loss at the fire was over $1,000,000, most of which was covered by insurance. This loss was shared by over one hundred and five business firms.

July 4, Engine Company No. 11 was called to extinguish a bonfire near a stable on Everett street, East Boston, which had been built by a mob, who assaulted the members of the company when trying to extinguish the same. On the 30th, a block of brick buildings located on Lewis street, East Boston, was destroyed. Three alarms were given for this fire; loss, $533,933.75; fully insured. Four alarms were given for a fire in the cordage factory of Sewall, Day, & Co., on Parker street, August 11; loss, $30,000; insurance, $15,575. Eighty-six horses were burnt to death October 11, at a fire at the corner of Berkeley and Appleton streets; loss, $51,000; insurance, $11.850. On the 29th, the granite buildings Nos. 213 to 219 State street, known as State-street block, were burned; loss, $51,000; insurance, $25.520. The same day the Court-House in Court square was damaged to the extent of $500 from a fire caught from a defective chimney in the judges' lobby in the Supreme Court. Monday, November 3, the brick buildings 41 and 42 Central wharf were burned; loss, $109,000; insurance, $71.452. At a fire at 17 Tileston street, December 23, a little girl was suffocated. Russell White, driver of Engine No. 4, was thrown from the apparatus while responding to a false alarm from Box 5, on the 25th, and severely injured.

On April 7, 1874, Chief Engineer Damrell was succeeded by Assistant Engineer William A. Green, and the number of assistant engineers was increased to thirteen, by an amendment of the ordinance on April 1. The city was divided into ten fire-districts, and the following gentlemen appointed in command: Joseph Dunbar, District No. 1; John Bartlett, No. 2; William H. Cunningham, No. 3; Samuel Abbott, Jr., No. 4; John W. Regan, No. 5; George Brown, No. 6; George C. Fernald, No. 7; John Colligan, No. 8; James Monroe, No. 9; J. Foster Hewins, No. 10; and Brown S. Flanders, inspector and aid to the chief. Assistant engineers in Districts 8 and 10 were aided by call-engineers, — the former by Charles A. Holbrook, and the latter by James F. Rogers; Henry W. Longley, Charles R. Classen, and B. F. Underhill, Jr., were appointed clerks to the board. By the annexation of Charlestown, West Roxbury, and Brighton, the following pieces of apparatus were added to the department: Charlestown, Steam-engine No. 1, Elm street, built by Amoskeag Manufacturing Company; Hose-carriages No. 1, Main street; No. 2, Main street; No. 3, Winthrop street; No. 4, Bunker Hill street; Ladder No. 1, Main street. West Roxbury: Steam-engine No. 1, Centre street, Jamaica Plain, built by Hunneman & Co., January 1, 1871; No. 2, Centre street, Jamaica Plain, built by the same company, June 25, 1872; Hand-engine No. 2, Centre street, Jamaica Plain, built by the same firm in 1859, and No. 3, corner of Shawmut avenue and Poplar streets, built during 1856; Ladder No. 1, Centre street, in house with engine, built by Hunneman & Co., December 21, 1870. Brighton: Steam-engine No. 1, Chestnut Hill avenue, built by Hunneman & Co., and Ladder 1, in the same house, built by the same firm. The fire-alarm system was connected with these districts, except in Brighton, which, on account of the large expense the construction would incur, a telegraph line was run to the engine-house in that district, and a double connection with the City Hall established.

Engine No. 26 was put in service during the year, in a house on Mason street. Other apparatus added were: Ladder No. 11 and Engine 29, at Chestnut Hill avenue, Brighton, January; Chemical-engines No. 2 on Church street, April 25; No. 3 on Longwood avenue, July 27; and No. 5 at Walnut park, November 21. One Skinner extension-ladder was also purchased. Engines Nos. 4, 9, 25, and 26 were ordered never to be sent out of the city, and No. 5 never to cross the ferry unless especially sent for. The custom of receiving and entertaining visiting firemen by members of a company, or visiting other fire departments as a company, was forbidden April 17.

On the 29th, the board adopted a style of uniform to be worn by the members of the permanent department. The coat for the chief was a double-breasted, close-fitting sack-coat, of dark-blue cloth, cut to button close to the neck, with rolling collar; to have eight medium-size department-buttons of white metal on each breast, grouped in pairs. The length of the coat to be in proportion to the height of the man, — for a man six feet, twenty-nine inches. For assistant engineer, same as chief, except the buttons on the breast were placed equidistant. For company officers, the same, except that the coat was single-breasted, with eight buttons. For members, same as company officers, except that the coat had six instead of eight buttons. For summer wear, the coat was to be made of dark-blue flannel, without lining. The pants of the same material, to fit loose around the thighs and legs. Vest for the chief, single-breasted, with standing collar, to button close to the neck with eight small department-buttons. Assistant engineers were to wear the same pattern, except that the buttons were to be placed equidistant, while those of the members were made without a collar. The overcoat of the chief was a double-breasted frock, with rolling collar, of dark-blue cloth, in length to reach two inches below the knee, to button close up to the neck with single large buttons, grouped in pairs; three on each skirt behind, and three small size on each cuff; the skirt to be closed behind. One large outside pocket on skirt, and a small one on the left breast, to be covered with lapels, and one inside pocket on the right breast. Assistants were to have the same, except that there were but seven buttons, placed equidistant. Same for members, except the lining was of blue flannel.

The chief and assistants were allowed to wear a white-linen shirt, with narrow rolling or standing collar; other members, a double-breasted blue-flannel shirt with rolling collar. A small necktie of black silk to be worn by the engineers; the officers a black-silk cravat, to pass once around the neck and tie with a double bow or a flat knot in front, the ends to extend not more than six inches from the knot. ' Gloves, when worn, of white Berlin lisle-thread or wash-leather. Fire caps: for the chief, a leather cap, entirely white, with sixteen combs, the front of white patent-leather supported by a gilt eagle-head; the letters indicating his office were black on a white ground, over which the insignia, to show on black ground, and under all the word " Boston." Assistants, same as chief, except that there were twelve combs, the rim and cape black on both sides, and the letters white on a red ground, as also the insignia; the initials of the wearer's name were to be placed. Company officers, a black-leather cap with eight combs; a white patent-leather front, the number of the company, in plain block figures, cut out of the centre; insignia of office, same as on coat collar, above the figure, and the number of the corporation badge below; the number of company, insignia of office, and number of badge were black patent-leather. For members of engine companies, same as above, except that the front was black with white figures. For officers of ladder companies, same as for engine companies, except that the number and insignia was in red, and the upper half of the skull painted red. For members of ladder companies, same as above, except that the front was black instead of white. Fatigue cap: chief, of blue cloth, same as the uniform coat, of the United States Navy pattern, with a plain patent-leather visor, one small button on each side; insignia of office same as on collar, placed in the centre of the front. Assistants, same as chief, except the insignia. Foremen, same as above, except the insignia and the number of the company in block figures one-half inch long, embroidered in silver upon a circle of light-blue cloth. Assistant foremen, the same, only the change in insignia. For members, the same, except the device, which was of white metal. In stormy weather a cover of oiled skin, so constructed that the device would remain in view, was worn over these caps. The insignia of office consisted of the following: For chief, a six-pointed gilt star, measuring one and a quarter inches in diameter, to be worn upon the front corners of the collar of the uniform coat. Assistants, the same as above, except that the star was silver, one inch in diameter. Foremen, a five-pointed silver star as above; assistant foremen, two five-pointed silver stars joined, measuring three-fourths of an inch (each) in diameter.

May 1, the pay of the members of the department was fixed as follows: Chief, $3,300; superintendent of fire alarms, $2,500; assistant engineers, $1,600. Permanent force: foremen, $1,250; assistants, $1,100; engine-men, $1,200; assistant engine-men, $1,100; hosemen and ladder-men, $1,100; chemical engineers, $1,100. Fire-boat: captain, $1,368.75; mate, $1,186.25; engineer, $1,368.75; assistant, $1,186.25; other hands, $1,000. Call-force: permanent foremen, $1,000; call-foremen, $300; hosemen and ladder-men, $225 each per annum.

May 13, the board forbid the granting of leaves of absence on legal holidays. On July 2 an order was passed that on the 3d, 4th, and 5th of the month ensuing, two men from each company were to be detailed for street patrol, while call-members were requested to be within the district to which they belonged; those who reported at the houses of their respective companies at 9 o'clock P.M. on the 3d, and remained at or near the same during the day, were entitled to an additional compensation of $1.50.

The same day it was ordered that straw hats should be worn by members from June 15 to September 15; also that white cotton or linen shirts, instead of those of flannel, should be worn, but on all occasions of ceremony the blue-flannel shirt should be substituted. Permission was also given to make arrangements to attend church service during Sunday, provided it did not interfere with the necessary work of the day. The cap-device worn by members was ordered, September 12, to consist of a Greek cross of white metal, with a circular shield. marked with the number of the wearer. (See stamp on cover of this book.) It was to be attached to the centre of the front of the cap.

The call-members attached to Engine Company No. 28 and Ladder Company No. 10, of West Roxbury district, reported. through their foreman. that they should resign and do no duty after 12 o'clock. Friday, P.M., November 20, on account of the smallness of their compensation. The commissioners, therefore, assigned Assistant Foreman E. A. Whitehead of Engine No. 6, and Hosemen C. Ingersoll of Engine No. 7, T. L. Whalen of Engine No. 8. and C. N. Allison of Engine No. 26, to take charge of the deserted engine, in connection with the permanent men of the company; while Assistant Foreman E. B. Smith of Ladder No. 8, and Hosemen B. H. Bayley of Engine No. 4, C. A. Smith of Engine No. 25, and T. C. Soesman of Engine No. 3 were detailed to take charge of Ladder No. 10, in connection with the permanent men attached. Chemical Engine No. 5, under the charge of H. D. Phillip of Chemical No. 1, and W. H. Gay of Chemical No. 5, was placed in the house of this company.

Smoking on the streets by members was forbidden, December 1, as was riding on the apparatus when returning from fires. Horses were ordered, on the 11th, to be exercised for two hours daily, except on those days when they were called out upon an alarm of fire. In exercising they were not to be taken beyond a radius of one-eighth of a mile from their respective houses. In the event of the bursting of any street water-pipe, the superintendent of the eastern division of the Boston Water Works was authorized to require the temporary service of a steam fire-engine. A physical examination was required to be passed by all applicants for the position of firemen, which examination was made by Dr. S. A. Green, city physician. Ex-Chief Damrell was presented with a silver service, valued at $3,000, at a public meeting at Tremont Temple on April 28, the presentation speech being made by ex-Mayor the Hon. William Gaston. Speeches were also made by several prominent citizens. Ex-Chief Engineer John Stanhope Damrell is a native of Boston, having been born at the North End, on June 29, 1828. He was left an orphan at the age of seven years, and found himself dependent upon his own energies for the means of subsistence. Having neither money nor influential friends, his self-reliant nature was at once called into action, and as quickly asserted itself. Experience soon taught him that to succeed he must do whatever he undertook with thoroughness, alacrity, and intelligence; that he must be master of, or master in, whatever calling he might choose. This showed him the necessity of an education, and by the most diligent industry and the strictest economy he was able to save enough for support while attending the grammar school, from which he graduated at the age of fourteen years.

He then entered upon an apprenticeship with a carpenter, in which he continued four years, when he was engaged as a journeyman, with full wages, and for eight years he was engaged as workman or foreman. In 1856 he went into business for himself as master-builder, achieving remarkable success and a competent fortune. In 1877 he received the appointment of Inspector of Buildings of the City of Boston, from Hon. F. O. Prince, who was then Mayor, and has held that important office ever since.

Early in life Captain Damrell developed a taste for fire duty. He first joined Hero Engine Company No. 6, located on Derne street, and upon the disbandment of that company entered the ranks of the City Hose Company. Subsequently he allied himself with Cataract Engine Company No. 4, and in it he held every office in the gift of his comrades. As company commander he was popular throughout the whole department, particularly with his own company, which, on July 4, 1856, presented him with a solid-silver trumpet. Resigning his position as foreman in 1867, he was elected a member of the Common Council from Ward 6, and in that body was active and useful.

During his term of office as foreman of the Cataract company, the committee of the City Council to nominate a chief engineer unanimously tendered to him that office, which he declined. He was subsequently chosen assistant engineer of the fire department, to which position he was reëlected for ten consecutive years, when he was called to the office of chief engineer. The election which led to this result was one of the most exciting local struggles in the history of the department, or that ever occupied the attention of the City Council. His competitor was Assistant Engineer Chamberlain, for the nomination of whom a petition was presented to the Committee on Nominations; and this, together with the influence of political friends, had the desired effect, — thirteen of the fifteen members of the committee giving their support to Mr. Chamberlain. But, upon the thirty-seventh ballot on the part of the Board of Aldermen, Captain Damrell was declared elected, and he was reëlected for eight consecutive terms. Captain Damrell has been presented with a number of valuable gifts from the members of the department and friends. The City Council gave him a solid-silver trumpet January 4, 1869.

The number of alarms from November, 1873, to April, 1874, was three hundred and eighty-six, including one hundred and thirty-seven still; loss to property, $1,074,091.26; insurance, $1,698,021.10. The first fire of importance occurred January 4 in the Clarendon-street Baptist Church, situated at the corner of Clarendon and Montgomery streets; loss, $34,674; insurance, $75,500. This fire was followed, two days later, by the destruction of a brick building at the corner of Green and Chardon streets. Mr. Joseph Hodet of Ladder No. 1, and J. A. Fynes of Babcock No. 1, were burned about the face, and Mr. Charles Neyersohn, a citizen, died from the effects of an explosion of a carboy of sulphuric acid, while assisting the chemical-engine company up the stairs with their pipe. Loss to property, $200. On the 13th, the five-story brick building, Nos. 70 to 74 Sudbury street, was destroyed; loss, $126.000; insured. On the 22d, a fire at the corner of Franklin and Federal streets. Loss, $1,577. A. H. Towne, driver of Engine No. 10, was thrown from his seat while going to this fire and badly injured.

Fire broke out in the brick building at the corner of Franklin and Congress streets, February 3; loss, $32,000; insured. On the 4th, the Eastern Railroad wharf at East Boston was consumed; loss, $24,800; no insurance. Four alarms were sounded for this fire. On the 11th, while on the way to a fire in the building 31 and 33 Plympton street, Hose-carriage No. 25 collided with Engine No. 7, whereby W. H. Hill, substitute on Engine Company No. 25, was thrown on the curbstone and instantly killed. Henry S. Worrall of the same company was injured in the foot and ankle in such a manner that amputation was necessary. Charles Dunton and Albert L. Pearson of the same company were also injured by the collision. Loss to property, $51,800; insurance, $42,000. Hardly had the department returned from this fire, when they were called to another of equal proportion at the corner of Commercial and South Market streets, where James C. Singleton of Engine Company No. 10 was severely injured on the leg by the falling walls. Loss to property, $10,000; insured. The Charlestown State Prison was destroyed on the 21st; loss, $242,661; insurance, $88,810. On the 28th, the wooden building at the corner of Meridian and Central squares, East Boston, was burned. Three alarms were sounded; loss, $4,450; insured. A man was arrested for setting this fire. At a fire at 5 Exeter place, July 1, Assistant Engineer B. S. Flanders, and William Brown, hoseman of Engine No. 26, were badly burned. Loss, $6,000; insured. Engines were sent from this city July 24 to assist at a fire in Hudson, Mass. Mrs. Harrington was burnt to death by her clothes taking fire in a building at 4 Newton court, August 4. A general alarm was given the next day for the burning of the South Boston car stables, Broadway and Fourth streets, South Boston; loss, $46,304; insured. Francis P. Mahan of Ladder 8 had his foot badly cut while at a fire at 8 and 10 Pitts street, on the 25th. Loss, $22,772.64; fully insured. On the 27th, Hoseman L. L. La Pierre, of Engine 26, while driving the hose-carriage to a fire on First street and Dorchester avenue, South Boston, was thrown from the seat and seriously injured. Patrick Lyden, a citizen, was burned to death at this fire. Loss, $7,746; insured. Three alarms were given for a fire in a large wooden building on Weeks' wharf, Sumner street, East Boston. on October 9; loss, $8,894; insured.

The conflagration to which the department was called at 10.55 P.M., Monday, December 14, was one ever to be remembered by them. On this date nine large wooden and brick buildings on Plympton, Wareham, and Albany streets, occupied as wood-working factories by twenty-nine firms, were destroyed. The night was one of extreme coldness, and every member suffered more or less from frost-bites, while some were severely frozen. Six alarms were sounded for this fire; loss, $391,100; insurance, $272,200. While this fire was raging, another of equal fury burst out at 5.50 A.M., the 15th, at Hittinger's wharf; five alarms were sounded for this, and assistance called from Somerville and Cambridge; loss, $137,075; insurance, $82,000. On the 18th, a block of two and one-half story brick buildings on Lawrence street was partly destroyed; loss, $4,295; insured.

Robert G. Fitch
Chairman
John R. Murphy
Thos. N. Marc
Mayor
Richard F. Tobin
Louis P. Webber
Chief

CHAPTER II.

1875–1880.

DURING the year 1875 the care of the houses in the department devolved on the commissioners, they having previously been looked after by the department of public buildings. On assuming the control of these structures, the board took advantage of the labor of the mechanics in the fire department who were detailed to do any work necessary when not interfering with the effective force. These members were required to work ten hours per day, reporting to the officer of the house to which they were assigned, who was to make a record of the time they were employed and the kind of work they did, also the time of their return to their own company. The detailed man was relieved from patrol duty and all other service except that of answering alarms with his own company at fires. If, however, the place of his employment was more than one mile distant from the fire, he was not to leave his work unless a second alarm sounded. He was also permitted to sleep at home, but must be within the sound of the alarm and within one mile of his quarters.

A repair-shop, in which all necessary repairs to apparatus, etc., could be done under the supervision of the department, was established in the building used by Ladder Company No. 3 on Harrison avenue, in which a plant was placed costing $6,241.45, although the City Council had appropriated $9.000 for this purpose. A hose and harness repair-shop was also established during September in unoccupied rooms of the new house of Ladder Company No. 8 on Washington square. Chemical Engine No. 4 was organized January 20. and placed at Washington street, Roslindale. Four light pungs, one two-wheel hose-carriage, two Concord wagons, were purchased, and eighteen pungs were fitted to carry a reel of hose. Steam-heaters were also provided for the engines. By means of these appliances, steam could be kept in the boilers of the engines at a pressure of thirty pounds ; but five pounds were found more practical, as the pressure could be carried up to the working-point by the time the engine was called into service. All the locks on the fire-alarm boxes were changed, on account of the keys being held by irresponsible people and frequent false alarms sounded. More caution was afterwards used in their distribution.

January 29, call-engineers were authorized to exercise a general supervision over the companies and districts under their command. All communications from the companies were to pass, both to and from headquarters, to them, after having first passed the hands of the permanent engineer. Their services were required outside of their district only when some part of their command was called for. House-patrol was to be maintained day and night in call-companies where three or more permanent men were employed. Members of the call-force were ordered to report at their houses and remain there twenty minutes, whenever second alarms were sounded from boxes to which their companies would respond on third alarm. On this date, Hoseman Joseph M. Gargan, acting as driver of the chief's wagon, was authorized as messenger to that official. His fire-hat had the combs painted white, and at night he carried the red lantern of the chief.

On May 29, the fatigue-cap and insignia of office of the chief and his assistants were modified as follows: In place of the cap a black-felt hat was in order: that of the chief had a black-and-gold cord, with gold acorns in the centre of the front. One and three-quarter inches above the rim was worn the insignia of office, which was the letter E, five-eighths inch long, surrounded by a wreath embroidered in gold. These were also worn on the front corner of the collar of the uniform coat. Those of the assistant engineers were the same, except that they were embroidered in silver. The daily roll of the permanent companies was ordered to be called at 10 o'clock A.M., when every member should appear in uniform.

June 5, a revised running-card was issued, and printed on a large card. Leave of absence was strictly forbidden on the sixteenth, seventeenth, and eighteenth days of June. Members of the call-force who reported for duty and remained at the house during this period were paid $5, or at that rate for such proportion of the time as each man was on duty. When an alarm was sounded, one member from each company in the city proper and Charlestown was ordered to precede the apparatus and give warning to the crowd and prevent collision or accident. An extra steamer or chemical engine was ordered to be placed in the Charlestown district, with a force sufficient to manage it, to be on duty from 6 o'clock in the evening of the 16th until 6 o'clock in the morning of the 18th. Epizootic appeared among the horses again this year, and orders were issued October 4 for company commanders to at once report cases of this disease among their horses.

The pay-roll of members in the West Roxbury district was established as follows: Permanent foremen, $1,000; call-foremen, $100 and $150; engineman, $1,000; driver, $720; hosemen on steam-engine, $100, chemical engine, $50, and hand-engine, $25; ladder-men, $100. In the Brighton district, call-foremen $100, and members $50, per year. The Charlestown engine on Elm street was numbered 27; West Roxbury engine on Centre street, No. 28; and the Brighton engine on Chestnut Hill avenue, No. 29. Hose companies in Charlestown were placed on the roll as follows: No. 1, Main street; No. 2, Main street; No. 3, Winthrop street; No. 4, Bunker Hill, corner of Tufts, street. Ladder companies: No. 9, Main street; No. 10, Centre street, Jamaica Plain; No. 11, Chestnut Hill avenue. Fire Commissioner David Chamberlin was reappointed for a term of three years. The salary of the members of the board was increased to $4,000 per annum.

The number of alarms from May 1, 1874, to April 30, 1875, was seven hundred and two, — the largest number known in this city. Loss, $1,228,403 ; insurance, $3,677,008. February 4, three alarms were sounded for the burning of a large wooden building in the rear of Sherman square and Dorrance street ; loss, $15,000 ; insurance, $5,000. T. L. Whalen, hoseman of Engine 8, fell from a ladder and was badly injured. March 3, a large building on First street, South Boston, was destroyed ; loss, $68,870 ; insurance. $50,500. On the 18th, buildings Nos. 101 and 103 Friend street were burned ; loss, $34,830 ; insured. A five-story brick building at 16 to 20 Beverly street was destroyed April 14 ; the loss, $23,532 ; insurance, $19,500. On Wednesday, May 26, at 6.30 P.M., the four and one-half story brick building at the corner of Washington and La Grange streets was entirely demolished by an explosion within the building. Subsequently, a slight fire broke out among the ruins, but was quickly extinguished. Four citizens were killed and twelve injured by the explosion.

A two-story building on Kemble street, occupied as a manufactory for fireworks, was demolished June 16 by an explosion of powder, by which John H. Kelley, a member of Ladder Company No. 4, and five other citizens, were killed, and ten badly injured. On the day following, Mrs. Grimes, of 11 Moulton street, Charlestown, was fatally burned by an explosion of a lamp. A three-story wooden building at 162 to 174 Canal street was badly burned on the 23d ; loss, $5,000 ; insurance, $6,500. W. S. Orrok of Ladder 8 and Engineman Travers of Engine 6 were injured by a falling building. Henry Fay, employed at a stable at 154 Cabot street, which was destroyed October 2, was burned to death. The Rice School-house, at the corner of Dartmouth and Appleton streets, was consumed December 20 ; loss, $20,000 ; no insurance. On the 25th, eleven horses, in a stable in Derby place, were burned to death ; loss, $4,000 ; insurance, $1,520.

Mr. Alfred P. Rockwell, chairman of the Board of Fire Commissioners, reappointed for three years from May 1, 1876, resigned October 5, 1876. Mr. Greeley S. Curtis was elected to serve out this term. Timothy T. Sawyer, appointed for one year from May 1, 1876, resigned July 24 of the same year. Charles H. Allen was appointed on October 5 to serve the unexpired term. David Chamberlin was appointed for two years from May 1, 1876, and chairman for one year. Mr. Granville A. Fuller was appointed call-engineer in District 8, and Mr. Classon resigned his position as assistant clerk to the engineers.

The building for Engine Company No. 22, on Dartmouth street, was completed during the year, and the company placed on a permanent basis. Chemical Engine No. 5 was located in a new house at Egleston square. No. 6 was placed in service May 21, and stationed at South Harvard street, Brighton, and No. 7 was put in commission September 21, and lodged in Mt. Vernon street, West Roxbury, taking the place of the hand-engine in that district, by which the last company manning one of these old-time machines was disbanded. A new ladder-truck for No. 8 was constructed at the repair-shop and placed in service February 7, while an aerial ladder, built by the Aerial Ladder Company, was placed in their care. A Bangor extension-ladder was stored ready for immediate use in the Derne-street house. A plan was adopted whereby a standard size was fixed upon for all wearing-parts of the apparatus in the service, so that duplicates were always ready to take the place of broken parts, rendering a saving in delays otherwise occasioned for making repairs.

January 12, the board discontinued the custom of imposing a fine of $1 upon members of the call-companies for tardiness or absence in case of alarm of fire, and allowing the amount of such to be paid into the companies. Instead of this method, charges were to be preferred against the delinquent member, and the commissioners imposed a penalty if they thought proper, the fine thus imposed being deducted from the pay-roll. Any member becoming too ill for duty was obliged to furnish a substitute, who was to be paid at the same rate as that received by the regular member. A revision of the running-card was made November 17. On the 21st, orders were issued to the assistant engineer for them not to leave their respective districts except in response to an alarm of fire, or leave of absence from the board or the chief. Morning reports were to be taken to headquarters from permanent companies by special messengers, and from call-companies by the police.

A new style in uniforms was ordered by the board December 4. No change was made in the coat or pants. The vest had the collar removed, so as not to interfere with the white collar of the shirt. White-linen shirts were to be worn from June 15 to September 15 by the company officers and members; during the rest of the year the blue-flannel shirt was in order. On the fire-hats of members of engine companies the letter H was placed over the figure to distinguish the hose companies, and the letter C, the chemical companies. The company on the fire-boat was the same as above, except the captain and mate were to wear, in place of the number of the engine on the fatigue-caps, the word " Fire-boat," embroidered with silver under the star.

The number of alarms from May, 1875, to April 30, 1876, was four hundred and eighty-three; loss, $541,272; insurance, $3,076,483. At a fire in a wooden building at 55 to 59 Palmer street, February 7, 1876, Hoseman J. W. Chase of Engine 3 and C. H. Masury of No. 14 were badly injured by the falling of the roof and upper floor. Loss, $5,873; insurance, $5,100. On the 27th, the Home for Destitute Children, at 780 Harrison avenue, was damaged to the extent of $4,000; insured. John Knights of Engine No. 3 was injured by the falling of the ceiling. The fire-department repair-shop, on Harrison avenue, corner of Wareham street, was slightly damaged March 6. April 29, the piano manufactory of W. P. Emerson, on Albany and Wareham streets, was damaged to the extent of $15,486; insured. Thomas E. Simonds had his ankle fractured in attempting to take his seat on the engine, while at a fire on Tremont street, May 12; and on the 28th, William Blake of Chemical

No. 3 was injured by being thrown from the engine while going to a fire on Tremont street; on the 24th, the Cummings & Carlisle building on Wareham street was destroyed. Loss, $28,000; insured.

At an explosion of gasoline at the Boston & Providence Railroad depot, August 7, W. A. Gaylord of Chemical No. 2 was badly burned, and John Ewers of Engine No. 22 was thrown from the hose-carriage and sustained a fracture of his leg. December 6, William K. Lewis of Chemical Engine No. 4, while driving to a fire on Terrace street, was thrown from his seat and broke his leg.

January 4, 1877, the board issued an order enjoining the members of the permanent companies to pay strict attention to their dress. The corporation badge was to be worn on the centre of the left breast of the coat, in full view, by all when doing house or street patrol. No part of the uniform was to be laid aside until bedtime, except by permission. Members were forbidden to appear on the main floor, except in the performance of duty. All necessary work in and about the house, stable, and apparatus was to be done before roll-call, except when prevented by unforeseen emergencies. February 19, orders forbade any person other than members riding on the apparatus; in the permanent force, three men, in addition to the driver, were allowed to ride on the engine in going to a fire, and six on the hose-carriage; but no one, except the engineman or his assistant, was allowed to remain on the apparatus when returning to quarters.

After April 2 the horses were to be exercised daily, one hour in the morning, from 6 to 7 o'clock, attached to their respective apparatus, and one hour in the afternoon, led or under the saddle. They were never to go beyond calling of their quarters. On Sundays and during very bad weather the exercise was to be omitted, if deemed expedient by the officer in charge; and such omission entered in their reports and sent to headquarters.

In view of the few working fires attended by the call-companies, they were, on April 23, ordered, on and after May 1 and until September 1, to be drilled once in two weeks for a period of one hour. A new running-card was issued June 1. A ribbon device for officers and men was supplied June 11, to be worn on the straw hat in place of the insignia of metal. During leave of absence the device on these hats was to be removed, and the hat worn with citizens' clothes.

The term for which Commissioner Charles H. Allen was appointed expired May 6, 1877, and the vacancy filled on the 25th, by the nomination of Mr. Henry W. Longley.

The number of alarms sounded from May 1, 1876, to April 30, 1877, was five hundred and nine; loss, $481,354; insurance, $2,827,528. The first fatality reported for the year was the burning of Mrs. Angier, at her dwelling in Cushman avenue, January 13. On the 26th, a workman employed in the kerosene-oil factory on E street, South Boston, was killed, while a fire was in progress in the building, and Thomas Wilson, of Ladder No. 5, injured. Loss to property, $36,000; insurance, $25,500. The Codman building, on Hanover street, was destroyed March 15; loss, $37,765; fully insured. Monday, June 25, Engines Nos. 6 and 7, and a detail of ladder-men from Ladders Nos. 1 and 8, under the command of Engineers Abbott and Flanders, were sent to the assistance of the Marblehead department. Assistant Engineman George H. Wentworth was thrown from the carriage and badly injured, while going to a fire on Suffolk avenue, July 25; and on August 7, John Pendoley of Ladder No. 8, and Thomas W. Strand of Ladder No. 1, were injured at a fire in Purchase street.

September 12, at a fire in Unity court, J. Kimball, of Chemical No. 1, was thrown from the driver's seat and severely injured. On the 27th, a large four-story brick building, at Nos. 9 to 17 Green street and 1 Pitts street, occupied by seventeen tenants, was burned; loss, $12,087.04; insurance, $78,689. The same day, at 8.40 P.M., assistance was called for from Providence, R.I., but was not needed. Monday, October 1, at 9.59 A.M., Milton, Mass., called for assistance. Engines Nos. 16, 18, 19, 20, and Ladder Company No. 6, responded. Mr. C. H. Willett, of Engine No. 4, had his back severely injured by a bale of rags, at a fire on Charlestown street, November 7. On the 17th, Foreman Hussey, of Engine No. 23, was thrown from a buggy, and severely injured, while going to a fire at 130 Canal street. Mrs. Mehegan was fatally burned by the explosion of a lamp at her residence, 144 B street, South Boston, December 23.

Commissioner Greeley S. Curtis resigned his office March 25, 1878, and the former commissioner, Charles H. Allen, was nominated to fill the vacancy, and confirmed April 1 ensuing. Commissioner Chamberlin was reappointed on the expiration of his term, May 4, for the ensuing three years. A general reduction of the compensation of the officers and members was made during the year; that of the Board of Commissioners was placed at $3,000; chief, $3,000; superintendent of alarms, $2,300; assistant engineers, $1,500; captain of fire-boat, $1,250; engineer, $1,200; assistant engineer, $1,100, per year. Petitions were received during the year from the permanent and call members of the West Roxbury and Brighton districts, asking to be paid the same amount as allowed the Dorchester and Roxbury members. The board then decided to equalize the compensation according to the amount of duty performed by the call-companies, therefore reduced the pay of the call-members of Dorchester to $175, and the firemen to $225; while that of the call-members in West Roxbury, attached to the engine and ladder companies, was increased to $150; call-foremen of ladder companies, $200; call-members of chemical companies, $75; members in the Brighton district, $75; call-foremen, $125; assistant engineers in West Roxbury and Brighton, $1,100; and permanent drivers, $1,000, per annum.

David L. Adamson was appointed a clerk at headquarters during the year. The second story of Chemical Engine-house No. 4, in Roslindale, used for primary-school purposes, was vacated, and afterwards fitted up as a residence for the driver of the chemical engine. Houses Nos. 2, 3, 5, 6, and 7 were built on the same principle, the tenants, of course, paying a rental for the same to the city. Bangor extension-ladders were supplied to all the ladder companies, and relief valves were attached to each engine. By this appliance a gate, or "shut-off," was constructed in the hose-pipe nozzle, which could be closed, thus shutting off the water supply without stopping the working of the engine; thereby doing away with the shouting of orders to stop the passing of water, and saving a large amount of damage occasioned by water. Two of the reserve engines, "Old 1" and "Old 7," being unfit for further service, were broken up. "Old 9" was also condemned, and "Old 6" was sold, as was also the old hand-engine at West Roxbury. Eighteen fuel and three supply wagons, from the factories of Messrs. J. T. Ryan, Holt & Steadman, A. Dixon, and G. H. Bird, were in the service of the department at this time. The number of hydrants controlled was two thousand one hundred and sixty-one Lowry, one thousand five hundred and ninety Boston, and three hundred and eighty-seven Post; also two hundred and thirty-eight reservoirs.

April 29, the line dividing fire districts Nos. 9 and 10 was changed by the board, so that it continued through Bowdoin and Commercial streets to Dorchester avenue; thence due east to the water, thereby including Engine Company No. 17 and Ladder Company No. 7, in District No. 10. On May 14, the duty of winding and keeping in correct time the twenty-nine public clocks throughout the city was assigned to the members of the department, instead of the men engaged in the fire-alarm service. Arrangements were made, July 19, with the chief engineers of the fire departments of Cambridge, Somerville, and Brookline to render aid to each department when so requested, by the presentation of a card officially signed by them. A copy is shown herewith:—

CAMBRIDGE, ...18..........

ASSISTANCE WANTED.

Chief Engineer.

Engineers and captains of companies were authorized, upon its presentation, to turn in an alarm from the box nearest the locality calling for it. The police commissioners issued similar instructions to the officers and patrolmen of their departments. A new running-card was issued August 22.

The Boston Veteran Firemen's Association was reorganized at the American House, Boston, April 9, 1878. Any person heretofore connected with the Fire Department of Boston, and suburbs annexed to the city of Boston, prior to 1873, or having a membership in the present Fire Department of five successive years previous to the time of making his application, was eligible to membership. The gentlemen who have presided as presidents of this organization from the above date are as follows: Otis Munroe, April 9, 1878, to November 18, 1880; James Quinn, November 18, 1880, to November 1, 1881; Hon. John M. Clark, November 1, 1881, to November 14, 1882; Joseph Lovett, November 14, 1882, to November 21, 1883; Gardner B. Chapin, November 21, 1883, to 1884; Bailey T. Mills, 1884 to 1885; John S. Damrell, 1885 to 1886; William H. Cunningham, 1886 to 1887; Robert (Father) Kemp, 1887 to 1888; Charles W. Blake, present incumbent.

The number of alarms from May 1, 1877, to April 30, 1878, was five hundred and fourteen; loss, $516,009; insurance, $3,803,910. Mr. Frederick A. W. Gay, a member of Ladder Company No. 3, while responding to an alarm from 63 East Brookline street, on Saturday, January 5, was caught between the door-post of the ladder-house and the hub of the wheel of the ladder-truck, and injured so severely that he died during the evening of the same day. On the 20th, the granite building at 4 Way street and 284 Harrison avenue was badly damaged. Robert Young, a young man residing on the premises, was smothered. The Odd Fellows' building, on Tremont street, was slightly damaged on the 23d. The most disastrous conflagration of the year broke out at 7.31 P.M., on Thursday, the 31st, in the large six-story brick building 121 Medford street, Charlestown, occupied by F. M. Holmes & Co. as a furniture factory. A storm of snow and sleet, driven by a gale of wind, was raging at the time, which greatly impeded the progress of the apparatus. A general alarm was sounded, and most nobly did the men battle with the flames, which threatened at one time to sweep over a considerable territory. As it was, nine buildings were destroyed and thirteen badly damaged; loss, $214,622; insurance, $157,056. Hoseman Charles Furlong, of Hose No. 2, had a leg broken by falling walls. Hosemen Owen Tully and George Phelps, of the same company, and John Cassidy, of Hose No. 3, were injured.

February 1, a third alarm was given by mistake for a fire in a wooden building at the corner of Dorchester avenue and Commercial street. The snow was so deep at the time that several of the engines were stuck in the drifts. On the 11th, at 12.15 P.M., a call for assistance was received from East Cambridge. Engines Nos. 6 and 27, also Hose No. 3, responded, under command of Engineer Bartlett. A call was also made for assistance from Somerville, Sunday, May 19, at 3 A.M. Engine No. 27 and Hose No. 2, under command of Engineer Bartlett, was despatched to the scene.

T. F. Fitzgerald, engineman of Engine No. 15, was thrown from the engine and injured at a fire at Downer's Oil Works, on First street, East Boston, June 21. On August 2, Dennis Kilduff, member of Engine No. 14, was injured by a falling beam at a fire on Boylston street, Jamaica Plain.

September 8, the spice-mill of H. L. Pierce, on Washington, corner of Adams street, was burnt; loss, $24,600; insured. The Merchants' Bank building, 28 State street, was damaged to the extent of $12,000, on the 17th; insurance, $400. Miss Mary Coughlin was burned to death by the explosion of a lamp at her residence, 86 Warrenton street, on the 20th. A cotton-waste factory, 128 to 148 Tudor street, was partially destroyed on October 5; loss, $35,600; insurance, $19,750. The Baptist church located at the corner of Stoughton and Sumner streets, East Boston, was damaged to the extent of $6,950, October 30; insurance, $9,000. The Boston Dye-wood and Chemical Works, at East Boston, was burnt November 9; loss, $27,750; insurance, $161,700. Chief Dyke, of Chelsea, responded with Engine Co. No. 1. Hoseman O. J. Booker, of Engine No. 23, was thrown from the hose-carriage and badly injured while responding to an alarm at the corner of Albany and Northampton streets, December 10. On the 28th, the Emerson piano factory and other buildings were badly damaged; loss, $75,158; fully insured.

Orders were issued by the board, January 11, 1879, whereby permanent members were allowed short leave of absence of not more than one and one-half hours' duration at any one time. On April 18, it was ordered that each permanent company should consist of a captain, one engineman and assistant engineman, and such number of hosemen, not exceeding eight, including a "senior," as the board may appoint. The number of laddermen was placed at nineteen, and the office of assistant foreman was abolished; those filling that position were appointed senior hosemen. The order went into effect on the 21st. Orders were given, on September 12, that all the bells, gongs, etc., connected with the department were to be struck for alarms of fire in every part of the city.

The house built for Ladder Company No. 4, on Dudley street, near Blue Hill avenue, was turned over to the Department of Public Buildings, and the apparatus returned to its old quarters on Eustis street, the second story of which building was arranged as a dwelling for the driver. A new engine was added to the reserve force, and one supply-wagon was purchased.

Mr. John E. Fitzgerald was appointed on the Board of Commissioners, May, 1879, *vice* Charles H. Allen. After a painful illness, David Chamberlin, then chairman of the board, died at North Adams, on September 4, after a period of thirty-seven years' connection with this department. The vacancy on the board occasioned by his death was filled, October 9, by Mr. Edward A. White.

On November 21, permission was given members of the permanent force to wear in stormy weather a rubber overcoat, rubber boots, and rubber cap-covering.

The large fires and serious accidents for 1879 were as follows : January 20, a young child of Mr. Callahan was smothered, and another nearly so, at a fire in their dwelling, 113 South street. Five alarms were given for a fire in the lumber-sheds Nos. 242 and 254 Albany street and 100 Lehigh street, on March 3 ; loss, $14,100 ; insured. Hoseman Chandler Griffin, of Engine No. 4, was badly injured at a fire in the rear of 22 Beach street, on the 10th, by falling through a scuttle. The Tremont Temple was destroyed Thursday, August 14, by fire which originated from some unknown cause in the rear of the organ. The flames extended to the buildings Nos. 70, 72, 90, 94 Tremont street and 3 Montgomery place, which were badly damaged. Hosemen Cushing, Bartlett, and Kelly, also substitute Pingree, of Engine No. 4, were badly burned, and Hosemen Bayley and Egerton, of Engine No. 10, were injured by timber and glass. The most disastrous fire, from the extent of life lost, broke out at 11.50 P.M., Wednesday, 17th, at 128 Gold street, South Boston. Fernald Meyroth was killed by jumping from a window ; Miss Amelia Meyroth, Mrs. George Holderied, Christian Pfieffer and her daughter Rose, were suffocated, and George Holderied burned to death. October 6, J. Barcaloupo and Andrew Jainstin were burned, the latter fatally, at their dwelling, 28 Ferry street.

The largest conflagration of the year occurred on Sunday evening, December 28, at 10.58 P.M., in the building Nos. 91 and 93 Federal street, occupied by Rice, Kendall, & Co. and others. The first, second, and third alarms were sent in, in quick succession. In the mean time the telegraph wires had fallen on the wires of the fire-alarm telegraph, cutting off all communication with the central office. When this fact was discovered, a messenger was despatched to the City Hall, and a general alarm ordered. The delay caused by this accident was a serious detriment to the department in arresting the flames, and they spread with frightful rapidity to the buildings Nos. 69, 71, 75, 105, and 107 Federal street, 236, 238, 240, and 250 Devonshire street, 106 Franklin street and 202 Devonshire street, also corner of Franklin and Devonshire streets ; loss, $905,393 ; insurance, $1,963,418. Laddermen C. D. Boardman of Ladder 1, E. B. Smith and Eugene Cummings of Ladder No. 8, J. H. Lafavor of Engine No. 3, and Walter N. Benton of Ladder 3, were severely injured. At this fire the system of concentrating into one stream the water from two or three engines, by the Siamese connection, was first adopted, when a three-way connection was used with splendid effect, by Engine No. 3 and engines from Cambridge and Chelsea, on the Cathedral building.

The number of alarms from May 1, 1878, to April 30, 1879, was five hundred and sixty-three ; loss, $403,451 ; insurance, $3,591,948.

All the houses of the call-companies were provided during 1880 with a room for the use of the members, where they were obliged to assemble once a week, between the hours of 7 and 9 o'clock P.M., for the purpose of reading the rules and general orders of the board. In many of these rooms the members, at their own expense, placed billiard tables. The commissioners made arrangements with the patentee of the Speedy swinging-harness to use it in this department. By the use of this appliance, a saving in the wear and tear of harness was effected, while the necessity of keeping the horses of the department constantly harnessed was obviated. The Scott-Uda Aerial Ladder was lodged in old Engine-house No. 3, on Washington street, near Dover, and a permanent driver appointed. A hospital for sick horses was also established in Hose No. 7's house, on Tremont street, under the charge of Mr. George F. Stimson, — a member of that company, who was later on appointed veterinary surgeon to the department. July 30, Hook and Ladder Company No. 12 was organized, and located in the house with Hose Company No. 7. A new engine of the Silsby pattern was purchased and put in service September 1, in charge of Engine Company No. 25. One buggy, for the use of the commissioners, two wagons, and a ladder-truck, for Ladder Company No. 12, were purchased, — the latter from Ryan Bros. of this city. Three ladder-trucks in the city proper were each provided with a calcium-light apparatus, which proved very useful.

Inspector Brown S. Flanders was appointed, January 2, Superintendent of Fire Alarms, *vice* John F. Kennard. A ball in aid of the Firemen's Relief Fund was given at Music Hall on the evening of March 31, the sale of tickets being made by the members of the department. Quite a large sum of money was realized. These entertainments were renewed each year, by which several thousand dollars were annually added to the fund of the Relief Association. June 18, it was ordered that a substitute serving for a member was to be paid by him during an absence of only twenty-four hours or less ; for a longer period the name of the substitute was entered on the pay-roll, and the amount of said services deducted from the pay of the member for whom he served.

All leave of absence from officers and permanent members was, after June 25, decided by the board. Application was made in writing, stating the reasons for making the request, and sent through the regular channels twenty-four hours in advance, with the opinion of intermediate officers, approving or disapproving, with reasons endorsed thereon. When a member found, from sudden sickness, that he was unable to do duty, or was called away, he was at once to notify the district engineer of the fact, who could temporarily grant him the leave of absence required, — the engineer or officer in command employing a substitute to fill the vacancy.

The Legislature, on March 17, passed the following act, pensioning members of the department : —

Be it enacted by the Senate and House of Representatives in General Court assembled, and by the authority of the same, as follows : —

SECTION 1. The board of fire commissioners of the city of Boston, by the affirmative vote of all the members, and with the approval of the mayor, may retire from office in the fire department any permanent or call member thereof, who has become disabled while in the actual performance of duty, or any permanent member who has performed faithful service in the department for a period of not less than fifteen consecutive years, and place the member so retired upon a pension roll. No such member shall be placed on the pension roll unless it shall be certified to the board in writing, by the city physician, that such member is personally incapacitated, either mentally or physically, from performing his duty as a member of the department. In case of total permanent disability, caused in or induced by the actual performance of his duty, the amount of annual pension shall be one-half of the annual compensation allowed to the permanent men of the grade in which said member served, or such less sum as the said board may determine. The pension of members of the permanent force who have served fifteen or more consecutive years shall be an amount not exceeding one-third the annual salary or compensation of the office from which said members are retired, or such less sum as the board may determine.

Sect. 2. If any member of the said fire department shall die from injuries received while in the discharge of his duties, and shall leave a widow, or if no widow, any child or children under the age of sixteen years, a sum not exceeding three hundred dollars may be paid by way of annuity to such widow so long as she remains unmarried, or to any such child or children so long as he or they continue under the age of sixteen years, and the board of fire commissioners may from time to time order such annuity to be reduced.

Sect. 3. For the purpose of carrying out the provisions of the foregoing sections, the board of fire commissioners may, with the mayor, expend such sums as may be specially appropriated therefor by the city council, for the relief of widows or children of members of the fire department who have been killed in the execution of their duty, or have died from the effect of injuries received in the execution of their duty. For the payment of the pension hereinbefore authorized the board of fire commissioners may draw, from time to time, upon the city treasurer of Boston, any sum which may be specially appropriated therefor by the city council.

Sect. 4. The mayor of the city of Boston for the time being (and his successors in office), the board of fire commissioners of the city of Boston for the time being (and their successors in office), shall together continue a body corporate for the purpose of receiving and holding all sums of money, and real and personal estate, not exceeding in the aggregate two hundred thousand dollars. which may be given, granted, bequeathed, or devised to it for either members of the Boston Fire Department, or their families, requiring assistance, or for the benefit of any person, or the families of any person who have been such members, requiring assistance. The property so held shall be known as The Boston Fireman's Relief Fund. The said body corporate shall have authority to manage and dispose of the same thereof, according to their best discretion, subject to the provision of any and all trusts which may be created for the purpose aforesaid. Such corporation shall have all the powers and privileges, and be subject to all the duties, restrictions, and liabilities set forth in all general laws, which now are or may hereafter be in force relating to similar corporations.

During the year the corporation was organized, and the chief engineer, as chairman of the committee of the firemen's ball, placed the sum of $9,000 in their care, to be used for the purpose aforesaid.

During 1877, Mr. Albert C. Lynn, a member of Ladder Company, No. 9, started the movement to have call-members enjoy the same privileges in case of disability, etc., as provided in the above act for the permanent members : and after a hard fight the desired result was obtained during 1888, whereby section one of the act was amended so as to include the call-force, and the following clause was added : —

The pension of members of the call force who have served fifteen or more consecutive years shall be an amount not exceeding one-half the annual salary or compensation of the offices from which said members are retired, or such less sum as the board may determine.

District Engineer Samuel Abbott, Jr., resigned his office July 1, to accept the position of Superintendent of the Protective Department; his place was filled by the appointment of William T. Cheswell. An order was issued on September 23, to the effect that any driver of the department driving over a line of hose, unless it could not be avoided, should be dismissed. The quarters occupied by Engine No. 12, on the corner of Dudley and Winslow streets, were moved to the premises of Ladder Company No. 4, on Dudley street, near Blue Hill avenue. These houses were both renovated, and adapted to the use of their companies; the stalls were changed, enabling the horses to face the apparatus, and swinging-doors provided, so that on the alarm, the latch fastening the doors being pulled, they quickly opened, allowing the horses to move rapidly forward in a straight line to the pole of the apparatus. This change was also made in the houses of Engines Nos. 6, 22, 3, 13, 14, 9, 11, and 18; also in Ladder Houses 8, 3, 4, and 5. A sliding pole was also placed in Engine House No. 4, connecting the sleeping apartments with the main floor, by which the members could slide from the upper to the lower story, thereby saving the time of going downstairs. These improvements were placed in all the other houses soon after. An act was passed by the Legislature April 15, 1880, entitled an " Act relative to the better means of egress from manufacturing establishments."

The loss by fire from May 1, 1879, to April 30, 1880, was $1,260,490; insurance, $4,602,591. Five hundred and seventy-one alarms were given during this period. A severe conflagration broke out Sunday, February 1, in the lumber and lime sheds at Nos. 468 to 498 Albany street, by which four buildings were totally destroyed and one badly damaged; loss, $32,303; insurance, $44,500. Laddermen Wilson, Darling, Clapp, and Bennett of Ladder No. 3, Foreman Riley and Hosemen Chase and Melzard of Engine No. 3, also Hosemen Whitney and McAllister of Engine No. 15, were severely burnt at this fire. On the 11th, Hoseman Cummings, substitute of Engine No. 4, was badly burnt at a fire at 14 to 20 Sudbury street. The day following, three alarms were given for a fire at 146 to 158 Blackstone street. One building was destroyed and two badly damaged; loss, $9,325; insured. The large five-story brick and freestone building, Nos. 79 to 81 Milk street, occupied by the Wright & Potter Printing Company and others, was destroyed Monday, February 23; loss, $37,912; insured. Engineer Colligan was badly injured in the right eye at a fire in the building Nos. 10 to 20 Elmwood street, March 17. The " Boston Journal " building was badly destroyed on the 21st; loss, $21,656; insured. A general alarm was given for this fire. Hosemen Douglass of Engine No. 25, Keyes of Engine No. 4, and Ladderman Wells of Ladder No. 1, were injured. Several of the inmates of the tenement-house Nos. 18 to 28 Travers street had a narrow escape from death, April 19, they being rescued by the firemen in an exhausted condition. L. F. Stevens, of Ladder No. 1, was badly injured the same day by falling from the roof of a shed in the rear of 24 Travers street.

Three alarms were given May 6 for a fire in the five-story granite building, No. 3 Winthrop square, occupied by Whitten, Burdett, & Young and others; loss, $491,781; insurance, $934,000. Captain Knight and Hosemen Sharkey and Kilduff, of Engine No. 14, were thrown from a ladder and badly injured at a fire at the corner of Harrison avenue and Hunneman street. June 1. Miss Josie Wanders, of 47 Prentiss street, was fatally burnt by the explosion of a kerosene-oil can on the 29th. July 12, J. L. McLaughlin, of Engine No. 4, was thrown from the hose-carriage and broke his leg while responding to a fire at 70 Beverly street. On the 20th, Hoseman M. B. Reardon, of Engine No. 25, broke his leg by falling through a scuttle, and Captain Griffin, of Ladder No. 8, severely injured his leg by falling through a hole in the floor while at a fire at 36 Central wharf. The lumber-sheds of W. H. Leatherbee, of 268 Albany street, were destroyed on the 22d; loss, $11,873; insured. The day following, Mr. John Murphy, a citizen, was run over and killed by Engine No. 4, on North Bennet street, while going to a fire on the same street. Two alarms were given for a fire at 42 and 44 Summer street, in a five-story building occupied by several tenants; loss, $122,643; insured. On the same day the building occupied as a carriage warehouse by Sargent & Hamm and others, at 26 to 30 Bowker street, was destroyed: loss, $16,963; insured. Hoseman W. M. Pierce, of Engine No. 8, was badly cut with glass at a fire at 4 Park street, September 17; loss to property, $6,727; insured. On the same day, at a fire at 412 Albany street, Hosemen Tobey, Kelley, and Enwright, of Engine No. 25, were injured by falling *débris;* loss to property, $31,900; insured. The department was called out, October 11, to extinguish a fire in a large quantity of coal at 588 Albany street, which had been burning three weeks. Captain Abbott and Laddermen Alexander, Poland, and Cummings, of Ladder No. 3. rescued Katie Williams and Mary Lehan from a burning building at 18 Seneca street, November 13.

The attention of the City Council being called to the large water-tax charged by the water department for each hydrant and reservoir located in the city, viz., $30 per hydrant and reservoir. this tax increasing from $59,730 in 1872 to $128,940 in 1880. — an amount altogether out of proportion to the cost of water used or the price paid by private citizens, — a special committee was appointed by the City Council during 1881 to look into the matter, which resulted in a reduction of $10 per hydrant and reservoir; but even this amount was considered insufficient, as the board contended that if the rate was fixed the same as for private citizens, — two cents per hundred gallons, — $3,000 would more than suffice to pay the total cost.

CHAPTER III.

1881–1888.

THE Commissioners' report for 1881 contained the following statement:—

The building laws in operation for the past eight years, and the appointment of competent inspectors to enforce the same, are a great improvement on former systems, over what might be termed the "build-as-you-please" style of combustible architecture. By this method many blocks of houses in the dwelling localities of the city have been constructed, and in such a manner as to insure communication by fire from one dwelling to another in the shortest space of time. If the architects and builders who constructed these blocks designedly erected them for the purpose of rapid destruction by fire, they could not have succeeded better; for while they have provided hollow spaces behind furrings and floors, and under roofs, by which fire can travel from basement to attic, and thence by the concealed spaces in the roof, from house to house in a block, they have admirably protected the fire from the water of the steam-engine. And this style of building is by no means confined to the poorer or middling classes of houses in the city. It is to be found in Beacon street equally with the wooden blocks in East or South Boston. . . .

Since the great fire in 1872 all the buildings in the burnt district have been built, and although they have not all the defects mentioned, they have others that are equally disastrous in case of fire, and which are beyond the reach of building laws, but which men and architects can remedy, if they will, at a very little cost. The bulk of our fire loss is in the business section of the city, and is occasioned by defects in the internal construction of the buildings, by which fire and smoke can communicate from the first to the sixth story through every floor, and occasion a loss of hundreds of thousands on the contents, though the loss on the building itself may be very small. In many large buildings in the "burnt district" there are as many kinds of business carried on as there are stories in the building, each story being under the control of a different occupant. These floors, instead of being separated from each other as much as possible, are usually connected by elevator shafts without automatic hatches or other appliances to cut off communication, by wooden stairways, and glass doors and windows at the head of each stairway,—all excellent conductors of flame and smoke, and calculated to produce the largest amount of loss in case of fire. A little additional expense, the use of a little more sheet-tin around elevators and doors,—the expense a mere trifle,—would save thousands yearly in this city and State. The estimated losses by fire in the whole State during the past year aggregate $4,454,221, and one-quarter of the above loss occurred in this city. In no other part of the civilized world is so much of the capital of the country destroyed through fire as in the United States, the amount averaging each year $75,000,000; and all this, notwithstanding the fact that in no countries are its large cities so well supplied with fire apparatus, men, and water-hydrants to fight fire as in the United States. If Boston, New York, or Chicago had only the facilities which the large cities of London or Paris have to combat fire, the loss here would be enormous. The difference in loss is due to the methods of building in vogue here and in European cities; carelessness in construction, carelessness in the supervision of goods stored in buildings, and over-insurances, are the fruitful seeds of large conflagrations.

Of the whole number of fires during the year in this State 40 per cent. are reported as incendiary or unknown.   This city during the past year has been visited by many serious incendiary fires, especially in lumber-yards, and all efforts to detect the perpetrators have thus far proved unavailing.   Many of these fires have been discovered in season, and before much damage was done, the places selected being stores in the " burnt district."   Broken panes in basement windows in our large warehouses afford ample facilities for the incendiary to perform his work; and owners and occupants should see that their basement windows are in good condition, especially during the night.   If every fire in this city could be investigated by some person authorized to act, and empowered to send for persons and papers, and take evidence in the nature of a fire inquest when necessary; if the result of these inquests were published, and the origin, cause, and course of each fire given to the public, the official exposure of those faulty methods of construction which make fires so disastrous, would bring about a reform in the building of warehouses, dwellings, etc., in the city, more effectually than even the building laws, because it would tend to remedy, through public opinion, that which the building laws could not reach.   Last year the City Council petitioned for authority to create the office of Fire Marshal, whose duty it should be to investigate the origin of all fires in this city; but the act failed, principally because of a disagreement between the representatives of the insurance companies and the city as to how this officer should be paid, — whether by the city or the insurance companies.   A more expeditious method than the roundabout way now prescribed by statute for a fire inquest is necessary.

Commissioner Edward A. White was reappointed on the board for a term of three years.   By order of the board one hoseman or ladderman of each company was designated assistant foreman, without additional compensation. On March 28, instructions were given the members to report immediately for duty on the floor after the first stroke of the alarm; the horses were to be hitched up, and the company prepared to leave quarters upon the word " Go ! " to be given by the officer in command, at the instant he is assured that the company, under the rule, is obliged to respond to the box indicated.   If the company was not to respond to that alarm, but obliged to do so on the alarm next succeeding, the horses were to remain hitched twenty minutes.   On inspection by the board it was found that eleven and a half seconds was the length of time required from the time of ringing the alarm until the company was ready to go, even when all the men, except the patrol, were in bed.   The uniform coat of the officers and crew of the fire-boat was ordered, December 12, to be of the pattern described as " reefer," and the assistant engineers were to wear a turn-down white collar instead of a standing one.   Ladderhouse No. 17 had its position changed, during the year, to a site adjoining the house of Engine 17.

Alarms from May 1, 1880, to April 30, 1881, aggregated seven hundred and thirty-one; loss, $1,183,818: insurance, $6,543,006.   The first accident which occurred during the year was received by Mr. George LeCain, of Engine 23, he being badly ruptured by lifting a pung while at company quarters. Wednesday, February 2, Mrs. Hanlan, aged seventy, and her son, aged thirty years, perished in the flames at a fire in a building on Commercial street. Engineer Hewins and several members of the department were severely frost-bitten. A number of wooden tenement-houses, Nos. 159 to 177 Chelsea street, East Boston, were badly damaged, on the 3d; loss, $6,954; building insured, but contents were not. A fire broke out Tuesday, 15th, at 9.55 P.M., in the lumber-sheds at 433 Harrison avenue, and at 10.37 P.M. another was discovered at 100 Lehigh street, among the lumber-yards. A general alarm was sounded; loss at the first, $4,240, and at the second, $8,400; insured. At this fire, Daniel Weston, of Ladder No. 5, fractured his hip, by falling from some lumber. An alarm was given Thursday, March 17, at 9.45 A.M., for a fire at the City Hospital, which was caused by a kettle of rosin boiling over. Mr. John Cleary was severely burned. The Brighton abbatoir caught fire Saturday, April 2; loss, $3,136; insured. Thomas J. Tobey, a deck-hand on the fire-boat, was injured, on the 15th, by being jammed between the draw of the Meridian-street bridge and the boat, while returning from a fire in an oil-tank at 496 Chelsea street, East Boston, and died the same day. May 4, the building Nos. 409 to 413 Atlantic avenue was destroyed; loss, $28,792; insured. And on the 12th, three alarms were given for a fire at 28 to 39 Charlestown street, and 2 to 8 Stillman place; loss, $39,028; insured. Hosemen W. W. Carsley and J. Strangman, of Engine No. 16, were severely injured by being thrown from a ladder while at a fire in a building on Minot street, occupied by New Era Coffee Co. and others; loss to property, $2,754; insured.

Commissioner J. E. Fitzgerald was reappointed on the board for three years, from May, 1882, as chairman. By the death of Assistant Engineer George Brown, September 13, Captain L. P. Abbott, of Ladder Company No. 3, was promoted, October 2, to fill the vacancy. One second-class Amoskeag engine, to replace Engine No. 23, was put in service October 10. Three hose-wagons, one sleigh, one pung, one open buggy, one top-buggy, and a water-tower were purchased during the year. The latter piece of apparatus was built by Mr. A. Greenleaf, of Baltimore. It is a portable stand-pipe, carried on a truck, and weighing about seven thousand five hundred pounds. Three sections of pipe are carried on the side of the truck, and of such lengths that the water-tower can be used at elevations of twenty-nine, thirty-six, forty-three, or fifty feet. It has, at the end of the highest section, a flexible pipe, to which nozzles can be attached one and one-fourth, one and one-half, one and three-fourths, or two inches in diameter; also, an elbow connection at the foot of the pipe, and seven feet of leading-hose, three and one-half inches in diameter, from the foot of the ladder, connecting with a four-way "Siamese," thereby enabling two or three engines to play a powerful stream through the tower. It is worked from the truck by one man. The stand-pipe has a rotary motion, and the nozzle attached can be directed perpendicularly or horizontally, and thus a stream can be thrown in any direction on a burning building, and at any angle of elevation. This tower was placed in the house of Ladder No. 8 on March 20.

Arrangements were made by the board with the proprietors of India wharf for a berth for the fire-boat at the end of the wharf, and for the accommodation of the officers of the boat a new house was built. The old location was in the vicinity of an outlet of one of the main sewers. The house formerly occupied by Hose No. 12 was fitted up as an engine-house, and made the quarters of Engine No. 2, May 10; and the old house of Engine No. 2 was taken possession of by Hose Company No. 12. An order was issued March 21 forbidding any member of the department assigning their wages to money-brokers and others as security for money lent them at usurious rates of interest; a violation of this rule was deemed sufficient cause for dismissal. On the 28th it was ordered that two-thirds of the members belonging to each permanent company should be present during meal hours. It was made compulsory, May 13, for the members whose apparatus was obliged to move from their quarters to that of another company during the progress of a fire to accompany said apparatus and be governed by the running-card of the company whose place they take. A new running-card was issued July 25, and an " all-out " signal was to be given after all alarms, indicated by striking two blows three times on the tappers in the engine-houses. It was ordered, on October 13, that on and after that date any member found guilty of intoxication would be immediately dismissed from service. The former fine of ten days' pay did not have the desired effect; hence the above.

A new manual of the department was issued, dated 1882, which went into effect December 20. This contained a revision of the rules and regulations, as well as the statutes and ordinances, necessary to the proper discharge of the duties of each member.

The Barnicoat Fire Association was reorganized during January, 1882. Any former member or volunteer of Barnicoat Engine Company No. 11, or volunteer of Barnicoat Engine Company No. 4, previous to April 7, 1874; the sons of former members of volunteers of Barnicoat Engine Companies Nos. 11 and 4, and past or present members of Engine Company No. 4 and their sons, — were eligible to membership. Upon the death of a member an assessment of $1 was levied on each surviving member, which sum was paid to the widow or heirs of the deceased member, by the board of trustees. The past presidents are as follows: John A. Fynes, 1882; Christopher C. Tracy, 1883; Thomas P. Bagley, 1884; William T. Cheswell, 1884; Samuel Abbott, Jr., 1885; Dexter R. Deering, 1886; Fred W. Barry, 1887–1888.

The first fire of any magnitude for the year 1882 broke out on Wednesday, February 1, in the building occupied by C. D. Cobb & Brothers and others, at 65 and 67 Union street; loss, $23,428; insured. Mrs. Mary Wall was fatally burned at her residence, 108 Warrenton street, on the 6th. Charles F. Poor, of Engine No. 22, broke his arm while driving to this fire. On the 10th, the building occupied by Doe, Hunnewell, & Co., 577 Washington street, was badly damaged; loss, $44,739: insured. C. W. Dixon, of Ladder No. 8, was badly injured by a falling floor at a fire at 120 Fulton street, April 18; loss, $30,800; insured. The building 82 and 84 Lenox street, occupied by the Union Carpet Lining Company, was destroyed May 2; loss, $24,235; insurance, $24,000. Thursday, June 8, an extensive conflagration originated in a building on Marginal street, East Boston, occupied by the Simpson Dry Dock Company, and before it was got under control the flames spread to twenty-three other buildings, many of which were totally destroyed; loss, $17,921; insured. Hoseman S. L. Fowle, of Engine No. 9, was badly hurt at this fire. On the 12th, another large fire was discovered in the lumber-sheds at 17 to 25 Wareham street; loss, $58,214; insured. Captain George Fern, of Engine No. 25, had a rib broken by falling through a scuttle. The plumbing-shop in the United States Navy Yard at Charlestown was damaged to the extent of $1,120, on the 15th. On the 17th, the building occupied as a wool warehouse, at 60 Hampshire street, was destroyed; loss, $14,155; insured. While several of the members were at work in this building the upper floor gave way, burning them in the *débris*, and severely injuring Hosemen W. Pierce of Engine No. 12, B. E. Handy and C. A. Straw of Engine No. 13, Captain C. F. Poor and Hosemen John Divoll and Edward Kelley of Engine No. 14, Laddermen W. E. Guerrierre of Ladder No. 4, W. H. Flavell of Ladder No. 8, T. F. Killion, W. H. Whitney, G. L. Swift. W. C. M. Howe, and C. H. Webber of Ladder No. 12. On the 27th, three alarms were given for a fire at 131 Border street, East Boston. The flames soon spread to 122 and 126 Liverpool street and 4 and 8 Decatur street; loss, $7,288; insured.

The large building 603 Washington street, occupied by several firms, was badly damaged August 16; loss, $19,268; insured. W. B. Lottridge, of Ladder No. 1, was thrown from the truck and badly injured while going to a fire at 8 Beacham street, on the 8th. William Rathburn, of Engine No. 6, was ruptured while at a fire at 141 Portland street, October 27. Four alarms were given by mistake for a fire at Stetson's wharf, 480 East First street; loss, $8,361; insured. J. F. McWhirk, of Engine 15, was run over by a hose-carriage at this fire, and received a severe injury to his back. November 25, at a fire at 4 Leverett street, Assistant Engineman C. C. Wilson and W. J. Gaffey, of Engine No. 10, were severely injured by the overturning of the apparatus. The building occupied by John P. Lovell & Sons and others, 147 Washington street and 11 Cornhill, caught fire from a gas explosion, December 19. At this fire Ladderman George Hutchinson entered the burning building and rescued a canister of powder. Captain Bickford, Foreman Egan, Laddermen Johnson, Holmes, Grady, and Boardman, were with him at the time of this heroic act; loss to property, $121,096. Messrs. Lovell & Co.'s loss was $104,522; insurance, $77,500. On the 26th, the building, 212 Camden street, occupied by W. B. Gleason & Co., was destroyed; loss, $29,641; insured. The building occupied by the Mystic Rubber Company, 159 Pearl street, was badly damaged on the 30th; loss, $25,000; insured. Number of alarms from May 1, 1881, to April 30, 1882, aggregated five hundred and ninety-three; loss, $615,836; insurance, $4,849,246.

On June 30, 1883, a ladder-truck of the Hayes pattern was placed in commission at quarters on Washington, near Dover street, which was formerly assigned to the aerial ladder, which apparatus was transferred to the house of Ladder 8, the water-tower being assigned quarters in the central house between Engine-house No. 4 and Chemical-house No. 1. Companies were organized for both. The former was called Ladder Company No. 13, and the latter, Ladder Company No. 14. July 10, a steam fire-engine was placed in service in quarters formerly occupied by Chemical-Engine Company No. 7, in the West Roxbury district; that company was disbanded, and a company was organized as Engine Company No. 30. Permanent foremen were assigned on the same date to Engine Companies Nos. 21 and 24, *vice* the call-foremen assigned to position of senior call-hosemen. July 21, the position of Inspector was abolished, and the powers and duties appertaining to the repair of apparatus, and the charge of the department repair-shop, were assigned to the foreman of the shop, Mr. Henry R. Demary, under the title of Superintendent of Apparatus Repairs, with a salary of $1,500 per year. On the same day an order went into effect whereby a permanent substitute corps was organized, and assigned to some permanent company for duty, subject to detail. They were uniformed similar to the members of the permanent force, and were governed by the same rules and regulations, and entitled to the same privileges, their compensation being fixed at $720 per annum, to be in full for all service rendered. All applicants for positions in the permanent force were compelled to serve as substitutes before being appointed to said force. August 1, the position of Inspector of Hose and Harness was created, with authority to examine into the condition of hose and harness, and have general charge of repairs of same. Assistant Engineer J. W. Regan was appointed to this position, with an increase of salary of $400 per annum.

Commissioner H. W. Longley was reappointed in the board for three years from May, 1883, and elected chairman. November 28, Hoseman George W. Stimpson, of Hose Company No. 7, was appointed Hospital Surgeon, with headquarters at Hose-house No. 7. His duty was to attend all second alarms, and look after the horses; also to have full control of the care of sick horses, giving such medical and surgical aid as may be required; examine all horses offered for purchase or hire to this department; and was to visit the various houses, and inspect the horses, stables, shoeing, feed, etc. The new-style hose-carriage, or wagon, was fast taking the place of the old-fashioned " jumper," or reel. It was only a matter of a few years when they were almost universally adopted in this department. The apparatus purchased during the year were: Two Hayes extension-ladder trucks; one third-class Silsby, one Hunneman, and one second-class Amoskeag steam-engine; four Ryan hose-wagons; two coal-wagons; two supply-wagons, one of which was made at the repair-shop; one buggy, and one engineer's wagon.

Number of alarms from May 1, 1882, to April 30, 1883, 727: loss, $814,154; insurance, $7,299,353. The first fatality occurred January 4, when

Miss L. Barry was burnt to death, her clothes catching fire from standing too near a stove, at her residence, 3 Bulfinch place. Mr. B. F. Underhill, clerk at headquarters, while assisting Engine Company No. 27 at a fire in 3 and 5 Water street, on the 5th, fell through the floor and broke his arm. A child of Mrs. Devlin was burnt to death by falling on a stove at her residence, 6 Emmet street, on the 13th. Captain Sawyer, of Ladder Company No. 12, rescued the body of Peter Bannon from the flames, at a fire in the rear of 581 Shawmut avenue, on the 20th. A call for assistance was received from Hyde Park, at 10 A.M., Thursday, 8th; Engine No. 19 responded. The building on Codman street, occupied as a factory, was damaged, on March 11, to the extent of $3,025; insured. On the 18th, the building 149 Milk street, occupied by several tenants, was destroyed; loss, $49,686; insured. Hotel Berkeley, corner of Berkeley and Boylston streets, was discovered on fire at 4.10 P.M., Friday, April 6, the loss on which was $59,727; insured. May 26, the building 32 and 34 Hawley street, occupied by G. H. Morrill for printing-inks, etc., was burnt; loss, $42,775; insured. On June 7, there was an explosion of naphtha in a car attached to Forepaugh's circus, which was lying at Huntington avenue. Foreman Cummings and Ladderman Wood, of Ladder No. 3, were severely burned, as were also J. Williams and William Stockman, employees of the circus, the latter dying from his injuries, a few days later. On the 16th, fire in the building Nos. 9 to 15 Chardon street damaged property to the extent of $98,102; insured. Mrs. McAllister was fatally burned while filling a lighted lamp at her residence, 28 Wapping street, July 23. Three alarms were given for a fire at 112 and 118 Orleans street and 2 Percival place, on the 27th; loss, $8,965; insured. Sunday, August 26, at 2.39 A.M., the dwelling-house No. 6 Thacher court caught fire. Mrs. F. Savage and her infant daughter, together with George and Katie and Thomas McLaughlin, aged respectively 13, 12, and 7 years, were suffocated, or injured so severely that death ensued. Mrs. McLaughlin and two children were severely burned, as were Fred and John Savage; cause of fire was the breaking of a kerosene lamp. Joseph Marquette was fatally burned at a fire in 214 Friend street, September 10. On the 12th, fire in the buildings Nos. 103 to 109 West Canton street damaged property to the extent of $28,854; insured. The breaking of a carboy of acid at 34 Bromfield street, on the 17th, caused the death of Mr. C. H. Codman; and, on October 5, Joseph King was fatally burned at a fire in 138 Richmond street. Mr. McDonald, of 6 Island street, while in a fit, October 20, dropped a lamp, which set the bed, etc., in a blaze, resulting in his death. On November 16, while at a fire at 61 Haverhill street, Driver Smith and Hoseman Graves, of Engine No. 4, were slightly, and Hoseman Hurley severely, burned, and Hoseman Leonard, of Engine No. 6, asphyxiated. At a fire in the building corner of First and L streets, December 7, property was destroyed to the extent of $35,500; insured. On the 8th, at 46 to 50 Federal street, and 143 to 147 Congress street, the loss aggregated $83,175; insured. On the 22d, the Cambridge Street Railroad Company's stable, corner of Winship and Washington streets, was badly damaged ; loss, $16,104 ; insured.

The term of office of Commissioner White having expired April 30, 1884, the Mayor appointed Chief Engineer W. A. Green to the office. By the vacancy occasioned by the appointment of Commissioner Green, assistant engineer of District No. 8, Louis P. Webber, was promoted his successor, on October 23, six weeks after. Mr. Webber was promoted assistant engineer, *vice* John Colligan, transferred to Engine Company No. 18 as foreman. Capt. Edward H. Sawyer, of Ladder Company No. 12, succeeded Mr. Webber, on November 1, as assistant engineer.

Chief Louis P. Webber was born in Long Island, N.Y., November 18, 1843. His first duty as fireman began when he became a member of Tremont Engine Company 7, of the Roxbury Fire Department. When the old-time hand-engine gave way to the modern steam one, he was appointed a hoseman on Dearborn Steamer 1, which subsequently, when Roxbury was annexed to Boston, became Engine Company 14. In 1868 he was elected assistant fore-man, and two years later was chosen to take charge of the command. At the time of the reorganization of the Boston Department, in 1874, the Fire Commissioners made him permanent foreman of this company. He retained this position until May 13, 1880, when his qualifications as a foreman, coupled with the excellent record he had made, induced the commissioners to transfer him to a more responsible field of duty, and he was given charge of Engine Company No. 3, located on Harrison avenue, in the dangerous lumber district. Here " Phil " Webber, as his intimate friends are wont to call him, made his mark, and when a vacancy occurred in the Board of Assistant Engineers he was selected to fill it, and was assigned to the eighth fire district. He had hardly settled down to his work in Roxbury, amid the scenes of his first duties as a fireman, when the seat in the Board of Fire Commissioners left vacant by the retirement of Mr. Edward A. White was filled by the selection of Chief Engineer William A. Green. Then the question came before the commissioners of who should be the chief engineer. District Chief Webber was elected by a unanimous vote, beginning his duties as such October 23, 1884, six weeks after his promotion to take charge of a district. From the time of his advent to the most prominent position in the department he has had to cope with a number of disastrous fires ; but his method of handling them has, in nearly every case, been above comment, and he has had uniform success since his inauguration. One of his strongest points is his popularity among his men, all of whom hold him in the highest esteem, and would do all in their power for him. Chief Webber never sends his men where he is unwilling to go himself, and at no time will he allow the men to " carry the pipe " into a spot where there is immediate danger.

Mr. A. Charles Scott was appointed during the year a clerk at head-quarters. Engine Companies Nos. 1, 9, 12, 13, and 27 were reorganized during September as permanent companies, of nine men each, and per-

Latest Improved Steam Fire-Engine. — Page 330.

manent captains were substituted for call-foremen in Engine Companies Nos. 2, 5, 11, 18, and 20, and Ladder Companies Nos. 2, 4, 5, 9, and 12. Hose Company No. 2 was disbanded March 17, and its members reinstated as members of Engine Company No. 32, which was organized on that date; at the same time call-foreman William E. Delano, of Engine Company No. 27, was promoted call-engineer of District No. 2.

During the year the following new apparatus was purchased: Two Silsby second-class engines, one Hayes extension ladder, one chemical engine, seven hose-wagons, six engineers' wagons, one coal-wagon, and four pungs. The extension ladder was placed in service April 25, at Fort Hill square, under charge of Ladder Company No. 14, the aerial ladder, previously used, being found of no value. By an order of the City Council permanent hosemen and laddermen received a salary at the rate of $1,000 per annum for the first two years of service, and $3 per day thereafter. An order was issued January 15 whereby the crew of the fire-boat were reorganized on the same basis as engine companies of the permanent force, and designated Engine Company No. 31. The assistant foreman, or lieutenant, as this officer was generally termed throughout the department, was, in addition to his regular duty as hoseman, to act as pilot of the boat, under the direction of the captain. The board, after an investigation of the many cases of collision that occurred during the year between the apparatus of the department, and also with private citizens and members of this service, were convinced that reckless driving was the principal cause; an order was, therefore, passed June 26, that the board would "hold all drivers of apparatus alone responsible for their safety in going to and returning from fires, and that drivers shall have exclusive control, and will be held responsible for the speed of the apparatus on these occasions, without interference from any person whatsoever, and any evidence of lack of judgment on their part, or reckless driving, will be followed by fine, removal, or dismissal." They were also reminded that, by a decision of the Supreme Court, the city is not liable for any injury to person or property resulting from their acts, but that they personally were civilly and criminally liable therefor.

All the houses in the department were, on August 13, ordered to be draped in mourning for thirty days, in respect to the memory of Hoseman Joseph Pierce and permanent substitute James Quigley, of Engine Company No. 4, who, on the morning of August 13, while at work on the roof of the burning building 108 to 112 Beach street, were killed by the falling in of the roof, whereby they were thrown into the flames.

The style of uniform overcoat for members of the department was changed October 1. The new coat was to be made of Middlesex beaver, thirty ounces weight, double-breasted; to button clear to the neck, with five buttons on a side, equidistant apart: three on each sleeve, with a slash at the cuff; whole back, with a vent in the side seam, open one and a half inches; flap on each breast, and pocket under left one; side pockets covered with flaps; edge turned in, double-stitched one-half inch; seams lapped and stitched raw, the same width. The sack-coat was as heretofore mentioned, except the length was to be one and a half inches shorter than the overcoat.

The Massachusetts State Firemen's Association was organized at New Era Hall, Boston, May 10, 1881, and incorporated May 10, 1883. From the articles of incorporation we clip the following: —

John S. Damrell, H. H. Esterbrook, Samuel Abbott, Jr., Z. T. Merrill, George S. Willis, F. H. Humphrey, A. P. Leshure, W. M. Snow, C. A. Hemenway, J. W. Morse, J. D. Hilliard, E. D. Donnell, James M. Gould, and E. P. Russell have associated themselves with the intention of forming a corporation under the name of the " Massachusetts State Firemen's Association," for the purpose of the mutual benefit and protection of its members, and the establishment of a fund to aid the widows, orphans, or other relatives and dependents of deceased members, and have complied with the provisions of the Statutes of this Commonwealth in such case made and provided, as appears from the certificate of the President, Secretary, Treasurer, and Executive Committee of said corporation, duly approved by the Commissioner of Corporations, and recorded in this office.

The first officers were : President, Ex-Chief John S. Damrell, Boston. Vice-presidents, Chief C. M. Whipple, Westfield; Chief H. L. Bixby, Newton; Chief E. R. Seaver, Stoneham; Chief W. E. Heald, Lawrence; Chief Frederick Macy, New Bedford. Secretary, H. H. Easterbrook, of Hose 7, Newton. Treasurer, Captain Samuel Abbott, Jr., Protective Department, Boston. Executive committee, Chief William C. Davol, Fall River; Capt. John Allen Root, Engine 2, Pittsfield; J. M. Gould, Hose 2, Somerville; Chief A. C. Moody, Lynn; Chief A. P. Leshure, Springfield; Chief S. E. Combs, Worcester; Ex-Chief W. H. Turner, Haverhill.

Its several conventions have been held as follows: Second, Springfield, October 11, 12, 13, 1881; third, Faneuil Hall, Boston, September 26, 27, 28, 1882; fourth, New Bedford, October 9, 10, 11, 1883; fifth, Fall River, October 14, 15, 16, 1884; sixth, New Era Hall, Boston, October 13, 14, 15, 1885; seventh, Pittsfield, August 31, September 1, 2, 1886; eighth, Taunton, September 7, 8, 9, 1887; ninth, Haverhill, September 5, 6, 7, 1888.

Its three principal officers since its organization have been: Ex-Chief John S. Damrell, of Boston, 1881–85; Chief Walter M. Snow, of Middleboro', 1886; G. S. Willis, of Pittsfield, 1887; Chief Abner Coleman, of Taunton, 1888; Chief Edward Charlesworth, of Haverhill, 1889; Superintendent Samuel Abbott, Jr., of the Boston Protective Department, 1889–90. Secretaries : H. H. Easterbrook, of Hose 7, Newton, 1881–85; Samuel Abbott, Jr., Boston, 1886–87; Capt. E. F. Martin, of Engine 7, Boston, 1888: D. Arthur Burt, of Hose 5, Taunton, 1889–90. Treasurers : Samuel Abbott, Jr., Boston, 1881–84; Chief C. M. Whipple, of Westfield, 1885–90.

Total number of alarms from May 1, 1883, to April 30, 1884. seven hundred and ninety-three; loss, $998,554; insurance. $7,981,807. January 4. the Home for Destitute Children, on Harrison avenue. was damaged to the extent of $2,413; insured. Lieutenant Hibbard, of Engine No. 3, had his right arm broken by a falling hose-pipe, at a fire corner of Berkeley street and Columbus avenue, on the 17th. February 9, Lieutenant John Grady, of Ladder No. 1, was severely injured by being thrown from a ladder at a fire in Chelsea and Gray streets. William Andrews was rescued from the building Nos. 456 to 464 Harrison avenue, which caught fire on the 15th; loss, $19,302; insured. On the 19th, Mr. Patrick Howard was rescued from the building No. 16 Tileston street, but died shortly after. At a fire in 21 Pearl and 138 Congress streets, May 8, the loss to property amounted to $23,391; insured. Two alarms were given for a fire in the old prison-yard, which originated in a pile of shavings; loss, $2,421; insurance, $1,421. On the 29th, fire at 406 Border street (McKay's wharf) caused a damage to property of $27,500; insured. Several members of the department were badly burned by an explosion of hot air at a fire in 152 to 158 Congress street, June 12; loss, $261,879; insured. On the day following, lumber-sheds, corner of Lehigh and Albany streets, were damaged to the extent of $32,588; insured. Owing to a collision of apparatus, while responding to a fire at 108 Fulton street, the 16th, Hosemen McLaughlin and Stevens, of Engine No. 4, and a citizen named F. C. Douglass, were severely injured. Assistant Engineer Imbert, of Engine No. 11, was severely injured by falling from a wharf to a float-stage, at a fire in New street, East Boston, the 17th. Engines Nos. 6, 10, 32, and Hose Companies Nos. 1 and 8, responded to a call for assistance from Somerville, on the 20th; and on the 22d, Engine No. 16 and Ladder 6 responded to a call from Milton. Ladderman M. Murnan, of Ladder No. 8, was severely injured by falling from the truck while responding to an alarm from 51 and 53 High street, on the 29th. July 4, Charles Schworm, a member of Protective Company No. 1, fell through the floor of a building at 37 Central wharf, and was seriously injured. A fire on the 23d, in the buildings Nos. 262 to 268 Dover street, occupied as a shoe-factory, caused a damage of $44,550; insured. A call for assistance from Chelsea was received on the 28th. Mrs. Hannah Wheelan was burned to death at her residence, 11 Davenport street, August 10.

The large buildings Nos. 108 to 112 Beach street, occupied by several tenants, caught fire Wednesday, August 13, at midnight. It was at this conflagration that Hosemen Pierce and Quigley, of Engine 4, were burned to death. Loss to property, $51,866; insured. Mrs. Regan was fatally burned by building a fire with kerosene oil, at her residence, 7 Fayette street, on the 18th. September 10, Miss Kate Connelly met with the same fate from a similar cause, at her residence, 128 Gold street. Mr. V. Sneider was seriously burned while trying to extinguish the flames in her clothing. Three alarms were given on the 25th, for a fire in Taylor street; loss, $51,609. Mrs. Elizabeth Kelly and Thomas Kane were rescued from the burning building Nos. 2 to 6 Everett court, October 25. Mrs. Kelly died from her injuries. William Stewart, watchman in the planing-mill 137 Border street, which was destroyed November 18, was burned to death. Mr. Sawyer, together with his daughters Esther and Ida, lost their lives by suffocation from smoke, in a fire in their dwelling, 62 Castle street, on the 20th.

Commissioner John E. Fitzgerald was reappointed on the board, and chosen chairman for three years, dating from May 1, 1885. Captain John A. Mullen, of Engine Company No. 15, was promoted to the position of assistant engineer, August 20, and assigned to District No. 6, *vice* Assistant Engineer L. P. Abbott, transferred to District No. 3, in the place of assistant Engineer W. H. Cunningham, resigned. A new building was erected during the year, at the corner of Albany and Bristol streets, for a repair-shop. The building is of brick, and gives accommodation for all the work to be done on apparatus, hose, and harness, and affords room for storage of supplies, etc. A large yard and building adjoining, on Bristol street, gives additional storage-room for lumber and other articles. During the four winter months extra horses were placed in service, under agreement with the owners that such service should be without cost to the city other than the care and feed, the same as is given the regular horses of the department. The new apparatus purchased during the year consisted of the following: One Manchester (Amoskeag) and one Silsby second-class engines, two ladder-trucks, one chemical engine (for Chemical Company No. 1), one hose-wagon, one coal-wagon, and one pung.

The first extensive fire during 1885 broke out January 18, at 8.44 P.M., in the building Nos. 45 to 63 Eastern avenue, occupied by the Bay State Sugar Refinery: loss, $222,278; insured. An overheated furnace in the building 230 to 234 Beacon street, on the 29th, caused a loss of $23,094; insured. James W. Sweetser, member of Protective Company No. 1, was instantly killed by the falling of a ladder while at a fire at 43 India square, March 8. Three alarms were sounded for a conflagration at the factory of the Boston Machine Company, located on First and Granite streets, on the 20th: loss, $180,649; insurance, $122,700. Fifty-eight workmen lost their tools, valued at $2,750; no insurance. On the 21st the Continental Sugar Refining Company had their buildings destroyed; loss, $24,201; insured. The building occupied by the Boston Dyewood and Chemical Company, 317 Border street, was burned on the 18th; loss, $39,239; insured. Miss Flora Evans was fatally burned, April 7, by her clothing taking fire from a lamp thrown at her by a visitor at her dwelling, 19 Lyman street. Annie Curran, aged six years, was run over and killed on Prince street, Saturday, 18th, by the hose-carriage of Engine No. 8, while responding to an alarm from 218 to 222 Main street. Miss Helen Fitzgerald, of 268 Eustis street, was fatally burned, May 27, by her clothes taking fire from building a fire with kerosene oil. Her mother and Miss Maggie Finney were severely burned while extinguishing the flames. At a fire in the "Youth's Companion" office, 41 Temple place, on the 28th, property was destroyed to the extent of $28,904; insured. Mrs. E. E. Alley, of 35 Vernon street, was fatally burned, June 14, by her clothes taking fire from a stove near which she was standing. A large conflagration occurred Monday, 22d, at 8.21 P.M., in the large building Nos. 89 to 93 Franklin street, occupied by Abraham French & Co. ; loss, $82,670 ; insured. John Bacon, an employé of the Maverick Oil Works Company, was fatally burned at a fire in their works on Chelsea street, July 2. Engine No. 15 was despatched to the assistance of the Norwood, Mass., department, Saturday, 19th. On the 21st, Mrs. L. Fliegel, of 130 Longwood avenue, was fatally burned by building a fire with kerosene oil. The Standard Dyewood Company and others lost $28,561 from a fire in the building Nos. 12 and 13 Sargent's wharf, Tuesday, 28th. A fire, August 10, in the buildings 33 to 38 Lewis wharf, occupied as United States bonded warehouses, caused a damage to property of $115,010 ; insured. The Smith organ factory, corner of Montgomery and Clarendon streets, was destroyed on the 18th ; loss, $45,632 ; insured. Three alarms were given for a fire at 34 and 36 Sargent street, occupied as dwellings and stables ; loss, $9,597 ; insured. Total number of alarms from May 1, 1884, to April 30, 1885, nine hundred and twenty-seven ; loss, $1,593,394 ; insurance, $8,068,295.

Mr. Robert G. Fitch succeeded Commissioner H. W. Longley, May 1, and on the resignation of Commissioner J. E. Fitzgerald, August 18, was appointed chairman of the board, and Mr. John R. Murphy received the appointment of commissioner. Mr. Fitch was reappointed by Mayor Thomas N. Hart, from May, 1889, for three years.

Mr. Thomas Norton Hart, Mayor of Boston, was born on January 20, 1829, at North Reading, Mass. His father was a farmer ; his mother, a woman of great refinement, was of the Nortons at Royalston. Mr. Hart's grandfather on his mother's side, Major John Norton, fought in the Revolutionary war. It will thus be seen that the chosen representative of the people is not a born aristocrat, for his father was poor, and, when a mere stripling, young Hart came to Boston to earn his living. He found employment in the dry-goods store of Wheelock, Pratt, & Co., on Kilby street, and lived with the family of the senior partner, who is still living. After a short experience in the Boston store, Mr. Hart returned to his native town to complete such an education as could then be had in a country school. After a term thus spent, he returned to Boston, more than forty years ago, and entered a hat, cap, and fur store on Hanover street. The store was kept by C. B. Grinnell and S. B. Proctor, with whom Mr. Hart stayed until 1850, when he entered the wholesale and retail store of Philip A. Locke, on Dock square. In 1855 he was admitted as partner ; the business was transferred to Elm street, the firm name being changed to Philip A. Locke & Co. In 1860 Mr. Hart founded the house of Hart, Taylor, & Co., his partners being Mr. Frederick B. Taylor and the late Orin B. North. This firm, also devoted to the hat, cap, and fur business, rose to be the greatest of its kind in New England, and one of the three or four largest in the country. The firm began business in August, 1860, finally erected a building of its own in Chauncy street, and retired on December 31, 1878, — selling out to Dyer, Taylor, & Co. The firm of Hart, Taylor, & Co. did not formally dissolve until 1885.

Mr. Hart's exceptional success in business brought him in contact with many people, and in 1878 he yielded to the importunities of Mr. Phineas Peirce, Mr. Charles H. Allen, Mr. Alanson W. Beard, and others, to enter the Common Council, where Mr. Hart served in 1879, 1880, and 1881 ; in 1882, 1885, and 1886 he served as alderman, representing first the South End, then the Fifth Aldermanic District. Since retiring from active business Mr. Hart has assumed the presidency of the Mt. Vernon National Bank, and brought it up to a good degree of prosperity. In politics he has always maintained the principle of national unity and union ; also the principle of national protection, of free public schools, and of equal rights for all American citizens, without making a distinction of race, color, nation, or creed. Though living a quiet and retired life with his family, he is a member of several clubs and an occasional attendant. He has always been a liberal contributor to benevolent enterprises, and at times has given them much personal attention.

Mr. Hart was a constant attendant at the famous Fisher Hill investigation. He opposed the granting of a franchise to the Bay State Gas Company to enter the streets of Boston for the sole purpose of making money, and he has had many a tilt, and occasionally a hard fight, with the elements then controlling our municipal affairs. These struggles for clean government, in the interests of the people, are a matter of public record, and Mr. Hart's political opponents have never questioned his integrity, his ability, and exuberant good-nature. Contrary to his wishes, he was nominated for Mayor in 1886, and renominated in 1887. The nomination of 1888 came to him unsolicited. His letter of acceptance, substantially like that of 1887, states that fact.

In 1886 Mayor Hart was the nominee of the Republicans only ; in 1887 and 1888, of the regular Republican and the Citizens' conventions. Although himself a Republican, Mayor Hart has taken, both as a candidate and as Mayor, a distinct stand for the non-partisan principle of government. His acts as Mayor are in harmony with this principle.

Robert G. Fitch, Chairman of the Board of Fire Commissioners, first saw the light in the town of Sheffield, Mass., March 19, 1846. He fitted for college at New Marlboro', Mass., and in 1866 entered Williams College, from which he graduated during 1870. Having a love for journalism, he moved to Springfield, Mass., and entered the office of the " Springfield Republican," where he began from the first rung of the ladder, filling the position of copyholder, proof-reader, local reporter, etc., until January 1, 1872, when he was assigned to Boston as legislative correspondent. His success in that capacity is well known, the articles contributed by him being recognized as the most authentic and able reports of the legislative proceedings published. He held that position until May, 1872, when he was offered, and accepted, an editorial position on the " Boston Post." His superior abilities as a journalist were soon recognized. In 1878 he was made managing editor, and in 1881 he assumed the chair of editor-in-chief. Under his management the paper became a power in political matters, its leading editorials being at all times fearless and impartial. He held that office until 1885, and in 1886 was appointed on the Board of Fire Commissioners by Mayor O'Brien. Chairman Fitch is a gentleman highly esteemed in both social and political circles, and in his duties on this board is at all times in favor of progress; at the same time, never hasty in his decisions. He is a strict disciplinarian, but does not expect impossibilities; in fact, a gentleman highly qualified to fill his office.

Commissioner John R. Murphy is the junior member of the board, and the youngest man to hold this office that has ever been appointed. He was born at Charlestown District, Boston, Mass., August 25, 1856. He attended the public schools of that section, and at an early age graduated from the Harvard Grammar and the Charlestown High schools. During 1873 he began his business career by entering the commission house of Messrs. Silsbee & Murphy, of this city, where he remained until 1876, when he was engaged in the business department of the "Pilot,"—one of the best-known weekly newspapers published in Boston. Two years and six months later he was engaged as business manager, in which capacity Mr. Murphy met with signal success, the business affairs of the paper being in a most prosperous condition. He was elected a member of the Legislature from Ward 5 during 1883, 1884, and 1885, and a member of the Senate from Charlestown District the year following, when he was appointed by Mayor Hugh O'Brien a member of the Board of Fire Commissioners, in which office his services have proved of special benefit. Mr. Murphy is a member of several social organizations, including the Royal Arcanum and the Foresters.

A new house for the accommodation of Ladder Company No. 9 and Hose Company No. 1 was erected the ensuing year on Main street, Charlestown. A new house was also erected at the corner of Saratoga and Byron streets, East Boston, for Chemical Company No. 7, which was organized and put in commission September 27. A new ladder-truck for Ladder Company No. 3 was put in service June 21. The system of giving public alarms on the bells in the West End and in the city proper north of Dover street, with the exception of the bell on Faneuil Hall, was discontinued during the year.

Orders were issued July 9 to the effect that weekly payments had been adopted in the department. This new order of things necessitated a change in making out certificates of time. The absentee reports were abolished, and the time of each member was entered on the roll. Leaves of absence, when less than for twenty-four hours, were granted for six, twelve, and eighteen hours. The officers of permanent companies and members in charge of quarters of call-companies were held responsible for making out and forwarding the rolls.

Mr. Charles W. Whitcomb was appointed to the office of Fire Marshal November, 1886, with headquarters at No. 5 Pemberton square. The act establishing this office was passed October 30, and accepted by the Common Council October 6.

An Act to establish the Office of Fire Marshal·of the City of Boston.

Be it enacted, etc., as follows: —

Section 1.   The governor of the Commonwealth, by the advice and with the consent of the council, shall appoint an officer to be known as the fire marshal of the city of Boston, who shall be a citizen of said city, to hold office for a term of three years from the date of his appointment, or until his successor is appointed.   Said fire marshal may be removed at any time by the governor.

Sect. 2.   It shall be the duty of said fire marshal to examine into the cause, circumstances, and origin of fires occurring within the municipal district of Boston, by which any building, vessels, vehicles, or any valuable personal property shall be accidentally or unlawfully burned, destroyed, lost, or damaged wholly or partially; and to especially examine and decide whether the fire was the result of carelessness or the act of an incendiary. The said fire marshal shall, when in his opinion said proceedings are necessary, take the testimony, on oath, of all persons supposed to be cognizant of any facts or to have means of knowledge in relation to the matters herein required to be examined and inquired into, and cause the same to be reduced to writing, verified and transmitted to the district attorney of the county of Suffolk, and to the board of fire commissioners of the city of Boston.   Said fire marshal shall report in writing to the owners of property, or other persons interested in the subject-matter of investigation, any facts and circumstances which he may have ascertained by such inquiries and investigation which shall in his opinion require attention from said person or persons, and it shall be the duty of said fire marshal, whenever he shall be of opinion that there is evidence sufficient to charge any person with the crime of arson, to cause such person to be arrested and charged with such offence, and furnish to the district attorney all the evidences of guilt, with the names of witnesses and all the information obtained by him, including a copy of all pertinent and material testimony taken in the case; and he shall specially report to the board of fire commissioners, as often as such board shall require, his proceedings and the progress made in all prosecutions for arson, and the result of all cases which are finally disposed of.

Sect. 3.   The fire marshal shall have power to subpœna witnesses and to compel their attendance before him in like manner and effect as trial justices to testify in relation to any matter which is, by the provisions of this act, a subject of inquiry and investigation by said fire marshal.   The said fire marshal shall be and is hereby authorized to administer and verify oaths and affirmations to persons appearing as witnesses before him, and false swearing in any matter or proceeding aforesaid shall be deemed perjury and shall be punishable as such.   The said fire marshal shall have authority, at all times in the day or night, in performance of the duties imposed by the provisions of this act, to enter upon and examine any building or premises where any fire shall have occurred, and the buildings and premises adjoining and near to that in which the fire occurred.

Sect. 4.   The compensation of the fire marshal shall be a salary of three thousand dollars per annum, which shall be paid in monthly instalments by the treasurer of the city of Boston.   Such salary, and all expenses incurred by said fire marshal in making inquests for the purpose of determining the origin of fires, shall be included in the expenses of the county of Suffolk.

Sect. 5.   It shall be the duty of the board of fire commissioners of the city of Boston to supervise and direct, whenever it shall be of opinion that the public interests will be subserved thereby, the investigations, examinations, and proceedings of said fire marshal, and make all needful and proper rules and regulations in relation to the duties of the office and the manner of performing the same, and to determine the necessary expenses, and to audit the accounts of said fire marshal.

Sect. 6.   On the first of May of each year, on presentation of proper vouchers and accounts, the treasurer of the Commonwealth shall pay to the treasurer of the city of Boston the salary of the said fire marshal, and the expenses incurred during the preceding calendar year in prosecuting his investigations in the manner above mentioned: *provided, however,* that the said payment made by the treasurer of the Commonwealth shall in no case exceed in amount twenty-five per cent. of the tax collected by the Commonwealth on premiums received by insurance companies for writing fire-risks in the city of Boston during the preceding calendar year.

SECT. 7. The fire marshal shall submit, each year in the month of May, a detailed report of his official action to the city council of the city of Boston.

SECT. 8. All acts inconsistent with this act are hereby repealed.

SECT. 9. This act shall take effect when accepted by the city council of the city of Boston.

Mr. Whitcomb was born at Boston, Mass., July 31, 1855. After graduating from the public schools he entered Dartmouth College, during 1876, from which he entered the Boston Law School, graduating during 1880, and was soon after admitted to the bar. He then entered the University of Gottingen, Germany, where he applied himself to his studies and received two first prizes, — one for the best essay, the other for general athletics. On his return to Boston he studied in the office of Mr. J. H. Benton, Jr. Mr. Whitcomb was elected a member (Republican) of the Common Council from Ward 18 during 1883 and 1884, during which time he received the well-known cognomen of "Boss" Whitcomb. He was also appointed secretary of the Republican Ward and City Committee for the years 1883 to 1886, when he was appointed to the office of fire marshal by Governor Robinson, being the first person to hold that position in the State. The success that he has attained in this new field of labor clearly shows his legal and executive abilities.

The salary of the veterinary surgeon was increased during the year to $1,600 per annum. Mr. Straw, member of Hose No. 7, was detailed as clerk in the apparatus repair-shop during the year.

Number of alarms from May 1, 1885, to April 30, 1886, 795; loss, $821,848; insurance, $7,082,541. The first fire of importance occurred Tuesday, January 12, at 61 to 81 Clinton street, occupied by S. T. Fletcher, produce dealer; loss, $107,006; insured. The American House, on Hanover street, caught fire March 6; loss, $31,370; insured. Box No. 4 was rung in on the 30th, to call assistance for the purpose of rescuing persons buried in the ruins of a fallen building, No. 235 Portland street. Three alarms were given for a fire at the Metropolitan Street Railroad Company's stable, on Roxbury street, April 24; loss, $5,604; insured. The Boston and Albany Railroad Company's stock-yard was burnt May 22. Engines from Cambridge, Newton, and Watertown rendered assistance; loss, $31,644; insured. June 18, Mrs. L. Ferri, rear of No. 19 Clark street, was fatally burned trying to kindle a fire with kerosene oil. A large fire broke out Saturday, 20th, at 7.12 P.M., at Nos. 590 to 594 Washington street, occupied by the Emigrant Savings Bank and others; loss, $60,689; insured. The most terrible conflagration of the year occurred Monday, 21st, at 2.20 P.M., in the New England Fair building, on Huntington avenue, and occupied as repair-shop by the Metropolitan Railroad Company. The fire originated from the boiling over of a glue-pot, which communicated to a pile of shavings, and with astonishing rapidity the flames spread over the entire building. The exit by the doors was soon cut off, and the windows being grated, six employés, prevented from making their escape, perished in the flames. Their names were: J. R. Taylor, Oliver Frost, William Campbell, Patrick Lyons, Julius Hunckle, and Henry W. Mason. Several others had very narrow escapes. Loss to property, $150,000; insured.

July 6, a woman was fatally burned at 23 Genesee street, trying to build a fire with kerosene. The buildings on Seventh street occupied by the Bradley Fertilizer Company were destroyed on the 22d; loss, $113,634; insured. David Kinsman, aged 14, a deaf-mute, was run over and killed by Engine No. 2, while responding to this fire. Mrs. Sophia Miller was fatally burned, September 12, at her dwelling, 8 Albert street, in attempting to remove a kerosene stove that had exploded. Hoseman W. A. McKenzie, of Engine No. 15, rescued George Towle, a lad of 15 years, from a smoky room in the building 160 Dorchester avenue, on the 21st. On the 29th, at 19 Indiana place, Miss Esby Abbott, a sick lady, fell upon a lighted kerosene stove, burning herself so badly that death ensued shortly after. November 25, Ladderman William H. Flavell, of Ladder Company No. 8, was suffocated by smoke at a fire in the building Nos. 232 to 234 Friend street: loss at this fire, $13,151: insured. Another large fire broke out on the 28th, at 79 Sumner street, East Boston, occupied by the Lockwood Manufacturing Company, machinists; loss, $98,917; insured. Engine Company No. 15 was despatched to the assistance of the Brockton, Mass., department, December 2.

Commissioner W. A. Green was succeeded by Mr. Richard F. Tobin, May 1, 1887.

Ex-Chief Engineer William A. Green was born at Clarendon, Vt., November 6, 1823. He came to this city during 1842, and was employed as wharfinger until he entered the Fire Department as a salaried officer. His first connection with the service dates from May, 1847, at which time he became a member of Boston Engine Company No. 15, of which he was elected foreman during October, 1851. February, 1858, he was appointed on the Board of Assistant Engineers, which office he held until April, 1874. During this period Captain Green organized, and was appointed superintendent of, the Boston Protective Department, combining the offices of assistant engineer and superintendent until the above date, when he succeeded Captain Damrell as chief engineer, and was appointed on the Board of Fire Commissioners during 1884 to May, 1887, having occupied every position in the department from hoseman to commissioner.

Commissioner Richard F. Tobin was born at Boston, Mass., November 20, 1844. At the age of sixteen he was a resident of Cambridge, Mass., and soon after began his apprenticeship to the trade of iron-moulding, with the firm of Lyman, Kinsley, & Co. During the Rebellion his greatest ambition was to enlist in the service of the United States: but his age was against him, being but sixteen years old. Once only did he succeed; but his glory was of short duration. It was during the call for three-months men, and a company was recruited in Cambridge and ordered to report at Faneuil Hall, Boston. Leaving his work one afternoon, he proceeded to headquarters; but "no admittance" was the order. Proceeding around the corner of the building in hopes of finding an entrance, he climbed the conductor and reached one of the second windows of the hall; but the first object that came to his view was the figure of a sentinel on duty at the open window. As soon as the would-be soldier caught sight of the guard he put himself in such a position as would appear as though he was retreating; he was seen and dragged into the hall, where in a few moments he was enlisted. His company was ordered home and disbanded within the twenty-four hours, and that settled his soldiering career. But he was determined to do service in the defence of the Union, and he shipped in the navy, on board the United States ship-of-war "Preble." After the destruction of that vessel he was transferred to the frigate "Potomac," and later to the gunboat "Pinola," all of which rendered effectual service under Admiral Farragut, in West Gulf squadron. At the expiration of his service, in 1863, he returned to this city, and was elected a member of the Cambridge City Council during 1873, and was for several years engaged in the fire department of that city, starting as hoseman, and at the time he resigned was assistant engineer. During 1885 and 1886 he was twice elected a member of the State Legislature from South Boston, and his record in that branch as the champion of the Soldiers' Exemption Bill, and other measures of interest to G.A.R. members, is well known. He was employed in the Walworth Manufacturing Company's iron-works at City Point, South Boston, for about twenty years, eight of which he was superintendent, which position he held when, in May, 1887, he was tendered his present office as a member of the Board of Fire Commissioners, which position he is most ably qualified to fill. Commissioner Tobin has held the various offices in the G.A.R., and was elected, during the meeting of 1886, Department Commander of the Department of Massachusetts.

March 15, Foreman Patrick E. Keyes, of Engine Company No. 6, was promoted to the position of assistant engineer, and assigned to District No. 6, *vice* Assistant Engineer Fernald, transferred to the position of foreman of Chemical Company No. 6. Hose Company No. 9 was disbanded October 28, and Chemical-Engine Company No. 8 organized and put in commission in its place. By a vote of the commissioners a limit age was established for call-members. This limit was fixed at fifty-seven years, it being thought neither advantageous to the city, nor properly considerate of the safety of the men themselves, to retain them in the hazardous service after that age. By this order nearly twenty call-members were retired, also several permanent men; the latter, having done over fifteen years of faithful service, received pensions equal to one-third the salaries which they were paid at retirement. August 30, the titles of the officers of the department were changed as follows: That of chief engineer to chief of department, assistant engineer to district chief, foreman and assistant foreman to captain and lieutenant. April 12, orders were issued to the effect that the list of vacations should be sent to headquarters on or before May 1, and that every permanent member should be allowed fourteen days' vacation, to include one of his days off.

August 15, the style of uniform of the officers and members was again changed. The uniform sack-coat consisted of a double-breasted close-fitting garment, with square corners of dark-blue cloth, cut with three seams in the back; to have eight medium-size department buttons of white metal in each breast, grouped in pairs; to be made with a turn-down collar that would roll two rolls and button six; on each breast a blind flap, five and a quarter by two and a quarter inches, and with slightly rounded corners, placed in a line with the bottom of arm-scye, beginning at one inch from scye and extending straight across (not slanting); a pocket six inches wide by seven deep on inside of left breast. The length of coat to be eight inches above centre of knee-pan. The edges of the turn-down collar to be finished with a double row of stitching, three-eighths of an inch wide. Those of the district chiefs and company officers were the same, except that the former had the buttons on the fronts placed equidistant, and in the latter only six buttons were placed in each row, so that it would roll one over and button five buttons. For other members the coat was single-breasted, straight-front sack, square corners, standing breast, six buttons in front placed equidistant. No change was made in the style of pantaloons or vests. The overcoat for the chief was of a double-breasted frock pattern, of dark-blue cloth, with turn-down collar; length of skirt two inches below the knee; to button close to neck. The front of coat to be cut in one piece, without lapel seam, but skirt cut separately, with eight large department buttons on each breast, grouped in pairs; on back skirt side edges, three buttons each side; three small buttons on each sleeve at cuff. The distance between these two rows of buttons on front was five and one-half inches at top and three and one-half inches at bottom; one large outside pocket-flap on each skirt, without pocket; a small outside pocket on the left breast, covered with a flap; one inside pocket on the right breast, and two back skirt-pockets inside. The edges were double-stitched one-half inch wide, and all seams plain. The same style was adopted for all other members, except that seven large buttons were placed on each breast. The fatigue-cap for all members was of blue cloth, same pattern as shown in illustrations. The Greek-cross device, as worn by the members, had the letter E for those worn by enginemen, and A for the assistant enginemen. The basis of the insignia of office for all officers was made of gold bullion. For chief, the insignia consisted of five trumpets crossed, to be surrounded by a gold-embroidered circle, and worn on the cap and on each corner of the collar of the uniform coat; for assistant chief, three trumpets; for district chief, two crossed trumpets; captains, two perpendicular and parallel trumpets on oblong background, with the number of the company placed between the trumpets for the cap device; this was to be worn on the hat and coat-collar;

for lieutenants, same as captain, except that there was only one trumpet, and that placed horizontally with number above the cap device. The background of the insignia for officers of ladder companies was red ; that of all others blue. Officers of hose companies and chemical companies were designated by H and C, respectively, above their numbers.

Total number of alarms from May 1. 1886. to April 30, 1887, 827 ; loss, $911,999 ; insurance, $6,771,654. The House of Correction, on East First street, South Boston, was slightly damaged February 1. Capt. H. T. Bowers and Hoseman P. C. Twiss, of Hose No. 10, were seriously injured while responding to this alarm, by being thrown from the apparatus. Box 528 was rung in Monday, March 14, at 7.23 A.M., for the terrible railroad disaster at Bussey bridge, where so many lives were lost. Slight fires were extinguished in three of the derailed cars by Chemical No. 4, and valuable assistance was rendered by members of the department in removing the dead and injured ; the hose-wagon of Engine No. 30 was used as an ambulance in conveying the injured to their homes. Three alarms were given for a fire at Clark's Hotel, 577 Washington street, on the 18th ; loss, $19,970 ; insured. April 4, at a fire in a building at Western avenue and Market street, Joseph Littlefield, aged fifty years, lost his life by suffocation. On the 6th, the building Nos. 96 to 102 Milk street. occupied by the Wright & Potter Printing Company and others, was destroyed, loss $85,652 ; insured. Several members were injured while working at this fire. Three alarms were sounded for a fire in the school-house on East Fifth and L streets ; loss, $5,515 ; no insurance. Two members of Engine Company No. 1 and three of Ladder No. 5 were more or less injured by the falling of a portion of the school-house roof. Box 47 was sounded at 11.11 A.M., Tuesday, May 10, for the purpose of exhibiting the department to Queen Kapiolani and suite of the Sandwich Islands. Mrs. Catherine Welch, of 19 Livingston street, was fatally injured June 25. An alarm was given for help on the 27th. occasioned by the falling of a building on Cambridge street, which buried two men in the ruins. Hugh Gallagher, of 6 Cooper street, was burned to death July 4 by the explosion of a kerosene lamp. An explosion of naphtha on board the schooner " War Eagle," lying at Foster's wharf, Chelsea, on the 7th, set fire to the city of Boston's bridge, and killed two men ; also injured two others.

Commissioner J. R. Murphy was reappointed for three years from May 1, 1888. Engine Company No. 33 and Ladder Company No. 15 were organized as permanent companies, and placed in commission, the former February 20, and the latter April 28, in the elegant new house located at the corner of Boylston and Hereford streets, in the Back Bay district. July 17, Chemical Company No. 9 was organized, and placed in commission in the house of Ladder Company No. 9, Charlestown. Hose Company No. 1 was, therefore, disbanded. October 12, Ladder Company No. 16 was organized, and placed in commission in the new building occupied by Chemical Company No. 4, at Roslindale ; and, November 3, Engine Company No. 34 was organized, and placed in service at the new house on Western avenue, Brighton district. The ladder for Ladder Company No. 15 was of the Babcock turn-table pattern, and cost $3,800. A new third-class Clapp & Jones engine was purchased for Engine Company No. 24. The preliminary steps for the construction of a new fire-boat, to take the place of the old one, was taken during the year, and on July 1, 1889, it was placed in service. Four new hose-wagons replaced the old-style carriage.

May 5, the order relative to the duties of assistant chief was rescinded, and after the above date he was governed by the following rules: "He shall, when ordered by the board, test the hose at a pressure not exceeding 100 lbs., and at once report the result to the board, stating the number of each piece, its date of being put in service, kind, maker, length, and at what pressure it burst; and by such report the board will be guided in their condemnation and replacement of the hose." Fabric hose, when wet or damp, was not to remain on the reel or wagon longer than twenty-four hours; and hose that had been on these vehicles without being used for ten days should be changed, and the fact noted in the company journal.

Permanent members of the department were permitted the privilege of free conveyance on the cars of the West End Horse Railroad Company after June 1, provided said members were in full uniform, and rode on the front platform of the car.

The salary of the commissioners and the chief was increased during the year to $3,500; assistant chief engineer, $2,400; assistant engineers, $2,000; assistant call-engineers, $400; superintendent of apparatus repairs, $1,800; department clerks, $1,500; clerk at apparatus repair-shop, $1,800; veterinary surgeon, $1,800; foremen, $1,400; assistant foremen, $1,300; enginemen, $1,300; assistant enginemen, hosemen, and laddermen, $1,200; others at $1,100 and $1,000; call-foremen, $400; call-men at $250, $200, and $175; permanent substitutes, $900 and $720; chief engineer's driver, $900; hostler, $720. Fire-alarm service: Superintendent, $3,200; assistant superintendent, $2,000; foreman of construction, $5 per day; three operators, $1,600; one repairer, $4; one, $3.75; six, $3.25; and three assistant repairers, $2.75, per day, respectively; and one battery man, $75 per month. In accordance with a request made by the board the City Council extended the limit of the number of men who may constitute the Fire Department from 700 to 1,000. This was made necessary by the fact that the former limit provided by the ordinance of 1873 was reached, and further expansion was impossible without new legislation.

The number of horses in the department April 30, 1888, was 180; 25 were purchased, 10 sold or exchanged, 4 died, and 2 were killed. Around the neck of each horse was attached a brass check, with its number.

The total number of hydrants in the city May 1 was 5,204. In addition to these hydrants there were 238 fire reservoirs in different sections of the city, that contain from 300 to 500 hogsheads of water, and can be used in an emergency. The number of hydrants added during the year was as follows: 67 Lowry, 139 Post, 1 Boston, and 43 Boston Lowry. The amount paid by this department for water, and the care and maintenance of hydrants, was $91,217.60, or at the rate of $20 per hydrant.

Amount of hose in use and in storehouse April 30, 1888: Cotton, in use, 48,371 feet; in store, 5,750 feet. Rubber, in use, 4,390 feet; in store, 1,000 feet. Leather, in use, 937 feet. Linen, in use, 450 feet. Chemical, in use, 5,135 feet; in store, 100 feet. Suction, in use, 1,162 feet; in store, 108 feet. Hand, in use, 2,436 feet; in store, 100 feet. Total, in use, 62,881 feet; in store, 7,058 feet. In each fire district a spare hose-carriage, with hose, was kept at department houses.

The following property was in charge of the Board of Commissioners of the Fire Department : —

ENGINE–HOUSES.

	Location.	No. of feet in lot.	Remarks.
No. 1..	Dorchester street	5,698	Addition built, 1874. Municipal Court, South Boston, and two classes Bigelow School, in this building.
2..	Cor. of O and Fourth streets	4,000	
3..	Bristol street and Harrison avenue	4,000	Ladder No. 3 in this building.
4..	Bulfinch street	6,098	Chemical Engine No. 1, Lancers' armory, and water-tower in this building.
5..	Marion street, E. B.	1,647	
6..	Wall street	1,372	
7..	East street	1,893	
8..	Salem street	2,568	
9..	Paris street, E. B.	4,000	
10..	River street	1,886	
11..	Sumner street, E. B.	4,010	Remodelled, 1870. Ladder No. 2 in this building.
12..	Dudley street	7,161	Formerly occupied by Ladder No. 4.
13..	Cabot street	4,305	Remodelled, 1870.
14..	Centre street	5,627	
15..	Dorchester avenue	2,843	
16..	River street, Dorchester Dist.	12,736	Ladder No. 6 in this building.
17..	Meeting-house hill, Dorchester Dist.	....	Old engine-house on this lot.

	Location.	No. of feet in lot.	Remarks.
No. 18..	Harvard street, Dorchester Dist...	10,225	
19..	Norfolk street, "	7,683	
20.	Walnut street, "	9,000	
21..	Boston street, "	9,355	
22..	Dartmouth street...............	4,463	
23..	Northampton street............	3,445	
24..	Cor. Warren and Quincy streets..	4,186	
25..	Fort Hill square...............	4,175	Ladder No. 8 and Ladder 14 in this building.
26..	Mason street	6,385	
27..	Elm street, Charlestown Dist. ...	2,600	
28..	Centre street, W. Roxbury Dist..	10,377	Ladder No. 10 in this building.
29.	Chestnut Hill ave., Brighton Dist..	14,350	Ladder No. 11 in this building.
30..	Mt. Vernon street, W. Roxbury Dist.	16,275	
32..	Bunker Hill street.............	8,000	Built 1883–84.
33..	Cor. Boylston and Hereford sts...	5,646	Ladder No. 15 in this building.
	Church street	3,412	Wardroom No. 11 in this building. Occupied by Chemical Engine No. 2.
	Cor. Longwood and Brookline avenues	5,400	Occupied by Chemical Engine No. 3.
	Poplar street, cor. Washington, W. Roxbury	14,729	Occupied by Chemical Engine No. 4.
	Washington street, between Atherton and Beethoven...... ..	3,848	Occupied by Chemical Engine No. 5.
	Harvard avenue, near Cambridge street, Brighton Dist.	6,112	Occupied by Chemical Engine No. 6.
	Centre street, near Highland station, W. Roxbury Dist.....	1,682	
	Saratoga and Byron streets.. ...	10,000	Occupied by Chemical Engine No. 7.
	B street	1,804	Occupied by Chemical Engine No. 8.

HOSE–HOUSES.

	Location.	No. of feet in lot.	Remarks.
No. 2..	Main street, Charlestown Dist....	1,592	Changed to coal depot, 1884.
3 .	Winthrop street	5,230	Armory in building.
4..	Monument street	5,668	
.5..	Shawmut avenue	889	
6..	Chelsea street.................	1,346	
7..	Tremont street	4,350	Ladder No. 12 and Department Hospital in this building.
8..	North Grove street	3,918	
10..	Washington Village	1,610	
12..	Fourth street..................	3,101	Remodelled, 1870.

HOOK–AND–LADDER HOUSES.

	Location.	No. of feet in lot.	Remarks.
No. 1..	Friend street..................	1.676	
4..	Dudley street..................	3,923	Formerly occupied by Eng. No. 12.
5..	Fourth street....	2.469	
7..	Meeting-house Hill.............		
19..	Main street, Charlestown........	2,430	Hose No. 1 in this building.
13..	Washington, near Dover street...	1,007	
15..	Boylston, cor. Hereford street...	....	Engine No. 33 in this building.
	Harrison avenue................	3,755	Formerly occupied by H. & L. No 3. Now used as a repair-shop.
	Eustis street..................	700	Occupied as a storehouse.
	Bristol street.................	....	Occupied as a storehouse.

Fuel-house, Salem street, 417 feet of land.
Repair-shop, corner of Albany and Bristol streets, 20,547 feet.

The following table shows the number of dwellings, hotels, etc., in the city, taxable valuation, and loss by fire : —

Year.	Dwellings.	Hotels.	Stores.	Miscellaneous.	Erecting.	Family Hotels.	Total Taxable Valuation.[1]	Loss by Fire.
1867......	19,516	55	....	....	.....	......	$444,946,100	$402,115
1868......	23,051	58	....	....	......	......	493,573,700	401,106
1869......	24,181	59	2,453	1,327	602	......	549,511,600	437,723
1870......	27,457	73	2,670	2,690	460	.....	584,089,400	855,571
1871......	28,880	80	2,661	2,811	...	......	612,663,550	704,329
1872......	29,736	70	2,398	2,645	734	......	682,724,300	1,516,549
1873......	30,461	73	1,284	1,727	734	......	693,831,400	2,680,953
1874......	39,106	72	2,778	2,764	446	21	798,755,050	941,483
1875......	39,707	74	2,669	3,262	398	27	793,961,895	1,228,403
1876......	39,804	100	2,915	4,274	172	57	748,996,210	541,272
1877......	39,170	111	3,172	4,476	132	89	686,840,586	481,354
1878......	41,467	120	3,074	4,360	146	80	630,446,866	516,009
1879......	41,652	88	3,319	4,258	139	114	613,322,692	403,451
1880......	41,975	75	3,254	4,653	194	136	639,462,495	1,260,490
1881......	41,903	70	2,994	4,622	170	147	665,554,597	1,183,818
1882......	42,267	68	2,987	4,935	218	152	672,497,961	814,154
1883......	43,986	76	3,347	5,102	209	153	682,432,671	998,554
1884......	44,196	88	2,965	4,970	289	178	682,648,000	1,593,393
1885......	45,137	81	2,998	5,057	282	211	682,656,000	821,848
1886......	46.042	78	2,973	4,801	292	264	710,621,400	911,999
1887......	47,380	73	3,278	5,663	385	298	747,642,500	784,667
1888......	....	......	......	....	......	......	......	1,078,333

[1] Not including property exempt from taxation at an estimated annual value of $60,000,000.

Total number of alarms from May 1, 1887, to April 30, 1888, 975 ; loss, $784,667 ; insurance, $10,165,625. The Post-Office building, Post-Office square, was damaged to the extent of $100 by a fire January 21. Mary Gainey, of 20 South Margin street, broke a kerosene lamp while intoxicated. on the 24th, and was fatally burned. Three alarms were given February 6 for a fire in the building 121 Medford street, occupied by Messrs. F. M. Holmes & Co. as a furniture factory; loss, $25,529; insured.   March 13, the carriage factory of J. T. Smith & Co., 2174 Washington street, was destroyed; loss, $47,977; insurance, $32,000.   At a fire in the building Nos. 155 and 157 High street, April 13, Hosemen Phœnix, Hearn, O'Brien, and Substitute Murphy, of Engine No. 25, together with Hoseman Kenney and Sub. Riley, of Engine No. 26, were severely burned; loss to property, $24,879; insured.   Mrs. Bergan, of 77 Brighton street, was fatally burned, on the 17th, by the explosion of a kerosene lamp.   The Atlantic Works, corner of Maverick and Border streets, East Boston, were nearly destroyed on the 26th; loss, $78,549; insured.   Robert Cassidy was rescued, fatally burned; two other employees were severely burned.   Capt. J. H. Elliott and Ladderman R. J. Bartlett, of Ladder No. 2, were severely burnt Tuesday, May 20, while rescuing females from a building at 278 Sumner street, East Boston.

Three alarms were sounded May 16 for a fire at 6 to 12 Haymarket place and 605 Washington street, occupied by Messrs. Cashman & Keating and others; loss, $35,430; fully insured.   On the 18th, the building at 134 Tudor street, occupied by Messrs. Adams Bros., was destroyed; loss, $7,648; insured.   The premises occupied by the Edison Electric Light Company and others, 3 Head place and 178 and 179 Tremont street, were burnt June 2; loss, $39,196; insured.   Mrs. Rachael Ginskly and her infant were fatally burnt, on the 6th, while attempting to kindle a fire with kerosene oil; and on July 22 a child of Mrs. Wolfe was burned to death by the upsetting of a kerosene stove, at 2 Salem place.   September 13, the warehouse at 361 and 365 Atlantic avenue, occupied by Secomb, Kehew, & Co. and others, was damaged to the extent of $19,686; insured.   The succeeding day a serious conflagration occurred in the building No. 390 Albany street, occupied by Mr. A. F. Leatherbee and several other lumber dealers; loss, $75,929; insured. Mrs. Hannah Hannon was fatally burned while trying to light a fire with kerosene, at 24 Winchester street, on October 3.   Saturday, the 6th, the building No. 411 and 413 Atlantic avenue, occupied by several leather dealers, was consumed; loss, $22,937; insured.   The next serious conflagration of the year broke out Sunday, October 21, at 9.28 A.M., in the building 37 and 38 Lewis wharf, and, before it was controlled, property to the extent of $66,011 was destroyed, which loss was shared by eighteen firms.   C. E. Phœnix, H. A. Fox, and T. J. Lannery, of Engine Company No. 25, were injured at the fire.   A number of female employees in the building 193½ Union street were rescued by members of the department. December 15.   The same day, the building Nos. 22 to 34 Mercantile street was blown to atoms by a gas explosion.   The surrounding property was considerably damaged, and every light of glass in Mercantile block was broken.   Horticultural Hall, 100 Tremont street, was damaged to the extent of $5,700; several occupants lost property to an aggregate value of $2,051; insured.

CHAPTER IV.

CLERKS AT HEADQUARTERS.

THE well-known features of FREDERICK W. SMITH, Jr., private clerk of the Board of Fire Commissioners, will be readily recognized on page 351, in Figure 1. He was born at Boston, Mass., November 4, 1838, and received his education in the public schools, after leaving which he learned the gold-beater's trade, at which he was employed until 1862. At the call for men to serve in the war of that date he enlisted in Company C, Forty-fourth Massachusetts Volunteers, in which he served for nine months, and during which time he was wounded in the breast at Rawles Mill, N.C., November 2, 1862. Soon after his return to this city he was appointed clerk to the Board of Assessors of Boston, which position he held for eight years. At the time the Board of Fire Commissioners was reorganized, and the placing of the department on its present basis, Mr. Smith was offered the position as private clerk, which he accepted, and has filled that office with the highest honor. Always courteous and ready to extend a kindness to all, he has made himself one of the most popular men in this department. Mr. Smith is a member of Firemen's Relief Association, Dorchester Lodge 541, K. of H., Everett Lodge 7, A. O. U. W., and Dorchester Council 437, R. A.

BENJAMIN E. UNDERHILL, Jr. (Fig. 2), senior clerk, was born at Boston, Mass., September 17, 1846. When he was very young his parents moved to Marlboro', Mass., where he attended the public schools, and during 1862 came to this city, where he obtained employment in the jewelry business. He soon after became connected with this department, and on October 4, 1864, he was one of the volunteer members attached to Engine Company No. 4, on which he remained until 1868, when he was enrolled a member of the call-force of the Protective Department at the time that service was organized. He was appointed a clerk in Chief Engineer Damrell's office on November 12, 1872, and on April, 1874, severed his connection with the Protective Department and devoted his whole time to the duties at this office, being transferred from the commissioners' office. His duties are very confining and varied. Besides attending to the regular duties of correspondence, etc., of the chief of department, embracing the Firemen's Relief Association, he has charge of the store-room; also the telephone board from 9 A.M. to 5 P.M. Mr. Underhill was considered a very swift runner. While a member of the department, at one time, on a wager, he ran around the outside of the Common in six minutes and twenty-seven seconds, on January 3, 1883. He broke his left wrist while working at a fire in Charlestown, which is the only accident he received.

Fire Marshal, Veterinary Surgeon, and Clerks. — Page 351.

He is secretary of Joseph Warren Council 8, Home Circle; collector of Monument Council No. 35, Royal Arcanum; secretary and treasurer Bunker Hill Yacht Club; and a member of Mishawum Tribe 30, Red Men, and the Barnicoat Association.

DAVID L. ADAMSON, the principal in the famous surgical case of 1876, will be readily recognized in Figure 3. He was born at Halifax, N.S., May 11, 1848, and in April, 1851, came to this city with his parents. After leaving school, in 1859, he was apprenticed to learn the gas and steam fitting trade, after finishing which he entered the printing business. His fire experience in this department dates from February, 1868, at which time he joined Engine Company 11 as a substitute, and on July, 1873, was enrolled a member. It was while hoseman in this company that he met with the accident that is so well known, the particulars of which are as follows: March 14, 1876, while on the roof of a burning building with the pipe, he slipped off the icy roof and landed in the branches of a peach-tree, on which he was impaled. Two companions, in trying to lift him from his terrible position, broke off the branch so that a portion of it remained in his body. The late Dr. William H. Thorndyke was called to attend him, and performed the operation of cutting into the back and removing the piece of limb. Two weeks later an injured artery burst, causing profuse hæmorrhage, and necessitated cutting down through the abdominal walls, removing the bowels, and ligating the internal iliac artery, to save his life. The case was one of the most dangerous and difficult in surgery, it being previously only performed seven times throughout the world, and in only one case, besides Mr. Adamson's, did it prove successful. He was confined for ninety-three days in one position, and it was five months before he could go around alone. On June 14, 1877, he was transferred to headquarters, to his present position. October 24, 1878, he met with another severe accident, by being caught between the East Boston ferry-boat and drop, and had his right leg crushed so as to necessitate amputation four inches below the knee, — which was also performed by Dr. Thorndyke. He now wears an artificial limb. He is a member of the Masonic fraternity since 1874, and is present Ruler of Maverick Assembly 18, R. S. of E. B.

Mr. A. C. SCOTT, book-keeper for the board, for some reason known only to himself, refused to furnish any data concerning his life or to allow his photograph to be inserted. Mr. Scott was one of the most severely injured men at the Sammett Mattress Factory fire on Hanover street, while a member of Hose Company No. 2. The position of clerk at the apparatus repair-shop was created, and he was appointed to that office, where he remained until his promotion to his present position.

CHARLES W. STEVENS (Fig. 4) was born at Wells, Me., July 19, 1858. He came to this city when but a child, but returned to his native town soon after, where he finished his education. He again came to this city during 1880, where he was engaged in the jewelry business until July 2, 1883, when he was appointed a substitute on Ladder Company No. 1.   October 21, 1883, he was promoted to be a permanent member, and assigned to Engine Company No. 4.   At a fire on December 8, 1883, he had the cords of his right hand severed by falling through a window.   June 16, 1884, in a collision of Engine 6 and Hose 4, on Blackstone street, the wheel of the engine passed over his left leg, just above the ankle, crushing it severely, so as to render him unfit for duty for thirty-two weeks.   On July 7, 1886, he was detailed to the position of clerk in the office of the board, where he still remains.   Mr. Stevens is a member of Barnicoat's and a life member of Firemen's Charitable Association.

GEORGE W. STIMPSON, veterinary surgeon, was born at Boston, January 2, 1846 ; consequently is forty-two years of age.   He entered the department in January, 1867, as a call-man on Hose Company No. 7.   July 1, 1870, he was appointed a permanent member of the same company, and detailed as driver.   He remained in that capacity until November 20, 1880, at which time he was appointed veterinary surgeon.   He was the first man appointed to this service, the work having formerly been done by various surgeons ; but the large amount of work to be attended to convinced the board that it was advisable to make it a permanent position, and he received the appointment. Dr. Stimpson is a member of the order of Red Men, Soangetaha Camp 21.

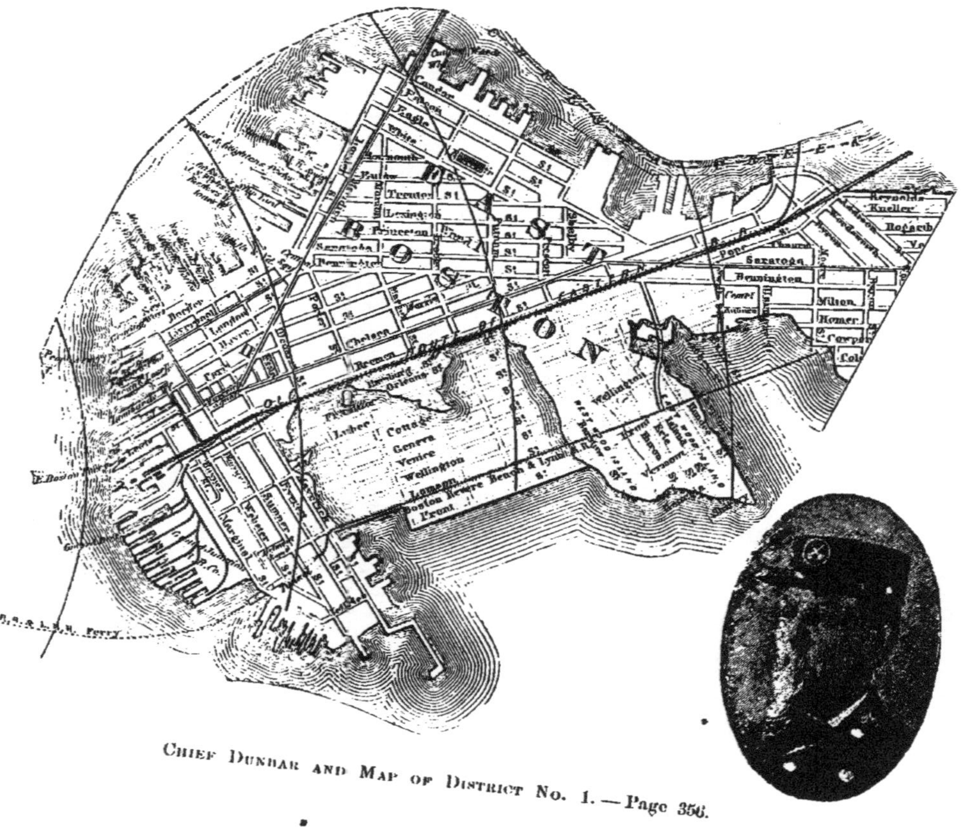

CHIEF DUNBAR AND MAP OF DISTRICT No. 1. — Page 356.

CHAPTER V.

DISTRICT 1.— EAST BOSTON.

EAST BOSTON — formerly the " Noddle's Island " frequently mentioned in early histories of Boston — comprises a tract of land of about a thousand acres, situated at the head of Boston harbor, and only a third of a mile from the main-land. During the first two centuries following the settlements in Massachusetts Bay, it was used chiefly as farming and pasturage land, and its inhabitants were only the families and servants of its successive owners; but in 1833 the entire island came into the possession of the East Boston Land Company, and from that time its growth and prosperity began.

The island was divided into house-lots, upon which houses, stores, and buildings for business purposes were soon erected; trees were planted; bridges, wharves, ship-yards, churches, school-houses, etc., were built; whatever was needed to meet the growth of a population which has increased from eight persons, as shown by a census of 1833, to about thirty-two thousand in 1888.

The advisability of connecting East Boston with the main-land by a bridge has been warmly discussed many times; but it has never been executed, and travel is carried on by means of the boats which ply between the two ferries. The North, running from the foot of Battery street to Sumner street, East Boston; and the South, from Eastern avenue to Lewis street. A boat leaves each ferry every seven minutes, and they are built sufficiently large and strong to accommodate all vehicles, besides the foot-passengers.

There is also another ferry, belonging to the Revere Beach & Lynn Railroad, which is run for the accommodation of its passengers, from Marginal street, East Boston, to the foot of High street and Atlantic avenue.

East Boston, being situated at the head, and in the most protected part of the harbor, and being surrounded by deep water, affords unusual facilities for shipping interests of all kinds. This was brought into use as early as 1839, when the Cunard Steamship wharf was built; and the following year the S.S. " Britannia " was moored at the wharf, which for nearly fifty years has received the passengers and cargoes of this celebrated line.

Between the years 1840 and 1850 the ship-building interest steadily increased, and ship-yards, wharves, and lumber-wharves were built all along the shores. Many celebrated vessels have been built here, and among them the " Flying Cloud," built by Donald McKay, which in 1854 made the quickest passage from New York to San Francisco which had ever been known. At the present time the principal wharves which are in use are the Cunard, Grand Junction, National Dock, and Eastern Railroad, and there are numerous smaller ones along the southern and western shores.

The grain elevator, which is an immense building one hundred and thirty-seven feet high, is located at the Grand Junction wharf, and is the property of the Boston & Albany Railroad. This is one of the largest grain elevators in the country. The Boston Sugar Refinery, on Lewis street, is another large building, eight stories high, which was built in 1834, and has been in operation since that time. Quite near it, on the westerly side of Maverick square, is the hotel known as the Maverick House, six stories high, and covering an area of a third of an acre. A large portion of the Island is occupied by dwelling-houses, most of them wooden; but the streets which border on the water are used almost entirely for manufacturing or business purposes. There are two large iron-works, — the Boston Forge Works, on Maverick street, and the Atlantic Works, at the corner of Maverick and Border streets. Bardwell & Anderson's furniture manufactory, at Jeffries' Point, and the Boston Dyewood Company's establishment, on Border street, are both buildings of great size, where many men are kept busily at work the entire year.

Following the shore toward the north are the New England Pottery and the Glendon Company's planing-mill and lumber-yard, and at the eastern end of the Island — which is now designated as the Fourth Section — are located the extensive Maverick Oil Works.

There are scattered over the Island thirteen churches and ten public-school buildings, nearly all of which are ornamental structures; a Masonic building on Central square; and a club-house on Meridian street, recently built, and occupied by the Jeffries Winter Club. Three steam railroads cross East Boston, — the Boston & Albany, Boston & Maine, and the Revere Beach & Lynn; and the residents are accommodated by the West End Street Railway, which has run its tracks in three different directions, and which has two stables here, — one on Meridian street and one at Winthrop Junction. Besides the connection by the ferry-boats, the Island is joined to the mainland by three bridges, — two of which are open thoroughfares to Chelsea, while the third joins Winthrop to East Boston. Of these, the Meridian-street bridge is the most important, the horse-cars running across it, and an almost uninterrupted stream of vehicles and people going in both directions during day and evening. A place so closely built with wooden dwellings, and having so many mills and lumber-yards, would necessarily be visited by many fires; and this has certainly been the case in East Boston, although the record of extensive conflagrations seems very small when we note the nature of its industries, and the exposure of the Island to winds from every direction.

During the first five years that the Land Company had possession, only five fires are recorded, and none of those at all serious; yet feeling that the safety of the place demanded protection, a petition was presented to the Mayor and Aldermen, in 1835, asking that an engine be placed in their charge to be used in case of fire. The petition was met favorably, and in 1836 a brick engine-house was built on Paris street, and in it was placed an old engine, furnished by the city, and called "Governor Brooks, No. 11." At the first serious fire, this engine was proved to be unserviceable, and great dissatisfaction was manifested, both by the members of the engine company and by the citizens. Frequent meetings and discussions were held, and as the result, a new engine, called the "Maverick, No. 11," was placed in the house in 1839, — when also a new company was organized.

In 1842 another company was formed, and an engine called the "Old North" was located in a building on Saratoga street, near Central square. The increasing number of fires on the Island induced the citizens to petition for a third engine, on the volunteer plan, and this was granted, — the new company organizing under the name of "Protection, No. 4." At the same time a company was formed to take charge of the hook-and-ladder carriage.

In 1846 it was deemed necessary to appoint an assistant engineer, and Mr. Thomas French was selected, who held the office until the time of his death. In 1855 a new engine, called the "Dunbar 10," took the place of the "Old North," and another company, the Webster Engine Company, No. 13, was formed.

The first destructive fire which visited East Boston was on July 4, 1861, and was caused by a fire-cracker. A large fire was then in progress on Albany street, Boston proper, and the assistance could not be given which was needed. The fire started on Weeks' wharf, at the foot of Sumner street, and burnt an area of eleven acres. At this time was consumed the Sectional Dock, — one of the finest dry-docks in the country, — also numerous dwelling-houses, planing-mills, stores, mills, etc. At the very spot where the fire of 1861 was stopped, another conflagration originated on July 25, 1871, and swept over about the same amount of territory, destroying two churches, planing-mills, many stores, and dwelling-houses. Since that time there have been many large losses from fire, but although often under most unfavorable circumstances, they have always been confined to a small area; and it is noticeable that they usually extend only to mills and workshops, — very few dwelling-houses having been destroyed.

There have been many changes of apparatus since the early days of the volunteer force; and at the present time there are located in East Boston three steam fire-engines: Engine No. 5, on Marion street; Engine No. 9, on Paris street; Engine No. 11, on Sumner street; one Chemical Engine, No. 7, corner Saratoga and Byron streets; one Hose Carriage, No. 6, on Chelsea street; one Hook and Ladder Carriage, No. 2, on Sumner street. The engineers who have had charge of this district were: Thomas French, 1846–1848; Anson Ellms, 1848–1851; Nathaniel Seaver, 1851–1853; Joseph Dunbar, 1853 to present time; Joseph Barnes, 1869–1874.

District Chief JOSEPH DUNBAR has held the position of assistant engineer for a greater number of years than any other member of this department. He was born at Boston, Mass., July 20, 1824, and after leaving school learned the shipwright trade. His fire experience dates from January, 1839, when he became connected with the Franklin Engine Company No. 7, of the Charlestown department, in the capacity of torch-boy, and in the following year was chosen a member. He remained there until 1843, when he left the service and went to China, but returned to East Boston during 1848, and joined Engine Company No. 19, of East Boston, as a call-member, and during 1853 was promoted to the position he now holds.

In June, 1885, the Dunbar Engine Company was organized and named after him. Chief Dunbar was thrown from the hose carriage while going to Box 19, October 29, 1876, and had several ribs broken. He was also laid up for several weeks from the effects of smoke, etc., at the S.S. "Cephalonia" fire, September 26, 1883. He is a member of Temple Lodge of Masons.

ENGINE COMPANY NO. 5.

NAMES OF MEMBERS SINCE 1874.

GEORGE N. TUCKER, foreman; J. S. Battis, engineman; R. Gallagher, asst. engineman, promoted and tr. to Engine 32, March 17, 1884; Daniel Curtis, driver; L. P. Bailey, call-hoseman; Lewis Keen, call-hoseman, resigned June 12, 1889; J. C. Phillips, call-hoseman; J. F. Barber, call-hoseman, resigned 1876; F. C. Douglas, call-hoseman, tr. to Engine 4, 1875; C. P. Cottle, call-hoseman, pensioned 1887; J. E. Wharton, call-hoseman; A. Furnald, call-hoseman, joined 1875, resigned 1882; William H. Gay, asst. engineman, joined March 17, 1884; tr. January 1, 1886, to Engine 14; H. Blount, call-hoseman, joined 1876, died 1882; E. V. Blount, call-hoseman, joined 1882; T. L. Dunbar, call-hoseman, joined 1882.

PRESENT MEMBERSHIP.

Capt. GERSHOM SHERMAN (Fig. 1) was born at Marshfield, Mass., April 25, 1827. He came to Boston when sixteen years of age, where he learned the ship-calking trade. His fire experience dates from 1848, at which time he joined old North Engine Company No. 19. He was enrolled a member of this company during 1860, but was transferred to Engine Company 9, and appointed a permanent member during 1872. He was promoted to his present position during 1884.

Engineman JOSIAH BATTIS (Fig. 2) was born at Winthrop, Mass., November 14, 1834. He came to East Boston when but a child. Soon after learning the machinist trade he began his experience as a fireman, joining Hose Company No. 6 during November, 1856, which makes him one of the oldest members in the department. He remained there until January, 1857,

Engine Company No. 5. — Page 362.

when he was promoted assistant engineman, and assigned to Engine Company No. 8. January 1, 1857, he was transferred to Engine Company No. 9, and on August of the same year was promoted to his present position and assigned to this company. Mr. Battis is a member of the Eastern Star Lodge, I. O. O. F., and the Firemen's Charitable Association.

Assistant Engineman GEORGE W. BROWN (Fig. 3) is another old member of the department. He was born at Concord, N.H., August 12, 1836, and during 1858 came to this city and learned the mechanical engineer trade. April 2, 1860, he entered this department, at which time he was appointed a permanent driver of Engine Company No. 8. He remained there until December 16, 1862, when he was transferred to this company, in the same position. On June 6, 1866, he was promoted to assistant engineman, and assigned to Engine Company No. 11, and on October 1, 1872, was transferred to Engine Company 9. He served with that company until October 21, 1883, when he resigned. He remained out of the department until November 10, 1884, when he was appointed assistant engineer in Engine Company No. 14, where he remained until January 1, 1885, when he was transferred to this company. Mr. Brown is a member of Mt. Tabor Lodge of Masons, Legion of Honor, the Pilgrim Fathers, and the Firemen's Charitable Association.

DANIEL CARTER (Fig. 4), driver, was born at Brookfield, Nova Scotia, October 25, 1833. During 1849 he moved to Bath, Me., and from 1853 to 1857 was a member of Deluge Engine Company No. 3 of that town as a torch-boy. During 1857 he came to Boston, and was employed as a teamster. When the war broke out he enlisted in Company I, Forty-seventh Massachusetts Regiment, in September, 1862, and served until 1863 ; and in 1864 reinlisted in Company H, Sixth Massachusetts Regiment, in which he served until 1864. He entered this department September 1, 1863, as a call-member of Engine Company No. 7, and on June 6, 1866, was appointed a permanent member, and assigned to this company in his present position.

GEORGE A. TUCKER (Fig. 5) was born at Saulsbury, Mass., March 22, 1830, and came to this city when seventeen years of age. He learned the ship-carpenter's trade, and during 1849 entered this department as a member of Engine Company No. 19, on which he served about three years, when he was enrolled a member of Dunbar Engine Company No. 10, in which he was elected assistant foreman, and in 1853 was chosen foreman, which position he held until the disbandment of the hand department. September 1, 1860, he was appointed call-foreman of this company, and held that office until he was succeeded by the present permanent captain, November 1, 1884, since which time he has acted as senior call-hoseman.

J. G. PHILLIPS (Fig. 6) was born at Abington, Mass., August 13, 1837. He came to this city during 1840, and learned the shipwright's trade. He entered this department, during 1858, as a member of Dunbar Engine Company No. 10, on which he remained until disbanded, when he was appointed a call-substitute in this company, and remained such until 1870, at which time he was promoted a call-member. He is a member of the Firemen's Charitable Association.

LEWIS KEEN (Fig. 7) was born at Marshfield, Mass., June 19, 1835, and came to Boston during 1850, where he learned the ship-carpenter's trade. His fire experience dates from 1854, at which time he was admitted a member of Webster Engine Company No. 13, where he remained about one year. During 1858 he joined Dunbar Engine Company No. 10, and served until it disbanded. At the outbreak of the war he enlisted in unattached company, Seventh Mass. Regiment, on May, 1864, and was discharged in October. He became a member of this company during 1870. He is a member of Post 35, G. A. R.

JOHN S. WHARTON (Fig. 8) was born at Charlestown District, Boston, Mass., April 10, 1847, and is a calker by trade. He first began fire duty as a call-substitute in this company during 1870, and remained such until March, 1873, when he was appointed a call-member. During the war he served in Company F, Fourth Connecticut Regiment, from April 30, 1861, to July 25, 1863. He is a member of Amo Lodge 194, K. of H., and Post 35, G. A. R.

L. P. BAILEY (Fig. 9) was born at Alma, Me., October 28, 1845, and came to this city during 1866, where he learned the carpenter's trade. His fire experience dates from June 1, 1874, at which time he was admitted a member of this company. While at a fire in Chelsea, Mass., May 31, 1882, Mr. Bailey had his arm severely injured.

EUGENE V. BLOUNT (Fig. 10) was born at Nantucket, Mass., February 18, 1848, and during June, 1861, came to this city, where he learned the iron-moulder's trade. He entered this service during 1879 as a call-substitute in this company, and June 6, 1882, was made a call-member. He is a member of Amo Lodge 194, K. of H.

THOMAS L. DUNBAR was born at Rye, N.H., July 16, 1858, and came to Boston when very young, and has been employed as a clerk. His fire duties began during 1878, when he joined Engine Company No. 9, in which he remained until January 20, 1882, when he was enrolled a member of this company.

ENGINE COMPANY NO. 9.

NAMES OF MEMBERS SINCE 1874.

This company was organized during 1874 with the following: Gershom Sherman, foreman, tr. as captain, Engine No. 5, October 30, 1884; George W. Brown, engineman, resigned October 21, 1883; William Hall, Jr., assistant engineman; Albert Bailey, driver; Samuel L. Fowle, tr. to Engine No. 11, September, 1884; John W. Smith; William Clay (see record of Engine No. 25); Norman R. Smith, tr. and promoted to the permanent force, September, 1877; Thomas E. Simonds, tr. and pro-

Engine Company No. 9. — Page 366.

moted to Ladder No. 1, June, 1875; Charles F. Smith, no record; I. E. Wells, tr. and promoted to Ladder No. 1, August, 1874; Joseph Brown, appointed May, 1875, tr. to Ladder No. 2, September, 1884; Frank Allard, no record; James Downer, no record, discharged September, 1884.

Reorganized and made a permanent company September 3, 1884. Gershom Sherman, captain, tr. to Engine No. 5, November, 1884; Albert Bailey, driver, tr. to Chemical No. 7, September, 1886.

PRESENT MEMBERS.

Captain E. B. SMITH (Fig. 1) was born at Dorchester District, Boston, Mass., April 3, 1845. He enlisted in Co. H, Eighteenth Massachusetts Volunteers, August 24, 1861, and on January 1, 1864, reenlisted, and was wounded May 8 of the ensuing year. November 5, 1865, he was discharged. He enlisted in the State Militia, in Co. I, First Massachusetts Regiment, and was soon after promoted corporal. July 21, 1868, he was made second lieutenant, and on October 5, 1869, promoted to first lieutenant, and remained such until his discharge, September 5, 1870. After the war he learned the wood-carving trade. His first experience in the Fire Department dates from 1865, when he became a member of Fountain Company No. 1, of Dorchester, where he remained until the annexation of that town, when he was made a member of Ladder Company No. 6, and on January 1, 1871, was promoted foreman. May 11, 1874, he was transferred to Ladder Company No. 8, and was promoted assistant foreman of that company. He was promoted to his present position November 1, 1884, and assigned to this company. Captain Smith had a very narrow escape at the Rice & Kendall fire, with his brother, a member of Ladder Company No. 11, and ex-Captain Cummings; he got out of it with a badly sprained back and ankle. On July 1, 1883, he was laid up with a sprained knee for three weeks. He is a member of Post 68, G. A. R., Dorchester Lodge 168, I. O. O. F., Abenakis Tribe 46, Red Men, and the Firemen's Charitable Association, and honorary member National Lancers.

Engineman WILLIAM HALL (Fig. 2) was born at Marshfield, Mass., April 16, 1831. He came to Boston during 1846, and soon after learned the shipwright trade. On May 1, 1853, he first became connected with this department, joining Dunbar Engine Company No. 10, in which he was made steward, December, 1856, and remained in that position until April, 1858; then hose-man, until the company was disbanded, December 31, 1859. He joined Engine Company No. 5, as a call-man, on September 1, 1860; and on February 1, 1873, was promoted to assistant engineman, and transferred to Engine Company No. 9; and on October 21, 1883, was promoted to his present position. Mr. Hall is a member of Lodge 356 of the Iron Hall, and a life member of the Firemen's Charitable Association.

Assistant Engineman ISAAC B. NOBLE (Fig. 3) was born at Derby, England, October 18, 1848, and came to Boston during 1855, where he soon after learned the machinist business. On May 2, 1864, he enlisted in Ninth Co., Unattached Infantry, and served until August 11, 1864; and on September 5, 1864, he again enlisted, in Co. B, Sixty-first Massachusetts Regiment, and served until June 17, 1865. Taken prisoner December 14, 1864, at 9 P.M.. and escaped on the 15th at about 5 P.M., and returned to his regiment on the night of the 16th of December, 1864, being a prisoner twenty hours. (See Adjutant-General's Report, 1863.) He entered this service on February 15, 1882, as a substitute, and April 1 of the ensuing year he was appointed ladderman, and assigned to Ladder Company No. 8. On October 21, 1883, hewas promoted to his present position. Mr. Noble is a member of Post 23, G. A. R., and past commander; a member of Baalbec Lodge of Masons, John Alden Colony of Pilgrim Fathers, Maverick Association, R. S. G. F., Abenakis Tribe 46, Red Men, and Firemen's Charitable Association.

CHARLES P. SMITH (Fig. 4) was appointed a call-member of this company June 1, 1874, and on September 8, 1884, was promoted a permanent member.

THOMAS W. ADAMS (Fig. 5) was appointed on this department April 6, 1875, as a substitute in this company, and on September 8, 1884, was promoted a permanent member.

JOHN W. SMITH (Fig. 6) was born at Esther, Mass., February 17, 1839, and, when a child, came to this city, where he learned the house-painter's trade. He enlisted on September 3, 1861, in the navy, and served two years. On February 1, 1872, he entered this department as a call-man in this company, in which he was appointed a permanent member, September 3, 1884. Mr. Smith is a member of Post 35, G. A. R.

CORNELIUS H. LEARY (Fig. 7) was born at Boston, Mass., October 1, 1850. He is a calker by trade, to which he added the duties of fireman, July 7, 1874, when he was made a call-man in this company, and on September 3, 1884, was appointed a permanent member. Mr. Leary is a member of General McClennan Assembly 127 of R. S. G. F. and the Firemen's Charitable Association.

ROBERT A. RITCHIE (Fig. 8) was born in New York city, October 30, 1855, and came to this city during 1872 and learned the boat-builder's trade. He became connected with this department during 1883 as a call substitute in Engine Company No. 11, in which he remained until September 3, 1884, when he was appointed a permanent member of this company. Mr. Ritchie is a member of General McClennan Assembly 127, R. S. G. F., Abenakis Tribe 46, Red Men, and Firemen's Charitable Association.

WILLIAM J. KILLION (Fig. 9) was born at Roxbury District, Boston, Mass., February 10, 1859, and, after leaving school, learned the wool business. He was appointed on this department February 16, 1888, and detailed to this company as permanent substitute.

C. F. CURRAN (Fig. 10) was born at East Boston, Mass., May 14, 1858.

ENGINE COMPANY No. 11. — Page 370.

He is a harness-maker by trade, at which he was employed until February 23, 1883, at which time he entered this department as a member of Engine Company No. 25, as a permanent member, in which he served until September 27, 1886, when he was transferred to this company. Mr. Curran is detailed in the harness and repair shop of this department.

D. J. HEDRINGTON (Fig. 11) was born at East Boston, Mass., December 11, 1859. He was employed as a teamster until appointment in this service, September 13, 1888, and detailed to this company as a permanent substitute.

ENGINE COMPANY NO. 11.

NAMES OF MEMBERS SINCE 1874.

ALANSON C. KEEN, call-foreman, joined company January 1, 1886, resigned 1883, since died; Joseph Sherman, joined department January 1, 1886; Henry R. Demary, joined April 10, 1868, ap. supt. of repair-shop; Charles E. Nutter, joined July 20, 1869; David L. Adamson, joined February 20, 1870, clerk at headquarters; Clarence O. Poland, permanent foreman, joined August 8, 1882, tr. January 1, 1884; captain Engine Company No. 25; James E. Burg, tr. Hose Company No. 6; Samuel L. Fowle, joined company, 1884.

PRESENT MEMBERS.

Captain GEORGE W. WARREN (Fig. 1) first saw the light at Portsmouth, N.H., February 26, 1831, and on June 1, 1852, came to this city and learned the carpenter's trade. On November 1, 1854, he became connected with this department, at which time he was admitted a call-member of Franklin Ladder Company No. 3, in which he remained until February, 1859, when he left the department, but returned again in September, 1872, to the same company. He was promoted to the position of captain, February 1, 1875, and assigned to Engine Company No. 10, and on January 1, 1881, was transferred to this company. Captain Warren had his arm broken at a fire on Tremont street, July 5, 1856. His brother, Charles T. Warren, of Ladder Company No. 3, was killed at a fire in Barber alley, July 29, 1856. Captain Warren is a member of the Boston Veterans and the Firemen's Charitable Association.

Engineman WALTER H. STURTEVANT (Fig. 2) was born at Dexter, Me., November 27, 1830, and during 1848 came to this city and learned the machinist trade. He began fire duty during the spring of 1853, and was made a member of Dunbar Engine Company No. 10, in which he remained until steam was introduced. November 17, 1863, he was promoted to assistant engineman, and assigned to Engine Company No. 5, in which he remained until January 1, 1866, when he was promoted to his present position and assigned to this company. Mr. Sturtevant had two fingers of his left hand taken off by the engine during 1869, and the third finger of the right hand frozen, so as to lose the use of it, at the Wareham-street fire. He is a member of Maverick Council Royal Arcanum, and a charter member of the Iron Hall; also a member of the Boston Veterans and the Firemen's Charitable Association.

Assistant Engineman GEORGE L. INBERT (Fig. 3) was born at Nantucket, Mass., January 10, 1833. He came to Boston during December, 1856, and was employed at the express business. His fire experience dates from June 1, 1857, when he joined Mellville Engine Company No. 6, in which he remained until September, when he was appointed a member of Extinguisher No. 5, in which he served until 1858, when he was transferred to Tremont Engine Company No. 12. When it was disbanded he joined Engine Company No. 7, as a member, July 1, 1860, and during 1864 was promoted to call-foreman, which position he held until January 1, 1866, when he was assigned a driver of this company, at his own request, and January 1, 1873, was promoted to his present position. Mr. Inbert has met with several very serious accidents. At a fire at the Eastern depot he had his left eye tore out by a stream from the hose. He was thrown from the engine on Blackstone street, and badly injured his back. During 1867 he was buried by a falling wall, at a fire on Border street, East Boston, and badly hurt; and on the night of June 17, 1884, was almost killed at Whidden's wharf fire, when he tripped over a rope and fell over the wharf on to a float, a distance of eighteen feet; when found he was nearly drowned, besides having four ribs broken and other injuries, which laid him up four months. He is a member of King Philip's Lodge 33, K. of P., and the Boston Veterans and Firemen's Charitable Association.

JOHN BICKFORD (Fig. 4), driver, was born at Boston, Mass., February 12, 1851. After leaving school he worked at the express business until his appointment on this department, which occurred January 1, 1873, when he was made a permanent member and assigned to this company as driver. Mr. Bickford is a member of Thorndike Council 262 of United Friends and the Firemen's Charitable Association.

WILLIAM BAKER (Fig. 5) was born at Exeter, England, January 9, 1838. He is a harness-maker by trade, he being now engaged in that business at East Boston. He entered this department January 1, 1866, as a call-member of this company. Mr. Baker was injured at a fire on the corner of Hanover and Blackstone streets, February 27, 1873.

LEONARD F. MERRILL (Fig. 6) was born at Falmouth, Me., October 20, 1838, and came to this city during 1859, when he learned the calker's trade. He was appointed a call-member of this company, August 5, 1869.

JOSIAH M. NOTTAGE (Fig. 7) was born at Boston, September 22, 1838, and is a cabinet-maker and upholsterer by trade, which business he carries on at East Boston. He became connected with this department, June 6, 1873, as a call-member of this company. Mr. Nottage froze his feet at the Clinton-street fire.

HERBERT N. KEEN (Fig. 8) was born at East Boston, Mass., June 13,

1848. He is employed in the grocery business. June 13, 1873, he was admitted a call-substitute in this company, in which he was promoted a call member, May, 1875. Mr. Keen is a member of the Boston Veterans and the Firemen's Charitable Association.

WILLIAM E. STAPLES (Fig. 9) was born at Newburyport, Mass., September 22, 1852. He is a carpenter by trade, to which he added the duties of fireman, June 9, 1880, as a call-member of this company.

HENRY WOODBURY (Fig. 10) was born at Swampscott, Mass., August 3, 1862. He learned the calker's trade, and on December 21, 1883, was appointed a call-man in this company.

LADDER COMPANY NO. 2.

NAMES OF MEMBERS SINCE 1874.

ALDEN S. TURNER, ap. June 1, 1857, discharged November 7, 1887; David H. Jones, ap. October 1, 1858, discharged May 31, 1882; James W. Seavey, ap. July 1, 1851, discharged February 26, 1881; George W. Fowle, ap. March 1, 1874, discharged November 16, 1878; Thomas W. Conway, ap. November 21, 1878, tr. October 21, 1881; Benjamin D. Hill, ap. March 1, 1875, tr. November 1, 1877; Edward A. Cook, ap. October 2, 1882, discharged June 11, 1887; Charles H. Colburn, ap. June 1, 1874, deceased December 25, 1888; Thomas E. Simonds, ap. October 21, 1881, tr. June 25, 1887; George H. Stinson, ap. June 25, 1887, tr. April 19, 1889; Joseph Nolan, ap. June 6, 1882, tr. February 25, 1886; Charles E. Simmons, ap. June 1, 1874, discharged August 20, 1882; John Otis Taber, ap. February 16, 1888, tr. July 2, 1888; John E. F. Griffin, ap. April 19, 1889, tr. April 23, 1889; William F. Hayes, ap. November 1, 1865, in service; George A. Brown, ap. May 1, 1863; John H. Elliott, ap. October 1, 1858; Richard S. Keen, ap. May 1, 1859; Charles W. Morse, ap. June 1, 1874; Sylvanus Currant, ap. July 12, 1874; William F. Seaver, ap. June 1, 1875; John H. Crafts, ap. August 4, 1874; Martin Moore, ap. June 1, 1874; Robert J. Bartlett, ap. June 1, 1874; George David Vinal Smith, ap. August 4, 1874; Thomas H. Pike, ap. June 20, 1876; Alexander Saunders, ap. March 5, 1881; Fred W. Battis, ap. March 1, 1886; Joseph H. Brown, ap. September 3, 1884.

PRESENT MEMBERS.

The well-known features of Captain JOHN H. ELLIOTT will be readily recognized in Figure 1, on page 375. He was born at Ware, N.H., September 6, 1837, and soon after came to Boston. After leaving school he learned the calker's trade, and during 1858 began fire duty, when he joined this company as a call-member, and remained such until June 27, 1887, when he was promoted to the position of call-foreman. On December 26, 1883, he was appointed to his present position. Captain Elliott is a member of the Boston Veterans, and a life member of the Firemen's Charitable Association.

George H. Stinson (Fig. 2), driver, was born at Rockport, Me., May 7, 1855, and came to this city when but a child. He was employed as a teamster up to the time of his appointment in this department, which occurred in June, 1881, when he was made a substitute, and assigned to Engine Company No. 26, as driver. He was appointed a permanent member during October, and assigned to Engine Company No. 25, where he remained until June 22, 1887, at which time he was transferred to this company. Mr. Stimson was thrown from the truck while going to a fire during February 15, 1887, and very seriously injured about the head and back.

William F. Hayes (Fig. 3) was born at Limerick. Me., December 10, 1831, and when but a child came to this city, where he learned the house-painting trade. He enlisted in Company E, Forty-first Massachusetts Regiment and Third Cavalry, on August 22, 1862, and served until May 20, 1865. His fire experience dates from November 1. 1851, when he entered this department, as a member of this company. Mr. Hayes is a member of Post 159, G. A. R.

Richard S. Keene (Fig. 4) was born at Boston, Mass., December 1, 1833. He is a shipwright by occupation. At an early age he began his fire experience as a member of Webster Engine Company No. 13, where he served until 1859, when he joined this company. Mr. Keene had his left foot broken at the box-factory fire in East Boston, from which he was laid up five weeks.

Joseph H. Brown (Fig. 5) was born at Waterborough, Me., April 10, 1849, and when but a child came to this city, where he learned the barber's trade, at which he is now employed. He entered this service on April 6, 1874, as a call-man in Engine Company No. 9, in which he remained until September 3, 1888, when he was transferred to this company as a call-member. Mr. Brown is a member of the Firemen's Charitable Association.

Robert J. Bartlett (Fig. 6) was born at Mt. Desert, Me., September 5, 1850, and came to this city when but a child, and after leaving school entered the grocery business. He became connected with this department November 1, 1872, as a call-substitute in this company, and during June, 1874, was appointed a member. Mr. Bartlett had his feet severely burned while on the ladder at the Summer-street fire, April 26, 1888. He is a member of the Firemen's Charitable Association.

Martin Moore (Fig. 7) was born at Portsmouth. N.H., July 24, 1847, and came to this city during April, 1867, where he learned the file-cutter's trade. During the war he enlisted in Company K. Thirteenth New Hampshire Regiment, serving from August, 1862, to July, 1865, he being one of the first Union soldiers to enter Richmond on April 3, 1865. He has done fire duty from May 30, 1873, at which time he was appointed a member of this company. Mr. Moore was injured at the fire on board the steamship "Cephalonia," September 26, 1883, also at a fire in Orleans street, March 8, 1878.

Thomas H. Pike (Fig. 8) first saw the light at Roxbury District, Bos-

Ladder Company No. 2. — Page 375.

ton, Mass., December 21, 1838. He is a mast and spar maker by occupation. When the war broke out he enlisted in Company T, Thirty-second Massachusetts Regiment, on August 13, 1862, and served three years, during which time he was twice badly wounded. He entered this service during 1860 as a member of Hancock Engine Company No. 1, of Charlestown, in which he remained until 1861, when he joined Red Jacket Hose Company, and served until he enlisted in the war. On his return he joined Massachusetts Ladder Company, in which he served as foreman for two years. He left the department soon after, but rejoined this company as a call-member during 1876. Mr. Pike is a member of Geo. L. Stevens Post 159, G. A. R., and the Charlestown Veterans.

WILLIAM F. SEAVER (Fig. 9) was born at East Boston, August 15, 1845. He is a calker by trade, and, when a youth, became connected with this company as a torch-boy. He was appointed a substitute during 1861, and on June 1, 1874, was made a member. Mr. Seaver is a member of the Boston Veterans, Joseph Webb Lodge of Masons, Signet Chapter, Scottish Rights, and the Pilgrim Fathers. He was injured at the fire on the steamer " Cephalonia," September 26, 1883.

GEORGE D. V. SMITH (Fig. 10) was born at Boston, Mass., September 8, 1836. His trade is that of a calker, to which he added the duties of a fireman during 1854, at which time he became connected with Webster Engine Company No. 13, as a substitute, where he remained eighteen months. He joined this company as a call-member on August 3, 1874. Mr. Smith is a member of the Boston Veterans.

JOHN H. CRAFTS (Fig. 11) was born at Boston, Mass., April 7, 1836. He is a calker by trade. When the war broke out he enlisted in Company K, Twenty-ninth Massachusetts Regiment, on April 18, 1861, and served three years. His fire experience dates from 1850, when he joined the Salem, Mass., department, in Reliance Engine Company No. 1 and Constitution Engine Company 9, in which he served two years. During 1854 he entered this department, in Webster Engine Company No. 13, as a call-substitute. In August, 1874, he joined this company as a call-member. Mr. Crafts is a member of Post 23, G. A. R., and Maverick Council, Good Fellows.

CHARLES W. MORSE (Fig. 12) was born at Portland, Me., August 21, 1846. He is an upholsterer by trade. On July 21, 1864, he enlisted in Company C, Forty-second Massachusetts Regiment, and served until the close of the war. He entered this department on June 1, 1873, as a call-member of this company. Mr. Morse is a member of Post 23, G. A. R.

GEORGE A. BROWN (Fig. 13) was born at Belfast, Me., January 2, 1833. He came to Boston during 1856, and worked at his trade as ship-joiner. He became connected with this department during 1859, as a call-substitute in Dunbar Engine Company No. 10, where he served until 1860. He then left the service until 1868, when he was appointed a member of this company. Mr. Brown is a member of the Firemen's Charitable Association.

WILLIAM B. GARDNER (Fig. 14) was born at Medford, Mass., October 18, 1837. He came to this city during 1852, and learned the calker's trade. He has been doing fire duty about fifteen years in various companies, and during 1884 joined this company as a call-substitute.

ALEXANDER SAUNDERS, call-ladderman, was born at Boston, Mass., March 2, 1851. He is a calker by trade. March 5, 1881, became a member of this company.

FRED S. PETERS (Fig. 15) was born at East Boston. After leaving school he engaged in the mercantile business, and in 1883 was appointed a call-substitute in this company.

CHARLES H. COLBURN, call-ladderman, was born at Blue Hill, Me., April 24, 1836. He came to Boston during 1840, where he learned the plumber's trade. His fire experience dates from 1854, when he became connected with Webster Engine Company No. 13 as a call-substitute, from which he went to Maverick Engine Company No. 9, where he remained a short time, when he left the service. He returned again, during June, 1874, and became a member of this company. He had his knee-pan broke at a fire at the Eastern Railroad wharf, February 12, 1876. Mr. Colburn died December 20, 1888.

HOSE COMPANY NO. 6.

NAMES OF MEMBERS SINCE 1874.

Porter E. Chase, call-member, no record, promoted to Ladder Company No. 8; Albert R. Johnson, call-member, no record, resigned April 26, 1881, promoted to permanent substitute; John L. Jemerson, call-member. no record, resigned April 21, 1883; Charles Brooks, permanent member, ap. 1871, resigned March, 1878, deceased; Charles H. Brooks, permanent member, March, 1878, resigned June 1, 1880; Albert Bailey, permanent member. May 1, 1865, pensioned April 15, 1888.

PRESENT MEMBERS.

Capt. JOHN H. WESTON (Fig. 1) is one of the oldest call-captains in the department. He was born at Salem, Mass., November 14, 1831. He joined Rapid Engine Company 2 of that city when a boy, where he served two years. He soon after came to this city and learned the calker's trade, and on December 28, 1856, entered this service as a member of this company, then called Hydrant Hose Company 6. When the war broke out he enlisted in the Third Massachusetts Cavalry as second lieutenant. on July, 1863, and served fifteen months, when he was discharged for disability. On April 1, 1869, he was elected foreman of this company, and has held that position ever since. Captain Weston was injured at the Young's fire, August 19, 1887. He is commander of Post 23, G. A. R., and a member of the Firemen's Charitable Association.

GEORGE B. ATWOOD (Fig. 2), driver, was born at Boston, Mass., February 22, 1851. He was employed in mercantile business, and in January,

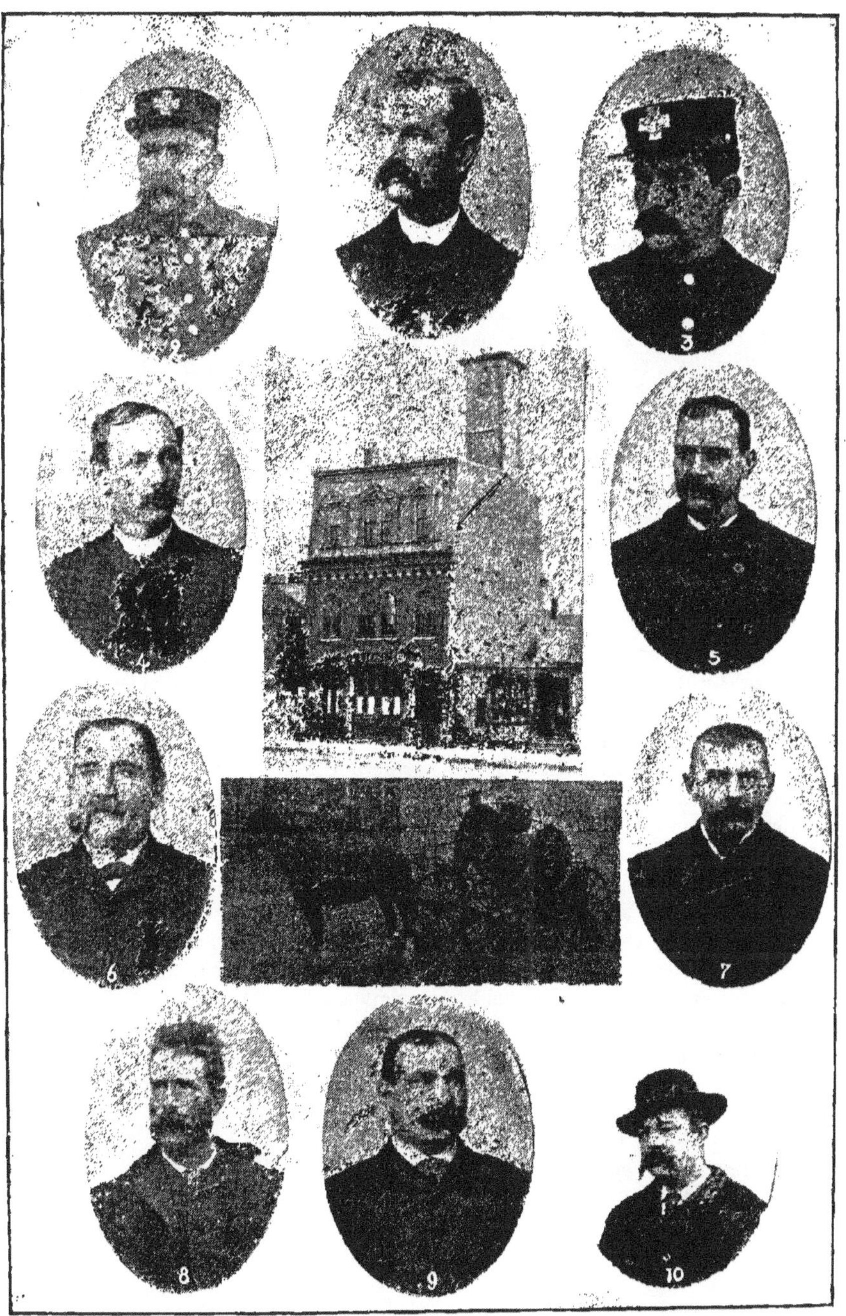

HOSE COMPANY No. 6. — Page 380.

1875, became connected with this department as a call-substitute on Engine Company No. 11, and on June 23, 1877, was promoted a call-member, where he remained until June 1, 1880, when he was appointed a permanent member and assigned to this company. Mr. Atwood is a member of Maverick Council No. 169, Royal Arcanum, the Boston Veterans, and Firemen's Charitable Association.

JAMES E. BURG (Fig. 3) entered this department April 5, 1878, as a substitute in Engine Company No. 11, and was promoted a permanent member and assigned to Engine Company No. 4, October 8, 1886. April 13, 1888, he was transferred to this company.

IRVING W. CAMPBELL (Fig. 4) was born at Watertown, Mass., November 16, 1845, and during 1863 came to this city. He enlisted in Company E, Third Massachusetts Cavalry, on January 5, 1864, and served until October 8, 1865. He was wounded at Winchester, Va., September 19, 1864, after which he learned the house-painter trade. On June 11, 1869, he entered this department, joining this company as a member. Mr. Campbell is a member of Post 23, G. A. R., and the Firemen's Charitable Association.

EDWARD A. MISENER (Fig. 5) was born at Halifax, N.S., January 24, 1842, and during 1849 he came to this city, where he learned the paper-hanging trade. He enlisted in Company B, First Massachusetts Infantry, July, 1862, and served until May, 1864. During 1868 he entered this service as a call-substitute in this company, and on December 1, 1872, was appointed a call-member. Mr. Misener is a member of Post 23, G. A. R., and Firemen's Charitable Association.

GEORGE S. SMITH, Jr. (Fig. 6), was born at Boston, Mass., January 26, 1842. He is a mast and spar maker by trade. His fire experience dates from 1872, when he became a call-substitute in this company, and in the following June was appointed a call-member.

G. W. W. PEARSON (Fig. 7) was born at Portsmouth, Mass., December 29, 1849. He is a merchant by occupation, to which he added the duties of a fireman, during 1872, as a call-substitute in this company, and on June 1, 1874, was admitted a call-member. Mr. Pearson is a member of Boston Veterans and Firemen's Charitable Association.

JOHN H. WHEELER (Fig. 8) was born at Portland, Me., June 27, 1852, and when but a child came to this city, where he learned the calker's trade. He became connected with this department as a call-member of this company on October 10, 1875.

E. D. LOCKE (Fig. 9) was born at Burlington, Mass., January 28, 1856, and came to this city during 1873, where he learned the spar-making trade. His fire experience dates from April 21, 1883, when he was admitted as call-member of this company. Mr. Locke is a member of the Firemen's Charitable Association.

WILLIAM H. MISENER (Fig. 10) was born at Halifax, N.S., August 28, 1848, and came to this city during 1875, where he learned the paper-hanging trade.   He entered the department as a call-man in this company April 26, 1881.

CHEMICAL ENGINE COMPANY NO. 7.

NAMES OF MEMBERS SINCE SEPTEMBER 27, 1886.

Albert Bayley, ap. September 27, 1886. tr. Hose No. 6, June 24, 1887; T. E. Simonds, ap. June 25, 1887; died February 15, 1889.

PRESENT MEMBERS.

Lieutenant JOHN W. GODBOLD (Fig. 1) was born at East Boston, Mass., April 3, 1856.   After leaving school he learned the ship-carpenter's trade, at which he was employed until his appointment in this department as a permanent substitute, June 21, 1881.   After serving in that capacity in several companies, he was promoted a permanent member on October 27 of the ensuing year, and assigned to Ladder Company No. 3, where he remained until September 22, 1886, at which time Chemical Engine Company No. 7 was organized, and he was placed in charge.   Lieutenant Godbold had his arm poisoned at the Smith Organ factory fire, January 24, 1883, from which he was laid up two weeks.   He is a member of the Firemen's Charitable Association.

JOSEPH NOLAN (Fig. 2) was born at Boston, Mass., October 1, 1850.   He learned the calker's trade, and on March, 1881, was appointed a call-substitute on Ladder 2, and on June 6, the year following, was made a call-man. He served in this company until February 25, 1886, when he was promoted a permanent member, and assigned to Engine 26, where he remained until March 2, 1888, when he was transferred to this company.

WARREN R. SMITH (Fig. 3) was born at Portsmouth, N.H., July 6, 1852. He came to this city when but a boy, and learned the machinist trade.   During 1873 he began fire duty as a call-substitute on Engine Company No. 9, and on June 1, 1874, was promoted a call-member.   December 4, 1877, he was appointed a permanent member, and assigned to Engine Company No. 7; and on March 17, 1877, was transferred to Engine Company 26.   On January 1, 1879, he was promoted assistant engineman, and assigned to Engine Company No. 14, from which he was transferred to Engine Company No. 20, in which he remained until February 20, 1886, when he was transferred to Engine Company No. 15; and on September 27, 1886, he was transferred to this company in his present position.   Mr. Smith is a member of Temple Lodge of Masons.

CHEMICAL ENGINE COMPANY No. 7. — Page 383.

CHAPTER VI.

DISTRICT 2. — CHARLESTOWN.

THE conflagration which attended the battle of Bunker Hill reduced the town of Charlestown to ashes, and the inhabitants from affluence to poverty; and it was not until after the evacuation of Boston, in March, 1776, that a portion of the former inhabitants began to return and to repair their waste places. The British "Annual Register" for 1775 observed that Charlestown was large, handsome, and well built, both in respect to its public and private edifices. It contained about four hundred houses, and had the greatest trade of any port in the province except Boston.

Dr. Josiah Bartlett, in his "Historical Sketch of Charlestown," says concerning the rebuilding of the town: "A few . . . were able to erect convenient dwellings, whilst others, like their hardy predecessors, were only covered with temporary shelter. . . . The principal streets were widened, straightened, and improved, and the market square was regularly laid out soon after the opening of the town, in 1776, to facilitate which a lottery was granted, and the State taxes were remitted for seven years. The first dwelling erected after the destruction of the town, June 17, 1775, was the Edes house, on Main street, which is now standing. In 1783 the roadway over Bunker Hill was opened. During 1785 an act was obtained by Charles Russell, Esq., and others, to build a bridge across Charles river, where the ferry was then established. This bridge was completed in 1786, and opened June 17. It was one thousand five hundred and three feet long and forty-three feet wide. In March, 1828, an act creating the Warren Bridge Corporation was passed by the Legislature ordering the corporation to erect another bridge; but this measure was strongly opposed by the Charles River Bridge Corporation, who carried the matter before the Supreme Court of the United States. The decision of that tribunal, however, was against them. The new bridge was toll free to foot-passengers."

The Middlesex canal, one terminus of which was in this town, at the Neck, was chartered in 1793. The roadway was completed in the summer of 1794, and the canal was navigable in 1803. In 1856, Boston avenue, now known as Warren avenue, was laid out. The same year the Charlestown Wharf Company and the Charlestown Branch Railroad were incorporated. The former was authorized to hold the water front from the Navy Yard to Lynde's Point. The Fitchburg Railroad Company, chartered in 1842, succeeded to the Branch Railroad, and acquired much of the Wharf Company's property. The Middlesex Horse Railroad Company was incorporated April 19, 1854.

In 1800 the national government established a naval station in the town. This marked an epoch in its history. The ruin and desolation caused by the war had given place to prosperity, and the town had assumed the aspect of an enterprising and successful community. The public buildings had been rebuilt, the streets improved, and the principal ones furnished (1795) with sign-boards. But it was not until 1826 that the streets generally were named and the numbering of the houses begun. The churches and schools were reëstablished on firm foundations, and were in a flourishing condition; the Fire Department was well organized and well regulated; and the finances, which had occasioned much solicitude, were in a satisfactory condition. An act incorporating the Bunker Hill Monument Association was passed June 7, 1823, and Gen. John Brooks was chosen its first president, June 17. Plans were soon matured to raise the funds necessary to buy the site of the battle-field on Breed's hill (which had been secured by Dr. John C. Warren), and to build the monument. On the fiftieth anniversary of the battle the corner-stone of the obelisk was laid, with Masonic ceremonies, in the presence of Lafayette, and an oration pronounced by Mr. Webster, who was also the orator at the completion of the monument, in 1843. This obelisk is about two hundred and twenty feet high. The architect was Solomon Willard. Recently a marble statue of Gen. Joseph Warren, and one in bronze of Col. William Prescott, have been placed in the grounds.

In 1804–5 the State Prison was built at Lynde's Point. Later on this institution was removed to Concord, and the building used as a city jail. Lamps in the streets were first lighted during August, 1815. October 6, 1818, the McLean Asylum for the Insane was opened; June 18, 1825, the Bunker-hill Bank was chartered; and February 21, 1829, the Warren Institution for Savings was incorporated. Lyceum Hall was incorporated March 4, 1831. This year the first Charlestown Directory appeared.

In 1824 the project of establishing as a separate town all that part of Charlestown which lay "without the Neck" was first considered in town-meeting. January 26, 1842, the town voted to accede to the petition of Guy C. Hawkins and others, to set off as the town (now city) of Somerville. The act incorporating the new town was passed March 3. April 22 following, Charlestown was newly divided into six wards.

January 5, 1846, the town considered a petition of the Hon. Henry P. Fairbanks and others, that application be made to the General Court for a city charter. November 9, 1846, the selectmen were authorized, by a vote of 798 to 774, to petition for a charter. One was granted February 22, 1847, and accepted by the town March 10, — the vote standing 1,127 in favor of the act, and 868 against it. March 20, the town was divided into three wards, as provided in the charter. April 19, upon a second trial, Mr. George C. Warren was elected Mayor. The Public Library was established, by a city ordinance passed June 5, 1860. The library was opened January 7, 1862.

The Mystic Water-Works were constructed under a legislative act

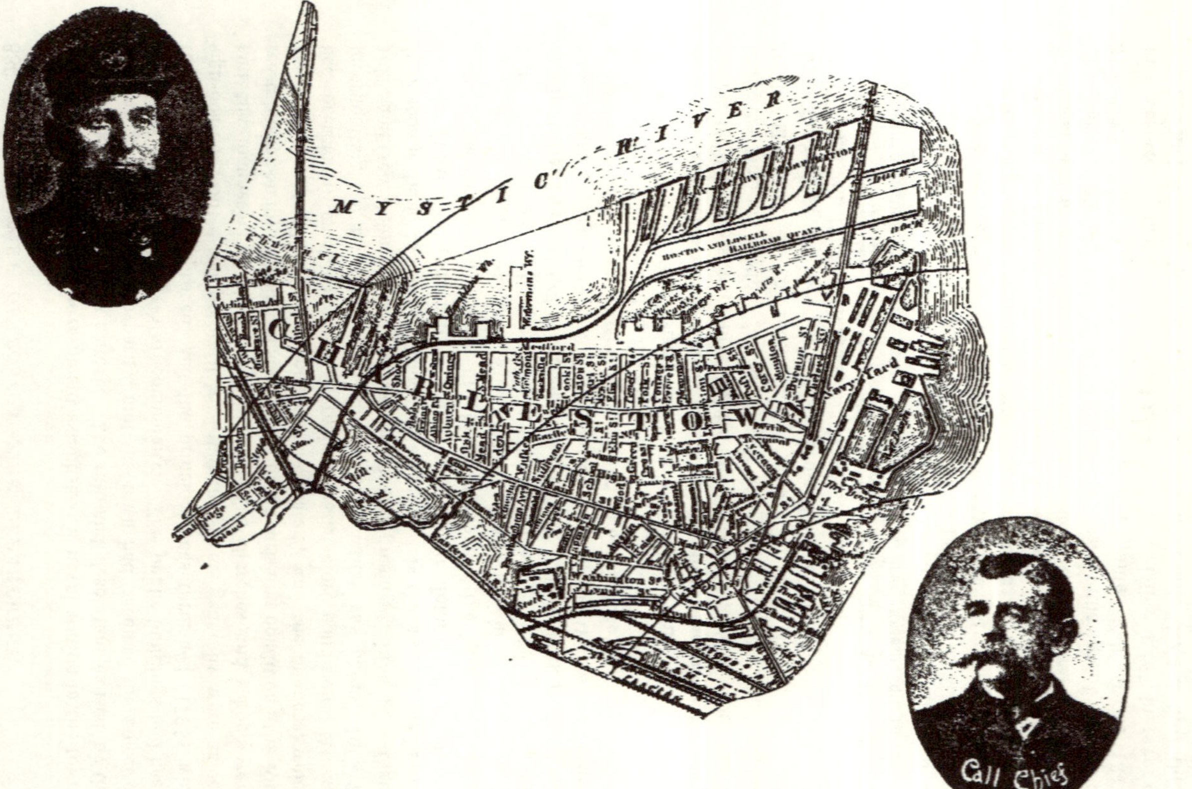

CHIEF BARTLETT AND CALL-CHIEF DELANO AND MAP OF DISTRICT No. 2.— Page 387.

passed in March, 1861, which was accepted by the people September 10. September 21, 1862, work was begun on the reservoir on Walnut Hill, Somerville. The water was formally introduced into the city, with imposing ceremonies, November 29, 1864. The Mystic Water Board was created the next year, 1865, and continued to manage the water department until it was merged with the Cochituate Water-Works in the Boston Water Board. The Winchester House for Aged Women was founded by Mrs. Nancy (Phipps) Winchester, October 3, 1865

The annexation of Charlestown to Boston was brought before the former city, on petition of Oliver Holden and others, as early as November 14, 1836, when the matter was "indefinitely postponed." At a town-meeting held January 28, 1845, a preamble and resolution opposing the scheme, which had been received, was presented by Mr. Richard Frothingham, Jr., and adopted. April 29, 1854, an act to unite the two cities was passed by the Legislature, and accepted by the people ; but it was set aside on account of a flaw in its provisions. The measure was again agitated in 1860 and in 1870. On May 14, 1873, another act was passed. It was accepted by both cities on the first Tuesday in October ; and on the first Monday in January, 1874, Charlestown became a part of the city of Boston. Charlestown at this time contained about thirty thousand inhabitants, and covered an area of five hundred and eighty-six square acres.

The Charlestown Veteran Volunteer Firemen's Association was organized at Monument Hall, Charlestown, June 23, 1884. The gentlemen who have served as officers from its organization to the present time are as follows : Presidents, 1884 to 1888, Messrs. George O. Wiley ; 1888 to 1889, Charles Field ; 1889, Henry W. Woodbury. Recording secretaries, 1884 to 1886, Thomas P. Smith ; 1886 to 1887, H. W. Woodbury ; 1887 to 1889, B. McNellis. Financial secretaries, 1884 to 1886, Joseph H. Bryant ; 1886 to 1889, Joseph F. King. Treasurers, 1884 to 1888, J. J. McCarthy ; 1889, Tobias Beck.

It was not until 1724 that the town purchased its first fire-engine. On the 18th of May £30 was appropriated for this purpose. In 1735 a second engine was paid for at a cost to the town of £117 2s. 2d. November 8, 1743, the Ancient Fire Society was formed. In 1758 their three engines were manned by twenty-four men, who were employed by the selectmen. In 1760 the town voted to build an engine-house in the green before Cape Breton Tavern, which at that time was kept by Zachariah Symmes, and stood at the junction of what is now Main and Essex streets. The site of the tavern is now occupied by Samuel D. Sawin, as a grocery. April 8, 1773, the "Massachusetts Spy," in describing a fire in Boston, mentions that the engine from Charlestown, which rendered assistance, was esteemed the best in America. The names of the engineers and company officers since 1847 — at which time a systematic record of the roll of members was first kept — are as follows : —

1846.

Engineers. — Joseph F. Boyd, chief ; Ames Drake, 1st asst. ; Thomas J. Elliott, 2d asst. ; Henry Conn, 3d asst. ; James M. Gardner, 4th asst.

Hancock Engine Company No. 1. — Stephen L. Kelley, foreman ; John A. Foley, 1st asst. ; George Hamlin, 2d asst. ; Joseph T. Walker, clerk.

Bunker Hill Engine Company No. 2. — John Howard, foreman ; John C. Tenney, 1st asst. ; Joseph Swan, 2d asst. ; Francis C. Savage, clerk.

Howard Engine Company No. 3. — Jesse Gay, foreman ; William H. Caswell, 1st asst. ; Lewis Wheeler, 2d asst. ; J. C. Deland, clerk.

Warren Engine Company No. 4. — James C. Poor, foreman ; James Caswell, 1st asst. ; Bernard Cooley, 2d asst. ; Isaac B. Trask, clerk.

Washington Engine Company No. 5. — Samuel F. Tilden, foreman ; Barker Bailey, 1st asst. ; Franklin Gardner, 2d asst. ; Charles Sanderson, clerk.

Franklin Engine Company No. 7. — Henry P. Gardner, foreman ; F. J. Almeder, 1st asst. ; Marshall A. Page, 2d asst. ; Martin Burkess, clerk.

Harvard Hook and Ladder Company. — H. W. McFarland, foreman ; Rufus K. Clark, asst. ; Kendall Bailey, clerk.

Hose Company No. 1. — William T. Bryant, foreman ; C. M. Bryant, clerk.

1847.

Engineers. — Joseph F. Boyd, chief ; Ames Drake, 1st asst. ; Stephen P. Kelley, 2d asst. ; Henry Conn, 3d asst. ; James M. Gardner, 4th asst.

Hancock Engine Company No. 1. — David S. Tucker, foreman ; Nathaniel S. Paine, 1st asst. ; Isaac S. Trask, clerk.

Bunker Hill Engine Company No. 2. — John Howard, foreman ; Joseph Swan, 1st asst. ; Francis C. Savage, 2d asst. ; Lyman O. Chase, clerk.

Howard Engine Company No. 3. — Thomas Barker, foreman ; Forbes Oakman, 1st asst. ; James B. Hatch, 2d asst. ; Lorenzo Garey, clerk.

Warren Engine Company No. 4. — James C. Poor, foreman ; Joseph Hayden, 1st asst. ; Charles T. Frost, 2d asst. ; Royal K. Monroe, clerk.

Washington Engine Company No. 5. — Samuel F. Tilden, foreman ; Franklin Gardner, 1st asst. ; Samuel Buckley, 2d asst. ; Charles Sanderson, clerk.

. *Franklin Engine Company No. 7.* — Henry P. Gardner, foreman ; F. J. Almeder, 1st asst. ; Marshall W. Page, 2d asst. ; Martin Burkess, clerk.

Harvard Hook and Ladder Company No. 1. — Isaac Kendall, foreman ; S. P. Hill, 1st asst. ; Peter Johnson, 2d asst. ; Augustus Whittemore, clerk.

Hose Company No. 1. — E. W. Brackett.

1848.

Engineers. — Henry Conn, chief ; Stephen P. Kelley, 1st asst. ; James M. Gardner, 2d asst. ; Isaac Cook, 3d asst. ; Robert Todd, 4th asst.

Hancock Engine Company No. 1. — David S. Tucker, foreman ; Isaac B. Trask, 1st asst. ; Enos Varney, 2d asst. ; Thomas Mason, clerk.

Bunker Hill Engine Company No. 2. — John Howard, foreman; Joseph Swan, 1st asst.; John C. Tenney, 2d asst.; F. O. Savage, clerk.

Howard Engine Company No. 3. — Jesse Gay, William C. Caswell, Lewis S. Wheeler, George W. Hammond.

Warren Engine Company No. 4. — James C. Poor, foreman; Joseph Hayden, 1st asst.; Charles T. Frost, 2d asst.; John W. Devereaux, clerk.

Washington Engine Company No. 5. — William Barry, foreman; John Mitchell, 1st asst.; Charles Sanderson, 2d asst.; Elias Crafts, clerk.

Franklin Engine Company No. 7. — Henry P. Gardner, foreman; F. J. Almeder, 1st asst.; Marshall W. Page, 2d asst.; Henry P. Gardner, clerk.

Harvard Hook and Ladder Company No. 1. — Augustus Whittemore, foreman; S. P. Hill, 1st asst.; Peter Johnson, clerk.

Hose Company No. 1. — Disbanded.

1849–50.

Engineers. — Henry Conn, chief; Stephen P. Kelley, 1st asst.; James M. Gardner, 2d asst.; Robert Todd, 3d asst.; Isaac Cook, 4th asst.

Hancock Engine Company No. 1. — George Hager, foreman; Samuel K. Brintnall, 1st asst.; Isaac B. Trask, 2d asst.; Thomas French, clerk.

Bunker Hill Engine Company No. 2. — John Howard, foreman; F. O. Savage, 1st asst.; John G. Abbott, 2d asst.; William Fiske, clerk.

Howard Engine Company No. 3. — Wm. H. Caswell, foreman; Reuben Goff, 1st asst.; John Scates, 2d asst.; C. H. Freeman, clerk.

Warren Engine Company No. 4. — James C. Poor, foreman; Joseph Hayden, 1st asst.; George Jackson, 2d asst.; John W. Devereaux, clerk.

Washington Engine Company No. 5. — Benjamin F. Tyler, foreman; B. V. Dennis, 1st asst.; Asphel P. Copps, 2d asst.; Elias Crafts, clerk.

Franklin Engine Company No. 7. — Henry P. Gardner, foreman; F. J. Almeder, 1st asst.; Marshall W. Page, 2d asst.; H. P. Gardner, clerk.

Harvard Hook and Ladder Company. — Nahum Chapin, foreman; Richard A. Stoddard, asst.; George S. Hammond, clerk.

Hose Company No. 1. — George W. Hobart, foreman.

1851–52.

Engineers. — Stephen P. Kelley, chief; Robert Todd, 1st asst.; James M. Gardner, 2d asst.; E. T. Rand, 3d asst.; J. A. D. Worcester, 4th asst.

Hancock Engine Company No. 1. — George Hager, foreman; Eben S. Gardner, 1st asst.; Isaac B. Trask, 2d asst.; Augustus Wilson, clerk.

Bunker Hill Engine Company No. 2. — John Howard, foreman; William Fernald, 1st asst.; Joseph Swan, 2d asst.; John Gardner, clerk.

Howard Engine Company No. 3. — H. V. V. Blanchard, foreman; William Mason, 1st asst.; Charles Gabriel, 2d asst.; George H. Jacobs, clerk.

Warren Engine Company No. 4. — George Jackson, foreman ; Joseph Hayden, 1st asst. ; Enoch J. Clark, 2d asst. ; Samuel C. Hunt, clerk ; Andrew Jackson, treasurer.

Washington Engine Company No. 5. — David S. Tucker, foreman ; B. V. Dennis, 1st asst. ; Charles A. Babcock, 2d asst. ; Elias Crafts, clerk.

Franklin Engine Company No. 7. — Edward A. Costigan, foreman ; Thomas M. Brintnall, 1st asst. ; John F. Powers, 2d asst. ; H. P. Goodwin, clerk ; E. R. Estes, treasurer.

Harvard Hook and Ladder Company No. 1. — Nahum Chapin, foreman ; Joseph H. Till, asst. ; Samuel C. Hunt, clerk.

Hose Company No. 1. — George W. Hobart, foreman ; Joseph Welsh, asst. ; Octavius Barry, clerk.

1853–54.

Engineers. — Stephen P. Kelley, chief ; James M. Gardner, 1st asst. ; H. P. Gardner, 2d asst. ; Nahum Chapin, 3d asst. ; E. T. Rand, 4th asst. ; George Hobart, 5th asst.

Hancock Engine Company No. 1. — George Hager, foreman ; Eben S. Gardner, 1st asst. ; Isaac B. Trask, 2d asst. ; Augustus Wilson, clerk.

Bunker Hill Engine Company No. 2. — William Fernald, foreman ; Daniel R. Beckford, 1st asst. ; Joseph Swan, 2d asst. ; John Gardner, clerk and treasurer.

Howard Engine Company No. 3. — H. V. V. Blanchard, foreman ; Oliver Pratt, 1st asst. ; William H. Jones, 2d asst. ; George H. Jacobs, clerk and treasurer.

Warren Engine Company No. 4. — William Mason, foreman ; George W. Prescott, 1st asst. ; George Jackson, 2d asst. ; Ed. E. Winslow, clerk ; Andrew Jackson, treasurer.

Washington Engine Company No. 5. — David S. Tucker, foreman ; Moses G. Webster, 1st asst. ; George E. Rogers, 2d asst. ; Elias Crafts, treasurer.

Franklin Engine Company No. 7. — Edward A. Costigan, foreman ; Thomas Brintnall, 1st asst. ; Daniel S. Gardner, 2d asst. ; H. P. Goodwin, clerk.

Harvard Hook and Ladder Company No. 1. — William H. Caswell, foreman ; Joseph H. Till, asst. ; Samuel C. Hunt, clerk.

Red Jacket Hose Company No. 1. — George W. Hobart, foreman ; Thomas Turner, asst. ; Amos B. Morse, clerk.

1855.

Engineers. — Henry P. Gardner, chief ; James W. Gardner, 1st asst. ; John Howard, 2d asst. ; James C. Poor, 3d asst. ; David S. Tucker, 4th asst.

Hancock Engine Company No. 1.—George Hager, foreman; Eben S. Gardner, 1st asst.; Isaac B. Trask, 2d asst.; Augustus Wilson, clerk.

Bunker Hill Engine Company No. 2.—Joseph Swan, foreman; William Fernald, asst.; John Gardner, clerk.

Howard Engine Company No. 3.—Abraham P. Pritchard, foreman; H. V. V. Blanchard, asst.; Gustavus Hall, clerk.

Warren Engine Company No. 4.—George W. Prescott, foreman; Richard Raymond, 1st asst.; E. W. Bean, 2d asst.; E. E. Winslow, clerk; Andrew Jackson, treasurer.

Washington Engine Company No. 5.—George W. Peirce, foreman; Moses G. Webster, 1st asst.; George E. Rogers, 2d asst.; Elias Crafts, clerk and treasurer.

Franklin Engine Company No. 7.—E. A. Costigan, foreman; Thomas Brintnall, 1st asst.; John F. Powers, 2d asst.; H. P. Goodwin, clerk; F. J. Almeder, treasurer.

Harvard Hook and Ladder Company No. 1.—William Caswell, foreman; Enoch J. Clark, asst.; Samuel C. Hunt, clerk.

Red Jacket Hose Company No. 1.—Ed. T. Barstow, foreman; Thomas Turner, asst.; Joseph Welsh, clerk.

1856.

Engineers.—James C. Poor, chief; David S. Tucker, 1st asst.; Ed. A. Costigan, 2d asst.; Henry A. Davis, 3d asst.; John M. Devereaux, 4th asst.

Hancock Engine Company No. 1.—Isaac B. Trask, foreman; George Hager, 1st asst.; John Nolan, 2d asst.; Augustus Wilson, clerk.

Bunker Hill Engine Company No. 2.—Joseph Swan, foreman; William Fernald, 1st asst.; Joseph W. Davis, 2d asst.; John Gardner, clerk and treasurer.

Howard Engine Company No. 3.—Samuel C. Hunt, foreman; William T. Bryant, 1st asst.; George Hammond, 2d asst.; Robert Stimpson, clerk; Marcellus Carpenter, treasurer.

Warren Engine Company No. 4.—George W. Prescott, foreman; Benjamin Williams, 1st asst.; Richard R. Raymond, 2d asst.; William E. Delano, clerk; Andrew Jackson, treasurer.

Washington Engine Company No. 5.—George W. Peirce, foreman; George E. Rogers, 1st asst.; Benjamin Brintnall, 2d asst.; Elias Crafts, treasurer.

Franklin Engine Company No. 7.—Thomas Brintnall, foreman; H. P. Goodwin, 1st asst.; John F. Powers, 2d asst.; Nelson Clapp, clerk; F. J. Almeder, treasurer.

Red Jacket Hose Company No. 1.—Ed. F. Barstow, foreman; E. R. C. Murray, asst.; J. J. Edmands, clerk.

Hook and Ladder Company.—Disbanded.

1857.

Engineers. — James C. Poor, chief ; D. S. Tucker, 1st asst. ; E. A. Costigan, 2d asst. ; Henry A. Davis, 3d asst. ; John W. Devereaux, 4th asst.

Hancock Engine Company No. 1. — Samuel R. Brintnall, foreman ; Daniel R. Beckford, 1st asst. ; Samuel C. Weston, 2d asst. ; James W. Simpson, clerk ; William L. Bond, treasurer.

Bunker Hill Engine Company No. 2. — Joseph Swan, foreman ; N. W. Robinson, 1st asst. ; William Fernald, 2d asst. ; George E. Tyler, 3d asst. ; John Gardner, clerk.

Howard Engine Company No. 3. — A. W. Copps, foreman ; Augustus Frost, 1st asst. ; James J. Johnson, 2d asst. ; J. Mason Mills, clerk.

Warren Engine Company No. 4. — George W. Prescott, foreman ; E. W. Bean, 1st asst. ; James B. Hatch, 2d asst. ; William C. Delano, clerk ; Andrew Jackson, treasurer.

Washington Engine Company No. 5. — George E. Rogers, foreman ; Benjamin F. Gardner, 1st asst. ; Albert Chandler, 2d asst. ; J. H. Bryant, clerk ; Elias Crafts, treasurer.

Franklin Engine Company No. 7. — Thomas Brintnall, foreman ; H. P. Goodwin, 1st asst. ; James F. Wilson, 2d asst. ; Nelson P. Clapp, clerk.

Hook and Ladder Company No. 1. — Enoch J. Clark, foreman ; Thomas Hay, asst. ; George Robertson, clerk.

Red Jacket Hose Company No. 1. — Amos Morse, foreman ; M. Wilder Rice, asst. ; J. J. Edmands, clerk.

1858.

Engineers. — E. A. Costigan, chief ; David S. Tucker, 1st asst. ; Samuel L. Mason, 2d asst. ; Thomas Brintnall, 3d asst. ; S. R Brintnall, 4th asst.

Hancock Engine Company No. 1. — John McCloud, foreman ; Thomas R. Armitage, 1st asst. ; John W. Holt, 2d asst. ; Augustus Wilson, clerk.

Bunker Hill Engine Company No. 2. — Joseph Swan, foreman ; James Stevens, 1st asst. ; George E. Tyler, 2d asst. ; John Gardner, clerk.

Howard Engine Company No. 3. — William T. Bryant, foreman ; William J. Hobill, 1st asst. ; William F. Rowe, 2d asst. ; Lee Melcher, clerk and treasurer.

Warren Engine Company No. 4. — George C. Prescott, foreman ; E. W. Bean, 1st asst. ; George O. Wiley, 2d asst. ; William E. Delano, clerk ; Andrew Jackson, treasurer.

Washington Engine Company No. 5. — Albert Chandler, foreman ; Benj. Brintnall, 1st asst. ; Moses F. Webster, 2d asst. ; J. H. Bryant, clerk ; Elias Crafts, treasurer.

Franklin Engine Company No. 7. — Henry P. Goodwin, foreman ; James F. Wilson, 1st asst. ; John Bartlett, 2d asst. ; H. N. Clapp, clerk ; F. J. Almeder, treasurer.

Massachusetts Hook and Ladder Company No. 1. — Enoch J. Clark, foreman ; Thomas H. Hay, asst. ; J. J. Edmands, clerk.

Red Jacket Hose Company No. 1. — Amos B. Morse, foreman ; M. Wilder Rice, asst. ; John Brower, clerk.

1859.

Engineers. — Edward A. Costigan, chief ; David S. Tucker, 1st asst. ; Samuel L. Mason, 2d asst. ; Thomas Brintnall, 3d asst. ; Samuel R. Brintnall, 4th asst.

Hancock Engine Company No. 1. — Thomas R. Armitage, foreman ; John W. Holt, 1st asst. ; George Bass, 2d asst. ; Augustus Wilson, clerk and treasurer.

Bunker Hill Engine Company No. 2. — John Howard, foreman ; James Stevens, 1st asst. ; George E. Tyler, 2d asst. ; John Gardner, clerk and treasurer.

Howard Engine Company No. 3. — Augustus Frost, foreman ; Charles L. Davis, 1st asst. ; John Bartlett, 2d asst. ; E. A. Roulstone, clerk.

Warren Engine Company No. 4. — George W. Prescott, foreman ; B. H. Simonds, 1st asst. ; George O. Wiley, 2d asst. ; William E. Delano, clerk ; Andrew Jackson, treasurer.

Washington Engine Company No. 5. — Benjamin Brintnall, foreman ; Bartlett T. Drew, 1st asst. ; Alfred Morse, 2d asst. ; Mark P. Smith, clerk ; Elias Crafts, treasurer.

Franklin Engine Company No. 7. — H. P. Goodwin, foreman ; James F. Wilson, 1st asst. ; Frank A. Nichols, 2d asst. ; James F. Farrington, clerk.

Massachusetts Hook and Ladder Company No. 1. — Enoch J. Clark, foreman ; Frank A. Chase, asst. ; J. J. Edmands, clerk.

Red Jacket Hose Company No. 1. — M. Wilder Rice, foreman ; Samuel T. Vaughan, asst. ; George E. Morrill, clerk.

1860.

Engineers. — E. A. Costigan, chief ; David S. Tucker, 1st asst. ; Thomas Brintnall, 2d asst. ; Samuel R. Brintnall, 3d asst. ; Israel P. Magoun, 4th asst.

Hancock Engine Company No. 1. — Thomas R. Armitage, foreman ; John W. Holt, 1st asst. ; George A. Bass, 2d asst. ; Augustus Wilson, clerk.

Bunker Hill Engine Company No. 2. — James Stevens, Jr., foreman ; Augustus W. Kimball, 1st asst. ; Joseph E. Bennett, 2d asst. ; John Gardner, clerk and treasurer.

Howard Engine Company No. 3. — William H. Caswell, foreman ; Timothy McCartney, 1st asst. ; George H. Farmilo, 2d asst. ; William Stollery, clerk.

Warren Engine Company No. 4. — George W. Prescott, foreman ; George

O. Wiley, 1st asst. ; Laban W. Turner, 2d asst. ; William E. Delano, clerk ; Andrew Jackson, treasurer.

Washington Engine Company No. 5. — Benjamin Brintnall, foreman ; B. F. Gardner, 1st asst. ; Alfred Morse, 2d asst. ; Mark P. Smith, clerk ; Elias Crafts, treasurer.

Franklin Engine Company No. 7. — H. P. Goodwin, foreman ; Frank A. Nichols, 1st asst. ; Joseph H. Till, 2d asst. ; James S. Farrington, clerk.

Massachusetts Hook and Ladder Company No. 1. — Enoch J. Clark, foreman ; D. R. Beckford, 1st asst. ; Artemas H. Baldwin, 2d asst. ; J. J. Edmands, clerk.

Red Jacket Hose Company No. 1. — M. Wilder Rice, foreman ; Isaac N. Burroughs, asst. ; George E. Morrill, clerk.

1861.

Engineers. — Edward A. Costigan, chief ; David S. Tucker, 1st asst. ; Thomas Brintnall, 2d asst. ; S. R. Brintnall, 3d asst. ; Israel P. Magoun, 4th asst.

Hancock Engine Company No. 1. — Thomas R. Armitage, foreman ; John W. Holt, 1st asst. ; John Boynton, 2d asst. ; Augustus Wilson, clerk.

Bunker Hill Engine Company No. 2. — James Stevens, Jr., foreman ; A. W. Kimball, 1st asst. ; Joseph E. Bennett, 2d asst. ; John Gardner, clerk and treasurer.

Howard Engine Company No. 3. — John Bartlett, foreman ; Timothy McCartney, 1st. asst. ; Edward Farmilo, 2d asst. ; William Stollery, clerk.

Warren Engine Company No. 4. — George W. Prescott, foreman ; George O. Wiley, 1st asst. ; George C. Sawyer, 2d asst. ; William E. Delano, clerk ; Andrew Jackson, treasurer.

Washington Engine Company No. 5. — Mark P. Smith, foreman ; Benjamin F. Gardner, 1st asst. ; Alfred Morse, 2d asst. ; J. H. Bryant, clerk ; Elias Crafts, Jr., treasurer.

Franklin Engine Company No. 7. — Henry P. Goodwin, foreman ; Frank A. Nichols, Joseph H. Till, James S. Farrington.

Red Jacket Hose Company. — William Wilder Rice, foreman ; E. R. C. Murray, asst. ; George E. Morrill, clerk.

Massachusetts Hook and Ladder Company. — Daniel R. Beckford, foreman ; Artemas Baldwin, asst. · J. J. Edmands, clerk.

1862.

Engineers. — David S. Tucker, chief ; Thomas Brintnall, 1st asst. ; Samuel R. Brintnall, 2d asst. ; Enoch J. Clark, 3d asst. ; B. V. Dennis, 4th asst.

Hancock Engine Company No. 1. — Thomas R. Armitage, foreman ; Charles E. Dennett, 1st asst. ; Allen Stone, 2d asst. ; Augustus Wilson, clerk.

Bunker Hill Engine Company No. 2. — John Howard, George E. Tyler, Charles L. Kimball, John Gardner.

Howard Engine Company No. 3. — John Bartlett, foreman ; Edwin Farmilo, 1st asst. ; William Stollery, clerk.

Warren Engine Company No. 4. — George O. Wiley, foreman ; Benjamin H. Simonds, 1st asst. ; George C. Thompson, 2d asst. ; William E. Delano, clerk ; Andrew Jackson, treasurer.

Washington Engine Company No. 5. — Benjamin Brintnall, foreman ; B. S. Drew, asst. ; J. H. Bryant, clerk ; Elias Crafts, treasurer.

Franklin Engine Company No. 7. — H. P. Goodwin, foreman ; J. H. Till, 1st asst. ; William F. Bibram, 2d asst. ; James S. Farrington, clerk.

Massachusetts Hook and Ladder Company. — Artemas Baldwin, foreman ; George O. Plaisted, 1st asst. ; Ira A. Worth, 2d asst. ; J. J. Edmands, clerk.

Red Jacket Hose Company. — John W. Holt, foreman ; Thaddeus Harrington, asst. ; W. S. Oakman, clerk.

1863.

Engineers. — David S. Tucker, chief; Thomas Brintnall, 1st asst. ; B. V. Dennis, 2d asst. ; Israel P. Magoun, 3d asst. ; Henry P. Goodwin, 4th asst.

Hancock Engine Company No. 1. — Charles H. Dennett, foreman ; John Boynton, 1st asst. ; Robert Denver, 2d asst. ; Augustus Wilson, clerk.

Bunker Hill Engine Company No. 2. — James B. Boswell, foreman ; George E. Tyler, 1st asst. ; William H. Norris, 2d asst. ; John Gardner, clerk.

Howard Engine Company No. 3. — George T. Currier, foreman ; Clark D. Garey, 1st asst. ; J. H. Reed, 2d asst. ; Albert C. Barrell, clerk and treasurer.

Warren Engine Company No. 4. — George O. Wiley, foreman ; George W. Sawyer, 1st asst. ; Seth F. Sawyer, 2d asst. ; William E. Delano, clerk ; Andrew Jackson, treasurer.

Washington Engine Company No. 5. — Edward E. Turner, foreman ; B. S. Drew, 1st asst. ; George H. Gardner, 2d asst. ; J. H. Bryant, clerk ; Elias Crafts, Jr., treasurer.

Franklin Engine Company No. 7. — Henry P. Gardner, foreman ; Samuel Dwight, 1st asst. ; James F. Wilson, 2d asst. ; F. J. Almeder, Jr., clerk.

Massachusetts Hook and Ladder Company No. 1. — Artemas Baldwin, foreman ; Ira A. Worth, asst. ; J. J. Edmands, clerk.

Red Jacket Hose Company No. 1. — John W. Holt, foreman ; J. H. Sanderson, asst. ; John P. Loring, clerk.

1864.

Engineers. — D. S. Tucker, chief; Thomas Brintnall, 1st asst.; B. V. Dennis, 2d asst.; Israel P. Magoun, 3d asst.; Henry P. Goodwin, 4th asst.

Hancock Engine Company No. 1. — Isaac Gibbs, foreman; Charles H. Dennett, 1st asst.; Andrew Sargent, 2d asst.; Augustus Wilson, clerk.

Bunker Hill Engine Company No. 2. — George E. Tyler, foreman; William H. Norris, 1st asst.; H. W. Kimball, 2d asst.; William Fernald, clerk.

Howard Engine Company No. 3. — Edwin Farmilo, foreman; George Chell, 1st asst.; H. L. Stone, 2d asst.; Albert Barrell, clerk. Disbanded Nov. 10, 1864.

Warren Engine Company No. 4. — George O. Wiley, George W. Sawyer, Seth F. Sawyer, William E. Delano, Andrew Jackson.

Washington Engine Company No. 5. — Edward E. Turner, foreman; B. S. Drew, 1st asst.; George H. Gardner, 2d asst.; J. H. Bryant, clerk; Elias Crafts, treasurer.

Franklin Engine Company No. 7. — James F. Wilson, foreman; Nelson Cutler, Jr., 1st asst.; William F. Bibram, 2d asst.; E. A. Roulstone, clerk.

Massachusetts Hook and Ladder Company No. 1. — E. J. Clark, foreman; Ira A. Worth, 1st asst.; T. J. Whittemore, 2d asst.; A. W. Whittemore, clerk.

Red Jacket Hose Company No. 1. — John W. Holt, foreman; William H. Gladden, asst.; John P. Loring, clerk.

Howard Steam Fire Engine Company No. 1. — Organized December 19, 1864. Henry L. Whiting, foreman; Albert Seavey, clerk; Joseph R. Gilbert, engineman; I. W. Brackett, asst. engineman.

1865.

Engineers. — Samuel R. Brintnall, chief; B. V. Dennis, 1st asst.; Israel P. Magoun, 2d asst.; H. P. Goodwin, 3d asst.; George E. Rogers, 4th asst.

Hancock Engine Company No. 1. — Isaac Gibbs, foreman; C. H. Dennett, 1st asst.; Lewis Carville, 2d asst.; James J. Dennett, clerk. Disbanded as Hand Engine Company, April 30, 1865.

Bunker Hill Engine Company. — George E. Tyler, foreman; William H. Norris, 1st asst.; C. L. Kimball, 2d asst.; John Gardner, clerk. Disbanded as Hand Engine Company, March 5, 1866.

Warren Engine Company No. 2. — George W. Sawyer, foreman; George O. Wiley, 1st asst.; Seth F. Sawyer, 2d asst.; William E. Delano, clerk; Andrew Jackson, treasurer.

Washington Engine Company No. 3. — Ed. E. Turner, foreman; B. S. Drew, 1st asst.; George H. Gardner, 2d asst.; Joseph H. Bryant, clerk; Elias Crafts, Jr., treasurer. Disbanded as Hand Engine Company, October 16, 1865.

Franklin Engine Company No. 7. — James F. Wilson, foreman ; Nelson Cutler, 1st asst. ; William F. Bibram, 2d asst. ; E. A. Roulstone, clerk. Disbanded as Hand Engine Company, September 30, 1865.

Massachusetts Hook and Ladder Company No. 1. — Enoch J. Clark, foreman ; D. R. Beckford, 1st asst. ; T. J. Whittemore, 2d asst. ; Converse F. Rand, clerk.

Red Jacket Hose Company No. 1. — James E. Wright, foreman ; E. C. Jacobs, asst. ; F. Robie, clerk.

Howard Steam Fire Engine Company No. 1. — H. L. Whiting, foreman ; William E. Delano, clerk ; I. R. Gilbert, engineer ; I. W. Brackett, asst.

Hose Companies, Organized 1865.

Bunker Hill Hose Company No. 2. — George E. Tyler, foreman ; William Norris, asst. ; L. B. Kimball, clerk ; John Gardner, treasurer. Organized from members of Engine Company No. 2.

Washington Hose Company No. 3. — George H. Gardner, foreman ; David McNulty, asst. ; John F. Rand, clerk ; Elias Crafts, Jr., treasurer. Organized from members of Washington Engine Company.

Franklin Hose Company No. 4. — William F. Bibram, foreman ; Samuel Williams, asst. ; E. A. Roulstone, clerk. Organized from members of Franklin Engine Company.

1866.

Engineers. — Samuel R. Brintnall, chief ; B. V. Dennis, 1st asst. ; Israel P. Magoun, 2d asst. ; H. P. Goodwin, 3d asst. ; George E. Rogers, 4th asst.

Howard Steam Fire Engine Company No. 1. — William E. Delano, foreman ; C. O. Richardson, clerk ; Marcellus Carpenter, treasurer.

Massacuhsetts Hook and Ladder Company No. 1. — Enoch J. Clark, foreman ; T. J. Whittemore, clerk ; D. R. Beckford, clerk and treasurer.

Red Jacket Hose Company No. 1. — M. Wilder Rice, foreman ; William J. Jordan, asst. ; George H. Green, clerk.

Bunker Hill Hose Company No. 2. — George E. Tyler, foreman ; William H. Norris, asst. ; William Fernald, clerk.

Washington Hose Company No. 3. — George H. Gardner, foreman ; William J. Marr, asst. ; Charles A. Page, clerk ; Elias Crafts, treasurer.

Franklin Hose Company No. 4. — Samuel Amsden, foreman.

1867.

Engineers. — George E. Rogers, chief ; B. V. Dennis, 1st asst. ; Israel P. Magoun, 2d asst. ; H. P. Goodwin, 3d asst. ; William E. Delano, 4th asst.

Howard Steam Engine Company No. 1. — Charles O. Richardson, foreman ; D. K. Wheelock, asst. ; Ezra B. Kenah, clerk ; Marcellus Carpenter, treasurer.

Massachusetts Hook and Ladder Company. — George B. Edmands, foreman; Charles E. Cutter, asst.; George E. Flint, clerk; D. R. Beckford, treasurer.

Red Jacket Hose Company No. 1. — Joseph O. Rice, foreman; Daniel Mason, asst.; Augustus Wilson, clerk.

Bunker Hill Hose Company No. 2. — George E. Tyler, foreman; Charles L. Kimball, asst.; John Gardner, clerk and treasurer.

Washington Hose Company No. 3. — George H. Gardner, foreman; Ed. E. Turner, asst.; Charles A. Page, clerk; Elias Crafts, treasurer.

Franklin Hose Company No. 4. — Samuel Amsden, foreman; William J. Jordan, asst.; Jesse Oakley, clerk.

1868.

Engineers. — George E. Rogers, chief; B. V. Dennis, 1st asst.; Israel P. Magoun, 2d asst.; William E. Delano, 3d asst.; John Bartlett, 4th asst.

Howard Steam Fire Engine Company No. 1. — Frank M. Estee, foreman; T. J. Whittemore, asst.; Ezra B. Kenah, clerk; Marcellus Carpenter, treasurer; William L. Butts, engineman; Isaac Brackett, asst.; D. K. Wheelock, driver.

Red Jacket Hose Company No. 1. — Charles M. Glazier, foreman; George J. Moore, asst.; Aug. Wilson, clerk.

Bunker Hill Hose Company No. 2. — George E. Tyler, foreman; C. L. Kimball, asst.; William E. Story, clerk; John Gardner, treasurer.

Washington Hose Company No. 3. — Thomas E. Smith, foreman; David McNally, asst.; Charles A. Page, clerk; Elias Crafts, Jr., treasurer.

Franklin Hose Company No. 4. — William J. Jordan, foreman; John F. Murphy, asst.; Charles H. Almeder, clerk; B. F. Stacy, treasurer.

Massachusetts Hook and Ladder Company No. 1. — George B. Edmands, foreman; C. E. Cutter, asst.; William Handy, clerk; D. R. Beckford, treasurer.

1869.

Engineers. — George E. Rogers, chief; Israel P. Magoun, 1st asst.; William E. Delano, 2d asst.; John Bartlett, 3d asst.; Edward E. Turner, 4th asst.

Howard Steam Engine Company No. 1. — William A. Whittemore, foreman; Charles E. Hayden, clerk; Marcellus Carpenter, treasurer; William J. Butts, engineman; Isaac W. Brackett, asst.

Massachusetts Hook and Ladder Company. — John Loner, foreman; Thomas H. Pike, asst.; Joseph Jepson, asst.; Thomas Reed, clerk.

Red Jacket Hose No. 1. — Charles M. Glazier, foreman; Thomas M. Paine, asst.; E. W. Gibbons, clerk; W. W. Bullock, treasurer.

Bunker Hill Hose Company No. 2. — Leonard McKinley, foreman; George A. Caldwell, asst.; L. B. Kimball, clerk; John Gardner, treasurer.

Washington Hose Company No. 3. — N. E. Abbott, foreman; David McNully, asst.; P. J. Donovan, clerk; Elias Crafts, treasurer.

Franklin Hose Company No. 4. — Edmund Goodwin, foreman; John F. Murphy, asst.; C. H. Almeder, clerk; B. F. Stacy, treasurer.

1870.

Engineers. — Israel P. Magoun, chief; William E. Delano. 1st asst.; John Bartlett, 2d asst.; Ed. E. Turner, 3d asst.; John Loner, 4th asst.

Howard Steam Fire Engine Company No. 1. — James W. Poor, foreman; William A. Whittemore, 1st asst.; Ezra B. Kenah, clerk; Marcellus Carpenter, treasurer; Albert C. Smith, engineman; Isaac W. Brackett, asst.; D. K. Wheelock, driver.

Massachusetts Hook and Ladder Company. — Thomas H. Pike, foreman; George Williamson, asst.; Thomas W. Strand, clerk; William S. Wiley, treasurer.

Red Jacket Hose Company No. 1. — Thomas M. Paine, foreman; George H. Huff, asst.; John S. Tuck, clerk; Charles O. Richardson, treasurer.

Bunker Hill Hose Company No. 2. — L. B. Kimball, foreman; George A. Caldwell, asst.; E. A. Roulstone, clerk; John Gardner, treasurer.

Washington Hose Company No. 3. — John McNulty, foreman; P. J. Donovan, asst.; W. E. Bridgett, clerk; Elias Crafts, Jr., treasurer.

Franklin Hose Company No. 4. — Morris Mead, foreman; Michael Carroll, asst.; James Murphy, clerk; B. F. Stacy, treasurer.

1871.

Engineers. — Israel P. Magoun, chief; William E. Delano, 1st asst.; John Bartlett, 2d asst.; Ed. E. Turner, 3d asst.; James W. Poor, 4th asst.

Howard Steam Fire Engine Company. — Israel T. Crafts, foreman; William A. Whittemore, asst.; E. F. Gross, clerk; James W. Clark, treasurer: Albert C. Smith, engineman; Isaac W. Brackett, asst.; D. K. Wheelock, driver.

Red Jacket Hose Company No. 1. — Thomas M. Paine, foreman; Henry G. Dwight, asst.; Augustus Wilson, clerk; Thaddeus Harrington, treasurer.

Bunker Hill Hose Company No. 2. — L. B. Kimball, foreman; William E. Story, asst.: E. A. Roulstone, clerk; John Gardner, treasurer.

Washington Hose Company No. 3. — John McNulty, foreman; C. H. Bridges, asst.; William H. Bridgett, clerk; Elias Crafts, treasurer.

Franklin Hose Company No. 4. — William J. Jordan, foreman; M. A. Carroll, asst.; George Getchell, clerk; N. G. Perkins, treasurer.

1872.

Engineers. — William E. Delano, chief; John Bartlett, 1st asst.; James W. Poor, 2d asst.; John Loner, 3d asst.; Enoch J. Clark, 4th asst.

Red Jacket Hose Company No. 1. — Allen Stone, foreman; Henry G. Dwight, asst.; Jesse M. Stone, clerk.

Bunker Hill Hose Company No. 2. — Walter W. Wyman, foreman; L. B. Kimball, asst.; C. E. Miner, clerk; A. W. Tilden, treasurer.

Washington Hose Company No. 3. — John McNulty, foreman; W. E. Bridgett, asst.; S. A. R. Burroughs, clerk; Elias Crafts, treasurer.

Franklin Hose Company No. 4. — T. J. Almeder, foreman; Joseph Riley, asst.; Jesse T. Oakley, clerk; B. F. Stacy, treasurer.

Massachusetts Hook and Ladder Company No. 1. — John Mears, foreman; B. J. Fish, asst.; Frank Fall, clerk; William S. Wiley, treasurer.

Howard Steam Fire Engine Company No. 1. — John W. Gale, foreman; J. J. Bridgett, asst.; James W. Clark, clerk and treasurer; John B. Cilley, engineman; I. W. Brackett, asst.; William H. Conn, driver.

1872.

PAID DEPARTMENT.

October 1, 1872, the department was reorganized on a paid basis, with the following members: —

Engineers. — William E. Delano, chief; John Bartlett, 1st asst.; James W. Poor, 2d asst.; John Loner, 3d asst.; Enoch J. Clark, 4th asst.

Hose Company No. 1. — Allen Stone, foreman; Warren B. Prescott, asst. and clerk; Charles S. Stone, Gilbert J. Lewis, George H. Neal, George W. Dennis, Charles F. Poor, Wendal S. Staples, Jesse M. Stone, Daniel W. Wilson, George S. Rich, George S. Garland, hosemen; D. K. Wheelock, driver.

Hose Company No. 2. — Walter W. Wyman, foreman; William F. Caldwell, asst. and clerk; L. B. Kimball, driver; Cornelius Leary, J. H. Fuller, C. J. Jennings, Theophilus Huckins, Moses B. Kelton, T. H. Emerson, hosemen.

Hose Company No. 3. — P. J. Donovan, foreman; A. J. McDonough, asst.; William A. Whittemore, driver; Charles Kendall, Michael McCafferty, A. Q. Clark, John D. Gallagher, Martin Turnbull, Edward Nagle, James Turnbull, James F. McAvoy, hosemen.

Hose Company No. 4. — F. J. Almeder, foreman; Joseph Riley, asst.; Samuel Amsden, driver; Charles Almeder, Frank Turnbull, James McLaughlin, George L. Almeder, William Todd, John Uart, George Getchell, Thomas Williams.

Steam Fire Engine Company No. 1. — George F. Titus, foreman; Samuel J. Bridgett, driver; John B. Cilley, engineman; Isaac W. Brackett, asst.; William H. Conn, driver; E. B. Kenah, James W. Clark, John W. Gale, Thomas H. Wright, Charles E. Hayden, William H. Dennis, George A. Newhall, Walter S. Dodge, John S. Gardner, hosemen.

Hook and Ladder Company No. 1. — David S. Tucker, foreman; C. H. W. Pope, asst.; Henry S. Pike, driver; Samuel Dwight, Augustus Wilson, Alexander Morely, Henry G. Dwight, Thomas W. Conway, John Mears,

William Selby, James W. Sweetser, I. K. P. Williams, C. A. Winslow, Charles D. Boardman, Henry E. Wright, I. N. Burroughs, William T. Crosby, George Plaisted, Thomas H. Pike, Benjamin J. Fish, David Johnson, J. C. Hutchins.

1873.

Engineers. — William E. Delano, chief ; John Bartlett, 1st asst. ; E. J. Clark, 2d asst. ; P. J. Donovan, 3d asst. ; David S. Tucker, 4th asst.

Hose Company No. 1. — George Rich, foreman ; Charles F. Poor, asst. ; D. K. Wheelock, driver.

Hose Company No. 2. — George E. Tyler, foreman ; M. B. Kelton, asst. ; L. B. Kimball, driver.

Hose Company No. 3. — A. J. McDonough, foreman ; J. T. McEvoy, asst. ; William H. Conn, driver.

Hose Company No. 4. — Joseph Riley, foreman ; George Getchell, asst. ; Samuel Amsden, driver.

Steam Engine Company No. 1. — George F. Titus, foreman ; S. J. Bridgett, asst. ; J. B. Cilley, engineer ; Isaac W. Brackett, asst. ; William A. Whittemore, driver ; B. V. Dennis, spare driver.

Hook and Ladder Company No. 1. — Samuel Dwight, foreman ; C. H. W. Pope, foreman ; Henry G. Dwight, asst. ; Henry S. Pike, driver.

1874.

On January 1, 1874, the city of Charlestown, by vote of the citizens of both cities, was annexed to the city of Boston ; and Chief Engineer William E. Delano turned over all property and a list of members late of the Charlestown Fire Department to Chief Engineer John S. Damrell, of Boston, who, on the first day of January, 1874, assumed charge of the department, the officers and men acting in the same capacity until May 1, when the Boston department was reorganized.

District Chief JOHN BARTLETT, of District No. 2, will be readily recognized on page 384, as he is one of the oldest members in the service. He was born at Charlestown District, October 4, 1830. He is an engineer by trade, and when sixteen years of age he became connected with the fire department of that section, joining Forest Engine Company No. 8, as a torch-boy, from whence he went to Franklin Engine Company No. 7, as a volunteer. In 1851 he moved to California, but soon returned, and joined the same company, as a member, and during 1858 was elected third foreman. He then joined Harvard Ladder Company No. 1, in which he remained one year. During 1860 he joined Howard Engine Company No. 3, as foreman, where he remained until the war. He enlisted July, 1861, in Company I, Thirty-second Massachusetts Regiment, and served eighteen months, at which time he was discharged, for sickness. On March 1, 1869, he was elected on the Board of Engineers of the Charlestown Department, and on the reorganization, in 1874, he was appointed to his present position. Chief Bartlett is a member of King Solomon Lodge of Masons, Signet Chapter Cœur de Leon Commandery Knights Templars; Egyptian Knights Templars, the Charlestown Veterans, and the Firemen's Charitable Association.

Call District Chief WILLIAM E. DELANO is probably one of the best known firemen in the Charlestown District; in fact, he has been prominently identified with this service for the past quarter of a century. He was born at Charlestown District, Boston, Mass., August 25, 1832, and in 1848 began his first fire duty, as a volunteer in Warren Engine Company No. 4, of that district, and on April 25, 1850, was chosen a member, and in 1855 was elected clerk, and served in that capacity until the disbandment of the company, March, 1865. March 1, 1865, transferred to Howard Steam Fire Engine Company No. 1, — now Engine Company No. 27, — as a member, and elected foreman March 1, 1866. In March, 1867, was elected assistant engineer, and served in that position until March, 1872. March 1. 1872, was placed as chief engineer of the Charlestown department, which position he held until April 1, 1874, when, on annexation, he transferred the department over to Chief Engineer Damrell, of the Boston department. He was tendered the position of chief or engineer of that district, but declined, and accepted captain's position of Engine No. 27. He was appointed to his present position March 17, 1884. Chief Delano is a member of Howard Lodge, I. O. O. F., and the Boston and Charlestown Veterans.

ENGINE COMPANY NO. 27.

NAMES OF MEMBERS SINCE 1874.

Engineman John B. Cilley, ap. May 2, 1874, died June 5, 1875; Albert C. Smith, ap. June 13, 1875, resigned Dec. 3, 1860. Asst. Engineman William J. Goodwin, ap. Dec. 16, 1880, resigned March 27. 1886. Hosemen: Samuel J. Bridgett, ap. June 1, 1885, resigned June 23, 1880; Thomas H. Wright, ap. May 2, 1874, resigned May 1, 1875; John S. Gardner, ap. May 2, 1874, resigned April 5, 1880; Joseph S. G. Sweatt, ap. May 2, 1874, resigned May 7, 1881; James W. Sweetser, ap. May 2, 1874, resigned October, 1874; James W. Poor, ap. May 2, 1874, resigned January, 1876: Howard W. Sargent, ap. November, 1874, resigned February 10, 1882; Eli S. Richardson, ap. May, 1875, died June 11, 1882; Henry S. Pike, ap. April 1, 1882. resigned December 26, 1882; William H. Conn, ap. June 25, 1880, died August 11, 1884.

PRESENT MEMBERS.

Captain GEORGE F. TITUS will be readily recognized in Figure 1. He was born at West Cambridge, Mass.. January 9, 1847. After leaving school he learned the whitener's trade. In July, 1864, he enlisted in Company H. Fifth Massachusetts Regiment, and served three months. He entered this depart-

ENGINE COMPANY No. 27. — Page 406.

ment as a member of Hose Company No. 3, during 1867, and on December 28, 1868, joined this company. He left the department July 29, 1869, but returned during March, 1870. March, 1872, was elected secretary, and in June, 1872, was elected foreman, which position he held until the reorganization of the department, May 2, 1874. April 24, 1875, was appointed senior hoseman, and served in that position until March 24. 1880, when he was appointed permanent hoseman, and assigned to Engine Company No. 22, from where he was transferred to Engine Company No. 4, April 13, 1882, and eight days later was promoted to the position of lieutenant, where he remained until March 17, 1884, at which time he was promoted to his present position, and assigned to this company. Captain Titus is a member of Henry Price Lodge of Masons, Howard Lodge 22, I. O. O. F., Boston Council 4, Royal Arcanum, Abraham Lincoln Post 11, G. A. R., Charlestown Veterans, and the Barnicoat Association.

Engineman ROBERT J. GALLAGHER (Fig. 2) was born at Calais, Me., September 26, 1845. His fire experience dates from 1859, when he was enrolled a member of Washington Engine Company No. 3 of that city, and served there until 1862, at which date he came to this city, where he learned the machinist trade. During 1863 to 1865 he served in the West Roxbury department, and in the following year joined Engine Company 2 of South Boston, as a volunteer. and served two years. From 1870 to 1874 he was a substitute on Engine 2 and Hose 12; and on June 4, 1874, he entered this department, as assistant engineman of Engine No. 5, which position he held until March 17, 1884, when he was promoted engineman of Engine Company 32; and on December 26, 1885, was transferred to this company. He is a member of Maverick Council, Royal Arcanum.

Assistant Engineman WILLIAM H. CLAY (Fig. 3) was born at Boston, Mass., March 26, 1850, and is a machinist by trade. He entered this department in April, 1874, as a call-member of Engine Company No. 9, in which he remained until 1878, when he resigned, and was appointed assistant engineman, June 3, 1880, and assigned to Engine Company No. 25. October 3, 1883, was promoted to engineman, and assigned to Engine Company No. 6. On March 28, 1886, was transferred, as assistant engineman. at his own request, to this company. Mr. Clay had his arm broken while on patrol duty, June 18, 1887. He is a member of Temple Lodge of Masons.

HENRY G. DWIGHT, senior hoseman (Fig. 4), was born at Charlestown District. Boston. Mass., May 17, 1845. When the war broke out he enlisted in the navy on gunboat " Kettenney," and " W. G. Anderson " on October, 1861, and served until October, 1864. He entered the Charlestown Fire Department during May, 1866, as a member of Red Jacket Hose Company No. 1, and in October, 1872, joined Ladder Company No. 1 of that district, when he was promoted assistant foreman. which position he held a short time when he was transferred to Hose Company No. 4, from which he was appointed a permanent member of Engine Company 25 of this department, on April 5, 1875.

He was again transferred June 1, 1881, as a call-member of this company, and on its reorganization, September 3, 1884, was made a permanent member. He is a member of Bunker Hill Lodge No. 14, I. O. O. F.

GEORGE D. BULLARD, driver (Fig. 5), was born at Boston, Mass., November 19, 1849. He was a teamster by occupation. When the war broke out he enlisted in the navy on the steamship " Whachuset," and served three years and five months. He also served two years in the Everett, Mass.. Fire Department. He entered this department during 1880, as a call-man on Engine No. 27, and transferred to Engine Company No. 8, as a driver. He was out of the department four months, when he returned, as a substitute in Ladder Company 8, being detailed as driver, which position he retained until October 23, 1885, when he was assigned to Engine Company No. 32, and on July 1, 1886, was appointed a permanent member and transferred to this company. Mr. Bullard is a member of Post 11, G. A. R.

LEONARD KNIGHTS (Fig. 6), driver of hose, was born at Lake Village, N.H., September 6, 1854, and during 1873 came to this city, where he learned the house-painting trade. He entered this department during 1874, as a call-substitute in this company, and, February 1, 1876, was appointed a call-man. During 1882 he was appointed a substitute in Engine Company No. 15, where he remained three months. when he was assigned to this company. On March 17, 1884, he was appointed a permanent member.

JOHN W. GALE was born at Alsted, N.H., May 22, 1847, and is a cabinet-maker by trade. He became connected with the Charlestown department during 1861, running as a volunteer on Warren Engine Company No. 4, and was made a member of the same two years later, and remained with it until it was disbanded. During 1868 he joined Howard Engine Company No. 1, and was elected foreman of that company, March, 1872, but resigned that office in the following June. Upon the reorganization of the department he was made a call-member of this company, and was appointed senior hoseman, in April, 1880, and remained such until September 3, 1884, when he was made a permanent member. He is a member of the Charlestown Veterans, Boston Veterans, Ivanhoe Lodge No. 13, K. of P., and Nonantum Tribe No. 73, Red Men.

NATHAN B. JACKSON (Fig. 8) was born at Portsmouth, N.H., May 10, 1849, and came to this city during 1863, where he learned the blacksmith's trade. He entered this department during 1878. as a call-substitute in this company, and on March 23, 1880, was appointed a call-member. September 3, 1884, he was assigned to his present position. Mr. Jackson is a member of Howard Lodge No. 22, I. O. O. F.

JOSEPH A. KELLEY (Fig. 9) was born at Boston, Mass., September 9, 1862. After leaving school he followed the sea for one and a half years, after which he was engaged in mining. January 13, 1888, was appointed substitute, and assigned to this company. January 4, 1889, was promoted hoseman.

H. H. ANDLESS (Fig. 10) was appointed November 23, 1888.

HOOK AND LADDER COMPANY NO. 9.
NAMES OF MEMBERS SINCE 1874.

T. W. Conway, ap. January 1, 1874, tr. March 28, 1886; C. D. Boardman, ap. January 1, 1874, tr. March 28, 1886; G. A. Newhall, ap. May 11, 1874, tr. September 3, 1884; E. C. Sargent, ap. May 11, 1874, tr. February 25, 1886; E. J. Tulley, ap. April 21, 1875, tr. October 8, 1886; T. A. Andrews, Jr., ap. April 21, 1875, tr. April 14, 1881; H. S. Pike, ap. January 1, discharged October 20, 1881; Augustus Wilson, ap. January 1, discharged November 11, 1887; M. S. Manning, ap. January 1, discharged May 20, 1881; John Mears, ap. January 1, 1874, discharged August 4, 1874; C. A. Winslow, ap. January 1, 1874, tr. June 1, 1881; C. H. Craige, ap. January 1, 1874, discharged September 10, 1874; D. W. Johnson, ap. January 1, 1874, discharged July 22, 1888; C. H. Marshall, ap. January 1, 1874, discharged July 21, 1875; H. W. Reed, ap. January 11, 1874, discharged August 27, 1877; M. G. Staples, ap. January 11, 1874, discharged January 1, 1875; C. L. Kendall, ap. January 21, 1874, discharged May 10, 1875; C. F. Woodbury, ap. January 8, 1875, discharged November 1, 1879; W. F. Butler, ap. May 10, 1875, discharged July 18, 1881; E. W. Jones, ap. July 21, 1881, discharged November 25, 1887; A. J. Davis, by tr. September 3, 1884, discharged November 23, 1888; F. P. Colby, ap. March 1, 1886, discharged July 13, 1888; F. P. Mahan, tr. from Ladder 8, March 28, 1885; October 21, tr. to Ladder 8.

PRESENT MEMBERS.

Capt. CHARLES H. W. POPE (Fig. 1) is another old member of this district. He was born at Boston, Mass., December 25, 1847, and began life as a cabinet-maker. His fire experience dates from September 30, 1870, when he entered the Charlestown department, as a member of Massachusetts Ladder Company No. 1. He remained in that capacity until October, 1872, when he was promoted to assistant foreman, and during April of the following year he was again promoted to the position of call-foreman. December 20, 1884, he was promoted to his present position, and in charge of Chemical 9 since its organization. Captain Pope had his eyes burned at the steamer "Venetian" fire, November 16, 1887, and was badly cut on the hands at a later fire. He is a member of Ivanhoe Council No. 13, K. of P., the Charlestown Veterans, and a trustee in the Firemen's Charitable Association.

M. B. REARDON (Fig. 2), driver, was born at Lynn, Mass., September 7, 1847. He came to this city when seventeen years of age, and worked at the livery business. July 1, 1880, he was enrolled a permanent member in this department, and assigned as driver of Engine Company No. 25, where he remained until October 19, 1881, when he was transferred to Hose Company No. 2. March 17, 1884, he was transferred to Engine Company No. 32, from which he was again transferred, October 21, 1885, to this company.

Mr. Reardon had his right leg broken by falling through a hatchway at a fire on India wharf on July 19, 1880.

Isaac M. Burrough (Fig. 3) was born at Philadelphia, Penn., June 17, 1835, and, when a boy, came to this city and learned the blacksmith's trade. His connection with the Charlestown department dates from October 26, 1855, when he became a member of Red Jacket Hose Company No. 1, in which he remained until 1862, when he enlisted in the Tenth Massachusetts Battery, and served until 1865. January 1, 1866, he became a member of Hose Company No. 1, and remained such until October 1, 1872, when he was transferred to this company. Mr. Burrough is a member of Post 11, G. A. R., Bunker Hill Lodge 14, I. O. O. F., Charlestown Veterans, and the Firemen's Charitable Association.

George O. Plaisted (Fig. 4) first saw the light at Boston, Mass., July 3, 1838. He is a furniture-packer by trade, and began his fire experience during 1854, as a volunteer in Howard Engine Company No. 3, in which he continued until 1857, when he joined Massachusetts Ladder Company, and during 1858 was admitted a member of this company, and elected second foreman, March, 1862. On September of that year he enlisted in Company H, Fifth Massachusetts Regiment, and served until July 2, 1863. February 29, 1864, he reënlisted in Sixteenth Massachusetts Battery, and was discharged, June 27, 1865. October 1, 1872, he again entered this department, as a member of this company. Mr. Plaisted is a member of Howard Lodge 22, I. O. O. F., Boston and Charlestown Veterans, and the Firemen's Charitable Association.

George J. Moore (Fig. 5) was born at Boston, Mass., November 26, 1840. He enlisted in Company G, First Massachusetts Regiment, May 25, 1861, and served until the close of the war. September 29, 1863, he joined Engine Company No. 4, in which he remained until it was disbanded, on March 28, 1865. He joined Red Jacket Hose Company No. 1, December 12, the ensuing year, and in April, 1872, joined Hancock Hose Company No. 1, as a call-substitute, in which he was admitted a member July 8, 1874, and on July 17, 1888, was transferred to this company. Mr. Moore is a member of the First Regiment Association and the Charlestown Veterans.

William J. Jordan (Fig. 6) was born at Charlestown District, Boston, Mass., September 18, 1837. He is employed as an expressman. His fire experience dates from August 27, 1860, when he became a member of Warren Engine Company No. 4. After running nine years as a call-substitute, he was, on March 1, 1864, transferred to Red Jacket Hose Company No. 1, and in the following year was elected assistant foreman, and twenty-eight days later was transferred to Franklin Hose Company No. 4, and promoted assistant foreman on June 1 of that year, and the following year was elected foreman, which position he held until the last of the ensuing year. June 31, 1870, was admitted a member of Franklin Hose Company No. 4, and promoted foreman the same year. On the disbandment of that company, October 1,

LADDER COMPANY No. 9 AND CHEMICAL ENGINE COMPANY No. 9. — Page 411.

1872, he was transferred to this company, as a call-member. At the Stickney & Poor fire he was severely injured by a falling board, and at the Medford-street fire, February, 1870, had his leg badly sprained. Mr. Jordan is a member of the Charlestown Veterans, Firemen's Charitable Association, and American Order of United Workingmen.

CHARLES J. JENNINGS (Fig. 7) was born at Boston, Mass., June 22, 1849. When thirteen years of age he enlisted as office-boy for ex-Mayor Martin, of this city, with the Massachusetts Battery, and served three years. In 1866 he entered Charlestown department, as a volunteer in Bunker Hill Hose Company No. 2, and July 27, 1868, was admitted a member, where he remained until October 11, 1874, when he was transferred to this company. Mr. Jennings is employed as a clerk, and is a member of the Charlestown Veterans.

J. CLARK HUTCHINGS (Fig. 8) was born at Charlestown District, Boston, Mass., September 3, 1840, and is a pattern-maker by trade. April 30, 1860, he joined the Charlestown department, as a member of Hancock Engine Company No. 1, in which he remained until April 30, 1865, when the company was disbanded; he was admitted in this company October 1, 1872. Mr. Hutchings is a member of Faith Lodge, Masons; Covenant Lodge No. 16, I. O. O. F.; Boston Lodge 3, K. of P.; Monticello Lodge 13, Workingmen; Bunker Hill Council 2, O. W. A. M.; Waverley Lodge 14, Pilgrim Fathers; American Lodge 24 of N. E. Order of Protection; and the Charlestown Veterans.

ALBERT C. LYNN (Fig. 9) was born at Portsmouth, N.H., July 23, 1848, and came to this city during 1868, where he learned the furniture business, in which he is now engaged. On November 19, 1869, he became a member of Massachusetts Ladder Company No. 1, in which he served until October 1, 1872; he then left the department, and returned again after three months' absence, doing duty as a substitute until July 1, 1873, when he was again appointed as a call-member of this company. Mr. Lynn had his arm broken at a fire in City square, September 29, 1888. He is a member of Monticello Lodge A. O. U. W., No. 13, Order of Workingmen; Olive Branch Lodge 73, I. O. O. F.; Bunker Hill Encampment, No. 5; B. H. Canton; Mishawum Tribe of Red Men; the Charlestown and Boston Veterans; honorary member Post 11, G. A. R.; Firemen's Charitable Association, and others.

THEODORE W. NELSON (Fig. 10) was born at Charlestown District, Boston, Mass., December 14, 1851. He is a wood-carver by trade, and on September 21, 1874, he entered this service as a call-member of this company.

JOHN K. WHEELOCK (Fig. 11) was born at Cambridge, Mass., August 1, 1859, and when a child came to this city. He is employed as a car-oiler, and on July 2, 1880, became connected with this department, as a call-substitute in Hose Company No. 1, in which he was admitted a call-member August 9 of the following year; and on July 17, 1888, was transferred to this company.

A. JUDSON DAVIS (Fig. 12) was born at Belfast, Me., June 19, 1848, and during 1863 came to this city, where he learned the painter's trade. During

1864 he enlisted in the First N. H. Battery, in which he served until the close of the war. April 21, 1883, he became a call-member of Engine Company No. 27, but was a call-substitute one year previous. September 3, 1884, he was transferred to this company. Mr. Davis is a member of Post 11, G. A. R. ; Howard Lodge 22, I. O. O. F. ; Windsor Castle No. 3, Golden Eagle, K. G. E. ; Mishawum Tribe 30, Red Men ; and the Firemen's Charitable Association.

EBEN H. WHEELOCK (Fig. 13) was born at East Cambridge, Mass., November 8, 1857. After leaving school he entered the express business, to which he added the duties of a fireman during 1879, as a call-substitute, in this company, and on July 28, 1880, was admitted a call-member.

NATHANIEL G. GLEASON (Fig. 14) was born at Charlestown District, Boston, Mass., February 5, 1857. His fire experience dates from February. 1881, when he joined this department as a call-substitute in this company, in which he was made a call-member April 17 of the ensuing year. Mr. Gleason is a city laborer.

JAMES M. ELLIOTT (Fig. 15) was born at Syracuse, N.Y., January 31, 1859, and when but a child came to this city, where he learned the paper-hanger's trade. May, 1881, he became connected with this department, as a call-substitute in this company, and on June 2 of the same year was admitted a call-member. Mr. Elliott had his hip dislocated, February 20, 1887, by the overturning of the truck while going to Box 457. He is a member of King Solomon Lodge 18, K. of P., Firemen's Charitable Association, and Windsor Castle No. 3, K. G. E.

ROBERT J. MITCHELL (Fig. 16) was born at Charlestown District, Boston, Mass.. February 22, 1858. He is a plasterer by trade, and during 1880 entered this department as a call-substitute in this company, in which he was made a call-member June 2, 1881.

R. J. RESTARICK (Fig. 17) was born at Charlestown District, Boston, Mass., November 16, 1859. He is a tinsmith by trade, and on June 20, 1887, entered the department, as a call-substitute in this company, and on January 14, 1888, was admitted as a call-member of Hose Company No. 1. On July 17, 1888, he was transferred as a call-man in this company.

WILLIAM H. SHUTE (Fig. 18) was born at Charlestown District, Boston, Mass., December 10, 1857. He began to do substitute duty in Hose Company No. 1 during 1881, and on October 8, 1886, was transferred as a member of this company. Mr. Shute is a member of Columbia Castle 4, Knights of Golden Eagle, and the Firemen's Charitable Association.

CHEMICAL ENGINE COMPANY NO. 9.

This company was organized July 17, 1888, to take the place of Hose Company No. 9. It is stationed in the same house with Ladder Company No. 9. The photographs are illustrated at bottom of plate.

DANIEL K. WHEELOCK (Fig. 1, at bottom of page), driver of Chemical

Engine Company No. 9, was born at East Cambridge, Mass., April 30, 1833, and is a house-painter by trade. His fire experience dates from August. 1853, at which time he joined Niagara Engine Company No. 3, of Cambridge, in which he remained until December 29, 1862, when he joined the Charlestown department, in Franklin Engine Company No. 7, in which he served until Howard Engine Company No. 1 was organized, December 19, 1864, when he was transferred to that company. On December, 1867, was appointed permanent driver, which position he held until 1872, when he was transferred to Hancock Hose Company No. 1, as driver, and on July 17, 1888, was assigned to this company. Mr. Wheelock had his leg broken at a fire in Clifton place, April 2, 1872, by being thrown off the hose-wagon. He is a member of the Boston and Charlestown Veterans, Firemen's Charitable Association, and Columbia Castle No. 4, Knights of the Golden Eagle. Messrs. J. K., E. H., and S. A. Wheelock, members of this department, are sons of this gentleman.

WILLIAM J. TOOMEY (Fig. 2, bottom of page), driver of Chemical Engine No. 9, was born at Roxbury District, Boston, Mass., March 18, 1857. After leaving school he began life as a teamster, at which he was employed until July 2, 1883, when he became connected with this department, as a substitute on Ladder Company No 1. March 21, 1884, he was appointed a permanent member, and assigned to Chemical Company No. 1, as driver, where he remained until July 17, 1888, when he was transferred to this company. Mr. Toomey is a member of Mishawum Lodge 113, R. G. F., and the Firemen's Charitable Association.

ENGINE COMPANY NO. 32.

NAMES OF MEMBERS SINCE MARCH 17, 1884.

This company was organized March 17, 1884.

R. J. Gallagher, engineman, ap. March 17, 1884, tr. Engine No. 27, December 26, 1885 ; M. B. Reardon, driver, ap. March 17, 1884, tr. Ladder No. 9, October 21, 1885 ; G. D. Bullard, driver, ap. October 21, 1885, tr. Engine No. 27, July 1, 1886 ; George E. Tyler, ap. March 17, 1884, died October 22, 1886 ; F. P. Cullinan, ap. March 17, 1884, resigned June 6, 1885 ; C. L. Kimball, ap. March 17, 1884, resigned November 11, 1887 ; P. T. Kimball, ap. March 17, 1884, resigned July 12, 1889.

PRESENT MEMBERS.

Captain MARTIN V. B. KIMBALL (Fig. 1) was born at Hill, N.H., April 7, 1835. When nine years of age he came to this city. He began life as a teamster, to which he added the duties of a fireman, September 1, 1855, when he became a member of Barnicoat Engine Company No. 11. In 1858 he was elected assistant foreman, which position he held until December 20 of the same year, when the company was disbanded. He then moved to Charlestown, and became a member of Washington Engine Company No. 5, during 1861. When war was declared he enlisted in Nimm's Battery, Second Massachusetts, on July 31, 1861, and served until August 14, 1864. After his return he was appointed a permanent member of this department, September 23, 1873, as a driver of Engine No. 25, which position he held until April 1, 1874, when he was promoted assistant foreman. May 1, of the ensuing year, was promoted to the position of captain, and assigned to Engine Company No. 6, where he remained until March 17, 1884, at which time he was transferred to this company. Captain Kimball fell from a ladder at the Wareham-street fire, and struck on his head, which resulted in paralysis, laying him up three months. October 6, 1859, he was badly burned at the post-office fire in this district. At a fire in Fulton street he fell through a hatchway and broke his shoulder-blade. Captain Kimball is a member of Oriental Lodge No. 10, I. O. O. F.; Columbia Lodge Masons; St. Andrew's Royal Arch Chapter, Boston Commandery Knights Templars; Lafayette Lodge Perfection, Rose Croix; Mt. Olive, Mass., Consistory; Giles F. Yates, Princess Jerusalem; Council No. 4, Royal Arcanum; Boston and Charlestown Veterans; and Barnicoat Association.

Engineman Isaac W. Brackett (Fig. 2) is another old member of the Charlestown department. He was born at Charlestown, Mass., July 16, 1835, and began life as a machinist. His fire experience dates from 1854, when he joined Warren Engine Company No. 4 of that district, and served in it until the war broke out, when, in August, 1862, he enlisted in Company D, Fifth Massachusetts Regiment, and served until June 30, 1863. On December 19, 1864, he was appointed assistant engineman, and assigned to Howard Engine Company No. 1 (now No. 27), and during 1880 was promoted to his present position. He remained there until December 26, 1885, when he was transferred to this company. Mr. Brackett had his right leg broken by the explosion of the boiler of the engine on Canal bank, which threw him over the furnace-grate, by which he received severe burns, from the effects of which he was laid up eleven months. He is a member of the Boston and Charlestown Veterans.

Assistant Engineman Octavius Donnell (Fig. 3) was born at Portsmouth, N.H., February 7, 1848, and during 1866 came to this city and learned the machinist trade. He enlisted in the war, September, 1864, in Company K, First New Hampshire Heavy Artillery, and served nine months. He joined this department as a call-man in Engine Company No. 27, October 3, 1881, in which he remained until March 17, 1885, when he was promoted to his present position and assigned to this company. Mr. Donnell is a member of American Order United Workmen, Monticello Lodge No. 13.

William A. Whittemore (Fig. 4), driver, was born at West Cambridge, Mass., December 27, 1839. He began life as a teamster, and in 1859 began to do duty as a fireman, at which time he became connected with Eureka

Engine Company No. 32. — Page 417.

Engine Company No. 1, of West Cambridge, as a torch-boy, and two years later was enrolled a member. He enlisted in December, 1861, in Company E, Twenty-fourth Regiment, and served until 1865. On his return he moved to Charlestown, and joined Howard Engine Company No. 1, in October, 1868. May 20, 1873, he was appointed a permanent member, and detailed as driver, which position he has since held. Mr. Whittemore is a member of King Solomon Lodge, K. of P., Nonantum Camp 73, Red Men, Windsor Castle, Knights of Golden Eagle, and the Charlestown Veterans.

CHARLES W. FURLONG (Fig. 5), senior hoseman, was born at Boston, Mass., September 6, 1854, and is employed as a book-keeper. He entered this department as a call-substitute in Bunker Hill Hose Company No. 2, during 1876, in which he was appointed a member December 20, 1878. He remained there until March 17, 1884, at which time the company was re-organized. He was appointed senior hoseman January 1, 1887. Mr. Furlong had his right leg broken at the Holmes fire, January 30, 1879, by a falling wall, from which he was laid up forty days. He is a member of Waverley Council No. 313, Royal Arcanum.

A. W. THOMS (Fig. 6) was born at Bangor, Me., December 16. 1843. and came to this city during 1866, where he was employed as a teamster. October, 1861, he enlisted in Company A, Seventeenth Massachusetts Volunteers, in which he served three years, and in October, 1872, entered this department as a member of Bunker Hill Hose Company No. 2, and on March 17, 1884, was transferred to this company.

MOSES B. KELTON (Fig. 7) was born at Northampton, Mass., May 13. 1838. When a child he came to this city. He enlisted in Company C, Third Heavy Artillery, on July 11, 1863, and served until September 28, 1865. He is employed as a teamster, and on October 1, 1872, entered this department, as a member of Bunker Hill Hose Company 2, and in 1873 was promoted to assistant foreman, in which position he remained until March 17, 1884, when he was transferred to this company. He is a member of Post 11, G. A. R., and the Charlestown Veterans.

HENRY N. HARDING (Fig. 8) was born at Charlestown, Mass., November 15, 1861. After leaving school he learned the steam engineer's trade, and on November 8, 1886, entered this department, as a call-man in this company. Mr. Harding is a member of Camp 82, Sons of Veterans.

WALTER W. WYMAN (Fig. 9) was born at Charlestown District, Boston, Mass., Oct. 14, 1848, and is a carpenter by trade. He began fire duty during 1871, as a member of Bunker Hill Hose Company No. 2, and remained such until 1872, when he was promoted to foreman, which position he held until March, 1873, when he left the department. He returned again during 1879, as a call-substitute, and was soon after made a member, where he remained until March 17, 1884, when he was transferred to this company. Mr. Wyman is a member of Bunker Hill Lodge No. 4, I. O. O. F., and Encampment No. 5, also T. P. Harlow Assembly No. 132, R. G. F., the Charlestown Veterans, and a trustee of the Firemen's Charitable Association.

EDMOND O. GOODWIN (Fig. 10) was born at Charlestown District, Boston, Mass., February 16, 1861. He is a son of Edmond Goodwin, of this company, and is a slater by trade. He entered this department as a call-substitute in Engine Company No. 27, May 1, 1882, and in December was appointed a member, in which he remained for a short time, when he was transferred to Franklin Hose Company No. 4, and later was transferred to this company. Mr. Goodwin was injured by a falling slate at Stickney & Poor's fire, November, 1884.

EDMOND GOODWIN (Fig. 11) was born at Sanford, Me., during 1835, and came to this city when young, and learned the slater's trade. He is one of the old " Vets," having entered the Charlestown department in June, 1854, as a member of Warren Engine Company No. 4, in which he remained until they were disbanded, in 1864. He then joined Franklin Hose Company No. 4, in which he was elected foreman, and served three years, when he joined Hancock Hose Company No. 1, in which he served as assistant foreman, and on the company being disbanded, July 17, 1888, he was transferred to this company as a call-member. Mr. Goodwin is a member of Monticello Lodge No. 13 American Order of Workingmen, Bunker Hill Council No. 2, Order of United American Mechanics, and the Firemen's Charitable Association.

JOHN H. WRIGHT (Fig. 12) was born at Charlestown District, Boston, Mass., Jan. 17, 1840, and is a carpenter by trade. He first began fire duty during 1857, as a volunteer in Washington Engine Company No. 5. He became a member of Massachusetts Ladder Company during 1860, from which he was transferred to Howard Engine Company No. 1 during 1865. He remained there until 1872, when he was transferred to Hancock Hose Company No. 1, and July 17, 1888, was transferred to this company. Mr. Wright is a member of the Charlestown Veterans.

PERCY T. KIMBALL (Fig. 13) was born at Randolph, Mass., November 9, 1857, and came to Boston during 1860. He is a box-maker by trade, and during 1879 entered this department as a call-substitute in Bunker Hill Hose Company No. 2, in which he was enrolled a member during 1881, and was transferred to this company March 17, 1884. Mr. Kimball is a member of Oasis Lodge No. 146, I. O. O. F.

JOHN C. MAHONEY (Fig. 14) was born at Cambridge, Mass., August 2, 1868, and came to Boston during 1876, where he learned the rubber-turning business. He was appointed a call-substitute in this company during October, 1888.

WILLIAM H. SMITH (Fig. 15) was born at Charlestown District, Boston, Mass., June 1, 1860. He is a carpet-layer by occupation, and during 1888 began his first fire duty as a call-substitute in this company.

HOSE COMPANY NO. 3.

NAMES OF MEMBERS SINCE 1874.

Captain, A. J. McDonough, resigned May, 1874; Charles Kendall, resigned May 19, 1874; M. McCafferty, resigned September 9, 1875; J. Waters, resigned November 21, 1874; D. McNulty, resigned May 9, 1874; captain, T. King, resigned October, 1880; S. G. Maloney, resigned May 2, 1874; A. Morse, resigned July 6, 1881; W. H. Conn, transferred to Engine Company No. 27, June 25, 1880.

PRESENT MEMBERS.

Call-captain OWEN TULLY (Fig. 1) was born at St. John, N.B., April 20, 1849, and came to this city twenty-three years ago, and learned the carpenter's trade. He entered the Charlestown department as a volunteer in Massachusetts Ladder Company No. 1, in which he remained until it disbanded, May 18, 1872, when he joined Hose Company No. 2, in which he was promoted assistant foreman, which position he held until November 1, 1881, when he was transferred to this company, in his present position. On October 12, 1878, he had his hip dislocated by falling walls at the Holmes fire; and in 1878 was badly suffocated at the church fire on Main street. He was ruptured at the Portland-street fire. Captain Tully is a member of the Charlestown Veterans and the Firemen's Charitable Association.

ROBERT J. C. BARTLETT (Fig. 2), driver, is a son of District Chief Bartlett, and was born at Charlestown District, Boston, Mass., April 13, 1856. He is a machinist by trade, and during 1875 entered this department as a call-substitute on Engine Company No. 27, and served as such for one year, when he was appointed a permanent substitute. June 25, 1880, he was promoted a permanent member, and assigned to this company as driver. Mr. Bartlett had his left arm burned at the Fitchburg Railroad fire, and was also badly overcome at the S. S. "Venetian" fire. He is a member of King Solomon Lodge of Masons.

CHARLES D. BOARDMAN (Fig. 3) is well known in this department. He was born at Boston, Mass., March 31, 1842. He was a mariner by occupation. On January, 1862, he enlisted in the navy, and served three months on line-of-battleship "Vermont," when he was discharged by reason of promotion to ex-officer of U. S. S. "Mercury," and served on several ships before he left, in July, 1863. He reënlisted in Fifth Rhode Island Artillery, and served fourteen months, when he was transferred on board ship "Tacony," on which he was engaged until 1865, when he was discharged. During 1867 he served in the Mexican War. He then went to New Orleans and entered the fire department of that city, joining Volunteer Engine Company No. 1. In 1870 he entered the Charlestown department as a member of Mass. Ladder Company No. 1, from which he was transferred to this company, January 1, 1874. July 20 of the ensuing year he was promoted a permanent member, and assigned to Ladder Company No. 1, on October 7, where he remained until February 15, 1885, when he was transferred to Ladder Company No. 8, and on June 25, 1887, was transferred to this company. Mr. Boardman was injured at the Rice & Kendall fire and the Russell House fire, also at the Hanes and Commercial street fires. He is a member of the Ancient Order of Workmen and the Charlestown Veterans.

Frank Kelley, Jr., (Fig. 4) allied himself with this department May 9, 1874, as a call-member of this company.

John E. Cassidy (Fig. 5) was born at Charlestown District, Boston, Mass., January 3, 1852. He is a locomotive blacksmith by trade, to which he added the duties of fireman during 1870, as a call-member of Franklin Hose Company No. 4, but for several years previous did duty as a call-substitute. During 1873 he was transferred to this company as call-member. Mr. Cassidy is a member of the Jackson Fishing Club, the Charlestown Artillery Association, and the Charlestown Veterans.

A. Q. Clark (Fig. 6) was born at Charlestown District, Boston, Mass., May 29, 1839, and is a printer by trade. He entered the Charlestown department during 1856 as a volunteer in Howard Engine Company No. 3, and in 1860 was made a member, where he remained until 1864, when the company was disbanded. He was then transferred to Washington Engine Company No. 5, as a volunteer, until it was organized into this company, during 1865, and in May, 1866, was appointed a call-member.

John E. McGowan (Fig. 7) entered this department as a call-member of this company July 12, 1881.

John D. Gallagher (Fig. 8) was born at Charlestown District, Boston, Mass., November 1, 1836. He enlisted in Company A, Fifth Massachusetts Regiment, in June, 1862, and served nine months. He is a mason by trade, and on March 12, 1860, joined this company as a call-member. At the Eastern Railroad wharf fire he received injuries which laid him up two months. Mr. Gallagher is a member of the Charlestown Veterans.

John H. Fuller (Fig. 9) was born at Charlestown District, Boston, Mass., August 26, 1847, and is a millwright by trade. He entered the Charlestown department as a member of this company July 16, 1888. Mr. Fuller is a member of Olive Branch Assembly No. 9, I. O. O. F.

E. P. Sholes (Fig. 10) was born at Charlestown District, Boston, Mass., June 23, 1861. He is a teamster by occupation, and on December 14, 1888, was admitted a call-substitute in this company.

James Turnbull, call-hoseman, was born at Bangor, Me., February 22, 1845, and came to this city when a child, where he learned the cooper's trade. He enlisted in the navy in March, 1861, and served nine months. On his return he joined Washington Engine Company No. 5 of this department, during 1863, in which he remained until this company was organized, when he was transferred to his present position.

James Reynolds, call-hoseman, was born in Ireland, April 1, 1838. He

Hose Company No. 3. — Page 423.

joined the Charlestown department September, 1863, as a member of Engine Company No. 5, where he remained three years, when he retired; but rejoined during 1868, doing duty in this company. During the war he served in the Fifth Massachusetts Regiment.

EDWARD PARKER HAMILTON, call-substitute, was born at Cohasset, Mass., March 3, 1859, and is a carpenter by trade. He entered this company March 6, 1882.

HOSE COMPANY NO. 4.

NAMES OF MEMBERS SINCE 1874.

Geo. L. Almeder, ap. January 7, 1874, resigned September 21, 1874; F. J. Almeder, ap. January 7, 1874, resigned June 1, 1874; Augustus M. Carroll, ap. January 1, 1874, resigned June 1, 1874; W. A. Caswell, ap. October 8, 1886, tr. Engine 4, February 16, 1888; Henry G. Dwight, ap. January 1, 1874, tr. Engine 25, April 5, 1875; Wm. Daley, ap. June 2, 1874, resigned September 21, 1875; Jas. W. Kimball, ap. August 4, 1874, tr. Chemical 1, November 6, 1875; Dominick Lavin, ap. October 13, 1875, resigned December 16, 1880; Jas. Murphy, ap. January 1, 1874, discharged June 1, 1874; Jas. Murphy, ap. April 14, 1875, resigned October 21, 1883; Wm. Todd, ap. January 1, 1874, discharged June 1, 1874; Thos. Williams, ap. January 1, 1874, discharged June 1, 1874; George Williams, ap. October 21, 1883, died September 26, 1886.

PRESENT MEMBERS.

Call-Capt. GEORGE N. F. GETCHELL (Fig. 1) was born at New Bedford, Mass., October 24, 1850, and on October 24, 1861, came to this city, where he learned the carpenter's trade. His fire experience dates from 1867, when he became a member of Protector Engine Company No. 2, of New London (Mass.) department, in which he remained a few months. During 1868 he was admitted a member of this company, in which he was chosen secretary, January 1, 1869, which office he held one year. January 1, 1873, he was promoted assistant foreman; and on June 1, 1875, was promoted to his present position. Captain Getchell is a member of the Charlestown Veterans. He enlisted when but thirteen years of age as messenger-boy in the navy, on board the S. S. "Rhode Island," and served from June 11, 1864, to June, 1865.

SAMUEL H. AMSDEN (Fig. 2), driver, is another old veteran in the Charlestown department. He was born at Boston, Mass., October 31, 1826. During 1846 he enlisted from New Orleans in the Mexican War, as first assistant wagonmaster in the quartermaster's department, in which he served eight months. December, 1847, he returned to this city, and was employed as a teamster, to which he added the duties of fireman. January 1, 1866, when this company was organized, with him as foreman. He held that position until

November of the following year, when he left the service, but was admitted a hoseman soon after. At this time he was employed at the navy-yard, and was connected with the fire apparatus of that place. He was appointed a permanent member, and detailed as driver of this company, October 1, 1872. Mr. Amsden was thrown off the hose-cart, on Main street, January 15, 1882, and severely injured his back and hip. He is a member of the Boston Veterans, King Solomon Lodge, Masons, Webster Lodge No. 14, K. of P., and Barnicoat Fire Association.

GEORGE R. CUMMINGS (Fig. 3) was born at New York City, January 19, 1857, and when but a child came to this city, where he learned the mason's trade. He entered this department, as a substitute in Engine Company 4, during 1879, and after one year's service was transferred to Engine Company No. 10. On May 19, 1880, he was appointed a permanent member of that company, in which he remained until June 25, 1887, at which time he was transferred to this company.

FRANK TURNBULL (Fig. 4) was born at Cork, Ireland, October 1, 1842, and when very young came to this city, where he learned the cooper's trade. He enlisted in the navy, on board the S. S. "Connecticut" and "Powhattan," during 1864, and served until July, 1868. During the latter part of that year he entered this service, as a member of this company, and was elected a trustee. Mr. Turnbull is a member of Post 149, G. A. R., Charlestown Veterans, T. F. Maars Commandery, Veterans' Union No. 3.

JOSEPH RILEY (Fig. 5) was born at Montreal, P.Q., June 6, 1840, and during 1859 came to this city, where he finished the boiler-maker's trade. April, 1872, he joined this company, as assistant foreman, and on March 1 of the same year was call-foreman, which position he held thirteen months. Mr. Riley is a member of the Charlestown Veterans, Urban Literary Association, Franklin Association, and Mushawum 113, R. S. G. F.

JOHN M. UART (Fig. 6) was born at Boston, Mass., March 30, 1845. He has been engaged in the barber business for a number of years. During 1862 he enlisted in the navy on board the sloop-of-war "Saratoga," on which he served until June, 1864. During the latter part of that year he reenlisted in Company M, Thirty-first Maine Volunteer Regiment, and was discharged July 16, 1865. He was wounded at Petersburg, April 2, 1865. September, 1866, he was admitted a member of this company. Mr. Uart was laid up for five weeks from injuries received at the big fire. At the stable fire on Warren street, August, 1870, he fell from the roof to the basement. He is a member of the Charlestown Veterans, Mushawum Assembly No. 113, R. S. G. F., and Franklin Associates.

JAMES H. McLAUGHLIN (Fig. 7) was born at Charlestown District, Boston, Mass., April 1, 1846. He is a mechanical engineer by trade, and on April 1, 1872, was admitted a call-member of this company. Mr. McLaughlin is a member of the Charlestown Veterans.

GEORGE H. KINCAIT (Fig. 8) was born at Charlestown District, Boston,

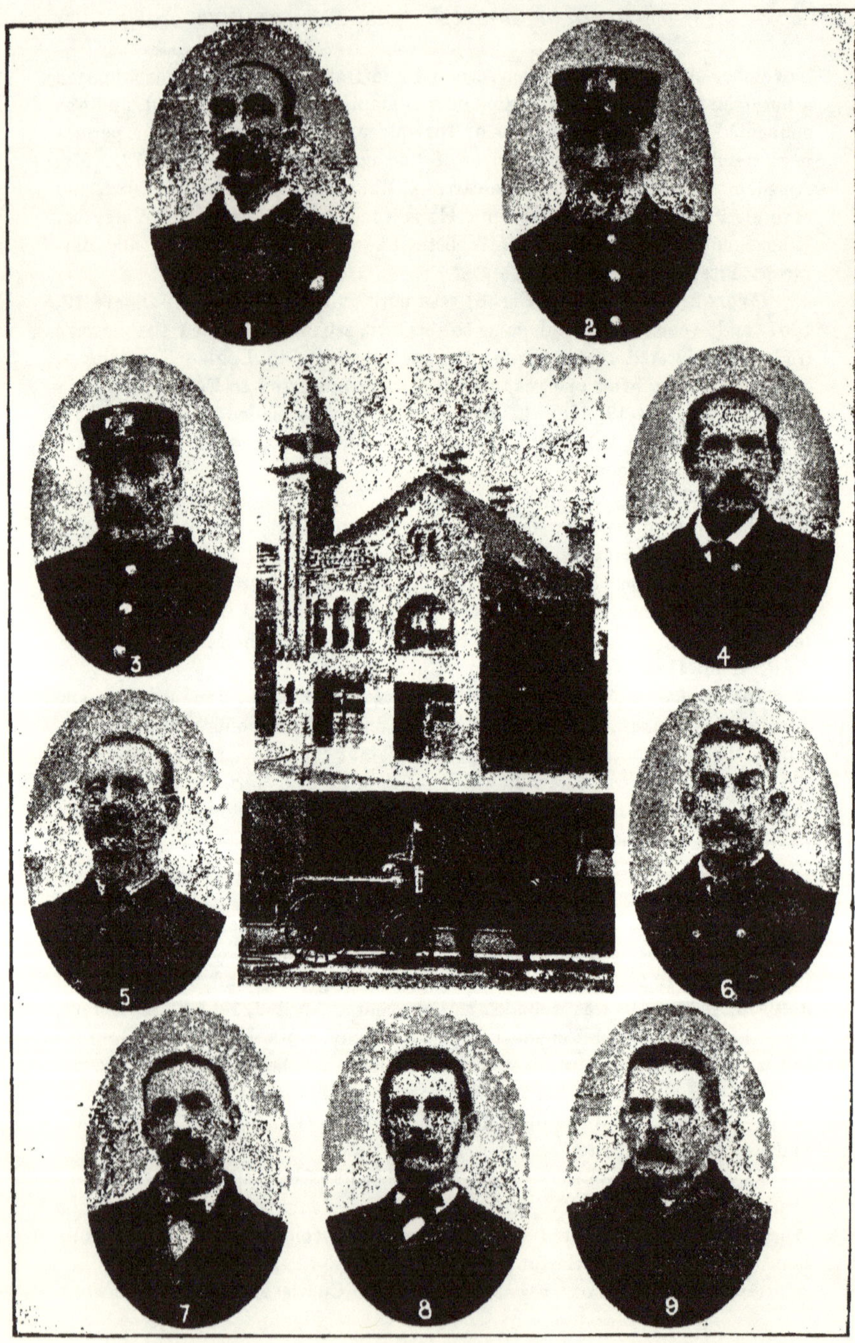

Hose Company No. 4. — Page 427.

Mass., February 24, 1839. He is a house-painter by trade. When but sixteen years of age he began his first fire duty on Warren Engine Company 4, as a call-substitute. Three years later he was admitted a member of Engine Company No. 5. Soon after he left the department, but was again enrolled a call-member, October 1, 1874, of this company. Mr. Kincait is a member of the Charlestown Veterans.

JAMES GRIFFIN (Fig. 9) was born at Charlestown District, Boston, Mass., March 4, 1853, and is an oil-finisher by trade. He entered the service during April, 1876, as a call-substitute in this company, in which he was made a member December 18, 1880. Mr. Griffin is a member of R. S. G. F. and the Franklin Associates.

CHAPTER VII.

DISTRICT NO. 3.

DISTRICT No. 3 is bounded by a line beginning at the Charlestown draw-bridge, and running through the centre of Charlestown street, Haymarket square, and Washington, to Summer street, and north of Summer street, and the N. Y. & N. E. R.R. passenger depot to the water. Within this boundary are the largest wharves, at which are moored sail and steam ships of all sizes, bringing the products of nations, which are stored in the immense warehouses in this territory. This district is what is called the wholesale section, in which are located many of the most famous landmarks, among which are the Old South Church, Faneuil Hall, Old State House, birthplace of Franklin, etc. Here are also to be found the principal banks, banking-houses, safe deposits, and insurance buildings. Newspaper row is also in this district, in which are published all the daily papers. Among the government buildings are the Custom-house, United States bonded warehouses, Post-office, etc. In a quarter in which so many industries are carried on, it is very hard to state which is the most important, but printing, and its kindred industries, will probably stand first on the list. It was over this section that the great fire of 1872 swept, although starting in District No. 5. The apparatus under charge are Engine Companies Nos. 8, 25, and 31 (fire-boat), and Ladder Companies Nos. 8 and 14. The headquarters for the District Chief is at the house of Ladder Company No. 8.

District Chief Lewis P. Abbott, of District No. 3, is a fireman of excellent ability. His judgment in the most trying moments is even, when determined at a moment's reflection, most effective, he possessing a natural ability for the planning of an attack on the flames. Always self-possessed, and ever ready to undertake the most perilous task, he is well qualified to fill the position he now enjoys. He was born in Bangor, Me., December 23, 1838, and is therefore fifty years of age. In 1857 he came to Boston, where he followed the carpenter's trade. When the war broke out he was among the first to offer his services, and in May, 1861, he enlisted in the detached service of the quartermaster's department as wagon-master. At the close of this great struggle he, in 1864, moved to Washington, D.C., where he remained until 1867, at which time he again returned to this city. His career in the fire department did not begin until April, 1873, when he was appointed a call-ladderman in Ladder Company No. 3. After a short service with this company, he, at the time of the reorganization of the department, left the force, and remained out of it until September, 1875, when he was appointed captain

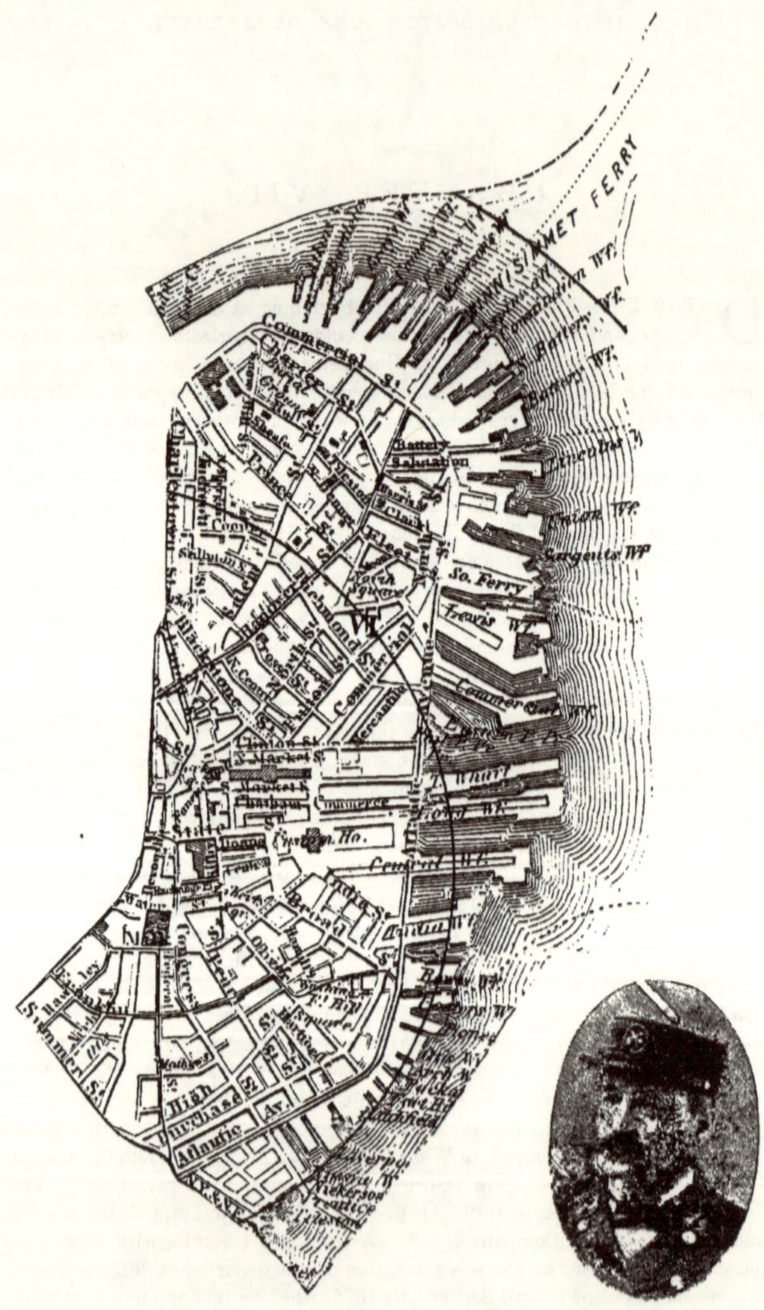

Chief Abbott and Map of District No. 3. — Page 431.

of Engine Company No. 22, he being the first foreman of that company. He remained there about one year, when he was transferred, as captain of Ladder Company No. 3, and October 2, 1882, was promoted to district engineer, and assigned to District No. 6, in South Boston. But his services were needed on more important work, and on August 3, 1885, he was assigned to District No. 3, which, as can be seen from the chapter preceding, is one of the most important and dangerous sections of the city. Captain Abbott is a strict disciplinarian, and when in charge of a fire his orders are few, but every point is covered. He is a member of the Grand Army of the Republic and the Knights of Honor.

ENGINE COMPANY NO. 8.

NAMES OF MEMBERS SINCE 1874.

Captain William Childs, ap. April 22, 1874, tr. to same position Chemical Engine No. 6, November 1, 1888; Lieutenant E. T. Smith, ap. April 23, 1874, tr. to Chemical Engine No. 6, November 1, 1888; Engineman R. E. Flanders, ap. April 22, 1874, discharged July 13, 1874; Assistant Engineman J. H. Marks, ap. April 22, 1874, tr. to Engine No. 7, May 8. 1874; Hosemen: C. W. Smith, ap. April 23, 1874, resigned September 6, 1881; Seth L. Low, ap. April 23, 1874, promoted to captain Engine No. 31, tr. January 1, 1884; Erwin C. Bowman, ap. April 23, 1874, tr. to Engine No. 4, September 29, 1888; Thomas L. Whalen, ap. April 23, 1874, resigned June 5, 1875; A. P. Smith, ap. April 23, 1874; William M. Pierce, ap. April 23, 1874. resigned March 31, 1885; J. D. Brown, ap. April 23, 1884; S. J. Bridget, ap. April 23, 1874; John Neal, ap. May 6, 1874, promoted to lieutenant and tr. to Engine No. 25, April 21, 1882; Assistant Engineman G. W. Barnard, ap. May 25, 1874, promoted to engineman and tr. to Engine No. 25, February 1, 1875; Engineman E. E. Jeffrey, ap. July 21, 1874, tr. to same position Engine No. 34, November 1, 1888; Assistant Engineman J. A. Shannon, tr. to this company from Engine No. 22, February 4, 1875, tr. to Engine No. 6, October 27, 1880; Hosemen: A. N. Ramsdell, ap. February 20, 1875, resigned October 5, 1882; G. W. Bullard, tr. from Engine No. 27 to this company, October 31, 1881, discharged December 28, 1882; Frank Douglass, tr. from Engine No. 25 to this company, April 21, 1882, resigned April 27, 1882; H. F. Wood, ap. June 27, 1882, tr. to Ladder Company No. 3, June 27, 1882; C. E. Phœnix, tr. from Engine No. 31 to this company, January 17, 1884, tr. to Engine No. 25, September 30, 1887; G. W. Edmunds, ap. March 28, 1885, tr. to Engine No. 15, March 11, 1887.

PRESENT MEMBERS.

Captain WILLIAM CHILDS. of this company. will be readily recognized in Figure 1 on page 435. He is one of the first members at the time reorganization. The old-time prestige of this company is not allowed to diminish in the least under his command. He was born in New York City,

N.Y., May 8, 1844, and is therefore 44 years of age. He came to this city during March, 1865, and worked in commercial business until April. 1865, and was admitted a call-hoseman in this company, March, 1866. February 4, 1873, he was promoted captain of this company, being the first foreman of the company after the reorganization of the department. Captain Childs is a member of the Masonic Order.

Lieutenant JOHN I. QUIGLEY (Fig. 2) was born at Philadelphia, Penn., July 27, 1855, and is therefore 33 years of age. When very young he came with his parents to this city. After leaving school he learned the pattern and model making trade, at which he worked until September 2, 1884, when he was appointed substitute in Engine Company No. 6. He was promoted a permanent member, and transferred to Ladder Company No. 1, March 27, 1885. From there he was transferred back to Engine Company No. 6, on January 16, 1886, and on Nov. 1, 1888, was promoted to his present position in this company. Mr. Quigley was severely injured at a fire May 25, 1888, by being jammed against a ballister, which resulted in a " lay off " for two weeks.

Engineman JOHN A. RYAN (Fig. 3) is one of the old fire-fighters of this city. He was born in Boston, Mass., January 25, 1845, and is therefore 43 years of age. He learned the distillery trade, and on the outbreak of the war enlisted in the navy, in 1862, on board the sloop-of-war " Brooklyn." He remained in the service until July, 1864, when he was discharged. The fire department claimed his attention, and on the reorganization, October 1, 1873, he was appointed permanent member and assigned to Ladder Company No. 8. He remained with that company one year, when he was transferred to Engine Company No. 25, and was nine years in the service as hoseman. He was promoted to assistant engineman during 1885, and on Nov. 1, 1888, he was promoted engineman and assigned to this company. He is a member of the Grand Army of the Republic.

Assistant Engineman WILLIAM HUDSON (Fig. 4) was born at Bath. Me., November 6, 1851, and is therefore 37 years of age. He joined this department February 1, 1872, at which time he was appointed assistant engineman and assigned to Engine Company No. 10. July 1. 1873, he left the service, but again returned, in September, 1874, as a substitute. He was appointed hoseman in Engine Company No. 10, December 7. 1875, and was transferred to Ladder Company No. 8, July 20. 1877. January 16, 1882, he was transferred and promoted to his present position.   •

JOHN FRANCIS O'CONNELL (Fig. 5), driver, was born at Brookline, Mass., March 11, 1861. He joined this force as a substitute, October 17. 1882, and on January 22, of the following year, was promoted a permanent member and assigned to this company, where he has since remained. The only accident he has met with was a severe sprain of his ankle while coming downstairs in the engine-house.

GEORGE W. DENNIS (Fig. 6) was born December 1, 1849. He entered

ENGINE COMPANY No. 8. — Page 435.

the Charlestown fire department during 1871, as call-man on an Engine Company, from which he was transferred to Hose Company No. 1, and then to the present company, and made a permanent member July 3, 1874. He was thrown off the apparatus and broke his leg while responding to an alarm. He is a member of the Howard Lodge, Odd Fellows.

Roscow E. HANDY (Fig. 7) first saw the light in Readville, Me., January 14, 1850, and is therefore 38 years of age. He came to this city during April, 1870, and February 4, 1876, was made a member of Engine Company No. 3 as call-man. He was appointed a permanent member October 2, 1882, and assigned to his present position. He was severely injured at a fire June 17, 1882, on Hampshire street, when he had his left shoulder broken. Some time later he was again off duty for four weeks from the effects of cuts from falling glass. He is a member of the Knights of Pythias, also a Mason.

JAMES F. DUFFY, hoseman (Fig. 8), was born at Lawrence, Mass., January 8, 1855; is therefore 33 years of age. He was for some time a resident of Fall River, and was a member of the fire department of that city, running with Hand Engine Company No. 1. He left that place and came to Boston, March 20, 1877, and worked at the South Boston Horse Car Paint Shops as painter. He was appointed a call-substitute in the South Boston force during 1878, and on May 22, 1882, was promoted a permanent substitute and assigned to this company, May 16, 1882. On October 16 was promoted a permanent member. He is a member of the Legion of Honor and the Ancient Order of Foresters.

PATRICK H. DISKEN will be recognized in Figure 9. He was born at the North End, this city, March 17, 1858, and is consequently 30 years of age. His career as a fireman began October 16, 1886, when he was appointed substitute. August 15 of the same year he was promoted a permanent member and assigned to this company October 30, 1887. He is a member of the Legion of Honor.

EDWARD J. MCKENDREW (Fig. 10) was born in New York City, April 24, 1859. He came to this city at an early age, where he learned the boiler-maker's trade, which business he followed until October 14, 1887, when he joined the force as a substitute and was assigned to this company.

W. H. MCDONALD (Fig. 11) was born at Boston, Mass., April 12, 1858; is therefore 30 years of age. He was employed as locomotive blacksmith previous to January 6, 1888, at which time he was appointed permanent member of this department and assigned to Engine Company No. 4, and in 1888 was transferred to this company. He is a member of the Order of American Firemen.

WILLIAM H. COBB (Fig. 12) was born at East Boston, April 29, 1858, and is therefore 30 years of age. His career as fireman dates from February 16, 1888, when he was appointed a substitute on this department and assigned to various engine companies, and during 1888 was detailed to this company.

ENGINE COMPANY NO. 25.

NAMES OF MEMBERS SINCE 1874.

Captain George W. Frost, ap. April 1, 1874, tr. April 28, 1885 ; Lieut.
M. B. Kimball, ap. October 1, 1873, tr. 1874 ; Engineman E. E. Jeffery, ap.
October 1, 1873, resigned May 20, 1874 ; Asst. Engineman J. A. Ryan, ap.
October 1, 1873, tr. November 1, 1888 ; J. W. Chase, ap. October 20, 1873,
tr. to Engine Company No. 3 ; D. McCarty, ap. October 1, 1873, tr. to Engine
Company No. 6, May 22, 1874 ; S. F. Ridler, ap. October 1, 1873, resigned ;
T. D. Kelley, ap. January, 1874, tr. to Hose Company No. 8 ; Frank Reed,
ap. October 1, 1873, tr. February 26, 1886 ; J. J. Hughes, ap. May 1, 1874,
tr. to Hose Company No. 9 ; N. E. Abbott, ap. May 8, 1874, discharged ; C.
D. Curtis, ap. May 10, 1874, tr. to Engine Company No. 28 ; Charles Miller,
no record, tr. to Engine Company No. 22 ; John Enwright, ap. October 1,
1873, tr. June 25, 1887 ; Charles Smith, ap. May 11, 1874, tr. to Engine
Company No. 3 ; G. H. Wentworth, ap. May 25, 1874, tr. to Engine Company No. 22 ; J. H. Maltd, no record, tr. to Engine Company No. 26 ; D.
Dennison ; H. D. Dwight, ap. April 5, 1875, resigned ; P. E. Keyes, no
record ; G. Guttermuth, no record ; D. J. O'Connell, no record ; Warren Flet-
cher, no record ; Frank Douglass, no record, tr. to Engine Company No. 8,
April 21, 1882 ; J. S. Tobey, ap. November 29, 1874, tr. May 31, 1889 ;
James Crosby, ap. April 12, 1877 ; William H. Clay, ap. June 1, 1880, tr. to
Engine Company No. 8 ; M. B. Reardon, ap. July 1, 1880, tr. ; Charles A.
Winslow, ap. June 1, 1883 ; George H. Stinson, ap. September 21, 1882, tr.
August 20, 1887 ; William J. Healey, ap. October 21, 1883, tr. November
23, 1885 ; E. F. Curran, ap. July 1, 1883, tr. September 26, 1886 ; J. F. Murray, ap. September, 1884, tr. September 27, 1886 ; F. H. Smith, ap. March
28, 1885, tr. July 1, 1886 ; M. J. Kennedy, ap. March 28, 1885, tr. December
26, 1885 ; J. F. McCarthy, ap. November 23, 1885, discharged April 11,
1887 ; H. W. Bauch, ap. February 25, 1886, tr. February 26, 1888 ; C. J.
Hearn, ap. February 16, 1888, tr. August 24, 1888 ; J. W. Murphy, ap. April
12, 1888, tr. January 4, 1889 ; William A. Caswell, ap. August 24, 1888, resigned October 19, 1888.

PRESENT MEMBERS.

Captain CLARENCE O. POLAND (Fig. 1), of this company, is an excep-
tionally fine man and commander. He was born in Winchendon, Mass.,
January 19, 1848, and is therefore 40 years of age. At an early age he
came to this city and learned the mason's trade. When the war broke out he
was among the first to offer his services, and enlisted in 1863 with Company
A, Forty-Second Massachusetts Infantry, and Company M, Third Massachusetts Cavalry. He remained until the close of the war, retiring in the latter
part of 1865. Ever ready to aid in the protection of the public, he entered
the force as call-man with Hook and Ladder Company No. 3, February 1, 1873.

May 1, 1874, he was promoted a permanent member, and promoted to captain of Engine Company No. 11, August 8, 1881. He remained there until January 1, 1884, when he was assigned to Engine Company No. 10. April 28, 1885, he was transferred to this company. Captain Poland has received a number of severe injuries while in the department, and has many times been praised by the Fire Commissioners, in their reports, for his bravery. Among the many accidents we will mention the following: Burned in the face and hands at a fire in Stearns' lumber wharf, September 26, 1883; he was overcome with gases in the hold of the English steamer " Cephalonia," and nearly smothered; February 12, 1885, he was severely injured in the breast by the explosion of an extinguisher. Reports of 1878 and 1881 mention his valuable services. He is a member of the Boston Veterans, Grand Army of the Republic, and the Odd Fellows.

Lieutenant JOHN NEAL (Fig. 2) was born in South Boston, January 8, 1843. After leaving school he engaged in the carpentry business, which he followed up to the time of the breaking out of the war, when he enlisted in 1861 in Company C, First Massachusetts Regiment, in the Pulaska Guards. He served two years as private, during which he was confined in Libby Prison four months. He returned to this city on the disbandment of his company. His career in the fire department dates from May 6, 1874, when he was appointed a permanent member, and assigned to Engine Company No. 8, where he remained eight years, after which he was promoted lieutenant and assigned to this company. Lieutenant Neal has a record of which he may well feel proud. He has been on the force for fourteen years, during which he has never missed but one alarm of fire when on duty. He has been very fortunate in escaping accidents, never having received any of a serious nature. He is a member of the Grand Army of the Republic, also of Howard Lodge I. O. O. F., Charlestown.

Engineman GEORGE W. BARNARD (Fig. 3) was born at Nantucket, Mass., April 12, 1845. He learned the machinist's trade, and came to Boston May 10, 1863. When the rebellion broke out he enlisted with Company C, Sixtieth Massachusetts Regiment, in 1863, and remained until disbanded, during 1864. He joined the fire department May 26, 1874, as assistant engineman in Engine Company No. 8. He remained with that company until February 1, 1875, when he was promoted engineman, and assigned to this company. He has been fortunate regarding accidents, the only one of a serious nature being in 1879, at the Stearns' fire, on Albany street. He has been a member of the Masonic Order for twenty years.

MARTIN H. RYAN (Fig. 4) was born at Boston, Mass., July 6, 1865. After leaving school he learned the mechanical engineer trade, and on August 29, 1888, was appointed in this company, to act as assistant engineman. He is a member of the Firemen's Charitable Association.

SAMUEL A. WHEELOCK (Fig. 5) was born at East Cambridge, Mass., April 28, 1862. He learned the slating trade, at which he worked until July

1, 1886, at which time he was appointed permanent substitute in this force. He had been a call-man from June 1, 1882, on Hose Company No. 1. His first assignment on the permanent force was as substitute on Engine Company No. 23, from which he was transferred July 27, 1886, to Engine Company No. 6; from there he was transferred to this company, September 27, 1886, and made a permanent hoseman. He was overcome by smoke in the fire at Clarke's Hotel, March 18, 1887, and laid up ten days; also from cuts received on the neck from falling glass, June 12, 1887, he was again unfit for duty for three weeks.

JAMES S. TOBEY (Fig. 6) was born in New Bedford, Mass., January 19, 1847. At an early age he learned the house-painting trade, and came to this city. He first began duty in this department as call-man in Engine Company No. 2, November 2, 1874. February 3, 1876, he was promoted a permanent member and assigned to this company, but was transferred to Hose Company No. 9 in 1884, where he remained 10 days, when he was again transferred to this company. He has been mentioned several times in the Commissioners' report, for bravery. At a fire on Albany street, September 17, 1880, he had his left leg broke, and was severely burned on the face and hands, and was again on the sick list one week, March 18, 1887, by being overcome by smoke. He is a member of the I. O. O. F.

HENRY A. FOX (Fig. 7) is a Boston boy, being born in this city, November 18, 1863. He joined the department October 15, 1886, as a substitute. He did fire duty in Engine Company No. 4 four months previous. July 29, 1887, he was promoted a permanent member and assigned to Engine Company No. 26, from which he was transferred to this company February 16, 1888.

JOHN J. O'BRIEN, hoseman (Fig. 8), is another Boston boy, he being born in this city, February 27, 1857, is therefore 31 years of age. His career as fireman dates from June 24, 1887, when he was appointed permanent substitute and assigned to this company, where he has since remained. He has in that short period been severely burned about the face and head, from the effects of which he was off duty seventeen days.

JAMES G. LOVELL (Fig. 9) was born in Boston, Mass., December 31, 1854; is therefore 34 years of age. His duties as a fireman began February 7, 1881, when he was appointed as call-man on Hose Company No. 5. June 18, 1887, he was made a permanent member and assigned to this company, where he has since remained. He was severely injured by a hot-air explosion, from the effects of which he was off duty three weeks.

THOMAS J. LANNARY (Fig. 10) is one of the very active men in this department. He was born at East Boston January 20, 1858; was employed as a ship-calker for several years, when he joined this force as a call-substitute, at East Boston, December, 1884. October 15, 1886, he was appointed permanent substitute and detailed to Engine Company No. 25. September 30, 1887, he was promoted permanent man and assigned to this company.

CHARLES E. PHŒNIX (Fig. 11) was born at Malden, Mass., May 12, 1856.

ENGINE COMPANY No. 25. — Page 441.

He was appointed substitute on Engine Company No. 1, May 1, 1872, where he remained until May 1, 1880. He then moved to East Boston, and in September of the same year run as volunteer with Engine Company No. 9. June 23, 1882, he was appointed substitute in the city proper, and did duty with most of the companies in this section. April 8, 1882, he was made permanent substitute, and on June 27 of the ensuing year was promoted permanent member and assigned to Engine 26. At his own request he was transferred to fire-boat "William M. Flanders" as hoseman. At a fire in the hold of Cunard S. S. "Cephalonia" he was severely overcome by smoke, which laid him up for seven days. January 17, 1884, he was transferred to Engine Company No. 8. While with this company he was obliged at one time to call on Engine Company No. 25 to play their water around him to prevent the flaming oil from burning him. August 26, 1887, he was transferred to this company. On the 13th of April, 1888, he was blown downstairs by a hot-air explosion at a fire in Fort Hill square, by which he was severely burned on the head and hands.

JOHN W. MURPHY (Fig. 12) was born at Boston, Mass., July 11, 1860, is therefore 28 years old. He was appointed substitute January 13, 1888, and assigned to Ladder 7, from which he was transferred on April 12 of the current year to this company. Mr. Murphy was badly burned on the face and hands on April 13 by a hot-air explosion, which necessitated remaining off duty seventeen days.

JOHN H. MURNAN (Fig. 13) was born at Boston, Mass., March 29, 1859. He is a carpenter by trade, at which he was employed until his appointment in this department, which occurred November 23, 1888, in this company. Mr. Murnan is a member of Catholic Order of Forresters.

HOOK AND LADDER COMPANY No. 8.
NAMES OF MEMBERS SINCE 1873.

Capt. George F. Griffin, ap. October 1, 1873; L. M. Clifford, ap. October 1, 1873, discharged July 18, 1874; C. H. Merritt, ap. October 1, 1873, discharged June 1, 1874; J. W. Chase, ap. October 1, 1873, tr.; W. B. Lottridge. ap. October 1, 1873, tr. September 21, 1876; A. Morse, ap. October 1, 1873, discharged May 9, 1874; H. K. Dole, ap. October 1, 1873, discharged December 11, 1874; S. W. Fletcher, ap. October 1, 1873; F. D. B. Hill. ap. October 1, 1873, discharged February 25, 1874; J. J. Hughes, ap. October 1, 1873, tr. May 1, 1874; C. E. Ramsdell, ap. October 1, 1873, discharged August 24, 1877; T. F. Lyons, ap. October 1, 1873. tr. March 24, 1879; A. H. Egerton, ap. October 1, 1873, tr. July 20, 1877; J. A. Ryan. ap. October 1, 1873, tr. July 30, 1874; Thomas Boggs, ap. October 1, 1873, tr. July 8, 1876; W. J. Large, ap. October 1, 1873, discharged June 20. 1881; E. B. Smith, ap. May 12, 1874, tr. November 9. 1884; Joseph Bell, ap October 1, 1873, discharged October 15, 1873; F. P. Mahan, ap. May 2, 1874, discharged June 24, 1887; J. H. Brown, ap.

January 8, 1874, died in service, December 20, 1877; Eugene Cummings, ap. June 6, 1874, tr. September 10, 1880; P. E. Chase, ap. April 5, 1875, discharged October 13, 1880; J. M. Nazro, ap. November 1, 1875, tr. July 20, 1877; W. J. Wilson, ap. November 21, 1875, discharged March 7. 1876; James Hines, ap. March 8, 1876, discharged June 13, 1876; R. McCarty, ap. March 9, 1876, discharged August 3, 1876; Thomas W. Rochfort, ap. June 19, 1876. discharged May 20, 1877; J. A. McLaughlin, ap. August 20, 1876, discharged December 23, 1876; John Pendoly, ap. September 21, 1876, tr.; William Hudson, ap. July 20, 1877, tr. January 16, 1882; E. E. Whiting, ap. August 27, 1877, tr. May 13, 1880; E. A. Smith, ap. December 21, 1877, tr. January 14, 1882; S. F. Ridler, ap. March 24, 1879, tr. August 12, 1880; B. D. Hill, ap. May 16, 1880, discharged October 3, 1882; O. M. Clapp, ap. September 10, 1880, discharged September 4, 1882; F. L. Wilson, ap. August 12, 1880, discharged October 3, 1882; William H. Flavell, ap. November 25, 1880. killed in service November 25, 1886; C. W. Dixon, ap. July 13, 1881, discharged May 20, 1885; M. Murnan, ap. April 1, 1882, tr. June 25, 1887; Isaac Noble, ap. April 1, 1882, tr. October 21, 1883; John Prendergast, ap. October 2, 1882, tr. June 21, 1889; T. B. Flanagan, ap. October 16, 1882, tr. January 7, 1889; William H. Hughes, ap. June 30, 1883, tr. July 1, 1886; P. F. McDonough, ap. October 21, 1883, tr. January 7, 1884; L. F. Stevens, ap. January 7, 1883, discharged October 13, 1884; D. J. Doherty, ap. February 16, 1885; tr. October 12, 1888; C. D. Bordman, ap. February 16, 1885, tr. June 24, 1887; L. Scallon, ap. March 28, 1885, tr. January 13, 1888; J. W. Groves, ap. February 25, 1886, discharged November 20, 1886; H. F. Woods, ap. January 4, 1886, discharged February 6, 1886; M. J. Kennedy, ap. July 1, 1886, tr. May 31, 1889; E. J. Tully, ap. December 5, 1886, tr. May 31, 1889; F. W. Battis, ap. February 4, 1887, tr. April 23, 1889; W. F. Watson, ap. February 4, 1887, discharged October 23, 1888; C. E. Kirby, ap. June 24, 1887, tr. 1888; J. N. Lally, ap. January 14, 1888, tr. 1888; P. J. McCarty, ap. February 16, 1888, tr. 1888.

Present Members.

Few men in this department have seen as much active service as Captain GEORGE F. GRIFFIN (Fig. 1), of Hook and Ladder Company No. 8. He has had a quarter of a century of fighting in the most inflammable sections, and his record is one worthy of pride. He was born in Gorham, N. H, April 18, 1838, and is therefore 50 years of age, but as vigorous and active as any on the force, despite the severe strains that have been put upon him. When about twelve years of age he began life as a sailor. November, 1863, he enlisted in the Fifty-sixth Massachusetts Regiment. and passed through three campaigns without a wound, returning with it to Boston, July, 1865. He then learned the carpenter's trade; in connection with it joined this force

October, 1868, as call-man in Ladder Company No. 1. He remained in that capacity until October, 1873, when he was promoted to captain of Ladder Company No. 8, which position he has since held. Besides the duties he performs in battling with the flames, he has for the past six years been making and repairing all the ladders used in the department, and, as may be supposed, this is no small item, as this department averages twelve hundred feet of ladders per year. In this service he has two assistants. Captain Griffin has also had assigned under his charge two pieces of apparatus at one time. Among these we will mention the old Areal ladder, Water Tower, and Hayes' ladder, and they have been handled as only a man of his experience could do. He has met with few accidents of a serious nature, the worst of them probably being received at the burning of the American House on Hanover street, when he fell through a dead-light in the floor and broke his knee-pan, from which accident he was laid up four months, and finding it did not get well he had to be again operated upon, from the effects of which he was off duty almost a year. He is a member of the Grand Army of the Republic and the I. O. O. F.

Lieut. JOHN S. KENNEY (Fig. 2) has had a varied experience in the service of the public. He was born in Boston, Mass., May 15, 1855. At the age of nineteen he enlisted in the cavalry for regular service, and was appointed under Gen. R. S. MacKenzie. During the five years in this service he was stationed at Fort Sill, Indian Territory; Camp Robinson, Nebraska; Fort Laramie, Nebraska; Fort Fetterman, Wyoming Territory; Fort Eliott, Texas, and other frontier points. He was in the famous Sioux and Cheyenne Indian fight in 1876, which lasted four days, during which he was wounded in the leg. This is only one of the many severe fights in which he participated. After his discharge, in September, 1879, he returned to Boston, and was employed in the weigher's department of the Custom-House. During October, 1882, he entered this department as substitute. January 8 of the following year he was appointed permanent member and assigned to this company. May 15, 1885, he was acting lieutenant in charge, in the absence of Captain Griffin, and September 4 of the ensuing year he was promoted lieutenant. Lieutenant Kenney is a member of the Barnicoat Fire Association, and past director in Pearl Council of the United Fellowship.

JOHN OTIS TABER (Fig. 3), driver, was born in Boston, Mass., June 24, 1863. He was employed as a driver of express and other wagons in this city until January 6, 1888, when he joined this department, and was appointed a substitute and assigned to Engine Company No. 9. February 16 he was transferred to Ladder Company No. 2, as driver, but was again transferred, July 2, to this company.

GEORGE A. NEWHALL (Fig. 4) was born in Lynn, Mass., October 5, 1850. He came to Boston during 1866, and soon after learned the machinist's trade. He joined the Charlestown (Mass.) department, October 1, 1872, as call-man in Engine Company No. 1. May 1, 1874, on the reorganization, he was transferred to Ladder Company No. 9, where he remained until September 3, 1884, when he was promoted a permanent member and transferred to this company; and on October 8 of the same year was transferred to Ladder Company No. 14, where he now is. Mr. Newhall had a narrow escape from death at the fire of Stickney & Poor's spice mill, November 21, 1883. He was on top of a forty-foot ladder when the wall fell, burying him under its *débris*, from which he was taken out in a terribly mangled condition; his leg was broken in two places, and many cuts and bruises covered his body; he was unable to attend duty for six months. September 9, 1884, he had the main artery in his thumb severed.

JOHN PRENDERGAST (Fig. 5) was born in Killarney, Ireland, March, 1850. He came to Boston in 1867, where he was employed in commercial work until the spring of 1871, when he enlisted in the United States navy, in which he served nine years, — three each on board the ship " Wabash," monitors " Ajax," and " Richmond." July, 1882, he joined the fire department, as substitute on Ladder Company No. 8; two months later he was appointed a permanent member and assigned to Ladder Company No. 14.

Many will recognize the well-known features in Figure 6 of THOMAS B. FLANAGAN. He was born in Boston, Mass., October 31, 1848. He learned the carpenter's trade, and during 1870 joined this force as call-man with Ladder Company No. 1, where he remained until November, 1875. He was assigned to this company during July, 1882. He has had some narrow escapes since becoming a member of the department, the most important being at a fire on Charlestown street, between Stillman and Cross streets. He, with Hosemen Kenney and Murnan, of Ladder Company No. 8, and Turner, of Ladder Company No. 1, was in the sixth story of a building, when they found the stairway cut off by the flames; turning to the windows they made the horrible discovery that these were heavily barred with iron; their axes were used, and soon the bars removed from one of them; but the leap to the ground would be death. Flanagan, ever self-possessed, would not permit his companions to make the jump until the last moment. When all hope was abandoned he discovered the dim outline of a roof a few feet from one of the windows, but several windows had to be spanned before the drop could be taken; but it was done, and they had barely reached the roof when the flames engulfed the floor from which they had just escaped. He has also been the means of saving several lives. He is a member of the Boston Veterans, also of the Barnicoat Association.

STEPHEN W. FLETCHER (Fig. 7) is one of the first members of this company. He was born at Medford, Mass., November 23, 1837, and came to this city at an early age, where he learned the carpenter's trade. He enlisted in Company C, Fifth Massachusetts Light Guards, of Medford, in April, 1861, and served three months. He reënlisted in October in Company C. Twenty-second Massachusetts Regiment, and served until the close of the war. His fire experience dates from 1855, when he joined Washington Engine Company

LADDER COMPANIES Nos. 8 AND 14. — Page 447.

No. 3, of Medford (Mass.) department, from where he went to Ladder Company No. 1, of Charlestown, Mass., where he served as a call-member until 1872, at which time he entered this department as a substitute in Ladder Company No. 3, and on October 1, 1873, he was promoted as a permanent member and assigned to this company. Mr. Fletcher was run over and badly injured by a horse-car while salting a hydrant on State street during February, 1886, and in 1873 had the first finger of his left hand taken off. He is a member of Tremont Lodge No. 15, of I. O. O. F., Sumner Lodge, K. of H., Charlestown Veterans, and the Firemen's Charitable Association.

JOHN FRANKLIN MITCHELL (Fig. 8) first saw the light in Portland, Me., January 1, 1853. He learned the carpenter's trade, in which he was engaged until December, 1882, at which time he joined this department as call-man, but was a substitute from December, 1879, in Ladder Company No. 4. He was promoted a permanent member 1887, and assigned to this company. He renders the department excellent service both in the calls of fire and assisting Captain Griffin in making and repairing ladders.

EDWARD J. TULLY (Fig. 9) was born in St. John, N.B., 1850. He learned the carpenter's trade and came to Boston in 1869. His career as a fireman began in 1871 as call-man in Ladder Company No. 1, Charlestown, which, after the annexation, was changed to Ladder Company 9. In 1886 he was transfered to Engine Company No. 26, and December 5, 1886, was transferred to this company, where he now remains. He has lost the use of his little finger by having the cords severed in a fire in 1886. On July 3, 1880, while at work dogging a ladder, a large slate fell from the top of the building and struck flat on his back, the force of which broke the slate. From this he was laid up three weeks. Another painful accident was received by running a nail through his foot. He has been instrumental in saving a lady's life at a fire in No. 1 Grant's court, Charlestown, in 1880.

MICHAEL J. KENNEDY (Fig. 10) was born in Boston, Mass., August 12, 1860. He attended the public schools, after which he was engaged in commercial business until March, 1885, when he was appointed substitute and assigned to this company, July 1, 1886. His only injuries so far has been by a fall of a ladder, the pick of which penetrated his foot.

CHARLES JOHN GIDDINGS (Fig. 11) was born in Bangor, Me., March 19, 1856. In 1870 he began going to sea, which vocation he followed until 1882. In 1884 he was appointed call-substitute in Ladder Company No. 4, and was promoted permanent substitute July, 1886, and twelve months later was appointed permanent member and assigned to this company. Mr. Giddings has been very fortunate in not meeting with severe accidents, although he has had a number of very painful wounds received while in some of the most dangerous parts of buildings. He is one of the most expert ladder-runners in the department. He was one of the four who assisted in the rescue of the only person that was saved in the Mechanics' Institute fire, June, 1886, and in trying to save the second man in the window he had a narrow escape from the falling walls.

FRED W. BATTIS (Fig. 12) was born in East Boston, February 20, 1863, and is therefore 25 years of age. He learned the machinist's trade, but the life of a fireman was more congenial, and he joined this department in 1886 as a call-man. February 4, 1887, he was made a permanent member and assigned to Ladder Company No. 2, East Boston, and was transferred to this company April 23, 1889.

STEPHEN J. RYDER (Fig. 13) was born in Boston, July 27, 1862. After a few years in the millinery business he joined the force, February 16, 1888, as substitute, and was assigned to Engine Company No. 24, a short time after which he was transferred to Engine Company No. 9, from which he was transferred to Engine Company No. 25, and during May, 1888, was assigned to this company.

JAMES J. FAY (Fig. 14) was born in Charlestown District, Boston, Mass., March 9, 1860, and is therefore 28 years of age. He was a clerk previous to his joining this force, which he did in July, 1887, when he was assigned to this company as permanent substitute.

PATRICK W. LANEGAN (Fig. 15) was born in Boston, Mass., December 7, 1860. He is a blacksmith by trade, and was appointed a substitute in this department Sept. 13, 1888, and detailed to Ladder Company No. 3, and was transferred to this company October 12.

M. A. MURPHY (Fig. 16) was born in Boston, Mass., October 12, 1865. He was employed as an expressman until his appointment in this department on September 13, 1888, when he was detailed to this company.

FIRE–BOAT OR ENGINE COMPANY NO. 31.
NAMES OF MEMBERS SINCE 1873.

George A. Scott, captain, ap. January 1, 1873, died December 16, 1883; Clark Doton, engineer, ap. January 1, 1873, resinged March 18, 1874; B. B. Wright, mate, ap. January 1, 1873, tr. to Ladder 16, October 12, 1888; L. Thompson, assistant-engineer, ap. April 1, 1874, resigned April 2, 1877; A. Smith, ap. January 1, 1873, resigned January 1, 1874; E. Whitchurch, steward, ap. January 1, 1873, resigned June 7, 1879; S. Abbott, ap. January 7, 1874, resigned August 16, 1874; T. J. Tobey, ap. September 1, 1873, died April 15, 1881; J. Cloutman, ap. August 16, 1874, resigned September 3, 1874; E. Ripley, ap. April 11, 1877, resigned July 10, 1881; E. Farren, ap. April 30, 1881, tr. to Engine 26, November 17, 1882; C. E. Phœnix, ap. November 27, 1882, tr. to Engine 8, January 15, 1884.

PRESENT MEMBERS.

The well-known features of Captain SETH L. LOWE, of this company, will be recognized in Figure 1 on the following page. He was born at Barre, Mass., July 18, 1841. He followed the trade of rigging vessels for

Engine Company No. 31 (Fire-boat). — Page 452.

about ten years. When the war broke out he was among the first to offer his services to his country, being enrolled July 12, 1861, in Company F, Fifteenth Massachusetts Volunteers, and served through the struggle. His career as a fireman began December 10, 1874, when he was appointed call-man in Engine Company No. 8. In March of the same year he was promoted a permanent member of the force, and remained with that company until January, 17, 1884, when his excellent and efficient services was rewarded by his promotion to captain of this company. He has been seriously injured but once. April 28, 1882, while at work on a fire, a large piece of iron fell and struck him on the knee, which rendered him unfit for duty for a year. Captain Lowe is a member of the Royal Arcanum.

Lieut. Bentley F. Healey (Fig. 2) was born at Rockland, Me., March 11, 1861. He came to Boston in 1863, and from the time of leaving school until his appointment on the force, January 15, 1884, he was employed on various steamboats. Just prior to his appointment he substituted for Captain Scott, of this company, from August 9 to the 15th of January. He was appointed a permanent member February 20, 1884, and assigned as second pilot of this boat, which position he held until August 29, 1888, when he was promoted to the position of lieutenant. He had the muscles of his back broken by a fall. He is a member of the Pilgrim Fathers Encampment, I. O. O. F.

Engineman George Walter Metcalf (Fig. 3) was born in Worcester, Mass., March 20, 1826, and is therefore 62 years of age. He is one of the oldest marine engineers running in this harbor, and is the oldest active engineman on the force. His life has been full of exciting interest, and despite his advanced age is very active. When a boy he began going to sea, which vocation he followed for ten years, when he settled in Buenos Ayres, as herdsman, having in charge thousands of head of sheep and cattle. After three years in this business he was pressed into the Buenos Ayres army, but only remained with it a few months. He returned to this country and enlisted in the navy, on board the frigate "Columbia," for three years and six months. In 1844 he enlisted in the Tennessee cavalry, under Generals Pillar and Patterson, and served two years in the Mexican War. On its closing, in 1846, he worked at his trade, of practical engineer. His services in the fire department dates from 1853, under Chief Barnicoat, on Engine Company No. 8. He remained with that company five years. He was appointed assistant engineman in this company, January 1, 1873. Eighteen months later he was promoted to his present position. Mr. Metcalf is a member of King Solomon Lodge of Masons.

Assistant Engineman Charles E. Small (Fig. 4) was born at Limington, Me., October 24, 1848. He came to this city at an early date, and was at one time employed as engineer on the Old Colony Railroad, also has had an experience on board ship for more than twelve years. He joined the department July 27, 1881, as a permanent member, and promoted to assistant engineman of this company. He is a member of Adams Lodge of the Royal Arch Chapter Hyannis, of the Masonic Order, and the Wachuset Lodgé 58, of the Order of Royal Good Fellows.

JAMES STUART KING (Fig. 5) was born in Boston, Mass., June 7, 1844. He joined this department in 1869 as call-man on Engine Company No. 7, where he remained until December, 1871, when he was transfered to Engine Company No. 10. September 4, 1874, he was again transferred to this company, where he has since remained. His first position in the boat was as fireman. From that he was made deck-hand, and in 1883 he was assigned to the position of hoseman. While riding on the steam propelling engine, on Mt. Vernon street, he was thrown off, and the wheels of the engine passed over his right foot, completely crushing it, but by the skill of his physicians it was saved from being amputated. He was unable to use it for sixteen mouths. Mr. King is a member of the Barnicoat Association, also of St. Paul Lodge, South Boston, and Queen Esther Chapter, Eastern Star of the Masons.

JOSEPH S. PINE (Fig. 6) was born in the island of Fayal, in the Azores, June 4, 1847, and is therefore 41 years of age. He came to this city when a boy, but went to sea until the rebellion, when he enlisted in the navy. He served in various war-vessels up to 1865, when he was mustered out and again went to sea, in the merchant-service. June, 1879, he was appointed a permanent member of this department and assigned to his present position. He is a member of the Grand Army.

THOMAS EDWARD EVANS (Fig. 7) is the youngest man in this company. He was born in Boston, Mass., November 18, 1864, and is therefore 24 years of age. His experience as fireman dates from September 23, 1887. when he was appointed a permanent member and assigned to this company, for which position he was well adapted, being previously employed in the tow-boats in Boston Harbor. He remained with this company until October 8, 1887. when he was transferred to Ladder Company No. 8, and a short time later was transferred to this company. Mr. Evans has been instrumental in saving several lives from drowning while employed in the harbor.

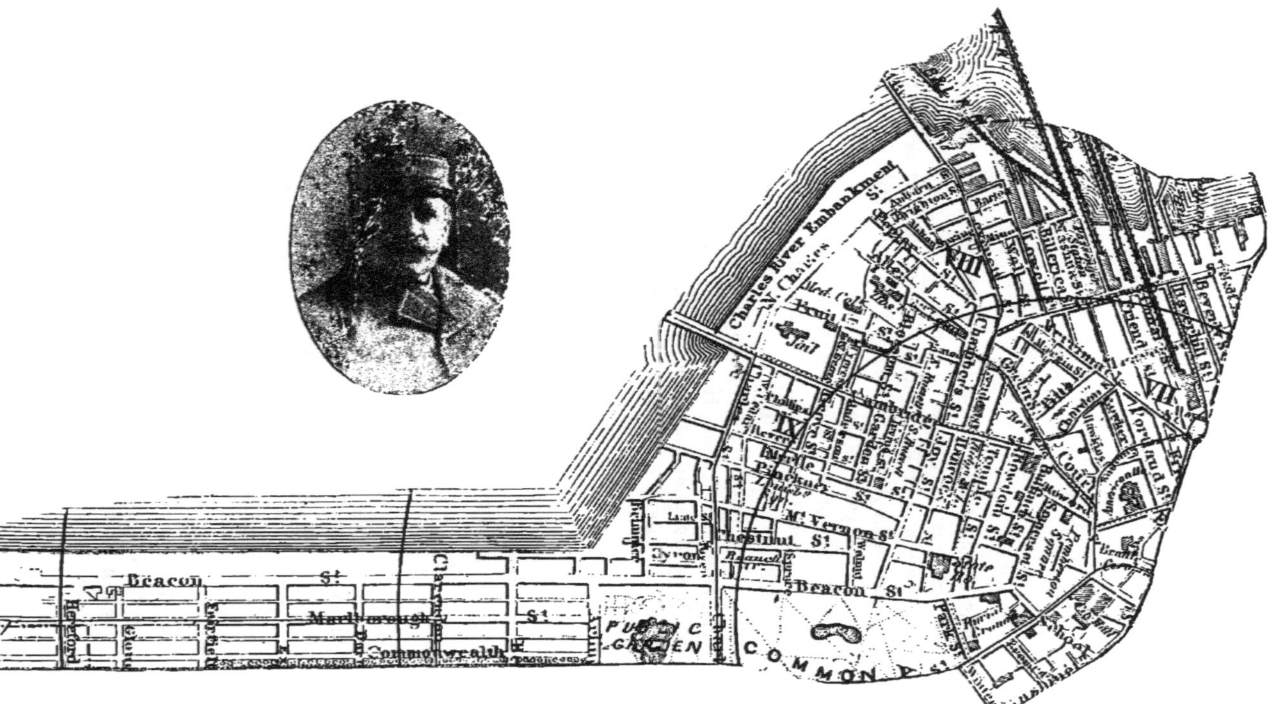

Chief Cheswell and Map of District No. 4. — Page 456.

CHAPTER VIII.

DISTRICT NO. 4.

THIS district is bounded as follows: Commencing at the draw of Charles-river bridge, west of Charlestown and Washington streets to Winter street; through the centre of Winter and Park streets, west side of Beacon to Arlington; through Arlington, west side of Commonwealth avenue to Chester park; through Chester park to the water (Charles river). Within this territory are embraced some of the largest warehouses, and other public and private buildings, to be found in the city. Of the public buildings we may mention the State House, City Hall, Registry of Deeds, Court House (Old and New), Suffolk County Jail, Massachusetts Hospital, Boston Athenæum, etc. Places of amusement: Music Hall, Horticultural Hall, Boston Museum, Howard Theatre, Dime Museum, and Nickelodeon. Hotels: Parker's, Young's, Tremont, American, Revere, Quincy, Coolidge, Crawford, Sherman, and Park's. Railroad depots: Boston & Maine, and its Eastern, Western, and Northern divisions, and the Fitchburg, Churches: King's Chapel. Park-street, Bowdoin-square, Mt. Vernon, First Congregational, West Church, Temple-street, and Saint Joseph's. Other notable buildings: Charity Buildings. Old Ladies' Home, Massachusetts Charitable Eye and Ear Infirmary, West City Stables, five public school-houses. etc.

One-half of the Common and the Public Garden are included in this section. After the fire of 1794, by which the several rope-walks on Pearl and Atkinson streets were burned, the inhabitants allowed them to be rebuilt on the flats at the foot of the Common, on condition that no rope-walks would be built upon the old site. By this act the old Round Marsh was lost to the town, which had always, from the first settlement, been a part of the Common, or training-field, and it was not until the first year of the elder Quincy's administration of city affairs that the lost estate was regained by paying the owners the sum of $54,000, and obtaining a conveyance of the land on February 25, 1824, it having been out of the town's possession for nearly thirty years, the grant from the town having been made September 1, 1794.

When the rope-walks were built, an open space was left at the southerly end, near the foot of Boylston street; but no street was laid out until Boylston street was extended westerly over the flats. September 25, 1837, Horace Gray and others petitioned for the use of the land for public gardens, which, in November, 1838, was granted, on certain conditions: one being that no building should be erected, except a greenhouse and a tool-house, and these not more than fourteen feet high. On February 1, 1839, Horace Gray, George

Darracott, C. P. Curtis, and others were incorporated as the proprietors of the Botanic Garden in Boston. They fitted up a conservatory for plants and birds, just north of Beacon and west of Charles streets, which was very attractive, until it was burned, during 1841; after that, efforts were fruitless to buy the garden. A place was designed for the City Hall upon Arlington street, on a line with Commonwealth avenue, the building facing due east and west; but this plan was given up, and the corner-stone of the present building was laid December 22, 1862, and dedicated September 18, 1865.

The apparatus in this district are: Engines Nos. 4, 6, 10; Chemical Engine No. 1, Ladder No. 1. Hose No. 8, and Water-Tower. The headquarters of the District Chief is in the house of Engine Company No. 4.

District Chief WILLIAM T. CHESWELL, of this district, is one of the best known men in the department. He was born in Boston. Mass., January 7, 1843, and is therefore 45 years of age. His experience in the fire department of this city dates from his boyhood, as in 1856 he joined the volunteer association connected with Extinguisher Engine Company No. 5, then located on East street, the site now occupied by Engine No. 7. In 1859 he was appointed a substitute on Steam Fire Engine No. 7, which was then located on Purchase street. April 1, 1863, he was appointed hoseman with the same company, where he remained until June 1, 1864, at which time he was transferred as driver of Barnicoat Engine No. 4. located in Scollay's building. January 1, 1871, he was promoted to assistant engineman, and April 4, 1874, was promoted to engineman, and three days later was promoted to captain of the same company. He was again promoted, July 1, 1880, to assistant engineer, the position he now holds. Chief Cheswell is a member of several organizations: Vice-president Veteran Firemen's Association; treasurer Firemen's Charitable Association; treasurer Boston Firemen's Burial Lot: past president Barnicoat Fire Association; also, a member in the Masonic fraternity, Odd Fellows, and other benevolent organizations.

ENGINE COMPANY NO. 4.

NAMES OF MEMBERS SINCE 1874.

W. T. Cheswell, promoted chief, 4th district. July 1, 1880; C. F. Deering, tr. September 1, 1882. to Engine Company No. 6; Frank Bowker, ap. 1874, tr. Engine Company No. 29; J. C. Harrington, resigned July, 1887, ap. August, 1874; M. Ahern. discharged December 15. 1875, ap. 1874; C. Griffin, died April 16. 1882, ap. 1874; F. P. Moriarty, discharged July 30. 1874. ap. 1873; Warren Blood, discharged April 30. 1874; J. D. Kelley, tr. to Ladder Company No. 3. April. 1882, ap. 1874; B. H. Bailey, tr. from Engine Company No. 10, discharged from Engine Company No. 4, 1879; M. Whelan, discharged August 10, 1874, ap. 1873; J. Brown, discharged September 11, 1874, ap. 1873; J. Kimball, tr. Chemical Engine Company No. 1, resigned August. 1885, ap. 1874: G. H. Knox. tr. Hose Company

No. 8, ap. September 1, 1874 ; C. C. Willett, promoted captain Engine Company No. 22, July, 1880, ap. September 1, 1874 ; F. C. Douglas, tr. Engine Company No. 25, December 15, 1875, ap. September, 1875 ; C. H. Cushing, discharged April, 1882, ap. December, 1877 ; Patrick Keyes, tr. Engine Company No. 22, April 13, 1882 ; B. E. Bartlett, ap. April 19, 1876, tr. Engine Company No. 1, 1882 ; G. R. Knights, ap. December 1, 1880, tr. Chemical Engine Company No. 1 ; Warren Fletcher, discharged December, 1880 ; Dennis O'Brien, discharged October 4, 1882, ap. September, 1881 ; William Gay, tr. Engine Company No. 10 ; George F. Titus, promoted captain Engine Company No. 27, March 17, 1884 ; F. W. Turner, resigned October, 1884, tr. from Engine Company No. 3, September 1, 1882 ; Walter Delano, resigned October 1, 1883, ap. October 14, 1882 ; John Graves, tr. Ladder Company No. 8, February 25, 1886 ; J. T. Byron, tr. Chemical Engine Company No. 5 ; C. H. Floyd, resigned September 19, 1885, ap. April, 1882 ; Edward B. Sproul, tr. Engine Company No. 10 ; Henry Coakley, tr. Engine Company No. 26, ap. 1881 ; Joseph Pierce, burned to death, August, 1884, ap. October, 1883 ; Joseph Newell, discharged November 29, 1882, ap. October, 1881 ; James Haley, tr. lieutenant Engine Company No. 10 ; William Chittick, tr. Engine Company No. 6 ; John McCarty, tr. Engine Company No. 12 (see Records Engine Company No. 25) ; John Travers, resigned October, 1882, tr. from Engine Company No. 6 to Engine Company No. 4, September 1, 1882 ; Daniel F. Hurley, ap. June, 1883, tr. Engine Company No. 7, January. 1886 ; William A. Rathburn, tr. Engine Company No. 4 from Engine Company No. 6, March 17, 1884, ap. October 21, 1883, tr. to Engine Company No. 34 ; C. W. Stevens, present member Engine Company No. 4, clerk at headquarters ; M. J. Crowley, tr. asst. engineman Engine Company No. 26 ; George H. Twiss, tr. hoseman Engine Company No. 1, ap. January 16, 1885 ; W. B. Bachelder, tr. Engine Company No. 15, ap. January 16, 1885 ; Frank H. Smith, tr. Engine Company No. 9, May 3, 1889 ; J. E. Burg, tr. Hose Company No. 6, ap. September 27, 1886 ; C. W. Harris, tr. Engine Company No. 33, ap. September 27, 1886 ; C. Herne, tr. Engine Company No. 10, ap. to Engine Company No. 4, August 23, 1888 ; Robert Carlton, tr. Engine Company No. 10, ap. September 3, 1884 ; Henry Phillips, discharged April 27, 1876 ; W. A. Caswell, tr. Engine Company No. 25, August 23, 1888, ap. February, 1888 ; J. L. McLaughlin, discharged, ap. 1874.

PRESENT MEMBERS.

Capt. HIRAM D. SMITH (Fig. 1) was born at Eastport, Me., October, 1844. He is a carpenter by trade, at which he was employed when the late war broke out. He was among the first to offer his services in this great struggle, and enlisted in the army in 1861. He remained in active service until 1864, when he was mustered out, and promoted a corporal. He came to Boston in 1865, and again worked at his trade, and joined the call force of the department, as assistant foreman of Ladder Company No. 3, during 1867.

On the reorganization he was transferred and promoted to captain of Engine Company No. 22. In 1880 he was transferred to his present company. He is a member of the Royal Arcanum, Odd Fellows, and the Grand Army of the Republic.

Lieut. J. P. DEAN (Fig. 2) was appointed a member of this department January 22, 1883, at which time he was detailed a hoseman in Engine Company No. 26. June 24, 1887, he was transferred to Engine Company No. 14, and on July 23, 1888, was transferred back to Engine Company No. 26. He was promoted to his present position, and assigned to this company November 1, 1888.

Engineman MICHAEL J. SLATTERY (Fig. 3) was born in Roxbury District, Boston, Mass., January 22, 1849. He is a machinist by trade, at which he was employed up to his appointment on this force, which occurred during 1870, as substitute on Engine Company No. 14. He was appointed hoseman on the same engine September 5, 1872, and reappointed to same position on the reorganization of the department, June 1, 1874, as a permanent member, and assigned driver of Hook and Ladder Company No. 11, September 21, 1879. He was promoted and transferred to assistant engineman of Engine Company No. 29, January 14, 1882. January 16, 1886, he was promoted and assigned to his present position. Mr. Slattery is a member of the Knights of Honor.

Assistant Engineman EBEN C. LOTHROP (Fig. 4) was born in Boston, Mass., May 26, 1860; is therefore 29 years of age. He is a machinist by trade, which vocation he followed until January 16, 1886, at which time he was appointed a substitute in the old Aerial Ladder Company; July, 1882, he was appointed a call-member in Hose Company No. 5, and was promoted to senior hoseman in charge in 1883. He was appointed a permanent member January 16, 1886, in this company, and transferred to Engine Company No. 23 April 1, 1886. During the ensuing year he was transferred to the repair-shop, but was again transferred, December 31, 1886, to this company as assistant engineman. Mr. Lothrop is a member of the Commercial Lodge of I. O. O. F.

W. B. WHITING (Fig. 5), driver of the water-tower apparatus, was born in Boston, Mass., August 17, 1850; is therefore 39 years of age. He enlisted in the navy in January, 1861, and served on the flagship "Melvin," under Admiral Porter; he was mustered out of service in 1863. April 1, 1885, he joined this department, as substitute in this company, and on June 24, 1888, was appointed a permanent member.

W. C. NEWDICK (Fig. 6), driver, was born in Georgetown, Me., February 29, 1856. He came to Boston in 1874, and joined this department. September 3, 1884, he was assigned to this company; from where he was transferred to Ladder Company No. 1, where he remained seven months, when he was transferred to his present position. Mr. Newdick is a member of the Order of American Firemen.

Top—Engine Company No. 4.   Bottom—Chemical Engine Company No. 1. — Page 461.

Edward C. Sargent (Fig. 7) was born in Portland, Me., December 19, 1845. He followed the sea previous to joining the Fire Department in 1873, at which time he was appointed a substitute. On the reorganization of the department he was appointed a permanent member, and in February, 1886, he was assigned to this company. He is a member of Bunker Hill Lodge of Odd Fellows, also of the Charlestown Veteran Firemen's Association.

Frank H. Smith (Fig. 8) first saw the light in Boston, Mass., December 26, 1859. He is a practical printer, which trade he pursued until becoming a member of this department. He was a call-substitute in Engine Companies Nos. 9 and 11 previous to his appointment as permanent substitute, on March 28, 1885, when he was assigned to Engine Company No. 25. July 1, 1886, he was made a permanent member, and transferred to this company. He is a member of the Firemen's Charitable Association.

Erwin C. Bowman (Fig. 9) was born in Littleton, N.H., September 22, 1850, and is therefore 38 years of age. He came to Boston in 1869, and was employed as clerk. April 23, 1874, he joined this department, and was assigned as permanent member to Engine Company No. 8, where he remained until September 29, 1888, when he was transferred to this company. During the fourteen years' service he has met with no severe accident. He is a member of the Odd Fellows and the Royal Arcanum.

C. J. Hearn (Fig. 10) was born in Boston, February 4, 1862, and is therefore 26 years of age. He entered the department as call-man, in Hose Company No. 5, January 19, 1886. He was made a substitute and assigned to Engine Company No. 25, February 16, 1888, and was promoted permanent member January 5, 1888; and on August 24, 1888, was transferred to this company. Mr. Hearn was severely burnt about the arms and face on April 13, 1888, by a hot-air explosion.

Thomas H. Ramsay (Fig. 11) was born in East Boston, July 14, 1859. He learned the plumber's trade, which he followed until February 16, 1888, at which time he joined this force, and was appointed substitute on Engine Company No. 29. He was assigned to this company April 13, 1888. Mr. Ramsay is a member of the Good Fellows and the Firemen's Charitable Association.

E. A. Burbank (Fig. 12) became connected with this department November 23, 1888, at which time he was appointed a substitute in this company.

J. F. F. Griffin (Fig. 13) first saw the light in Charlestown District, Boston, Mass., October 6, 1859. After leaving school he was employed as a teamster, which occupation he followed until November 23, 1888, when he was appointed a substitute in this department and detailed to Engine Company No. 1, from which he was transferred to this company, November 27, and assigned assistant driver of Chemical Engine No. 1.

CHEMICAL ENGINE COMPANY NO. 1.

JAMES C. K. HUMPHRY (Fig. 1, bottom of page), engineman of Chemical Engine Company No. 1, was born in St. John's, N.F., October 8, 1844. He came to Boston in 1850, and April 1, 1871, joined this force, being appointed a permanent member and assigned to this company. February 9, 1873, he was transferred and promoted to his present position. Mr. Humphry is a member of the Theatrical Mechanics' Association of this city, also of the Charitable, Veteran, and Barnicoat Fire Association.

JOHN J. FLANAGAN (Fig. 2, bottom of page) was born in Charlestown District, Boston, Mass., November 18, 1858. He entered this department as a substitute, in Engine Company No. 6, March 28, 1885; and on February 4, 1887, was promoted a permanent man; and on September 1, 1888, was transferred to this company.

JOHN B. HENNESSY (Fig. 3, bottom of page), of Chemical Engine Company No. 1, was born in Lawrence, Mass., March 3, 1860. He worked at his trade as house-painter until July 2, 1883, when he was appointed substitute and assigned to Engine Company No. 7, from where he was transferred to Engine Company No. 26 in the same year. He was appointed a permanent member May 1, 1884, and assigned to this company as hoseman. He is a member of the American Legion of Honor, also of the Firemen's Charitable Association.

ENGINE COMPANY NO. 6.

NAMES OF MEMBERS SINCE 1874.

M. B. Kimball, captain, ap. May 1, 1874, tr. March 17, 1884; E. A. Whitehead, lieutenant, ap. May 1, 1874, tr. September 1, 1882; J. C. Travers, engineman, ap. May 1, 1874, tr. September 1, 1882; C. C. Wilson, assistant engineman, ap. May 1, 1874, tr. September 1, 1882; C. W. Hodgdon, ap. May 1, 1874, tr. January 3, 1879; J. W. Groves, ap. May 1, 1874, tr. August 8, 1881; F. A. Bean, ap. May 1, 1874. tr. May 31, 1889; P. H. Freeman, ap. May 1, 1874, discharged November 3, 1876; W. C. Fogg, ap. May 1, 1874, resigned May 20, 1876; Z. S. Smith, ap. May 1, 1874, discharged June 20, 1876; L. G. Newman, ap. May 1, 1874, discharged May 14, 1876; F. L. Coats, ap. May 1, 1874, discharged July 31, 1876; D. McCarty, ap. May 24, 1874, discharged March 15, 1876; A. E. Cluff, ap. April 6, 1876, discharged August 20, 1876; P. J. Carey, ap. June 20, 1876, killed July 31, 1886; W. A. Rathburn, lieutenant, ap. August 29, 1876, tr. March 17, 1884; W. N. H. Knights, ap. August 29, 1876, tr. March 24, 1879; J. A. Kelley, ap. November 9, 1876, tr. December 1, 1875; L. La Pierre, ap. December 1, 1876, resigned April 2, 1879; Frank Norton, ap. January 3, 1879, discharged March 9, 1882; James Porter, ap. March 24, 1879. tr. November 6, 1885; Michael H. Barry, ap. April 30, 1879, discharged November 27, 1880; George Chapman, ap. December 15, 1880, tr. December 21, 1880; P. J. Farley, ap. December 21, 1880, died October 31, 1881; A. R. Johnson, ap. August 8, 1881, tr. October 27, 1881; J. A. Shannon, ap. October 27, 1881, tr. September 1, 1882; W. R. Adams, ap. November 7, 1881, resigned November 8, 1885; C. T. Deering, engineman, ap. September 1, 1882, discharged September 19, 1883; F. A. Greenleaf, assistant engineman, ap. September 1, 1882, tr. March 21, 1883; J. A. Haley, ap. September 1, 1882, tr. December 10, 1884; J. H. Metcalf, ap. October 2, 1882, resigned November 29, 1882; Silas Morse, Jr., assistant engineman, ap. March 21, 1883, tr. March 31, 1886; J. H. Marks, engineman, ap. October 8, 1883, resigned October 11, 1883; W. H. Clay, engineman, ap. October 21, 1883, tr. March 28, 1886; P. E. Keyes, captain, ap. March 17, 1884, promoted March 17, 1887; J. F. Ryan, lieutenant, ap. March 17, 1884, tr. February 16, 1888; P. H. Kenney, ap. September 24, 1886, tr. March 24, 1888; C. E. Mulloy, ap. January 16, 1886, tr. June 25, 1887; Eugene Cummings, captain, ap. April 1, 1887, discharged August 20, 1888; P. F. McDonough, lieutenant, ap. February 16, 1888, tr. August 31, 1888; John Bell, ap. January 22, 1883, tr. November 1, 1888; J. I. Quigley, ap. January 16, 1886, tr. November 2, 1888; J. J. Flanagan, ap. February 4, 1887, tr. October 19, 1888.

PRESENT MEMBERS.

Capt. JOHN F. RYAN (Fig. 1) was born in Boston, April 17, 1857, which makes him the youngest man holding a similar position in the department. After leaving school he worked at the steam-fitting business until May 15, 1880, when he entered this department, as a permanent member, and was assigned to Engine Company No. 7. January 22, 1883, he was transferred to Engine Company No. 26, and on March 17 of the following year he was promoted lieutenant and assigned to Engine Company No. 6. February 16, 1888, he was promoted to the position of captain, and assigned to Engine Company No. 33, and on August 30, 1888, was transferred to Engine Company No. 6. Captain Ryan was never severely injured, but has, like his colleagues, met with many narrow escapes from death. He, in company with District Chief Keyes, saved the life of an old lady from a building in North Bennet street. He is a member of the Blue Hill Assembly, Legion of Honor, and the Boston Veteran Firemen's Association.

Lieut. JOSEPH M. GARGAN (Fig. 2) was born in Boston, Mass., March 19, 1853, and is therefore 35 years of age. He began his career in this department on April 24, 1873, as driver for ex-Chief Engineer Damrell, and held that position until the administration of ex-Chief Engineer Green, in 1874, when he was appointed as messenger to that officer, and was appointed a permanent member of the force. He was transferred April 1, 1876, to officer in charge of Hose Company No. 8, and on June 1, 1882, was transferred to Engine Company No. 23, and was again transferred, May 4 of the same year, to Engine Company No. 10, as driver. He remained with that company until February 16, 1888, when his efficient services were recognized by promotion to lieutenant, and assigned to Engine Company No. 26, and on August 31, 1888, was transferred to this company. Lieut. Gargan has had some very narrow escapes from death, the most notable being at the Tremont Temple fire, when he with several firemen were at work inside the building at the time the roof fell in. Some of his comrades were buried under the *débris,* but were got out all right, while the more fortunate got under the gallery. In 1875, while driving ex-Chief Green to Box 67, they had a narrow escape from a collision with Ladder Truck No. 8.

Engineman JOHN H. McGARR (Fig. 3) was born in Donegal, Ireland, June 16, 1850. He came to this city June 29, 1861, but soon after went to Winchester, Mass., where he learned the machinist's trade. From there he came to Boston and entered the Boston police force, 1876, in which he served five years, when he went to Augusta, Ga., where he was foreman of a large machine-shop. While in that city he was a member of the Augusta fire department, acting as engineman and instructor of Richmond Steamer No. 7. He remained in that position two years and eight months. On his return to Boston he joined this department, October 8, 1883, as substitute, and was assigned to the repair-shop. In March he was transferred to Engine Company No. 10 as a permanent member. He remained there two years, when he was promoted to engineman and assigned to this company. Mr. McGarr met with a painful accident while going to a fire in April, 1885. His engine struck a horse-car, which threw him off his seat and pulled his arm out of joint. He is a member of the Royal Arcanum and of the Odd Fellows.

Assistant Engineman WILLIAM F. CROWLEY (Fig. 4) was born in St. John, N.B., November 1, 1855. He came to this city about eighteen years ago, and worked at the machinist's trade until October 24, 1883, when he was appointed a substitute in this force and assigned to Engine Company No. 3. From there he was transferred to Engine Company No. 23, and detailed to repair-shop; then back to Engine Company No. 3 again. He was promoted a permanent member February 16, 1885, and assigned to this company as assistant engineman, April 1, 1886. Mr. Crowley is a member of the Royal Arcanum.

FRANK A. BEAN (Fig. 5) is the oldest man in this company. He was born in Belfast, Me., July 18, 1839, and is therefore 49 years of age. He came to Boston in 1862, at which time he discontinued the occupation of mariner. He joined this department May, 1867, as call-man in this company, and in May, 1874, was promoted a permanent member. Mr. Bean has during this time never been seriously wounded. He is a member of America Lodge 191, of the Odd Fellows.

MICHAEL C. LEONARD (Fig. 6) was born in Jamaica Plain District, Boston, Mass., March 21, 1858. He is a plumber by trade, at which he was employed until his appointment as a substitute in this department, April 24, 1882, and detailed to this company; and on June 27 he was promoted to a

Engine Company No. 6. — Page 467.

permanent member.   He does a large amount of plumbing-work for the department.   Mr. Leonard was laid up for three weeks from injuries received by being run over by a hose-cart at a fire on Sudbury street, Box 21, May 10, 1885.

WILLIAM CHITTICK (Fig. 7) first saw the light in Boston, July 13, 1854. He is a brass-finisher by trade, at which he worked until 1882, when he was appointed a substitute and assigned to Engine Company No. 26, in which he was promoted a permanent member October 16 of the ensuing year.   He resigned January 22, 1883, but again returned May 2, 1884, as substitute in the company.   He was transferred to Engine Company No. 4, and made a permanent member December 10, 1884.   From there he was transferred to this company, and June 24, 1887, was again transferred to Engine Company No. 10, and was promoted assistant engineman, October 16 of the same year; but in August, 1887, he was transferred to this company to his present position.

ALFRED CHADBOURN (Fig. 8) was born in the Dorchester District, Boston, Mass., August 25, 1859.   After leaving school he was employed as a mill-hand; his appointment in this department dates from January, 1880, as a call-man in Engine Company No. 17.   February 25, 1885, he was promoted a permanent member and assigned to Engine Company No. 26, and on March 26, 1888, he was transferred to this company.

WILLIAM J. RILEY (Fig. 9) was born in Charlestown District, Boston, Mass., August 28, 1860.   He is a tin-roofer by trade, at which he worked until appointed a substitute in the department, June 24, 1887, and assigned to this company.   Mr. Riley was one of the men who were severely burned at the Fort Hill square fire.   He was laid up seven weeks.   He is a member of Hanover Assembly, Royal Good Fellows.

PETER CALLAHAN (Fig. 10) was born in Boston, Mass., July 5, 1858. He was employed as a machinist's helper until June 24, 1887, when he was appointed a substitute of the department and assigned to this company.

CORNELIUS DONOVAN (Fig. 11) was born in Dover, Mass., July 17, 1857. He was employed at the Norway Steel and Iron Works as teamster, until his appointment in this department as a substitute in Ladder Company No. 3, on February 4, 1887; and on January 6, 1888, was appointed a permanent member.   November 16, 1888, he was transferred to this company.

M. J. NORTON (Fig. 12) was born in Boston, Mass., July 27, 1864.   He is a cooper by trade, at which he was employed until his appointment in this department.   He first began fire service as a call-substitute on Hose Company No. 9, October 10, 1886, and soon after was transferred to Ladder Company No. 5.   He was promoted a permanent substitute February 16, 1888, and assigned to Ladder Company No. 1, and during 1888 was transferred to this company.   Mr. Norton fell from the top of a ladder while a member of Ladder Company No. 1, which company was exercising, July 28, 1888, on Friend street, and was very seriously injured.   He is a member of Sts. Peter and Paul's Temperance Society.

ENGINE COMPANY NO. 10.

NAMES OF MEMBERS SINCE 1874.

G. W. Warren, captain, ap. 1874, no record; Gilman Tyng, engineman, ap. 1874, resigned May 20, 1880; James E. Dooly, assistant, ap. 1874, resigned June 20, 1876; A. H. Towne, ap. 1874, resigned October 15, 1875; William Payne, ap. 1874, resigned February 15, 1875; C. H. Skimmings, ap. 1874, resigned December 7, 1875; J. L. Stimson, ap. 1874, resigned October 5, 1878; B. F. Bayley, ap. 1874, resigned May 20, 1880; Thomas Lally, ap. 1874, tr. to Engine Company No. 26, November 8, 1879; H. S. Worrell, ap. 1874, resigned March 27, 1886; A. P. Smith, ap. February 15, 1875, resigned November 7, 1881; Samuel Ridler, ap. November 1, 1875, tr. to Ladder Company No. 8, March 24, 1879; William Hudson, ap. December 8, 1875, tr. July 26, 1877; Frank A. Greenleaf, ap. August 25, 1876, tr. to Engine Company No. 23, September 1, 1882; Julius M. Nazro, ap. July 20, 1877, tr. to Engine Company No. 22, October 10, 1878; A. H. Egerton, ap. October 6, 1878, resigned April 10, 1880; A. W. Hutchings, ap. October 10, 1878, resigned March 28, 1881; Thomas F. Lyons, ap. March 24, 1879, resigned December 4, 1880; William. H. Knight, ap. March 24, 1879, tr. to Engine Company No. 6, November 6, 1885; Walter Restarick, ap. November 8, 1879, tr. to Engine Company No. 26, March 1, 1880; C. Allison, ap. March 1, 1880, died November 28, 1887; C. H. Tagan, ap. April 10, 1880, tr. to Engine Company No. 23, May 4, 1885; E. A. Perkins, ap. December 17, 1880, tr. as captain to Ladder Company No. 5, April, 1887; G. Cummings, ap. May 20, 1880, no record; W. J. Gaffey, ap. December 24, 1881, tr. to Ladder Company No. 13, no record; C. C. Wilson, ap. September 1, 1882, no record; March 17, 1884, Gay, ap. November 25, 1882, tr. to Engine Company No. 5; F. P. Carpenter, ap. October, 1883, resigned July 15, 1884; J. M. McGarr, ap. March 17, 1884, tr. to Engine Company No. 6, April 1, 1886; T. F. McDonough, ap. July 17, 1883, resigned November 26, 1884; C. H. Stevens, ap. March, 1885, tr. to Engine Company No. 4, January 19, 1889; C. O. Poland, captain, ap. April 28, 1885, tr. to Engine Company No. 25, April 28, 1885; G. W. Frost, captain, ap. April 28, 1885, tr. to Engine Company No. 33, August, 1888; J. M. Gargan, ap. May 4, 1885, tr. to Engine Company No. 6, April 1, 1887; S. Morse, assistant enginman, ap. April 1, 1886, resigned; G. F. Joyce, tr. to Ladder Company No. 3, October 30, 1888.

PRESENT MEMBERS.

Captain PETER F. McDONOUGH (Fig. 1) was born in Boston, Mass., August 7, 1856. His service in the department dates from July 1, 1883, at which time he was appointed a substitute in Ladder Company No. 8. September 24, 1883, he was assigned a permanent member in the same company. He was transferred January 7, 1884, to Ladder Company No. 1, from which

ENGINE COMPANY No. 10. — Page 472.

company he was transferred and promoted to the position of lieutenant, August 16, 1887, to Engine Company No. 26, where he remained until February 16, 1888, when he was transferred to Engine Company No. 6. His services were again recognized, and he was promoted captain and assigned to Engine Company No. 10. Captain McDonough is a member of the Firemen's Charitable Association.

Lieut. JAMES A. HALEY (Fig. 2) first saw the light in Boston, Mass., March 31, 1850, and is therefore 38 years of age. He is a slater by trade. He joined the force in August, 1876, as call-substitute in Engine Company No. 26, and was appointed a permanent member on June 2, 1880, and assigned to the same company. He was transferred, September 1, 1882, to Engine Company No. 6. From there he was transferred, December 10, 1885, to Engine Company No. 4. He was promoted lieutenant, and transferred to this company, February 18, 1888. Lieutenant Haley has been several times severely injured, but has recovered from their effects completely. He is a member of the Oliver Ames Lodge of Good Fellows, also the Charitable and Veteran Firemen's Associations.

Engineman JOSEPH R. GILBERT (Fig. 3) was born in Leeds, Me., August 7, 1833. He was a member of the Lowell, Mass., fire department in 1851, and in 1854 was a member of the department in Lawrence, Mass. He removed to Charlestown, and was employed in the Navy-Yard as a machinist in 1861, and joined the Charlestown fire department the same year. In 1866 he moved to Pawtucket, R.I., and was a member of the fire department of that city. During 1870 he again returned to this city and joined this department; was appointed engineman, and assigned to Engine Company No. 21, from where he was transferred to this company, June 1, 1880. Mr. Gilbert is a member of the Charlestown Veteran Firemen's Association.

Assistant-Engineman RICHARD T. TUSON (Fig. 4) was born in Ballardvale, Mass., September 2, 1858, and is therefore 30 years of age. He is a machinist by trade, at which he worked until February, 1886, at which time he was appointed a call-man in Hose Company No. 7. He was appointed a permanent member in June, 1887, and assigned to Engine Company No. 26, and on October 7, 1887, was transferred to this company.

WILLIAM HENRY BOUDWYN (Fig. 5), driver, was born in Boston, February 9, 1856. He was employed as a teamster, and on August 3, 1874, was appointed permanent driver in Engine Company No. 26, from where he was transferred to Ladder Company No. 3, and on October 30, 1888, was transferred to this company. Mr. Boudwyn was laid up two months with a fractured ankle, received at a fire at Edison Electric Light Works, June 2, 1888.

JAMES C. PORTER (Fig. 6), driver of the hose-carriage, was born in Bristol, England, December 7, 1830. He came to this city in May, 1847, and worked at his trade of basket-making. He left Boston in 1862, but again returned in 1863, which was the only time he was out of the department since December, 1853, at which time he joined Hand Engine Company No. 4, which was stationed in this house. He remained with it until the company was disbanded, and Hose Company No. 7 took their place, when he became a member of that company; and when the present company was organized, in 1874, he was among the number engaged. He was promoted captain of this company in 1872. Later on he was transferred to Engine Company No. 6, and soon after was assigned to his present position in this company.

JOHN HENRY BARUTIO, Jr. (Fig. 7), was born in Roxbury District, Boston, Mass., March 6, 1860. He is a house-painter by trade, and in October, 1886, was appointed a call-member in Engine Company No. 14. One year later he was promoted a permanent member, and assigned to this company. Mr. Barutio received a medal and twenty-fivedollars from the Humane Society for rescuing a man from drowning in the Charles river on the night of November 29, 1887.

JAMES M. WALTERS (Fig. 8) was born in Charlestown District, Boston, Mass., September 25, 1859, and is therefore 29 years of age. He was employed as a teamster previous to his appointment on the force, which occurred February 16, 1888, when he was assigned to Ladder Company No. 1, and on Jan. 1, 1889, was transferred to this company.

CHARLES H. STEVENS (Fig. 9) was born in Boston, October 5, 1858. After leaving school he was employed as driver of express and other wagons until March 28, 1885, when he was appointed substitute and assigned to this company.

ROBERT JOHN CARLETON (Fig. 10) was born in St. John, N.B., August 30, 1859, making him 29 years of age. He came to Boston during 1877, and worked at mercantile business until he entered this department as a substitute, July 1, 1883, in Engine Company No. 8. September 3, 1884, he was promoted a permanent member and assigned to this company. Mr. Carleton had his shoulder dislocated at the Sugar Refinery fire, on Eastern avenue, by the falling in of the floor; he was also burned about the face and hands at the Congress-street fire. He is a member of the Firemen's Charitable Association.

ROBERT CUMMINGS (Fig. 11) was born in St. John, N.B., November 24, 1857. He is a house-painter by trade, and came to this city ten years ago. He joined this department in 1885, as call-substitute in Hose Company No. 4, and was appointed permanent substitute, January 5, 1888, and assigned to this company.

EDWARD F. FITZGERALD was born in Boston, Mass., August 16, 1850. He worked at the printer's trade until his appointment in this department. His career as a fireman dates from 1871, at which time he was appointed a call-substitute. He left the force shortly after, but returned again in 1876 as a substitute; and on March 28, 1881, was promoted a permanent member and assigned to this company. He was laid up for three months by an injury to his legs, which occurred by being run over by a hose-carriage. Mr. Fitzgerald died February 25, 1889.

LADDER COMPANY NO. 1.
NAMES OF MEMBERS SINCE 1874.

D. C. Bickford, ap. May 2, 1874, tr. July 10, 1883; C. H. Knox, ap. May 2, 1874, tr. November 27, 1874; James Edwards, ap. May 2, 1874, tr. March 28. 1883; William Lewis, ap. May 2, 1874, tr. September 28, 1874; Joseph Hodet, ap. May 2, 1874, discharged July 4, 1874; P. A. Kimball, ap. May 2, 1874, discharged January 9, 1875; T. B. Flanagan, ap. May 2, 1874, resigned May 14, 1875; L. F. Stevens, ap. May 2, 1874, tr. January 14, 1884; J. Grady, ap. May 2, 1874, tr. July 26, 1884; L. A. Smith, ap. May 2, 1874, resigned April 5, 1877; T. W. Strand, ap. May 2, 1874, discharged March 30, 1885; J. Mahan, ap. May 2, 1874, discharged February 27, 1875; F. Norton, ap. May 2, 1874, tr. January 2, 1879; C. F. Reed, ap. May 2, 1874, discharged August 2, 1874; J. P. Fisher, ap. August 1, 1874, discharged August 7, 1874; I. Wells, ap. August 12, 1874, resigned September 30, 1882; H. A. Blanchard, ap. August 12, 1874, resigned June 1, 1876; C. D. Bordman, ap. October 9, 1874, tr. February 16, 1885; T. Roach, ap. January 14, 1875, discharged December 6, 1875; T. E. Simonds, ap. June 1, 1875, tr. October 21, 1881; C. H. Cushing, ap. December 9, 1875, tr. December 15, 1875; E. Whiting, ap. June 8, 1876, tr. September 21, 1876; W. B. Lottredge, ap. September 21, 1876, resigned October 28, 1885; C. W. Hodgdon, ap. January 2, 1879, discharged March 27. 1886; A. R. Johnson, ap. October 27, 1881, tr. April 29, 1887; A. C. Holmes, ap. October 2, 1882, tr. March 17, 1884; F. C. Turner, ap. July 10, 1883, tr. February 16, 1888; P. F. McDonough, ap. January 7, 1884, tr. August 27, 1887; E. Cummings, ap. July 30, 1884, tr. March 28, 1885; J. I. Quigley, ap. March 28, 1885, tr. January 15, 1886; George C. Swift, ap. January 15, 1886, tr. February 16, 1888; Charles C. Springer, ap. January 15, 1886, tr. September 27, 1886; F. P. Stengel, ap. January 15, 1886, tr. September 27, 1886; J. M. Fitzgerald, ap. September 27, 1886, tr. June 25, 1887; J. F. Mitchell, ap. June 18, 1887, tr. June 24, 1887; J. E. Mahoney, ap. June 24, 1887, discharged July 9, 1887.

PRESENT MEMBERS.

Captain JOHN FRANCIS EGAN (Fig. 1) was born in Boston, April 21, 1849, and is therefore 39 years of age. After leaving school he learned the roofer's trade, at which he was employed until he joined this department, February 3, 1876, when he was appointed a permanent member and assigned to Ladder Company No. 1. His whole career as a fireman has been with this company. He was promoted lieutenant April 18, 1882, and on July 10, 1883, he was again promoted, this time to captain. He is a gentleman of rare courage, and very popular in the department, while his affairs as captain of this company are carried on in a most systematic manner. He is a member of the Firemen's Charitable Association, also of the Royal Society of Good Fellows and the Total Abstinence Society.

Lieut. JAMES M. LITTLETON (Fig. 2) was born in Bellows Falls, Vt., July 31, 1851, and is therefore 37 years of age. He came with his parents to this city when he was very young, and after leaving school learned the carpenter's trade, at which he was employed until his appointment in this force, as a call-substitute. in Hose Company No. 7, May 14, 1871. August 1, 1871, became a call-member of that company. October 3, 1874, he was promoted to this company as a permanent member. In 1883 he was appointed driver of the truck, and was promoted to his present position April 29, 1887. He has met with several painful accidents, including a severe injury to his leg, caused by being run over by the truck, February 26, 1888. He is a member of the Charitable Association and the Boston Veteran Firemen's Association.

JOHN J. SHEA (Fig. 3), driver, was born in Boston, Mass., February 23, 1859. He was employed as a blacksmith before joining this department, which he did January 15, 1880; he was appointed a call-man in Hose Company No. 10, where he remained until January 16, 1885, when he was made a permanent member and assigned to this company. Mr. Shea was accidentally cut on the wrist with an axe by a comrade while at work at Wright & Potter fire, April, 1887, which laid him up two months. He is a member of the Firemen's Charitable Association.

GEORGE HUTCHINSON (Fig. 4) was born in Dunham County, England, August 7, 1839, and is therefore 49 years of age. He began going to sea when but 13 years of age, and from 1857 to 1860 was employed in a British man-of-war. He also did service in the Crimean War. In 1860 he came to this country, and before the breaking out of the Rebellion was in the South on a revenue cutter; but when war was declared this cutter was, like many others, fitted up as a gunboat. He then retired. and came North, going to Buffalo, N.Y., where he enlisted in the navy, joined the gunboat "Rhode 'Island," and later on the ship "Onward." He left the service in 1864, and was employed in the Ordnance Department at the Charlestown (Mass.) Navy-Yard. He also did rigging-work. His career as a fireman began January 14, 1875, as permanent member in this company. Mr. Hutchinson has had a very eventful life, and has met with some narrow escapes from death. In another part of this book will be found an item of interest regarding the John Lovell fire, in which he figured very conspicuously. He is a member of the Knights of Honor and a life member of the Firemen's Charitable Association.

JOHN P. McMANUS (Fig. 5) was born in Boston, Mass., January 20, 1856, and is therefore 32 years of age. He was a stationary fireman by occupation. He joined this department, September 3, 1884, as a substitute in Ladder Company No. 3. but was promoted a permanent member and as-

Ladder Company No. 1.—Page 477.

signed to this company, March 4, 1885. By mistake this gentleman's portrait is inserted twice, both in Figures 5 and 6.

WILLIAM H. HUGHES (Fig. 7) was born in Charlestown District, Boston, Mass., October 20, 1856. He is a baker by trade, at which he was employed until February 5, 1883, when he was appointed a substitute in this department. Previous to this, during 1880. he was a call-man in Hose Company No. 4. He was promoted a permanent member, and assigned to Ladder Company No. 8, June 30, 1883. He remained with that company until July 1, 1886, when, at his own request, he was transferred to this company. where he has since remained. Mr. Hughes is a member of the King Solomon Lodge, the St. Paul Royal Arch Chapter, of Masons, and the Bunker Hill Yacht Club. At a fire on board the steamer "Venetian" he was nearly suffocated by smoke.

PETER THOMAS MAGEE (Fig. 8) was born in Quebec, P.Q., July 3, 1852, and is therefore 36 years of age. He came to Boston in 1869, and was employed at the hotel business for three years and six months, when he engaged in the wood-turning business. He joined this department March 28, 1885, when he was appointed a substitute on Engine Company No. 8. He was transferred to this company and promoted a permanent member September 24. 1886. Mr. Magee is a member of the St. Stephen's Temperance Society, with which he has been identified for over fourteen years. During 1888 he had his leg cut off while responding to an alarm of fire, by a collision of the truck and a horse-car.

GEORGE P. DOWLING (Fig. 9) was born in Boston, Mass., May 26, 1856. He became connected with this department July 1, 1886, at which time he was appointed a call-member of Hose Company No. 10. July 29, 1887, he was promoted a permanent member, and assigned to this company. Mr. Dowling was severely injured July 25, 1888. by falling from a Bangor extension-ladder, a distance of thirty-five feet, when the company were exercising in front of quarters.

T. M. McLAUGHLIN (Fig. 10) allied himself with this department July 1. 1886. at which time he was detailed to Engine Company No. 28. from which he was transferred to this company October 7, 1887.

FREDERICK WALDEN LE CAIN (Fig. 11) was born in Boston, Mass., December 31, 1863, and is therefore 25 years of age. He is a carpenter by trade, but left it to become a fireman. he joining the force November 19, 1886. when he was appointed a call-man in Ladder Company No. 12. He was transferred and promoted a permanent member, October 7, 1887. in this company. He severely sprained his ankle July 16, 1887, by which he was laid up one month.

DANIEL J. COLDEN (Fig. 12) was born in Boston, Mass., October 18, 1860. He was employed as a teamster before his appointment in this department, on September 13. 1888. when he was detailed to this company. Mr. Colden is a member of St. James Total Abstinence Society and Catholic Order of Foresters.

John F. Morrison (Fig. 13) was born in Boston, Mass., January 29, 1861. He is a rigger by trade, which he learned after following the sea for a period of six years. He joined this department January 29, 1887, as a substitute, and assigned to Engine Company No. 26. He remained there until June, 1887, when he was transferred to this company, and in January 6, 1888, was promoted a permanent member. He is a member of the Theatrical Mechanics' Association of Boston, No. 2.

Timothy Leahy (Fig. 14) was born in Boston, Mass., June 17, 1865. He was employed as a teamster until his appointment in this department, as a substitute, January 18, 1889, and detailed to this company.

Charles H. Morrison, substitute, was born in East Boston, Mass., November 15, 1865. He is a rigger by trade, and on November 23, 1888, entered this department as a substitute in this company.

HOSE COMPANY NO. 8.

Names of Members since 1874.

Previous to May, 1875, this was a call-company, and there are no records of whom it was composed, other than the driver, Horatio Ely, who was pensioned and retired March 28, 1885. Some time in May, 1875, John F. Lewis and Eugene Boyle were sent to the company as permanent members; Lewis as hoseman and teamster, Boyle as hoseman and hostler. Lewis is a present member of company; Boyle was discharged; no record. Lieut. James Gargan, now of Engine Company No. 6, was sent to company as hoseman in charge, during 1875; tr. June 1, 1882. George H. Knox, tr. from Engine Company No. 4, as hoseman, April 21, 1882; resigned September 24, 1886. Capt. John Knights, tr. from Engine Company No. 14, as assistant foreman in charge, June 1, 1882; tr. May 1. 1885. Capt. E. F. Martin, tr. from Chemical Engine Company No. 2, May 1, 1885; tr. August 26, 1887.

Present Members.

Lieut. John H. Ewers (Fig. 1) was born in Hallowell, Me., January 24, 1848, and is therefore 40 years of age. He is an oil-cloth printer by trade, at which he was employed until October 14, 1873, when he was appointed a call-member of this department, and assigned to Engine Company No. 22, as a hoseman, which was then located on Parker street, previous to its being made a permanent company. It was removed to Dartmouth street, August, 1875, and established as a permanent company, September 27, 1875. He was promoted to lieutenant in April, 1881, in that company, and transferred to Engine Company No. 26, July 26, 1883. He was again transferred, 26th of August, 1887, to his present quarters. Lieutenant Ewers was thrown from the hose-carriage while responding to Box 63, August 7, 1876, on Columbus avenue, and received a fracture of his left leg in five places, from which he

HOSE COMPANY NO. 8. — Page 481.

was off duty five months. He is a member of the Royal Arcanum and the Firemen's Charitable Association.

EDWIN A. WHITEHEAD (Fig. 2) first saw the light in Boston, December 14, 1835, being one of the oldest men in the department. He began life as a gold-beater, but later on was assistant insurance messenger, and from that engaged in the umbrella business. His career as fireman dates from the hand-engine department, in which he was a volunteer. In 1861 he joined Engine Company No. 4, as a call-substitute, and in February 1, 1881, he was appointed a call-member of Engine Company No. 6, and was promoted a permanent member of the same company May 1, 1873. He was promoted assistant foreman of the company on the reorganization of the department, which position he held for three years, after which he was senior hoseman for five years. In 1882 he was transferred to Engine Company No. 26, where he remained four years and two months, when he was transferred to this company. Mr. White-head is a member of the Odd Fellows and the Royal Good Fellows.

JOHN F. LEWIS (Fig. 3), driver of Supply Wagon No. 1, was born in Boston, January 9, 1835. His career in the department dates from 1855, when he was appointed a call-driver in Ladder Company No. 3. He remained there until September, 1860, when he was promoted a permanent driver and assigned to Engine Company No. 4. In March, 1863, he was transferred to Engine Company No. 8. He left the department during 1865, and was engaged by the Adams Express Company as a driver in New York City. He again joined the force in August, 1874, as a driver in Engine Company No. 26, from where he was transferred, May 28, 1875, as hoseman of this company, and on May 1, 1875, was detailed to his present position.

PATRICK J. KELLEY (Fig. 4) was born in Ireland, January 12, 1848. He came to this city at an early age, and was employed in various industries. He joined the department January 8, 1874, as a permanent member, and was assigned to Engine Company No. 25. He was transferred to this company March 28, 1885. Mr. Kelley has met with several severe accidents, the most notable of which was at a fire on Commercial street, when he had several of his ribs broken.

CHAPTER IX.

DISTRICT NO. 5.

DISTRICT No. 5 is covered by an area of three hundred acres, and lies in the retail section of the city, embracing all that part south of Districts 3 and 4 to the centre of Dover-street draw-bridge, and a line running through the centre of Dover, Berkeley, Boylston, east side of Commonwealth avenue to Arlington to Boylston streets. The principal industries carried on within these limits may be said to be retail dry-goods and wholesale leather and cotton-waste, although, as a matter of fact, almost every thing that enters into the make-up of the commerce of a city may there be found. Among the buildings devoted to the former industry may be mentioned Jordan, Marsh, & Co., R. H. White, C. F. Hovey, and, in fact, all the principal dealers in dry-goods. Places of amusement are features of importance. The Park, Globe, Boston, and Hollis theatres, World's Museum and Gaiety Theatre, are located within this boundary, as are many minor places of entertainment. Hotels are well represented by the United States, Adams, Clark's, Thorndyke, Vieth's, Richwood, Pelham, and Boylston, to say nothing of numbers of smaller ones. The Boston & Albany, Boston & Providence, New York & New England, and Old Colony railroads have their passenger and freight depots there, while the city buildings are represented by the Public Library and eight school-houses. We might also mention the Masonic Temple, Young Men's Christian Union, Young Women's Christian Union, St. Paul's Church, Paine and Parker Memorial buildings. It was in this district where the great fire of 1872 started, but swept over District No. 3. The apparatus in this district are Engines Nos. 7, 26, and Chemical No. 2. The quarters of the District Chief is in the house of Engine Company No. 26, where is also the private office of the Chief of the department.

Assistant Chief JOHN W. REGAN is in command of this district. For some reason known to himself he refused to furnish us with a photograph or any data concerning his life.

ENGINE COMPANY NO. 7.
NAMES OF MEMBERS SINCE 1874.

Daniel T. Marden, foreman, ap. May 21, 1874, tr. to Engine Company No. 13, August 26, 1887; John Marks, ap. May 21, 1874, tr. to Engine Company No. 26, July 29, 1875; George H. Bridge, ap. May 21, 1874, promoted to engineman, September 25, 1875; George M. Robinson, ap. May 21, 1874, resigned May 28, 1874; Charles Ingersoll, ap. May 21, 1874, promoted to

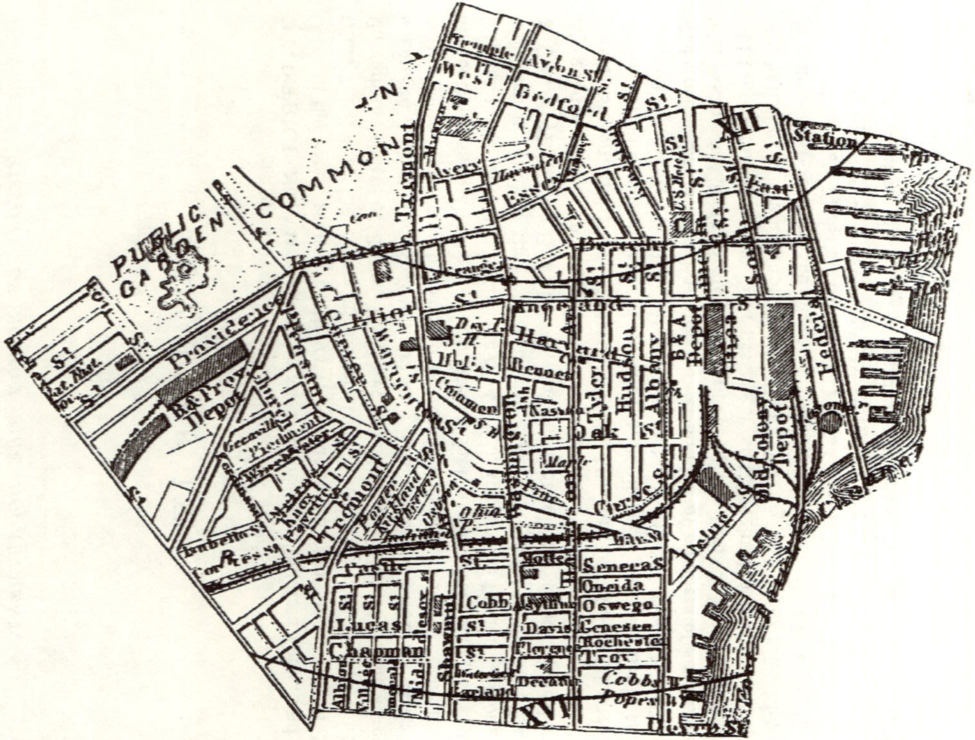

MAP OF DISTRICT No. 5. — Page 485.

lieutenant, tr. to Engine Company No. 33, February 16, 1888; William Norris, ap. May 21, 1874, died February 20, 1882; Charles E. Deering, ap. May 21, 1874, tr. to Engine Company No. 4, January 5, 1874; Bartholomew McCarthy, ap. May 21, 1874, promoted to captain Engine Company No. 12, August 2, 1883; Gilman F. Thyng, ap. May 21, 1874, tr. to Engine Company No. 10, January 5, 1874; T. H. Foster, ap. May 21, 1874, tr. to Engine Company No. 22, May 15, 1880; B. B. Brown, Jr., ap. May 21, 1874, resigned August 1, 1874; T. F. Kiley, ap. May 21, 1874, resigned March 30, 1875; George R. Williams, ap. May 21, 1874, tr. to Chemical Engine Company No. 3, April 13, 1888; Henry J. Hart, ap. June 3, 1874, promoted to lieutenant Engine Company No. 26, August 31, 1888; E. B. Haskell, ap. August 11, 1874, resigned November 22, 1878; Dennis B. Mahoney, ap. November 24, 1874, tr. January 20, 1875; Patrick J. Haley, ap. April 6, 1875, tr. March 5, 1884; Patrick M. Crotty, ap. September 28, 1875, tr. to Engine Company No. 22, July 10, 1883; Warren R. Smith, ap. December 4, 1878, tr. to Engine Company No. 26, March 24, 1879; Edward F. Martin, ap. March 24, 1879, April 29, 1881, tr. to Chemical Company No. 2, returned as captain, August 26, 1887; John F. Ryan, ap. May 15, 1880, tr. to Engine Company No. 26, January 22, 1883; W. R. Adams, ap. April 29, 1881, tr. to Engine Company No. 6, November 7. 1881; Joseph Smith, ap. November 7, 1881, tr. to Chemical Engine Company No. 2, July 10, 1883; John Montgomery, ap. July 10, 1883, resigned July 13, 1883; F. H. Bradbury, ap. July 10, 1883, tr. to Engine Company No. 30, January 21, 1884; J. M. Nugent, ap. July 13, 1883, resigned August 2, 1884; J. B. Hennessey, ap. July 21, 1883, tr. to Engine Company No. 26, November 5, 1883; Edward W. Clark, ap. October 11, 1883, tr. to Ladder Company No. 13, October 21, 1883; John Ready, Jr., ap. October 21, 1883, tr. to Engine Company No. 26, February 16, 1885; John A. Shannon, ap. January 21, 1884, resigned April 15, 1889; Charles W. Kennison, ap. March 5, 1884, July 1, 1884, tr. to Engine Company No. 23; M. F. Walsh, ap. April 9, 1884, tr. to Engine Company No. 22, June 25, 1887; P. H. Boleman, ap. September 3, 1884, August 1, 1885, tr. to Engine Company No. 2; George N. Dunn, ap. September 3, 1884, December 31, 1886, tr. to Ladder Company No. 3; W. F. Crowley, ap. February 16, 1885, March 28, 1885, tr. to Engine Company No. 23; Daniel B. Barrus, ap. June 24, 1887, tr. to Engine Company No. 26, March 24, 1888; John J. Shea, ap. September 5, 1888, tr. to Ladder Company No. 1, October 1, 1888; John F. Ryan, ap. October 1, 1888, tr. to Engine Company No. 25, November 1, 1888.

Present Members.

Captain EDWARD F. MARTIN (Fig. 1) was born in Brighton, Mass., April 17, 1850, and is therefore 38 years of age. He joined the fire department of that town at the age of sixteen, when he ran with the famous hand-engine "Butcher Boy," which is now in service at Braintree, Mass. This engine was awarded the prize of $200 in gold at the muster held at Hingham in 1875.

Captain Martin went there as a member of the old company, and held the pipe for the victorious " tub " against thirteen competitors.   At the annexation of Brighton with Boston, and the organization of the permanent force in this city, in 1874, he was assigned to Engine Company No. 25, as a permanent substitute, being a representative from Brighton District.   In 1875 he was promoted a permanent hoseman on Engine Company No. 26.   He remained in that company until March, 1879, when he was transferred, at his own request, to this company.   In April, 1881, he was promoted and transferred as hoseman in charge of Chemical Engine No. 2, where he rendered the most valuable service, and was in consequence appointed captain of the company. This took place July 20, 1883.   May 1, 1885, he was transferred to Hose Company No. 8, and August 16, 1887, was transferred to this company. During a fire in the printing-house of Rockwell & Churchill he was at work as hoseman in the fourth story.   It was a cold morning, and ice formed very fast : by a twist of the hose he was knocked over, and slid from the top down the entire four flights, out into the sidewalk, where he landed, covered with slush, etc., but without a scratch.   During an explosion of hot air in a fire on Pearl street in 1884 he was badly burned about the face and hands, and narrowly escaped death, the air coming through a shaft through from Pearl to Congress street, and was a very severe explosion.   He is a very able writer on fire matters.   His paper, read before the meeting of the Massachusetts State Firemen's Association, September 18, 1887, clearly shows the thorough manner in which he has studied this matter.   He was elected secretary of that association during 1887.   Captain Martin is pronounced an expert in handling chemical engines.

One of the most faithful servants in the employ of this department is Lieut. GEORGE W. STODDARD (Fig. 2), as his record of a quarter of a century fighting fires in Boston can testify.   He was born in Hingham, Mass., November 10, 1835.   He began his career on the force February, 1863, when he joined Hose Company No. 1, on Salem street.   In April, 1869, he joined this company as call-man, in which capacity he remained until the same month in 1871, when he was promoted permanent driver.   He held that position until the reorganization, in 1864, when he was promoted to his present position. Lieutenant Stoddard has attended every fire in his district since 1872, and has never met with any serious accident, although in the centre of danger, and passing through many narrow escapes.

Engineman GEORGE H. BRIDGE (Fig. 3) was born in Boston, Mass., December 16, 1845.   He entered the force January 5, 1874, as hoseman. April 27, 1874, he was promoted assistant engineman and assigned to this company.   His efficient service soon won recognition, and on September 25, 1875, he was promoted to his present position.

Assistant Engineman JOHN A. SHANNON (Fig. 4) was born in Boston, Mass., November 15, 1851.   His career as a fireman dates from August 1, 1873, as assistant engineman in Engine Company No. 10.   Six weeks after-

ENGINE COMPANY No. 7. — Page 490.

wards he was transferred to Engine Company No. 22, where he remained for three years. From there he was transferred to Engine Company No. 8, in which he served for eight years, when he was again transferred to Engine Company No. 6 as hoseman. One year was served with that company, when he was transferred to Chemical Engine No. 2, in which he worked for one year; and on July 10, 1883, he was assigned to this company, since which time he has been promoted to his present position.

Mr. JAMES MEEHAN (Fig. 5) was born in Lowell, Mass., April 16, 1856. He began fire duty during February, 1883, when he was appointed substitute on Hose Company No. 9, after which he was transferred to Hose Company No. 12, where he remained until January 5, 1888, when he was transferred to this company. He is now acting as driver.

M. J. MULLIGAN (Fig. 6) first saw the light in New York City, June 10, 1858. He came to this city when young, and was employed as a teamster until he joined this department, as a substitute, on March 28, 1885. He was promoted a permanent member on September 24, 1886, and assigned to this company. Mr. Mulligan was severely burned in the eye at Lewis-wharf fire, in 1885.

D. F. HURLEY (Fig. 7) was born in Boston, Mass., February 6, 1856. He was appointed permanent substitute February 15, 1883, and on June 30 of the ensuing year was promoted a permanent member and assigned to Engine Company No. 4, where he remained until January 16, 1886, at which time he was transferred to this company. Mr. Hurley had two of his ribs broken June, 1884, while going to a fire in Hanover street, by the collision of Engine No. 6 with the carriage of Engine No. 4. The bones were again fractured by a falling ladder while at a fire in Beach street, August 12, 1884.

J. MURRAY (Fig. 8) was born in Boston, Mass., December 21, 1848. He is a currier by trade. His experience as a fireman dates from 1871, at which time he joined hand-engine Fountain Company No. 1, of the Roxbury department, as captain. On December 10, 1874, he was made a call-man in Chemical Company No. 5, and on July 1, 1886, he was promoted a permanent member and assigned to this company.

THOMAS C. HANEY (Fig. 9) entered this department June 12, 1874, in Engine Company No. 2, and on May 10, 1882, was transferred to Hose Company No. 12, from which he was transferred to this company June 21, 1887. Mr. Haney is a carpenter by trade, and does a considerable amount of work in that line in the various houses in the department.

J. J. O'CONNOR (Fig. 10) was born in Boston, Mass., October 18, 1864. He was appointed January 6, 1888, in Chemical Engine Company No. 3, where he remained until April 15, when he was detailed to the present company.

JAMES F. MAGUIRE (Fig. 11) was born in Washington, D.C., September 12, 1862. He came to this city when but a child. He entered this service on September 12, 1888, as a substitute, and was detailed to this company.

MICHAEL MULLIGAN (Fig. 12) was born in New York City, N.Y., September 19, 1862. He came to Boston at an early age, and on October 6, 1887, became a member of the department, as substitute, and assigned to Engine Company No. 4, immediately after which he was transferred to Chemical Company No. 7. March 2, 1888, he was again transferred to Engine Company No. 26, where he remained three weeks, and March 24, 1888, was transferred to this company.

ENGINE COMPANY NO. 26.

NAMES OF MEMBERS SINCE 1874.

Samuel L. Harrington, ap. May 7, 1874, foreman, tr. November 27, 1874, to Engine Company No. 3 ; Winfield S. Lawrence, ap. May 7, 1874, assistant foreman, tr. January 14, 1876, to Engine Company No. 23 ; J. H. Adams, ap. May 7, 1874, engineman, resigned November 27. 1874 ; J. H. Maldt, ap. May 7, 1874, assistant engineman, tr. July 29, 1875, to Engine Company No. 22 ; A. W. Brown, ap. May 7, 1874, tr. July 28, 1880, to Engine Company No. 22, promoted to lieutenant ; J. S. B. Cloutman, ap. May 7, 1874, tr. August 18, 1874, to Engine Company No. 31 ; Mark W. Hayes, ap. May 7, 1874, killed July 31, 1874 ; George A. Kennison, ap. May 7, 1874, tr. May 1, 1876, to Chemical Engine Company No. 6 ; A. W. Turner, ap. May 7, 1874, resigned September 4, 1874 ; Louis L. La Pierre, ap. May 7, 1874, tr. December 1, 1876, to Engine Company No. 6 ; Frederick W. Knight, ap. May 7, 1874, resigned February 20, 1875 ; Charles N. Allison, ap. May 7, 1874, tr. May 1, 1880, to Engine Company No. 10 ; William H. Bowdwin, ap. August 3, 1874, tr. February 25, 1886, to Ladder Company No. 3 ; John F. Lewis, ap. August 25, 1874, tr. June 1, 1875, to Supply Wagon ; Walter Resterick. ap. September 21, 1874, tr. November 8, 1879, to Engine Company No. 10 ; Charles H. Knox, ap. November 27, 1874, foreman, tr. July 28, 1880, to Engine Company No. 12 ; Isaac A. Williams, ap. February 1, 1875. assistant engineman, tr. May 20, 1880, to Engine Company No. 15, promoted to engineman ; David J. O'Connell, ap. March 1, 1875, tr. June 21, 1875, to Engine Company No. 25, promoted to assistant engineman ; John Weldon, ap. June 1, 1875, resigned April 15, 1876 ; E. F. Martin, ap. June 21, 1875, tr. March 24, 1879, to Engine Company No. 7 ; John H. Marks, ap. June 29, 1875, engineman, tr. October 8. 1883, to Engine Company No. 6 ; J. F. McKenzie, ap. February 3, 1876, resigned May 13, 1877 ; William C. Lee, ap. April 15, 1876, tr. October 2, 1882, to Ladder Company No. 3, promoted to lieutenant ; George L. Spencer, ap. May 7. 1876, tr. June 2, 1881, to Engine Company No. 3 ; J. A. Kelley, ap. December 1, 1876, resigned February 15, 1878 ; Charles Miller, ap. May 20, 1877, tr. December 11, 1878, to Engine Company No. 22 ; James Bennett, ap. March 20, 1878, tr. October 21, 1878, to Ladder Company No. 3 ; Charles Windhorn, ap. October 4, 1878, chief's driver, tr. October 16, 1882, to Engine Company No. 28, promoted to assistant engineman ; Frederick E. Hibbard, ap. October 21, 1878, tr. June 1, 1882, to Engine Company No. 3, promoted to lieutenant ; Warren R. Smith, ap. March 24, 1879, tr. June 2, 1880, to Engine Company No. 14, promoted to assistant engineman ; Thomas P. Lally, ap. November 8, 1879, tr. March 1, 1883, to Chemical Engine Company No. 4, driver in charge ; Walter Resterick, ap. March 1, 1880, tr. October 21, 1880, to Chemical Engine Company No. 2 ; T. F. Fitzgerald, ap. May 20, 1880, assistant engineman, tr. May 25, 1881, to Engine Company No. 1 ; James A. Haley, ap. June 3, 1880, tr. September 1, 1882, to Engine Company No. 6 ; Thomas H. Welch, ap. October 21, 1880, tr. December 1, 1880, to Chemical Engine Company No. 2 ; Daniel H. Coakley, ap. December 1, 1880, resigned November 5, 1882 ; John Montgomery, ap. June 2, 1881, chief's driver, tr. July 10, 1883, to Engine Company No. 7 ; T. A. Andrews, ap. July 11, 1881, assistant engineman, tr. December 31, 1881, to Engine Company No. 16 ; A. B. Frye, ap. December 31, 1881, assistant engineman, tr. March 10, 1884, to Engine Company No. 22, promoted to engineman October, 1883 ; Charles E. Phoenix, ap. June 27, 1882, tr. November 27, 1882, to Engine Company No. 31 ; Edward A. Whitehead, ap. September 1, 1882, tr. October 8, 1886, to Hose Company No. 8 ; Thomas Boggs, ap. October 2, 1882, tr. September 22, 1884, to Engine Company No. 3 ; William Chittick, ap. October 16, 1882, resigned January 22, 1883 ; Edgar R. Farrin, ap. November 27, 1882, tr. June 24, 1887, to Engine Company No. 14 ; John F. Ryan, ap. January 22, 1883, tr. March 17, 1884, to Engine Company No. 6, promoted to lieutenant ; James P. Dean, ap. January 22, 1883, tr. November 1, 1888, to Engine Company No. 4, promoted to lieutenant ; Charles Kennison, ap. March 1, 1883, tr. March 5, 1884, to Engine Company No. 7 ; John H. Ewers, ap. July 28, 1883, lieutenant, tr. August 26, 1887, to Hose Company No. 8, lieutenant in charge ; William Lynch, ap. October 8, 1883, assistant engineman, tr. September 16, 1885, to Engine Company No. 15, promoted to engineman ; J. B. Hennessey, ap. October 21, 1883, substitute, tr. May 1, 1884, to Chemical Engine Company No. 1 ; Patrick Haley, ap. March 5, 1884, tr. February 25, 1886, to Engine Company No. 3 ; P. M. Crotty, ap. March 10, 1884, engineman ; A. T. Holmes, ap. March 17, 1884, died, January 24, 1887 ; John McCarthy, ap. May 16, 1884, tr. September 3, 1884, to Engine Company No. 4 ; Thomas Nugent, ap. September 3, 1884, resigned October 15, 1884 ; William Whalen, ap. September 3, 1884, tr. February 4, 1887, to Engine Company No. 23 ; Frank Stengel, ap. April 1, 1885, tr. September 3, 1885, to Engine Company No. 3 ; D. J. McInery, ap. September 16, 1885, assistant engineman, tr. December 10, 1886, to Engine Company No. 3 ; Joseph Nolan, ap. February 25, 1886, tr. March 2, 1888, to Chemical Engine Company No. 7 ; A. Chadbourn, ap. February 25, 1886, tr. March 22, 1888, to Engine Company No. 6 ; Edward Tully, ap. October 8, 1886, tr. December 5, 1888, to Ladder Company No. 8 ; Henry Fox, ap. December 31, 1886, tr. February 16, 1888, to Engine Company No. 25 ; Frank Morrison, ap. February 4, 1887, tr. June 20, 1887, to Ladder Company No. 1 ; Richard Tuson, ap. June 24, 1887, tr. October 7, 1888, to Engine Company No. 10 ; William J. Riley, ap. June 24, 1887, tr. September 6, 1888, to Engine Company No. 6 ; P. F. McDonough, ap. August 26, 1887, lieutenant, tr. February 16, 1888, to Engine Company No. 6 ; Edward Richardson, ap. 1888, tr. to Engine Company No. 14 ; Robert Cummings, ap. May, 1888, tr. July 24, 1888, to Engine Company No. 10 ; J. O'Brien, ap. April 11, 1888, resigned May, 1888 ; M. Mulligan, ap. March 2, 1888, tr. March 22, 1888, to Engine Company No. 7 ; William Cobb, ap. February 16, 1888, tr. July 24, 1888, to Ladder Company No. 1 ; J. M. Gargan, ap. February 16, 1888, lieutenant, tr. August 27, 1888, to Engine Company No. 6.

PRESENT MEMBERS.

Captain CHARLES C. WILLETT (Fig. 1) was born in Boston, Mass., September 1, 1851. He was obliged to leave school when about 15 years of age, on account of poor health, and went to sea, which occupation he followed until September 19, 1874, when he was appointed a permanent member of Engine Company No. 4. January 3, 1877, he was promoted to the position of lieutenant of the same company, and remained in that capacity until July 21, 1880, when he was promoted captain and assigned to Engine Company No. 22, and on July 20, 1883, transferred to this company. At a fire in a Canal-street stable, in 1876, a bale of hay, in falling, struck him between the shoulders, almost breaking his back. · At the Tremont Temple fire he had a most miraculous escape. He was inside the building, in charge, and while in the act of holding the hose, in which he was supported by five members of the company, a most terrific explosion of hot air knocked him and the men a distance of several feet, all of whom were severely burned, but he was not scratched. While at work at a fire on Congress street, June 12, 1884, he received severe burns in the face, neck, and hands, which resulted in blood-poisoning, and necessitated his laying off duty nine weeks. June 22, 1885, he was badly burned about the eyes, which laid him up several weeks. During 1877, in company with an ex-member of the department, " Spike " Sullivan, he rescued a woman from a three-story tenement, corner of Prince and Hanover streets. Captain Willett is a member of Franklin Lodge of Odd Fellows, the Pilgrim Fathers, the Boston Veteran Firemen's Association, and the Barnicoat Association.

Lieutenant H. J. HART (Fig. 2) was born in Fort Hill square, Boston. Mass., February 14, 1848. He enlisted in Company C, of the Massachusetts Heavy Artillery, in 1864, and was mustered out in 1865. He entered this service, as substitute at this station, in 1871, after which he was transferred to Hose Company No. 2, where he remained until appointed a permanent member and assigned to this company, in 1874, when he was transferred to Engine Company No. 7, and on August 31, 1888, was promoted to the position of lieutenant and assigned to this company. Lieutenant Hart was severely

ENGINE COMPANY No. 26. — Page 496.

injured at a fire at the corner of High and Federal streets by falling through a plate-glass window; his legs were badly lacerated. While going to a fire in South Boston he was knocked off the hose-carriage to the street, and had several cords in his left arm broken. He has rendered yeoman service in the department, and drove the hose-carriage of Engine No. 7 for a long time. He is a member of Post 91, G. A. R.

Engineman PATRICK M. CROTTY (Fig. 3) was born in Ireland in February, 1848. His family came to this city when he was but two months old. After attending the grammar school he learned the machinist's trade. October 13, 1873, he was appointed a permanent member of the department and assigned to Engine Company No. 7, as hoseman. He was promoted to assistant engineman in Engine Company No. 19, during January, and in 1874 was transferred to Engine Company No. 21, from which he was, on September 28, 1875, again transferred to Engine Company No. 7, as assistant engineman. He was promoted engineman and assigned to Engine Company No. 22, July 10, 1883, from which he was transferred to his present company March 10, 1884.

Assistant Engineman MICHAEL J. CROWLEY (Fig. 4) was born in Newton, Mass., May 28, 1852. He is a machinist by trade, at which he worked a number of years. While at Newton he joined that fire department as a substitute on August, 1871, on Engine Company No. 2, and was promoted assistant engineman, May, 1872. He remained with that department until 1880, when he came to this city. March 1, 1881, he was appointed a substitute on this force and assigned to Engine Company No. 1. He was promoted a permanent member on April 21, 1882, and assigned to Engine Company No. 3; and on August 21, 1884, was promoted to assistant engineman in Engine Company No. 4, where he remained until December 31, 1886, when he was transferred to this company.

JOHN READY (Fig. 5), driver, was born in Brighton District, Boston, Mass., November 12, 1854. He joined the department February 20, 1882, as a call-man in Ladder Company No. 11. July 10, 1883, he was appointed a substitute and assigned to Engine Company No. 7. He was promoted a permanent member, October 20, 1883, and assigned to that company, and on February 11. 1885, he was transferred to this company as driver of engine. Mr. Ready is a member of No. 5 Assembly of the Order of Royal Good Fellows.

PHILIP G. FLYNN (Fig. 6) first saw the light in Brighton District, Boston, Mass., September 12, 1861. His career in the department dates from January 23, 1886, at which time he was appointed call-man in Engine Company No. 29. On October 7, 1887, he was promoted a permanent member and assigned to this company as driver of hose-carriage. Mr. Flynn is a member of the Massachusetts Catholic Order of Foresters.

JAMES P. DEAN (Fig. 7) was born in Boston, Mass., July 15, 1855. He is a trunk-maker by trade, at which he was employed at the time of his appointment in this department, which occurred July, 1882, as a substitute, and January 23, 1883, he was promoted a permanent member and assigned to this company. On June 25, 1887, he was transferred to Engine Company No. 14, but was returned to this company again July 23, 1888.

Joseph M. Garrity (Fig. 8) was born in Boston, Mass., January 29, 1862. He is a house-painter by trade, at which he was employed until his appointment on the permanent force. He first entered the department as a call-man in Ladder No. 12, and was promoted a permanent member June 18, 1887, and assigned to Ladder Company No. 3, from which he was transferred to this company, June 25, 1887.

Edward Sproul (Fig. 9) was born in Boston, Mass., February 2, 1855. He is a carpenter by trade. He entered this service October 17, 1882, in Engine Company No. 4, in which he remained until February 5, 1888, when he was transferred to Engine Company No. 10. He was transferred to this company July 24, 1888.

Patrick H. Kenney (Fig. 10) was born in Boston, Mass., July 23, 1861, He is a blacksmith by trade. He joined this department as a substitute, December, 1883, in Engine Company No. 14. September 24, 1885, he was promoted a permanent member and assigned to Engine Company No. 6, from where he was transferred, March 24, 1888, to this company.

Daniel B. Barrus (Fig. 11) was born in Roxbury District, Boston, Mass., August 9, 1859. He is an oil-cloth printer by trade. He joined the department as call-substitute in Engine Company No. 13 in 1880, and was appointed a call-man in Ladder Company No. 12, August 10, 1884. July 23, 1887, he was appointed a substitute and assigned to Engine Company No. 7, and was soon after transferred to this company. He was severely burned on the face and hands at a fire in Lincoln street.

Walter M. McLean (Fig. 12) was born in Boston, Mass., September 29, 1865. He entered this department September 12, 1888, in this company. He was employed as a general carriage-fitter before his appointment.

E. J. Shallow (Fig. 13) was appointed in Engine Company No. 26, November 23, 1888.

Daniel W. Stevens (Fig. 14), driver for Chief Engineer Webber, was born in St. John, N.B., December 15, 1867. He came to Boston when but a child, and after leaving school began driving for ex-Chief Engineer Green July 21, 1883, and when the present chief of the department was appointed he continued in the same position. He is on the roll of Engine Company No. 26, although his duty is entirely with the chief.

CHEMICAL ENGINE COMPANY NO. 2.

NAMES OF MEMBERS SINCE 1874.

Williston A. Gaylord, ap. July 3, 1874, hoseman in charge, promoted to captain of Engine Company No. 12, April 4, 1881; Conrad Rosemere, ap.

CHEMICAL ENGINE COMPANY No. 2. — Page 500.

September 21, 187–, tr. to Chemical Engine Company No. 3, February 1, 1875; T. Henry Weltch, ap. February 1, 1875, tr. to Engine Company No. 26, October 21, 1880, ap. again December 1, 1880, tr. to Chemical Engine Company No. 3, July 21, 1882; Walter Restarrick, ap. October 21, 1880, resigned November 27, 1880; Edward F. Martin, hoseman in charge, ap. April 4, 1881, promoted to captain July 20, 1883, tr. to Hose Company No. 8, May 1, 1885; John A. Shannon, Jr., ap. September 1, 1882, promoted to assistant engineman and tr. to Engine Company No. 30, July 10, 1883.

Present Members.

Captain John Knights (Fig. 1) was born in Boston, August 15, 1847. He is a paper-hanger by trade. When the late war broke out he enlisted in Company C, Forty-fifth Massachusetts Regiment, June, 1862, and was mustered out July 7, 1863. He reënlisted in Company A, Volunteers, Forty-second Regiment, and served 100 days. He joined this department as call-substitute in 1871, in Engine Company No. 3, and in 1873 was appointed a call-man. May 7, 1874, he was promoted a permanent member with the same company. He was driver of Hose Company No. 2, May 30, 1874, and was transferred back to Engine Company No. 3, May 1875, as hoseman. May 1, 1880, he was promoted captain of Engine Company No. 14, from which he was transferred to Hose Company No. 8, June 1, 1882, and was transferred to his present position, May 1, 1885. Captain Knights was the first man to take a civil-service examination for promotion in this department, this occurred September 20, 1875. He has met with some most severe and painful accidents during his career as a fireman, some of which affect him to the present day. He is a member of the Grand Army of the Republic. Captain Knights invented the Scott Hose Hitch in 1875, also the Combined Chemical Engine and Hose Carriage, one of which is now used in Somerville, Mass.

Addison Getchell (Fig. 2), driver, was born in Alton, N.H., December 5, 1833. He came to Boston in 1852, and was employed as a teamster. His experience in the fire service dates from May 1, 1853, when he joined old hand-engine Tremont Company No. 12, as a call-man. He ran with that company until May 1, 1854, when he joined Extinguisher Company No. 5. On December 1 of the same year he left the department, but returned, in Tremont Engine Company No. 12, April 1, 1885. He remained with that company until July 1, 1860, at which time horses were introduced in the service. At this date he left the service, but again returned, on July 1, 1861, and joined Hose Company No. 8. July 1, 1867, he again left the department, and did not return until August 1, 1873, when he was appointed a permanent member and assigned to Hose Company No. 8. This company was transferred to North Grove street, May 7, 1874, and an extinguisher engine was put in its house, which remained until July 3, 1874, when the present company was organized, and Mr. Getchell detailed to his present position. He has been in this house fifteen years, and in the department, on and off, for thirty-five years. He is a member of the Odd Fellows.

JOSEPH SMITH (Fig. 3) was born in Boston, April 20, 1853. He was employed as a teamster until his appointment as a substitute in this department, November 23, 1880, in Engine Company No. 25. From there he was transferred twenty times, until October 7, 1881, when he was made a permanent member and assigned to Engine Company No. 7. He has served on nearly all the different apparatus in the force. On July 10, 1883, he was transferred to this company. Mr. Smith has met with several severe accidents, and had some narrow escapes. He is a member of the Boston Assemby No. 5 of the Royal Society of Good Fellows.

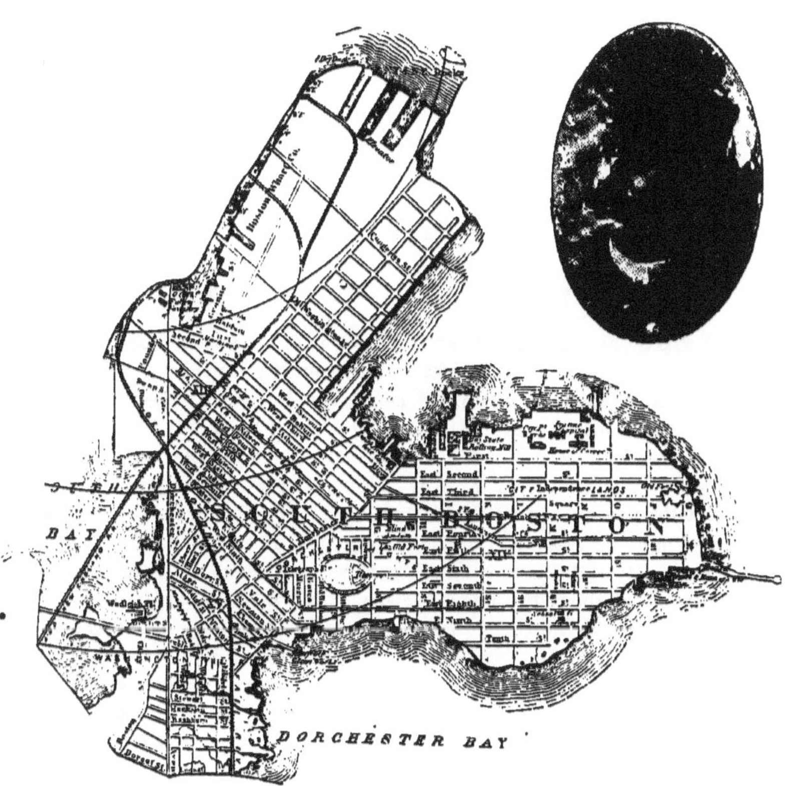

CHIEF MULLEN AND MAP OF DISTRICT No. 6. — Page 504.

CHAPTER X.

DISTRICT NO. 6.—SOUTH BOSTON.

THE Sixth Fire District comprises that part of Boston known as South Boston. It was set off from Dorchester by legislative enactment, March 6, 1804. It is bounded, south, by Dorchester Bay, and spreads about two miles on the south side of the harbor above the forts. It contains about eight hundred acres, and is laid out in regular streets and squares, the former running alphabetically from A to Q streets, and numerically from First to Tenth, with additional small streets and lanes. The surface of South Boston is exceedingly picturesque. In about the centre of this tract, and about two miles from City Hall, the memorable "Dorchester Heights" rear their heads one hundred and thirty feet above the sea, from which is presented a splendid view of Boston, its harbor, and the surrounding country. It is connected with old Boston by three bridges; viz., Congress street, Mt. Washington avenue, and Federal street. There are also two others, connecting it with the south or newer portion of the city ; viz., Broadway and Dover street, — making five in all. This part of Boston is rapidly increasing in population and wealth, its inhabitants numbering about 75,000, or almost one-sixth of the entire population of the city. It consists principally of wooden dwellings and stables, there being about seven thousand of the former, although the manufacturing interests are well represented. The district is considered a very dangerous one for fires, owing to the inflammable nature of its buildings. It has often been predicted that should a fire get a proper start here, it would be very apt to sweep the entire section ; but, owing to the efficiency of this branch of the department, with an increase of fire hydrants and modern improvements in the appliances for the extinguishment of fires, the above prediction has not as yet been fulfilled, although there have been some few serious conflagrations that have created considerable alarm for the time being.

There are located here seven fire companies, consisting of three steamers, one chemical engine, two independent hose-carriages, and one ladder-truck, situated at very advantageous points, so that any fire-box in the district can be reached by at least one of the above companies inside of two minutes. The district contains several public institutions, among them the Perkins Institution for the Blind, formerly the Washington House, near the Heights, which is famous for the advantages presented for the education of the blind. The manufacturing interests are represented by the South Boston Iron

Company, formerly "Alger's," where the business of casting heavy ordnance for the United States Government is carried on; also several other foundries and other iron industries, including machine-shops and the well-known concerns the Norway Iron and Steel Company, Bay State Iron Works, Whittier's, Walworth's, and S. A. Wood's machine companies. Two large sugar refineries, the Standard and Continental, are located here, the former nine stories in height and covering, with its storehouses and other buildings, several acres, the latter a five-story building, covering an entire square; also Shale's and Blake's furniture factories, Jenney's Oil Refinery, the Old Colony Railroad machine and car shops, and severallarge brewe ries. On the water-front, on the harbor side, are located the New York & New England railway and steamship piers. The land of the Boston Wharf Company is given up principally to warehouses and storehouses, and being situated in close proximity to the New York & New England piers and water-front, it offers splendid inducements to business firms; it is fast being built upon, and is adding greatly to the wealth of South Boston. The American Express Company and the Boston Hotel Coach and Phaeton Company have their stables here, the largest of the kind in the country. The wharves along here and the easterly side are occupied by lumber firms, coal-dealers, boat-builders, etc. At the foot of O street, adjoining Walworth's machine-shop, on East First street, is Lawley & Son's ship-yard, where were built the famous fast-sailing yachts "Mayflower," "Puritan," and "Sachem," and many others of the "Burgess" design. In a southerly direction from here is the large "North Point" stable and car-house of the West End Horse Railway; directly opposite, and running westerly, is the Marine park, overlooking the harbor, with its great iron pier reaching like an arm far out into the sea. This is a great summer resort; with cheap car-fares and the accommodations provided by the horse railway company it is not only frequented by the residents of South Boston, but it is a boon for the suburban residents and their families.

The West End Railway Company have at the Point three large stables and car-sheds, holding hundreds of horses, one of which — the K-street stable — was entirely destroyed by fire August 5, 1874, necessitating calling out the entire department. The other side of the peninsula, Dorchester Bay, is given up to boat-building and the anchorage of some five hundred or more pleasure yachts, owned by well-known residents of Boston. Three large yacht club-houses are located here, — the Boston, South Boston, and Bay View. The Boston Cordage Works cover an entire square at this point, giving employment to hundreds of hands. In the district, at the present time, are twenty school-houses and the same number of churches of all denominations.

The district has been in charge of the following-named district engineers since 1838 : —

Thomas B. Warren. 1838 to 1840; John Green, Jr., 1840 to 1847; Brewster Raynolds, 1847 to 1849; John Davis, Jr., 1849 to 1851; James

Wood, 1851 to 1852; George S. Thom, 1852 to 1856; George F. Hibbard, 1856 to 1859; George Brown, 1859 to 1882; Louis P. Abbott, 1882 to 1885; John A. Mullen, 1885, at present in charge. The companies in the district consist of the following: Engines Nos. 1, 2, 15; Chemical Engine No. 8; Hose Nos. 10, 12; and Ladder No. 5. The headquarters of the district chief is at the house of Engine Company No. 1.

District Chief JOHN A. MULLEN, of District No. 6, first saw the light in South Boston, June 2, 1851, and is the youngest man holding a similar position in the department, but despite his age none are more successful in their duties. After leaving school he learned the iron-moulder's trade, at which he was employed up to the time of assuming the business of a fireman. On June 12, 1874, he entered this department, at which time he was appointed a call-man in Engine Company No. 15, and on May 8, 1876, was appointed a permanent member and assigned to Engine Company No. 23, where he remained until August 8, 1881, at which time he was promoted to the position of captain, and again assigned to Engine Company No. 15. He held that position until August 20, 1885, when he was promoted to his present position. Chief Mullen is one of the oldest members of Engine Company No. 15, and by his long residence in South Boston is thoroughly familiar with that section. He is a member of the Boston Veteran Firemen's Association and a life member of the Firemen's Charitable Association, also a director in the Firemen's Mutual Relief Association, and a member of the Irish Charitable Association and of the Royal Arcanum.

ENGINE COMPANY NO. 1.

NAMES OF MEMBERS SINCE 1874.

Joseph W. Fowler, ap. July 1, 1862, foreman from July 13, 1874, assistant foreman from August 8, 1881, left December 8, 1883; Loring D. Shaw, ap. August 1, 1871, assistant engineman, left May 23, 1881; Temp. C. Twiss. ap. December 1, 1864, driver, left June 1, 1878; George Chapman, ap. June 13, 1874, left December 15, 1880; J. Willard Hayes, ap. June 13, 1874, left August 8, 1881; Charles K. Clark, ap. June 13, 1874, left July 16, 1884; Benjamin F. Donnell, ap. June 1, 1878, left June 28, 1887; George M. Gourley, ap. December 24, 1880, left November 25, 1883; Thomas F. Fitzgerald, ap. May 25, 1881, assistant engineman, August 16, 1887; George W. Edmonds, ap. December 10, 1883, left September 3, 1884; George J. Wall. ap. September 3, 1884, left April 10, 1889; Cornelius H. Lynch, ap. June 28. 1887, left October 27, 1888; Thomas J. Harty, ap. August 19, 1887, assistant engineman, left November 1. 1888.

On September 16, 1872. the present engine, built by the Amoskeag Manufacturing Company, was put into service. She was built originally for the New Orleans (La.) fire department, and on completion was sent by the

manufacturers to compete with other well-known builds of engines at the
Lowell (Mass.) Agricultural Fair. She threw a horizontal stream 311 feet
9 inches. and was purchased on the spot by Chief Engineer Damrell, of Boston, and sent immediately to be put into service. She appeared the following
day in the annual parade of the Fire Department. Her first working fire was
the " big fire " of November 9, 1872, when she performed good service.

Present Members.

Captain ROBERT E. BARTLETT (Fig. 1) was born in South Boston, Mass.,
October 8, 1853. He began life as a book-keeper. to which business he added
the duties of a fireman, joining this company as a call-substitute. August 9.
1871. June 13, 1874, he was appointed a call-hoseman. On April 29. 1876,
he was promoted a permanent member and assigned to Engine Company No. 4,
holding the position of senior hoseman from July 1, 1880, to August 8, 1881 ;
on the later date he was promoted to his present position and assigned to this
company. Captain Bartlett was severely injured at the Tremont Temple fire.
August 14, 1879, while at work in the building with Hosemen Cushing, Kelley.
and Pingree. He is a member of the Barnicoat Fire Association. the Boston
Veteran Firemen, and Puritan Assembly of the Royal Society of Good
Fellows.

Engineman JOHN RAY (Fig. 2) was born in Peru, Me., June 21, 1835.
He came to Boston during 1854 and learned the machinist's trade, in which
line he is an expert, and has rendered the department excellent service in
this capacity. Mr. Ray has the credit of being the first to introduce the relief valve, which was attached to his engine July, 1861. These valves are now
doing effective service on all engines in the city. He entered this department,
February 1. 1857. in Extinguisher Company No. 5, and was promoted clerk
of the company, February 1, 1859. He remained there until January 1,
1860. when he was promoted assistant engineman of Engine Company No. 7,
and one month later was promoted engineman. June 1, 1864, he was transferred, at his own request, to this company. where he has since remained.
Mr. Ray is a member of the Knights of Pythias, Washington Lodge No. 10.

Assistant Engineman THOMAS H. EVANS (Fig. 3) was born in Boston,
Mass., September 14, 1844. He is a machinist by trade. at which he was
employed for a number of years. On the outbreak of the war he enlisted,
during 1862, in Company C, Forty-Second Massachusetts Regiment, but returned in 1864, and again enlisted in Company F, Sixth Massachusetts Regiment. and remained to the end of the struggle. He joined the department
as a call-substitute on October 1. 1873, in this company. and May 21, 1876,
was made a call-man, and remained in that capacity until September 3,
1884, when he was promoted a permanent member. Mr. Evans was laid up
for eight weeks from injuries to his knee-pan received at the Gaston school-
house fire, on April 28, 1887, and was injured at Jenney's Oil Works fire,

ENGINE COMPANY No. 1. — Page 510.

January 26, 1877. He is a member of Post 32, G. A. R., the American Legion of Honor No. 141, the Pow-Wow Tribe No. 74 of Red Men, and the Boston Veteran Firemen's Association.

MELVIN PARKER MITCHELL (Fig. 4), driver, was born in Jamaica Plain District, Boston, Mass., February 10, 1859. His former employment was as a machinist. He joined the force during the fall of 1880 as a call-substitute in this company. November 27, 1883, he was appointed a call-man, and promoted a permanent member, September 3, 1884, and detailed as driver. Mr. Mitchell had a very narrow escape at the Plympton street fire, when an immense beam fell and struck the side of his fire-hat, throwing him quite a distance. He is a member of the Pow-Wow Tribe No. 74 of Red Men.

NICHOLAS J. FITZWILLIAM (Fig. 5) was born in Lowell, Mass., February 20, 1860. He left Lowell at an early age and came to Boston, and was employed in various occupations in Boston and New York City. He joined this force, February 16, 1888, as a substitute in Engine Company No. 12 ; April 16 he was transferred to Engine Company No. 26, and on April 19 was transferred to Ladder Company No. 3, where he remained until November 1, 1888, at which time he was assigned to this company.

WILLIAM HENRY CHAPMAN (Fig. 6) was born in Boston, August 20, 1840. He was for years employed as a building-mover. His experience in the Fire Department dates from 1870, when he joined this company as a call-substitute. October 1, 1873, he was made a call-man, and September 3, 1884, was promoted a permanent member. He was appointed to take charge in the absence of the captain.

JOHN R. CHAPMAN (Fig. 7) was born in South Boston. Mass., February 28, 1841. He was employed at various occupations previous to his entering this department. He began his fire record as a call-substitute in this company during 1873. On August 23 of that year he was made a call-man, in which capacity he remained until September 3, 1884, when he was promoted a permanent member. Mr. Chapman was injured at the Gaston school fire April 28, 1887.

GEORGE J. WALL (Fig. 8) was born in Boston, August 28, 1858. His trade is that of a carpenter. On July 7, 1879, he joined the department, as call-substitute, in Hose Company No 10, and remained in that capacity until December 7, when he was made a call-man. During December 5, 1883, he was appointed a substitute in Engine Company No. 3, from which he was promoted a permanent member and assigned to this company, September 3, 1884. Mr. Wall is a member of Howard Lodge No. 46 of the Royal Arcanum.

LAWRENCE SCALLON (Fig. 9) was born in Boston, September 5, 1842. He did ninety days' service in Company A, Fourth Battalion Rifles, during the war. He was a member of the Washington Hand-Engine Company No. 5, at Charlestown, Mass., and was made a call-man in Engine Company No. 1, January 13, 1874, where he remained until September 3,

1884, when he was transferred to Ladder Company No. 5. March 28, 1885, was appointed a permanent member of Ladder Company No. 8 and assigned to Engine Company No. 1, January 14, the ensuing year, where he remained until March 30, 1888, when he was transferred to Engine Company No. 15. October 28, 1888, he was transferred to this company.

GEORGE H. TWISS (Fig. 10) was born in Boston, Mass., March 24, 1860. After leaving school he worked at the house-painter's trade until December 29, 1881, when he joined the department as a call-member, and was assigned to Hose Company No. 12. Several months later he was transferred to Engine Company No. 2. January 16, 1886, he was transferred to Engine Company No. 4, and promoted as permanent hoseman. November 27, 1888, he was transferred to this company. Mr. Twiss is a member of the Order of Iron Hall.

ENGINE COMPANY NO. 2.

NAMES OF MEMBERS SINCE 1874.

On June 13, 1874, the company was reorganized with the following-named members: John Brown, call-foreman; D. H. Twiss, permanent driver; E. B. Swadkins, senior hoseman; hosemen: George H. Delano, George A. Jones, William Schofield, Thomas B. Doyle, C. H. Tayen, T. H. Young. In the year 1876 Foreman Brown left the department, and Senior Hoseman Swadkins was promoted to the position of call-foreman, and George H. Delano was made senior hoseman. In the year 1879 Foreman Swadkins left the department, and George A. Jones was promoted to the position of call-foreman. The following have been members of the old company. Engineman George O. Twiss was transferred to the repair-shop August 13, 1887, and was pensioned May 1, 1888. George H. Delano joined the department January 1, 1847, in Perkins No. 16, and remained in the department until November 11, 1887, having reached the age limit. The other members were John S. Cleverly, George H. Twiss, George E. Harkins, Charles H. Burgess, D. J. Fitzgerald. Driver D. H. Twiss died in May, 1885.

PRESENT MEMBERS.

Captain GEORGE A. JONES (Fig. 1) was born in Acton, Mass., August 1, 1845. He was a tinsmith by trade. On the outbreak of the war he enlisted in Company I, Thirty-eighth Massachusetts Infantry, August, 1862, and served with it until his discharge, July 16, 1865. He entered this department June 13, 1874, as a call-man in Hose Company No. 12, and was promoted a call-foreman of that company December 29, 1881. May 10, 1882, he was transferred to this company, and promoted to his present position, November 1, 1884. Captain Jones has been very fortunate as regards accidents, although having been in some very dangerous quarters. He is a member of Adelphi Lodge of Masons, the Bethesda Lodge of Odd Fellows, and the Boston Veteran Firemen's Association.

ENGINE COMPANY No. 2. — Page 514.

Engineman THOMAS F. FITZGERALD (Fig. 2) was born in New York City December 24, 1833. He came to this city when young, and began life as a locomotive engineer. He entered this department July 28, 1873, as assistant engineman in Engine Company No. 15, in which he was promoted to engineman, June 10, 1874. May 8, 1880, he was transferred to Engine Company No. 26, as assistant engineman, from where he was transferred to Engine Company No. 1, May 21, 1880; and on August 16, 1887, was promoted engineman and transferred to this company. Mr. Fitzgerald was severely injured by the engine running over his foot while on the way to Box 121, in 1875, he being thrown from the engine. At the Clinton-street fire he had both feet frozen while working at his engine; this caused him to lay off duty nine months. He is a member of Tremont Lodge of Odd Fellows and King Solomon Lodge of Masons, also the Charitable Firemen's Association.

Assistant Engineman HORACE F. FERRIN (Fig. 3) was born in South Boston, January 11, 1836. When the war broke out he enlisted, January 8, 1862, as a first-class fireman on board the United States man-of-war " Chocura." in which he served until the close of the great struggle, March 1, 1865. He then returned to his trade, that of a machinist, at which he was employed until January 1, 1870, when he was appointed to his present position.

PATRICK H. BOLEMAN (Fig. 4), driver, was born in Bridgewater, Mass., January 26, 1854. He was employed at the plumbing trade until he joined this department, July 1, 1883, at which time he was appointed a substitute in Engine Company No. 15. September 3, 1884, he was promoted a permanent member, and assigned to Engine Company No. 7, from which he was transferred to this company, August 1, 1885, and detailed to his present position. Mr. Boleman was laid up two months from the effects of a broken leg, received by a kick from one of the horses in August, 1886.

WILLIAM H. LEWIS (Fig. 5) was born in South Boston, Mass., May 28, 1860. He is a broom manufacturer, and combined with this the duties of fireman, May 10, 1882, at which time he joined Hose Company No. 12 as a call-substitute, and on January 23, 1885, was transferred to this company and promoted a call-member. Mr. Lewis is a member of Iron Hall.

WILLIAM SCHOFIELD (Fig. 6) was born in St. John, N.B., June 21, 1838. He came to this city during 1858, and learned the pattern-maker's trade, and on June 13, 1874, joined Hose Company No. 12, from which he was transferred to this company, May 10, 1882. Mr. Schofield is a member of Bethesda Lodge of I. O. O. F., The United Order of Workmen, and the Boston Veterans.

ROBERT McINTYRE (Fig. 7) was born in St. John, N.B., March 13, 1859. He came to this city during 1878, and learned the pattern-maker's trade. He joined this department as a call-substitute in this company, 1882, and was made a call-man July 1, 1886. He is a member of Hobah Lodge 53 of I. O. O. F., Puritan Assembly No. 8, Good Fellows, and Daughters of Rebekah.

PERCY W. GOWEN (Fig. 8) was born in Boston, Mass., Sept. 17, 1860. He is a machinist by trade, and on June 30, 1882, entered this department as a call-man, in Hose Company No. 9, in which he served until October 28, 1887, when he was transferred to this company. Mr. Gowen is a son of Captain Gowen, of Engine Company No. 21, and is a member of American Lodge, 191, I. O. O. F., Boston Council No. 4, of Royal Arcanum.

EDWARD M. SHINE (Fig. 9) was born in Boston, Mass., November 30, 1861. He is a machinist by trade, to which he added the duties of fireman, February 3, 1888, when he joined Ladder Company No. 5, in which he remained until June 1, 1888, when he was transferred to this company as a call-hoseman.

GEORGE W. THOMPSON (Fig. 10) first saw the light in South Boston, February 17, 1865. After leaving school he was employed as a teamster, and on December 1, 1886, he entered this department as a call-substitute in Ladder Company No. 5. He remained there until June 15, 1888, when he was appointed a call-member and assigned to this company.

JOSEPH W. HAYES was born in Boston, Mass., July 3, 1847. He is a jeweller by trade, and on June 13, 1874, became a member of this department, joining Engine Company No. 1 as a call-man. He remained there until August, 1881, when he was transferred to Hose Company No. 12, and from there was transferred to this company May 10, 1882.

ENGINE COMPANY NO. 15.

NAMES OF MEMBERS SINCE 1874.

Nicholas C. Cogley, ap. December 22, 1869, foreman, died March 12, 1875; Thos. F. Fitzgerald, ap. August 1, 1873, engineman, left May 20, 1880; Charles H. Smith, ap. August 15, 1871, assistant engineman, left February 1, 1886; Edward M. Grant, ap. March 10, 1873, driver, no record; Orestes L. Woods, ap. December 22, 1869, left December 1, 1884; James Bennett, ap. December 22, 1869, no record; Amos Marshall, ap. December 22, 1869, died July, 1876; Laurence H. Sexton, ap. May 5, 1873, no record; John A. Mullen, ap. June 12, 1874, left March 9, 1876; Frank H. Noonan, ap. June 12, 1874, left October 28, 1887; Timothy J. Sexton, ap. June 12, 1874, no record; John F. Scott, ap. September 1, 1874, left September 1, 1881; James Shields, ap. February 1, 1875, no record; Albert J. Breed, ap. February 5, 1875, driver, no record; Alexander Baith, ap. June 17, 1875, no record; Otis M. Clapp, driver, no record; Michael R. Mullen, ap. February 5, 1876, no record; John H. Frederick, ap. May 1, 1876, no record; Henry C. Whitney, ap. Sept. 21, 1876, left May 6, 1882; Richard Fitzgerald, ap. September 4, 1876, left October 4, 1877; Frank B. Dodge, ap. July 21, 1877, left June 10, 1880; William H. Flavell, ap. March 4, 1878, left July 27, 1880; Edwin W. Clark, ap. April 26, 1878, left May 12, 1880; John Flavell, ap. October 21, 1878, left April 21, 1882; Alexander N. Allen, ap. July 28,

1880, died February 25, 1882; William A. Emery, ap. August 5, 1880, left November 5, 1880; William A. McKenzie, ap. January 26, 1881, left October 31, 1881; James Foster, ap. November 2, 1881, left November 6, 1888; John A. Mullen, ap. August 8, 1881, captain, left August 20, 1885; Cornelius H. Lynch, ap. April 21, 1882, left June 28, 1887; William A. McKenzie, ap. May 6, 1882, left January 7, 1887; Michael Cook, ap. June 1, 1882, left May 31, 1889; William Loney, ap. April 21, 1883, left July 16, 1885; Warren R. Smith, ap. February 1, 1886, assistant engineman, left September 7, 1886; George W. Edmonds, ap. March 11, 1887, died April 13, 1889; John S. Cleverly, ap. August 3, 1887, left August 11, 1888; Daniel H. Sennott, ap. October 28, 1887, lieutenant, left August 11, 1888; Lawrence Scallan, ap. March 30, 1888, left October 28, 1888.

Present Members.

Captain Isaac Austin Williams (Fig. 1) was born in West Roxbury District, Boston, Mass., January 21, 1849. He is a machinist by trade, at which he was employed until his permanent appointment in this force. His career as a fireman dates from 1868, when he entered the hand department, joining Alert Engine Company No. 4, of Dorchester. On the annexation of that district with Boston, January 5, 1870, the engine was numbered No. 19, and he was appointed a call-hoseman of that company. April 1, 1871, he was promoted assistant engineman, from which he was transferred and promoted engineman of Engine Company No. 23, January 5, 1874. He remained there until May 1, 1874, when he left the department, but returned again as assistant engineman February 1, 1875, in Engine Company No. 26. He was promoted engineman, and transferred to this company May 20, 1880; and on September 4, 1885, was promoted to his present position. Captain Williams is a member of the Boston Veteran Firemen's Association and Boston Council No. 4, Royal Arcanum.

Lieut. F. H. Noonan (Fig. 2) was born in Boston, Mass., August 6, 1853. He was a laborer by occupation. His fire service began on July 12, 1874, as a call-man in this company, and on July 1, 1882, was promoted a permanent member. January, 1883, he was promoted to his present position, and in October, 1887, was transferred to Chemical No. 8, in charge. He remained there until October, 1888, when he was reinstalled in this company.

Engineman William M. Lynch (Fig. 3) was born in St. Johnsbury, Vt., August 25, 1856. He came to Boston during 1878, and learned the machinist trade, at which he was employed until February 2, 1883, when he was promoted a permanent member, and assigned to Engine Company No. 23, and detailed to the repair-shop. On October 13, 1883, he was promoted assistant engineman, and assigned to Engine Company No. 26, where he remained until September 15, 1885, when he was promoted to his present position, and assigned to this company. He was laid up five weeks from injuries received at the Swett-street fire. 1886.

Assistant Engineer WILLIAM R. BACHELDER (Fig. 4) was born in Bath, Me., August 8, 1851. He came to Boston in April, 1869, and learned the machinist's trade. On December 21, 1883, he was enrolled in this service as a call-man in Ladder Company No. 5, where he remained until January 16, 1886, when he was promoted a permanent member, and assigned to Engine Company No. 4, September 27, of the same year. He was transferred to this company and promoted to his present position, April 10, 1887. Mr. Bachelder is a member of Bethesda Lodge of Odd Fellows.

JAMES H. McALLISTER (Fig. 5), driver, was born in Methuen, Mass., December 12, 1841. When the war broke out he enlisted, during 1862, in Company G, Forty-Second Massachusetts Regiment, serving nineteen months. He was then employed as a teamster, and on December 21, 1878, he entered this department as a call-man in this company. May 12, 1880, he was promoted a permanent member, and assigned to this company in his present position. Mr. McAllister was severely injured February, 1880, at the Stearns' wharf fire, at which he was knocked from a floor on some lumber, and severely injured his spine, necessitating a most serious surgical operation, which laid him up three months.

MICHAEL COOK (Fig. 6), driver of hose-carriage, was born in Galway, Ireland, May 15, 1850. He came to this city when young, and was employed as a teamster. He entered this department at West Roxbury, working in hand-engine. May 14, 1871, he was appointed driver of Ladder Company No. 1, which is now No. 10, and remained there until June 1, 1882, when he was transferred to this company, and detailed driver of hose-carriage.

JOHN F. McWHIRK (Fig. 7) was born in Boston, February 4, 1855. He is a wood-turner by trade, and entered this department as a call-substitute during 1879, in this company. May 15, 1880, he was appointed a call-member, and on December 1, 1882, a permanent man, always serving with this company. His most serious accident occurred November 17, 1882, when he was run over by the hose-carriage, which injured his back, so as to render him unfit for duty for two weeks.

GEORGE W. EDMONDS (Fig. 8) was born in Boston, May 16, 1855. He is a machinist by trade. He entered the force as a call-substitute, August 5, 1875, in Hose Company No. 10, in which he was appointed a call-man, December 24, 1878; and during 1882 was transferred to Engine Company No. 1. September 3, 1884, he was promoted a substitute, and assigned to this company. He was appointed a permanent member March 28 of the same year, and assigned to Engine Company No. 8, but was transferred back to this company March 11, 1887.

JOHN ENWRIGHT (Fig. 9) was born in West Newcastle, Ireland, February 20, 1841. He came to this city when but eight years of age. He was employed as a fireman on stationary engines until October 16, 1873, when he

Engine Company No. 15. — Page 519.

was appointed a permanent member of this department, and assigned to
Engine Company No. 10. He remained there until May 12, 1874, when he
was transferred to Engine Company No. 25. From there he was transferred
to Hose Company No. 9, June 25, 1887, in which he remained until he
was transferred to this company. Mr. Enwright is a member of the Montgomery Light Guards and the Garfield Assembly of the Good Fellows.

CORNELIUS H. LYNCH (Fig. 10) was born in Albany, N.Y., March 5,
1849. He came to this city during 1865, and learned the cooper's trade.
He enlisted in this department April 21, 1880, as a call-man in Engine
Company No. 15, and on November 1, 1882, was promoted a permanent
member. June 28, 1887, he was transferred to this company.

JOHN JOSEPH RILEY (Fig. 11) was born in Newburyport, Mass., June 12,
1863. He came to Boston during 1880, and worked at the barber business
until his appointment in this department as a substitute, and was assigned to
Engine Company No. 18, September 13, 1888; a short time after he was
transferred to this company.

FITZGERALD M. O. LALOR (Fig. 12) was born in Boston, Mass., June 11,
1862. He is a carpenter by trade, and was appointed in this department, as
a substitute, December 14, 1888, and detailed to this company.

LADDER COMPANY NO. 5.

NAMES OF MEMBERS SINCE 1874.

Captains J. B. Hill, ap. January 1, 1870, discharged November 11, 1887
(he was captain of company from January 1, 1870, to March 28, 1885);
E. Cummings, tr. from Ladder No. 1, March 28, 1885, to Engine No. 6.
April 1. 1887; driver, B. F. Donnells, tr. from Hose No. 10, January 1,
1870; resigned March, 1874. The following were appointed January 1, 1870:
Albert E. Goodwin, discharged June, 1874; Appleton Lathe. discharged
November 11, 1887; David Kunus, discharged June, 1874; Alexander McKenzie, discharged June, 1874; Edward A. Perkins, discharged November
11, 1887; Joseph Bell, discharged June, 1874; Humphrey Choate. died July
30, 1878; Henry B. Fowler, discharged August 20, 1881; John H. Howard,
discharged August 1, 1874; John A. Hodgkins, discharged June, 1874;
Lyman Lock, discharged September 13, 1872; Charles Spear, discharged
June, 1874; William Sheene, discharged December 20, 1883; Frank B.
Sibley, discharged October 25, 1871; Daniel Weston, discharged May 1,
1883; Samuel H. Whitney, ap. July, 1870, discharged June, 1874; Anthony
Martin, ap. November, 1871, discharged June, 1874; John F. Currier, ap.
October, 1873, discharged February 8, 1886; S. Colley, ap. June 13, 1874.
died June 9, 1878; Daniel Nason, ap. June 13, 1874. discharged September
26, 1883; W. A. Emery, ap. June 13, 1874. discharged August 9. 1874;
George Gray. ap. June 13, 1874, died January 20, 1880; Henry Kohr, ap.
June 13. 1874, discharged July 20. 1874; Robert Dow, ap. June 13, 1874,

discharged January 7, 1887; F. Bamberg, ap. June 13, 1874, discharged June 13, 1882; T. Wilson, ap. September, 1874, discharged March, 1880; W. H. Mapes, ap. September, 1874, discharged April 11, 1879; L. G. Weeks, ap. October, 1874, discharged September 21, 1876; J. T. Weston, ap. August, 1876, tr. to Engine No. 22, September 8, 1884; W. F. Delano, ap. May 3, 1879, tr. to Ladder No. 1. October 5, 1882; Francis White, ap. March 31, 1880, discharged June 24, 1887; G. N. Dunn, ap. March 31, 1880, tr. to Engine No. 7, September 3, 1884; H. B. Sprowl, ap. October 11, 1881, discharged October 29, 1885; F. A. Hamilton, ap. July 1, 1882, discharged October 29, 1885; F. P. Stengel, ap. April 21, 1883, tr. to Ladder No. 1, March, 1888; W. R. Batchelder, ap. December 21, 1883, tr. to Engine No. 4, January 16, 1886; J. W. Currant, ap. June 4, 1884, discharged September 30, 1887; L. Scallan, tr. from Engine No. 1, September 2, 1884, tr. to Ladder No. 8, March 28, 1885; J. G. Mahoney, ap. January 16, 1886, tr. to Hose No. 1, October 29, 1886; F. P. Chapman. tr. from Hose No. 10, January 16, 1886; M. Cronin, ap. January 23, 1886, tr. to Ladder No. 3, June 18, 1887; J. H. Flaherty, ap. January 8, 1887, discharged August 19, 1887; Edward M. Shine, ap. June 1, 1888, tr. to Engine No. 2, June 8, 1888; Charles Sweetser, ap. June 1, 1888, tr. to Engine No. 2, June 8, 1888.

Present Members.

Capt. Edwin A. Perkins (Fig. 1) was born in Gilmonton, N.H., May 11, 1855. He came to Boston during 1863, and after leaving school learned the carpenter's trade. His career as a fireman dates from May 17, 1876, when he was made a call-man in Engine Company No. 21. December 17, 1880, he was appointed a permanent member, and assigned to Engine Company No. 10, and was promoted lieutenant of that company, April 21, 1882. April 1, 1887, his excellent services were again recognized, and he was promoted to his present position, and assigned to this company.

Francis S. Parson (Fig. 2), driver, was born in Norway, Me., August 31, 1836. He was employed as a teamster previous to entering this department, which he did as a call-man on Engine Company No. 7, during 1871. June 1, 1872, he was transferred to Hose Company No. 9, where he remained until January 11, 1874, when he was appointed a permanent member, and assigned to Engine Company No. 7. He was transferred March 31, 1874, to this company, and detailed to his present position April 31 of the same year. Mr. Parson was badly hurt at the Broad-street fire during 1871, when he fell through a building and hurt his back.

George F. Horne (Fig. 3) first saw the light in South Boston, Mass., July 27, 1846. He is a machinist by trade, and on October 1, 1872, entered this service as a member of this company. Mr. Horne is a member of Bethesda Lodge, 30, I. O. O. F., and Taylor Council, 87, American Legion of Honor.

LADDER COMPANY No. 5. — Page 524.

GEORGE H. VINAL (Fig 4) was born in Scituate, Mass., September 23, 1841, and came to Boston during 1858. He is a mason by trade, to which he added the duties of fireman March 1, 1870, when he was appointed a member of this company. Mr. Vinal had a narrow escape at the big fire May 30, 1873. He is a member of Knights of Pythias and Gate of Temple Masons, and a life member of the Firemen's Charitable Association.

SILAS B. CRANE (Fig. 5) was born in Canton, Mass., March 17, 1845. He came to Boston when but a child, and began life as a machinist. He enlisted in Company F, Twenty-Fourth Massachusetts Infantry, on October 21, 1861, and served until January 20, 1866. He entered this department June 13, 1874, when he was enrolled a member of this company. Mr. Crane was commander of Post 32, G. A. R., at the time the Soldiers' Monument on the Common was dedicated, and is now past-commander of that Post.

EDWARD F. CURRANT (Fig. 6) was born in East Boston, Mass., October 16, 1856. He is a pattern-maker by trade, and first began running to fires, when but a boy, in General Taylor Engine No. 4, of South Malden, Mass. (now Everett), but was first enrolled as a member in Pacific Engine No. 1, of Stoughton, Mass., during 1879; and in the following year steam was introduced, and he became a member of Steam Fire Engine Company No. 1, of that city, and acted as steward about a year, when he came to this city, and in 1888 was appointed a call-substitute in this company, in which he was promoted a member, May 1, 1883. He is a member of Soaugctaha Tribe 21 of Red Men.

FRANK P. CHAPMAN (Fig. 7) was born in South Boston, February 22, 1854. He is employed as a laborer, and began running to fires as a call-substitute in Engine Company No. 1 for about five years. He was appointed a call-member of Hose Company No. 9, October 20, 1876, from which he was transferred to Hose Company No. 10, July 16, 1885; and on January 16, 1886, was transferred to this company. Mr. Chapman was laid up for seven weeks, from burned feet, received at the fire at Bishop's Factory, on Tudor street. He is a member of the Firemen's Charitable Association.

DAVID J. FITZGERALD (Fig. 8) was born in New York City, May 16, 1854, and came to this city when a child. After leaving school he learned the house-painter's trade, and on November 24, 1881, joined Engine Company No. 2 as a call-substitute, from which he was transferred to Hose Company No. 12. July 10, 1882, he was transferred back to Engine Company No. 2, as a call-man, and on November 21, 1885, was transferred to this company.

LOUIS F. BOWERS (Fig. 9) was born in South Boston, May 24, 1862. He is a bricklayer by trade, and began attending fires January 1, 1886, in Hose Company No. 10, in which he was a call-substitute, and remained such until November 8 of the same year, when he was transferred to this company, and appointed a call-ladderman.

DANIEL KANE (Fig. 10) was born in Boston, Mass., August 17, 1849. He is a stone-cutter by trade, and entered this department during 1874 as a call-substitute in Hose Company No. 9, in which he was promoted a call-member, June 20, 1880; and in October 28, 1887, was transferred to this company.

WILLIAM LONEY (Fig. 11) was born in Cork, Ireland, October 6, 1856, and when but a child came to this city. He began his experience as a fireman during 1878 as a call-substitute in Engine Company No. 15, in which he was made a call-member April 21, 1883. July 16, 1885, he was transferred to Hose Company No. 9, and October 28, 1887, was transferred to this company. Mr. Loney was highly complimented for his services at the fire at Hotel Berkeley, when he held the hose on an aerial ladder three hours, without relief. He is a member of Catholic Order of Foresters and the Knights of St. Rose. He has been engaged in the coal and wood business for a number of years.

EDWARD SCHELL (Fig. 12) was born in East Boston, September 6, 1861. He first began fire duty on July 1, 1882, when he was appointed a call-substitute in Hose Company No. 9, in which he was made a call-member April 21, 1883, and on October 28, 1887, was transferred to this company. He was laid up two weeks from a cut in the head, received at a fire on Dorchester avenue, by the nozzle of a hose.

JOHN F. HUGHES (Fig. 13) was born in Boston, Mass., April 11, 1851. He is engaged in commercial work, and was appointed call-substitute in Hose Company No. 9, January, 1884; and May 6, 1884, was promoted a call-member, where he remained until October 28, 1887, at which time he was transferred to this company.

ELISHA W. GOLDTHWAIT (Fig. 14) was born in Randolph, Mass., January 29, 1862. He came to Boston when but a child, and is employed as a teamster. He became connected with this department in Hose Company No. 9, as a call-substitute, during 1883, in which he was promoted a call-member, January 21, 1884. He was transferred to this company October 28, 1887. He is a member of Soangetaha Tribe, No. 21, of Red Men.

JEREMIAH F. SULLIVAN (Fig. 15) was born in Lowell, Mass., November 4, 1858. He came to Boston when but a child, and learned the gas-fitting trade. February, 1887, he was appointed a call-substitute, and on December 30, 1887, was promoted a call-member, and was assigned to this company.

MICHAEL B. MULCAHY (Fig. 16) was born at Galasha, County Waterford, Ireland, September 26, 1860. He came to this city during 1879, and is employed as a moulder's helper. He entered this department December 30, 1887, being appointed a call-member of this company.

WILLIAM D. FITZGERALD (Fig. 17) was born in Boston, Mass., August 25, 1864, and is now employed as a blacksmith. He entered this department January 7, 1888, when he was appointed in this company as a call-substitute.

JOSEPH J. O'CONNOR (Fig. 18) was born in Boston, Mass., January 21, 1863. He is employed at commercial work, and became connected with this department March 28, 1888, when he was appointed in this company as a call-substitute.

P. W. DAY (Fig. 19) was born in Worcester, Mass. He came to Boston, February, 1887. His trade is that of a machinist, and he became connected with this force June 1, 1888, when he was appointed a call-substitute in this company.

A. S. MITCHELL (Fig. 20) was born in South Boston, September 20, 1861. He is now employed as a teamster, but entered this service, June 25, 1888, as a call-substitute, and assigned to this company.

WALTER H. WRIGHT (Fig. 21) was born in Clinton, Mass., December 31, 1862, and came to Boston during 1887. His trade is that of a machinist, and he became connected with this department September 14, 1888, when he was appointed in this company as a call-substitute. He was connected with the Clinton fire department for about two and a half years, and the Worcester department about six months.

HOSE COMPANY NO. 10.

NAMES OF MEMBERS SINCE 1874.

Frank A. Greenleaf, ap. June 13, 1874, call-foreman, tr. to Engine 10, no record; George W. Stone, ap. June 13, 1874, driver, discharged in 1875; Benj. F. Donnell, tr. from Ladder Company No. 5 to this company in 1875, driver, tr. to Engine Company No. 1, June 1, 1878; Jos. Wall, ap. June 13, 1874, no record; Charles H. Gill, ap. June 13, 1874, discharged, 1879; Lewis T. Lunt, ap. June 13, 1874, discharged July 5, 1889; James E. Stanley, ap. June 13, 1874, resigned June 15, 1887; Pelham W. Harloy, ap. June 13, 1874, call-foreman, discharged in 1882; Thomas J. Good, ap. June 13, 1874, tr. to Engine Company No. 3 in 1884; Robert Barnes, ap. June 13, 1874, no record; George F. Emmons, ap. November 20, 1876, was murdered November 25, 1886; John Shea, ap. April 13, 1880, tr. to Ladder Company No. 1, in 1887; George W. Emonds, no record, tr. to Engine 1, December 10, 1883; James L. Bartlett, ap. January 19, 1886, tr. to Hose Company No. 12; George Wall, ap. April 13, 1880, tr. to Engine 3, April 1, 1884; James Linerhan, ap. January 19, 1886, resigned May 12, 1886; George Dowling, ap. January 15, 1886, tr. July 25, 1887.

PRESENT MEMBERS.

Call-Captain HENRY T. BOWERS (Fig. 1) was born in Albany, N.Y., January 17, 1835. He enlisted on board the war-ship "Ohio" during the beginning of the war, and remained some time. He entered this department as a steward of Deluge Hose Company No. 1, October 31, 1861, where he remained until April, 1862, at which time he enlisted in the navy, after which he joined the same company, and remained there until 1874, when he resigned; but entered again during 1875, and has been with the company ever since. February, 1887, he was laid up six weeks, from the result of injuries received from being run over by the engine while going to Box 138. Captain Bowers is a member of the Boston Firemen's Veteran Association, Bethesda Lodge of Odd Fellows, Massachusetts Lodge No. 1 of the Order of Heptasops, and the Firemen's Charitable Association.

TEMPLEMAN C. TWISS (Fig. 2), driver, was born in Nashua. N.H., December 11, 1839, and came to this city in 1840. He joined this department March, 1857, as a member of Mazeppa Engine Company No. 1, and resigned December 19, 1859. He was reappointed January 1, 1865, as driver of Engine Company No. 1, where he remained until June 1, 1878, when he was transferred to this company at his own request. Mr. Twiss was thrown from the hose-carriage while responding to Box 138, February 1, 1887, and had his left leg broken in two places, also his right foot.

CHARLES E. MOLLOY (Fig. 3) was born in Boston, July 22, 1857. He first did fire-duty as a call-substitute in this company during 1879, and on April 1, 1884, was made a call-member. He was promoted substitute in Engine Company No. 15, April 7, 1885, and to his present position January 16, 1886, and assigned to Engine Company No. 6, from which he was transferred to this company June 24, 1888.

LEWIS T. LUNT (Fig. 4) was born in Boston, Mass., March 18, 1846, and is a machinist by trade. He served in the war until October 27, 1864, in Company F, Sixth Massachusetts Regiment. He joined this company during 1874 as a call-hoseman, and still holds that position. At the fire of the Norway Iron Works, January 24, 1877, he was seriously injured.

HENRY A. PECKHAM (Fig. 5) was born in Whitingsville, Mass., December 27, 1859, and came to this city during 1865, when he learned the electrician's trade. He entered the department as a call-substitute in this company during October, 1879, and on March 21, 1883, was admitted a call-member. He is a member of Commercial Lodge No. 97, Mt. Sinai Encampment No. 49, and Canton Mascot No. 12, I. O. O. F.

JAMES DOYLE (Fig. 6) was born in Boston, Mass., December 12, 1857, and is a machinist by trade. He entered this department in October, 1882, in Engine Company No. 15, and was transferred to this company, December 12, 1883, as a call-member.

CHARLES W. SWEETSER (Fig. 7) was born in Boston, Mass., July 25, 1866, and is a machinist by trade. He joined this department as a call-substitute in Ladder Company No. 5, June 1, 1888, and was transferred to this company, June 16, in the same capacity.

JOHN A. NOONAN (Fig. 8) was born in Boston, Mass., November 22, 1865. He is a teamster by occupation, and joined this department as call-substitute in this company, May, 1888.

HOSE COMPANY No. 10. — Page 529.

HOSE COMPANY NO. 12.

NAMES OF MEMBERS SINCE 1874.

D. Smith, ap. May 10, 1882, resigned November 11, 1887 ; E. Lamphier, ap. May 10, 1882, resigned November 11, 1887 ; T. C. Haney, ap. May 10, 1882, tr. June 24, 1887 ; J. Collins, ap. May 10, 1882, tr. February 16, 1888. D. McNerny, ap. May 10, 1882, tr. April 7, 1885 ; J. Meehan, ap. August 1, 1885, tr. January 31, 1888.

PRESENT MEMBERS.

Call-Captain ALBERT SCHELL (Fig. 1) was born in East Boston, Mass., January 28, 1855. After leaving school he learned the cabinet-maker's trade, and entered this service as a call-substitute in Hose Company No. 9, June, 1874, and on October 2, 1875, was appointed a call-member. March 3, 1882, he was promoted to the position of captain of that company, in which he remained until October 28, 1887, on its disbandment, when he was assigned to this company in his present position. Captain Schell is a member of the Boston Veterans.

MOSES A. JONES (Fig. 2), driver, was born in Alney, Me., July 19, 1833. He came to this city when but a child, and began life as an iron-moulder. His fire experience dates from 1855, at which time he entered the department in Hand-Engine Mazeppa No. 1, which was taken out of service during 1859, and Engine Company No. 1 was organized. September 17, 1860, he was appointed driver, and transferred to Engine Company No. 2. On the outbreak of the war he enlisted, February 1, 1864, in the Fourth Massachusetts Battery, in which he served until 1866, after which he returned to this city, and was installed in his former position, in which he remained until the reorganization, when he was assigned to this company. Mr. Jones is a member of the Puritan Assembly, Pilgrim Fathers, Royal Good Fellows, and Post 2, G. A. R.

BENJAMIN F. DONNELL (Fig. 3), senior hoseman, was born in Wells, Me., March 23, 1834. He came to Boston when young, and began life as a teamster. His experience as a fireman dates from 1853, as a call-substitute, and in 1855 he joined Hand-Engine Company Perkins No. 2, where he remained until 1859, at which date he left the department, but returned again during 1860, as a driver in Hose Company No. 9. He remained there until August 14, 1862, when he enlisted in Company D, Thirty-Fifth Massachusetts Regiment, and did service until 1865. On March 1, 1868, he again entered the service, joining Hose Company No. 10 as a driver. He was transferred January 1, 1870, to Ladder Company No. 5, where he remained until March 1, 1874, when he resigned. He again entered this service, May 9. 1876, in Hose Company No. 10, and remained there until June 1, 1878, when he was transferred to Engine Company No. 1. June 28, 1887, he was transferred to his present position. Mr. Donnell is a member of the Boston Veterans,

Firemen's Charitable Association, Post 2, G. A. R., Bethesda Lodge of Odd Fellows, and Mount Washington Encampment, and the Knights of Honor.

ALONZO PRATT (Fig. 4) first saw the light in South Boston, August 31, 1834. He is an iron-moulder by trade, at which he has worked for years. He entered this department as a call-substitute. October 1, 1865, in Engine Company No. 2. July 1, 1866, he was appointed a call-man, and remained in that company until the reorganization, when he was transferred to this company. Mr. Pratt was injured at the House of Correction fire by a falling plank, which laid him up for six weeks. He is a member of the Golden Rule Lodge No. 206, Knights of Honor, and the Boston Veterans.

CHARLES GRIFFIN (Fig. 5) was born in Bridgton, Me., November 27, 1849. He came to Boston during 1870, and learned the car-builder's trade. His experience as a fireman dates from September, 1872, when he was appointed a call-substitute in Engine Company No. 2. During June, 1873, he was promoted a call-hoseman, and transferred to this company.

EUGENE TRAFTON (Fig. 6) was born in Charlestown District, Boston, Mass., November 22, 1845. He is a wood-turner by trade. He enlisted in this service as a call-substitute, August. 1873, in Engine Company No. 2, and in February, 1874, was promoted a call-member, and transferred to this company. He is a member of Standish Lodge No. 141 of the Legion of Honor, and Iron Hall No. 353.

JAMES L. BARTLETT (Fig. 7) was born in South Boston, Mass.. October 6, 1861. He is a house-painter by trade, and entered this department as a call-substitute during October. 1883, in this company. He was appointed a call-hoseman January 23, 1886, and assigned to Hose Company No. 10, and was transferred to this company June 8. 1888.

FRANK M. PERKINS (Fig. 8) was born in Boston, Mass., December 31, 1852, and was a clerk by occupation. He entered this department during 1876 as a call-substitute in Ladder Company No. 5, and in August, 1885, was transferred to this company by District Chief Mullen, and was reappointed by the Board, July 11, 1887.

JAMES P. NOLAN was born in Roxbury District, Boston, Mass, 1867. July 11, 1887, he enlisted in this service as a call-substitute in this company.

CHEMICAL ENGINE COMPANY NO. 8.
NAMES OF MEMBERS SINCE OCTOBER 27, 1887.

Chemical Engine No. 8 was organized on Thursday October 27, 1887, at 10.30 A.M., under the command of Lieutenant Frank H. Noonan, tr. from Engine Company No. 15; hosemen: James J. Hughes, tr. from Hose Company No. 9; John Enwright, tr. from Hose Company No. 9. Company in service, Saturday, August 11, 1888: Lieutenant Frank H. Noonan and Hoseman John Enwright, tr. to Engine Company No. 15, Saturday, August 11; Lieutenant Daniel H. Sennott and Hoseman John S. Cleverly, tr. from Engine Company No. 15 to Chemical Engine No. 8.

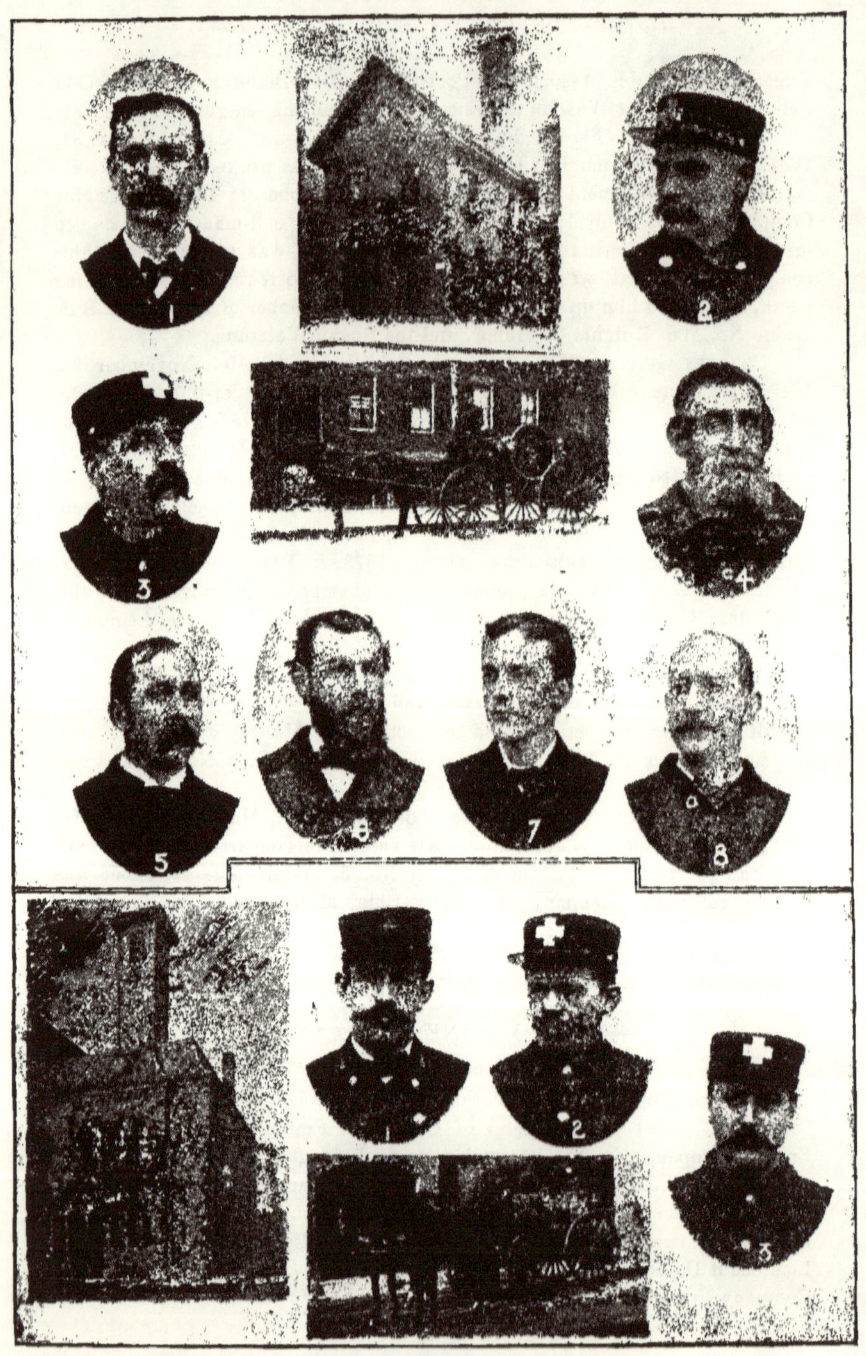

Top — Hose Company No. 12.   Bottom — Chemical Engine Company No. 8. — Page 533.

Present Members.

Lieutenant DANIEL H. SENNOTT (Fig. 1, bottom of page 533) was born in Charlestown District, Boston, Mass., May 26, 1860, being one of the youngest lieutenants in the department. After leaving school he worked at the express business, and in October, 1881, was admitted on this force as a call-substitute in Engine Company No. 27. June 15, 1882, he was appointed a call-man, and, September 3, 1884, was promoted a permanent member. He remained there until October 28, 1887, when he was promoted to his present position, and assigned to Engine Company No. 15, from which he was transferred, on August 11, 1888, to this company in charge. Lieutenant Sennott is a member of Bunker Hill Council of the Royal Arcanum.

JAMES J. HUGHES (Fig. 2, bottom of page), driver, was born in Boston, Mass., August 22, 1852. He is a printer by trade, at which he worked until October 1, 1873, when he was appointed a permanent boseman in this department, and assigned to Ladder Company No. 8, from which he was transferred, April 30, 1874, to Engine Company No. 25. July 21, 1883, he was transferred to Hose Company No. 9, and detailed as driver. He remained there until October 28, 1887, when he was transferred to this company on its organization. Mr. Hughes is a member of the Catholic Order of Foresters.

JOHN S. CLEVERLY (Fig. 3, bottom of page) was born in Quincy, Mass., July 30, 1851. He came to this city during October, 1878, and worked at the cabinet-maker's trade. He enlisted in this department as a call-substitute in Engine Company No. 2, August, 1879, and May 8, 1880, was appointed a call-man in Hose Company No. 12. May 10, 1882, he was transferred to Engine Company No. 2. February 25, 1886, he was promoted a permanent member, and assigned to Ladder Company No. 3, from which he was transferred to Engine Company No. 15, August 3, 1887, and, August 11, 1888, was transferred to this company. Mr. Cleverly received severe injuries to his neck and shoulders at a fire on Albany street, September 26, 1886, by falling from a ladder.

CHAPTER XI.

DISTRICT NO. 7.

THIS district comprises all that part of Boston south of District No. 5, to the centre of Albany street; thence through the centre of Albany and Northampton streets to Columbus avenue and Chester park, to east side of Commonwealth avenue, to centre of Berkeley to Dover street. In this radius we find the principal wealthy residential section. Here are located the aristocratic thoroughfares and the mansions of Boston's most wealthy citizens. These include the immense apartment hotels, and the famous Hotels Brunswick and Vendome. Scattered over this district are more churches than in any other, among which are the famous New Old South, Trinity, Church of the Unity, Brattle square, New Hollis street, First Church, Clarendon, Warren avenue, Cathedral, Immaculate Conception, and others; also the Young Men's Christian Association, Young Women's Christian Association, the Art Museum, Natural History Building, new Public Library. It has also the principal educational institutions, embracing Normal Art School, School of Technology, College of Pharmacy, Boston Medical College, Boston (Jesuit's) College, Conservatory of Music, the Boys' High and Latin Schools, also the Girls', together with many other public schools. Public institutions are also largely represented. Among them are the City Hospital, Homœopathic Hospital, Home for Destitute Children, Homes for the Aged, etc. The manufacturing industry is principally lumber, and the dreaded Wareham-street district is within these boundaries. At this section are located a number of planing and other wood-working mills, which are built in such a manner as to make a fire here the most dreaded of any other section. A large number of Boston's very poor, and their humble dwellings, can also be found in that section. Only two theatres — the Grand Dime Museum and the Grand Opera House — are within this district. The apparatus in this section are Engines Nos. 3, 22, 23, 33; Ladders Nos. 3, 13, 15; and Hose No. 5, — the headquarters of the chief of district being at Engine Company No. 3.

On the opposite page will be readily recognized the features of District Chief PATRICK E. KEYES, chief of District No. 7. He was born in Boston, Mass., March 19, 1850. As a fireman he has found his forte, for his success in battling with the destroying element is attested by his past record and his early promotions. He was formerly employed as a painter, but left that occupation to join this department as a permanent man, April 5, 1875, at

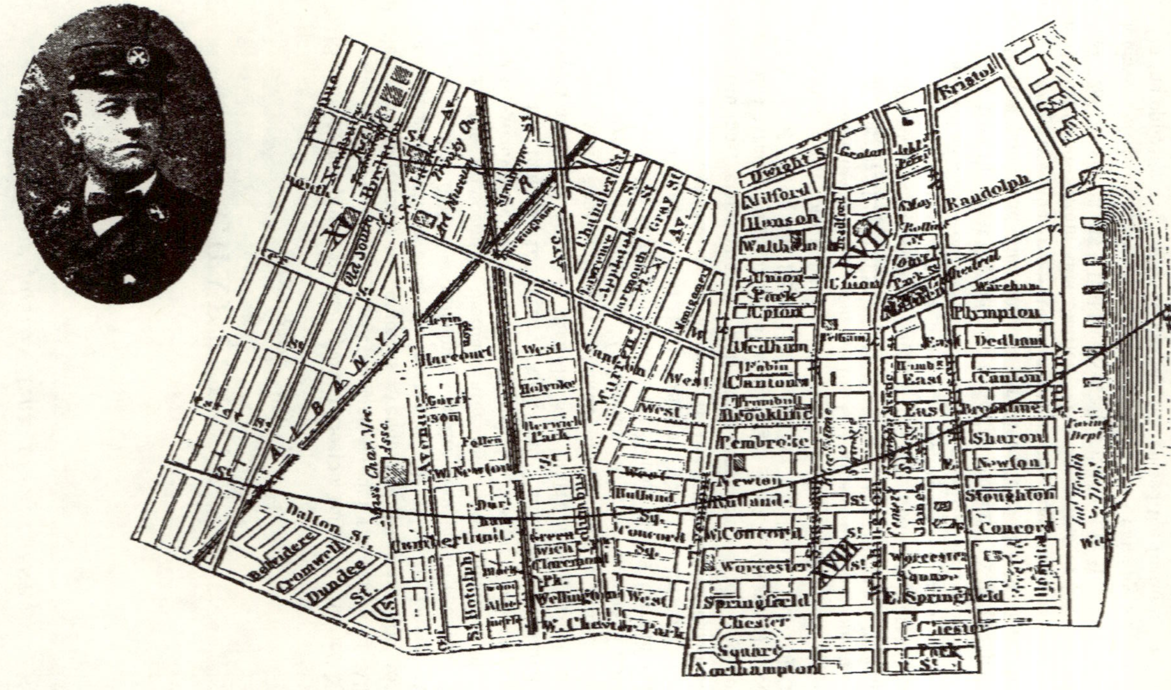

Chief Keyes and Map of District No. 7. — Page 537

which time he was assigned to Engine Company No. 25. From there he was transferred to Engine Company No. 4 on December 14, 1875. April 14, 1882, he was transferred to Engine Company No. 22, and March 17, 1884, was promoted to captain, and assigned to Engine Company No. 6, where he served until March 18, 1887, at which time he was promoted to his present position. Chief Keyes was the only one in this force that has ever been promoted from hoseman to captain of a permanent company, that came in under the new Board of Commissioners. He has met with several very painful accidents, but never been seriously hurt; although, as may be supposed, he has been in some very dangerous quarters.

ENGINE COMPANY NO. 3.

NAMES OF MEMBERS SINCE 1874.

F. M. Hines, foreman, resigned March 8, 1879; N. L. Hussey, assistant foreman, promoted to foreman, and tr. to Engine Company No. 23, March 1. 1875; A. H. Hamilton, assistant engineman, tr. to Engine Company No. 17, December 21, 1881; John Knights, promoted to captain, and tr. to Engine Company No. 14, May 30, 1880; E. F. Moody, resigned April 19, 1875; I. H. Melyard, resigned December 20, 1880; H. Heyman, promoted to assistant engineman, and tr. to Engine Company No. 28, January 1, 1881; G. F. Conant, resigned April 11, 1875; T. C. Soesman, resigned March 10, 1875; G. W. Lucas, resigned November 21, 1874; S. D. Harrington, from Engine Company No. 26, November 27, 1874, tr. to Ladder Company No. 13, March 11, 1887; R. B. Riley, assistant foreman, from Ladder Company No. 3, March 1, 1875, promoted to foreman March 8, 1879, resigned May 13, 1880; C. A. Smith, ap. April 5, 1875, tr. to Engine Company No. 23, March 21, 1877; T. H. Wright, ap. May 1, 1875, resigned January 8, 1876; E. W. Knowlton, ap. May 3, 1875, tr. to Engine Company No. 22, April 21, 1882; John Chase, ap. January 14, 1876, promoted to lieutenant, tr. to Ladder Company No. 13 in command June 30, 1883; W. A. Davis, ap. March 21, 1877, discharged, at his own request, April 24, 1879; D. Ruby, ap. May 5, 1879, promoted assistant engineman, and tr. to Engine Company No. 23, May 25, 1881; L. P. Webber, captain, from Engine Company No. 14, May 13, 1880, promoted to assistant engineer September 8, 1884; E. Whiting, ap. May 13, 1880, resigned May 20, 1881; G. W. Chapman, appointed December 21. 1880, resigned February 6, 1886; M. J. Crowley, ap. May 25, 1881, promoted to assistant engineman, and tr. to Engine Company No. 4, November 16, 1884; F. W. Turner, ap. August 7, 1881, tr. to Engine Company No. 4, October 16, 1882; G. L. Spencer, ap. June 3, 1881, tr. to Engine Company No. 14, March 2, 1888; G. F. Quimby, ap. January 1, 1882, tr. to Engine Company No. 14, April 1, 1882; C. H. Poor, lieutenant, ap. April 21, 1882, promoted to captain, and tr. to Engine Company No. 14, June 1, 1882; J. H. Maldt, assistant engineman, ap. November 8, 1882, promoted to engineman, and tr. to Engine

Company No. 23, December 10, 1886 ; T. Boggs, ap. September 22, 1884, tr. to Hose Company No. 5, May 31, 1889 ; W. F. Crowley, ap. December 9, 1884, tr. to Engine Company No. 7, February 16, 1885 ; J. T. Weston, ap. February 16, 1885, promoted to assistant engineman, and tr. to Engine Company No. 24, July 29, 1886 ; P. J. Haley, ap. February 26. 1886, resigned August 31, 1886 ; D. J. McNerney, ap. May 1, 1885, tr. to Engine Company No. 26, September 16, 1885 ; T. J. Good, ap. July 30, 1886, died December 10, 1886 ; F. H. McLaughlin. ap. June 24, 1887, tr. to Ladder Company No. 3, March 2, 1888 ; —— McKenzie, ap. January 7, 1887. promoted to assistant engineman, and tr. to Engine Company No. 12, February 15, 1888 ; E. R. Farrin, ap. March 2, 1888, resigned July 21, 1888 ; M. Ryan, ap. September 12, 1888, tr. to Engine Company No. 7, October 12, 1888 ; J. F. Maguire, ap. October 13, 1888, tr. to Engine Company No. 7, November 1, 1888 ; John B. Byrne, ap. January 18, 1889, tr. to Engine Company No. 8, January 26, 1889.

Present Members.

Captain James H. Lafavor (Fig. 1) is another old and experienced fireman. He was born in Boston, Mass., May 10, 1841. He worked at the roofing trade until the breaking out of the Rebellion, when he enlisted on April 17, 1861, in Company C, First Massachusetts Volunteers, which was detached shortly after, and he joined the Sixth Massachusetts Regiment, which company was changed from C to K. He only served three months with it, and reënlisted in the Forty-Second Regiment. He joined this department as call-man in Engine Company No. 3 in 1862. He was appointed a permanent member, August, 1872, in the same company, and November 20, 1884, he was promoted to the position of captain. Captain Lafavor is recognized by all as a man of excellent judgment. He is a member of the Grand Army and the Veteran Firemen's Association.

Lieutenant F. Emerson Hibbard (Fig. 2) first saw the light in Woodstock, Conn., November 13, 1845. He learned the carpenter's trade, at which he worked until he joined this department. In April, 1870, he came to this city, and on August 31, 1873, was appointed a call-substitute in Ladder Company No. 3. January 9, 1874, he was made a call-man in the same company, and on the reorganization of the department, May 7, 1874, was appointed a permanent member, and assigned to that company, from where he was transferred to Engine Company No. 26, October 21, 1878, as hoseman ; June 1, 1882. he was promoted, and assigned to his present quarters. Lieutenant Hibbard was struck by a falling hose. January 17, 1884, and had his arm broken. He is a member of the Boston Lodge No. 134 of the Knights of Honor, also the Boston Veterans.

Engineman Henry M. Hawkins (Fig. 3) was born in Dover, N.H., October 20, 1840. He came to Boston October 20, 1855, and learned the machinist's trade. September 1, 1861, he joined this department as call-

Engine Company No. 3. — Page 542.

hoseman in this company. He remained here until August 7, 1862, when he enlisted in Company C, First Massachusetts Heavy Artillery, and was discharged from service, July 8, 1864. He again engaged in this department, and was appointed assistant enginemen of this company, March 1, 1865. He held that position until May 1, 1873, when he was promoted engineman, and is senior member. He is at present detailed in the apparatus and repair shop. Mr. Hawkins is a member of the Grand Army, the Masonic Order, the Veteran Firemen's Association, and the Firemen's Charitable Association. He has been severely hurt several times, once while at a fire at the corner of Temple place and Washington street, and again by being kicked by a horse.

Assistant Engineman DENNIS J. McNERNEY (Fig. 4) was born in St. Williams, County Carlow, Ireland, July 2, 1848. He came to this city in 1852, and worked at the machinist's trade. He joined this department as a call-man in Engine Company No. 2, September 29, 1879, from which he was transferred to Hose Company No. 12. May 1, 1885, he was appointed permanent substitute, and assigned to Ladder Company No. 13, and transferred, May 1, 1885, to this company. September 16, 1885, he was transferred and promoted assistant engineman to Engine Company No. 26, and on December 10, 1886, was again transferred back to this company, in the same position. Mr. McNerney is a member of the Firemen's Charitable Association.

WILLIAM J. GAFFEY (Fig. 5), driver, was born in Boston, Mass., October 16, 1857. He was formerly employed as a teamster, and on December 3, 1881, joined the department as a substitute, being assigned to Engine Company No. 22, from where he was transferred to Engine Company No. 10. December 25, of the same year. He was promoted a permanent member April 1, 1882, and assigned to the latter company, where he remained until October 8, 1883, when he was transferred to this company, and appointed driver, March 11, 1887.

FRANK P. STENGEL (Fig. 6) was born in Boston, May 16, 1859. Before becoming a fireman he was employed as a teamster. His first experience in the service dates from November 28, 1881, when he became a call-substitute in Ladder Company No. 5. April 23, 1883, he was appointed a call-man in the same company, where he remained until March 28, 1885, when he was enrolled as a substitute in the permanent force and assigned to Engine Company No. 26, from which he was transferred to this company, September 16, 1885. He was promoted a permanent member January 16, 1886, and assigned to Ladder Company No. 1, from where he was again transferred to this company, September 26, 1886.

THOMAS F. BOGGS (Fig. 7) was born in Boston, Mass., January 10, 1850. He is a silver-plater by trade, at which he worked until October 15, 1873, when he joined this department as a permanent member of Ladder Company No. 8, which was the first to enter under the reorganization of the department. He was transferred to Ladder Company No. 3, March 8, 1876, and from there was again transferred to Engine Company No. 26,

October 2, 1882, from which he was transferred to this company, September 22, 1884. Mr. Boggs has been several times badly cut and burned. but has been fortunate in not being obliged to remain off duty for any length of time.

THOMAS J. DENNEY (Fig. 8) is a Boston boy, having been born in this city December 22, 1856. He is a bookbinder by trade, at which he was employed until July 3, 1880, when he joined this department as a substitute in Engine Company No. 23, and was substitute for a short length of time in every permanent company in the city proper. He was appointed a permanent man, and assigned to this company April 1, 1882. Mr. Denney has been badly burned and wounded during his career, but never to be laid up for any length of time.

TIMOTHY J. LEARY (Fig. 9) was born in Boston, Mass., September 1, 1850. He was employed as a teamster before his enlistment in this department. which occurred April 30, 1883. as a substitute, and detailed in several companies. He was promoted a permanent hoseman January 30, 1883. and assigned to this company. He was struck by a hose in the groin. April. 1887, at a trial of an engine, which laid him up four weeks : and in 1888 was thrown from the engine while on the way to a fire. and received severe internal injuries.

W. A. PACKARD (Fig. 10) was born in Dorchester District, Boston, Mass., April 13, 1860. His trade is that of a florist, at which he was employed until appointed a substitute, and assigned to Engine Company No. 18, December, 1880. He was promoted a permanent member February 16, and assigned to this company. Mr. Packard was instrumental in rescuing a lady, 72 years of age, at a fire on Waterlow street, not before, however, she had been fatally burned.

MAURICE HEFFERMAN (Fig. 11) was born in County of Limerick, Ireland, June 17, 1858. He came to this city, March, 1873, and worked at the woolgrader's trade. He joined this department July 1. 1886, as a substitute in this company, and on January 6, 1888, was promoted a permanent hoseman.

J. N. LALLEY (Fig. 12) was appointed a permanent substitute in this department August 17, 1888, and assigned to this company.

GEORGE O. LEEMAN (Fig. 13) was born in Woolwichton, Me., June 8, 1858. He came to this city when young, and began life as an engineer. His experience in the department dates from August 6, 1887, when he was appointed a substitute in Engine Company No. 10. He was transferred to this company March 3, 1887. and acted as assistant engineman for a long time.

LADDER COMPANY NO. 3.

NAMES OF MEMBERS SINCE 1874.

The following were appointed May 7, 1874 : Foreman J. B. Prescott. tr. to Chemical Engine Company No. 7, September 20, 1876 ; Assistant Foreman H. D. Smith, tr. to Engine Company No. 22, as assistant foreman,

September 20, 1876; C. O. Poland, tr. to Engine Company No. 11, August 8, 1881, as foreman; H. A. York, discharged August 30, 1874; J. A. Durling, tr. to Ladder Company No. 12, October 18, 1884; F. A. Desmond, resigned June 25, 1875; F. E. Hibbard, tr. to Engine Company No. 26. October 2, 1878; G. M. Carr, resigned October 18, 1878; J. Finnerty, resigned July 17, 1874; R. B. Riley, tr. as lieutenant to Engine Company No. 3, March 1, 1875; T. L. Wilson, tr. to Ladder 8, August 12, 1880; H. H. Walker, resigned March 6, 1875; F. A. W. Gay, killed January 5, 1878; G. H. Alexander, resigned September 19, 1881; S. Sawyer, ap. August 2, 1874, tr. to Engine Company No. 23, February 1, 1875; T. F. Turner, ap. February 1, 1875, resigned June 15, 1876; G. B. Riley, ap. March 6, 1875, tr. to Engine Company No. 12, June 1, 1878; J. R. Moore, ap. April 6, 1875, resigned February 12, 1876; O. M. Clapp, ap. September 22, 1874, tr. to Engine Company No. 15, January 13, 1875; W. N. Benton, ap. June 15, 1875, resigned April 20, 1882; C. F. Poor, ap. May 20, 1875, tr. to Engine Company No. 22, May 20, 1877; T. Boggs, ap. March 8, 1876, tr. to Engine Company No. 26, October 2, 1882; T. P. Carpenter, ap. June 16, 1876, tr. to Aerial Ladder Company No. 1, April 1, 1882; L. P. Abbott, ap. September 20, 1876, promoted district chief of District No. 6, October 2, 1882; E. O. Whiting, ap. September 22, 1876, tr. to Ladder Company No. 8, August 27, 1877; C. J. Burrill, ap. January 15, 1878, tr. to Ladder Company No. 12, September 25, 1884; C. J. Burrill, ap. October 18, 1884, resigned December 31, 1886; C. A. Smith, ap. June 1, 1878, resigned January 22, 1887; O. M. Clapp, ap. October 2, 1878, tr. to Ladder Company No. 8, September 10, 1880; J. Bennett, ap. October 21, 1878, resigned January 28, 1881; E. Cummings, ap. September 10, 1880, tr. to Ladder Company No. 1, July 26, 1884; W. Dunn, ap. February 4, 1884, resigned February 6, 1886; J. W. Godbold, ap. October 27, 1881, tr. to Chemical Engine Company No. 7, September 27, 1886; W. A. McKenzie, ap. October 31, 1881, resigned May 6, 1882; J. T. Byron, ap. April 1, 1882, tr. to Engine Company No. 4, April 20, 1882; J. D. Kelley, ap. April 21, 1882, tr. to Hose Company No. 5, January 25, 1889; T. Foster, ap. April 21, 1882, tr. to Engine Company No. 7, January 22, 1883; William Coulter, ap. June 27, 1882, tr. to Engine Company No. 23, January 26, 1886; H. F. Wood, ap. October 2, 1882, tr. to Ladder Company No. 8, January 4, 1886; G. H. Nichols, ap. May 24, 1883, tr. to Ladder Company No. 13, June 18, 1887; C. W. Kennison, ap. September 25, 1884, resigned February 6, 1886; C. H. Mouing, ap. March 28, 1885, tr. to Engine Company No. 14, June 18, 1887; J. S. Cleverly, ap. February 25, 1886, tr. to Engine Company No. 15, August 3, 1887; W. H. Boudwin, ap. February 24, 1886, tr. to Engine Company No. 10, October 30, 1888; C. Donivan, ap. January 6, 1888, tr. to Engine Company No. 6, November 16, 1888.

PRESENT MEMBERS.

Captain JOHN GRADY (Fig. 1) is one of the youngest captains in the department. He was born in Boston, Mass., July 12, 1854. After leaving the public schools he learned the mason's trade, at which he was employed for a number of years. His first experience in the department was during 1869, when he began running with Ladder Company No. 1, as a volunteer, and remained with that company until May 2, 1874, when he was appointed a permanent driver in Ladder Company No. 1. On July 10, 1883, he was promoted to lieutenant of the same company. His efficient services were soon recognized, and on July 26, 1884, was promoted captain and assigned to this company. Captain Grady has always had a great interest in the Fire Department, while the work done in the service by him clearly shows his ability. He has received some very severe injuries, one of which nearly cost him his life. It occurred while at a fire on Chelsea street, February, 1883, while at work on a ladder, which fell with him. An ugly scar over his eye is a constant reminder of this accident. He is one of the members who did service through the big fire during 1872.

Lieutenant WILLIAM C. LEE (Fig. 2) is a Boston boy, being born in this city, April 27, 1849. He attended the public schools of Brighton, after leaving which he learned the roofer's trade, at which he worked for a number of years. His first experience in the Fire Department was with the Wilson-Hose Company No. 1, of that district, in 1868, as clerk of the company. The house of that company was located under the town-hall, which has since been transferred to a police-station. He was with that company for two years. July 2, 1874, he was appointed a call-man in this department and assigned to Engine Company No. 29, where he remained until April 15, 1876, at which time he was promoted a permanent hoseman and assigned to Engine Company No. 26. October 2, 1882, he was promoted lieutenant and transferred to this company.

GEORGE N. DUNN (Fig. 3), driver, was born in East Boston, August 5, 1858. He was employed as a teamster at the time he was on the call-force of this department, which he joined as a call-substitute in Ladder Company No. 5, March, 1879. March, 1880, he was appointed a call-member in the same company, and September 3, 1884, was made a substitute and assigned to Engine Company No. 7, and was promoted a permanent hoseman in the same company, March 28, 1885, from which he was transferred to this company and detailed as driver, December 31, 1886. At the Stearns' lumber-yard fire in 1879, he and five comrades were thrown from a boat into the water and almost drowned.

SAMUEL F. RIDLER (Fig. 4), driver of Supply Wagon No. 3, was born in Boston, Mass., June 30, 1844. He enlisted in the United States navy, February 13, 1862, and remained until February, 1865. He then worked at the teamster's business, and entered this service as a call-man in Hose Company No. 1, July 1, 1867, where he remained until October 1, 1873,

LADDER COMPANY NO. 3. — Page 548.

when he was transferred to Engine Company No. 25, as a permanent member. November 1, 1875, he was transferred to Engine Company No. 10, and from there to Ladder Company No. 8, April 4, 1879, from which he was transferred to this company, August 12, 1880, and detailed to his present position. At the fire of Proctor & Drummey's lumber-yard, in 1880, he had the palm of his right hand torn open by a hook. Mr. Ridler had his ankle broken, and other injuries, May 9, 1885, by being thrown from his wagon, which was run into by a wagon of the Sewer Department of the city. September 15, 1885, he received a severe cut under the eye from a pick of a ladder. March 25, 1886, he fell down a hatchway, about twenty feet, on Way street (Box 65), and on August 26, 1887, at the Ham & Carter fire, he had his right eye burned out by lime. He is a member of Tremont Lodge No. 15 of the Odd Fellows, and a member of the Firemen's Charitable Association.

ROBERT ROONEY (Fig. 5) was born in Ireland, and came to this country when but a child. He was employed as a hackman until his appointment as a substitute in this department, March 28, 1885, and assigned to this company, in which he was promoted to a permanent member, October 8, 1887.

JOHN PENDOLEY (Fig. 6) was born in Genoa, Italy, November 17, 1843. He came to this city when very young, and, after leaving school, learned the harness-making trade. He joined the department September 20, 1876, as a permanent member, and was assigned to Ladder Company No. 8, from where he was transferred, January 4, 1885, to this company, and detailed in the hose and harness shop.

CHARLES T. ADAMS (Fig. 7) was born in Hampden, Me., December 9, 1851. He is a shipsmith by trade, at which he worked while on the call-force. His career as a fireman dates from 1870, when he joined the Bangor Fire Department as ladderman in Ladder Company No. 2. He was promoted captain January, 1880, and remained there until May, 1881, when he came to Boston, and was appointed a substitute on this force, March 28, 1885, in Ladder Company No. 1. He was transferred to this company, and promoted a permanent man, February 25, 1886. Mr. Adams is a member of Penobscot Lodge No. 7, of Bangor, Me., I. O. O. F.

FRANK P. LOKER (Fig. 8) was born in Huntsville, Texas, January 30, 1856. He came to this city at an early age, and learned the stair-builder's trade. He joined this department November 2, 1885, as call-man in Ladder Company No. 7, and was transferred to Engine Company No. 17, March 1, 1886, where he remained until September 27, 1886, at which time he was appointed a permanent member, and assigned to this company, September 27. The most severe injury he ever received occurred July 27, 1883, when he was struck by a ladder while the company were on exhibition drill, from which he was unfit for duty for ten weeks.

JAMES P. BOWLES (Fig. 9) was born in Dorchester District, Boston, Mass., December 20, 1853. He is a painter by trade, and is detailed at this work in the department most of his time. He entered this service July 30,

1880, in Ladder Company No. 12, as a call-man, and remained there until February 4, 1887, when he was promoted a permanent member and assigned to this company.

WILLIAM JOHN HICKEY (Fig. 10) was born in Lynn, Mass., July 17, 1863. He is a florist by trade. and on November 9, 1883, enlisted in the department as call-man in Engine Company No. 18. He was promoted a permanent member July 29, 1887, and assigned to this company.

MORTIMER M. CRONIN (Fig. 11) was born in Cork, Ireland, August 28, 1857. He came to this city in 1869, and worked at the currier business. He joined this department as call-man in Ladder Company No. 5, January 19, 1885, and was appointed a permanent member June 18, 1887, being assigned to this company. Mr. Cronin nearly lost his eye while at a fire on Washington street, May 8, 1887. The accident was caused by a falling line, forced by a stream from the engine.

GARODE F. JOYCE (Fig. 12) was born in Dublin, Ireland, July 11, 1866, and when but a child came to this city. His fire experience dates from October 5, 1887, when he was appointed a substitute in this company, in which he remained until October 14, at which time he was transferred to Engine Company No. 10. He was promoted a permanent member, March 2, 1888, and on August 10 was transferred back to this company.

PATRICK J. McCARTHY (Fig. 13) was born in Charlestown District, Boston, Mass., March 15, 1859. He worked at various pursuits until he joined the department as substitute in Ladder Company No. 8, January 6, 1888, and was transferred to this company July 2.

FRANK H. McLAUGHLIN (Fig. 14) was born in Boston, Mass., August 31, 1860. He was employed as a teamster until appointed in this department as a substitute June 24, 1887, and assigned to Engine Company No. 3. March 2, 1888, he was transferred to this company.

DANIEL J. BUCKLEY (Fig. 15) was born in East Boston, Mass., August 12, 1858. He followed the sea for a number of years, and on January 18, 1889, was appointed a substitute and detailed to this company.

ENGINE COMPANY NO. 22.

NAMES OF MEMBERS SINCE 1874.

The first twelve names are of those who were appointed when the company was organized as a call-company. L. P. Abbott was appointed foreman when the company was put on a permanent basis, September 27. 1875.

Rothenas E. Flanders, no record: John A. Shannon, no record; Alexander P. Hawkins, no record; Samuel L. Gilman, no record; Charles H. Robers, no record: B. F. Appleby, no record; R. A. Burgess, no record: William Tobin, no record; Samuel L. Gilman, ap. December 1, 1877; John Ewers, ap. July 28, 1883; John Toy, ap. December 7, 1878; A. H. Perry, ap. May 20, 1878, returned May 21, 1881, left June 1, 1882. L. P. Abbott, ap. September 27, 1875, tr. to Ladder Company No. 3, September 20, 1876; J. H. Hines, ap. September 7, 1875, tr. March 8, 1876; A. H. Hutchins, ap. September 7, 1875, tr. October 3, 1878, to Engine Company No. 10; Charles Miller, ap. September 7, 1875, tr. May 20, 1877, returned December 11, 1878; Silas Morse, ap. March 11, 1876, tr. May 15, 1880; H. D. Smith, ap. September 20, 1876, tr. July 1, 1880, to Engine Company No. 4; Charles F. Poor, ap. May 20, 1877, tr. and promoted April 21, 1882, to Engine Company No. 3; E. P. Cushing, ap. December 7, 1877, resigned October 12, 1882; J. M. Nazro, ap. October 3, 1878, tr. March 21, 1880, to Ladder Company No. 8; G. F. Titus, ap. March 24, 1880, promoted and tr. April 21, 1882, to Engine Company No. 4; B. F. Carpenter, ap. May 20, 1878, tr. May 25, 1881, to Engine Company No. 21; T. H. Foster, ap. May 15, 1880, tr. April 21, 1882, to Ladder Company No. 3; C. C. Willett, ap. July 1, 1880, tr. July 28, 1883, to Engine Company No. 26; C. Williams, ap. April 21, 1882, resigned May 22, 1883; E. W. Knowlton, ap. April 21, 1882, resigned May 2, 1882; P. E. Keyes, ap. April 13, 1882, promoted and tr. March 7, 1884, to Engine Company No. 6; Joseph Cox, ap. April 27, 1882, resigned March 26, 1883; T. Nannery, ap. June 1, 1882, tr. July 10, 1883, to Engine Company No. 30; F. S. Bradbury, ap. September 7, 1882, tr. July 10, 1883, to Engine Company No. 30; H. Heyman, ap. November 8, 1882, tr. February 16, 1888, to Engine Company No. 33; C. A. Straw, ap. October 16, 1882, tr. March 29, 1883, to Engine Company No. 13; T. Good, ap. July 10, 1883, tr. July 30, 1886, to Engine Company No. 3; G. W. Goodwin, ap. July 10, 1883, died July 3, 1886; P. Crotty, ap. July 10, 1883, tr. March 10, 1884, to Engine Company No. 26; A. B. Fry, ap. March 10, 1884, resigned June 30, 1886; J. H. Weston, ap. September 8, 1884, resigned February 16, 1885; C. H. Webber, ap. April 1, 1885, tr. June 25, 1887, to Ladder Company No. 3; J. Woodard, ap. July 1, 1886, tr. July 23, 1886; T. J. Hearty, ap. July 1, 1886, tr. August 19, 1887, to Engine Company No. 1; J. H. Murray, ap. August 26, 1887.

PRESENT MEMBERS.

Capt. WILLISTON A. GAYLORD will be readily recognized in the preceding plate in (Fig. 1). He was born in Boston January 12, 1844. In early life he was employed as an expressman, but his love for the excitement of working at fires led him to join Hose Company No. 5, nicknamed " Hardscrabble Hose Company No. 5," when a boy, as a volunteer. He worked in this capacity until the outbreak of the war, when, in August, 1862, he enlisted in Company I, Forty-Fourth Massachusetts Regiment, in which he served nine months. January 1, 1865. he again entered the department as a call-man in the same company. April 1, 1872, he was appointed driver of Extinguisher Wagon No. 2, which was consolidated as Chemical Company No. 2, July 31, 1874, when he was assigned to the position of engineman of that company. He remained there until April 1, 1881, when he was promoted captain of Engine Company No. 12, and on July 28, 1883, was transferred to this company. Captain Gaylord was laid off duty six weeks from the result of injuries received by falling through a floor at the American House fire in March, 1877, when he dislocated both his shoulders. He was also badly burned by a naphtha explosion in the Boston & Providence Railway yard, which laid him up four weeks. He is a member of Siloam Lodge No. 2 of the Order of Odd Fellows, Suffolk Council No. 37 of the Legion of Honor, Gettysburg Post No. 191, the Grand Army of the Republic, and the Firemen's Charitable Association.

Lieut. ANOR W. BROWN (Fig. 2) was born in Fairhaven, Conn., November 4, 1840. He was employed in various occupations until he joined this department. His first public service was during the late war; he enlisting in Company F, First Connecticut Regiment, in which he served three months. He reënlisted immediately after in Company F, Sixth Connecticut Regiment, and was discharged November 8, 1865. He came to Boston in December, 1872, and one year later joined Hose Company No. 8 as a substitute, but was promoted a permanent member May 7, 1874, and assigned to Engine Company No. 26 as a hoseman. May 17, 1882, he was promoted to lieutenant, and assigned to this company July 28, 1883. Lieutenant Brown lost the tips of two fingers at a fire (Box 68) September 19, 1874, and broke his wrist at another fire (Box 41). He is a member of G. A. R. Post No. 7, Mayflower Assembly of the Royal Society of Good Fellows, and the Firemen's Charitable Association.

Engineman JOHN H. MALDT (Fig. 3) was born in Boston, Mass., March 15, 1837. His career in the department began at an early age with the old hand-engines. He learned the machinist trade, at which he was employed until he entered the department in March, 1874, as a member of Engine Company No. 25. He was promoted assistant engineman and transferred to Engine Company No. 26, May 7, 1874; from which he was transferred to this company on its organization, July 1, 1875, in the same position, and during November, 1882, was again transferred to Engine Company No. 3. He was promoted engineman and assigned to Engine Company No. 23 on December 10, 1886, where he remained until February 16, 1888, at which time he was transferred to this company.

Assistant Engineman CHARLES MILLER (Fig. 4) was born in Brooklyn, N.Y., August 5, 1835. He worked at his trade, that of steam-fitting, until the war, when he enlisted in April, 1861, in the Fourteenth Brooklyn, N.Y., Regiment. He lost his right eye at the first battle of Bull Run and was discharged; but reënlisted in 1862 in the Key-Stone Battery of Philadelphia, Pa., and was discharged in 1864. He came to Boston during 1865 and worked at his trade, at the same time joining the Charlestown call-department. He entered this department as a substitute in Hose Company No. 7 during 1871. He was appointed a permanent member and assigned to Engine Company No. 25, May 21, 1874. He was transferred to this company September

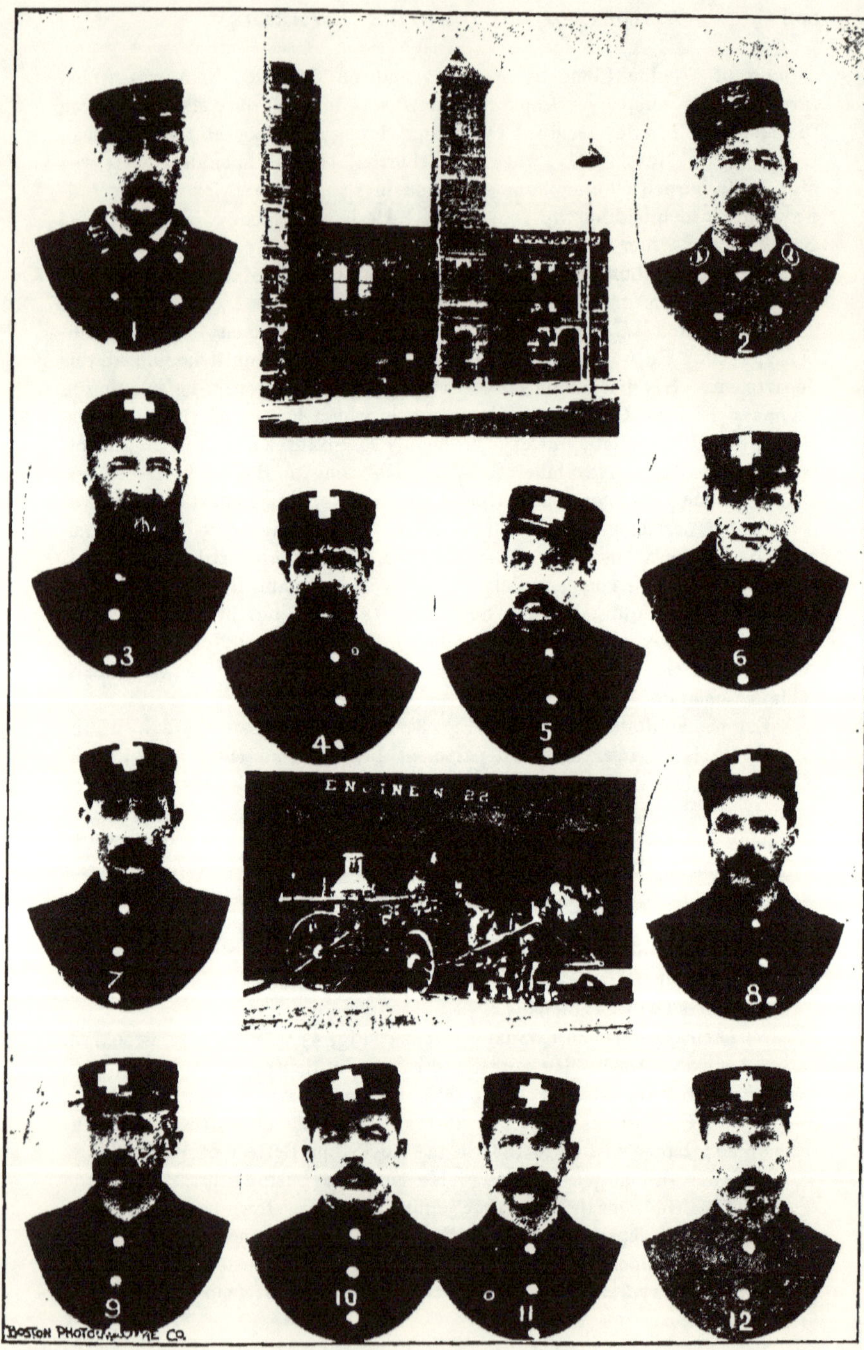

ENGINE COMPANY No. 22. — Page 553.

27, 1875, and was again transferred May 20, 1877, to Engine Company No. 26, from which he was transferred back to this company December 11, 1878, and promoted to his present position August 19, 1887. Mr. Miller is a member of G. A. R., Post No. 2, the Veritas Lodge of Odd Fellows, Philadelphia, Pa., the Joseph Webb Lodge of Masons, the Firemen's Charitable Association, and Boston Royal Arcanum.

FRED A. McILROY (Fig. 5), driver, was born in Medford, Mass., October 8, 1854. His employment, previous to entering this department, was that of a teamster. July 31, 1880, he joined this department as a call-man in Ladder Company No. 12. February 7, 1883, he was appointed substitute in this company, in which he remained until May 24, 1883, when he was promoted a permanent member, and assigned as driver. He was badly injured at the Hampden-street fire, June 17, 1882, he being in the building when it fell, and barely escaped with his life.

WILLIAM ANDREW MITCHELL (Fig. 6), driver of hose-carriage, was born in Charlestown District, Boston, Mass., September 24, 1860. He was employed at various pursuits until he joined this department as a substitute in Engine Company No. 4, September 24, 1882. He remained there until May 24, 1883, when he was promoted a permanent member and assigned to this company, and one year later was assigned driver of the hose-carriage.

WALTER POWERS (Fig. 7) was born in County Waterford, Ireland, April 7, 1854. He came to this city when a boy, and after leaving school was employed as a teamster. He joined this force on September 24, 1882, as a substitute, and was assigned to various companies until May 22, 1883, when he was promoted a permanent hoseman in this company. Mr. Powers had the ligaments of his knee broken at the Clinton-street fire, from the effects of which he was laid up six months.

JAMES H. VICTORY (Fig. 8) was born in Stoughton, Mass., August, 1853. July 31, 1880, he entered this department as a call-man in Ladder Company No. 12, where he remained until April 5, 1884, when he was made a substitute and transferred to this company; and on September 5, 1884, he was promoted a permanent member.

LEONARD MURDOCK (Fig. 9) was born in Pictou, N.S., August 31, 1856. He came to this city at an early age, and after leaving school learned the carpenter's trade. He entered this department as a call-substitute during 1882 in Engine Company No. 17, and in the following year was made a call-substitute in Ladder Company No. 7, and made a call-man during 1884, where he remained until July 1, 1886, at which time he was promoted a permanent member and assigned to this company. Mr. Murdock is a member of the Firemen's Charitable Association.

MICHAEL WALSH (Fig. 10) was born in Boston, Mass., September 1, 1855. He is a printer by trade, at which he was employed until he joined this department as a substitute in Engine Company No. 7, April 9, 1884. He was appointed a permanent member September 3 of the ensuing year, and assigned to the same company, from which he was transferred to this company, June 27, 1887. Previous to this he enlisted in the navy, in January, 1879, on the ship " Richmond," which was making the tour around the world with General Grant. He served in China three years and four months. He was also eighteen months on board the ship " Tennessee," in the North Atlantic stations.

CHARLES C. SPRINGER (Fig. 11) was born in Saxonville, Mass., June 14. 1859. He was employed in the piano business for seven years, and during September, 1880, he joined Ladder Company No. 12 as a call-substitute. November, 1882, he was enrolled a call-man in the same company. He remained there until January 16, 1886, when he was promoted a permanent member, and assigned to Ladder Company No. 1. September 27, 1886, he was transferred to this company.

JOHN S. MURRAY (Fig. 12) was born in Skowhegan, Me., March 31. 1855. He came to this city in 1871, and worked at the carpet-printing trade. and joined the department November 1, 1882, as call-substitute in Engine Company No. 13. September 3, 1884, he was appointed a substitute in Engine Company No. 25, and promoted a permanent hoseman March 28, 1885, and on August 26, 1887, was transferred to the present company. Mr. Murray had his knee-pan injured and wrist sprained while at a fire (Box 12), January, 1885.

ENGINE COMPANY NO. 23.

NAMES OF MEMBERS SINCE 1875.

Engine Company No. 23 was made a permanent company February 11, 1875, with the following officers and members : —

N. L. Hussey. captain ; J. H. Le Cain, assistant foreman ; B. W. Carpenter, engineman, tr. to Engine No. 22, May 20, 1878 ; Theodore Hutchings, assistant engineman, resigned March 30, 1875 ; B. F. Thayer ; William B. Marshall, resigned January 20, 1886 ; George Le Cain ; Samuel S. Sawyer, resigned March 29, 1875 ; J. F. Downs, tr. Engine No. 12, April 28, 1876 ; G. H. Wentworth, assistant engineman, ap. April 5. 1875, resigned December 31, 1878 ; David Dennison, ap. April 5, 1875, resigned December 11. 1875 ; W. S. Davis, ap. February 3, 1876, tr. to Engine No. 3, March 21, 1887 ; J. A. Mullen. ap. May 9, 1876, tr. and promoted foreman Engine No. 15, August 8. 1881 ; C. A. Smith, ap. March 21, 1877, tr. to Engine No. 3, June 1, 1878 : A. H. Perry. engineman, ap. May 20. 1878, tr. to Engine No. 22. May 25, 1881 ; O. J. Booker, ap. June 1, 1878 ; H. L. Whiting. ap. assistant engineman, January 1, 1879, resigned November 18. 1879 : F. M. Brown, ap. assistant engineman, November 24, 1879, resigned March 14, 1881 ; G. J. H. Gutermuth, engineman. ap. May 25, 1881, tr. to Fire-Alarm Telegraph, December 3, 1886 : Hoseman D. Ruby, of Engine No. 3, promoted to the position of assistant engineman, May 25. 1881, tr. to Engine No. 34. November 1, 1888; J. Newell, ap. August 8, 1881, died May 18, 1882; J. M. Gargan, ap. June 1, 1882, tr. to Engine No. 10, May 4, 1885; E. Kelley, ap. May 1, 1884, tr. to Engine No. 14, June 25, 1887; C. Littlefield. ap. May 1, 1884, tr. to Ladder No. 7, July 1, 1884; C. W. Kennison, ap. July 1, 1884, tr. to Ladder No. 8, September 25, 1884; W. F. Crowley, ap. March 28, 1885, tr. to Engine No. 6, May 31, 1886; T. J. Harty, ap. February 16, 1885. tr. to Engine No. 22, July 23, 1886; E. L. Brown, ap. February 16, 1885. tr. to Engine No. 13, March 28, 1885; C. H. Tagen, ap. May 4, 1885, tr. to Engine No. 13, June 25, 1887; F. S. Reed. ap. February 25, 1886, tr. to Hose No. 5, Jan. 25, 1889; E. C. Lothrop, ap. March 31, 1886, tr. to Engine No. 4. December 31, 1886; J. F. Woodward, ap. July 23, 1886; J. H. Maldt, engineman, ap. December 10, 1886, tr. to Engine No. 22, February 16, 1888; W. J. Whelan, ap. February 5, 1887; W. L. Eaton, ap. August 5, 1887: William Coulter, ap. November 9, 1888, tr. to Engine Co. No. 17 as hoseman; Substitute E. F. Richardson, of Engine Company No. 17, ap. November 9, 1888.

Present Members.

The well-known features of Captain Nathan L. Hussey will be recognized in Fig. 1, on page 559. He was born in Boston, Mass., December 3, 1845. After leaving school he learned the mason's trade, to which he added the duties of a fireman on January 14, 1862, as a call-substitute in Engine Company No. 3; and on July 1, 1870, he was appointed a member. He held that position until May 7, 1874, when he was promoted assistant foreman in Engine Company No. 3, and was promoted to his present position February 1, 1875, and assigned to this company. Captain Hussey dislocated his hip and shoulder by a fall through a scuttle at the Congress-street fire on August 26, 1871. May 24, 1887, he was injured in the back by a falling ladder at a fire on Tremont street, and was ruptured at the Albany-street fire, September 15, 1888. He is a life-member of the Firemen's Charitable Association and the Boston Veterans.

Lieutenant John H. Le Cain (Fig. 2) is another old veteran in the department. He was born in Annapolis, N.S., April 23, 1837. He learned the carpenter's trade, and came to this city in 1859, and worked at this business for years. His experience as a fireman dates from February 18, 1860, at which time he joined the department as a call-substitute in Hose Company No. 4. which was located at this house. In the spring of 1866 he was appointed call-man, which position he held until 1871, when he was promoted foreman of the same company. The old hose company was transferred on April 7, 1872, and the present company was organized, and he remained in that position until the reorganization of the department, when he was appointed to his present office. He has been detailed to do carpenter-work in the department, having done work in almost every station in this city. He is a member of the Firemen's Charitable Association, the Boston Veterans, and the Order of Red Men.   Lieutenant Le Cain has two members of his family in the service : his brother George, in this company, and his son Fred. W., in Ladder Company No. 1.

Engineman FRANK A. GREENLEAF (Fig. 3) was born in Nashua, N.H., May 21, 1849.   He is a machinist by trade, and came to this city in 1865. His first appointment in this department was as a call-foreman in Hose Company No. 10, June 13, 1874.   August 25, 1877, he was appointed a permanent member, and assigned to Engine Company No. 10, in which he was promoted assistant engineman, May, 1878.   He was transferred to Engine Company No. 6, September 1, 1884, and from that to Engine Company No. 12, March 22, 1885.   February, 1888, he was promoted to his present position, and assigned to this company.   He is a member of the John Hancock Council of the Royal Arcanum.

Assistant Engineman THOMAS J. HARTY (Fig. 4) was born in Boston, Mass, December 14, 1848.   He learned the machinist trade, at which he worked until joining the permanent force.   He first began working at fires as a volunteer in Hose Company No. 9, during 1883, and was appointed a call-man July 3, in the same year.   On May 3, 1884, he was appointed a substitute in this company, and on February 16, 1885, was promoted a permanent member.   He was transferred to Engine Company No. 22 on July 23, 1886, and promoted assistant engineman ; and on August 19, 1887, was transferred to Engine Company No. 1, and on Nov. 1, 1888, was transferred to this company.   He was also employed at his trade in the repair-shop of the Fire Department for two and a half years.

BENJAMIN F. THAYER (Fig. 5), driver, was born in St. Monmouth, Me., January 25, 1828, making him 60 years of age.   He came to Boston in January of 1848, and worked at his trade, that of a shoemaker ; and in 1849 began his duties as fireman, joining Hose Company No. 2 as a volunteer, where he remained until some time in 1850, at which time he joined Engine Company No. 18 as a substitute.   February 1, 1851, he became member of Hydrant Company No. 4, and October 1, 1851, joined Engine Company No. 12.   May 1, 1853, he joined Engine Company No. 3, and on January 1, 1859, he run with Hose Company No. 5.   August, 1860, he brought Chester Hose No. 4 to Northampton street, and was installed as driver.   He remained with that company until April, 1872, when the present engine was put in, and he was appointed driver, which position he has held ever since. Mr. Thayer has met with some very severe accidents ; the most serious being at a fire on Hampden street, in 1882, at which he broke his leg ; another injury was received by a kick from a horse attached to his engine, which smashed his fire-hat and fractured his skull.   A horrible scar attests to the severity of the blow.

GEORGE LE CAIN (Fig. 6) was born in Annapolis, N.S., November 18, 1845.   He learned the carpenter's trade, and came to this city in 1867.   He joined the force February 25, 1871, as call-man in old Chester Hose Com-

ENGINE COMPANY No. 23. — Page 559.

pany No. 4. He remained in that company until January 27, 1875, when he was promoted a permanent member and assigned to this company, where he has since remained. Mr. Le Cain had a narrow escape on February 27, 1873, at the Hanover-street fire. He, with three other men, were at work in the fourth story when the walls fell and buried them in the ruins; they were taken out for dead. Mr. Le Cain had all his ribs on one side broken, and was otherwise injured. He was also severely ruptured, which is to this day a great annoyance. He is a member of Boston Lodge No. 25 of the Odd Fellows, also a member of the Veteran Firemen's Association.

F. S. REED (Fig. 7). See records of Hose Company No. 5.

JOHN F. WOODWARD (Fig. 8) was born in Taunton, Mass., July 24, 1857. He is a florist by trade, and came to this city November, 1872. In 1879 he joined the department as call-substitute in Engine Company No. 24, and on May 21, 1881, was made a call-member in Engine Company No. 12, and transferred to Engine Company No. 24. He remained in this position until July 1, 1886, when he was appointed a permanent member and assigned to Engine Company No. 22, from which he was again transferred, August 1, of the same year, to this company.

WILLIAM COULTER (Fig. 9), hoseman, was born in Boston November 30, 1858. He learned the tinsmith's trade, at which he was employed until May 8, 1882, when he was appointed a substitute in the department, and served in Engine Companies Nos. 6, 23, and 26. January 27, 1882, he was promoted a permanent member and assigned to Ladder Company No. 3, and on January 26, 1886, was transferred to his present position as a hoseman and assistant driver. November 9, 1888, he was transferred to Engine Company No. 17 and appointed driver. Among the photographs of members of that company his portrait will also be found. Mr. Coulter was crushed by two ladder trucks which collided on their way to Box 53, in November, 1883. The injuries received nearly proved fatal, and he was laid up seven months. He is a member of Siloam Lodge No. 2, and Massasoit Encampment No. 1, of Odd Fellows.

W. G. CARLEY (Fig. 10) was born in Boston, Mass., December 11, 1858. He is an oil-cloth printer by trade, at which he worked for several years. During 1878 he joined this department as a call-substitute in Engine Company No. 13, in which company he was made a call-man October 4, 1881. September 3, 1884, he was promoted a permanent member, and on January 25, 1887, was transferred to this company. Mr. Carley is a member of the Junior Order of the United American Mechanics.

WILLIAM J. WHELAN (Fig. 11) was born in Roscommon County, Ireland, February 22, 1862. He came to this city in 1878, and was employed in various occupations until September 3, 1884, when he joined this department as a substitute, and was assigned to Engine Company No. 26, from which he was transferred, February 5, 1887, to this company; and on June 18, 1887, was promoted a permanent hoseman.

WALACE DEATON (Fig. 12) was born in Digby, N.S., September 15, 1860. He came to this city August 17, 1877, and was employed at his trade, that of wood-turning, until he entered this department as a substitute, August 5, 1887, and was assigned to this company.

GEORGE L. SPENCER (Fig. 13) was born in Putnam, Conn., June 21, 1847. He enlisted in the First Connecticut Heavy Artillery December 2, 1863, and served until October 2, 1865. He came to Boston during 1868, and learned the mason's trade. In 1873 he joined this department as a call-substitute in Hose Company No. 2. He remained there until 1874, when he left the service, but returned again May 9, 1876, as a permanent member, and was assigned to Engine Company No. 26. June 2, 1881, he was transferred to Engine Company No. 3, and from there was transferred to Engine Company No. 14, March 2, 1888, and was assigned to this company November 23, 1888. Mr. Spencer had his knee-joint shattered at a fire on School street, on September 1, 1878, which laid him up six months. He is a member of G. A. R. Post 7 and the Union Lodge of the Knights of Honor.

LADDER COMPANY NO. 13.

NAMES OF MEMBERS SINCE JUNE 30, 1883.

This company was organized Saturday, June 30, 1883, and the following members were appointed : —

Lieutenant J. W. Chase ; F. P. Mahan, tr. to Ladder 8 ; F. P. Carpenter, tr. to Engine 10 ; W. J. Gaffey, ap. October 11, 1883, tr. to Engine 3 ; S. D. Harrington, ap. March 11, 1887, tr. to Engine 16, since dead.

PRESENT MEMBERS.

Lieutenant JOHN WALTER CHASE (Fig. 1), in charge of this company, was born in Philadelphia, Pa., December 5, 1836. He joined the fire department of that city November 1, 1857, at which time he was appointed hoseman in the Spring Garden Fire Company No. 36. He remained there until 1865, when he came to this city and worked at his trade, that of Freestone carving. He joined this department as a substitute in Ladder Company No. 3, February 1, 1871, and remained there until October 1, 1873, when he was appointed a permanent man and assigned to Engine Company No. 25. He was transferred to Engine Company No. 3, December 15, 1875, and worked with that company until June 30, 1883, when he was promoted lieutenant and assigned in charge of this ladder, which the city had just bought. The first aerial ladder in this department was the " Skinner," which was purchased in 1872. It was placed in the house of Ladder Company No. 3, with which company Lieutenant Chase was working, and he was detailed as tiller-man, until it was sent in charge of Ladder Company No. 8, six months afterward. He has been very careful in keeping record of occurrences happening in the force, and his journals and scrap-books give some most valuable and interesting matter. He has been severely injured several times. On February 7, 1876, at a fire on Palmer street, the roof fell in and nearly killed him, and on June 29, 1885, he had a narrow escape by being struck on the head by a brass hose-coupling, while at work on a ladder. At a fire on Thaxter street, June 2, 1879, he was severely hurt by falling timber.

GUSTAVUS H. NICHOLS (Fig. 2) was born in Cohasset, Mass., July 10, 1860. He was formerly employed at general mercantile work up to the time of his appointment as a substitute on October 15, 1882, and assigned to different companies. May 24, 1883, he was promoted a permanent member and assigned to Ladder Company No. 3, in which he remained until June 25, 1887, when he was transferred to this company. Mr. Nichols is a member of Bethesda Lodge of Odd Fellows, Mt. Washington Encampment, Daughters of Rebekah, and Standish Council 146 of the American Legion of Honor.

EDWIN W. CLARK (Fig. 3), driver, first began his fire duties with Hose Company No. 9, about 1872, and he remained there as a call-substitute until April 25, 1878, at which time he was enrolled a call-member, and on October 21 was appointed driver of Engine Company No. 15, in which he remained until May 12, 1880, when he was transferred to this company as driver, February 20, 1882. He again entered the department as a substitute in Engine Company No. 23, and remained until October 1, 1883, when he was appointed a permanent member of Engine Company No. 7. On October 21 he was transferred to this company, and detailed as driver. He is a house-painter by occupation.

CHARLES H. WEBBER (Fig. 4) was born in Roxbury District, Boston, Mass., April 30, 1854. He is a baker by trade, at which he was employed for several years. January 13, 1881, he joined the department as call-man in Ladder Company No. 12. He was appointed a substitute March 24, 1885, and assigned to Engine Company No. 22, where he remained until June 18, 1887, when he was promoted a permanent member and assigned to this company. Mr. Webber was laid up for thirteen weeks from the effects of a cut received at a fire on Tremont street. in April, 1882. He is a brother of the chief of the department.

HOSE COMPANY NO. 5.

NAMES OF MEMBERS SINCE 1874.

Edwin H. Bright, resigned August 31, 1874; Thomas Crompton, ap. February 7, 1876, resigned February 3, 1881; George C. Fernald, promoted engineer, District No. 7, April 6, 1874; Alfred B. Fry, ap. June 24, 1887, promoted captain May 25, 1888, tr. to Hose Company No. 7, January 25, 1889; George C. Gardner, resigned September 30, 1875; Harry Heyman, tr. to Engine Company No. 3, May 7, 1874; C. J. Hearn, ap. January 23, 1886, tr. to Engine Company No. 25, February 16, 1888; James G. Lovell, ap.

February 7, 1881, tr. to Engine Company No. 7, June 18, 1887; Williard E. Manley, suspended January 25, 1889; George H. Melvin, ap. June 30, 1882, resigned November 29, 1882: Reuben J. Ryder, resigned May 9, 1874: Charles A. Smith, tr. to Engine Company No. 25, May 9, 1874; E. B. Lothrop, no record, tr. to Engine No. 4.

PRESENT MEMBERS.

Call-Captain ALFRED B. FRY (Fig. 1) was born in New York City, March 1, 1858. He was educated as a mechanical engineer. His first experience with this department dates from June, 1880, as a call-substitute in Engine Company No. 28, from which he was transferred to Engine Company No. 14, September, 1881, and two months later was enrolled a call-member. On December of the same year he was appointed a permanent member and assigned as acting assistant engineman in Engine Company No. 26, and was promoted to assistant engineman in March, 1882. October, 1883, he was again promoted, this time to engineman, serving in Engine Company No. 26 until March, 1884, when he was transferred to Engine Company No. 22. He served in that company until May, 1886, when he resigned to accept the appointment as chief engineer in the United States treasury service at the Treasury building at Boston. He again entered this service in June, 1887, as a call-hoseman in Hose Company No. 5, in which he was promoted to captain. Captain Fry is a member of the First Regiment Club, Boston Athletic Club, Town Club, First Corps of Cadets, Companion in the Loyal Legion, and the Order of the Cincinnati Society of Rhode Island.

JOHN D. KELLEY (Fig. 2) is a Boston boy, being born in this city June 30, 1843. January 19, 1863, he enlisted in Company C, Fourth New York Regiment, with which he remained until August 12, 1864. November 11 he joined Company A, Sixth Connecticut Infantry, which he left at the close of the war, August 25, 1865. He then went to work as a teamster, at which he remained until May 1, 1874, when he was appointed a permanent member of this department and assigned to Engine Company No. 4. April 20, 1881, he was transferred to Ladder Company No. 3, and on January 25, 1889, was transferred to this company in charge, Captain Fry being transferred to Hose Company No. 7. Mr. Kelley was badly injured by falling *débris* at the Tremont Temple fire. At the second fire of Smith Organ Factory he received a contusion of the shoulder by a falling slate. June 16, 1887, he fell from the sliding-pole to the floor, while responding to an alarm of fire, with such force as to receive a concussion of the spine, from the effects of which he has not as yet fully recovered.

The well-known features of SILAS LOVELL, driver, will be recognized on page 565 (Fig. 3). He was born in Boston, Mass., September 12, 1827, being one of the oldest men in the department. He is a machinist by trade, and his experience as a fireman dates from 1847, when he joined hand-engine Suffolk No. 1, in which he remained until this company was organized,

Top — Ladder Company No. 13.   Bottom — Hose Company No. 5. — Page 563.

and was assigned as driver during 1861, which position he has since held, responding to almost every alarm since that period. During this time he has never received any severe injuries, and has only been off duty three weeks from sickness.

F. S. REED (Fig. 4) was born in Hanover, N.H., June 11, 1831. He followed the sea about fifteen years before settling in this city, which he did during 1850. He was in the South during the war, doing service on board despatch-boat "C. W. Thomas," on which he remained seven months and fourteen days. He joined this department November 1, 1867, as a call-man, in Hose Company No. 1, where he served until October 1, 1873, when he was appointed a permanent member and assigned to Engine Company No. 25. He was transferred Feb. 25, 1886, to Engine Company No. 23, and on this company being placed on a permanent basis was assigned as hoseman.

ENGINE COMPANY NO. 33.

This company was organized February 16, 1888, with the following company, except Capt. George W. Frost, he succeeding Capt. J. F. Ryan, who was transferred to Engine Company No. 6, August 31, 1888 : —

Captain GEORGE W. FROST (Fig. 1) first saw the light in Hancock, Me., August 1, 1838. He went to sea from 1854 to 1862, when in September 19 of that year he enlisted in the United States navy on the frigate "Sabine," on which he was severely injured in the head by a falling block. He remained on board of this frigate until February, 1863, at which time he retired, but shortly after reënlisted and served on the ships "Vandalia," "Ohio," "Supply," and "Sabine" until 1867. After this he learned the trade of steam and gas pipe fitting, in which business he was soon established. April, 1868, he joined the Roxbury department. During 1872 he was promoted captain and assigned to Ladder Company No. 4. He was transferred from that company April 1, 1874, to Engine Company No. 25, and April 29, 1885, was transferred to Engine Company No. 10, where he remained until August 30, 1888, when he was transferred to this company. He was at work as hoseman in a building on Washington street during the "big fire," with several other members. He told his companions he did not like the looks of the wall from the inside, and would go out and look at it. Only one man followed him, and they had barely got outside when the wall fell, killing every man within. Captain Frost is a member of the Masonic Order, Knights of Honor, Royal Good Fellows, and the Boston Veterans.

Lieutenant CHARLES INGERSOLL (Fig. 2) was born in Boston, June 16, 1849. He was employed in the sewing-machine business for several years. His first experience as a fireman dates from 1870, at which time he began as a volunteer in Engine Company No. 3. December, 1872, he was appointed a call-man in Hose Company No. 2, and October 14, 1873, was appointed a permanent member and assigned to Engine Company No. 7. February 16,

1888, he was promoted lieutenant and assigned to this company. Lieutenant Ingersoll was severely injured at the Hanover-street fire by a falling wall. He had his wrist broken and the sinews of his legs torn off.

Engineman HENRY HEYMANN (Fig. 3) is a native of New York City. He was born June 13, 1853, and came to this city during 1870. He joined this department as a call-substitute in Ladder Company No. 3 during the fall of 1871, and July 1, 1873, was appointed a call-man in Hose Company No. 5. May 7, 1874, he was promoted a permanent member and transferred to Engine Company No. 3, and December 29, 1881, was promoted assistant engineman and assigned to Engine Company No. 28, where he remained until October 12, 1882, at which time he was transferred back to Engine Company No. 3. November 6, 1882, he was again transferred to Engine Company No. 22, and promoted engineman of that company July 1, 1886, and February 16, 1888, he was transferred to this company. Mr. Heymann was severely burned at the Children's Hospital fire in 1876. He is a member of the Siloam Lodge No. 2, I. O. O. F., the Boston Veterans, and the American Order of Firemen. The beautiful wood-carving at the fire-alarm office, City Hall, is the work of this gentleman.

Assistant Engineman JOSEPH F. COLLINS (Fig. 4) was born in Boston, Mass., January 2, 1854. He learned the engineer's trade, and joined this department as a call-man, September 21, 1874, in Engine Company No. 2. During May, 1882, he was appointed a permanent member; February 16, 1888, was transferred to this company. Mr. Collins is a member of the Iron Hall.

HARRY W. BAUCH (Fig. 5), driver, was born in New York City, December 28, 1860. He came to this city when young, and began life as a teamster. His experience as a fireman dates from September, 1878, when he joined Engine Company No. 18 as a call-substitute. During 1881 he was appointed a call-man. February 25, 1886, he was promoted a permanent man, and assigned to Engine Company No. 25, and detailed as driver. February 16, 1888, he was transferred to this company.

CHARLES W. HARRIS (Fig. 6), driver of hose-carriage, was born in Neponset, Mass., February 12, 1862. He was employed as a teamster, and on October 9, 1885, joined this department as a call-man in Engine Company No. 17. He was appointed a permanent member and assigned to Engine Company No. 4, September 24, 1886. February 16, 1888, he was assigned to this company, and detailed as driver of hose-carriage. Mr. Harris is a member of the Order of Iron Hall.

DANIEL J. GLENNON (Fig. 7) was born in Montpelier, Vt., February 10, 1852. He came to Boston at an early age, and began life as a carriage-smith. He entered this department as a call-man in Engine Company No. 14, on October 14, 1883, and was transferred to Ladder Company No. 12, June, 1886. He was appointed a permanent member January 5, 1880, and assigned to this company February 16 of the present year

Engine Company No. 33. — Page 569.

B. F. HAYES (Fig. 8) was appointed in this company August 17, 1888.

THOMAS F. HEDRINGTON (Fig. 9) was born in East Boston, March 21, 1862. He was employed as a machinist previous to January 13, 1888, when he was assigned to Engine Company No. 12, as a substitute. He was transferred to this company February 16, 1888.

WILLIAM F. RICE (Fig. 10) was born in Somerville, Mass., July 27, 1859. He was employed as a book-keeper until June 23, 1887, when he was assigned to Engine Company No. 12. He was transferred to Engine Company No. 22, July 5, 1887, and transferred to this company February 16, 1888.

LADDER COMPANY NO. 15.

This company was organized February 20, 1888, with the following members : —

Captain THOMAS W. CONWAY (Fig. 1) is a Boston boy, being born in this city May 19, 1842. His employment before entering the permanent department was that of a teamster. He was appointed on the said force as callman in Ladder Company No. 1, in Charlestown. November 27, 1878, he was appointed a permanent member, and assigned to Ladder Company No. 2, as driver, and was transferred to Ladder Company No. 9, October 11, 1881. March 28, 1885, he was promoted captain, and assigned to Ladder Company No. 12, and February 16, 1888, was placed in command of this company. Captain Conway is a member of the Firemen's Charitable Association, also the Boston and the Charlestown Veterans.

Lieutenant GASPER H. MONING (Fig. 2) was born in Berlin, Germany, December 16, 1853. He came to this country during 1855, and located at Plymouth, coming to Boston in 1871, and was employed as an oil-cloth printer. He joined the department September, 1876, as a call-substitute in Engine Company No. 13. July 30, 1880, he was appointed a call-man, and assigned to Ladder Company No. 12. September 3, 1884, he was promoted a permanent substitute, and assigned to Ladder Company No. 3. March 28, 1885, he was appointed a permanent man in the same company, and transferred to Engine Company No. 14. June 25, 1887, he was promoted lieutenant, and assigned to this company, February 16, 1888.

CHARLES E. KIRBY (Fig. 3), driver, was born in Fall River, Mass., August 3, 1862. His first experience as a fireman began when eighteen years of age, with the Fall River department, as a volunteer in Ladder Company No. 1, and remained with that company until 1881. He was a teamster for several years, and when he came to this city, April 14, 1882, he followed the business of car-driving until his appointment in the force as a substitute, June 24, 1887, as a driver in Ladder Company No. 8. February 16, 1888, he was transferred to this company in his present position.

FRANK C. TURNER (Fig. 4) was born in New York City, November 16, 1861. He came to this city when a boy, and, after attending the High

School, entered the druggist's business. With this he studied music, and is very proficient in that art. He enlisted in this department, as a substitute, in Ladder Company No. 1, February 22, 1883, and on June 30 was promoted a permanent member, and transferred to this company, February 16, 1888. Mr. Turner was severely burned about the face and hands by a hot-air explosion at the Congress-street fire.

GEORGE C. SWIFT (Fig. 5), tillerman, was born in Roxbury District, Boston. Mass., January 29, 1859. He is an oil-cloth printer by trade. He joined this force as a call-man in Ladder Company No. 12, July 30, 1880, and January 16, 1886, was appointed a permanent member and assigned to Ladder Company No. 1. February 16, 1888, he was transferred to this company. He was injured at a fire in Hampshire street, June 17, 1882, at which he had a very narrow escape from death.

J. M. FITZGERALD (Fig. 6) was born in Catch Harbor, N.S., April 22, 1858. He came to this city when very young, and started life as a basket-maker. He entered this department August 1, 1886, as a call-man in Ladder Company No. 12, and on September 27, 1887, was promoted a permanent member and assigned to Ladder Company No. 1, and was transferred to Engine Company No. 13, June 24, 1887. February 16, 1888, he was transferred to this company. He had three ribs crushed by being thrown from an ambulance while accompanying a friend to the hospital. He is a veteran member of the Independent Fusiliers, Company D, and the Roxbury Horse Guards.

DUNCAN MCLEAN (Fig. 7) was born in Pictou County, N.S., April 9, 1849. He came to Boston during 1868, and worked at the carpenter's trade. During 1877 he joined this department as a call-man in Ladder Company No. 4. He was transferred to Ladder Company No. 12, July 31, 1880, and February 20, 1888, was promoted a permanent man and assigned to this company.

DANIEL F. GREENLAW (Fig. 8) was born in Deer Isle, Me., May 16, 1854. He came to this city in April 16, 1872, and worked at the carpenter's trade. He joined this department as a call-substitute during July, 1883, in Ladder Company No. 12. April 16, 1884, he was appointed a call-man, and February 16, 1888, was promoted a permanent member and assigned to this company.

THOMAS HENRY FOX (Fig. 9) was born in West Roxbury District, Boston, Mass., October 14, 1862. He was employed as a carriage-driver. and on January 6, 1887, joined this force as a call-man in Ladder Company No. 10. February 16, 1888, he was promoted a permanent man and assigned to this company. Mr. Fox rendered most valuable service at the Bussey-bridge railroad accident, in rescuing the victims and providing for their comfort. until a regular physician could attend them.

CHARLES A. RODD (Fig. 10) was born in St. John, N.B., August 3, 1863. He came to Brighton. Mass., when a child, and after leaving the

LADDER COMPANY No. 15. — Page 573.

Brighton school learned the blacksmith's trade. He entered this department, November 11, 1886, as a call-man in Ladder Company No. 11, and February 16, 1888, was promoted a permanent member and assigned to this company. Mr. Rodd is a member of Norfolk Lodge No. 48 of the I. O. O. F.

GEORGE H. RANDALL (Fig. 11) was born in Charlestown District, Boston, Mass., November 23, 1856. He is a printer by trade. He entered this service April 19, 1871, as a volunteer in Franklin Hose Company No. 3, in which he remained six years. On January 8, 1887, he was appointed a call-substitute in Engine Company No. 14, and was assigned to Ladder Company No. 4 as a call-member June 25, 1887. May 16, 1888, he was promoted a permanent member and assigned to this company. Mr. Randall had his jaw-bone broken at the Merrimac-stable fire.

JOHN HUTCHINSON (Fig. 12) was born in Waterford, Ireland, May 10, 1863. He came to this country during 1880, and learned the iron-moulding trade. He was appointed in this department as a substitute and assigned to Engine Company No. 29, January 13, 1888, and transferred to this company on February 16, 1888.

CHAPTER XII.

DISTRICT NO. 8. — ROXBURY AND BRIGHTON.

DISTRICT No. 8 comprises all that part south and west of District No. 7, to the boundary line of West Roxbury and west of Washington street, to the Brookline boundary line, and including all of Ward 25, formerly Brighton, and is largely the residence of the middle-classes, although many of the largest manufacturing industries are carried on within this radius, among the most important being the Suffolk Iron Works; several large iron foundries and machine-shops; Hancock Inspirator Works; Chickering's immense piano factory; Hasting Church Organ factory; Roxbury Carpet, Boston Belting, Boston Rubber, and Tower's Oiled-clothing factories; Sewall & Day Cordage Works, covering over twenty acres of ground; Boston & Albany Railroad cattle-barns, repair and car works; Old Colony Railroad car-works; Dennison Tag factory; fifteen breweries; Boston Storage Warehouse; Brighton Abattoir; eight horse-railroad stables; car-houses and car-works of the West End Street Railroad; eighteen public schools; twenty churches; fifteen halls; fifty-two apartment hotels; Notre Dame Academy; Marcella-street Home; Children's Hospital; New England Hospital; Murdock's Hospital for Women, etc. A large section of this district contains some of the very poorest of the residents of the city, consequently cheap wooden buildings are crowded together in narrow streets. This is also a growing territory, the open country being rapidly built up with a very nice class of buildings, especially in the Brighton District.

By an act of the Legislature, dated February 24, 1807, the town of Brighton was formally incorporated. The town of West Cambridge, or Menotomy, the second parish, was incorporated the same month, and by the separation of the two, Cambridge lost a large portion of her territory. Brighton received another instalment of the mother town by annexation, January 27, 1816. The annexation of Brighton to Boston was effected January 5, 1874, the act of the Legislature authorizing it, dated May 21, 1873, having been accepted by the city and town October 8, 1873. To the city, the advantages of annexation were to be found in the protection of public health by inspection and supervision of her meat-supply, and by organizing under one head a general system of sewerage, and in the acquisition of territory for houses at a moderate cost. A point on the eastern part of Brighton, where the Boston & Albany railroad crosses Cambridge street, formerly known as Cambridge crossing, is now named Allston.

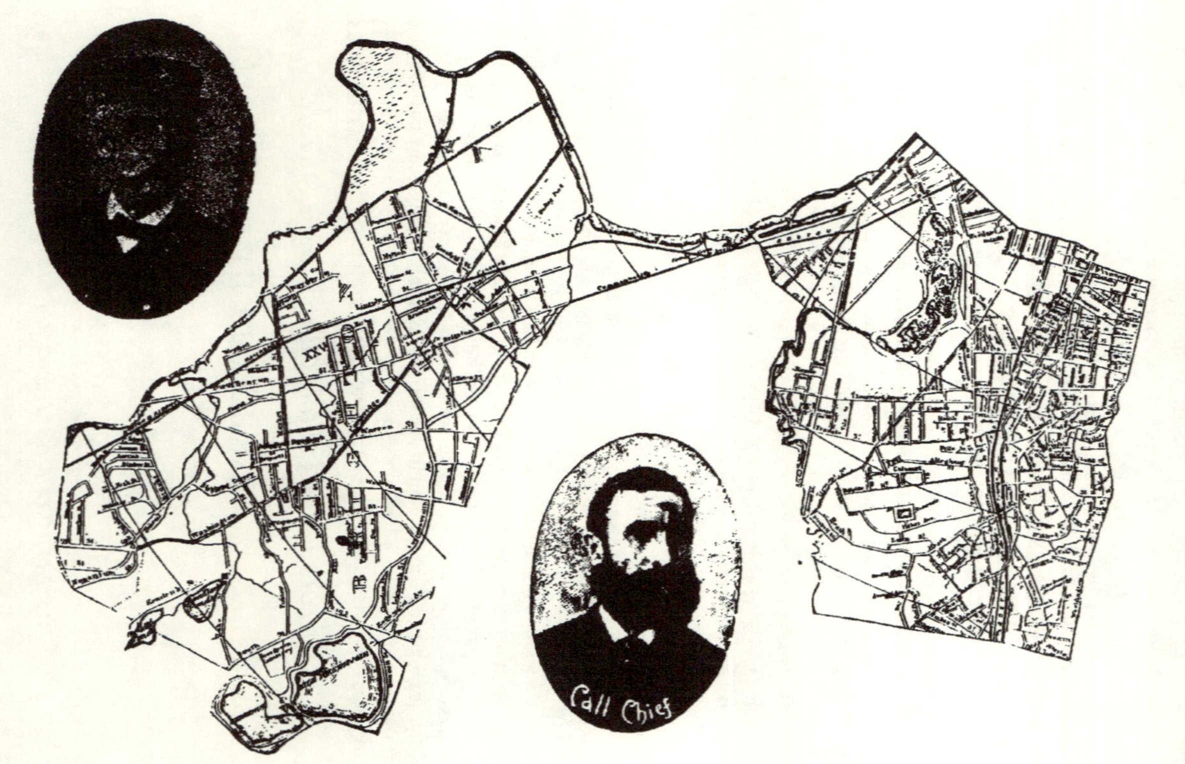
Call Chief

The number of pieces of apparatus in this district are Engines Nos. 13, 14, 29, and 34; Chemical Engines Nos. 3 and 6; Ladder Companies Nos. 11 and 12; and Hose Company No. 7. The headquarters of the district chief is in the house of Ladder Company No. 12.

District Chief EDWARD H. SAWYER, Chief of District No. 8, was born in Portland, Me., December 18, 1838. When but sixteen years of age he entered the Portland fire department as a torch-boy in Civic Engine Company No. 9. When twenty-one years old he became a regular member, attached to Company No. 8, in which he remained until it was disbanded. He left the department and enlisted on August, 5, 1862, in Company B, Tenth Maine Regiment, and served until his discharge, May 14, 1865, during which he was in all the battles of that victorious regiment. He came to Boston during March, 1869, and worked at his trade, that of carpenter, and was soon in business for himself, but left it to do service in this department. During 1872 he joined Ladder Company No. 4, as a call-substitute, and on October 1, 1873, was made a call-man, in which capacity he remained until April, 1877, at which time he was promoted assistant foreman of the company. July 31, 1880, he was promoted captain and assigned to Ladder Company No. 12, and November 1, 1884, was promoted to his present position. By reference to the "Roll of Merit" of the department it will be seen that Chief Sawyer has been the means of saving two lives, for which act he was highly complimented. His act of life-saving in the cases at 43 Fellows street, on August 14, 1882, and 581 Shawmut avenue, on January 20, 1883, is deserving of every praise. Chief Sawyer is a member of Mt. Pleasant Lodge 76, I. O. O. F., Roxbury Lodge Knights of Honor, Jewell Lodge 21 of Knights and Ladies of Honor, the Maine Veteran Firemen's Association, Post 26, G. A. R., and the Firemen's Charitable Association.

Call-District Chief GRANVILLE A. FULLER, of District 8, was born in Brighton District, Boston, Mass., March 13, 1837. After leaving school he engaged in the lumber business, in which he is engaged at the present time. He became identified with the fire department during 1856, at which time he became a member of Butcher Boy Engine Company No. 1, of which he was chosen foreman in 1859. The following year he was chosen foreman of Charles River Engine Company No. 2. In 1863 he was appointed Fire Warden, and in 1865 was appointed on the Board of Engineers of the Brighton Fire Department. January, 1874, he was appointed foreman of Ladder Company No. 11, which position he held until promoted to his present position. He was injured at a fire on Everett street; the roof of the piazza being covered with ice, he fell to the ground, a distance of twelve feet, and hurt his back. At a fire on Western avenue he was struck in the back by a stick of timber, the effects of which injuries he feels to the present time. He is a member of Bethesda Lodge of Masons.

ENGINE COMPANY NO. 13.

NAMES OF MEMBERS SINCE 1874.

J. McInerny, ap. January 6, 1888, tr. to Engine 26, July 19. 1888 ; J. P. Tobey, ap. February 16, 1888, tr. to Engine 25, May 5, 1888 ; E. F. Richardson, ap. January 14, 1888, tr. to Engine 17, October 12, 1888 ; C. H. Tagen, tr. to Engine 13, June 25, 1887 ; L. Thing, ap. October 21, 1882, tr. to Hose 7, June 25, 1887 ; W. G. Carley, ap. July, 1881, tr. to Engine 23, 1887 ; C. A. Straw, ap. 1875, tr. to Engine 22, October 16, 1882 ; Bart. Burgess, ap. 1870, resigned February, 1876 ; Francis Freeman, ap. 1872, tr. to Chemical 3, August 24, 1887 ; E. I. Roe, ap. 1872, resigned 1881 ; S. T. Horn, ap. 1872, tr. to Ladder 12, September 3, 1884 ; C. W. Lincoln, ap. 1870, resigned 1881 ; G. W. Gilman, ap. 1870, tr. to Hose 7, September 3, 1884 ; R. E. Hardy, ap. 1876, tr. to Engine 8, 1882 ; Whipple, died 1876.

PRESENT MEMBERS.

Captain DANIEL T. MARDEN (Fig. 1) was born in Rye Beach, N.H., March 3, 1836. He came to Boston during 1855, and on April 1 of the following year joined Barnicoat Engine Company No. 4. April, 1885, he joined Tremont Engine Company No. 12, until 1860, when he left the department and gave his attention to the dry-goods business. He again entered the service, September, 1862, joining Engine Company No. 7, and on January 1. 1868, was promoted to the position of captain. While there he became greatly interested in the antiquity of that old company, and during 1871 had the brass tablet on page 43 made and presented to the company. August 26, 1887, he was transferred to this company. He is a trustee of the Firemen's Charitable Association. Captain Marden won the first prize, a silver trumpet, March 18, 1865, given by Mr. John Stetson, manager of the old National Theatre, for a foot-race between members of the Fire Department.

Engineman FRANCIS SWIFT (Fig. 2) was born in Canton, Mass., March 5, 1831. He came to this city during 1848, and learned the morocco-currying trade. May, 1852, he joined American Engine Company No. 2 as a volunteer, and Dearborn Hose Company No. 2, in 1861, and in 1862 he succeeded Foreman George White. He left the department shortly after, and was engaged as fireman and later as an engineer on the Boston & Providence Railroad. where he remained until 1868, when he joined Roxbury Engine Company No. 3 as assistant engineman. He was promoted to his present position during September, 1872. Mr. Swift is a member of Highland Colony No. 12 of the Pilgrim Fathers, also the Massachusetts State Firemen's Association.

Assistant Engineman ELBRIDGE L. BROWN (Fig. 3) was born in Cape Elizabeth, Me., February 2, 1856. He came to Boston when a child, and began life as a mechanical engineer. He joined this department April 8. 1884, as a substitute, and was assigned to Engine Company No. 23, and

ENGINE COMPANY No. 13. — Page 582.

appointed a permanent member February 13, 1885. During March 28, 1885, he was promoted to his present position.

R. F. GARLAND (Fig. 4), driver, was born in Boston, Mass., November 16, 1840. He is a cabinet-maker by trade. During the war he enlisted in First Massachusetts Regiment, Company G, in 1861, and came out in 1864 and joined this department as a call-man in Ladder Company No. 1 during the ensuing year. He allied himself with the Protective Department as a driver during 1868, but left that service eighteen months later and entered this department as a member. He is a member of Franklin Lodge, I. O. O. F., and Post 15, G. A. R.

CHARLES LITTLEFIELD (Fig. 5) was born in Boston, Mass., October 19, 1843. He was a teamster by occupation. When the war broke out he enlisted in Company I, Forty-Second Massachusetts Regiment, on September 18, 1862, and served until August, 1863. During 1864 he joined Protector Engine Company No. 2, and July 20, 1884, was appointed a permanent member and detailed a driver. On October 12, 1887, he was transferred to this company.

HENRY P. PITCHER (Fig. 6) was born in London, England, June 29, 1840. He came to this country during 1856, and learned the carpenter's trade. In December, 1858, he entered this department, joining American Engine Company No. 2. When the war broke out he enlisted, on April 19, 1861, in the first three years' companies, Wighman's Rifles, which was mustered into the State service May 21, 1861, proceeded to Fortress Monroe and attached to the Third and Fourth Massachusetts Militia, which was afterwards known as the Twenty-Ninth Regiment. He was severely injured at the battle of Great Bethel, while trying to remove a piece of artillery, at which Lieutenant Grebble was shot. With his discharge he was given a letter signed by the commanding general, colonel, major, captain, and lieutenant of the regiment, in which he was rated as one of the bravest men under their command. While in Boston he underwent an operation, and recovered from his illness. He again enlisted, September 24, 1861, in Company C, United States Engineer Corps, and came out in September, 1864. He entered this department, joining Hose Company No. 1, in which he remained until May, 1865, when he went to London. While there he was presented by the "Royal Society for the Protection of Life from Fire, of London, England," with a silver medallion, for bravery in saving the lives of four persons at a fire at No. 76 St. George's road, London, May 19, 1869. He returned to this country in 1875, and on October 10, 1876, again entered this department, being appointed a call-hoseman in this company, and was appointed a permanent member September 3, 1884. On October 8, 1887, he was promoted to the position of senior hoseman. Mr. Pitcher is a member of Post 26, G. A. R., Lafayette Lodge of Masons, and the Association of U. S. Veteran Engineers, also the Firemen's Charitable Association.

JOHN GEORGE BALDNER (Fig. 7) was born in Roxbury District, Boston,

Mass., September 7, 1852. He began life as an upholsterer, and on June 18, 1882, entered this department as a call-man in this company, and was promoted a permanent member September 3, 1884, and assigned to this company. Mr. Baldner had a narrow escape at a fire at Box 244. While at work on a lower story a marble slab fell from the floor above and struck him on the back a side blow. He is a member of the Tremont Lodge 1480 of the Knights of Honor.

FRANCIS C. PRATT (Fig. 8) is a Boston boy, having been born in the Roxbury District May 5, 1844. He is a machinist by trade. In 1865 he joined this department as a call-man in Engine Company No. 3, of Roxbury, being appointed a permanent member September 3, 1884. Mr. Pratt has had several very narrow escapes, one of which was at the Hampshire-street fire.

JAMES A. McGEE (Fig. 9) was born in Boston, Mass., August 29, 1857. He is an upholsterer by trade. He entered this department as a substitute in this company January 6, 1888.

HENRY W. WALTER (Fig. 10) was born in Boston, Mass., April 6, 1863. He is a core-maker by trade, at which he was employed until his appointment in this department as a substitute on November 23, 1888.

ENGINE COMPANY NO. 14.
NAMES OF MEMBERS SINCE 1874.

The following members were appointed June 1, 1874 : —

Louis P. Webber, tr. May 13, 1880; Thomas Nannery, tr. June 1, 1882; G. J. H. Gutermuth, tr. June 20, 1880; Calvin W. Bates, tr. October 12, 1888; John H. Barutio, tr. June, 1880; Michael J. Slattery, no record; Dennis Kilduff, no record; George White, resigned December 20, 1881; Calvin Vose, no record; John R. Yendley, no record; John Divoll, no record; Joseph C. Barrus, no record; Thomas Downing, no record; William T. Brady, ap. August 21, 1879, resigned September 20, 1880; Warren R. Smith, ap. June 2, 1880, tr. February 6, 1882; F. W. Webber, no record, tr. July 31, 1880; James R. Sullivan, ap. August 18, 1880, tr. September 21, 1881; Edward Kelly, ap. June 25, 1887; James H. Sharkey, resigned November 20, 1887; Alfred B. Frye, no record; William C. Houseman, ap. January 14, 1882, resigned February 3, 1882; John W. Garrett, ap. May 16, 1881, resigned February 3, 1882; William Fearon, resigned September 20, 1882; Hugh Leonard, ap. September 20, 1882, no record; James H. Sullivan, no record; Daniel H. Glennon, ap. July 10, 1884, no record; C. H. Moning, ap. June 25, 1887, no record; F. W. Webber, ap. June 25, 1887, tr. August 26, 1887; E. R. Farren, ap. June 25, 1887, no record; James P. Dean, ap. June 25, 1887, no record; George L. Spencer, ap. March 2, 1888, tr. to Engine Company No. 23; George F. Quimby, ap. April 1, 1882, resigned November 1, 1884; Malachie Kilduf, no record, resigned December 31, 1886; William Monnahan, no record; John H.

Engine Company No. 14. — Page 586.

Barrito, Jr., ap. November 19, 1886, no record; George H. Randall, ap. January 8, 1887, no record; George W. Brown, ap. November, 1884, tr. January 1, 1886; John Knights, ap. May 30, 1880, tr. June 1, 1882.

PRESENT MEMBERS.

Captain CHARLES F. POOR (Fig. 1) was born in Charlestown District, Boston, Mass., April 26, 1852. Early in his life he began going to sea, and followed that calling for some time. During 1869 he joined Red Jacket Hose Company No. 1, of Charlestown, as a volunteer. January 1, 1873, he was promoted assistant foreman of Hancock Hose Company No. 1, and June 26, 1875, entered this department as a permanent member assigned to Ladder Company No. 3. He served with it until May 13, 1878, when he was transferred to Engine Company No. 22, as senior hoseman, and was transferred to Engine Company No. 3, and promoted lieutenant, April 21, 1882. He was promoted to captain and assigned to this company June 1, 1882. At a fire in Dartmouth street, on October 14, 1881, he fell down stairs with an extinguisher, and broke three ribs. A few days after recovering he broke his arm while going to Box 62. February 6, 1883, while at the Hampshire-street fire, he narrowly escaped being killed. He is a member of the Bunker Hill Lodge No. 5 of Odd Fellows, Bunker Hill Encampment No. 14 of the Royal Good Fellows, and the Massachusetts State Firemen's Association, Firemen's Charitable Association, and the Boston Veterans.

Engineman ALFRED H. PERRY (Fig. 2) was born in New Bedford, Mass., July 11, 1833. He came to this city in 1851, and learned the machinist trade. He joined the department during 1853, in Hand-Engine Tremont Company No. 7, where he remained until 1857, when he left the department. December 19, 1859, he joined Engine Company No. 1 as engineman. During the war he enlisted, December, 1863, in the navy, as engineer on board United States steamer "Malvin," on which he remained until May, 1865. He joined the Roxbury Fire Department, in Engine Company No. 3, June, 1865, and served there a few months, when he went West, but returned again on the force, October, 1865, joining Cochituate Hose Company No. 1 during 1866. In 1874 he again left the department, but returned February 4, 1875, joining Engine Company No. 22 as engineman. June, 1878, he was transferred to Engine Company No. 23, and in June, 1881, was transferred back to Engine Company No. 22. June 1, 1882, he was transferred to this company. Mr. Perry had his leg broken at the Warren-street fire, and on July 13, 1887, was thrown off the engine and badly hurt his head. He is a member of Tremont Lodge No. 15, I. O. O. F.

Assistant Engineman WILLIAM H. GAY (Fig. 3) was born in Roxbury District, Boston, Mass., March 1, 1845. He is a machinist by trade. He joined Torrence Engine Company No. 6 when a boy, and remained with it until it disbanded, and then became connected with Ladder Company No. 4 for a short term. He then joined Warren Engine Company No. 2, of Roxbury, and served until 1869, when he was enrolled a call-substitute in Engine Company No. 12. November 21, 1874, he was appointed a permanent member, and assigned to Chemical Company No. 5, and June 1, 1880, was transferred to Chemical Company No. 1. He was again transferred to Engine Company No. 4 during 1881, and detailed to Engine Company No. 10, as acting assistant, engineman, November 23, 1882; then to Engine Company No. 5, as assistant engineman, March 17, 1884. January 1, 1886, he was assigned to this company. Mr. Gay is a member of the Boston Veterans.

C. H. TAGEN (Fig. 4) was born in Lowell, Mass., December 9, 1852. He came to Boston when young, and, after leaving school, was employed as a teamster. In 1873 he joined the department, as a call-substitute in Hose Company No. 12. June 13, 1874, was appointed a call-man, and April 10, 1880, was promoted a permanent member and assigned to Engine Company No. 10. He was transferred to Engine Company No. 23, May 4, 1885. June 25, 1887, he was assigned to Engine Company No. 13, and to this company February 24, 1888.

EDWIN F. RICHARDSON (Fig. 5) was born in East Baldwin, Me., August 22, 1865, and came to this city during 1867, where he was employed as a teamster. His first experience in the department was as a call-substitute in Hose No. 5, August 19, 1887, and on January 6, 1888, he was made a permanent substitute. On December 31, 1888, he was promoted a member and assigned to this company.

EDWARD KELLEY (Fig. 6) was born in King's County, Ireland, September 15, 1853. He came to this city during 1859, and learned the house-painter's trade. He joined this department as a call-substitute during 1878, and during 1881 was appointed a call-member. July 18, 1883, he was made a substitute in Engine Company No. 23, and a permanent member during the ensuing year. June 24, 1887, he was transferred to this company. Mr. Kelley was badly cut and bruised at the Hampshire-street fire.

EDWARD H. WHITNEY (Fig. 7) first saw the light in Boston, Mass., January 22, 1845. He enlisted in Company D, Thirteenth Massachusetts Regiment, July 6, 1861, and served until July 16, 1864, and came out with the rank of sergeant. He joined the department as a call-substitute in this company during 1873, and was made a call-man June 26, 1874. August 3, 1874, he was promoted a permanent member, and assigned to Engine Company No. 17, as a driver. He remained there until January 28, 1885, when he was transferred to Ladder Company No. 7, also as driver, and on August 26, 1887, was assigned to this company. He is a member of the Ancient Order of United Workingmen.

DANIEL J. DOHERTY (Fig. 8) was born in Boston, Mass., October 6, 1856. He learned the carriage-finisher's trade, which he followed until September 3, 1884, when he was appointed a substitute in Ladder Company No. 8, and promoted permanent member January 15, 1885. He was transferred to this company October 12, 1888. Mr. Doherty broke his knee-pan during 1887.

HOSE COMPANY NO. 7. — Page 590.

At a fire March 3, 1886, he received a severe cut on the wrist, necessitating thirteen stitches to close it.

JOHN A. McINERNY (Fig. 9) was born in Boston, Mass., October 24, 1858. He was employed as a brakeman on passenger cars until his appointment in this department, January 6, 1888, as a substitute. Was assigned to this company July 21, 1888. He is a member of the Boston & Maine Railroad Relief Association.

JOSEPH A. DOLAN (Fig. 10) was born in Boston, Mass., April 14, 1864. He was employed as a teamster for a number of years previous to entering this department, which he did November 21, 1888, as a substitute, detailed to this company.

HOSE COMPANY NO. 7.

NAMES OF MEMBERS SINCE 1874.

C. G. Green, foreman, 1874, resigned 1888 ; G. W. Stimpson, promoted veterinary surgeon, November 28, 1883 ; J. R. Yendley, died 1886 ; G. C. Goodwin, ap. April 17, 1884 ; W. A. Copeland, resigned 1877 ; A. H. Perry, ap. 1877 ; J. H. Barutio, ap. September 3, 1884, tr. to Ladder Company No. 1, October 7, 1887 ; F. W. Webber, ap. July 31, 1880 ; Richard T. Tuson, ap. January 23, 1886, tr. to Engine Company No. 26, June 18, 1887 ; Captain A. B. Frye, ap. January 21, 1889, tr. from Hose Company No. 5 (see records of Hose Company No. 5), honorably discharged May 31, 1889.

PRESENT MEMBERS.

MICHAEL MURNAN (Fig. 1), driver in charge, was born in Boston, Mass., October 5, 1855. He is a boiler-maker by trade. July 30, 1880, he entered this service as a call-man in Ladder Company No. 8, and was appointed a permanent member April 1, 1881. June 24, 1887, he was transferred to this company. Mr. Murnan received a silver medal for life-saving, and has had several narrow escapes from death, probably the closest call being at the Charlestown-street fire, when he, with hosemen Flanigan and Turner, were cut off in the sixth story, and had to take to the windows, from which they managed to reach another building.

LEVI THING (Fig. 2), assistant driver, was born in Auburn, Me., July 29, 1852. He came to this city in May, 1872, and learned his trade, that of a carpet-printer. He joined this department August 29, 1881, as a call-man in Engine Company No. 13. September 3, 1884, he was promoted a permanent member, and on June 25, 1887, was transferred to this company.

EDWARD C. FRASER (Fig. 3) was born in Jamaica, West India Islands, August 7, 1833. He came to this city January, 1851, and learned the organ-making business. He entered this department June 10, 1871, as a call-man in this company.

BENJAMIN F. APPLEBY (Fig. 4) was born in Palmyra, Me., April 16,

1845. He enlisted in the Twenty-Second Maine Regiment, Company K, on the outbreak of the war, in 1861, where he remained until 1863. He came to Boston twenty-one years ago and learned the carpet-printer's trade, shortly after which he entered this department as a call-man in Engine Company No. 12, during 1874, when he was transferred to this company. He was struck on the head by a hose-pipe while at a fire, June 17. 1883. He is a member of Rebecca Lodge of Masons, Putnam Lodge, I. O. O. F., the Knights of Pythias, Lodge No. 42, and Gettysburg Post 191, G. A. R.

GEORGE W. GILMAN (Fig. 5) was appointed in Engine Company No. 12 before the reorganization, where he remained until September 3, 1884, when he was transferred to Ladder Company No. 12. March 28, 1885, he was assigned to this company. Mr. Gilman died April 24, 1889.

JOHN GOVER (Fig. 6) first saw the light in Millbury, Mass., July 30, 1845. During 1863 he enlisted in Company I, Fifty-Seventh Massachusetts Regiment, in which he served until 1864. During 1867 he entered the Millbury Fire Department, joining Hand-Engine Eagle Company No. 4, and in 1868 entered the Worcester, Mass., department, in Eagle Hose Company No. 3, which he left in 1871. He returned to this city and worked at the carpenter's trade, and entered this service August 24, 1876, as a call-man in this company. During 1881 he was appointed a permanent member and assigned to Engine Company No. 23, and in 1883 resigned. but came back again March, 1887, as a call-substitute in this company. Mr. Gover had the spike of a ladder enter his foot while at a fire. He is a member of Post 26, G. A. R.

LADDER COMPANY NO. 12.
NAMES OF MEMBERS SINCE JULY 31, 1880.

This company was organized as a call-company July 31, 1880, with the following members : —

E. H. Sawyer, captain by promotion, was made District Chief, November 1, 1884; J. F. Bowles, tr. to Ladder Company No. 3. February 4, 1887; C. H. Moning, tr. to Ladder Company No. 3, September 3, 1884; Duncan McLean, tr. to Ladder Company No. 15, February 20, 1888: G. C. Swift, tr. to Ladder Company No. 1, January 14. 1886: J. H. Victory, tr. to Engine Company No. 22: W. K. Whiting, resigned; M. Murnan, tr. to Ladder Company No. 8, July, 1881; George W. Gilman. ap. September 3. 1884, tr. to Hose Company No. 7, April 3. 1885; C. J. Burrill. ap. September 25, 1884, tr. to Ladder Company No. 3, October 18, 1884; Captain Conway, ap. March 25, 1885. tr. to Ladder Company No. 15, February 20, 1888; J. M. Fitzgerald, ap. August 1, 1885, tr. to Ladder Company No. 1, September 27, 1886; C. C. Springer, ap. January 14, 1886. tr. to Ladder Company No. 1; J. M. Garrity, ap. January 23, 1886, tr. to Engine Company No. 26. June 20, 1889: M. J. Dunn, ap. January 23, 1886, tr. to Engine Company No. 26, February 4, 1887; F. W. Le Cain, ap. November 19, 1886, tr. to Ladder

LADDER COMPANY No. 12. — Page 594.

Company No. 1, October 7, 1887; Daniel Glennon, ap. June 24, 1887, tr. to Engine Company No. 33, February 20, 1888; D. F. Greenlaw, promoted from Ladder Company No. 12, February 20, 1888, tr. to Ladder Company No. 15.

PRESENT MEMBERS.

Captain ALBERT R. JOHNSON (Fig. 1) was born in East Boston, Mass., February 15, 1849. After attending the public schools he began life as a sailor, following the sea until April, 1875. He entered this department April 21, 1875, as a call-man in Hose Company No. 6, and April 21, 1881, was made a substitute. On August 8 of the same year he was appointed a permanent member and assigned to Engine Company No. 6. October 27, 1881, he was transferred to Ladder Company No. 1, and November 28, 1885, was promoted lieutenant. March 28, 1887, he was transferred to Engine Company No. 10, and February 15, 1888, was promoted to his present position and assigned to this company. He was on the roof with Pierce and Quigley when they fell; he saved his life by jumping from the roof to a forty-foot ladder. He was also within a few feet of James Sweetser, and was on the roof of the same building on which Flavell met his death.

JOSEPH C. BARRUS (Fig. 2), driver, was born in Boston, Mass., March 8, 1852. He learned the painter and machinist trades, but was disabled from following the latter by an accident to his hand. He joined this department during 1871 as a call-substitute in Hose Company No. 7, and on October 28, 1876, was made a call-man in Engine Company No. 14. He remained there until January 2, 1877, when he was detailed as hostler in the Veterinary Hospital. He was appointed a permanent member January 26, 1877, and assigned to Hose Company No. 7, and transferred to this company July 31, 1881, as permanent driver. He broke his ankle by being thrown from the hose-carriage in 1878. He also broke his arm at the Lenox-street fire in 1883. He is a member of the Martha Washington No. 1 Rebekah Encampment; Putnam Lodge No. 81, I. O. O. F.; Paul Revere No. 57 Encampment; the Subrette Lodge; the Order of Royal Good Fellows; Boston Veterans; and the Admiral Winslow Camp 31 of the Sons of Veterans, G. A. R.

JOHN C. PELTON (Fig. 3) was born in Boston, Mass., June 26, 1848. He is a piano-polisher by trade. He entered this department as a call-substitute in Hose Company 2 during 1866. From 1867 to 1872 he was a substitute in Ladder Company No. 3. During 1872 he became a member of the protective force, in which he remained a short time. He left the department in 1874, but returned again July 31, 1880, as a call-man in this company. January 12, 1886, the wheel of the ladder-truck passed over his leg while going to a fire from Box 237, injuring it so as to make it shorter than the other. He is a member of the Boston Veterans.

DAVID CURRIE (Fig. 4) was born in Brooklyn, N.Y., May 4, 1861. He came to this city when young and learned the house-painter's trade. January 23, 1886, he was appointed a call-member in this company.

Samuel T. Horn (Fig. 5) was born in Lowell, Mass., January 23, 1850. He came to this city during 1864, and soon after learned the house-painter's trade. He entered this service January 1, 1873, as a call-member in Engine Company No. 13, from which he was transferred to this company October 3, 1884. Mr. Horn is a member of Admiral Winslow Post 31 of the Sons of Veterans, G. A. R., and the Boston Veterans.

George Joseph Reis (Fig. 6) was born in Boston, Mass., January 21, 1863. He is a teamster by trade, and joined this force September 17, 1886, as a call-man in Chemical Company No. 5. February 3, 1888, he was transferred to this company. Mr. Reis is a member of Eliot Council No. 2 of the Royal Arcanum.

James Daley (Fig. 7) first saw the light in Boston, January 15, 1860. He is a mason by trade. During April, 1882, he became connected with Engine Company No. 14, as a call-substitute, and was appointed a call-member October 10, 1882. June 30, 1884, he resigned, but did occasional duty for several months during 1885, and in August, 1886, returned again as substitute. January 8, 1887, he was again appointed a call-member, and on June 29 was transferred to this company.

Alfred A. Young (Fig. 8) is a Boston boy, being born in this city June 22, 1864. He is a telegraph operator by trade, and entered this department as a call-member of this company January 13, 1888.

Millen R. Joy (Fig. 9) was born in West Buxton, Me., June 10, 1865. He came to this city when young and learned the mason's trade. He entered this department February 24, 1888, as a call-man in this company. Mr. Joy is a member of Massachusetts Lodge No. 1226 of the Knights of Honor and the New England Order of Protection.

William C. M. Howe (Fig. 10) was born in South Reading, Mass., October 3, 1846. He enlisted, on December 1, 1863, in Company B, Fourth Regiment, Massachusetts Cavalry, and remained in service until June 2, 1865, during which he was a prisoner of war at Andersonville, Ga., and Florence, S.C. He came to Boston during September, 1868, and learned the oil-cloth-printing business. He entered this department July 18, 1876, as a call-substitute in Engine Company No. 13, and July 31, 1880, was appointed a call-member and assigned to this company. He was one of the unfortunates at the Hampshire-street fire, at which he received injuries to his ankle. He is a member of Putnam Lodge No. 81, I. O. O. F., Massachusetts Lodge No. 42 of Knights of Pythias, and Post 4, G. A. R.

William B. Dobbins (Fig. 11) was born in Boston, Mass., November 18, 1860. He is regularly employed as a teamster, but entered this department as a call-substitute in this company July, 1880. Previous to his appointment he was a volunteer in Engine Company No. 4. Mr. Dobbins is a member of the Barnicoat Association.

James J. Hardy (Fig. 12) was born in Boston, Mass., November 3, 1864. He is an iron-moulder by trade, and joined this department, January

16, 1887, as a call-substitute in Ladder Company No. 4. March 13, 1888, he was promoted a call-member and transferred to this company.

Charles C. Hutchinson (Fig. 13) was born in Chelsea, Mass., February 18, 1858. He is a sail-block-maker by trade. He entered this service March 13, 1882, as a call-substitute in Chemical Company No. 3, and January 29, 1885, was transferred to this company.

Thomas F. Killion, pensioned member, was born in Roxbury District, Boston, Mass., on April 12, 1852. After leaving school he learned the stone-cutter's trade. He entered this department as a call-substitute in Engine Company No. 14, in May, 1880, and in July was appointed a call-member of this company. At the fire on Hampshire street, August 17, 1882, he was one of the unfortunates who were maimed for life; his injury was to his left arm, the use of which he has entirely lost. He was pensioned November 16, 1884. Mr. Killion is a member of the Boston Veteran and the Firemen's Charitable Associations.

ENGINE COMPANY NO. 29.

Names of Members since 1874.

The Board of Engineers for Brighton for 1873 were: J. L. B. Pratt, chief; J. C. H. Lee, Joseph F. Bates, Charles Courier, and Richard Smart, assistants. The members of the engine company were: J. Griffin, captain; James Young, engineman; Peter Murphy, driver; hosemen: John Gardner, John Cross, Charles Fisher, Nicholas Roach, Dennis Ring, Henry S. Cook, Michael Featherston, Joseph Caldwell, Arthur Needham, Edward Welch, John Carigan, John Gaffy. On January 5, 1874, Brighton became one of the wards of the city of Boston and a part of Fire District No. 8, under the district engineership of Captain John Colligan and call-engineer Charles N. Holbrook. On June 8, 1874, Captain C. H. Champney was appointed and assigned to Engine Company No. 29. On June 20 a reorganization of the department of this district was effected by the discharge of all the original members and appointment of the following as members of the company from that date: Peter Murphy, driver; hosemen: Arthur Needham, resigned August 29, 1881; John Cross, resigned September 23, 1874; Henry S. Cook, resigned March 18, 1875; Michael Featherstone, resigned May 31, 1875; George H. Atwood, resigned February 21, 1878; Charles F. Fisher, resigned May 10, 1876; George A. Briggs, resigned February 6, 1879; Edward R. Davis; Dennis Ring, died February 23, 1881; William E. Fales, resigned April 1, 1875; James Young, engineman, resigned August 9, 1875; William C. Lee, ap. June 30, 1874, tr. to Engine Company No. 26, April 15, 1876; Daniel Carter, ap. November 20, 1874, resigned May 20, 1877; Thomas Minto, ap. April 1, 1875, tr. March 28, 1878; Lewis Humphrey, ap. June 14, 1875, resigned December 6, 1875; Charles E. Marshall, ap. May 1, 1876, resigned February 20, 1880; Hiram Hutchins, ap. May 1, 1876, resigned January 4, 1879;

Charles E. Browne, ap. June 10, 1876, resigned December 4, 1876 ; Thomas Morrisey, ap. July 8, 1877, resigned July 17, 1877 ; A. H. Cogswell, ap. March 28, 1878, tr. to Ladder Company No. 11, February 12, 1879 ; Fletcher Caldwell, ap. January 7, 1879 ; Frank Riddy, ap. February 12, 1879, tr. to Chemical Company No. 6, March 21, 1880 ; H. S. Osborn, ap. February 21, 1879, resigned January 20, 1880 ; J. W. Cushman, ap. April 15, 1880, resigned January 3, 1881 ; Charles Dixon, ap. July 16. 1880, tr. January 1, 1881 ; F. C. Nutter, ap. July 1, 1881, resigned September 13, 1881 ; H. F. Wood, ap. June 1, 1881, tr. April 15, 1882 ; F. C. Nutter, ap. January 14, 1882, resigned December 25, 1883 ; M. J. Slattery, ap. January 14, 1882, tr. to Engine Company No. 4, January 16, 1886 ; R. E. Kirkland. ap. February 14, 1882, resigned February 21, 1882 ; Richard Haggerty, ap. October 3, 1882, died October 30, 1884 ; P. G. Flynn, ap. January 23, 1886, tr. October 7, 1887, to Engine Company No. 26.

PRESENT MEMBERS.

Captain CHARLES H. CHAMPNEY (Fig. 1) was born in Brighton, Mass., August 16, 1834. He learned the trade of furniture-carving, and became a member of Butcher Boy Engine Company, August 2, 1853. December 1, 1857, he was elected clerk and treasurer, which he held until the disbandment of the company, in May, 1859. At a reorganization of the company, May 4, 1860, he was chosen second assistant foreman, and captain, May 6, 1861. August 5, 1862, he enlisted in Eleventh Massachusetts Battery for nine months ; on the 8th he resigned his position as captain of the engine company. He was mustered out of the United States service, as a corporal, May 29, 1863. June 1 he was tendered his former offer as captain of the engine company, but declined, and accepted the position of first assistant. September 7 he resigned. He was an active participant with the Light Battery at the Cooper-street riot, and on December 25, 1863, reënlisted in the Eleventh Battery, as sergeant, which was being again recruited for the war. He remained in service until June 16, 1865, when he was discharged. He was appointed to his present position June 8, 1874. He is a Past Grand Master of Nonantum Lodge No. 116, I. O. O. F. ; a charter member of Francis Washburn Post 92, G. A. R. ; a member of the Boston Veterans, also the Massachusetts State Firemen's Association.

Engineman FRANKLIN G. BURLEY (Fig. 2) was born in Exeter, N.H., June 9, 1839. He is a machinist by trade. August 9, 1875, he entered this department as a permanent member, and assigned to his present position. Mr. Burley is a member of the Maid in the Adelphia Lodge of Masons, the Nonantum Lodge No. 116, I. O. O. F., and Assembly No. 15, R. S. G. F.

Assistant Engineman FRANK BOWKER (Fig. 3) was born in Auburndale, Mass., June 26, 1852. He is a machinist by trade. He entered this department February 4, 1872, as a call-man in Hose Company No. 3. During

Engine Company No. 29. — Page 600.

1873 he was appointed a permanent member and assigned to Engine Company No. 4. March 4, 1874, he was promoted assistant engineman, and January 16, 1886, was transferred to this company. The ligaments of his leg were severely cut at a fire about ten years ago. Mr. Bowker is a member of the Royal Arch Chapter of Masons, and Franklin Lodge, I. O. O. F., the Sons of Veterans of the G. A. R., Post 89, the Charlestown and Boston Veterans, and the Barnicoats.

PETER MURPHY (Fig. 4), driver of engine, was born in Brighton, Mass., February 16, 1851. He joined this department in Butcher Boy Engine Company during 1867, and was appointed first assistant foreman. He then joined Wilson Hose Company, and when the T. C. Armory Engine was introduced in Brighton, on September 19, 1873, he was appointed a driver, also on the F. A. Whitney Engine Company No. 1, which succeeded it December 30, 1873. When this company was formed he was appointed to his present position. He was thrown off the horse while exercising, January 5, 1885.

CHARLES O. BARLOW (Fig. 5) was born in Roxbury District, Boston, Mass., February 19, 1839. During 1861 he enlisted in Company I, First Regiment, and served until 1862, when he enlisted in the navy and served two years. He is a carpenter by trade, and entered this service July 23, 1875, as a member of this company. Mr. Barlow is a member of Post 92, G. A. R.

EDWARD R. DAVIS (Fig. 6) was born in Brighton District, Boston, Mass., March 17, 1849. He is employed in the express business, and began his fire experience when seventeen years of age, joined Butcher Boy Engine Company, and later on the Wilson Hose Company, in which he remained until this company was organized, when he was appointed a member. He was injured by a chimney falling on him at a fire on Western avenue. Mr. Davis is a member of Bethesda Lodge, Masons, Nonantum Lodge No. 116, I. O. O. F., Brighton Lodge, K. of H., Iron Hall, Red Men, and Boston Veterans.

WALTER B. WOOD (Fig. 7) was born in Brighton District, Boston, Mass., Nov. 10, 1853. After leaving school he learned the carpenter's trade, and on November 20, 1874, was admitted a member of Ladder Company No. 11, and on April 1, 1881, was transferred to this company.

FLETCHER CALDWELL (Fig. 8) was born in Brighton District, Boston, Mass., January 1, 1858. He is a carriage-builder by trade, and entered this department as a member of this company January 7, 1879.

KIRK W. CALDWELL (Fig. 9) was born in Brighton District, Boston, October 26, 1859. He is a carpenter by trade, and during 1879 entered this department as a call-substitute in this company, in which he was promoted a member September 15, 1881.

CHARLES F. PARKER (Fig. 10) was born in Manchester, N.H., July 31, 1849, and came to this city during 1867. He is employed as a car inspector. He entered this department as a member of this company April 15, 1880.

Mr. Parker is a member of Nonantum Lodge No. 116, I. O. O. F., and William Bliss Assembly No. 196, R. S. G. F.

Daniel O. Riordan (Fig. 11) was born in West Rutland, Vt., July 29, 1852. He came to this city during 1876 and finished his trade as a plumber, and on April 10, 1882, entered this department as a call-member in this company.

William F. Cashman (Fig. 12) was born in Lexington, Mass., October 29, 1854, and during 1873 moved to Brighton District, where he learned the tin-smith's trade. He entered this department as a call-member in this company July 30, 1883. Mr. Cashman was injured at a fire on Shephard street, December 24, 1887, by falling through a hole in the roof of the building. He was also badly scalded while extinguishing a fire at J. Rhodes' plumbing-shop, where he was employed, July, 1888.

LADDER COMPANY NO. 11.

Names of Members since 1873.

Captain, Thos. Perry; driver, Thos. White; secretary, Thos. Parr; ladder-men: Edwd. F. Martin, Hugh Riley, Daniel Browne, Geo. S. Ring, Michael Tehan, Moses Murphy, Wm. Cunningham, John Russell, Edwd. Russell, Thos. Akin, Thos. Kelty, Michl. Conners. All the above were discharged at the time of the reorganization of the company June 21, 1874, and on June 30 the following members were appointed: Captain G. A. Fuller, ap. call-engineer January 25, 1876; Geo. G. Morrison, ap. captain January 25, 1876, resigned October 25, 1882; J. H. Towne, resigned June 5, 1875; C. E. Dennett, resigned September 1, 1874; C. P. Jones, resigned October 21, 1874; F. H. Langley, resigned August 8, 1881; F. M. Swett, resigned September 14, 1880; J. W. Cushman, resigned August 15, 1877; Henry H. Jones, resigned; J. T. Morrill, resigned September 9, 1881; Chas. Smart, resigned July 29, 1875; A. H. Norcross, tr. April 15, 1880, to Chemical Engine 6; H. F. Wood, ap. October 1, 1874, tr. June 1, 1881, to Engine 29; W. B. Wood, ap. November 20, 1874, tr. April 1, 1881, to Engine 29; C. E. Dennett, ap. August 10, 1875, resigned April 5, 1877; Geo. Carlton, ap. October 20, 1875, resigned October 20, 1876; S. M. Cofran, ap. June 24, 1876, resigned October 20, 1885; G. H. Crooker, ap. October 20, 1876, resigned April 2, 1877; Joseph Caldwell, ap. March 29, 1877, resigned February 5, 1879: John Cushman, ap. March 29, 1878, tr. March 20, 1880, to Engine 29; A. H. Cogswell, ap. February 12, 1879, resigned July 11, 1879; M. J. Slattery, ap. September 19, 1879, tr. January 14, 1882, to Engine 29; Wm. A. Carlin, ap. April 14, 1880, resigned April 4, 1881; Wm. F. Shaw, ap. June 10, 1880, resigned October 15, 1882; Chas. Smart, ap. April 20, 1881, resigned March 27, 1882; Matthew Watson, ap. July 1, 1881, died May 23, 1886; Chas. McKenzie, ap. August 21, 1881, died December 26, 1887; Forest Hall, ap. May 11, 1881, resigned December 26, 1882; Fred. Nutter, ap. January 14,

LADDER COMPANY No. 11. — Page 604.

1882, resigned December 29, 1883; John Ready, ap. March 20, 1882, tr. July 21, 1883, to Engine 26; C. H. Coyle. ap. July 28, 1883, resigned July 14, 1888; H. W. Coffin, ap. January 23. 1886, resigned July 31, 1886; Chas. A. Rodd, ap. November 26, 1886. tr. January 6, 1888, to Ladder 15.

PRESENT MEMBERS.

Call-Captain JAMES A. DOOLEY (Fig. 1) was born in Brighton District, Boston, Mass., July 13. 1850. He is a carpenter by trade. and entered the Brighton department during 1871 as a member of Butcher Boy Engine Company, in which he remained until it was disbanded. He entered this service as a member of this company, September 14, 1880, and on July 28, 1883, was promoted to his present position.

EDWIN A. SMITH (Fig. 2), driver, was born in Dorchester District, Boston, Mass., November 14, 1841; after leaving school he began life as a mechanical engineer. He entered this department as a substitute during the fall of 1876 in Ladder Company No. 8. December 21. 1877, he was appointed a permanent member. January 14. 1882, he was transferred to this company in his present position. Mr. Smith, with his brother, Captain Smith, of Engine No. 9, and ex-Captain Cummings of Engine No. 6, had a narrow escape at the Rice-Kendall fire, where they were buried by falling walls. He was also badly cut by falling glass at a fire on Purchase street, July, 1879, from the effects of which erysipelas resulted. He is a member of Neponset Lodge No. 84, I. O. O. F.

HENRY H. JONES (Fig. 3) was born in Smithfield, Me., January 25, 1844. He enlisted in Company F. Tenth Maine Regiment, May 3. 1861, from which he was discharged during 1863. He soon after enlisted in the navy and served sixteen months. He then enlisted in the Fourth Hancock V. M., of Augusta, Me., and was discharged one year later. He came to Boston and learned the stone-cutter's trade, and on July 2, 1874, entered this department as a member of this company. Mr. Jones is a member of Nonantum Lodge 116, I. O. O. F., Allston Council 68, Royal Arcanum, Post 92, G. A. R.

GEORGE T. ANDREWS (Fig. 4) was born in Hartford, Conn., October 9, 1851. and came to Boston during the spring of 1873, where he engaged in the butcher business. During 1867 he became a member of Chatham Engine Company No. 1, of Portland, Conn., in which he remained until 1869. During 1872 he entered the Winsted, Conn., department in Eagle Hose Company, and served one year. He became a member of this company, June 17, 1882. Mr. Andrews is a member of Brighton Lodge 1016, K. of H.

JOHN H. GREENLEAF (Fig. 5) was born in Boston. Mass., May 31. 1850. He is employed as a clerk. and in 1867 joined Butcher Boy Engine Company, and remained until they were disbanded. He was admitted a member of Wilson Hose Company on October 21. During 1882 he was appointed in this company. Mr. Greenleaf is a member of the C. O. Foresters.

WILLIAM J. VAN ETTEN (Fig. 6) was born in Albany, N.Y., June 28, 1854, and came to Boston during 1872, where he learned the wood-working trade. He was admitted a member of this company July 28, 1883. He is a member of C. O. Foresters.

WILLIAM E. WALLACE (Fig. 7) was born in Pittsburgh. Pa., March 15. 1852, and came to this city during 1869 and learned the car-builder's trade. He was admitted a member of this company July 28, 1883.

ELWYN BEARD GILBERT (Fig. 8) was born in Leeds, Me., January 29, 1857, and came to Boston during 1876, where he learned the steam-fitter's trade. He entered this department as a member of this company July 28, 1883, but did substitute service a few months previously.

THOMAS H. GRACE (Fig. 9) was born in Brighton District, Boston, Mass., November 15, 1863. After leaving school he learned the mason's trade, and on October 18, 1886, was admitted a member of this company.

SAMUEL J. WILDE (Fig. 10) was born in London, Eng.. January 31, 1860, and when five years of age came to this city, where he learned the tailor cutting trade. He entered the department January 6, 1888, as a member of this company. Mr. Wilde is a member of Nonantum Lodge 116, I. O. O. F. ; Brighton Degree 29, Daughters of Rebekah ; Boston Assembly No. 5, R. S. G. F. ; accountant of Local Branch 359, Iron Hall ; and Algonquin Tribe, Red Men.

CHARLES J. O'CONNELL (Fig. 11) was born in Brighton District, Boston, Mass., January 27, 1865. After leaving school he learned the plumber's trade, and entered this department as a member of this company January 14, 1888.

CHEMICAL ENGINE COMPANY NO. 3.

NAMES OF MEMBERS SINCE 1874.

This company was organized July 27, 1874, with T. H. Weltch as hoseman and William Blake as driver. Permanent members : Thomas H. Weltch, tr. to Chemical Engine Company No. 2, February 1, 1875 ; C. S. Rosemere, ap. February 1, 1875, resigned July 22, 1882 ; William Blake, pensioned April 13, 1888 ; call-hosemen : M. J. Conley, ap. January, 1874, resigned March. 1875 ; Louis Voight, ap. 1875 : E. J. Jourdain, resigned June, 1880 ; J. J. Harrington, ap. June, 1880, resigned August 20. 1882 ; William J. Healey, ap. November 24, 1882, tr. July 6, 1883, to Engine Company No. 25.

PRESENT MEMBERS.

Engineman THOMAS H. WELTCH (Fig. 1) was born in Boston, Mass., January 5, 1849. After leaving school he learned the machinist's trade. and on August 1, 1873, entered this department as a call-man in Hose Company No. 8. in which he served until April, 1874, in Hose Company No. 2. June

Top — Chemical Engine Co. No. 3.   Bottom — Chemical Engine Co. No. 6. — Page 608.

1, 1874, he was appointed a permanent member and assigned to Chemical
Engine Company No. 1, and later to Engine Company No. 26. February 1,
1875, he was transferred to Chemical Engine Company No. 2, in which he
remained until July 29, 1882, at which time he was promoted to his present
position. Mr. Weltch is a member of Siloam Lodge No. 2, I. O. O. F., and
Boston Assembly No. 5, R. S. G. F.

GEORGE R. WILLIAMS (Fig. 2), driver, was born in South Abington.
Mass., October 17, 1840. He came to this city when but a child, and after
leaving school entered the grocery business. February 1, 1868, he was
appointed a call-member of Engine Company No. 7. On July 25, 1873, he
was promoted a permanent member and detailed as driver of hose-wagon,
which position he held until April 13, 1888, when he was transferred to this
company. Mr. Williams is a director of the Firemen's Relief Fund for District No. 5, and a member of the Firemen's Charitable Association.

GEORGE R. KNIGHT (Fig. 3) was born in Portland. Me., November 17,
1849. When the war broke out he enlisted, February 10, 1865, in Company
C, Twenty-Ninth Maine Regiment, in which he served until February 10, 1866.
He came to Boston during 1868 and learned the painter's trade, and on December 1, 1880, entered this department, being appointed a permanent member and
assigned to Engine Company No. 4. October 21. 1881, he was transferred
to Chemical Engine Company No. 1, from which he was transferred to this
company April 16, 1884. Mr. Knight was ruptured at the Haymarket Block
fire, May 12, 1880, which laid him off duty nearly three months, and was
again ruptured on the other side at a fire, Box 21. He is a member of Post
15, G. A. R.

JOHN S. KEENAN (Fig. 4) was born in Roxbury District, Boston, Mass.,
November 2, 1860. He is an electrician by trade, and in November, 1879,
was appointed a call-substitute in this company, in which he was appointed
a call-hoseman July 10, 1883. Mr. Keenan is a sergeant in Company D, First
Regiment Infantry, M. V. M.

CHEMICAL ENGINE COMPANY NO. 6.

NAMES OF MEMBERS SINCE COMPANY WAS ORGANIZED, MAY 1. 1876.

F. R. Monto, ap. May 21, 1876, resigned June 20, 1878; J. H. Towne,
ap. June 6. 1876, resigned June 25, 1877; C. L. Smart, ap. June 14. 1876,
resigned April 26, 1880; W. H. Hall, ap. June 29, 1877, tr. to Engine Company No. 34, November 1, 1888; T. F. Monto, ap. March 28, 1878, resigned
November 6. 1879; G. F. Sparhawk. ap. November 21. 1879, resigned March
15, 1880; F. Ruddy, ap. March 21. 1880, tr. to Engine Company No. 34,
November 1. 1888; A. H. Norcross, ap. April 27, 1880, tr. to Engine Company No. 34. November 1, 1888; Captain George C. Fernald, ap. March 1,
1887, tr. to Engine Company No. 34, November 1, 1888.

PRESENT MEMBERS.

Lieutenant E. F. SMITH (Fig. 1) entered the department as a torch-boy. He was made a call-member of old Engine Company No. 8, January, 1856; resigned November, 1859; reappointed September, 1861, and discharged November of the same year. June, 1867, he was again appointed, and remained a member until 1882, when he was promoted lieutenant. November 3, 1888. he was transferred to this company as lieutenant in charge.

GEORGE A. KENISON (Fig. 2), driver, was born November 6, 1843. He came to Boston June 1, 1866, and during August, 1869, began his first fire duty with Ladder Company No. 3. He was admitted a member of Hose Company No. 26, May 6 of the year following. He served with it until May 1, 1886, at which time he was transferred to this company as driver in charge. June 5, 1875, he slipped from the seat of the engine while at the corner of State and Washington streets, while responding to an alarm of fire, and broke his leg. During the war he enlisted in Company A, Thirteenth Regiment, New Hampshire Volunteers, August 11, 1862, and served until June 30, 1865. He is a member of Oriental Lodge No. 10, I. O. O. F., and Post 92, G. A. R.

JOHN LEE (Fig. 3) was born in Boston, August 24, 1855. He was employed at the lathing trade until October 16, 1882, when he joined this department as a substitute in Engine Company No. 15. He remained there two weeks, when he was transferred to Engine Company No. 4, and later on was transferred to Engine Company No. 10. January 22, 1883, he was promoted a permanent member and assigned to Engine Company No. 6, and on November 3, 1888, was transferred to this company.

ENGINE COMPANY NO. 34.

This company was put in commission November 3, 1888.

PRESENT MEMBERS.

Captain GEORGE C. FERNALD (Fig. 1) was born in Boston, Mass., September 21, 1834, and when 17 years of age began to do fire duty as a torch-boy in Suffolk Engine Company No. 1. He is a house-painter by trade. He remained in that company until 1852, when he joined Hose Company No. 5 as a call-substitute, and on November 1, 1855, was admitted a member. January, 1856, he was promoted assistant foreman. and was elected foreman January, 1869. April 7, 1874, he was promoted chief of District No. 7, and on March 1, 1887, was transferred to Chemical Engine No. 6 as captain, and when this company went into commission, November 3, 1888, he was given command. January 31. 1862, at a fire at Box 42, he fell from a roof and broke his wrist and leg. December 7, 1869, he was badly ruptured at a fire in Commercial street. November 14, 1868, at a fire on Albion street, he was buried, with several others, by a falling wall, and was rescued by ex-Captain J. Fynes, of Engine Company No. 4; and on May 6, 1869, was badly burned.

ENGINE COMPANY No. 34. — Page 612.

Captain Fernald is a member of Siloam Lodge No. 2, I. O. O. F., and encampment, also the Boston Veterans, and a life member of the Firemen's Charitable Association.

Engineman ERASTUS E. JEFFREY (Fig 2) was born in Salem, Mass., January 2, 1833. He became connected with this department April, 1857, when he was appointed a call-man in Hand-Engine Company No. 8. He left the service during 1860, and worked at his trade, that of a mason, but returned again in 1864 as call-man in Engine Company No. 8. In April, 1865, he was promoted to permanent assistant engineman in Engine Company No. 8, and September, 1873, was transferred to Engine Company No. 25. He resigned May 1, 1874. July 1, 1875, he was again assigned to Engine Company No. 8, and promoted engineman. November 3, 1888, he was transferred to this company. He was run over by a hose-carriage on State street.

Assistant Engineman DANIEL RUBY (Fig. 3) was born in Taunton, Mass., May 30, 1841. He began life as a machinist, and when the war broke out he enlisted in the navy, December 19, 1862. He was discharged from the receiving-ship " Princeton," at Philadelphia, December 31, 1863. He re-enlisted August 19, 1864, and remained until May 21, 1865. He came to Boston in 1866, and worked again at the machinist's trade. May 5, 1879, he joined this department as a permanent member, and was assigned to Engine Company No. 3. He was promoted to assistant engineman, May 25, 1881, and transferred to Engine Company No. 23, and on November 3, 1888, he was transferred to this company. Mr. Ruby is a member of Post 7, G. A. R., and the Boston Veterans.

W. A. RATHBURN (Fig. 4), driver, is a Boston boy, being born in this city, August 18, 1847. He enlisted with the Tenth Massachusetts Battery January 15, 1861, and was transferred to the navy January 5, 1865, and while at Fort Fisher was shot in the face. After the close of the war he followed his trade, that of cigar-making, until August 11, 1874, when he joined this department as a permanent member, and was assigned as hoseman in Engine Company No. 6. August 10, 1876, he was promoted to driver, and April 7, 1887, promoted to lieutenant. He was transferred to Engine Company No. 4, March 17, 1884, and on November 3, 1888, was transferred to this company and assigned as driver, at his own request. At a fire, December 2, 1886, he had his shoulder broken. He was ruptured at a fire on Portland street, February 17, 1876. Mr. Rathburn is a member of Oriental Lodge, I. O. O. F., and the Barnicoat Fire Association.

ALBERT H. NORCROSS (Fig. 5) was born in Hallowell, Me., January 21, 1841. During his early life he followed the sea, first sailing as a boy, and at the time of his retiring was first officer. During July, 1856, he made a voyage around the world, and has been as far north as 71°. He enlisted in Company B, Sixteenth Maine Infantry, July 22, 1862, and was transferred April, 1864, to the navy, and served until June 15, 1865. During 1869 he accepted a position on the Boston & Albany Railroad, and became connected with this department, July 2, 1874, as a member of Ladder Company No. 11, from which he was transferred to Chemical Company No. 6, April 2, 1880, and remained there until November 3, 1888, when he was transferred to this company. Mr. Norcross is a member of Post 92, G. A. R., Nonantum Lodge 116, I. O. O. F., Branch 359, Iron Hall, Brighton Degree 29, Daughters of Rebekah, and William Bliss Assembly 196, R. S. of G. F.

JOHN W. S. CROSSMAN (Fig. 6) was born in Portland, Me., December 19, 1861. He came to this city during 1869, and since leaving school he has been employed as clerk, to which he added the duties of a fireman on November 3, 1888, when he was enrolled a member of this company.

WILLIAM H. HALL (Fig. 7) was born in Danvers, Mass., April 9, 1843, where he learned the carpenter's trade, and came to Boston September 29, 1873. He enlisted May 11, 1861, in Company F, Second Regiment, M.V., and was transferred October 24, 1862, to Company E, Fourth Regular Artillery, and was discharged at expiration of service, May 11. 1864, but again enlisted in Third Massachusetts Cavalry, and was discharged August 29, 1865. He first did fire duty on Chemical Engine Company No. 6, June 27, 1879, when he was appointed a call-hoseman; on November 3, 1888, was transferred to this company. Mr. Hall is a member of Nonantum Lodge 116, I. O. O. F., and Bethesda Lodge, Masons.

JOHN J. RILEY (Fig. 8) was born in Boston. Mass., January 15, 1866. After leaving school he learned the plumber's trade, and on November 3, 1888, was admitted a member of this company. Mr. Riley is a member of Court 65, C. O. Foresters.

JOSEPH W. BROWN (Fig. 9) was born in Boston, Mass., February 23, 1864, and is a car-builder by trade. He entered this department November 3, 1888, as a call-member of this company.

FRED. E. COREY (Fig. 10) was born in Brookline, Mass., June 4, 1861. He is a plumber by trade, and during 1876 first began fire duty as a call-substitute in Chemical Company No. 6, where he remained until November 3, 1888, at which time he was transferred to this company.

JAMES W. SHAPLEIGH was born in Brighton District, Boston, Mass., February 22, 1863. He is a coach-builder by trade, and on November 3, 1888, was appointed a member of this company. Mr. Shapleigh is a member of Royal Arcanum and Order of Iron Hall.

FRANK RUDDY was born in Canada, June 1, 1846. He is a car-builder by trade. February 12, 1878, he was enrolled a member of Engine Company No. 29, where he remained until May 21, 1880, at which time he was transferred to Chemical Company No. 6, and on November 3, 1888, was transferred to this company.

Chief Munroe and Map of District No. 9. — Page 616.

CHAPTER XIII.

DISTRICT NO. 9. — ROXBURY.

AT the close of the Revolutionary war, and for nearly half a century afterward, Roxbury was still a suburban village, with a single narrow street, and dotted with farms, many of which were yet held by the descendants of original proprietors. Its population at this period was probably under ten thousand. The eastern, central, and western portions, respectively, known as the First Parish, Jamaica Plain, and Spring Street, constituted, prior to 1820, when parochial divisions had all disappeared, the First, Second, and Third Parishes. Punch-Bowl Village was at Muddy river, now Brookline; Roxbury precinct included the westerly side of Parker Hill and vicinity; and Pierpont Village clustered around the mill, whose site is now the Roxbury station of the Boston & Providence Railroad.

Slight alterations were made in the boundary lines by the legislative acts of 1836, 1838, and 1859. In 1857 a decision of the Supreme Court of Massachusetts deprived her of seventy-one acres of Back-bay land, which had belonged to her from time immemorial, and declared it to be the property of the State. Much of this territory, formerly covered with water, has been reclaimed, and now constitutes the finest portion of the city. The Back-bay park, with the exception of a small portion belonging to Brookline, is included in the Roxbury tract. In 1838, eighteen hundred acres of Newton, bounded upon Charles river, were set off to Roxbury. That part of the town lying between Muddy river and the Brook, its original boundary, was annexed to Brookline in 1844. The filling of Roxbury canal, the extension of Swett street and of East Chester park, have slightly enlarged the area of the town on its eastern side. A canal fifty feet in width, from the wharf at Lamb's Dam creek, nearly, to Eustis street, just east of the burying-ground, was built in 1795, the line between Boston and Roxbury passing through its centre. This canal was recently filled up by the city.

In 1795 the Jamaica Pond Aqueduct Company was incorporated; in 1851 the Boston Water Board bought the right of this company for $45,000. In 1856 the city sold it for $32,000 to the present corporation, on condition that they should not bring water into the city proper. The Boston & Roxbury Mill Corporation was chartered June 4, 1814, and in 1818 work was begun on the Mill-dam, on Western avenue, the first of the artificial roads connecting the peninsula of Boston with the mainland. It was opened July 2, 1821, with a public parade.

In 1824 Roxbury street was paved and brick sidewalks laid. In 1825 all the existing roads, to the number of forty, received names from the town authorities. The streets were first lighted in May, 1826, lamps being provided by the inhabitants. During this year hourly coaches began to run from the town-house to the Old South Church in Boston. Tremont street was opened to Roxbury from its Boston terminus, near Chickering's piano-forte factory, September 10. 1832, the work being carried on chiefly by private subscription.

The town of Roxbury became a city by legislative enactment March 12, 1846. The act was accepted by the inhabitants on the 24th of the same month, eight hundred and thirty-six voting in the affirmative, while one hundred and ninety-two voted in the negative. The old board of selectmen was replaced by a mayor (John Jones Clark), eight aldermen, and twenty-four councilmen. The territory of the town was divided off into eight wards. West Roxbury was set off in 1851 ; it took parts of Wards 4 and 5, and all of Wards 6, 7, and 8, with the exception of Brook Farm and Forest Hills Cemetery, both between the territorial limits of the new town. A horse railroad was put in operation in 1856, running at first from Guild row only to Boylston street. Washington street was widened during 1855.

During 1700 the idea of dividing the town was first expressed, when petitions to the General Court from the eastern section prayed that the western part of the town might form a separate precinct. It accordingly became the Second Parish in 1711. An unsuccessful attempt was made in 1777 to incorporate the Second and Third Parishes into a district to be called Washington. Efforts for separation were renewed in 1817, again in 1838, 1843, and 1844, and finally in 1850, when they were successful, the act setting off and incorporating West Roxbury taking effect May 24, 1851. The dividing line was Seaver street. from Blue Hill avenue to Washington street, thence running in the same direction to Brookline, crossing Centre street at its junction with Day and Perkins streets. By this division Roxbury lost four-fifths of her territory. which was reduced to two thousand one hundred acres.

The project of annexing Roxbury to Boston, broached in the year 1851, was for a long time strenuously opposed. Voted down in 1853 (262 yeas, 399 nays), it was carried by the people in 1857, — 808 yeas to 762 nays : but in view of the small majority, the city authorities declined to act upon it. In 1859 the Legislature gave the petitioners leave to withdraw. In 1864 the proposition was rejected in the Senate. The commissioners of both cities had previously reported in favor of the measure. It was accordingly adopted by the voters of the two cities on the second Monday of September, and annexation took effect January 6, 1868. The vote of Roxbury was 1,832 for, and 592 against. The majority of votes for it in Boston was also very large.

The fire department of Roxbury has always been remarkable for its promptitude. skill, and efficiency. In 1784 its first fire-engine was located in

Roxbury street, opposite Vernon, the site of the old Grey Hound Tavern. Daniel Munroe was its captain; William Bosson, Jr., clerk and treasurer. Its members were: John Swift, David Swift, John Williams, Jr., Elijah Weld, Joseph Weld, Joseph Richardson, William Dorr, Joshua Felton, Amos Smith, Aaron Willard, Abel Hutchins, Capt. Samuel Mellish, Ensign R. H. Greaton, Jeremiah Gove, Jesse Doggett, and Blaney. Firewards were also chosen. A new fire-engine was established in 1787, near the Punch-Bowl Tavern. The members of this company were: John Ward, Isaac Davis, Joseph Davenport, Joseph Crehore, James Pierce, Samuel Barry, Capt. Belcher Hancock, and Lieut. William Bosson. In 1802 the Torrent Engine No. 2 was accepted, and its company of twenty-one men appointed. A new engine was purchased by subscription in 1819 for Engine Company No. 1, and the town was asked for land on the northerly corner of the burying-ground on which to build its house. In 1831 Roxbury had seven fire-engines, with four hose-reels attached, — Enterprise No. 1, corner of Dudley and Warren streets (new house); America No. 2, Centre street, by Poor House; Jamaica No. 3, corner of Centre and Day streets; Elliott No. 4, Centre street, near Pond, Jamaica Plain; Salamander No. 5, Spring street; Torrent No. 6, Eustis street (new house); No. 7, "Norfolk," at Punch-Bowl Village (Brookline). In 1842 Tremont No. 7 was organized, and stationed on Ruggles street; Warren, afterwards Washington, Ladder Company No. 1, organized in 1846, corner of Warren and Dudley streets; Cochituate Hose Company No. 1, corner of Tremont and Roxbury streets.

The first siamese-pipe was made by Messrs. Allen & Gay, coppersmiths, members of this department, during 1855. Engine Companies Nos. 6, 7, and 2 were the first to play through it. Engine No. 6 was the first to have a vacuum or suction. A member of the company by the name of Green was the inventor. This department was also the first to introduce the two and one-half inch hose, which is now the standard size. It was formerly called the "Roxbury size," and was first made by Messrs. Hunneman & Co. during 1845.

Among the most noticeable manufactories in the district are the Roxbury Carpet Company, Roxbury Rubber Company, L. Prang & Co.'s lithographic manufactory, Howard Watch and Clock Company, several large breweries, Cook's Organ Factory, Smith Cordage Factory, Boston Lead Works, Pearson Cordage Works, New England Piano Factory, Bay State Gas Works, sewer pumping-station, etc. Thirteen large churches, a number of the largest apartment hotels in the city, schools, etc. The boundary line of District No. 9 is from the centre of the Roxbury canal at Albany street to Northampton street, to Washington street, to Seaver street, to Blue Hill avenue, to Columbia street, to Geneva avenue, to Olney street, to Bowdoin street, to Commercial street, to Dorchester avenue, following the water-line to South Boston. Apparatus in district: Engines Nos. 12, 17, 21, 24; Chemical No. 5; Ladder Companies Nos. 4 and 7. The headquarters of the district chief is in the house of Ladder Company No. 4.

The chief engineers since 1830 were : Samuel Doggett, 1830 ; Joshua B. Fowle, 1830 ; Daniel B. Green, 1832 ; Stephen Williams, 1832 ; Samuel Knowr, 1835 : John Webber, 1836 ; Joshua Seaver. 1837 : Ephraim Harrington, 1841 ; Edwin Lemist, 1842 ; William G. Eaton, 1844 ; Edwin Lemist. 1845 ; Abraham Parker, 1847 ; John L. Stanton, 1855 ; Samuel F. Train. 1856 ; James Munroe, 1858 to 1868.

District Chief JAMES MUNROE was born in Charlestown District, Boston. Mass., September 3, 1818, making him 70 years of age. After leaving school he was apprenticed to a morocco-dresser, with whom he learned his trade, and when but eighteen years of age began his experience as a fireman. June, 1836, he joined Engine Torrent No. 6, of Roxbury, as a brakeman. and in 1839 was elected foreman, which position he filled until the following year, when he moved to Charlestown. While in that section he joined Warren Engine Company No. 4. During 1842 he again returned to Roxbury, and joined his former company as second foreman. and one year later was chosen its leader. During 1850 and 1851 he was elected a member of the Roxbury city government, and in April, 1855, was appointed to the position of assistant engineer. and was again promoted, in November, 1858, to chief engineer of the Roxbury department, which position he held until annexation, when he was appointed to his present position. Chief Munroe has served more years in active duty than any other member of the force, having worked at all the large fires, including the Hollis-street Church fire in 1839. He is a member of Wampatuck Camp of Red Men, the Boston and Charlestown Veterans, and a life member of the Charitable Association.

ENGINE COMPANY NO. 12.

NAMES OF MEMBERS SINCE 1874.

Company reorganized June 9, 1874, as follows : —

Captain, O. J. Booker, tr. to Engine 23, June 1, 1878 ; assistant engineman, T. W. Bradley, died January 24, 1876 ; driver, J. M. Huggins, resigned June 11, 1876 : M. N. Hubbard, tr. to Engine 24, no record : L. L. Caswell, resigned 1876 ; Geo. W. Downs, resigned July 5, 1882 ; Malachi Killduff, tr. to Engine 14. 1876 ; John Lavey, Jr., resigned 1876 : Sam. S. Sawyer. promoted to permanent member, tr. to Ladder No. 3 : Caleb L. Sturgis, tr. to Ladder No. 4, September 3, 1885 ; Wm. H. Gay, ap. to Chemical 5, as driver : James G. Hooper, resigned 1880 : Edgar R. Farren. no record : Chas. Masurey, tr. to Engine Company 14. January 5. 1876 ; Duncan McLean. no record : Frank P. Loker, ap. June 30, tr. September 3, 1884 : Geo. B. Reiley, ap. captain June 1. 1878. tr. to Engine 28. April 4, 1881 : W. A. Gaylord, ap. April 4. 1881, tr. to Engine 22, July 28, 1883 ; Chas. Knox, captain. ap. July 28, 1883, resigned August 1. 1883 ; assistant enginemen : Thomas W. Bradley. died January 24. 1876. ap. 1865 : Harry Gerry. ap. May 31. 1875, resigned May 16, 1876 ; John Collicut, ap. May 16. 1876. tr. to Engine

Company 24, May 15, 1880 ; Silas Morse, ap. May 15, 1880, tr. to Engine 6. March 20, 1883 ; Frank A. Greenleaf, ap. March 20, 1883, promoted engine-man and tr. to Engine 23, February 16, 1888 ; drivers : James M. Huggins, ap. June, 1864, resigned June 11, 1875 ; Alva D. Snow, ap. June 21, 1875, resigned April 20, 1876 ; John F. Downs, ap. April 28, 1876, resigned September 20, 1882 ; call-hosemen : W. E. Hammett, ap. May, 1875, died October 13, 1880 ; Moses N. Hubbard, no record ; Levi L. Caswell, no record ; Sam S. Sawyer, no record ; John H. Barutio, tr. to Hose Company No. 7, September 3, 1884 ; Wm. H. Brown, tr. to Hook and Ladder No. 4. September 3, 1885 ; Chas. B. Wood. tr. to Hose No. 5, September 4, 1884 ; Fred E. Carleton, resigned September 3, 1884 ; Thos. E. Spear, resigned September 3, 1884 ; John J. Goff, ap. call-substitute May, 1882 ; Wm. O. Keefe, ap. August, 1883, resigned June, 1884 ; permanent substitutes : Thomas F. Hedrington, ap. January 13, 1888, tr. to Engine 33 ; Nicholas F. Fitzwilliams ; John J. Brooks, Jr., ap. December 14, 1888, tr. to Hose Company 7, August 27, 1889 ; John F. McCarthy, ap. May, 1884, tr. November, 1885.

PRESENT MEMBERS.

Captain BARTHOLOMEW McCARTHY (Fig. 1) was born in Boston, Mass., June 1, 1848. After leaving school he began life as a teamster. October 13, 1873, he was made a permanent member of Engine Company No. 7. He remained there until August 2, 1883, when he was promoted to the position of captain and assigned to this company. He is a member of the American Legion of Honor, Order of Foresters, and the Irish Charitable Association.

Engineman JAMES T. COLE (Fig. 2) was born in Boston, Mass., February 3, 1836. He is an iron-moulder by trade. May 1, 1855, he joined the Roxbury department in Hand-Engine Torrent No. 6, and was foreman of hose during 1856. The year following he was promoted assistant foreman of engine, and the following year was elected foreman, but soon after resigned to the position of assistant foreman, which he held until December, 1860, when he joined Dearborn Engine Company No. 1. June 1, 1862, he was appointed assistant engineman. August 1, 1864, he was promoted engineman and assigned in charge of Warren Engine Company No. 2, which was reorganized during annexation to this company. Mr. Cole, with several comrades, saved the lives of a woman and several children at a fire in Cherry alley, now Quincy street, during 1858.

Assistant Engineman WILLIAM A. McKENZIE (Fig. 3) was born in Yarmouth, N.S., January 6, 1846. He came to this city during 1865, and enlisted in the Charlestown fire department in July of the following year as a call-man in Massachusetts Ladder Company. During 1869 he left the department and moved to Fitchburg, Mass. In 1876 he entered the department of that town, joining Rollstone Hose Company, in which he remained until 1880. He entered this service October 3 of that year as a call-man in Engine Company No. 15. He was appointed a permanent member November 14, 1881, and assigned to Ladder Company No. 3. May 1, 1882, he resigned to the position of call-man, but joined Engine Company No. 15 as a permanent member, May 1, 1884, and was transferred to Engine Company No. 3, October 15, 1886. February 16, 1888, he was promoted to his present position.

MATTHEW BURNS (Fig. 4), driver, was born in St. John, N.B., February 28, 1850. He came to this city during 1860, and after leaving school learned the carpenter's trade. He entered the fire service in the Brookline, Mass., department, May 1, 1872, joining Hose Carriage Company "Good Intent," in which he remained until May, 1877. May 17, 1882, was appointed as a substitute in this department, and was promoted a permanent member and assigned to this company, October 2, 1882, and detailed as driver. Mr. Burns was thrown from the engine while leaving the house, May 28, 1887, and received a fracture of the right ankle and other bruises. He is a member of Massachusetts Lodge 1226 of the Knights of Honor.

JOHN J. GOFF (Fig. 5) was born in Boston, Mass., April 22, 1861. He began life as a machinist, and entered this service May 3, 1882, as a call-substitute in this company. September 3, 1884, he was appointed a permanent substitute, and on March 28, 1885, was promoted a permanent member. Mr. Goff is a member of the American Legion of Honor and Order of Foresters.

HADWIN SAWYER (Fig. 6), senior hoseman, first saw the light in Portland, Me., September 16, 1849, and came to this city June, 1869. He is a painter by trade, and entered this department September 10, 1874, as a call-man in Engine Company No. 14. January 5, 1876, he was transferred to this company, and September 3, 1884, was appointed a member. Mr. Sawyer is a member of the Boston Veterans.

WALTER PIERCE (Fig. 7) is a Boston boy, being born in Roxbury District, June 23, 1858. He is an iron-moulder by trade, and enlisted in this service February 7, 1880, as a call-man in Engine Company No. 24. May 16, 1881, he was transferred to this company, and September 3, 1884, was appointed a permanent man. Mr. Pierce was injured at the Hampshire-street fire.

WILLIAM J. HEALEY (Fig. 8) was born in Lowell, Mass., September 22, 1861. He came to Boston when but a child, and began life as a telegrapher. He entered this department November 3, 1881, as a call-member of Chemical Company No. 3. June 17, 1882, he was appointed a substitute, and October 2, 1882, was promoted a permanent member and assigned to Engine Company No. 25, from which he was transferred to this company, November 21, 1886.

CHARLES F. EATON (Fig. 9) was born in Oxford County, Me., April 14, 1856. He came to this city March 31, 1871, and learned the carpenter's trade. During 1878 he entered the department as a call-substitute in Engine Com-

Engine Company No. 12. — Page 623.

pany No. 21, and May 6, 1880, was appointed a call-man. September 3, 1884, he was promoted a permanent member and assigned to this company. Mr. Eaton is a member of the Ancient Order of the United Workmen.

ENGINE COMPANY NO. 17.
NAMES OF MEMBERS SINCE 1874.

Charles C. Lane, ap. 1866, as engineman, resigned August 17, 1874; Patrick Freeman, ap. 1867, as driver, resigned July 6, 1874; Augustus Nickerson, ap. April 15, 1876; Edward N. Whitney, ap. permanent member August, 1874, tr. to Ladder Company No. 7, January 27, 1885; Walter Chadbourn, ap. May 27, 1874, resigned February 7, 1881; James E. Finley, ap. January 3, 1879, resigned February 7, 1881; James H. Banks, ap. April 24, 1876, resigned October 6, 1882; Charles Littlefield, ap. call-hoseman May, 1874, assigned to Engine Company No. 6, July 21, 1883; William N. Barker, ap. February 26, 1881, tr. to Fire-Alarm Department, October 15, 1884; Samuel B. Littlefield, ap. July 28, 1883, resigned October 5, 1885; Marshall S. Smith, ap. November 26, 1884, resigned May 26, 1885; Charles W. Harris, ap. call-hoseman October 9, 1885, made permanent September 24, 1886, tr. to Engine Company No. 4; Frank P. Loker, ap. March 1, 1886, made permanent September 24, 1886, tr. Ladder Company No. 3; William Jones, ap. May 29, 1869, resigned August 30, 1886; Charles Littlefield, ap. January 27, 1885, tr. to Engine Company No. 13, October 12, 1888; Edward Richardson, ap. October 12, 1888, tr. November 9, 1888; Gustavus H. Nichols, no record.

PRESENT MEMBERS.

Captain ALEXANDER GLOVER (Fig. 1) was born in Dorchester District, Boston, Mass., July 14, 1847. After leaving school he began life as a cabinet-maker. During 1865 he joined Protector Engine Co. No. 2 (since reorganized to this company). On annexation he was appointed in this department as a hoseman. May 26, 1873, he was promoted to his present position. Captain Glover is a member of Parker Hill Council of the Royal Arcanum and the Boston Veterans.

Engineman NATHANIEL H. BIRD (Fig. 2) was born in Dorchester District, Boston, Mass., July 8, 1835. When eighteen years of age he joined hand engine, Protector Engine Company No. 2, as a torch-boy. During 1856 he was appointed a hoseman, and working at his trade, that of a cabinet-maker. He enlisted in Company I, Forty-Second Massachusetts Regiment, on September 18, 1862, and served until August, 1863. On his return to this city he joined Steam Protector Engine Company No. 2 as steward and fireman, and was appointed assistant engineman, June 6, 1874. April 21, 1880, he was promoted to his present position. Mr. Bird is a member of Post 68, G. A. R., and the Boston Veterans.

Assistant Engineman ALVAN HAMILTON (Fig. 3) first saw the light in

Roxbury District, Boston, Mass., February 2, 1837. After leaving school he learned the machinist's trade, and entered this department in Hand-Engine Company No. 9, at East Boston, as a volunteer, in which he remained at various times until 1870, when he worked in Engine Company No. 4, from which he joined the Protective Department as a substitute. During April, 1872, he was appointed a member of both the Protective and this department, but chose the latter, and was assigned to Engine Company No. 3, on May 1, 1873, as assistant engineman. December 21, 1881, he was transferred to this company. Mr. Hamilton is a member of the Boston Veterans and Barnicoat Associations.

WILLIAM COULTER (Fig. 4), driver. See record and photographs with those of Engine Company No. 23.

JOHN F. GREENWOOD (Fig. 5), senior hoseman, was born at Ipswich, Mass., December 29, 1841. He came to this city at an early age, and learned the mason's trade. He became a fireman during 1862, when he joined Protector Engine Company No. 2. He was elected foreman soon after, which position he held until the reorganization, after which he became a member. Mr. Greenwood is a member of the Boston Veterans.

ALBERT FRANCIS LAKE (Fig. 6) was born in Boston, Mass., December 27, 1841. He is a mason by trade, and his fire service dates from 1862, when he joined old Protector Engine Company No. 2. Mr. Lake is a member of the Boston Veterans.

STEPHEN H. HOWE (Fig. 7) was born in Dorchester District, Boston, Mass., on July 14, 1847, and after leaving school learned the carpenter's trade. He entered the department in Protector Engine Company No. 2. Mr. Howe is a member of the Union Lodge of Masons, Kitchamankin Tribe 42 of Red Men, and the Boston Veterans.

JOHN H. RILEY (Fig. 8) is a Boston boy, being born in this city April 29, 1851. He is a wood-finisher by trade. April 9, 1882, he was appointed a call-substitute in this company, and on October 21, 1882, was made a call-member. Mr. Riley was thrown from the engine while driving to a fire at Box 321, on February 1, 1884, and received severe injuries to his head and hips.

JOHN T. DONAHOE (Fig. 9) was born in Boston, Mass., August 26, 1858. He is a stair-builder by trade, and joined this department on October 8, 1886, when he was appointed a call-member of this company. Mr. Donahoe is a member of the C. O. Foresters.

JAMES E. GAFFEY (Fig. 10) first saw the light in Boston, Mass., January 16, 1862. He is a house-painter by trade. During the fall of 1884 he was appointed a call-substitute in Engine Company No. 21, and on October 8, 1886, was promoted a call-man and assigned to this company.

EDWARD F. DOODY (Fig. 11) was born in Dorchester District, Boston, Mass., January 1, 1862. Since leaving school he has been employed as a clerk, and on October 8, 1886, was appointed a call-member of this company.

Engine Company No. 17. — Page 627.

ENGINE COMPANY NO. 21.

NAMES OF MEMBERS SINCE 1874.

L. H. Bridgham, resigned July 22, 1884; Jesse M. Brown, ap. June 8, 1874; Charles J. Beebee, ap. December 21, 1880, resigned May 16, 1881; James Crosby, tr. to Engine Company No. 25, April 12, 1887: Oliver Davenport, resigned May 1, 1874; J. N. Dixon, ap. October 21, 1874; George R. Donnelly, ap. October 2, 1882; George W. Everett, ap. November 21, 1874, resigned February 26, 1876; Charles F. Eaton, ap. May 17, 1881, tr. to Engine Company No. 12, September 3, 1884; Joseph R. Gilbert, tr. to Engine Company No. 10, June 1, 1880; James B. Graham, resigned April 1, 1874; Robert T. Glidden, resigned May 2, 1874; Theodore Hersey, resigned March 3, 1874; Charles T. Heald, ap. May 6, 1874, resigned February 25, 1877; R. H. Lawler, resigned September 20, 1876, reap. September 11, 1884, resigned December 18, 1888; Warren A. Lewis, ap. June 11, 1874, resigned March 21, 1882; M. D. McLean, ap. March 26, 1882; E. A. Perkins, ap. May 17, 1876, tr. to Engine Company No. 10, December 16, 1880; George Richardson, resigned May 1, 1874; Walter Restarick, ap. May 6, 1874, tr. to Engine Company No. 26, September 21, 1874; W. H. Rice, ap. October 21, resigned April 12, 1876; J. F. Williams, resigned April, 1874; William G. Whiting, resigned October 6, 1874; H. L. Whitney, ap. March 17, 1876. tr. to Engine Company 23, January 1, 1879; G. A. Gutermuth, ap. engineman June 1, 1880, tr. to Engine Company No. 23, May 25, 1881.

PRESENT MEMBERS.

Captain THOMAS W. GOWEN (Fig. 1) was born in Dorchester District, Boston, Mass., March 10, 1830. He began life as a carriage-painter. May 1, 1848, he joined Hand-Engine Company Tiger No. 6. May 1, 1853, he resigned and left the city, and was gone until December 1, 1854, and on December 1, 1859, joined Hand-Engine Company Perkins No. 2, of South Boston. December 1, 1859, it disbanded, and on November 1, 1860, he joined Hose Company No. 9, and August 11, 1862, was appointed driver. July 10, 1883, he was promoted to his present position. He is a member of Washington Council No. 10, Knights of Pythias, and the Boston Veterans.

Engineman BENJAMIN W. CARPENTER (Fig. 2) was born in Hardwick, Mass., March 8, 1835. He came to Boston in 1853, and learned the machinist's trade. He enlisted in Company G, Twelfth Massachusetts Regiment, June 26, 1861, and on November 12, 1862, had several ribs broken by a bursting shell, at the battle of Antietam, from which cause he was discharged. He returned to Dorchester, and joined Independence Company No. 5, during 1864. January 1, 1870, he was assigned to Engine Company No. 20 as callhoseman, and May 1, 1872, was promoted assistant engineman and assigned to Engine Company No. 15. August 1, 1873, he resigned, and May 21, 1874, was promoted engineman and assigned to Engine Company No. 23, from which he was transferred to Engine Company No. 22, May 21, 1878. May 25, 1881, he was transferred to this company. Mr. Carpenter was severely injured on the shoulder at a fire on West Canton street. He is a member of the Masons, Neponset Lodge No. 4, I. O. O. F., Boston Council No. 4 of the Royal Arcanum, and the Firemen's Charitable Association.

Assistant Engineman M. A. LYNCH (Fig. 3) was born in Ireland during 1850, and came to this city when but nine months old. Some time after he moved to St. Johnsbury, Vt., where he learned the machinist's trade. During 1863 he joined Ladder Company No. 1 of that town as assistant steward. The following year he was admitted a member of Engine Company No. 3, also of that place, which company was composed of boys of about his age. During 1868 he was enrolled a member of Ocean Hose Company No. 1, of Lowell, Mass. During 1870 was appointed a call-member in the Boston Protective Department, in which he remained three years, when he resigned and entered business. On September 28, 1875, he was appointed to his present position. September 20, 1878, he was severely injured by being tramped upon by one of the engine horses in the stall. Mr. Lynch is a member of Mt. Pleasant Lodge No. 176, I. O. O. F.; Everett Lodge No. 7, A. O. U. W.; Upham Assembly No. 61, R. S. G. F.; Boston Council No. 4, R. A.; President of Washington Mutual Benefit Association; Barnicoat Association; Boston Firemen's Charitable Association, of which he is one of the trustees, also one of the Relief Committee.

GEORGE R. DONNELLY (Fig. 4), driver, was born in Boston, Mass., April 16, 1854. His business was that of a teamster, and during 1874 he entered the department as a call-substitute in Ladder Company No. 4, in which he remained until the fall of 1876, when he left the service. He returned in the Protective Department as a call-man, October 1, 1878, and was assigned to Ladder Company No. 4. July 1, 1882, he resigned and was appointed in this department as a permanent substitute in this company, in which he served as driver until October 2, 1882, when he was made a permanent driver. He had both feet badly burned at the " lime fire " on Albany street, Sunday, February 1, 1880. Mr. Donnelly is a member of Boston Council No. 4 of the Royal Arcanum and Upham Assembly No. 61, I. O. O. F.

JOHN A. DE SORGHER (Fig. 5) was born in Ooste, Belgium, November 6, 1848. He came to this city during 1868, and learned the carpenter's trade. In 1869 he joined Tiger Engine Company No. 6. During 1870 he resigned, but on May 6, 1874, again entered the service, joining this company.

CLARENCE H. COFFIN (Fig. 6) was born in Barrington, N.S., December 5, 1848. He came to this city about fourteen years ago, and soon after learned the machinist's trade. He entered the department as a call-substitute in this company during 1876, and on October 13 of the same year was promoted a call-member. Mr. Coffin is a member of Massachusetts Lodge 1226, Knights of Honor, and the Firemen's Charitable Association.

ISAAC N. DIXON (Fig. 7) first saw the light in Boston, Mass., August

Engine Company No. 21. — Page 631.

31, 1843. He is a carpenter by trade. May 1, 1863, he joined Warren Engine Company No. 1, of Roxbury, and October 2, 1874, joined this company. Mr. Dixon is a member of Boston Council No. 4, Royal Arcanum, and the Boston Veterans.

MURDICK D. McLEAN (Fig. 8) was born in Prince Edward Island, March 17, 1855. He came to this city May 11, 1876, and worked at the blacksmith's trade. He entered the department January, 1882, as a call-substitute, and on March 24 of the same year was made a call-member. Mr. McLean is a member of Upham Assembly 61 of Royal Good Fellows.

WALTER BIRD (Fig. 9) was born in Boston, May 7, 1857. He is a house-painter by trade, and entered this department as a call-substitute in this company during 1881, and on March 1, 1882, was made a call-member.

JARVIS S. PERKINS (Fig. 10) was born in Sanford, Me., April 10, 1850. He came to this city during 1864, and worked at the grocery business. During 1878 he entered this department, joining this company as a call-substitute, and on January 1, 1879, was appointed a call-member.

FRANK W. BROWN (Fig. 11) was born in Exeter, Me., December 8, 1857. He is a machinist by trade, and during 1884 came to this city. He entered this department during 1888 as a call-substitute. Mr. Brown is a member of Elizabeth Council No. 4, I. O. O. F.

JAMES J. BYRNE (Fig. 12) was born at Birkenhead, England, July 4, 1862, and came to this city August, 1868. He is by occupation a hair-dresser, and in 1880 was admitted a member of Engine Company No. 1, of Marlborough, Mass. July 7, 1887, he joined this company as a call-substitute. Mr. Byrne is a member of Upham Assembly No. 61, Royal Good Fellows.

ENGINE COMPANY NO. 24.

NAMES OF MEMBERS SINCE 1873.

This company was organized December 10, 1873, with the following members: Charles O. Jones, driver, ap. June 1, 1874, died April 19, 1879; William W. Wilkinson, assistant engineman, ap. June 1, 1874, resigned April 29, 1876; John B. Burges, ap. June 1, 1874, resigned January 1, 1879; William M. Payne, tr. to Engine Company No. 10, June 1, 1874; John F. Lynsky, resigned July 15, 1874; Edwin W. Beal, ap. June 1, 1874, resigned February 1, 1880; Henry H. Brown, ap. June 1, 1874, tr. January 1, 1876, to Engine Company No. 12; Albert T. Holmes, ap. August 1, 1874, tr. July 8, 1882; John A. Collicott, ap. May 15, 1880, resigned June 16, 1886; Walter Pierce, ap. February 1, 1880; Charles W. Soule, ap. July 8, 1882, resigned September 11, 1884; Moses N. Hubbard, ap. January 1, 1876, resigned September 1, 1879; John T. Woodward, ap. May 16, 1881, tr. July 15, 1886.

Present Members.

Captain DANIEL CLARK BICKFORD (Fig. 1) was born in Richmond, Me., March 12, 1827. He came to this city during the spring of 1847, and learned the blacksmith's trade. He was one of California's "Forty-niners," and remained in that State four years. After his return he engaged in the blacksmith business for himself, which he carried on for twenty years on Beverly street. He entered this department as a call-ladderman in Ladder Company No. 1, September 1, 1861, and early in 1872 was promoted a call-captain. On the reorganization he was appointed permanent foreman of that company. July 12, 1883, he was transferred to this company. Captain Bickford, on February 1, 1888, while going to Box 225, was thrown from the pung and severely injured his hand and other parts of his body. He is a member of Oriental Lodge No. 10 of the Odd Fellows, also of the Firemen's Charitable Association and Boston Veterans.

Among the old working veterans will be recognized Engineman CHARLES RILEY (Fig. 2). He was born in Pomfret, Vt., February 17, 1833. He went to Lowell, Mass., during 1846, and learned the machinist's business. He joined the fire department of that city during 1850, on Hand-Engine Company No. 3. During 1858 he left the service, and came to this city during 1862, and on November 7, 1863, entered this department as an assistant engineman in Engine Company No. 7; May 31 of the following year was promoted to engineman. December 10, 1873, this company was organized and he was put in charge. Mr. Riley is a member of Franklin Lodge 23, I. O. O. F., the Beneficial Association, and a life member of the Firemen's Charitable Association.

Assistant Engineman JOHN T. WESTON (Fig. 3) was born in South Boston, Mass., February 18, 1855. He is a machinist by trade, and entered this department as call-man in Ladder Company No. 5, October 15, 1876. September 1, 1884, he was made a substitute and transferred to Engine Company No. 22. He was promoted assistant engineman July 30, 1886, and assigned to this company. Mr. Weston was laid up two weeks from injuries received from falling through a scuttle at the Walcott Hotel fire at South Boston.

FREDERICK W. HAYES (Fig. 4), driver, first saw the light in Portland, Me., December 26, 1854. He came to Boston when but a child, and after leaving school was employed as an expressman. He entered this department as a call-substitute June, 1873, in Ladder Company No. 4, and on June 10 of the following year was made a call-man of that company, and was detailed for several months in Engine Company No. 22. December 26, 1878, he was assigned to this company as driver in place of Charles E. Jones, the regular driver, who was sick, and on his death, April 21, 1874, was appointed permanent. Mr. Hayes was injured in the arm at a fire on Albany street during 1875.

ENGINE COMPANY No. 24. — Page 636.

Joseph F. Bolton (Fig. 5), senior call-hoseman, was born in Boston, Mass., February 17, 1843. He is a paper-hanger by trade. In May, 1863, he enlisted in the Eighth Massachusetts Battery, in which he served until the end of that year. During 1856 he joined Hose Company No. 3 (now Hose Company No. 8) as a substitute. He served there until it was disbanded, when he joined Melville Engine Company No. 6 in 1857; returned to Hose Company No. 3 in 1859. He was made a member on September 1, 1861, and was transferred to this company December 10, 1873. He was promoted call-captain June 10, 1874, and held that position until the permanent captain took his place.

Samuel C. Lord (Fig. 6) was born in Bath, Me., January 31, 1832. He is a carpenter by trade. His first fire duty was done in that place in Kennebec Engine Company in 1850. He came to this city during 1859, and joined the Roxbury department during 1861, in Dearborn Engine Company No. 1, in which he served as assistant foreman from November 2, 1863, to May 1, 1865, when he joined Warren Engine Company No. 2. in which he was a member until 1868. He was admitted a member of this company December 10, 1873.

Charles D. Sampson (Fig. 7) was born in Duxbury. Mass., December 6, 1831. He went to Lawrence, Mass., during 1848, and joined Essex Engine Company No. 1, in which he remained one year. He then went to Ogdensburg, N.Y., and from there to Plymouth, Mass., and was a member of Torrent Engine Company No. 4. During 1855 he came to this city and joined Mazeppa Engine Company No. 1, and in 1858 was enrolled in Hose Company No. 4. In 1860 he joined Dearborn Engine Company No. 1, and in 1863 allied himself with Warren Engine Company No. 2. On annexation he was enrolled a member of this company, December 10, 1873. Mr. Sampson is a member of Montezuma Lodge No. 33, I. O. O. F., and Boston Veterans.

John P. Ego (Fig. 8) was born in Cambridge, Mass.. July 10, 1856. He is a florist by trade, to which he added fireman's duties, July, 1881, when he entered this department as a call-substitute in this company, and on September 16, 1886, was appointed a call-member. Mr. Ego is a member of the Catholic Order of Foresters.

John C. Kelly (Fig. 9) was born in Roxbury District, Boston, Mass., October 29, 1848. He is a plumber by trade, to which he added the duties of fireman, as a call-member of Warren Engine Company No. 1, of Roxbury. February 1, 1870, he joined Engine Company No. 12. He left the department during 1874, and February 1, 1879, joined this company. Mr. Kelly is a member of the Pilgrim Fathers, Pawnee Tribe No. 61. Red Men, Dearborn Lodge, United Order Workmen, Tremont Lodge No. 1480, K. of H., and the Boston and Roxbury Veterans.

George E. Gardner (Fig. 10) first saw the light at Lyme, N.H., October 21, 1840. He came to this city when but a child, and is employed as a stair-builder. He enlisted in Company C, Thirteenth Massachusetts Volunteers, in which he served until 1862, when he joined a Reserve Corps, and served until 1865. He entered this department when a boy, in Hose Company No. 5, and on his return served until 1874. He then left the service, but came in again as a call-substitute, and was shortly after made a call-member. Mr. Gardner was ruptured at the Hayes-stable fire. He is a member of Post 26, G. A. R., and the Boston Veterans.

JOHN F. LYNSKY (Fig. 11) is a Boston boy, being born in the Roxbury District, August 1, 1849. He is a painter by trade. December 10, 1873, he joined this company as a call-member. He resigned July 15, 1874, but returned again soon after as a call-substitute, and on April 11, 1884, was appointed a call-member. Mr. Lynsky is a member of Tremont Lodge No. 1480, K. of H., and Pawnee Tribe No. 61, Red Men.

ALBERT BALL (Fig. 12) was born in Roxbury District, Boston, Mass., January 28, 1851. After leaving school he learned the carriage business. and on December 10, 1873, entered this department as a call-member of this company.

CHARLES B. WOOD (Fig. 13) was born in Gardner, Me., August 13, 1852, and came to this city during 1856. He entered this department in November, 1877, in Engine Company No. 12, as a call-man. August 29, 1884, he was transferred to Hose Company No. 5. and in 1889 he was transferred to this company. He was internally injured at the Hampshire-street fire by being struck on the back; was also injured about the head at the Swett-street planing-mill fire, 1879. Mr. Wood is at present employed as business manager of the Boston Industrial Home, and the assistant superintendent of the Appleton Temporary Home; also treasurer of the Shawmut Universalist Church. In secret orders he is a member of the Bay State Council No. 48, Royal Arcanum, and Shawmut Lodge No. 37, I. O. O. F.

LADDER COMPANY NO. 4.

NAMES OF MEMBERS SINCE 1873.

Robert McQuesten, ap. January 1, 1873. resigned March 1, 1876 : Alfred W. Howard, ap. January 1, 1873, resigned October 19, 1880; Thomas C. Soerman. ap. February 1, 1873, resigned August 15, 1873 ; Edgar R. Farren, ap. May 1, 1873, resigned November 20, 1874: Geo. L. Saville, ap. May 1, 1873, resigned September 20, 1873; Henry L. Whiting. ap. May 1, 1873, resigned May 1, 1874 ; Samuel S. Sawyer, ap. September 1. 1873, resigned June 9, 1874 ; Edward H. Sawyer, ap. October 1, 1873, resigned August 1, 1880; Chas. E. Hill. ap. November 1, 1873, resigned December 1, 1875; Wm. B. Lottridge, ap. August 15, 1873, resigned October 15, 1873 ; Chris. J. Burrill, ap. October 15, 1873, resigned January 15, 1878 ; Albert W. Choate, ap. December 15, 1873, resigned January 10, 1876 : Phineas D. Allen. ap. April 15, 1874, resigned March 2, 1877 ; Fred. E. Gardner, ap. June 10, 1874, resigned October 15, 1876 ; Frank Whittemore, ap. June 10, 1874, resigned November, 1880 ; Fred. W. Hayes, ap. June 10, 1874, resigned April, 1879 ; Geo. B. Reiley, ap. September 1, 1874, resigned November 1, 1875 ; Geo. W. Morse, ap. September 1, 1874, resigned September 1, 1875 ; David McLaren, no record, resigned December 1, 1876 ; Robert W. Devonshire, ap. October 10, 1875, resigned September 5, 1878 ; Isaac C. Leade, ap. December 20, 1875, resigned September 20, 1877 ; Elijah H. Eldredge, ap. June 20, 1876, resigned May 31, 1889 ; Duncan McLean, ap. September 20, 1877, resigned April, 1879 ; Harry E. Munroe, ap. October, 1876, resigned January 20, 1877 ; Chas. A. Hinckley, ap. January 15, 1878, resigned September, 1882 ; Charles E. Hill, ap. September 18, 1878, resigned October 28, 1882 ; Geo. W. Knights, ap. May 3, 1879, resigned January 15, 1883 ; Frank J. Mitchell, ap. October, 1882, resigned June, 1887.

PRESENT MEMBERS.

Captain JOHN M. POWERS (Fig. 1) was born in Georgetown, Me., December 26, 1833. He left that town during 1847 nd went to Bath, Me., where he began his experience as a fireman, joining Torrent Engine Company No. 2 during 1855. During 1858 he came to this city and worked at the carpenter's trade, and in 1869 he joined this department, being appointed a call-substitute in this company. October 12, 1871, he was made a call-member, and in December, 1872, was elected assistant foreman, which position he filled until March 31, 1877, when he was promoted call-captain, and on March 28, 1885, was appointed permanent foreman. Captain Powers had a narrow escape at the " big fire," he being in the building on Washington street in which the ten men were killed, but he fortunately got out in time. He was struck on the ear with a stream of water at the fire on Boston street, on December 22, 1872, which severely affected his sense of hearing. He is a member of the Washington Lodge of Masons, Firemen's Charitable Association, and Boston Veterans.

ALBERT D. SNOW (Fig. 2), driver, was born in Sharon, Mass., October 20, 1840. He came to Boston when but a child. He enlisted in Company K, First Massachusetts Volunteers, on May 23, 1861, and served until May 23, 1864. On his return he worked as a teamster. May 1, 1865, he joined Engine Company Dearborn No. 1, of the Roxbury department, as a call-man. In 1871 he was appointed a permanent member. April 1, 1873, he left the permanent and joined the call force in Engine Company No. 12, but was, in 1875, again made a permanent member. He again left this force, and joined the call-men in this company, on December 16, 1876, and on January 15, 1878, was placed on the permanent list and detailed as driver. Mr. Snow is a member of Post 26, G. A. R., and Millmont Assembly No. 68, R. S. G. F.

HENRY L. BARTLETT (Fig. 3) was born in Dedham, Mass., July 4, 1830. He came to Boston during 1856, and learned the iron-moulder's trade. Two years later he entered this department as a member of this company, in which he has since served, and is the only member of the company of that time in the service.

Joseph E. Sawyer (Fig. 4) was born in Portland, Me., May 24, 1842. After leaving school he learned the carpenter's trade, and on the outbreak of the war enlisted in Company H, Twenty-Fifth Maine Regiment, on September 29, 1862, from which he was discharged July 11, 1863, after which he served on board the U.S. revenue cutter " J. C. Dobbins " for one year. He came to this city twenty years ago, and on November 5, 1878, entered this department as a call-substitute in this company, in which he was made a member May 3, 1879. Mr. Sawyer is a member of Lincoln Council No. 11 of American Legion of Honor, Post 26, G. A. R., and Boston Veterans. He is a brother of District Chief Sawyer, and of H. Sawyer, of Engine Company No. 12.

William E. Guerrier (Fig. 5) was born in London, Eng., February 14, 1845, and during 1860 came to this city, where he learned the house-painter's trade. June 10, 1874, he was appointed a call-member of this company. Mr. Guerrier was injured at the Hampshire-street fire, June 17, 1882, when he fell with the building and was taken from the ruins. He is a member of Elliot Council No. 2, Royal Arcanum, Suffolk Lodge No. 36, Knights of Honor, Washington Lodge. F. and A. M., Mt. Vernon Chapter, Joseph Warren Commandery of Masons, and Massachusetts Rifle Association.

Frank W. Munroe (Fig. 6) is a Boston boy, being born in the Roxbury District, June 20, 1846. He enlisted on July 14, 1864, in Company D, Forty-Second Massachusetts Regiment, and served until the close of the war. On his return he learned the machinist's trade. He entered this department in March. 1867, as a call-substitute in this company, and on March 15, 1872, was appointed a call-member. Mr. Munroe is a son of Chief Munroe, of District No. 9 ; and is a member of Post 26, G. A. R. ; Jewell Lodge No. 21, and Past Protector, of K. and L. of H. ; Roxbury Lodge. K. of H. ; the Roxbury Artillery Veteran Association ; and the Boston Veterans.

E. H. Eldridge (Fig. 7) was born in Dennisport, Mass., October 28, 1845. He followed the sea previous to his coming to Boston, which he did during 1872, when he learned the clock-maker's trade. He entered this service on January 20, 1876, in this company, as a call-man. Mr. Eldridge is a member of Massachusetts Lodge No. 1, I. O. O. F., and Roxbury Lodge No. 205 of K. of H.

Caleb L. Sturgis (Fig. 8) was born in West Dennis, Mass.. June 23, 1846. He is a machinist and engineer by trade, and came to this city May 5, 1872. He entered this service June 5, 1874, as a call-member of Engine Company No. 12, where he remained until September 4, 1884, at which time he came to this company. Mr. Sturgis had his arm broken by the overturning of the hose-carriage of Engine Company No. 12 at the corner of Adams and Yeoman streets. He is a member of Mt. Horeb Lodge of Masons, Boston Lodge No. 25, I. O. O. F., Samoset Tribe, Red Men, De Soto Lodge, K. of P., the Firemen's Charitable Association, and Boston Veterans.

LADDER COMPANY No. 4. -- Page 641.

C. B. GILBERT (Fig. 9) was born in Phippsburg, Me., July 30, 1849. He came to Boston in November, 1867, and learned the carpenter's trade. August, 1873, he joined this company as a call-substitute, and on June 10, 1874, was made a call-member. Mr. Gilbert is a member of the Roxbury Artillery Association, Boston Veterans, Roxbury Lodge, No. 205. K. of H. Jewell Lodge No. 21, Knights and Ladies, Millmont Assembly No. 68, Royal Society of Good Fellows, Enterprise Lodge No. 22, New England Order of Protection, and Boston Janitors' Association.

JOHN DIVOLL (Fig. 10) was born in Boston, Mass., September 30, 1852. He is employed as a watchman, and on June 26, 1874, was appointed a member of Engine Company No. 14, where he remained until 1887, when he was transferred to this company. Mr. Divoll had his back injured at the Hampshire-street fire. He is a member of the Boston Veterans.

ALBERT S. McINTOSH (Fig. 12) was born in Roxbury District, Boston, Mass., May 21, 1849. He is a watch-maker by trade, and in February, 1876, entered this department, joining this company as a call-substitute. March 8, 1876, he was appointed a call-member. Mr. McIntosh was badly cut on the hand, October 30, 1878, at a fire in Dorchester. He is a member of Roxbury Lodge No. 205, K. of H.

JAMES A. MOSHER (Fig. 13) first saw the light in South Boston, January 20, 1853. He is a machinist by trade. In August, 1875, he joined this company as a call-substitute, and on November 19 was appointed a call-man. He is a member of the Royal Arcanum.

WALTER HENRY STANLEY (Fig. 14) was born in Vergennes, Vt., September 4, 1857. He came to Boston when but a child, and learned the clock-maker's trade. He entered this service in February, 1880, as a call-substitute, and on November 13 was appointed a call-member. Mr. Stanley is a member of Massachusetts Lodge 1226, K. of H., and the Boston Veterans.

PATRICK KEVAN (Fig. 15) was born in Ireland. He joined this company June 27, 1875, as a call-ladderman.

GEORGE C. HANES (Fig. 16) was born in Northfield, Minn., October 23, 1860. He came to this city during 1880, and worked at his trade, that of clock-making. On February 7, 1881, he entered this department as a call-substitute in this company, and on November 8, 1882, was appointed a call-member. Mr. Hanes is a member of Millmont Assembly 68 of R. S. G. F. and Washington Lodge of Masons.

W. F. DAVIS (Fig. 17) was born in Turner, Me., November 21, 1864, and came to this city March 1, 1882. He joined this company June 10, 1883, as a call-substitute.

DAVID W. MORSE (Fig. 18) was born in Boston, Mass., July 21, 1859. He is employed in mercantile business, and on July 21, 1885, entered this department as a call-substitute in this company, and on February 1, 1887, was granted call-man's pay on account of injuries. Mr. Morse had his collar-bone broken and head fractured at a fire in a box factory on Farnum street, February 1, 1888, by a falling brick wall, from which he lay six weeks in a most critical condition.

CHARLES A. HINCKLEY (Fig. 19) was born in Nantucket, Mass., May 26, 1854, and when quite young came to this city. He is a clock-maker by trade. August, 1877, he entered this department as a call-substitute. and on January 15, 1878, was appointed a call-member in this company. Mr. Hinckley is a member of De Soto Lodge No. 21, Knights of Pythias, Uniform Rank K. of P., Millmont Assembly 68, R. S. G. F., and the Patriotic Order Sons of America. By mistake this gentleman's portrait appears in Fig. 11.

BELLVILLE L. RANDALL, call-ladderman, was born in Monmouth, Me., July 17, 1837. He came to this city December 1, 1861, and learned the car-building trade. He entered this department August 21, 1862, as a call-member of this company. Mr. Randall was seriously injured by falling from a Bangor ladder while exercising. He is a member of I. O. O. F. and Encampment, the Knights of Pythias, and the Chevaliers of Pythias.

LADDER COMPANY NO. 7.

NAMES OF MEMBERS SINCE 1874.

John Murphy, ap. January 23, 1888, tr. April 15, 1888; H. Buck, driver, ap. 1874, resigned 1884: E. H. Whitney, driver, no record, tr. August 26, 1887; J. Garrot, no record; G. W. Elms, ap. June 9, 1874, resigned September 1, 1884; R. N. Elms, ap. June 9, 1874, resigned September 1, 1884; J. Curtis, no record; L. Murdock, ap. September 9, 1884, tr. to Engine Company No. 22, July 1, 1886: F. P. Loker, ap. November 2, 1885, tr. to Engine Company No. 17, March 1, 1886; J. D. Coffey, ap. August 16, 1885, resigned August 24, 1885; C. W. King, ap. March 28, 1883, resigned July 29, 1885; T. J. Gill, ap. March 1, 1886, resigned September 2, 1887; G. F. Oliver, no record, resigned January 22, 1883; J. W. Bird, ap. October 21, 1877, resigned January 1, 1878; W. H. Gordon, ap. October 21. 1877, resigned October 1, 1883.

PRESENT MEMBERS.

Captain LEWIS P. BIRD (Fig. 1) was born in Dorchester District, Boston, Mass., May 25, 1833, and when eighteen years of age joined Protective Engine Company No. 2 as a torch-boy. Three years later he was appointed a member, and in 1853 was elected clerk. During 1862 he was elected steward and then foreman of the company. On the reorganization he was transferred to this company as second foreman, which position he held until March, 1881, when he was promoted to his present position. Captain Bird has been carrying on a provision business for a number of years. He is a member of Union Lodge of Masons and the Boston Veterans.

FERDINAND WILLIAM WEBBER (Fig. 2), driver. is a Boston boy, being born in Roxbury District, January 31, 1856. After leaving school he learned the machinist trade, and in February, 1877, entered this department as a

LADDER COMPANY NO. 7. — Page 646.

call-substitute in Engine Company No. 14, and January 4, 1878, was made a call-man. July 31, 1880, he was appointed a permanent member and assigned as driver of Hose Company No. 7. June 26, 1887, he was transferred back to Engine Company No. 14. While driver of the hose-carriage, July, 1887, on the way to Box 232, Engineman Perry of that company was thrown from the engine in front of his horse; but Mr. Webber was equal to the emergency, and by a quick movement pulled his horse to one side with such force as to throw him off his feet, which undoubtedly saved the life of Mr. Perry. Mr. Webber was highly complimented by the board for his presence of mind and judgment. On August 26, 1887, he was transferred to this company as driver. He is a member of the Boston Veterans.

JOSEPH H. KENNEY (Fig. 3) was born in Boston, Mass., September 25, 1858. He was a teamster by occupation, and was appointed a permanent substitute November 23, 1888, and detailed to this company.

WILLIAM LANDELLS (Fig. 4) was born in Bathurst, N.B., August 24, 1847. He came to this city during 1867, and learned the carpenter's trade. He entered this service as a call-substitute in this company during the fall of 1879, and on February 9, 1881, was appointed a call-member. Mr. Landells is a member of the Boston Veterans.

WILLIAM L. MOULTON (Fig. 5) was born in Dorchester District, Boston, Mass., January 1, 1837, where he is employed as a carpenter. During the Rebellion he served in Company E, Twenty-Second Massachusetts Infantry, from 1861 to 1862. He joined Protector Engine Company No. 2 during 1855, in which he served three years, when he resigned, but joined this company about twenty years ago. Mr. Moulton is a member of Post 68, G. A. R.

RUSTES GORDON (Fig. 6) was born in Rockland, Me., November 5, 1845. He came to Boston during 1858, and engaged in the express business. During 1863 he joined Protector Engine Company No. 2. January 1, 1870, it was changed to Engine Company No. 17, and on May 1, 1872, he was appointed a permanent member and detailed as driver of hose-carriage. April 28. 1874, he resigned and became a call-member in this company. Mr. Gordon is a member of Union Lodge and St. Stephen's Royal Arch Chapter of Masons, Norfolk Lodge 48 and Siloam Encampment No. 12, I. O. O. F., also Boston Veterans.

JASON GORDON (Fig. 7) was born in Dorchester District, Boston, Mass., June 17, 1849. He is engaged in the florist business. During 1863 he joined Protection Engine Company No. 2. When that company was changed he was appointed permanent driver of Ladder Company No. 7, in which he remained until 1874, at which time he resigned and became a call-member of this company.

JOHN I. GURNEY (Fig. 8) was born in St. Johnsbury, Vt., October 26, 1853. He came to this city during the fall of 1873, and engaged in the florist business. In 1881 he joined this force in this company as a call-substitute, and during the fall of 1883 was enrolled a call-member.

EDMOND FRUEAN (Fig. 9) first saw the light in Dorchester District. Boston, Mass., October 10, 1844. He joined this company during 1860, as a call-member. Mr. Fruean is a member of Dorchester Lodge 541, K. of H.

GEORGE W. WOODWORTH (Fig. 10) was born in Cornwallis. N.S., October 18, 1858. He came to Boston when but a child. He is a provision dealer. He enlisted in this department in November, 1881, as a call-substitute in this company, and during May 23, 1882, was appointed a call-man. Mr. Woodworth was badly injured at a fire at Neponset during 1881. He is a member of Washington Council No. 10. Royal Arcanum, and Upham Assembly. R. S. of Good Fellows.

EDWARD M. FEENEY (Fig. 11) was born in Dorchester District, Boston, Mass., April 17, 1866. He is a furniture-polisher by trade. October 15, 1886, he joined this company as a call-member.

ALLEN J. McDONALD (Fig. 12) was born in Cape Breton, N.S.. March 20, 1864. He came to this city during 1882, and worked at the house-painter's trade. June, 1886, he entered this department as a call-substitute in this company, and on December 30, 1887, was made a call-member.

CHEMICAL ENGINE COMPANY NO. 5.

NAMES OF MEMBERS SINCE 1874.

Permanent hoseman, William H. Gay, ap. 1874; call-hosemen: J. Murray, ap. December 10, 1874; J. R. Waterman, ap. 1874: G. W. Stevens, ap. October 21, 1878, resigned May 31, 1879; George G. Byron, ap. August 20. 1881, resigned December 20, 1881, reappointed July 9. 1884, resigned October 8, 1884; W. W. Ellis. ap. May 21. 1882, resigned July 7, 1883; H. F. Perkins, ap. June 9. 1882. resigned May 7, 1887; A. A. Jordan. ap. July 7, 1883. resigned March 14, 1884: G. Reis. ap. September 17. 1886, tr. to Ladder Company No. 12, February 3. 1888.

PRESENT MEMBERS.

Engineman JOHN T. BYRON (Fig. 1) was born in Roxbury District. Boston, Mass., December 5. 1859. He is a leather currier by trade. December 24, 1879. he joined this company as a call-member, in which position he remained until August 4. 1881, when he was appointed a substitute, and on April 1. 1882. was promoted a permanent member and assigned to Ladder Company No. 3, and on the 21st of that month was transferred to Engine Company No. 4. June 10 he was detailed as driver of the water-tower. in which he remained until October 8, 1886, when he was transferred to this company in charge. Mr. Byron is a member of Egleston Council No. 42 of the American Legion of Honor.

CHARLES E. WILSON (Fig. 2), driver, was born in Boston, Mass., March 13. 1842. He was a teamster by occupation. He enlisted in the Eleventh Massachusetts Battery. in August, 1863. and served until May, 1864. and on

CHEMICAL ENGINE COMPANY No. 5. — Page 649.

December 1, 1865, joined this department in Hose Company No. 3 — now No. 8 — as a member. During September he was transferred to Engine Company No. 6, and April 1, 1871, was appointed a permanent member, and detailed as messenger and driver for ex-Chief Damrell. He was transferred soon after as driver of Extinguisher No. 1, and in February, 1873, was transferred as driver of Chemical Engine Company No. 1. June 1, 1880, he was transferred to this company. Mr. Wilson had his leg broken by a kick from a horse while at the last annual parade, September 18, 1872, and on Christmas-day 1887, had his arm broken by falling down stairs while at a fire in Blossom street. He is a member of Suffolk Council No. 60, Royal Arcanum.

EDWIN AMSDEN (Fig. 3) was born in Boston, Mass., March 22, 1864. He is a clerk by occupation, and on March 28, 1885, was appointed a call-member of this company. Mr. Amsden is a member of Battery A, M.V.M.

CHAPTER XIV.

DISTRICT NO. 10. — DORCHESTER AND WEST ROXBURY.

UNTIL 1793 Dorchester was a part of Suffolk County, and thus practically joined to Boston in all judicial matters; but more than fifty years before this time an agitation was begun for a separation from Boston, the complaint being made that the people who had business at the courts in the city were long detained, to the great expense of time and money. The town therefore voted, in 1743, that it was desirous that the country town-meeting be separated from Boston and erected into a district and county by itself. In 1784 this vote was reaffirmed. When the separation was finally made, in 1793, the citizens presented a memorial to the Legislature protesting against the division of the County of Suffolk, and praying that Dorchester might be annexed thereto. The town began to be encircled by the arms of Boston during 1803, when Dorchester Neck, now known as South Boston, was taken. We say taken, for the bill for annexation was passed by the Legislature, despite the opposition vote of the inhabitants against the measure, March 6, 1804.

In 1836 the inhabitants of Little Neck (Washington Village) petitioned to be joined to Boston. The town of Dorchester opposed the annexation, and the committee of the General Court reported against it; but the matter was only delayed, for Washington Village was formally annexed to Boston, May 21, 1855. Roxbury was the next to succumb, during 1868. In 1867 the subject of annexing Dorchester was more or less agitated by the citizens themselves, who brought the matter before the Boston city government, and secured the appointment of a board of commission, to confer with commissioners appointed by the town. No immediate action followed, but a year later the matter was taken up, this time from the Boston side; and by order of the City Council, passed December 22, 1868, the Mayor was requested to appoint a commission of three discreet and intelligent persons, carefully to examine the subject. The result of this examination was a unanimous report for annexation. In May, 1869, the subject came up before the Legislature. The Mayor and City Council urged the annexation. An act was passed by the Legislature annexing the town, provided that a majority of legal voters in Boston and in Dorchester were in favor of it. A special election was held simultaneously in both places, on June 22, 1869. There were 928 votes for the project and 726 against. The annexation took place on the first Monday in January (4th), 1870.

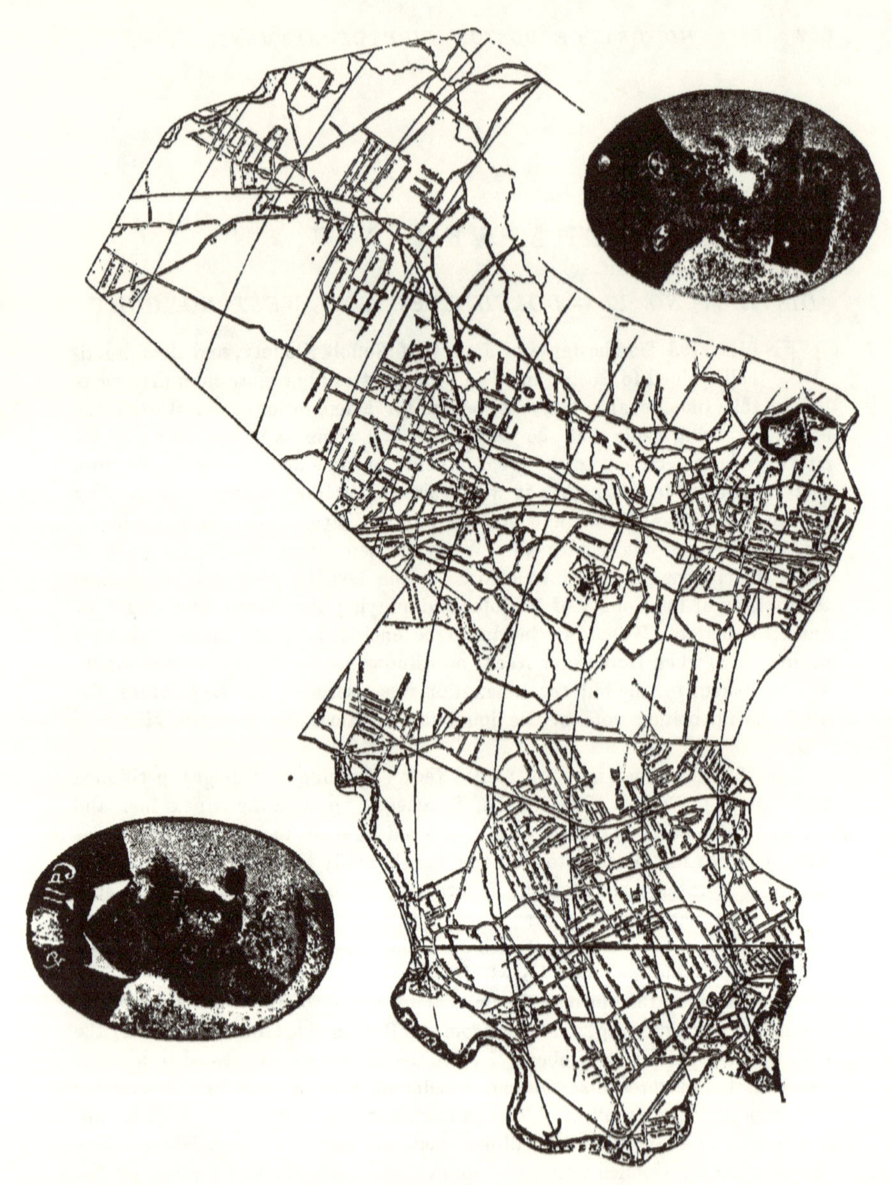

By this act the area of Boston, which, with the annexation of Roxbury, amounted to 5,370 acres, was nearly doubled, — Dorchester adding 4,532 acres. If we add the area which Boston acquired by annexing South Boston and Washington Village, — 908 acres, — the total acreage she obtained from Dorchester was 5,432. West Roxbury followed the example of her older sister, January 5, 1874, which added a territory embracing an area of 7,848 square acres, with a population aggregating 9,000 people.

Four large factories are in operation in this district, the most noticeable being the chocolate mills, and several paper mills. The whole territory being devoted, and will continue to be so for years to come, as a residential section for those who do business in the city proper. Regarding the fire department of the early days we have no data at hand to enable us to write an accurate account; we know, however, that the old " fire laddies " of this place were equally zealous and enterprising as those of the neighboring towns, and kept pace with the improvements in apparatus, — at the time of annexation there being one steam fire-engine and several hand-engines, besides ladder-trucks and hose-carriages. (See under date 1873, this volume.)

The district is bounded as follows: All the southerly part of Boston south of districts 8 and 9, including West Roxbury. The apparatus in the district are Engines Nos. 16, 18, 19, 20, 28, 30; Ladders Nos. 6, 10, and 16; and Chemical No. 4. The headquarters for the district chief is at the house of Engine Co. No. 18.

District Chief J. Foster Hewins was born in Dorchester District, Boston, Mass., April 5, 1838. After leaving school he was employed in the grocery business. He first did fire duty when but seventeen years of age, as a member of the volunteer company attached to Torrent Engine No. 3, where he remained until it was disbanded. He enlisted in 1862 in Company I, Forty-Second Massachusetts Regiment, as sergeant, and served nine months, and was taken prisoner at Galveston, January 1, 1863. On his return he organized a volunteer company, of which he was made captain, which was in service until steam was introduced, when he was appointed foreman of Torrent Engine Company No. 18, which position he held until April 7, 1874, when he was promoted to his present office. Chief Hewins is assisted by Call-Chief J. F. Rogers.

Call District Chief James F. Rogers will be recognized on page 653. He first saw the light, July 20, 1832, in Langdon, N.H. In April, 1851, he came to this city and entered into mercantile business. During the late war he served in Company E, Fifth New Hampshire Volunteers, from November, 1861, to October, 1862, during which time he was wounded at Fair Oaks. Ten years after his discharge he was appointed chief engineer for the town of West Roxbury. During 1873 he retired, and remained out of the service until January 20, 1875, at which time he was appointed to his present position. Chief Rogers is a member and P. G. of Quinobequin Lodge 74,

I. O. O. F., and Eliott Lodge of Masons. He is engaged as superintendent of the Jamaica Plain Gas-Light Company.

ENGINE COMPANY NO. 16.
NAMES OF MEMBERS SINCE 1874.

Samuel O. Hebard, driver, ap. October, 1869, resigned August 24, 1887; Eugene H. Freeman, engineman, ap. October, 1869, resigned March 31, 1877; Charles F. Hall, assistant engineman, resigned; William Shields, assistant engineman and hoseman from 1869 to 1887; William W. Carsley, foreman, ap. 1869, resigned December 6, 1882; Horace N. Plummer, ap. 1869, resigned 1876; Jacob H. Taylor, ap. 1869, resigned 1871; David S. Black, tr. to Ladder Company No. 6; Thomas Strangman, resigned in 1872; David J. O'Connell, engineman, ap. April, 1877, tr. May 1, 1880, to Engine Company No. 28.

PRESENT MEMBERS.

Captain EDWIN R. MERRILL (Fig. 1) was born in Concord, N.H., August 11, 1841. He came to this city during 1863, and was employed as a teamster. December 1, 1872, he was assigned to this company as permanent driver of hose-carriage. He was only fourteen months in that position when he was promoted to captain.

Engineman RUFUS L. MASON (Fig. 2) was born in Northampton, N.H., May 3, 1838. During 1855 he joined Mascoma Engine Company No. 2, at Lebanon, N.H., in which he worked until 1858. He came to this city the following year, and worked at the machinist's trade, and during January, 1870, began running as a call-substitute in this department. In May, 1871, he was appointed a call-man in this company, and on April 15, 1876, was promoted to assistant engineman and transferred to Engine Company No. 28, and did the duties of engineman until May 1, 1880, when he was promoted to his present position and transferred back to this company, the transfer being at his own request. Mr. Mason is a member of Dorchester Lodge 158 of I. O. O. F.

Assistant Engineman THOMAS A. ANDREWS, Jr. (Fig. 3), is a Boston boy, being born in this city, February 20, 1851. He is a machinist by trade, and during the spring of 1872 joined Howard Engine Company No. 1, of Charlestown District. November 13, 1879, he was transferred as call-man in Ladder Company No. 9, and resigned to accept the position of a substitute engineman. On May 25, 1881, he was promoted assistant engineman and assigned to Engine Company No. 26, from which he was transferred, January 31, 1881, to this company. Mr. Andrews is a member of the American Order United Workmen and the Charlestown Veterans.

SAMUEL DANA HARRINGTON (Fig. 4), driver, was born in Westboro', Mass., September 30, 1834. He came to this city when but a child, where

Engine Company No. 16. — Page 658.

he began life as a piano-polisher, and during August, 1857, he joined Hose Company No. 2, then located on Hudson street. He remained in it until 1859, and in March, 1862, he joined Engine Company No. 3. He enlisted, in July, 1862, in Company C, First Heavy Artillery, in which he served until 1864. On his return he rejoined Engine Company No. 3. May, 1874, he was transferred to Engine Company No. 26 as captain, and in October of the same year was transferred to Engine Company No. 3 as hoseman. September 16, 1887, he was transferred to this company in his present position. Mr. Harrington is a member of Mount Lebanon Lodge of Masons.

JOHN HUTCHINSON (Fig. 5) was born in Dorchester District, Boston, Mass., May 17, 1842. He is a wood-moulder by trade. He enlisted in Battery A, First Light Battery, September 5, 1861, and served until October 3, 1864. He joined Fountain Engine Company No. 1 during the spring of 1865, and remained there until January 1, 1870, when he joined this company. He is a member of Norfolk Lodge No. 48, I. O. O. F., and Post 68, G. A. R.

JEDEDIAH STRANGMAN (Fig. 6) first saw the light in Prince Edward Island, August 29, 1839. He went to Newburyport, Mass., when but a child, and on January 2, 1854, came to this city and worked at his trade, harness-making. He enlisted on May 25, 1861, in Company E, First Massachusetts Infantry, and served three years. He joined Fountain Engine Association during 1857. After his return he joined Fountain Engine Company No. 1, and January 1, 1870, became a member of this company. Mr. Strangman is a member of Post 102, G. A. R., the R. S. G. F., Uncataquisset Tribe of Red Men, Dorchester Lodge of I. O. O. F., Ellison Encampment, and the Firemen's Charitable Association.

MINOT B. THAYER (Fig. 7) was born in Milton, Mass., June 23, 1839. He entered this department in Hose Company No. 1, of Dorchester, as a call-man, during 1868. January 1, 1870, he joined this company. Mr. Thayer is employed as a janitor.

JOHN BAWMEISTER (Fig. 8) was born in Boston, Mass., December 13, 1846. He enlisted in Company A, Fifth Regiment, on July 12, 1864, and served until November, 1864. He then returned, and worked at his trade, that of cabinet-making, and entered this department in the spring of 1865, in Fountain Engine Company No. 1. January 1, 1870, he joined this company. Mr. Bawmeister is a member of Norfolk Lodge No. 40 of I. O. O. F.

WILLIAM SCHREIDER (Fig. 9) was born in Milton, Mass., February 3, 1848. He enlisted in Company F, Fifty-Sixth Infantry, on November 24, 1863, and served until June 6, 1865. On his return he learned the cabinet-maker's trade, and during the fall of 1865 joined Fountain Engine Company No. 1 as a volunteer. He joined this company, as a call-member, June 6, 1874. Mr. Schreider is a member of Post 68 of G. A. R.

AUGUSTUS NICKERSON (Fig. 10) was born in Brewster, Mass., November 5, 1846. He came to this city when eighteen years of age, and learned the cabinet-maker's trade. He was appointed a call-man in Engine Company No.

17, during 1869, and served until 1871, when he left the department, but returned in Engine Company No. 17, during August, 1874, and joined this company April, 1876. Mr. Nickerson is a member of Dorchester Lodge No. 158, I. O. O. F., and Temple Lodge No. 9 of American Order of United Workmen.

SYLVESTER H. HEBARD, Jr. (Fig. 11), was born in Dorchester District, Boston, Mass., February 9, 1845. He enlisted in Company I, Forty-Second Regiment, in 1864, and served one hundred days. On his return he worked at the express business, and during 1876 joined this company as a call-substitute, and six months later was appointed a call-member.

LEBEUS G. SMITH (Fig. 12) was born in Dorchester District, Boston, Mass., October 31, 1856. After leaving school he learned the cabinet-maker's trade, and on December 21, 1882, entered this department as a call-member of this company.

ENGINE COMPANY NO. 18.

NAMES OF MEMBERS SINCE 1874.

Lewis Briggs, tr. to Engine Company No. 20, May, 1880, died January 5, 1882 ; Henry W. Bauch, ap. July 21, 1882, tr. to Engine Company No. 25, February 25, 1886 ; Charles R. Classon, resigned June 6, 1874 ; John Connell, ap. June 6, 1874, tr. to repair-shop May 11, 1875 ; Timothy Donahoe, resigned, by limit of age, November 11, 1887 ; Henry Fobes, resigned, limit of age, November 11, 1887 ; Samuel Gleason, ap. June 6, 1874, resigned March 20, 1877 ; Maurice Hallihan, resigned April 19, 1877 ; William J. Hickey, ap. November 9, 1884, promoted permanent member and tr. to Ladder Company No. 3, July 29, 1887 ; H. J. McNabb, ap. August 1, 1874, resigned July 21 1882 ; Edward Moffatt, ap. July 1, 1877, resigned November 7, 1882 ; John E. Munn, ap. May 16, 1886, resigned September 21, 1888 ; W. A. Pickard, ap. November 8, 1882, tr. to Engine Company No. 3, February 16, 1888 ; J. J. Riley, ap. September 13, 1888, tr. to Engine Company No. 15.

PRESENT MEMBERS.

Captain JOHN COLLIGAN (Fig. 1) was born in Watertown, Mass., December 20, 1827. He came to this city when but a child and began life as a carpenter. During 1842 he became connected with the Roxbury department, joining Torrent Engine Company No. 6. In 1874 he was elected a regular member, and the following year assistant foreman ; a year later he was chosen foreman. He nominally resigned during 1852, but did active duty when called upon, and returned again in 1857, and was elected assistant engineer of the Roxbury department, which position he held through its various changes. September 8, 1884, he was assigned captain of this company. He was injured March 17, 1880, in Roxbury, and again at Temple-place fire, December 23, 1872. He is a charter member of the United Workmen and the Royal Arcanum.

Engine Company No. 18. — Page 662.

Engineman FRED H. BRONSDON (Fig. 2) first saw the light in Milton, Mass., June 23, 1838. He began life as a machinist, and on August 26, 1862, enlisted in Company H, Thirty-Ninth Regiment, in which he served until he was wounded in the ankle, at Hatches' Run, February 6, 1865 ; discharged May 26. May, 1857, he became a member of Independence Engine Company No. 5, of Neponset, in which he served until Engine Company No. 20 was put in commission, May 15, 1875 ; he was promoted assistant engineman and assigned to that company. May 20, 1880, he was promoted to his present position.

Assistant Engineman DAVID RIPLEY (Fig. 3) was born in Hingham, Mass., April 30, 1830. He came to this city during 1848 and learned the britannia business, and in May, 1849, joined Torrent Engine Company No. 3, of Dorchester, as a member. He was elected steward during 1850, and held that position until 1860, when he left the city, but returned one year later, and on April 1, 1871, was promoted to his present position. Mr. Ripley is a member of Norfolk Lodge, I. O. O. F., Siloam Encampment, Boston Council, K. of H., and Boston Veterans.

WILLIAM H. COOPER (Fig. 4), driver, was born in Boston, Mass., August 26, 1847. He was employed as a teamster. During 1865 he joined Torrent Engine Company No. 3, of Dorchester District. December 25, 1869, he was transferred to this company as a permanent driver.

GEORGE L. PITMAN (Fig. 5) was born in Boston, Mass., November 28, 1840. He is engaged in the provision business. He enlisted in Company I, Forty-Second Massachusetts Regiment, in August, 1862, and served until August 20, 1863. During 1855 he entered this department as a torch-boy in Torrent Engine Company No. 3, of Dorchester, in which he remained until annexation, when he came to this company as a call-member. Mr. Pitman was severely injured at the fire at Thayer's house. He is a member of Norfolk Lodge No. 48, and Siloam Encampment No. 12, I. O. O. F., and Benjamin Stone, Jr., Post 68, G. A. R.

JAMES F. MCINTOSH (Fig. 6) was appointed a call-member of this company July 1, 1877.

PETER F. CONNORS (Fig. 7) was born in Roxbury District, Boston, Mass., March 11, 1865. He is employed as a teamster, and on October 2, 1888, was appointed a call-member of this company.

PETER WHITE (Fig. 8) was born in County Roscommon, Ireland, August 13, 1861, and came to this city on May 16, 1879, where he engaged in the periodical business. He was appointed a call-member of this company November 14, 1888.

WALTER H. MIXER (Fig. 9) was appointed a call-man in this company April 11, 1889.

ENGINE COMPANY NO. 19.

NAMES OF MEMBERS SINCE 1874.

P. M. Crotty, assistant engineman, ap. June 7, 1874, tr. to Engine No. 21; George H. Bird, ap. June 7, 1874, resigned October 15, 1887; H. B. Tucker, ap. June 7, 1874, resigned May 10, 1889; E. D. Towner, ap. June 7, 1874, died June 7, 1878; Joseph Abenzeller, ap. June 7, 1874, resigned January 8, 1875; William Walker, ap. June 7, 1874, resigned; George L. Burt, ap. June 7, 1874, resigned; C. E. Stevenson, ap. June 7, 1874, resigned; I. A. Williams, ap. June 7, 1874, tr. to Engine No. 23; Warren Berry, no record; Joseph Apperceller, no record; George H. Bird, ap. June 7, 1874, resigned, 1887; William Hart, assistant engineman, no record.

PRESENT MEMBERS.

Captain GEORGE F. FENNO (Fig. 1) was born in Wrentham, Mass., December 14, 1834. He came to this city when but a child, and soon after learned the carriage-making trade. While a boy he began running with Alert Engine No. 4, and when eighteen years of age became a member of that company. He was a suction-hoseman the first year; in the second he was elected foreman of the leading-hose, and after that, second foreman of the company; shortly after was appointed steward, and two years later was elected foreman. He enlisted in the Second Company, Andrew Sharpshooters, October 20, 1861, and remained three years. On his return he joined his former company, and during 1868 was promoted assistant engineer of District No. 4, of West Roxbury, which he held until annexation, and in May of the same year he was enrolled as a call-member of this company, and promoted call-foreman, May 1, 1872. November 16, 1884, he was promoted permanent captain. Captain Fenno was thrown from the hose-cart while going to Box 353, on July 28, 1888, and struck on his head, which badly injured his left eye. He is a member of Norfolk Lodge, I. O. O. F., Siloam Encampment, Hyde Park Lodge No. 537, K. of H., and the Massachusetts Firemen's Association.

Engineman EZRA B. HEBARD (Fig. 2) was born in Mattapan District, Boston, Mass., August 22, 1836. After leaving school he learned the mechanical engineer's trade. When eighteen years of age he joined Alert Engine No. 4, in which he served until 1861. He enlisted in January, 1862, on board frigate "San Jacinto," and was discharged seventeen months later, for sickness. On his return he was employed in the tow-boat service, and entered this department again December 27, 1870, and one week later was promoted engineman and assigned to this company. Mr. Hebard is a member of Winnisipet Lodge No. 24, I. O. O. F., and Equity Council No. 50, Knights of Honor.

Assistant Engineman EDWARD R. STERN (Fig. 3) was born in Boston, December 17, 1861. After leaving school he learned the machinist's trade.

ENGINE COMPANY No. 19. — Page 666.

February, 1882, he was appointed a call-substitute in this company, and December 26, 1883, was appointed a permanent substitute and detailed on special duty. November 16, 1884, he was made a permanent hoseman, and two years later was promoted to his present position. While at the Lewis fire, September, 1887, he fell and hurt his wrist.

LUTHER M. KNOX (Fig. 4), driver, was born in Leventon, Me., January 28, 1829. During his youth he joined the department at Dover, N.H., as a member of Protector Engine Company No. 2. He came to this city about thirty years ago, and worked at the shoemaker's trade, and soon after joined Alert Engine Company, in which he was promoted to foreman of the leading-hose. On the reorganization he was appointed a permanent member and detailed as driver of this engine. Mr. Knox was severely injured, during 1878, while exercising the horses.

HENRY B. TUCKER (Fig. 5), senior call-hoseman, was born in Dorchester District, Boston, Mass., December 30, 1846. He is a blacksmith by trade, and during 1864 he joined Alert Engine Company No. 4 as a member, and was shortly after elected a member on section-hose. On annexation he was appointed a call-hoseman.

JONATHAN BAKER (Fig. 6) was born in Yarmouth, N.S., October 26, 1837. He came to Boston during 1857 and learned the carpenter's trade, and during 1858 joined Torrent Engine Company No. 3, and on annexation became a member of this company. He enlisted during September, 1862, in Company I, Forty-Second Massachusetts Regiment, in which he served eleven months. He is a member of the American Legion of Honor.

JOHN D. SCANNELL (Fig. 7) was born in Cork, Ireland, March 18, 1845. He came to this city during 1866 and learned the blacksmith's trade, and soon after entered this department as a member of Alert Engine Company No. 4. He enlisted in Company I, First Massachusetts Militia, during 1862, and served two years. Mr. Scannell was badly injured by the spike of the ladder.

JAMES A. HERSEY (Fig. 8) first saw the light in Dorchester District, Boston, Mass., October 26, 1843. During the fall of 1862 he enlisted in Company B, Forty-Fifth Massachusetts Regiment, and served until July, 1863. On his return he worked at his trade, that of a blacksmith, and on June, 1874, joined Alert Engine Company No. 4. Mr. Hersey is a member of American Legion of Honor, Hyde Park Lodge 437, K. of H., and Norfolk Lodge 48 of I. O. O. F.

NICHOLAS BURCKHART (Fig. 9) was born in Germany, November 10, 1846, and during April, 1855, came to this city and worked at the starch-making business. During 1866 he joined Alert Engine Company No. 4. On annexation he left the service, but came back two years later and worked as a call-substitute six years, when he was made a call-member. He is a member of Equity Council 50, American L. of H.

L. A. WITHINGTON (Fig. 10) was born in Dorchester District, Boston,

Mass., February 27, 1853. He became connected with this company February, 1885, and is a member of American L. of H. and Red Men.

ENGINE COMPANY NO. 20.

NAMES OF MEMBERS SINCE 1874.

Fred H. Bronsdon, reap. June 8, 1884, tr. to Engine Company No. 18, May 20, 1880; Warren R. Smith, ap. February 6, 1882, tr. to Engine Company No. 15, February 1, 1886; G. W. Simpson, reap. June 8, 1884, resigned; W. O. Swan, reap. June 8, 1884, resigned; G. G. Dennison, reap. June 8, 1884, resigned May 21, 1882; Stephen Moulton, reap. June 8, 1884, resigned December 21, 1880; Edwin F. Field, reap. June 8, 1884, resigned February 4, 1887; George W. Richardson, reap. June 8, 1884, resigned October 1, 1888; Lewis Briggs, ap. May 20, 1880, died January 15, 1882.

PRESENT MEMBERS.

Captain WILLIAM G. BLANCHARD (Fig. 1) was born in Dorchester District, Boston, Mass., January 10, 1838. He entered this department May 19, 1855, as a member of Independence Engine Company No. 5, and in 1860 left the service, but returned again on October 6, 1862. February 6, 1865, he was elected call-foreman, and on May 6, 1867, was appointed clerk. May 4, 1868, he was chosen clerk and treasurer, and was made senior hoseman of Engine Company No. 20, April 24, 1875, and call-foreman May, 1882, and on November 16, 1884, was promoted to his present position. Captain Blanchard was in the carpenter business for a number of years. He is a member of Neponset Lodge 84 of I. O. O. F., Firemen's Charitable Association, and the Home Circle.

Engineman FRANKLIN MUZZY (Fig. 2) was born in Gardner, Me., April 2, 1828. When 18 years of age he became a member of Fire King Engine Company No. 3, of that town, and five years later came to this city and worked at the machinist's trade. He entered the service October 6, 1862, in Independence Engine Company No. 5, of Dorchester, as a member. On annexation he was promoted to his present position. Mr. Muzzy was run over by the hose-carriage, which seriously hurt his arm; he was also badly hurt on the back by being thrown from the engine against the curbstone. He is a member of Boston Lodge 134, K. of H., Neighborly Club of Neponset, and the Firemen's Charitable Association.

Assistant Engineman CHARLES H. SMITH (Fig. 3) was born in Portsmouth, N.H., April 4, 1844, and came to this city when but a child. After leaving school he learned the machinist's trade. He enlisted in Company E, Sixteenth Massachusetts Regiment, on July 12, 1861, and served three years; and on April 13, 1871, entered this department as a call-member of Engine Company No. 15, and on July 21, 1874, was promoted to the position of as-

ENGINE COMPANY No. 20. — Page 670.

sistant engineman. February 1, 1886, he was transferred to this company. Mr. Smith was one of the unfortunates at the Sammet mattress factory fire, where he was crushed by falling walls, which broke his left leg and severely injured his head and back. He is a member of Post 34, G. A. R., and Boston Veterans.

GEORGE R. TARBELL, driver, entered this department March 21, 1874, as a member of Engine Company No. 2, and on May 10, 1882, was transferred to Engine Company No. 4, from which he was transferred to this company, January 16, 1886.

FRANKLIN C. P. EMERY (Fig. 4), senior call-hoseman, was born in Rockland, Me., June 20, 1842, and came to this city when very young. He is a house-painter by trade. He enlisted in Company I, Forty-Fourth Massachusetts Regiment, and served nine months, after which he became a member of Independence Engine Company No. 5, and soon after was enrolled a member of this company. Mr. Emery is a member of Union Lodge Masons, Neponset Lodge No. 84, I. O. O. F., Boston Lodge No. 134, K. of H., Post 68, G. A. R., Boston Veterans, and Firemen's Charitable Association.

WILLIAM R. PILLSBURY (Fig. 5) first saw the light in Dorchester District, Boston, Mass., July 27, 1839. He is a carpenter by trade. During 1857 he became a member of Salamander Engine Company No. 2, of West Roxbury, and on February 2, 1863, joined Independence Engine Company No. 5, of Dorchester, and upon annexation was made a member of this company. December 13, 1871, he was elected secretary and treasurer, and continued so until the creation of the Board of Fire Commissioners, when this office was abolished. Mr. Pillsbury is a member of Boston Lodge No. 134, K. of H., Neponset Lodge No. 84, I. O. O. F., and the Firemen's Charitable Association.

GEORGE W. BERRY (Fig. 6) was born in Kittery, Me., December 14, 1836, and when a boy came to this city. When thirteen years of age he acted as torch-boy in Protector Engine Company No. 2, and later on was promoted foreman of leading-hose of Independence Engine Company No. 5, of Neponset, and during 1871 was elected a call-substitute in this company. On the reorganization he was appointed a call-member. Mr. Berry had the cord of his right hand severed, by which he has lost the use of his second finger, at a fire on Richmond street. He is a blacksmith by trade.

GEORGE S. BLAISDELL (Fig. 7) was born in Quincy, Mass., January 12, 1845. He first began fire duty in that town when young, joining Tiger Engine Company No. 2, and remained until 1861, when he moved to this city, and in 1867 joined an engine company of Dorchester. He joined this company, as a call-substitute, some time after, and December 21, 1880, was appointed a call-member.

JOSEPH H. HOYT (Fig. 8) is a Boston boy, being born in Dorchester District, Boston, Mass., February 4, 1848. During 1877 he joined Independence Engine Company No. 5, as a member, and on the reorganization he was made a call-substitute, but was appointed a call-man on May 20, 1882. Mr. Hoyt has been in the provision business for a number of years, and is a member of Neponset Lodge No. 84, I. O. O. F., Boston Lodge No. 134, K. of H., the Neighborly Club of Neponset, and the Firemen's Charitable Association.

GARDNER DENNISON (Fig. 9) was born in Dorchester District, Boston, Mass., August 23, 1856. He is a house-painter by trade, and on December 28, 1880, entered this service, as a call-substitute in this company, and on October 12, 1888, was appointed a member. Mr. Dennison is a member of Soangetaha Tribe No. 21 of Red Men.

HENRY D. MURPHY (Fig. 10) was born in Dorchester District, Boston, Mass., November 5, 1860, and, after leaving school, learned the harness-making trade. He was appointed a call-substitute in this company on June 6, 1882, and on October 12, 1888, was appointed a call-man. Mr. Murphy is a member of Neponset Lodge No. 84, I. O. O. F.

ELMER H. HEATH (Fig. 11) was born in Belfast, Me., April 6, 1862. He joined the Belfast department during 1880, in Hydrant Engine Company No. 2, and remained until 1883. He came to this city during 1885, and worked at the wood-working business, and on October 12, 1888, joined this company. He is a member of Neponset Lodge No. 84, and Ellison Encampment No. 54, I. O. O. F., and Camp No. 30, Sons of Veterans, Millmont Assembly No. 68, R. S. G. F.

ENGINE COMPANY NO. 28.

NAMES OF MEMBERS SINCE 1875.

This company was reorganized January 21, 1875, with the following officers and members : —

Captain Samuel Abbott, resigned March 25, 1881 ; Engineman Charles D. Curtis, resigned April 6, 1876 ; William Condry, tr. to Engine No. 30, July 10, 1883 ; John Lynch, tr. to Ladder No. 10, June 1, 1882 ; Frank Coston, no record ; Conn. Clap, died May 8, 1875 ; Gus. Fuller, resigned December 1, 1875 ; James McDonald, died October 11, 1878 ; Robert Green, resigned December 20, 1875 ; William Gleason, tr. to Engine No. 18, June 4, 1875 ; Sewal D. Balkam, resigned June 20, 1885 ; B. M. Murry, resigned October 6, 1876 ; P. H. Henderson, ap. December 10, 1875, resigned June 10, 1877 ; E. S. Wetherbee, ap. June 12, 1875, resigned April 1, 1878 ; William P. Kerby, ap. December 20, 1875, resigned September 1, 1876 ; William H. Stevens, ap. April 4, 1876, resigned March 1, 1877 ; F. A. Hartford, ap. December 1, 1876, resigned June 10, 1886 ; John S. Handy, ap. January 21, 1877, resigned March 20, 1880 ; Joseph Goodnow, ap. January 1, 1878, resigned February 1, 1883 ; R. L. Mason, engineman, ap. April 15, 1876, tr. to Engine No. 16, May 1, 1880.

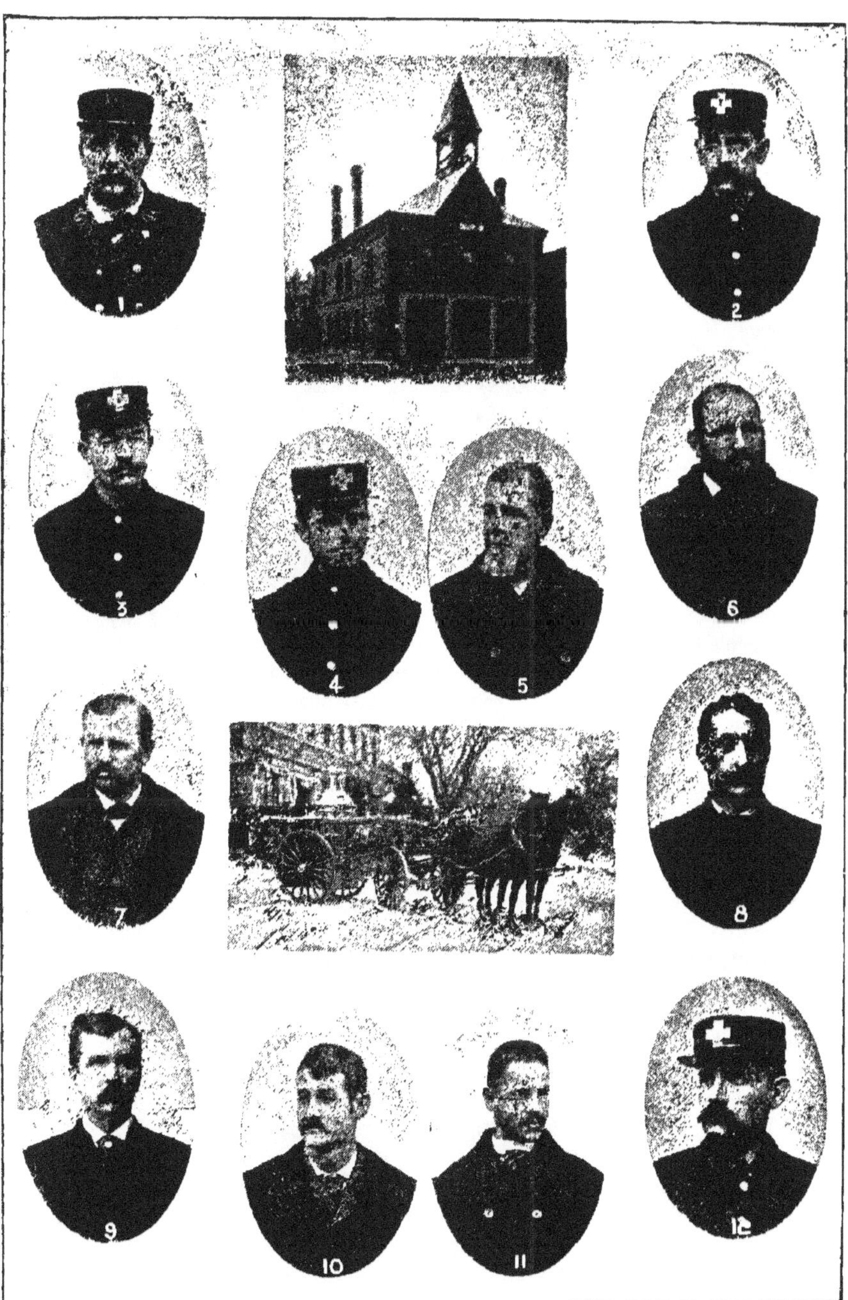

Engine Company No. 28. — Page 674.

PRESENT MEMBERS.

Captain GEORGE B. REILEY (Fig. 1) came to Boston from Portland, Me., during September, 1869, and worked at the carpenter's trade. September 21, 1874, he was admitted a member of Ladder Company No. 4, and on March 6, 1875, was transferred to Ladder Company No. 3 as a permanent man. He remained in that position until September 20, 1876, when he was promoted to the position of assistant foreman of that company. June 1, 1878, he was promoted to captain, and assigned to Engine Company No. 12, and April 4, 1881, was transferred to this company. Captain Reiley is a member of the Masonic Order.

Engineman DAVID J. O'CONNELL (Fig. 2) was born in Roxbury District, Boston, Mass., August 19, 1846. After leaving school he learned the machinist's trade, and on March 1, 1875, was appointed a permanent hoseman in Engine Company No. 26. June 21, 1875, he was promoted assistant engineman and assigned to Engine Company No. 25, and April 10, 1877, was transferred to Engine Company No. 16, and acted as engineman, from which he was promoted to his present position, May 1, 1880. Mr. O'Connell was laid up ten days in consequence of injuries received at Box 521, April 10, 1881. He is a member of Brookline Assembly No. 87, R. S. G. F., and the Firemen's Charitable Association.

Assistant Engineman CHARLES WINDHORN (Fig. 3) was born in Hanover, Germany, April 7, 1856. He came to this city about twenty years ago, and learned the machinist's trade. March 4, 1874, he joined Engine Company No. 26, and was appointed driver for ex-Chief Engineer Green. June 2, 1881, he was promoted a permanent member, and was transferred, October 16, 1882, to this company, and promoted to his present position. He was thrown from the hose-carriage while going to Box 532, on April 11, 1885, and severely injured his spine. Mr. Windhorn is a member of Boston Council No. 93 of the American Legion of Honor and the Barnicoat Association.

JOHN GLENNON (Fig. 4), driver, first saw the light in Jamaica Plain District, Boston, Mass., March 21, 1859. He began life as a teamster, and on February 25, 1883, entered this department as a substitute. July 9, 1883, he was appointed a permanent member and assigned to this company as driver of engine.

ALFRED A. BESTWICK (Fig. 5) was born in Dedham, Mass., July 19, 1834, and came to this city when a boy. He is a harness-maker and trimmer by trade. During 1865 he became a member of the Francis Head Engine Company of West Roxbury, in which he was elected foreman during 1867. The following year he left the department, and remained out until January, 1875, when he was admitted a member of this company. He enlisted, August, 1861, in Company F, Eighteenth Massachusetts Regiment, and served one year. Mr. Bestwick broke his arm, on December 23, 1885, at the Centre-street fire. He is a member of Franklin Assembly 28, R. S. G. F.

Frank G. Rhodes (Fig. 6) was born at Walpole, Mass., November 8, 1853, and came to Boston during 1869, where he learned the roofer's trade. He entered this department, January 1, 1875, as a member of this company. Mr. Rhodes had his feet frozen at a fire on Centre-street, December 20, 1885.

Nicholas Albrecht (Fig. 7) was born in Rien, Germany, January 21, 1846, and came to this city during 1865. He is a barber by trade, and during 1868 became a member of Jamaica Engine Company No. 3, and in the following year joined Ladder Company No. 1, of West Roxbury. March 20, 1880, he joined this company. Mr. Albrecht had his shoulder dislocated at a fire, March 20, 1885. He is a member of Lodge 70, I. O. O. F., and the Boston Veterans.

Eugene Ayers (Fig. 8) was appointed a call-member of this company January 1, 1874.

John B. McKay (Fig. 9) was appointed in this department, as a call-member of this company, September 10, 1887.

William T. McCormack (Fig. 10) was born in Jamaica Plain District, Boston, Mass., December 6, 1852. He is a carpenter by trade, and on March 23, 1880, entered this department as a member of this company. Mr. McCormack is a member of the Roxbury Veterans.

George Alexander (Fig. 11) was born in Boston, Mass., June 27, 1865. He is a house-painter by trade, and entered this department as a call-substitute in this company, November 16, 1887.

Thomas J. Fitzgerald (Fig. 12) was born in Concord, Mass., November 18, 1859, and came to this city when but a child, where he was employed as a teamster until his appointment on this department, as a permanent substitute, January 18, 1889.

CHEMICAL ENGINE COMPANY NO. 7.

Names of Members since September 21, 1876.

Henry Colburn, resigned March 20, 1879 ; Albert Hutchins, resigned April 30, 1881 ; Abijah Draper, resigned November 15, 1877 ; E. B. Wetherell, ap. March 2, 1880, resigned July 20, 1881 ; W. H. Hutchins, ap. May 24, 1881, resigned November 20, 1882 ; F. A. Brock, ap. April 15, 1882, resigned June 17, 1882 ; F. A. Morrill, ap. December 9, 1882, resigned April 5, 1889.

This company went out of commission July 10, 1883, the members of the company being transferred to

ENGINE COMPANY NO. 30.

John E. Shannon, Jr., ap. July 10, 1883, tr. to Engine Company No. 7, January 1, 1884.

ENGINE COMPANY No. 30. — Page 678

PRESENT MEMBERS.

Captain JAMES B. PRESCOTT (Fig. 1) was born in Newport, Me., October 8, 1836. He came to this city during 1852, and worked at the carpenter's trade. December 1, 1856, he joined Franklin Ladder Company No. 3, as a member, and during January, 1860, was promoted driver, which position he held until October, 1874, at which time he was promoted foreman. September 10, 1876, he was transferred to Chemical Company No. 7, and July 10, 1883, was transferred to his present position. Captain Prescott is a member of Siloam Lodge No. 2, I. O. O. F., and a life member of the Firemen's Charitable Association.

Engineman THOMAS NANNERY (Fig. 2) was born in Boston, Mass., May 2, 1837. He is a machinist by trade. February 22, 1864, he was appointed engineman in Engine Company No. 7. April, 1866, he was transferred to Engine Company No. 10, and on October, 1871, was promoted engineman and assigned to Engine Company No. 14. June 1, 1882, he was transferred to Engine Company No. 22, and July 10, 1883, was transferred to this company. Mr. Nannery is a member of Tremont Lodge 1480, K. of H., and C. O. Foresters.

Assistant Engineman FRANK S. BRADBURY (Fig. 3) first saw the light in Yarmouth, N.S., October 1, 1848. When nine years of age he came to this city. He is a machinist by trade. September 7, 1882, he was appointed a hoseman in Engine Company No. 22, and July 10, 1883, was promoted to his present position and assigned to this company. Mr. Bradbury is a member of Marion Lodge No. 66 of American Order United Workmen.

WILLIAM T. CONDRY (Fig. 4), driver, was born in West Roxbury District, Boston, Mass., October 24, 1851. He began life as a teamster. He was appointed driver of Francis Head Engine Company No. 1, of West Roxbury, and on reorganization was transferred to Engine Company No. 28. July 10, 1883, he was transferred to this company.

WALTER F. SPEAR (Fig. 5), senior call-hoseman, was born in Quincy, Mass., October 24, 1844. He is a carpenter by trade. September 10, 1868, he joined Salamander Engine Company No. 2, of this district, as a substitute, and on January 20, 1875, was transferred to Chemical Engine Company No. 7, and was made a member, and has been in this house ever since.

GEORGE B. PRESCOTT (Fig. 6) was born in Boston, Mass., August 2, 1862. He is a clock-maker by trade, and on February 2, 1882, became connected with this department as a member of Chemical Engine Company No. 7, and was transferred to this company on its organization. He is a member of Elliot Council No. 2 of the Royal Arcanum. He is a son of Captain Prescott.

JOHN PETERS (Fig. 7) was born in Boston, Mass., August 9, 1866, and learned the farming business. He became connected with this department on October 19, 1888, as a call-member of this company.

FRED A. MORRELL, call-hoseman, was born in Boston, Mass., April 3, 1853. He is a house-painter by trade, and on December 9, 1882, entered this department as a member of Chemical Engine Company No. 7, and was transferred to this company on its organization.

LADDER COMPANY NO. 6.

NAMES OF MEMBERS SINCE 1874.

The company was organized January, 1870, as follows: Henry Crane, foreman; Samuel Bridget, assistant, died Jan. 19, 1873; John E. E. Goward, James H. Bourne, Edmond B. Smith, Henry Crane, Jr., Charles E. Skinner, Samuel B. Locklin, E. Piper, and Warren Wild; W. C. Bourne, ap. June, 1874, resigned August 20, 1877, died June 30, 1880; Jacob H. Taylor, ap. June 10, 1874, resigned April 4, 1883, and John Taylor ap. same date, resigned January 1, 1881. Walter Jenkins, P. B. Packard, and Granville Young were ap. July 13, 1873; there is no record of the date they resigned.

PRESENT MEMBERS.

Call-Captain GEORGE S. BOURNE (Fig. 1) was born in Falmouth, Mass., February 17, 1853. He came to Boston during 1870, and learned the house-painter's trade. June 10, 1874, he was appointed a call-member of this company, and on December 6, 1887, was appointed to his present position. Captain Bourne is a member of Dorchester Lodge 158, I. O. O. F., and Ellison Encampment No. 54, Daughters of Rebekah, American L. of H., Riverside Lodge 91, R. S. G. F., and the Firemen's Charitable Association.

DAVID S. BLACK (Fig. 2), driver in charge, was born in Dorchester District, Boston, Mass., April, 7, 1838. After leaving school he was employed as a teamster. January 1, 1870, he was appointed a permanent driver of hose-wagon in Engine Company No. 16; when this company was organized he was assigned as driver. Mr. Black was severely injured on February 7, 1885, while exercising the horses. He was laid up eleven weeks at that time, and three weeks during 1877, from the same cause. He is a member of Blue Hill Council 451 of K. of H.

CHARLES T. NEEDHAM (Fig. 3) was born in Dorchester District, Boston, Mass., October 2, 1848. He is a paper-maker by trade, and in May, 1864, enlisted in Company H, Sixty-Second Massachusetts Regiment, in which he served until the close of the war. December 1, 1870, he was made a call-substitute in this company, and on June 10, 1874, was appointed a call-member. Mr. Needham is a member of Blue Hill Lodge 142, K. of H., May Flower Lodge 52, American Order of Workmen, and Improved Order of Red Men.

WARREN T. WILD (Fig. 4) was born in Charlestown District, Boston, Mass., September 19, 1842. He is a cabinet-maker by trade. He enlisted

LADDER COMPANY No. 6. — Page 682.

in Company E, Seventh Massachusetts Regiment, on June 15, 1861, and served until June 27, 1864. January, 1870, he joined this company as a call-man, and in June of the same year was enrolled a call-substitute. During 1871 he moved West, but returned again, and joined this company as a call-substitute. June 10, 1874, he was appointed a call-member. Mr. Wild is a member of Dorchester Lodge 158, I. O. O. F., and Post 68, G. A. R.

JAMES H. BOURNE (Fig. 5) was born in Falmouth, Mass., April 1, 1845, and during 1867 came to this city, where he engaged in the painting business. During the war he was attached to the U.S. transport "Cosmopolitan," doing service on the South Atlantic coast, as quartermaster and second officer, and served until 1866. December 1, 1870, he was appointed a member of this company. He was promoted to lieutenant in 1873, and served in that capacity until 1888, when the change was made to have the drivers of Call Ladder Companies act in that capacity. Mr. Bourne is a member of Shawmut Council 309, Royal Arcanum.

ALFRED G. BAYNTON (Fig. 6) was born in Dorchester District, Boston, Mass., July 18, 1851. He is a mechanical engineer by trade. June 10, 1874, he was admitted a call-member of this company. Mr. Baynton is a member of Union Lodge, Masons, Dorchester Lodge 158, and Ellison Encampment 54, I. O. O. F., and Daughters of Rebekah, also the Firemen's Charitable Association.

FRANCIS H. CRANE (Fig. 7) was born in Dorchester District, Boston, Mass., March 2, 1853. He is a carpenter by trade. June 10, 1874, he was appointed a call-man in this company.

JOHN A. LOCKLIN (Fig. 8) was born in Underhill, Vt., March 6, 1848, and during 1864 moved to Lowell, and came to this city during the same year, and learned the cabinet-maker's trade. He entered this service in Fountain Engine Company No. 1 as a call-man, during September, 1867. June 10, 1874, he joined this company as a call-substitute, and was appointed a member June 6, 1881. Mr. Locklin is a member of Dorchester Lodge 158, I. O. O. F., and Ellison Encampment No. 54.

ELMER BAYNTON (Fig. 9) is a Boston boy, being born in Dorchester District, Boston, Mass., January 25, 1862. He is a plumber by trade, and on April 21, 1883, he entered this service and was appointed a call-member of this company.

HORACE R. CRANE (Fig. 10) first saw the light in Dorchester District, Boston, Mass., January 3, 1861. He was a call-substitute in this company, and on April 21, 1883, was appointed a call-member. Mr. Crane has been engaged in the livery-stable business for a number of years, and is a member of Improved Order of Red Men.

ALONZO P. BAYNTON (Fig. 11) was born in Dorchester District, Boston, Mass., August 29, 1859. After leaving school he learned the house-painter's trade, and on April 21, 1883, was appointed a call-substitute in this company.

F. S. ROWE (Fig. 12), substitute, was born in Laconia, N.H., June 4,

1858, and came to this city about ten years ago, and worked at the house-painting trade.   July 1, 1883, he joined this company as a call-substitute. Mr. Rowe is a member of Dorchester Lodge 158, I. O. O. F., Riverside Assembly 91, R. S. G. F., and the Red Men.

LADDER COMPANY NO. 10.
NAMES OF MEMBERS SINCE 1874.

E. S. Abbott, ap. January 20, 1875, resigned November 21, 1876; Joseph Brown, ap. January 1, 1874, resigned November 21, 1874; C. K. Bullock, ap. January 11, 1875, resigned December 31, 1886; Wm. Buchanan, ap. December 21, 1876, resigned January 9, 1880; Michael Cork, ap. January 1, 1874, resigned April 1, 1874; Wm. Condry, ap. June 1, 1882, tr. to Engine 30, July 10, 1883; Wm. Curley, ap. June 1, 1874, resigned November 21, 1874; John Curty, ap. January 1, 1874, resigned November 21, 1874; Nicholas Cormack, ap. January 1, 1874, resigned November 21, 1874; Wm. Conrick, ap. January 1, 1874, resigned November 21, 1874; C. J. Cook, ap. January 20, 1875, resigned March, 1881; C. J. Colbath, ap. January 20, 1875, resigned August 20, 1875; M. Davis, ap. January 20, 1875, died December 19, 1887; Peter Harvey, ap. January 1, 1874; B. Judge, ap. January 1, 1874, resigned November 21, 1874; M. Kenny, ap. January 1, 1874, resigned November 21, 1874; Joseph Larkins, ap. January 1, 1874, resigned November 21, 1874; John McCarthy, ap. January 1, 1874, resigned November 21, 1874; John H. Moulton, ap. January 20, 1875, resigned May 14, 1875; W. F. Mahn, ap. September 21, 1875, resigned December 20. 1876; Daniel O'Brien, ap. January 1, 1874, resigned November 21, 1874; Patrick Parlow, ap. January 1, 1874, resigned November 21, 1874; Chas. Tulley, ap. January 1, 1874, resigned August 20, 1874; Geo. P. Trott, ap. January 20, 1875, resigned December 31, 1886.

PRESENT MEMBERS.

Call-Capt. JOHN F. BOOTHBY (Fig. 1) was born in Limerick, Me., March 9, 1846, and came to Boston during 1866, where he learned the carpenter's trade.   December 26, 1876, he was appointed a call-member in this company, and on January 13, 1888, was promoted to his present position.   Captain Boothby is a member of Forrest Lodge 148, I. O. O. F., and Anawan Tribe 75, Red Men.

JOHN LYNCH (Fig. 2), driver, was born in Lawrence, Mass., December 15, 1851.   He came to Boston during 1869, and worked at the teamster's business. October 8, 1873, he was assigned to Engine Co. No. 28 as driver.   June 15, 1882, he was transferred to this company.   Mr. Lynch had both of his ankles sprained in October, 1873, by the overturning of the hose-carriage.

F. A. N. PEABODY (Fig. 3) was born in Salem, Mass., September 13. 1850, and when but a child came to this city, where he learned the house-

LADDER COMPANY No. 10. — Page 685.

painter's trade. He entered this department January 21, 1875, as a member of this company. Mr. Peabody was injured at the Egleston-square fire five years ago.

ANDREW THANISCH (Fig. 4) was born in Germany, December 17, 1850, and came to this city November 16, 1877, where he learned the carriage-smith's trade. April 16, 1875, he entered this department as a call-member of this company. Mr. Thanisch is a member of Tremont Lodge, I. O. O. F., and Quinobequin Tribe 70, Red Men.

CHARLES G. LYNCH (Fig. 5) was appointed in this company May 21, 1875, as a call-member.

JEREMIAH F. SHEA (Fig. 6) was born in Boston, Mass., March 11, 1857. He is a gardener by trade, and in December 29, 1887, entered the service as a call-member of this company.

ALFRED A. BESTWICK, Jr. (Fig. 7), was born in Dedham, Mass., November 25, 1862, and when nineteen years of age came to this city and learned the carpenter's trade. He entered this department during 1882, as a call substitute in Engine Co. 28, in which he remained until February 7, 1886, when he was transferred to this company.

JAMES MURRAY (Fig. 8) was born in Liverpool, Eng., December 28, 1860, and came to this city during 1869, where he learned the tinsmith's trade. He entered this department as a call-substitute in this company September 5, 1884. He is a member of Samoset Tribe 20, Red Men, and General Warren Colony, Pilgrim Fathers.

ALBERT A. AYERS, call-ladderman, was born in Brookline, Mass., Feb. 19, 1840, and is a carpenter by trade. He entered this department during 1864, as a member of Jamaica Engine Company No. 3, in which he served four years, when he left the department. He returned again on January 14, 1884, as a call-member of this company. Mr. Ayers is a member of Tribe 75, Red Men, Massasoit Lodge No. 1, I. O. O. F., and Encampment.

A. W. SPRAGUE, call-ladderman, was born in Hingham, Mass., March 25, 1849, and came to this city during 1863, where he has been employed as a clerk. He entered this department January 1, 1875, as a call-member of this company.

LADDER COMPANY NO. 16.

COMPANY ORGANIZED AUGUST 24, 1888.

PRESENT MEMBERS.

Lieut. BENJ. B. WRIGHT (Fig. 1) was born in Halifax, N.S., May 15, 1824. He came to Boston when but fifteen years of age, but followed the sea for a number of years, sailing out of Boston and New York, after which he engaged in the rigging business, in which he was employed in the Navy-Yard before and after the late war. He also served as special police officer in the Court-House for some time. February, 1858, he was admitted a member of Ladder Company No. 3, and was promoted assistant foreman January 1, 1869. January 1, 1873, he was promoted, and assigned, at his own request, to the position of mate and second pilot on board the fire-boat, and a short time after was promoted first pilot, and served in that capacity until August 24, 1888, when, at his own request, he was transferred as lieutenant in charge of Ladder Company No. 16 and Chemical Company No. 4. He is a member of the K. of P. and the Boston Veterans.

CALVIN W. BATES (Fig. 2), driver, was born in Roxbury District, Boston, Mass., December 23, 1836. He was employed in various occupations before taking up this business, which he commenced by running to fires with American Engine Company No. 2, when but a boy. During 1860 it was disbanded, and Dearborn Engine Company No. 1 was organized. He was appointed hoseman in 1863, and driver of the hose-carriage in 1867. Five years later he was appointed driver of Engine No. 14, and held that position until 1888, when he was transferred, at his own request, to this company. He is a member of the Gate of Temple Lodge of Masons.

D. C. WHITTEMORE (Fig. 3) was born in Boston, Mass., May 9, 1860. He is at present engaged in the coal and wood business, and on the organization of this company was enrolled a call-member. Mr. Whittemore is a member of Bay State Lodge, W. A. M.

BENJAMIN COBLEIGH, Jr. (Fig. 4), was born in Waltham, Mass., July 2, 1859, and when but a child came to this city, where, after leaving school, he learned the plumber's trade. He entered this department at the time this company was organized. He is a member of Bay State Lodge, W. A. M.

GRANVILLE F. SEAVERNS (Fig. 5) was born in Roslindale District, Boston, Mass., December 29, 1858. He is engaged in the grocery business, and when this company went into commission was admitted a call-member. Mr. Seaverns is a member of Bellevue Lodge 460, K. of H., and Quinobequin Tribe 70, Red Men.

THOMAS B. MULQUEENY (Fig. 6) first saw the light in Cheshire County, England, October 16, 1863, and came to this city when but a child. He is a stone-mason by trade, and was enrolled a call-member of this company on its organization.

P. HAVEY, Jr. (Fig. 7), entered this department October 12, 1888, as a call-member of this company.

CHEMICAL COMPANY NO. 4.

NAMES OF MEMBERS SINCE 1874.

Wm. Lewis. ap. September 28, 1874, died January 16, 1883 ; R. Weeks, ap. January 20, 1875, resigned November 11, 1887 ; Wm. R. Southern. ap. January 20, 1875, resigned June 15, 1885.

Top—LADDER COMPANY NO. 16.   Bottom—CHEMICAL ENGINE COMPANY NO 4.—Page 689.

PRESENT MEMBERS.

THOMAS P. LALLY (Fig. 1, bottom of page 689), driver, was born in Boston, Mass., May 28, 1846, and is a mason by trade. He entered this department as a call-substitute in Engine Company No. 7 during 1865, and was admitted a call-man January 1, 1867. July 31, 1873, he was appointed driver of hose-carriage, and on October 13 was transferred to Hose Company 2. He resigned October 1, 1874, but returned again as a permanent member of Engine Company No. 10, February 1, 1875, from which he was transferred, at his own request, to Engine Company 26, November 8, 1879, where he remained until March 1, 1883, at which time he was transferred to this company. He is a life member of the Firemen's Charitable Association.

JAMES EDWARDS (Fig. 2) has served more consecutive years in this department than any other person, with one exception. He was born in Robinson, Me., January 9, 1824, in which town he remained until 1840, when he came to this city and learned the leather-currier's trade. September 27, 1847, he joined Lafayette Engine Company No. 18, in which he served five years, when he was transferred to Ladder Company No. 1, and during 1884 was transferred to this company. Mr. Edwards is a member of Joseph Warren Lodge, Masons, and a life member of the Firemen's Charitable Association.

G. W. COBLEIGH (Fig. 3) was appointed a call-member of this company May 27, 1882.

W. C. ORALL (Fig. 4) entered this department January 1, 1874, as a member of Engine Company No. 8, and on January 20, 1875, was transferred to this company.

CHAPTER XV.

THE ELECTRIC FIRE-ALARM SERVICE.

IN Boston, as in all other cities, the old-time method of giving an alarm of fire was by ringing as many bells as the town afforded. This was adequate for a small town, as it was an easy matter to locate the fire ; but as the place grew, it became a constant source of annoyance, and the confusion and delay in ascertaining the location of the conflagration was the means of many heavy losses. It was not until June, 1845, that the idea of utilizing the telegraph for giving alarms of fire was thought of. At that date it was first made known by Dr. William F. Channing, of Boston, a gentleman well known in medical and scientific circles of this city. It appears that to his medical training is due the first suggestion of the thought of his great plans, which are clearly expressed in his address delivered before the Smithsonian Institute at Washington, shortly after the successful introduction of the system in Boston.

It is not to be supposed, however, that Dr. Channing had a smooth road to success ; far from it, and it was only by the most energetic, patient, and persistent efforts on his part that the many obstacles were overcome. Notwithstanding these great personal qualifications, he might have failed had not Mr. Moses G. Farmer, also of this city, come to his assistance, and by his practical knowledge in electrical science was enabled to develop and put on a practical basis his great scheme. By this coöperation it became known as the Channing and Farmer system. Its first publicity attracted little if any attention, as it was considered a visionary or " cranky " scheme, without the slightest possibility of utility. Fortunately for them, Boston had for its Mayor during 1848 Josiah Quincy, who became greatly interested in the plan, and urged upon the City Council to investigate its merits, which resulted in the passage of an order for the construction of two machines for the striking of the city bells from a distant point. These were constructed under the supervision of Mr. Farmer, and one of them was placed in the belfry of the old City Hall, and was connected with a line of telegraph wires extending to New York City, where the operator, following his instructions, opened and closed the circuit by means of his " key," resulting in a series of blows on the bells in this city, which, according to the papers of that date, " caused a false alarm of fire." It was not, however, until 1851 that any further developments or exertions to adopt it were made, but at that date the bill was formally laid before the City Government, with plans and specifications, and they resolved to give it a trial, appropriating $10,000 for its construction, — a decision much to their honor, as it was an experiment, being without precedent in the world. The entire construction of the system was intrusted to Mr. Farmer, and the plant, consisting of forty miles of wire, forty-five signal-boxes or stations, and sixteen-alarm bells, was formally accepted by the city at noon on the 28th day of April, 1852. The first box or station is illustrated on page 699, and, like the entire system, had an open circuit. This box, with the one of 1853, which latter is the improvement, or first closed-circuit box, are in the possession of the department, and are the only ones existing. The first boxes, as can be seen, were very crude affairs, and were operated by a crank, which was turned fast or slow, backward or forward, according to the degree of excitement under which the individual operating it might be laboring; but this objection was soon remedied, and the next station was made so that the crank could only be turned in the proper direction. In the first construction a double set of wires were used: one for the signal-boxes, on which to receive the alarm, the other with which to strike the bells. These stations had each a set of characters, as the city was divided into districts, and only the district number was struck on the bells. The box number, sounded separately in the boxes, as, for instance, three dots, and, after a pause, a dash and three dots, thus: ... — ... coming in from a station, indicated district three, station six, so that, on the first sound of the city bells, the firemen had to run to the box and listen for the box number. When it was proposed to improve on this method by striking the box number direct on the bells, and omit the district, then went up a great cry from those interested, as they thought it was impossible to indicate so many numbers; but, like many other improvements, it was accomplished. Mr. Farmer was appointed superintendent of the service, with four assistants, their first duty dating from April 29, or the day after the system was completed, when an alarm of fire was given from District 1, Station 7, now Box 12, located at that time on the Cooper-street Church. The original plan for supplying the electric force necessary to run the plant consisted of a Grove battery for the signal circuits, and a large magneto-electric machine turned by water-power, and later by hand, for the bell circuits. Mr. Farmer continued in charge until October 8, 1853, when he was succeeded by Mr. Joseph B. Stearns, under whose management several changes and improvements were made, consisting of the introduction of the method of giving the box number, instead of district number, as above alluded to. He did away with the double-circuit system, and placed the alarm-bells on a single circuit, so that the alarms were received and given on the same circuit. September 30, 1863, the electric wires were extended to East Boston by means of a cable, at an expense of $5,000. December 26 of the same year the circuit was extented to South Boston, the boxes being placed at the corner of Eighth and K streets, First and I streets, and Sullivan street.

During February, 1867, Mr. Stearns resigned, and was succeeded by Mr. John F. Kennard. under whose administration, during 1868, was introduced the automatic instead of the crank signal-box ; the first of these boxes being numbered 84. But the growth of the city, by annexation and otherwise, necessitated a large increase of circuits and apparatus, which were added from time to time. During 1874 the fire department was reorganized, and the Board of Fire Commissioners established, under whose administration this service was placed ; and on January 1, 1880, a reorganization of the system was effected. Capt. Brown S. Flanders was appointed superintendent, and the positions of assistant superintendent and foreman of construction were created, to which Cyrus A. George and William H. Godfrey were respectively appointed. The old, antiquated apparatus in the City Hall dome gave place to new machines of the most approved form of construction. The circuits were reconstructed in the most thorough manner, and were increased in number, and run on new and carefully selected routes, with a view of protecting the city by more than one circuit. Perhaps the most important improvement added by Captain Flanders, July 26, 1884, was the box-gong service, by which the alarms were given directly to the various houses from the signal-boxes, thereby saving much time in reaching the fire. This result is obtained by running independent circuits to the houses, which are connected with a set of apparatus at the central office, the action of which transfers the work from any box into the entire group of gong circuits ; thus giving a simultaneous and almost instantaneous alarm to all the houses in the city.

The operations of our present great system may be briefly stated as follows : The central office is located in the dome of the City Hall, from which radiates in many directions the various circuits to all parts of the city. This system is called Metallic Circuit ; *i.e.*, each circuit consists of a wire running from the central office and returning again, so that, in case of a break. the whole system can be put in condition for use, each station still being connected with the City Hall. For this reason. the entire city is divided into sections, which has an independent circuit, numbered, for convenience in operation. Distributed on the buildings, in as public and convenient a position as possible. are attached iron cottage-shaped boxes. $10\frac{1}{2} \times 17$ inches in dimensions, painted red, with bronze numbers on a black background, no two numbers of which are alike, except on those that are termed " duplicates," which are located in a dangerous section, to facilitate reaching the boxes quickly, and are placed so near that each one locates the scene of destruction with sufficient accuracy. Over each box is a tin sign, painted in white letters on a black background, giving the address of the person under whose charge the key remains. (Some boxes, however, that are located in the thickly business sections, merely have a handle. which, by a notice on the box, instructing the alarmist to turn, opens the outer door, at the same time sounds a gong, so that the attention of those passing is attracted to it, thus preventing false alarms.) The door open, all that is seen is an inner door, painted black, with a brass hook projecting through, it and the words : " Pull the hook down once and let go." This is all that is necessary to give the alarm ; but on opening this second door the most beautiful and delicate machinery is exposed (see illustration on page 699), confined in a space one foot square and four inches deep, contained in which is a circular box, in which is a simple piece of clock-work, the motive-power being a clock-spring. There is also an electro-magnet and a small telegraph key. The object of the clock-work is to revolve a small wheel having a metal rim, one edge of which is continuous, the other having little pieces (more or less in number) cut out. To this wheel, through the magnet, are connected the circuit wires, and the hook in the door is so arranged that the pulling it down tightens the spring and sets the clock-work in motion, revolving the wheel ; the effect of which is to break the circuit just so many times, and no more, as there are breaks in the metal rim. Connected with each circuit at the central office is a register, so called, which records every break that is made in the circuit. Hence it follows that the pulling of the hook in any box starts the clock-work, and a strip of paper comes out of one side of the glass case, in the office, on which the registering pen will have made a row of marks, corresponding to the breaks in the wheel. Thus, -- --- ----- indicates 235 as the box. As the paper comes out of the register it passes over the automatic time-stamp, put in the office December 22, 1885, which the operator presses, and on the paper will be printed a clock-dial, with the hands indicating just the time the stamp was pressed.

All the bells in the city connected with this office have attached to them mechanism similar to the striking parts of a town-clock, which is used for regulating the movement of a heavy hammer that strikes the bell. This appliance is easily controlled by the current switched on from the office (each circuit having its own switches, which are systematically arranged by a series of small brass switches). The repeater is next used. This is a complicated piece of clock-work : with three dials, fifteen inches in diameter, with figures from 1 to 12 arranged around the circumference, and with two hands similar to a clock. With this machinery are connected the wires running to the bells, etc. The operator sets the short-hand of the dial to the number he wishes to strike, presses a small lever, and immediately all the bells in the city commence their warning notes ; and repeats it three times, making a regular pause of three and one-half seconds between each blow, eight seconds between the figures, and twenty seconds between each series of blows, or " round." These dials facilitate striking boxes of more than one figure ; as, for instance, for Box 3 the hand on the right-hand dial is set at 3 and the lever pressed ; if 37, then the middle dial is set at 3 and the right at 7 ; if 372, the left-hand dial is set at 3, the centre at 7, and the right at 2, but only one pressure of the lever is necessary. The long-hand on each dial records the total number of blows the dial to which it is attached has struck. The current being sent through the wire to the bell apparatus, the magnet attracts the armature, which in turn throws up a small lever, and this liberates a detent which releases the machinery, causing the hammer to strike one blow; and, the wheels revolving, the detent and lever catch again as they come round, and the machinery is all ready for another impulse to set it free. The machinery itself is run by a weight, similarly to any clock, which weight is raised and the machine wound up by hand.

To keep this great system in perfect order at all times, and to remedy any damage within the shortest possible time, requires other machines. On each circuit is an electric bell and annunciator at the central office, so constructed that as soon as any part of it is tampered with in the least degree it will, by these instruments, give notice at headquarters, where, by means of galvanometers and testing, the repairer can be at once notified, and he can keep up any conversation necessary by means of a telegraph key located in each box. The latest device placed in the boxes is the apparatus introduced by the Boston Auxiliary Fire-Alarm Company. This is connected with the other machinery of the box in such a manner that, while it in no way interferes with the regular action itself, it will operate, by effect of electric current transmitted from a distant point, as certainly and as quickly as when the box is pulled by hand. This is illustrated in the right-hand corner of the large box on page 699.

At the office is a watch-clock, through which each circuit is connected, and which is so constructed that every circuit must be tested, in regular order, by the operator once every twenty minutes. The automatic fault-detector, added to the equipment during 1885, is run by clock-work, by which a hand is rotated like an hour-hand, making the round in an hour. Every minute and a half it passes over a piece of copper connected with one of the circuits. If that circuit is crossed or grounded, a vibrating bell will be started, and kept going until the operator stops it. Sleeping-rooms are provided for the operators at headquarters, and that every possible precaution may be taken against the operator falling asleep, dropping in a fit, or dying suddenly, a vibrating bell is set going in the bedroom by the ringing in of an alarm. The one on duty must, therefore, turn the switch to save his companion from getting up and investigating. All these instruments and circuits are run by batteries in the battery-room, in the second story of the dome. Here are fifteen hundred cells of a modified form of the Serson-Kauffer battery, — a combination of the gravity and the Daniells. These are arranged on racks, joined in sets of fifty, more or less, each set being called a battery. The cells have to be renewed about every eight months; but it keeps one man busy all the time attending to them.

There are 464 fire-alarm boxes, divided as follows, viz.: Boston, 140; South Boston, 51; East Boston, 43; Roxbury, 61: Dorchester, 62; Charlestown, 38; West Roxbury, 40; Brighton, 28; Chelsea, 1.

The wires of the service are also connected with the dwelling-houses of each member of the telegraphic force and other officials.

Two new switch-boards, of elegant design and construction, have been provided for telephone service. They are mounted on black-walnut desks, which were made for the purpose, and are in use, one at headquarters and the other in the office of the Chief Engineer; the former being in general use during the night, the latter during the day. There are thirty-seven bells or gongs throughout the city connected with this service, also a machine for blowing the Abattoir whistle in Brighton.

During the latter part of 1886 and the beginning of 1887, eleven bells belonging within the limits of the city were cut off. The department has also thirty-seven tower-clocks under their charge, stationed throughout the city.

The gentlemen who have served in this department from 1852 are as follows: Operators, 1852, Messrs. Coffin, Browham, Shapleigh, Cushing, Edson, and Brooks; 1853, Edward Rogers; 1855, Mr. Clay; January, 1856, Adam McAfee; March, Mr. Cutting; April, George S. Thom; January, 1857, Charles S. Stearns; July, Frank Bedger; December, 1858, Mr. Wyman; June, 1859, E. S. Doe; August, 1862, J. H. Stevens; 1864, J. N. George, Jr.; December, 1864, Alfred S. Manson; March, 1865, G. S. Mendall. Repairers: June, 1876, William B. Green; January, 1872, Benjamin Barchsted; April, 1881, David Freeman.

PRESENT MEMBERS.

The portrait of Superintendent BROWN S. FLANDERS will be found on page 699. He was born in Hopkinton, N.H., September 30, 1836. After leaving school he went to Concord, N.H., and from there to Manchester, where he entered the works of the Amoskeag Manufacturing Company, with whom he learned his trade, that of a machinist. He joined Engine Company No. 1, of that city, during 1852, in which he remained until 1855, when he joined Engine Company No. 6, and in the following year was elected foreman. During March, 1860, he was elected in the Board of Engineers, and remained in that office until 1862. In the fall of the following year he came to Boston, and shortly after became a member of Engine Company No. 7, and on July, 1864, was promoted assistant engineman. February 1, 1865, he was promoted to engineman and assigned to Engine Company No. 8. On the reorganization he was appointed aid to the chief, and inspector and master mechanic of the department, with headquarters in the chief's office at City Hall. January 2, 1880, he was chosen Superintendent of Fire Alarms, and held these positions three years, when, during 1883, he was relieved of the duties of aid to the chief and master mechanic, and his whole attention was given to this service. While a member of the various engine companies he received some severe injuries. Superintendent Flanders is a member of Zetland Lodge of Masons; the Massachusetts Mechanics' Charitable Association; Past Exalted Ruler of the Boston Order of Elks, now a member; and a life member of the Firemen's Charitable Association. .

Assistant Superintendent CYRUS A. GEORGE will be recognized on page

699. He was born in Plaistow, N.H., March 26, 1839. After leaving school he began life in mercantile business, and May 25, 1865, came to this city and entered this department as operator, since which time he has become identified with the fire-alarm service of Boston. He has worked with his superintendent in perfect harmony, and to these gentlemen Boston owes her perfect system of fire-alarms. From the position of operator Mr. George was promoted, January 1, 1880, to his present office. He is a member of Lafayette Lodge of Masons.

CHARLES M. CHAPLIN, operator (see portrait on page 699), was born in Worcester, Mass., December 6, 1846, and came to this city when but a child. After leaving school he engaged in mercantile business, and on November 21, 1866, entered this service as a repairer. Two months later he was put in charge of the batteries, and was assistant operator. January 1, 1872, he was promoted to his present position, being on duty at the central office from 10 P.M. to 3 A.M. Mr. Chaplin is a member of Joseph Warren Lodge, Signet Chapter, and Cœur de Lion Commandery of the Masons.

UZZIEL PUTNAM, operator, was appointed a permanent repairer during 1864, but worked when called upon from 1859. He was promoted operator, January, 1876.

JAMES L. CROWLEY, operator, was born in Boston, Mass., September 23, 1855. He was appointed a battery-man August 23, 1879, and promoted to his present position June 30, 1881.

JAMES L. GETHINS, battery-man (see portrait), was born in Boston, May 31, 1864. After leaving school he was for some time employed in the Boston Public Library, and on March 16, 1882, was engaged in this department and placed in charge of the batteries.

Superintendent of Construction WILLIAM H. GODFREY (Fig. 1) was born in Taunton, Mass., January 25, 1842, and came to this city during 1855, where he was employed in mercantile business. During 1864 he joined Hose Company No. 9, and three years later was engaged as a lineman in this service. He resigned his position in the hose company in January, 1871, and during 1873 was put in charge of the Southern Division of the Electric Fire Alarm. During 1880 he was promoted to his present position. Mr. Godfrey has charge of the construction and repairs of all the fire-alarm wires and apparatus throughout the city. He is a member of St. Paul Lodge, Masons, St. Matthew Royal Arch Chapter, St. Omer Commandery of Knights Templars, Powwow Tribe 74, Red Men, and the South Boston Yacht Club.

G. J. GUTERMUTH (Fig. 2), repairer, was born in Konigsberg, Prussia, April 5, 1845, and came to this city during 1855, where he learned the machinist's trade. He was appointed a member of Engine Company No. 25, March 1, 1874, and on April 1 of the same year was promoted to assistant engineman and assigned to Engine Company No. 14. June 1, 1880, he was promoted to engineman and assigned to Engine Company No. 21, and was

FIRE ALARM DEPARTMENT. — Page 699.

transferred to Engine Company No. 28, May 25, 1881. He remained there until December 2, 1886, when he was assigned to his present position, he having charge of all repairing of the electrical instruments of this service. Mr. Gutermuth is a member of the Royal Arcanum and the German Turners.

GRANVILLE S. MENDELL (Fig. 3), repairer, was born in Great Falls, N.H., October 13, 1834, and during 1859 came to this city, where he was engaged in the grocery business. He entered this service in April, 1865, being one of the senior members in this department. Mr. Mendell is a member of Chickering Lodge 856, K. of H.

ISSACHAR WELLS (Fig. 4), repairer, was born in Kennebunkport, Me., April 10, 1842, and during 1866 came to this city. He enlisted in the navy, January, 1863, and served until July, 1866. During 1873 he was appointed a permanent member of Engine Company No. 9, in which he served but a short time, when he was transferred to Ladder Company No. 1, and during 1880 was promoted lieutenant. In 1882 he resigned, and soon after was appointed to his present position. Mr. Wells was injured at a fire on Haverhill street. He is a member of Post 159, G. A. R.

CHARLES PENNY (Fig. 5), repairer, first saw the light in Wilton, Eng., July 19, 1852, and came to this city during 1879. He was employed as a mariner previous to his appointment in this service, which occurred on April 19, 1883. Mr. Penny is a member of Powwow Tribe 74 of Red Men.

HIRAM W. CHERRINGTON (Fig. 6), repairer, is a Boston boy, being born in this city January 18, 1862. He was formerly foreman in the works of the Bay State Iron Company. During February, 1885, he was appointed to his present position. Mr. Cherrington is a member of Powwow Tribe 74 of Red Men.

JOSEPH W. BIRD (Fig. 7), repairer, was born in Boston, Mass., September 21, 1846. When the war broke out he enlisted in the navy, August 3, 1864, and served until July 4, 1865. He was then engaged in the photographic business until February 23, 1876, when he was appointed to his present position. Mr. Bird is a member of Post 7, G. A. R.

JOHN FLAVELL (Fig. 8), repairer, was born in Dorchester District, Boston, Mass., June 8, 1855. After leaving school he was engaged in the milk business, and in 1879 was admitted a call-member of Engine Company No. 15. April 21, 1882, he was appointed to his present position. Mr. Flavell is a brother of the unfortunate William H. Flavell, of Ladder Company No. 8, who was killed Thanksgiving-day, 1886.

JACOB SCHAFFER (Fig. 9), repairer, is a native of East Boston. He was born July 11, 1852. After leaving school he was engaged in several trades. He followed the sea for ten years, after which he was employed on the Boston & Providence Railroad. A few years later he was employed by the Western Union Telegraph Company. He was engaged with the Telephone Dispatch Company, and worked for them as lineman in this city. When the long-distance telephone was introduced Mr. Schaffer was the first to go out as builder, going to New York to take charge of their lines in that city, and on his return to Boston was engaged by the same company in the Suburban Division. June, 1887, he was appointed in this department, and did active service until November 17, 1887, when he received injuries that incapacitated him from further duty.

WILLIAM H. BARKER (Fig. 10), repairer, was born in Brunswick, Me., July 2, 1855, and on May 3, 1873, came to this city. He is a carpenter by trade. February 26, 1880, he was appointed a call-man in Engine Company No. 17, and April 2, 1883, was detailed to this department. Mr. Barker is a member of Powwow Tribe No. 74 of Red Men.

DAVID ISAACS (Fig. 11), repairer, was born in Boston, Mass., May 8, 1854. He is a boiler-maker by trade, at which he was employed until his appointment in his present position, May 12, 1883. Mr. Isaacs is a member of Boston Lodge 80 of the Sons of Benevolence.

JONATHAN M. MORRIS (Fig. 12), repairer, was born in Cambridge, Mass., June 6, 1856, and was employed in the brush trade. He entered this service during April, 1880.

Repair Shop. — Page 704.

CHAPTER XVI.

REPAIR-SHOP.

SUPERINTENDENT HENRY R. DEMARY (Fig. 1) was born in Weathersfield, Vt., September 6, 1836. During 1861 he enlisted in the Mechanicsfield, N.H., Ranks, and served three months : he then served with Sherman's Express at Port Royal, four months. He finished the machinist's trade at Manchester, N.H., where he became a member of Niagara Engine Company No. 2. located at the machine-shop. He came to this city during 1862. and joined Engine Company No. 11, during May, 1868, as a call-man. September 21, 1877, he was transferred to this department, in the machine-shop, in which he was promoted assistant foreman July 15, 1883, and two years later was promoted to his present position. He has charge of all repairing of the apparatus in the department, and must be at the scene of fires on the second alarm. Superintendent Demary was ruptured at the mattress factory fire, also had his knee-pan and hip fractured. He is a member of King Philip Lodge 33, K. of P.

CHARLES A. STRAW (Fig. 2) store-keeper and clerk, was born in Newbury, N.H., March 2, 1854, and came to this city when but a boy. After leaving school he was employed in mercantile business, and September 28, 1874, joined Engine Company No. 13 as a call-member. October, 1882, he was appointed a permanent member and assigned to Engine Company No. 22. He was transferred to Engine Company No. 13, from which he was transferred to Hose Company No. 7. He is still a member. While at work at the fire on Hampshire street, his spine and back were severely injured, from the effects of which he never fully recovered. He was detailed to his present position April 5, 1885. Mr. Straw is a member of Washington Lodge 5, I. O. O. F., Massachusetts Lodge 42, K. of P., and Boston Veterans.

JAMES SLATTERY (Fig. 3), machinist, was appointed in this department during February, 1880.

JOHN H. MARKS (Fig. 4), machinist, was born in Boston, Mass., February 25, 1849. He entered this department as assistant engineman in Engine Company No. 8, during 1873, and later on was promoted to the position of engineman and assigned to Engine Company No. 7, where he remained several months. He was transferred to Engine Company No. 26, from which he was transferred to Engine Company No. 6 in 1883, but resigned. He was out of the department until September 7, 1885, when he came to this shop. Mr. Marks had the second finger of his left hand amputated at the repair-shop in May, 1886. He is a member of Boston Council No. 4, Royal Arcanum.

EDWARD F. HOYE (Fig. 5), machinist, was born in Franklin, N.H., November 27, 1848, and when but a child came to this city. He was appointed to his present position November 12, 1880. Mr. Hoye is a member of Boston Council 4, Royal Arcanum.

ARTHUR K. PARADISE (Fig. 6), machinist, was born in Boston, Mass., January 15, 1860. He entered the department May 1, 1882. Mr. Paradise is a member of Assembly 49, Pilgrim Fathers.

JOHN E. NOLAN (Fig. 7), machinist, was born in County of Tipperary, Ireland, February 14, 1849, and during 1880 came to this city. He entered this department September 7, 1885. Mr. Nolan is a member of the Amalgamated Society of Engineers.

JEREMIAH J. O'BRIEN (Fig. 8), machinist, was born in Boston, Mass., January 2, 1850. He entered this department October 15, 1886. Mr. O'Brien is a member of Massachusetts Catholic Order of Foresters.

PATRICK B. HANNON (Fig. 9), harness and hose-maker, was born in Boston, Mass., March 17, 1845. He entered the fire department September 1, 1874, and was assigned to his present position some time later. Mr. Hannon is a Franklin-medal graduate of the old Boylston School of the Class of 1859.

THOMAS F. TURNER (Fig. 10), foreman of paint-shop, was born in Macclesfield, England, February 1, 1847, and when but a child came to this city, where he learned the painter's trade. During 1868 he became a member of Dearborn Engine Company No. 1, of Roxbury. During 1873 he was transferred to Hose Company No. 7. The same year he was made a permanent member and assigned to Ladder Company No. 3. and in June, 1876, was assigned to his present position. Mr. Turner is a member of Boston Council No. 4, Royal Arcanum, and Boston Veterans.

MICHAEL KYLE (Fig. 11), wheelwright, was born in Sligo, Ireland, August 8, 1843, and came to this city during 1863. March 30, 1885, was engaged in this department.

PATRICK WELCH (Fig. 12), wheelwright, was born in County of Westmeath, Ireland, February 6, 1827, and when but a child came to this city. He entered this department during May, 1877.

JOHN CONNELL (Fig. 13), blacksmith, was born in Dorchester District, Boston, Mass., May 16, 1850. He was appointed to his present position during 1875. Mr. Connell was a member of Engine Company 18, previous to this time, for a period of three years.

THOMAS BUCKLEY (Fig. 14), blacksmith, was born in Georgetown, Mass.. May 3, 1854. He was a member of Washington Engine Company No. 1, of that city, for four years before he came to Boston, and was engaged in this department during 1875. Mr. Buckley is a member of Boston Council No. 4, Royal Arcanum.

WILLIAM BOWERS (Fig. 15), blacksmith, was born in Pictou, N.S., September 21, 1850, and came to Boston when a boy. He entered this department May 24, 1875.

PATRICK McDAVITT (Fig. 16), blacksmith, was born in County Donegal, Ireland, March 14, 1849, and came to this city during 1868. He entered this department January 24, 1887.

THOMAS H. WRIGHT (Fig. 17), blacksmith, was born in Charlestown District, Boston, Mass., March 9, 1844. He enlisted in 1862 in the navy on board the S.S. "Housatonic," and was discharged, for sickness, during 1864. He reënlisted in Company K, Fifty-Eighth Massachusetts Regiment, and served until the close of the war. During 1867 he joined Howard Engine Company No. 1, and during 1873 was transferred to Engine Company No. 3 as a permanent member, and remained until reorganization. January 24, 1887, he was engaged in his present position. Mr. Wright had his arm broken and received a severe contusion of the skull while at work with Hose Company No. 1, at a fire on Water street, during 1885, when he fell from a second-story window. He is a member of Columbia Castle, Knights of the Golden Eagle, and the Charlestown Veterans.

FRANK P. ELLIOTT (Fig. 18), blacksmith, was born in Raymond, N.H., January 8, 1853. He came to Boston July, 1882, and entered this department. Mr. Elliott was a member of Niagara Engine Company at Maverick, Mass., during 1878 to 1882.

JAMES QUINN (Fig. 19), machinist, was born in Waltham, Mass., October 24, 1841, and came to Boston October 10, 1876. He enlisted on January 12, 1862, in Ninty-Ninth New York Regiment, and was discharged January 13, 1865. During 1858 he joined Neptune Engine Company, of Waltham. He was engaged in this department May 2, 1887. Mr. Quinn is a member of Post 7, G. A. R.

JOHN DURLING (Fig. 20), hostler, was appointed a call-member of Ladder Company No. 12, October 17, 1884, and March 16, 1885, was assigned as hostler, at the same time doing duty in the repair-shop. Mr. Durling died August 21, 1889.

OLIVER J. BOOKER (Fig. 21), watchman, was born in Boston, Mass., August 29, 1834. His occupation was that of a seaman previous to hi sentering this department. During the war he enlisted in the navy, on board the S.S. "Tuscarora" and "Macedonia," September 10, 1863, and served until the following year. April 6, 1865, he joined Warren Engine Company No. 2, of Roxbury, as a permanent member, and was promoted foreman June 4, 1874. Shortly after he was transferred to Engine Company No. 23 as a hoseman, and September, 1882, was detailed to his present position. Mr. Booker received serious injuries to his eye and spine during 1878, at a fire on Ham's wharf. At a fire in Chadwick street he had several ribs broken by being thrown from the engine. He is a member of Roxbury Lodge 205, K. of H., and the Boston Veterans.

C. C. WILSON (Fig. 22), watchman, was born in Windham, N.H., April 2, 1828, and is a granite-carver by trade. He came to Boston when a boy, and entered this department as leading hoseman in Melville Engine Company No. 13, September 1, 1851. December 1, 1855, he was transferred, at his own request, to Ladder Company No. 1, and on June 1 the following year was transferred back to Engine Company No. 6. The next month he was appointed clerk, and January 1, 1857, was promoted foreman, serving as such until January 1, 1859, when the company was disbanded, and Steam Engine "Eclipse" was put in its place, on trial for one year, he being installed as foreman. September 1 he was appointed assistant engineman. He was transferred, on account of injuries received at a fire on Foster's wharf, July 4, 1860, to Engine Company No. 10, September 1, 1882, and on November 25 was injured at the corner of Cambridge and Chambers streets, by the capsizing of the steamer; and on June 28, 1883, still being unable, on account of said disability, to do fire duty, was sent to Chemical Engine Company No. 7, when he slipped and broke both bones in his left wrist. May 10, 1884, he was sent to Engine Company No. 10 to do floor duty, and on September 1, 1885, was detailed to his present position.

CHAPTER XVII.

THE BOSTON PROTECTIVE DEPARTMENT.

PREVIOUS to 1849 the destruction to property by water amounted to almost as much as that by fire, which loss had to be carried by the fire insurance companies. It was during that year that the old firm of insurance agents, Messrs. Dobson & Jordan, of 50 State street, had two canvas bags made, each of which contained three small oil-cloth covers, which were in charge of Assistant Engineer F. A. Coburn, who, being provided with a key to their office, would, on an alarm of fire, rush to headquarters, and pressing into the service anybody he could find, run with these coverings to the scene of destruction. This was the origin of the Boston Protective Department. The first fire at which these covers were used was in the dry-goods store of Fortune & Pelletier, located on Washington street, where the Adams House now stands. This means of covering was carried on until 1858, when the insurance people made arrangements with the Fire Department to allow six oil-cloth covers to be carried in a box attached to Ladder Company No. 1, the members of that company spreading the covers when not engaged in their regular duties, the compensation being fixed at fifty cents per hour per man. But this system was inadequate to meet the demands, therefore, on October 1, 1868, the first company was organized, the members being appointed by Chief Engineer John S. Damrell from the members of the Fire Department, but under pay of the fire underwriters. This company was composed of the following : Assistant Engineman W. A. Green, in charge ; J. W. C. Prescott, captain ; Robert F. Garland, driver ; George P. Kingsley, James Shannon, B. F. Underhill, Jr., Alvah Morse, M. A. Lynch, J. W. Randall, H. W. Longley, and T. Hall, members ; the driver being the only permanent man. An old milk-wagon was procured, which served as a means of transportation, and was housed in old Engine Company No. 8's quarters, on North Bennet street. This, with twenty-five covers, several brooms and shovels, constituted the equipment with which they did such excellent service within the following seven months, responding to 221 alarms of fire, during which they spread 338 covers and worked 366¼ hours.

The great advantage of this system became apparent to most of the insurance firms, and the amount of saving to property wrought by this department during 1869 and part of 1870 convinced them that it was no longer an experiment, but a success, and one that they could not afford to dispense with. On September 1, 1870, a suitable wagon was ordered from the Abbott-Downing Company, of Concord, N.H., and put in service, the company's quarters being moved to the house of Engine Company No. 7, on East street, and the membership was increased by the following additions: S. C. Smith, James H. Huff, Charles C. Snow, M. F. Packard, J. K. P. Reed, and John C. Pelton; J. W. Randall having been promoted to assistant captain. During 1874 a charter was granted by the Legislature.

A meeting was held March 11, and the act of the Legislature was accepted, a code of by-laws adopted, and the following gentlemen were elected the first Board of Directors: J. W. Kingsley, George A. Curtis, H. B. White, George F. Osborne, W. B. Sears, C. E. Guild, and J. F. Hovey. The first meeting of this board was held during the same day, and the following officers were elected: President, J. W. Kingsley; vice-president, W. B. Sears; treasurer, G. F. Osborne; secretary *pro tem.*, O. Howes, Jr.

The first meeting of the Boston Protective Department was held Thursday, March 29, at room 84, Mason Building, 70 Kilby street, when a vote was taken to continue the active duties of said department for the ensuing year; also to establish the fiscal year commencing April 1, and ending April 1 the following year. The maximum amount for expenditure was fixed at $30,000. The meeting of the directors held April 1 was for the purpose of appointing a committee to examine the districts to be covered by the department, and recommend a location for the two wagons. The wagon located in Bulfinch street was designated as Wagon No. 1, and the company was established by the appointment of five permanent men and four call-men, viz.: Foreman, D. R. Dearing; driver, R. W. Hitchcock; permanent men, G. E. Smith, J. B. Shannon, and Russell White; call-men, Timothy Hall, M. F. Packard, J. H. Huff, and Joseph Pierce, — with a salary corresponding to those holding similar positions in the Fire Department.

At the directors' meeting, April 8, the committee on securing locations for the wagons recommended that the building at the corner of Franklin and Hamilton streets be secured for the use of Wagon No. 1; they were authorized to hire the same. The rules and regulations submitted by the committee were adopted. An addition was made in the permanent ranks by the appointment of R. F. Garland. At the directors' meeting, April 11, Captain J. Stover Jacobs was appointed superintendent of the department, at a salary of $1,500 per annum. S. E. Smith was appointed assistant foreman. Directors Kinsley, Hovey, and Curtis were appointed a committee to procure a fire badge. Three hundred copies of the Charter, By-Laws, and Regulations were ordered printed for distribution. On April 18 another company was formed and designated Company No. 2, and the following promotions, transfers, and appointments took place, viz.: Promotions, J. H. Huff, assistant foreman of Company No. 2; M. F. Packard, permanent member, Company No. 2; Russell White, driver, this company; Timothy Hall, permanent man in this company. Transfers, R. W. Hitchcock, driver; R. F. Garland, to Company No. 2. Appointments, Samuel P. Poole, James Mills, and W. E. Wright, call-men in this company. This company was instructed not to respond to first alarms south of Dover street. Messrs. Kinsley, Curtis, and Hovey were appointed, at the meeting held May 5, a committee to confer with the officers of the Charitable Association of the Fire Department, and urge upon them the necessity of changing, by some amendment, the act of incorporating the association, so that the men attached to this department might obtain assistance from it in case of accident. May 8, O. Howes, Jr., was elected secretary of the Board of Directors. At this meeting the pay of the call-men was fixed at $300 per annum. May 13, Messrs. Osborne, Guild, and White were appointed an auditing committee. May 10, it was voted to put the permanent members of the department in uniform. It was also voted to obtain for the active members the advantages arising from the Firemen's Mutual Relief Association.

June 20, Treasurer George F. Osborne resigned, and C. E. Guild was elected to fill that office. Fire-badges were distributed on that date. C. E. Wadleigh and W. G. Reed were appointed call-substitutes, at the same time Call-man Joseph Pierce resigned. The Rules and Regulations went into effect July 1. Substitute C. E. Wadleigh was appointed call-man July 8, and on the 21st J. H. Howard was appointed call-man and assigned to South Boston, at a salary of $300 per year. T. Finley was appointed a substitute, to take effect August 1. Five rubber covers, 12 × 12 feet, for each of the four ladder companies, *i.e.*, 11, 7, 9, and 5, were ordered to be purchased. August 22, the Watkins' Automatic Fire Alarm was authorized to locate in this company's house. On December 10 the city was districted so that each company would have a certain section to look after. For this company was assigned West Boston Bridge, Cambridge, Bowdoin, Beacon, Park, Tremont, Winter, Washington, Essex streets, Harrison avenue, and Beach street to the water-front. The permanent force was increased by the appointment of George W. Thompson and J. Mackenzie, to date from December 1. James Sweetser was appointed a call-man in Charlestown, to take effect November 17, 1874. January 1, 1875, Mr. Thomas P. Bagley was appointed captain of the department, without command or pay. W. E. Wright was promoted a permanent man, *vice* J. B. Shannon resigned. J. E. Thayer was appointed call-man for East Boston.

The second annual meeting of this corporation was held March 1, 1875. It was voted to continue the active duties of the department for the ensuing year, with an appropriation of $40,000. The old Board of Directors were reëlected. Immediately after the adjournment of this meeting, the Board of Directors organized, with the choice of the following officers: President, J. W. Kinsley; vice-president, W. B. Sears; treasurer, C. E. Guild; and secretary, O. Howes, Jr. Driver Russell White resigned on April 14, to take effect April 1, and George W. Thompson was promoted to fill the vacancy; James W. Sweetser was also promoted a permanent man, and Charles Waldron appointed. May 13, R. F. Garland resigned. James F. Mackenzie resigned June 10; J. L. Huff was appointed a permanent man, to take effect May 18, and J. M. Hutchins, to the same position, on June 10; H. C. Packard was appointed a call-man.   At the directors' meeting, July 14, the pay of call-men in West Roxbury District was increased to $100 per year.   Call-man J. H. Howard died June 20, and J. W. Sweetser resigned on June 30, which vacancies were filled by the promotion of D. W. Brown, permanent, to take effect July 1, and Joseph Bell, call-man in South Boston, to go into effect June 20.   T. Finley resigned as substitute.   It was voted, September 8, that the entire department be put under the command of Captain Bagley, to take effect October 1.   He was given a salary of $1,500 per annum, and assigned for duty as fire marshal.   The first inspection drill was held September 13.   The superintendent was authorized to pay substitutes twenty-five cents per hour for actual fire service, and to detail watchmen to remain at fires when the property of the department was left.   At the meeting held November 9, the first report of the fire marshal was read. These reports were ordered to be printed and distributed to members of the corporation.   On this date J. B. Shannon and C. F. Tinkham were appointed substitutes.   Call-man P. D. Allen resigned December 8, and Charles E. Hill was appointed in his place.

March 8, 1876, the members of the corporation held their third annual meeting, at which it was voted to continue the active services of the department for the ensuing year, for which $40,000 was appropriated.   A change was adopted by increasing the number of directors from seven to nine, and electing three for three years, three for two years, and three for one year, resulting in the following election: George A. Curtis, Joseph W. Kinsley, and W. B. Sears, for three years; George F. Osborne, J. F. Hovey, and C. E. Guild, for two years; H. B. White, S. G. Rogers, and George O. Carpenter, for one year.   The auditing committee was composed of Messrs. Isaac Sweetser, Richard Pope, and Cyrus Brewer.   On the following day the Board of Directors organized as follows: President, J. W. Kinsley; vice-president, William B. Sears; secretary, O. Howes. Jr.; treasurer, C. E. Guild.   Substitutes W. E. Reed and G. H. Jones were discharged.   June 14 it was voted that the department should not respond to first alarms from boxes beyond the corner of Austin and Main streets, Charlestown; corner of E street and Broadway, South Boston; Maverick square, East Boston; Guild row and Police Station 10. Roxbury; also the entire Dorchester District. The inconveniences arising from crossing the East Boston ferries was settled at this date, the directors of the ferries according the same privileges to this service as given to the Fire Department in case of alarms of fire.   An inspection of the entire service was held September 16.   On November 14 the directors lost, by death, S. G. Rogers.   President Kinsley sent in his resignation as president and director, December 5.   At the following meeting, December 13, the existing vacancies in the board were filled by the election of Isaac Sweetser, *vice* Kinsley, and Thomas W. Tucker, *vice* Rogers.   Call-man James Mills resigned February 14. 1876, and his position was filled by promotion of J. B. Shannon, to take effect March 1. The directors elected Vice-President Sears president, at their meeting, March 2, and Director H. B. White, vice-president. The introduction of the Champion Fire Extinguisher in this service occurred March 14. W. H. Skinnings was appointed substitute.

March 22, 1877, found the members in session at their fourth annual meeting, when the vote to conduct the active duties of the department for the ensuing year, at an expenditure of the sum previously appropriated, was voted, after which they adjourned, to meet on April 5. At the meeting held on this date the following officers were elected: Geo. F. Osborne, Charles E. Guild, and James F. Hovey, for three years; Geo. A. Curtis, Isaac Sweetser, and Henry B. White, for two years; and Geo. O. Carpenter, Thos. W. Tucker, and Richard Pope, directors for one year. It was at this meeting that the regular morning reports of fires was voted for. The following day the directors organized, with the choice of the following officers: President, H. B. White; vice-president, Richard Pope; treasurer, C. E. Guild; secretary, O. Howes, Jr. Five hundred copies of the revised edition of the By-Laws, Rules, and Regulations were ordered printed. It was agreed, May 9, that the directors assume the responsibility of damages to books taken from the Public Library by the members. Both houses of this department were connected by telegraph with the house of Engine 7, on September 12. The rules adopted by the Board of Directors were issued on September 15, for the first time, under the term General Orders, and numbered; No. 1 of which defines the mode of issuing votes for the government of the department. The uniforms for the active members were adopted September 25.

Nothing of importance occurred until the fifth annual meeting, held March 28, 1878, at which it was voted to continue as heretofore for another year, with the same appropriation of funds. The directors elected were Thos. W. Tucker, J. Edward Hollis, and Richard Pope. At the directors' meeting, ten days later, H. B. White was elected president; R. Pope, vice-president; O. Howes, Jr., secretary; April 10, C. E. Guild was reëlected treasurer. Callman J. B. Shannon resigned, and his place was filled by Substitute W. H. Skinnings, Jr. At this time the expense of the department caused some dissatisfaction. It was decided, therefore, that an investigation be made, with a view of reducing it. A committee was chosen at this meeting, the result of whose labor was made known at the next session, May 8, when the following reductions of salaries were adopted: Superintendent, $1,400; fire marshal, $1,400; captain, $1,200; lieutenants, $1,000; privates, $900; call-men in city proper, Roxbury, East Boston, South Boston, and Charlestown, $250; and in Dorchester, $150, each, per annum, to take effect June 1. It was also decided that when the office of lieutenant became vacant it should be abolished. Jas. H. Jacobs was appointed a substitute. The superintendent and fire marshal, who had heretofore worn no uniform, were authorized, at this date, to procure them. January 8, Timothy Hall and Call-man Wadleigh resigned. On February 3, the building now occupied was leased. The following changes in the company occurred February 12 : Call-man J. H. Jacobs promoted permanent man, to date from July 9 ; Substitute George H. Carter promoted call-man ; and C. M Williams, substitute.

The sixth annual meeting was held March 26, 1879, at which it was voted to expend $35,000 for the ensuing year. The directors elected were Isaac Sweetser, Henry B. White, and Jas. Swords. On the 29th of the same month the directors organized, with the following choice of officers : H. B. White, president ; Pope, Guild, and Howes, Jr., were reëlected. A new committee was formed, *i.e.*, on appointments and discharges. The death of Call-man S. P. Poole was announced July 9. September 10, it was voted to suspend that part of orders in reference to officers wearing white shirts. Call-man Waldron resigned, February 11, 1880, and his place filled by J. W. Sweetser. On May 10 the houses of Companies Nos. 1 and 2 were connected by telephone with the General Exchange.

The seventh annual meeting occurred March 25, 1880. Thirty-five thousand dollars was the limit voted for expenses. Chas. E. Guild, Samuel Appleton, and Robt. H. Wass were elected directors. March 29, the Board of Directors reëlected their president and vice-president, and on May 12 the reëlection of treasurer and secretary occurred. It was also voted to combine the offices of superintendent and fire marshal, and to increase the number of permanent men. Geo. Donnelly resigned, and J. W. Eldridge was appointed, June 9. June 15, the directors elected Samuel Abbott, Jr., to be superintendent and fire marshal, at a salary of $2,250, to take effect July 1, 1880, on which date Superintendent Jacobs and Fire Marshal Bagley resigned. A new order in relation to uniforms was adopted July 14. The fire commissioners, the same day, were requested to allow members of this department assigned to ladder companies to sleep in the house of those companies, which was granted. A new wagon was ordered on this date for the superintendent. August 11, the following general orders were issued : No. 16, relative to the promulgation to the force of general and special orders. No. 17, in relation to the discipline to be observed going to and at a fire. No. 18 referred to the duty of house patrol, and the drill of men and horses. No. 19, in relation to the call-men sleeping in the house of the Fire Department ; and the superintendent was authorized to procure the necessary bedding and furniture to conform to this order. October 13, H. S. Kendall and A. McInnis, Jr., were elected call-men. The old horses of this company were transferred to Company No. 2, and two new ones purchased. Vice-President Pope died December 2. December 8, F. W. Pierce was promoted call-man, *vice* A. McInnis, resigned ; S. W. Ronimus, call-man, *vice* W. H. Skinnings, Jr., resigned, to take effect December 1, 1880.

March 25, 1881, the eighth annual meeting of the department was held. Thirty-five thousand dollars was appropriated. J. Edward Hollis, George C. Stearns, and H. V. Freeman were elected directors for three years, and W. A. Wheeler, *vice* R. Pope, deceased, for two years. March 28, the directors organized as follows: H. B. White, president; James Swords, vice-president; C. E. Guild and O. Howes, Jr., were reëlected. A. J. Osborne was appointed a substitute, April 13, on which date changes were made in the house of this company by placing the horses abreast of the wagon, as recommended by the superintendent. May 10, F. W. Pierce resigned. On this date it was voted to increase the salaries of the department, viz.: Captain, $1,250; all other permanent men, $1,000; call-men in city proper, South and East Boston, Charlestown, and Roxbury, $300; in West Roxbury, $150. A. J. Osborne was promoted call-man, June 8, and G. H. Carter, substitute. The salaries of call-members in the West Roxbury and Brighton Districts were increased $25 each per annum. July 13, Lieutenant Smith had his salary increased $50 per year. November 9, George R. Rogers was elected a director, *vice* H. R. White, who ceased to be a member, owing to the company he represented retiring from business. A horse was purchased, December 14, for the special use of the superintendent. Vice-President James Swords was elected president, and J. E. Hollis, vice-president. January 11, 1882, a billiard table was placed in the house. The first quarterly exhibit of the property of the department was also held. March 9, C. W. Williams resigned, and J. C. Bense appointed. This house was connected by telephone with City Hall on that day.

The ninth annual meeting was held March 29, 1882, when $35,000 was appropriated for the year's expenses. Messrs. F. E. Sweetser, James Swords, and G. R. Rogers were elected as directors for three years. March 30, Mr. Swords was elected president, J. E. Hollis, vice-president, Charles E. Guild, treasurer, and Osborne Howes, Jr., secretary. March 29, 1883, the tenth annual meeting was held, at which $40,000 was appropriated for the year. Charles E. Guild, Samuel Appleton, and B. B. Whittemore were elected directors for three years. The old board of officers were reëlected, April 3. It was voted, April 11, that it was expedient to substitute permanent men in the place of call-members in the city proper, and May 9 the following were appointed on the permanent force: Arthur T. Osborne, James W. Sweetser, George H. Carter. Samuel W. Rónimus, Joseph C. Bense, Charles H. Cushing, Michael J. Tully, and Porter E. Chase; Andrew F. Hall, appointed a call-man in Charlestown, and Moses F. Packard was promoted lieutenant of Company No. 2, — all to take effect May 10, 1883. July 11, the superintendent submitted a set of new rules and regulations to govern the active working of the department, which were printed and distributed, August 8. W. E. Wright resigned December 24, and Charles Schwarm was promoted permanent. The eleventh annual meeting was held March 27, 1884. The same amount of money was appropriated, and J. Edward Hollis, H. C. Bigelow, and H. V. Freeman were elected directors for three years. The officers were reappointed.

The lease of the house of Company No. 1 expired June 30, and was renewed for five years, at a rental of $1,600 and taxes per annum. The first issue of the fire marshal's daily reports was distributed May 23, 1884. Both houses were draped in mourning August 13, in memory of the death of Messrs. Pierce and Quigley, members of Engine Company No. 4, who were killed August 12, 1884. November 12, the superintendent was authorized to detail men for this company to inspect storage of merchandise in buildings. December 10, the committee arranged a scale of prices to be charged for the placing of covers, when they were asked to protect the property of those who had suffered from loss by fire. The charge was placed at $10 for five covers or less, and for service of men, whether spreading, removing, or as watchmen, at the rate of twenty-five cents per hour. James H. Jacobs resigned January 14, 1885. Director Samuel Appleton resigned February 11. James W. Sweetser was killed by a falling ladder, at 48 India wharf, March 8, 1885. Mr. N. Foster, Jr., succeeded Director Samuel Appleton, March 11. The same date, Henry W. Kimball and James T. Fitzgerald were promoted permanent members. March 31, 1885, the twelfth annual meeting was held; Messrs. James Swords, George R. Rogers, and F. C. Sweetser were elected directors for three years. No change occurred in the board of officers. George H. Perry and Andrew F. Hall were appointed permanent substitutes, April 8, being the first to hold this office in this department. Charles H. Ferrier was appointed call-man in Charlestown. Three water-funnels and four canvas roof-covers, 20 × 25 feet in dimensions, were purchased July 8. New style helmets were provided the members September 9. The total number of covers in the possession of the department October 14, 1885, was four hundred and five. George H. Perry and Porter E. Chase resigned on this date. A. F. Hall was promoted permanent member, and F. O. Hinckley and J. J. McCarthy promoted permanent substitutes.

The thirteenth annual meeting was held March 30, 1886. Messrs. Charles E. Guild, N. Foster, Jr., and E. D. Blake were elected directors for three years. New insignias of office were adopted June 9, 1886. M. J. Tully resigned July 14, and August 11 J. J. McCarthy was promoted a permanent member. October 13, Henry E. Thompson was appointed a permanent substitute. Joseph C. Bense resigned January 12, 1887. F. O. Hinckley was promoted March 9. Alarm-receiving registers were placed in the houses of Companies Nos. 1 and 2, owing to the discontinuing of the public bell-alarm in the city proper.

March 31, 1887, the fourteenth annual meeting was held. Messrs. J. Edward Hollis, H. V. Freeman, and Thomas F. Temple were elected directors for three years. The salaries of the members were increased, April 1, as follows: Captain, $1,500; lieutenant, $1,250; patrolmen, first year's service, $1,000, after two years' service, $3 per diem; substitutes, first six months, $750, after first six months, $900, per annum. The members were requested to join the Boston Firemen's Mutual Relief Association. A new floor was laid in the house of Company No. 1, October 12, and a new pung was purchased. The fifteenth annual meeting was held March 29, 1888, when $50,000 was appropriated for the year's expenses. Messrs.

SUPERINTENDENT ABBOTT AND PROTECTIVE COMPANY No. 1. — Page 718.

George R. Rogers, F. H. Stevens, and G. P. Field were elected directors for three years. J. Edward Hollis was elected president, March 30, and George R. Rogers, vice-president. April 11, the salaries of the call-members of Dorchester, West Roxbury, and Brighton were increased to correspond with those paid by the Fire Department; the charges for watch duty were increased to fifty cents per hour.

The well-known features of Superintendent SAMUEL ABBOTT, Jr., will be recognized on page 717. He was born in Boston, Mass., October 23, 1846. When fourteen years of age he went to sea, coasting in South America. He was in the merchant ship "Haverlock," which was the first merchantman that entered New Orleans after it was taken, in 1862. During the following year he enlisted in the quartermaster's department as driver, which position he held a few months, when he was promoted to wagon-master. During April, 1864, he enlisted in the navy, and was in both engagements at Fort Fisher. He was discharged during 1866. In 1856 he became connected with Hydrant Hose Company No. 2, as torch-boy, in which position he remained until the war; after returning from which he was admitted on the roll of Eagle Engine Company No. 3, as a call-substitute, and on August 1, 1866, was appointed a call-member. February 12, 1874, he was promoted to the position of captain and assigned to Engine Company No. 4, he being one of the first to receive a commission under the new organization. On April 6 of the ensuing year he was promoted to district chief of District No. 4. June 30, 1880, he resigned, to accept his present position. On his resignation he was highly complimented by the Board of Fire Commissioners for his faithful service. July 1, 1887, he began his duties as superintendent of this department. Superintendent Abbott was tendered the office of fire commissioner by Mayor O'Brien, but his services were considered too valuable as head of this department, consequently he was prevailed upon by its directors to remain with them. At the Jordan-Marsh fire, September 17, 1875, he fell through the roof of the elevator. He has been thrown from his wagon several times, but escaped with but slight injuries. He is a member of and filled several offices in Lafayette Lodge, Masons, Oriental Lodge 10, I. O. O. F., John Hancock Council 452, R. A., Bay State Assembly 71, R. S. G. F., Commonwealth Council 37, P. F.; Vice-President of Firemen's Charitable Association and B. F. M. R. Association; ex-President of the Barnicoat Association; ex-Secretary Massachusetts S. F. Association, and Boston Veterans.

COMPANY NO. 1.

PRESENT MEMBERS.

Captain DEXTER R. DEARING (Fig. 1) was born in the Charlestown District, Boston, Mass., May 7, 1835. After finishing his education, he served an apprenticeship at the mason's trade, and in May, 1853, was appointed a member of Hydrant Hose Company No. 2, in which he remained until he was transferred to Tiger Engine Company No. 7. He was then transferred to Cataract Engine Company No. 4, as leading hoseman, from which he was transferred to Franklin Hose Company No. 3, remaining until promoted to the position of assistant engineman of Barnicoat Engine Company No. 4; some time afterward he was promoted to the position of engineman. On the reorganization he resigned to accept his present position. At a fire on Union street, April 27, soon after his appointment, he was injured by driving the sharp point of an axe into his knee-cap. In 1875 he was injured by falling through the scuttle on the roof of the quarters, while responding to an alarm of fire, receiving broken ribs and other injuries. He is a member of America Lodge No. 191, I. O. O. F., Mount Sinai Encampment No. 49; a charter member of the Barnicoats; one of the directors of the B. F. M. R. Association; and on the relief committee of the Firemen's Charitable Association.

Lieutenant SAMUEL E. SMITH (Fig. 2) is a Boston boy, being born in this city, June 7, 1849. After completing his education he learned the occupation of a stationary engineer. In May, 1869, he entered this department, serving as a substitute until the 1st of September, 1872, when he was appointed a member of the Fire Department, and assigned to this department as a call-man. On the reorganization he was appointed a member of the permanent force, and on April 11, 1874, was appointed to his present position. He was injured at a fire on Congress street, in September, 1872, also at a fire on Chauncy street, April 11, 1876; and was thrown from the apparatus, by the breaking of the hind axle, while responding to Box 19, December 7, 1885, receiving a broken wrist, fractured ribs, and internal injuries. He is a member of America Lodge 191, I. O. O. F., and the Boston Veterans.

GEORGE W. THOMPSON (Fig. 3), driver, was born in Boston, Mass., July 18, 1835. He was a teamster by occupation. During 1858 he joined Ladder Company No. 1 as a call-substitute, and two years later was admitted a call-member. He enlisted in Company G, First Massachusetts Infantry, during 1861, from which he was discharged for disability three months later. During 1862 he again joined the Ladder Company, and was appointed driver. November, 1874, he was appointed in this company as a patrolman, and was assigned to his present position during March, 1875. He was seriously injured while going to Box 19, December 7, 1885, by the wagon breaking and throwing him, with several others, in the street. He is a member of Pilgrim Fathers, Boston Veterans, Barnicoat Fire Association, and a life member of the Firemen's Charitable Association.

HENRY W. KIMBALL (Fig. 4), patrolman, was born in Boston, Mass., November 30, 1858. He was engaged in mercantile business. During 1880 he was appointed a call-substitute in the fourth district of the Fire Department. Two years later he was appointed a permanent substitute in this department, and on March 11, 1884, was promoted to his present position.

ARTHUR T. OSBORNE (Fig. 5), patrolman, was born in Milford, Mass., March 16, 1857, and came to this city February 22, 1881. He is a machinist by trade, and April 3, 1881, entered this department as a call-substitute, and May 11, 1881, was appointed a call-member and assigned to this company. May 10, 1883, he was promoted to his present position. Mr. Osborne fell through a scuttle, a distance of twenty feet, at a fire, Box 53, in Fayette court, August 16, 1882, and severely injured his back and hips. He was also injured severely at a fire on Portland street, December 20, 1883. He is a member of Montezuma Lodge 33, I. O. O. F.

JOHN J. MCCARTHY (Fig. 6), patrolman, was born in Waltham, Mass., June 20, 1853. He came to this city when young and began life as a clerk. On November, 1884, he was appointed a call-member and assigned to Ladder Company No. 11, and October 23, 1885, was promoted to his present position. Mr. McCarthy had the main artery of his leg severed while at work at a fire, January 4, 1885.

ANDREW F. HALL (Fig. 7), assistant driver, was born in Charlestown District, Boston, Mass., November 17, 1853, and is a ship-joiner by trade, and was employed for years in the Navy-Yard. May 10, 1883, he was appointed a call-member and assigned to Ladder Company No. 9, where he remained some time, when he was appointed a permanent substitute in the Fire Department and detailed to Engine Company No. 2, April 7, 1885. He was promoted to his present position October 19, 1885. Mr. Hall is a member of the Firemen's Charitable Association and Knights of the Golden Eagle.

D. WEBSTER BROWN (Fig. 8), patrolman, was born in the Charlestown District, Boston, Mass., December 23, 1851. After leaving school he was employed in mercantile business. In 1868 he joined Howard Engine Company No. 1 of that district. May 1, 1875, he was appointed in the permanent force of this department. During his term of service Mr. Brown has met with several accidents. He is a member of the Boston Veterans and the Firemen's Charitable Association, Oriental Commandery 76, U. O. G. C., of East Boston, and the Imperial Lodge of the same district.

JAMES T. FITZGERALD (Fig. 9), patrolman, was born in Boston, Mass., August 2, 1859. After leaving school he entered mercantile business until his appointment in this department as a substitute in this company, during 1882, from which he was transferred to Engine Company No. 2, and on March 11, 1884, was promoted a permanent member and assigned to this company. Mr. Fitzgerald dislocated his arm and received internal injuries at a fire, July 2, 1886.

CHARLES SCHWARM (Fig. 10), patrolman, was born in Germany, March 29, 1857, and came to this city when but a child. He is a wood-carver by trade, and during 1878 joined this department as call-substitute, and on January, 1881, was made a call-member in the South Boston District. January 15, 1884, he was promoted to his present position. His back was injured by falling through a hatchway while at a fire at Box 37, July 4, 1884.

Henry E. Thompson (Fig. 11), substitute, was born in Brooklyn, N.Y., March 11, 1860, and during 1878 moved to Somerville. Mass., and from 1880 to 1884 resided in the Charlestown District, when he came to this city. He is an electrotyper by trade. During 1883 he joined Ladder Company No. 1, of Somerville. He entered this department in his present position October 13, 1886. Mr. Thompson is a member of Ivanhoe Lodge, K. of P.

Joseph E. Thayer (Fig. 12), call-member, was born in Roxbury District, Boston, Mass., June 11. 1830. He is a calker by trade, and in March, 1854, joined Webster Engine Company No. 13 as a member. Eighteen months later he was appointed a permanent driver of Ladder Company No. 2. and during 1874 he joined this department as a call-member for District No. 1. Mr. Thayer is a member of the Boston Veterans.

COMPANY NO. 2.

(The records of the meetings of the corporation and the board of directors will be found in the annals of Company No. 1, many of the orders of which refer to both companies; they were consequently omitted from the records of this company, to avoid repetition.)

At a meeting of the directors, held April 18, 1874, it was voted that another company should be added to the department, which resulted in the organization of this company, which was designated No. 2. The members appointed were as follows: J. H. Huff, assistant foreman; R. W. Hitchcock, driver; M. F. Packard and R. F. Garland, permanent members; J. L. Huff and James Mackenzie, call-men. They were instructed not to respond to first alarms north of Hanover street. The office of foreman was filled, May 8, 1874, by the appointment of J. W. Randall. June 10, P. D. Allen was appointed call-man; and on July 8 Alonzo Huff and John Gillon were enrolled as substitutes. The following additions were added to this company, July 21: Geo. H. Peck, Brighton, at $50 per year; Benj. Bird and George Needham, Dorchester District, $225 per annum; and on August 12 E. L. Weatherbee was admitted a call-man in West Roxbury. The district allotted to this company on December 10 were all points south and west of the line covered by Company No. 1, including South Boston, Roxbury, Dorchester, West Roxbury. and Brighton. E. L. Weatherbee resigned at this date, and W. W. Coleman was appointed in his place, to date December 1, 1874. February 10, 1875, Walter Dalrymple was appointed substitute, *vice* Alonzo Huff, resigned. John Gillon and Walter Dalrymple were appointed call-men, May 5. to take effect May 1. J. L. Huff promoted permanent, June 9, to take effect May 18, and Hubbard C. Packard call-man. Joseph Bell appointed call-man in South Boston, July 14. to take effect January 20; also S. C. Curran and R. Collins, substitutes. The pay of West Roxbury call-men was increased to $100. P. D. Allen resigned December 8, and was succeeded by Chas. E. Hill. December 13. 1876, R. Collins resigned, and on May 9, 1877, Geo. H. Carter was admitted a substitute. It was voted at the directors' meeting, July 11, to allow Messrs. J. H. Huff and M. F. Packard to receive $40, presented by the merchants of Boston for saving lives at the Shawmut-avenue fire. S. C. Curran resigned, and W. H. Gillon appointed. Walter Dalrymple resigned September 25, 1877; S. C. Curran promoted in his place.

April 17, 1878, Capt. J. W. Randall was discharged for absence without leave. May 8, Lieut. J. H. Huff was promoted to the position of captain of this company. June 12, 1878, it was voted to limit the leave of absence of members of this company to twelve hours in ten days. August 14, 1878, M. F. Packard was appointed senior member of this company. W. H. Keenan was appointed call-man, and assigned to West Roxbury, *vice* W. W. Tolman, resigned September 11. October 9, G. R. Donnelly was admitted call-man, *vice* Chas. E. Hill, resigned September 18. February 12, 1879, Moses Regal is recorded as substitute, and on March 12 J. F. Stetson was appointed call-man in Brighton, *vice* G. H. Peck, resigned.

April 9, the members of this company petitioned the board of directors for an extension of leave of absence, as provided by Order No. 8. A petition from Blodgett Bros., to put in the alarm of their electric fire detector, was also received. J. F. Stetson resigned February 11, 1880, to take effect March 1. June 9, Geo. Donnelly was discharged, and J. W. Eldridge appointed in his place. October 13, Moses Regal, G. F. Williams, and E. A. Coats were appointed call-men, to take effect September 1, 1880, *vice* H. C. Packard, J. E. Gillon, S. C. Curran, and G. H. Carter; F. W. Pierce was admitted a substitute. December 8, F. W. Pierce was promoted call-man and assigned to Company No. 1, *vice* A. McInnis, Jr., resigned. J. Bell died January 7, 1881, and Chas. Schwarm was appointed, to take effect February 1, 1881. The call-men in South Boston and Roxbury had an increase of salary to $300, and those in West Roxbury to $150, May 10; and June 8, the call-man in Brighton had his salary increased $25 per year. October 12, Geo. A. Needham resigned, and G. W. Dalton was appointed to fill his place.

George R. Donnelly resigned July 12, and was succeeded by Fred. O. Hinckley. The building No. 11 Pine street was leased August 9, for ten years, for this company. Five thousand dollars was expended in making alterations. R. W. Hitchcock resigned November 8, and H. S. Kendall was promoted permanent. Frederick Coates resigned December 13, 1882; J. C. Bense promoted; George H. Carter promoted a call-member. Fred C. Byrnes was appointed a call-man in South Boston, February 13, 1884. The salaries of call-members in Brighton District were increased to $100 per annum. A canvas tunnel was purchased, May 21, 1884. S. A. Coombs resigned November 12, and J. J. McCarthy appointed. A new pair of horses were purchased, January 14, 1885. Paul A. Garcia was appointed call-man in Roxbury District, October 14, 1885, and Henry Malone in the Brighton District. Joseph W. White appointed a permanent substitute, February 9, 1887. Henry E. Malone died April 4; John J.

O'Keefe appointed in Brighton District, April 13. C. A. Woods was appointed in West Roxbury, August 10, *vice* Keenan, deceased. Extensive alterations were made in the house of this company, June 13, 1888. B. C. Bird resigned October 10, and Edmund Fruean, Jr., was appointed a call-man. Sherman S. Bearse was appointed in the West Roxbury District. Joseph W. White resigned, December 12, and was succeeded by Samuel Abbott, 3d, January 9, 1889.

Present Members.

Captain JAMES H. HUFF (Fig. 1) was born in Boston, Mass., August 14, 1846, and duing 1857 moved to Maine, where he learned the mason's trade. In July, 1862, he enlisted in Company E, Nineteenth Maine Regiment, and served until 1865. He returned to Boston during 1866, and in September, 1872, entered this department as a call-man. April 25, 1874, he was made a permanent member, and on the organization of this company was promoted to the position of lieutenant. May 1, 1878, he was promoted to his present position. Captain Huff is a member of Joseph Warren Lodge and St. Andrew's Chapter, Boston Council and Commandery, and Scottish Rites, of the Masons.

Lieutenant MOSES F. PACKARD (Fig. 2) was born in Dixfield, Me., August 26, 1843. He is a mason by trade. He served in Company K, Fifth Maine Regiment, from March, 1861, until November of the same year, when he was discharged for disability. During 1869 he moved to this city, and shortly after joined Hose Company No. 8, as a call-substitute. September, 1871, he was made a call-man in this department, and March 1, 1874, was appointed a permanent member and assigned to this company, and on May 13, 1883, was promoted to his present position. Lieutenant Packard was laid up three months from injuries received at the Sammett Mattress Factory fire. He is a member of Dahlgren Post 2, G. A. R., Tremont Lodge 15, I. O. O. F., Tremont Lodge 50, Good Templars, Wendell Phillips Council 23, R. C., K. of H.

ISAAC M. HUTCHINS (Fig. 3), driver, was born in Lee, Me., April 20, 1845. He enlisted, December 27, 1861, in the Fourth Maine Battery, in which he served until January 20, 1865. He came to this city soon after, where he was employed as a teamster. June 9, 1875, he was appointed a permanent member of this company. Mr. Hutchins is a member of Massachusetts Lodge of Masons, and Howard Lodge 20, I. O. O. F.

CHARLES H. CUSHING (Fig. 4), assistant driver, was born in Groton Junction, Mass., November 6, 1848, and when young came to this city, where he was employed as a teamster. He was admitted a call-man in Red Jacket Hose Company No. 1, of Charlestown department, and later was made a call-substitute in Engine Company No. 10. Two years later he was appointed a permanent member of Ladder Company No. 1, from which he

PROTECTIVE COMPANY No. 2. — Page 726.

was transferred to Engine Company No. 4. He left the department some time after, and May 11, 1883, was made a permanent member of this company. Mr. Cushing is a member of the Barnicoat Fire Association. He was one of the three that were injured in the Tremont Temple fire.

JOHN L. HUFF (Fig. 5), patrolman, was born in Carver, Mass., March 23, 185C, and came to this city when young, where he learned the mason's trade. He entered this department as a call-man in this company March 24, 1874, in which he was made a permanent man, May 19, 1875, and is at present senior patrolman. Mr. Huff had his arm broken, March 14, 1886, by being thrown from the wagon. He is a brother of Captain Huff, and is a member of the Firemen's Charitable Association.

HARRY S. KENDALL (Fig. 6) was born in Brooklyn, N.Y., June 5, 1846, and came to this city when but a child, where he learned the house-painter's trade. During 1864 he was admitted a member of Hose Company No. 1, of the Roxbury department, and was transferred to Engine Company No. 13, January, 1871. He was enrolled a call-member of this department, September, 1880, in Company No. 1; and on November 12, 1882, was transferred to his present position, and has been driver for Superintendent Abbott for the past seven years, during which he has met with several narrow escapes. Mr. Kendall was made a member of Lafayette Lodge of Masons, March 8, 1869; he is also a member of the Barnicoat Association, Boston Veterans, trustee of the Firemen's Charitable Association for this company, treasurer of Protective R. A., Boston Protective Department.

SAMUEL W. RONIMUS (Fig. 7), patrolman, was born in Boston, Mass., January 19, 1854, and is a paper-hanger by trade. He entered this department December 1, 1880, as a call-man in Company No. 1. May 10, 1883, he was appointed a permanent member and assigned to this company. Mr. Ronimus, while at a fire, had his ankle dislocated. He is a life member of the Firemen's Charitable Association.

GEORGE H. CARTER (Fig. 8), patrolman, was born in Boston, Mass., July 9, 1848. After leaving school he was employed as a clerk. He was a call-man in Ladder Company No. 1, and during 1874 left the Fire Department. Soon after he was admitted a substitute in Company No. 1, of this department, and on May 10, 1883, was made a permanent member and assigned to this company. Mr. Carter's father was killed during 1860, at the Manning-Glover fire in Merchants row, while a member of Ladder Company No. 1.

FRED O. HINCKLEY (Fig. 9), patrolman, was born in Nantucket, Mass., August 27, 1859, and came to this city when but a child, where he learned the clock-making trade. April 18, 1880, he was appointed a call-substitute in Ladder Company No. 4, and July 10, 1882, was made a call-man in Company No. 1 of this department and assigned to District No. 9. October 19, 1885, he was appointed a permanent substitute. January 12, 1887, he was promoted a permanent member of this company. Mr. Hinckley was laid up one year from injuries received at a fire, August 25, 1887, by falling through a glass floor. He is a member of Millmont Assembly 68, R. S. G. F., and De Soto Lodge 21, K. of P.

SAMUEL ABBOTT, 3d (Fig. 10), substitute, is a Boston boy, being born in this city, October 23, 1867. After leaving school he went to sea, following that vocation for several years, and on March 1, 1887, entered this service as a call-substitute, and January 9, 1889, was promoted to his present position and detailed to this company. Mr. Abbott fell three stories through a scuttle, while at a fire on Beverly street, October 28, 1888, receiving a dislocated ankle and a fracture of leg. He is a member of Shawmut Tribe 4, Red Men, and the Barnicoat Association.

PAUL A. GARCIA (Fig. 11) was born in Cadiz, Spain, April 6, 1854, and came to this city during 1863, where he learned the clock-maker's trade. He was appointed a call-member of Ladder Company No. 4, February 28, 1882. October 9, 1885, he was appointed a call-member of this department and assigned to this company, detailed to Ladder Company No. 4. Mr. Garcia is a member of De Soto Lodge 21, K. of P., Uniform Rank, Boston Division. By an oversight this gentleman's portrait is inserted (Fig. 20) among those of members of Ladder Company No. 4.

FRED C. BYRNES (Fig. 12), call-member, was born in South Boston, Mass., December 22, 1857. He is employed as a teamster, and during 1877 began his fire experience as a call-substitute in Hose Company No. 9. April 3, 1880, he was appointed a call-member, and January 20, 1884, was appointed a call-member of this department and detailed to Ladder Company No. 5.

EDMUND TRUEAN, Jr. (Fig. 13), call-member, was born in Dorchester District, Boston, Mass., September 20, 1865. He is a tin and sheet-iron worker by trade. During 1885 he joined Engine Company No. 21 as a call-substitute, and later worked with Ladder Company No. 7, until he received his present appointment in this department and was assigned for duty in Ladder Company No. 7, November 1, 1888.

GEORGE W. DALTON (Fig. 14), call-member, was born in Milton, Mass., September 27, 1838, and is a blacksmith by trade. He enlisted in Company E, First Massachusetts Regiment, on May 25, 1861, and served nineteen months. He joined Fountain Engine Company No. 1, of Dorchester department, during 1856. in which he served six years, when he was admitted a volunteer of Torrent Engine Company No. 3, in which he remained a short time, when he moved back to Milton, and there joined Granite Ladder Company, in which he was elected foreman, and served in that capacity two years. He then came to Dorchester and did duty, as a call-substitute in Engine Company No. 16. for seven years. He was appointed to his present position during 1880 and assigned to Ladder Company No. 6. Mr. Dalton is a member of Post 68, G. A. R., Blue Hill Lodge 457, K. of H., the Boston Veterans, and the Firemen's Charitable Association.

C. A. WOOD (Fig. 15) became connected with th
11, 1887, at which time he was appointed a call-member and assigned to this company, detailed to Ladder Company No. 10.

JOHN J. O'KEEFE (Fig. 16), call-man, was born in Grafton, Mass., January 5, 1852, and came to Boston during 1866. He is employed as a teamster, and in April, 1887, was appointed a member of this company and assigned to Ladder Company No. 11. He is a member of M. C. O. of Foresters.

CHARLES H. FERRIER (Fig. 17) was born in Boston, Mass., January 14, 1860. After leaving school he was employed as a clerk. January, 1881, he was admitted a call-substitute in Hose Company No. 3. May, 1883, he joined Engine Company No. 27 in the same capacity, until the company was made permanent, when he left the department. He was admitted a call-man in this department April 9, 1885, and assigned to Charlestown District, in Ladder Company No. 9. Mr. Ferrier is a member of Company No. 1, among the members of which his portrait should be placed, but by an oversight it was inserted with Company No. 2.

STEPHEN S. BEARSE (Fig. 18), call-man, was born in Chatham, Mass., October 28, 1864, and came to Boston during 1866, where he has been employed as a teamster. He entered this department November 17, 1888, as a call-man, assigned to Protective Company No. 2, and detailed to Ladder Company No. 16.